PENGUIN BOOKS

THE REGENERATION TRILOGY

'A new vision of what the First World War did to human beings, male and female, soldiers and civilians. Constantly surprising and formally superb' A. S. Byatt, *Daily Telegraph*

'What Barker does in all three novels is explore with gritty realism – and absolute clarity of vision – the whole dirty, glorious and horrific business of war' Kate Chisholm, *Sunday Telegraph*

'One of the few real masterpieces of late 20th-century British fiction' Jonathan Coe, *W* (the Waterstone's magazine)

'Pat Barker's Great War trilogy is distinguished by its compassion, intelligence and astonishing control of tone and technique' Anthony Quinn, *Harpers and Queen*

'One of the most distinguished works of contemporary fiction' Barry Unsworth, *Sunday Times*

'She has produced a trilogy which is right up there with other classics of First World War literature. I could not recommend it more highly' Charlotte Joll, *Spectator*

ABOUT THE AUTHOR

Pat Barker was born in Thornaby-on-Tees in 1943. She was educated at the London School of Economics and has been a teacher of history and politics. Her books include *Union Street* (1982), winner of the 1983 Fawcett Prize, which has been filmed as *Stanley and Iris*; *Blow Your House Down* (1984); *Liza's England* (1986), formerly *The Century's Daughter*; *The Man Who Wasn't There* (1989); and the highly acclaimed *Regeneration* trilogy, comprising *Regeneration*, *The Eye in the Door*, winner of the 1993 Guardian Fiction Prize, and *The Ghost Road*, winner of the 1995 Booker Prize for Fiction. *The Man Who Wasn't There* and all three volumes of the *Regeneration* trilogy are published in Penguin. Her latest novel, *Another World*, is published by Viking.

Pat Barker is married and lives in Durham.

PAT BARKER

The Regeneration Trilogy

PENGUIN BOOKS

PENGUIN BOOKS

Published by the Penguin Group
Penguin Books Ltd, 27 Wrights Lane, London W8 5TZ, England
Penguin Putnam Inc., 375 Hudson Street, New York, New York 10014, USA
Penguin Books Australia Ltd, Ringwood, Victoria, Australia
Penguin Books Canada Ltd, 10 Alcorn Avenue, Toronto, Ontario, Canada M4V 3B2
Penguin Books (NZ) Ltd, 182-190 Wairau Road, Auckland 10, New Zealand

Penguin Books Ltd, Registered Offices: Harmondsworth, Middlesex, England

Regeneration first published by Viking 1991
Published in Penguin Books 1992
The Eye in the Door first published by Viking 1993
Published in Penguin Books 1994
The Ghost Road first published by Viking 1995
Published in Penguin Books 1996
Published in one volume as *The Regeneration Trilogy* by Viking 1996
Published in Penguin Books 1998
1 3 5 7 9 10 8 6 4 2

Set in 11/13.25 pt Monotype Bembo
Printed in England by Clays Ltd, St Ives plc

For David,
and in loving memory of Dr John Hawkings
(1922–1987)

CONTENTS

REGENERATION

Part One

ONE

Finished with the War
A Soldier's Declaration

I am making this statement as an act of wilful defiance of military authority, because I believe the war is being deliberately prolonged by those who have the power to end it.

I am a soldier, convinced that I am acting on behalf of soldiers. I believe that this war, upon which I entered as a war of defence and liberation, has now become a war of aggression and conquest. I believe that the purposes for which I and my fellow soldiers entered upon this war should have been so clearly stated as to have made it impossible to change them, and that, had this been done, the objects which actuated us would now be attainable by negotiation.

I have seen and endured the suffering of the troops, and I can no longer be a party to prolong these sufferings for ends which I believe to be evil and unjust.

I am not protesting against the conduct of the war, but against the political errors and insincerities for which the fighting men are being sacrificed.

On behalf of those who are suffering now I make this protest against the deception which is being practised on them; also I believe that I may help to destroy the callous complacence with which the majority of those at home regard the continuance of agonies which they do not share, and which they have not sufficient imagination to realize.

S. Sassoon
July 1917

Bryce waited for Rivers to finish reading before he spoke again. 'The "S" stands for "Siegfried". Apparently, he thought that was better left out.'

'And I'm sure he was right.' Rivers folded the paper and ran his fingertips along the edge. 'So they're sending him here?'

Bryce smiled. 'Oh, I think it's rather more specific than that. They're sending him to *you*.'

Rivers got up and walked across to the window. It was a fine day, and many of the patients were in the hospital grounds, watching a game of tennis. He heard the *pok-pok* of rackets, and a cry of frustration as a ball smashed into the net. 'I suppose he is – "shell-shocked"?'

'According to the Board, yes.'

'It just occurs to me that a diagnosis of neurasthenia might not be inconvenient confronted with this.' He held up the Declaration.

'Colonel Langdon chaired the Board. *He* certainly seems to think he is.'

'Langdon doesn't believe in shell-shock.'

Bryce shrugged. 'Perhaps Sassoon was gibbering all over the floor.'

' "Funk, old boy." I know Langdon.' Rivers came back to his chair and sat down. 'He doesn't *sound* as if he's gibbering, does he?'

Bryce said carefully, 'Does it matter what his mental state is? Surely it's better for him to be here than in prison?'

'Better for *him*, perhaps. What about the hospital? Can you imagine what our dear Director of Medical Services is going to say, when he finds out we're sheltering "conchies" as well as cowards, shirkers, scrimshankers and degenerates? We'll just have to hope there's no publicity.'

'There's going to be, I'm afraid. The Declaration's going to be read out in the House of Commons next week.'

'By?'

'Lees-Smith.'

Rivers made a dismissive gesture.

'Yes, well, I know. But it still means the press.'

'And the minister will say that no disciplinary action has been taken, because Mr Sassoon is suffering from a severe mental breakdown, and therefore not responsible for his actions. I'm not sure *I*'d prefer that to prison.'

'I don't suppose he was offered the choice. Will you take him?'

'You mean I *am* being offered a choice?'

'In view of your case load, yes.'

Rivers took off his glasses and swept his hand down across his eyes. 'I suppose they *have* remembered to send the file?'

*

Sassoon leant out of the carriage window, still half-expecting to see Graves come pounding along the platform, looking even more dishevelled than usual. But further down the train, doors had already begun to slam, and the platform remained empty.

The whistle blew. Immediately, he saw lines of men with grey muttering faces clambering up the ladders to face the guns. He blinked them away.

The train began to move. Too late for Robert now. Prisoner arrives without escort, Sassoon thought, sliding open the carriage door.

By arriving an hour early he'd managed to get a window seat. He began picking his way across to it through the tangle of feet. An elderly vicar, two middle-aged men, both looking as if they'd done rather well out of the war, a young girl and an older woman, obviously travelling together. The train bumped over a point. Everybody rocked and swayed, and Sassoon, stumbling, almost fell into the vicar's lap. He mumbled an apology and sat down. Admiring glances, and not only from the women. Sassoon turned to look out of the window, hunching his shoulder against them all.

After a while he stopped pretending to look at the smoking chimneys of Liverpool's back streets and closed his eyes. He needed to sleep, but instead Robert's face floated in front of him, white and twitching as it had been last Sunday, almost a week ago now, in the lounge of the Exchange Hotel.

For a moment, looking up to find that khaki-clad figure standing just inside the door, he thought he was hallucinating again.

'Robert, what on earth are *you* doing here?' He jumped up and ran across the lounge. 'Thank God you've come.'

'I got myself passed fit.'

'Robert, *no*.'

'What else could I do? After getting *this*.' Graves dug into his tunic pocket and produced a crumpled piece of paper. 'A covering letter would have been nice.'

'I wrote.'

'No, you didn't, Sass. You just sent me this. Couldn't you at least have *talked* about it first?'

'I thought I'd written.'

They sat down, facing each other across a small table. Cold northern light streamed in through the high windows, draining Graves's face of the little colour it had.

'Sass, you've got to give this up.'

'Give it up? You don't think I've come this far, do you, just to give in now?'

'Look, you've made your protest. For what it's worth, I agree with every word of it. But you've had your say. There's no point making a martyr of yourself.'

'The only way I can get publicity is to make them court-martial me.'

'They won't do it.'

'Oh, yes, they will. It's just a matter of hanging on.'

'You're in no state to stand a court-martial.' Graves clasped his clenched fist. 'If I had Russell here now, I'd *shoot* him.'

'It was my idea.'

'Oh, pull the other one. And even if it was, do you think anybody's going to understand it? They'll just say you've got cold feet.'

'Look, Robert, you think exactly as I do about the war, and you *do . . . nothing*. All right, that's your choice. But don't come here lecturing *me* about *cold feet*. This is the hardest thing I've ever done.'

Now, on the train going to Craiglockhart, it still seemed the hardest thing. He shifted in his seat and sighed, looking out over fields of wheat bending to the wind. He remembered the silvery sound of shaken wheat, the shimmer of light on the stalks. He'd have given anything to be out there, away from the stuffiness of the carriage, the itch and constriction of his uniform.

On that Sunday they'd taken the train to Formby and spent the afternoon wandering aimlessly along the beach. A dull, wintry-looking sun cast their shadows far behind them, so that every gesture either of them made was mimicked and magnified.

'They won't *let* you make a martyr of yourself, Sass. You should have accepted the Board.'

The discussion had become repetitive. For perhaps the fourth time, Sassoon said, 'If I hold out long enough, there's nothing else they can do.'

'There's a lot they can do.' Graves seemed to come to a decision. 'As a matter of fact, I've been pulling a few strings on your behalf.'

Sassoon smiled to hide his anger. 'Good. If you've been exercising your usual tact, that ought to get me at least two years.'

'They won't court-martial you.'

In spite of himself, Sassoon began to feel afraid. 'What, then?'

'Shut you up in a lunatic asylum for the rest of the war.'

'And that's the result of your string-pulling, is it? Thanks.'

'No, the result of my string-pulling is to get you another Board. You must take it this time.'

'You can't put people in lunatic asylums just like that. You have to have *reasons*.'

'They've got reasons.'

'Yes, the Declaration. Well, that doesn't prove me insane.'

'And the hallucinations? *The corpses in Piccadilly?*'

A long silence. 'I had rather hoped my letters to you were private.'

'I had to persuade them to give you another Board.'

'They won't court-martial me?'

'No. Not in any circumstances. And if you go on refusing to be boarded, they *will* put you away.'

'You know, Robert, I wouldn't believe this from anybody else. Will you *swear* it's true?'

'Yes.'

'On the Bible?'

Graves held up an imaginary Bible and raised his right hand. 'I swear.'

Their shadows stretched out behind them, black on the white sand. For a moment Sassoon still hesitated. Then, with an odd little gasp, he said, 'All right then, I'll give way.'

In the taxi, going to Craiglockhart, Sassoon began to feel frightened. He looked out of the window at the crowded pavements of Princes Street, thinking he was seeing them for the first and last time. He couldn't imagine what awaited him at Craiglockhart, but he didn't for a moment suppose the inmates were let out.

He glanced up and found the taxi-driver watching him in the mirror. All the local people must know the name of the hospital, and what it was for. Sassoon's hand went up to his chest and began pulling at a loose thread where his MC ribbon had been.

For conspicuous gallantry during a raid on the enemy's trenches. He remained for 1½ hours under rifle and bomb fire collecting and bringing in our wounded. Owing to his courage and determination, all the killed and wounded were brought in.

Reading the citation, it seemed to Rivers more extraordinary than ever that Sassoon should have thrown the medal away. Even the most extreme pacifist could hardly be ashamed of a medal awarded for *saving* life. He took his glasses off and rubbed his eyes. He'd been working on the file for over an hour, but, although he was now confident he knew all the facts, he was no closer to an understanding of Sassoon's state of mind. If anything, Graves's evidence to the Board – with its emphasis on hallucinations – seemed to suggest a full-blown psychosis rather than neurasthenia. And yet there was no other evidence for that. Misguided the Declaration might well be, but it was not deluded, illogical or incoherent. Only the throwing away of the medal still struck him as odd. That surely had been the action of a man at the end of his tether.

Well, we've all been there, he thought. The trouble was, he was finding it difficult to examine the evidence impartially. He *wanted* Sassoon to be ill. Admitting this made him pause. He got up and began pacing the floor of his room, from door to window and back again. He'd only ever encountered one similar case, a man who'd refused to go on fighting on religious grounds. Atrocities took place on both sides, he'd said. There was nothing to choose between the British and the Germans.

The case had given rise to heated discussions in the MO's common room – about the freedom of the individual conscience in wartime, and the role of the army psychiatrist in 'treating' a man who refused to fight. Rivers, listening to those arguments, had been left in no doubt of the depth and seriousness of the divisions. The controversy had died down only when the patient proved to be psychotic. That was the crux of the matter. A man like Sassoon would always be trouble, but he'd be a lot less trouble if he were ill.

Rivers was roused from these thoughts by the crunch of tyres on gravel. He reached the window in time to see a taxi draw up, and a man, who from his uniform could only be Sassoon, get out. After paying the driver, Sassoon stood for a moment, looking up at the building. Nobody arriving at Craiglockhart for the first time could fail to be daunted by the sheer gloomy, cavernous bulk of the place. Sassoon lingered on the drive for a full minute after the taxi had driven away, then took a deep breath, squared his shoulders, and ran up the steps.

Rivers turned away from the window, feeling almost ashamed of having witnessed that small, private victory over fear.

TWO

Light from the window behind Rivers's desk fell directly on to Sassoon's face. Pale skin, purple shadows under the eyes. Apart from that, no obvious signs of nervous disorder. No twitches, jerks, blinks, no repeated ducking to avoid a long-exploded shell. His hands, doing complicated things with cup, saucer, plate, sandwiches, cake, sugar tongs and spoon, were perfectly steady. Rivers raised his own cup to his lips and smiled. One of the nice things about serving afternoon tea to newly arrived patients was that it made so many neurological tests redundant.

So far he hadn't looked at Rivers. He sat with his head slightly averted, a posture that could easily have been taken for arrogance, though Rivers was more inclined to suspect shyness. The voice was slightly slurred, the flow of words sometimes hesitant, sometimes rushed. A disguised stammer, perhaps, but a life-long stammer, Rivers thought, not the recent, self-conscious stammer of the neurasthenic.

'While I remember, Captain Graves rang to say he'll be along some time after dinner. He sent his apologies for missing the train.'

'He *is* still coming?'

'Yes.'

Sassoon looked relieved. 'Do you know, I don't think Graves's caught a train in his life? Unless somebody was there to *put* him on it.'

'We were rather concerned about you.'

'In case the lunatic went missing?'

'I wouldn't put it quite like that.'

'I was all right. I wasn't even surprised, I thought he'd slept in. He's been doing a . . . a lot of rushing round on my behalf recently. You've no idea how much work goes into *rigging* a Medical Board.'

Rivers pushed his spectacles up on to his forehead and massaged the inner corners of his eyes. 'No, I don't suppose I have. You know this may sound naïve but . . . to *me* . . . the accusation that a Medical Board has been rigged is quite a serious one.'

'I've no complaints. I was dealt with in a perfectly fair and reasonable way. Probably better than I deserved.'

'What kind of questions did they ask?'

Sassoon smiled. 'Don't you know?'

'I've read the report, if that's what you mean. I'd still like to hear your version.'

'Oh: "Did I object to fighting on religious grounds?" I said I didn't. It was rather amusing, actually. For a moment I thought they were asking me whether I objected to going on a crusade. "Did I think I was qualified to decide when the war should end?" I said I hadn't thought about my qualifications.' He glanced at Rivers. '*Not true*. And then . . . then Colonel Langdon asked *said* "Your friend tells us you're very good at bombing. Don't you still dislike the Germans?"'

A long silence. The net curtain behind Rivers's head billowed out in a glimmering arc, and a gust of cool air passed over their faces.

'And what did you say to that?'

'I don't remember.' He sounded impatient now. 'It didn't matter what I said.'

'It matters now.'

'All right.' A faint smile. '*Yes*, I am quite good at bombing. *No*, I do not still dislike the Germans.'

'Does that mean you once did?'

Sassoon looked surprised. For the first time something had been said that contradicted his assumptions. 'Briefly. April and May of last year, to be precise.'

A pause. Rivers waited. After a while Sassoon went on, almost reluctantly. 'A friend of mine had been killed. For a while I used to go out on patrol every night, looking for Germans to kill. Or rather I told myself that's what I was doing. In the end I didn't know whether I was trying to kill them, or just giving them plenty of opportunities to kill me.'

'"Mad Jack."'

Sassoon looked taken aback. 'Graves really *has* talked, hasn't he?'

'It's the kind of thing the Medical Board would need to know.' Rivers hesitated. 'Taking *unnecessary* risks is one of the first signs of a war neurosis.'

'Is it?' Sassoon looked down at his hands. 'I didn't know that.'

'Nightmares and hallucinations come later.'

'What's an "unnecessary risk" anyway? The maddest thing *I* ever did was done under orders.' He looked up, to see if he should continue. 'We were told to go and get the regimental badges off a German corpse. They reckoned he'd been dead two days, so obviously if we got the badges they'd know which battalion was opposite. Full moon, not a cloud in sight, *absolutely mad*, but off we went. Well, we got there – eventually – and what do we find? He's been dead a helluva lot longer than two days, and he's French anyway.'

'So what did you do?'

'Pulled one of his boots off and sent it back to battalion HQ. With quite a bit of his leg left inside.'

Rivers allowed another silence to open up. 'I gather we're not going to talk about nightmares?'

'You're in charge.'

'Ye-es. But then one of the paradoxes of being an army psychiatrist is that you don't actually get very far by *ordering* your patients to be frank.'

'I'll be as frank as you like. I did have nightmares when I first got back from France. I don't have them now.'

'And the hallucinations?'

He found this more difficult. 'It was just that when I woke up, the nightmares didn't always stop. So I used to see . . .' A deep breath. 'Corpses. Men with half their faces shot off, crawling across the floor.'

'And you were awake when this happened?'

'I don't know. I must've been, because I could see the sister.'

'And was this always at night?'

'No. It happened once during the day. I'd been to my club for lunch, and when I came out I sat on a bench, and . . . I suppose I must've nodded off.' He was forcing himself to go on. 'When I woke up, the pavement was covered in corpses. Old ones, new ones, black, green.' His mouth twisted. 'People were treading on their faces.'

Rivers took a deep breath. 'You say you'd just woken up?'

'Yes. I used to sleep quite a bit during the day, because I was afraid to go to sleep at night.'

'When did all this stop?'

'As soon as I left the hospital. The atmosphere in that place was really terrible. There was one man who used to boast about killing German prisoners. You can imagine what living with *him* was like.'

'And the nightmares haven't recurred?'

'No. I do dream, of course, but not about the war. Sometimes a dream seems to go on after I've woken up, so there's a a kind of in-between stage.' He hesitated. 'I don't know whether that's abnormal.'

'I hope not. It happens to me all the time.' Rivers sat back in his chair. 'When you look back now on your time in the hospital, do *you* think you were "shell-shocked"?'

'I don't know. Somebody who came to see me told my uncle he

thought I was. As against that, I wrote one or two good poems while I was in there. We-ell . . .' He smiled. '*I* was pleased with them.'

'You don't think it's possible to write a good poem in a state of shock?'

'No, I don't.'

Rivers nodded. 'You may be right. Would it be possible for me to see them?'

'Yes, of course. I'll copy them out.'

Rivers said, 'I'd like to move on now to the . . . thinking behind the Declaration. You say your motives aren't religious?'

'No, not at all.'

'Would you describe yourself as a pacifist?'

'I don't think so. I can't possibly say "*No* war is ever justified", because I haven't thought about it enough. Perhaps some wars are. Perhaps this one was when it started. I just don't think our war aims – *whatever they may be* – and we don't know – justify this level of slaughter.'

'And you say you *have* thought about your qualifications for saying that?'

'*Yes.* I'm only too well aware of how it sounds. A *second-lieutenant*, no less, saying "The war must stop". On the other hand, I have *been* there. I'm at least as well qualified as some of the old men you see sitting around in clubs, cackling on about "attrition" and "wastage of manpower" and . . .' His voice became a vicious parody of an old man's voice. '"*Lost heavily in that last scrap.*" You don't talk like that if you've watched them die.'

'No intelligent or sensitive person would talk like that anyway.'

A slightly awkward pause. 'I'm not saying there are no exceptions.'

Rivers laughed. 'The point is you hate civilians, don't you? The "callous", the "complacent", the "unimaginative". Or is "hate" too strong a word?'

'No.'

'So. What you felt for the Germans, rather briefly, in the spring of last year, you now feel for the overwhelming majority of your fellow-countrymen?'

'Yes.'

'You know, I think you were quite right not to say too much to the Board.'

'That wasn't my idea, it was Graves's. He was afraid I'd sound too sane.'

'When you said the Board was "rigged", what did you mean?'

'I meant the decision to send me here, or or somewhere similar, had been taken before I went in.'

'And this had all been fixed by Captain Graves?'

'Yes.' Sassoon leant forward. 'The point is they weren't going to court-martial me. They were just going to lock me up somewhere . . .' He looked round the room. '*Worse* than this.'

Rivers smiled. 'There *are* worse places, believe me.'

'I'm sure there are,' Sassoon said politely.

'They were going to certify you, in fact?'

'I suppose so.'

'Did anybody on the Board say anything to you about this?'

'No, because it was –'

'All fixed beforehand. Yes, I see.'

Sassoon said, 'May I ask you a question?'

'Go ahead'

'Do *you* think I'm mad?'

'No, of course you're not mad. Did you think you were going mad?'

'It crossed my mind. You know when you're brought face to face with the fact that, yes, you did see corpses on the pavement . . .'

'Hallucinations in the half-waking state are surprisingly common, you know. They're not the same thing as psychotic hallucinations. Children have them quite frequently.'

Sassoon had started pulling at a loose thread on the breast of his tunic. Rivers watched him for a while. 'You must've been in agony when you did that.'

Sassoon lowered his hand. 'No-o. *Agony's* lying in a shell-hole with your legs shot off. I was *upset*.' For a moment he looked almost hostile, then he relaxed. 'It was a futile gesture. I'm not particularly proud of it.'

'You threw it in the Mersey, didn't you?'

'Yes. It wasn't heavy enough to sink, so it just' – a glint of amusement – '*bobbed* around. There was a ship sailing past, quite a long way out, in the estuary, and I looked at this little scrap of ribbon floating and I looked at the ship, and I thought that me trying to stop the war was a bit like trying to stop the ship would have been. You know, all they'd've seen from the deck was this little figure jumping up and down, waving its arms, and they wouldn't've known what on earth it was getting so excited about.'

'So you realized *then* that it was futile?'

Sassoon lifted his head. 'It still had to be done. You can't just acquiesce.'

Rivers hesitated. 'Look, I think we've . . . we've got about as far as we can get today. You must be very tired.' He stood up. 'I'll see you tomorrow morning at ten. Oh, and could you ask Captain Graves to see me as soon as he arrives?'

Sassoon stood up. 'You said a bit back you didn't think I was mad.'

'I'm quite sure you're not. As a matter of fact I don't even think you've got a war neurosis.'

Sassoon digested this. 'What have I got, then?'

'You seem to have a very powerful *anti*-war neurosis.'

They looked at each other and laughed. Rivers said, 'You realize, don't you, that it's my duty to . . . to try to change that? I can't pretend to be neutral.'

Sassoon's glance took in both their uniforms. 'No, of course not.'

Rivers made a point of sitting next to Bryce at dinner.

'Well,' Bryce said, 'what did you make of him?'

'I can't find anything wrong. He doesn't show any sign of depression, he's not excited –'

'Physically?'

'Nothing.'

'Perhaps he just doesn't want to be killed.'

'Oh, I think he'd be most insulted if you suggested *that*. To be fair, he did have a job lined up in Cambridge, training cadets – so it isn't a question of avoiding being sent back. He could've taken that if he'd wanted to save his skin.'

'Any trace of . . . er . . . religious *enthusiasm*?'

'No, I'm afraid not. I was hoping for that too.'

They looked at each other, amused. 'You know, the curious thing is I don't think he's even a pacifist? It seems to be entirely a matter of horror at the extent of the slaughter, combined with a feeling of anger that the government won't state its war aims and impose some kind of *limitation* on the whole thing. That, and an absolutely corrosive hatred of civilians. *And* non-combatants in uniform.'

'What an uncomfortable time you must've had.'

'No-o, I rather gather I was seen as an exception.'

Bryce looked amused. 'Did *you* like *him*?'

'Yes, very much. And I found him . . . much more *impressive* than I expected.'

Sassoon, at his table under the window, sat in silence. The men on either side of him stammered so badly that conversation would have been impossible, even if he had wished for it, but he was content to withdraw into his own thoughts.

He remembered the day before Arras, staggering from the outpost trench to the main trench and back again, carrying boxes of trench mortar bombs, passing the same corpses time after time, until their twisted and blackened shapes began to seem like old friends. At one point he'd had to pass two hands sticking up out of a heap of pocked and pitted chalk, like the roots of an overturned tree. No way of telling if they were British or German hands. No way of persuading himself it mattered.

'Do you play golf?'

'I'm sorry?'

'I asked if you played golf.'

Small blue eyes, nibbled gingery moustache, an RAMC badge. He held out his hand. 'Ralph Anderson.'

Sassoon shook hands and introduced himself. 'Yes, I do.'

'What's your handicap?'

Sassoon told him. After all, why not? It seemed an entirely suitable topic for Bedlam.

'Ah, then we might have a game.'

'I'm afraid I haven't brought my clubs.'

'Send for them. Some of the best courses in the country round here.'

Sassoon had opened his mouth to reply when a commotion started near the door. As far as he could tell, somebody seemed to have been sick. At any rate, a thin, yellow-skinned man was on his feet, choking and gagging. A couple of VADs ran across to him, clucking, fussing, flapping ineffectually at his tunic with a napkin, until eventually they had the sense to get him out of the room. The swing doors closed behind them. A moment's silence, and then, as if nothing had happened, the buzz of conversation rose again.

Rivers stood up and pushed his plate away. 'I think I'd better go.'

'Why not wait till you've finished?' Bryce said. 'You eat little enough as it is.'

Rivers patted his midriff. 'Oh, I shan't fade away just yet.'

Whenever Rivers wanted to get to the top floor without being stopped half a dozen times on the way, he used the back staircase. Pipes lined the walls, twisting with the turning of the stair, gurgling from time to time like lengths of human intestine. It was dark, the air stuffy, and sweat began to prickle in the roots of his hair. It was a relief to push the swing door open and come out on to the top corridor, where the air was cool at least, though he never failed to be depressed by the long narrow passage with its double row of brown doors and the absence of natural light. 'Like a trench without the sky' had been one patient's description, and he was afraid it was only too accurate.

Burns was sitting on his bed, while two VADs helped him off with his tunic and shirt. His collar bones and ribs were clearly visible beneath the yellowish skin. The waistband of his breeches gaped.

One of the VADs tugged at it. 'There's room for two in there,' she said, smiling, coaxing. 'Have I to get in with you?' The other VAD's frozen expression warned her of Rivers's presence. 'I'll get this sponged down for you, Captain.'

They hurried past Rivers, bursting into nervous giggles as they reached the end of the corridor.

Burns's arms were goose-pimpled, though the room was not cold. The smell of vomit lingered on his breath. Rivers sat down beside him. He didn't know what to say, and thought it better to say nothing. After a while he felt the bed begin to shake and put his arm round Burns's shoulders. 'It doesn't get any better, does it?' he said.

Burns shook his head. After a while Rivers got up, fetched Burns's coat from the peg behind the door and wrapped it round his shoulders. 'Would it be easier to eat in your own room?'

'A bit. I wouldn't have to worry about upsetting other people.'

Yes, Burns *would* worry about upsetting other people. Perhaps the most distressing feature of his case was the occasional glimpse of the cheerful and likeable young man he must once have been.

Rivers looked down at Burns's forearms, noting that the groove between radius and ulna was even deeper than it had been a week ago. 'Would it help to have a bowl of fruit in your room?' he asked. 'So you could just pick something up when you felt like it?'

'Yes, that might help.'

Rivers got up and walked across to the window. He's agreeing to make me feel useful, he thought. 'All right, I'll get them to send something up.' The shadows of the beech trees had begun to creep across the tennis courts, which were empty now. Rivers turned from the window. 'What kind of night did you have?'

'Not too good.'

'Have you made any progress with what we talked about?'

'Not really.' He looked up at Rivers. 'I can't make myself think about it.'

'No, well, it's early days.'

'You know, the worst thing is . . .' – Burns was scanning Rivers's face – 'that it's a . . . a joke.'

'Yes.'

After leaving Burns, Rivers went up a further short flight of stairs and unlocked the door to the tower. Apart from his own bedroom, this was the only place in Craiglockhart he could hope to be alone for more than a few minutes. The patients weren't allowed out here, in case the hundred-foot drop to the path below should prove too tempting an exit from the war. He rested his arms on the iron balustrade and looked out towards the hills.

Burns. Rivers had become adept at finding bearable aspects to unbearable experiences, but Burns defeated him. What had happened to him was so vile, so disgusting, that Rivers could find no redeeming feature. He'd been thrown into the air by the explosion of a shell and had landed, head-first, on a German corpse, whose gas-filled belly had ruptured on impact. Before Burns lost consciousness, he'd had time to realize that what filled his nose and mouth was decomposing human flesh. Now, whenever he tried to eat, that taste and smell recurred. Nightly, he relived the experience, and from every nightmare he awoke vomiting. Burns on his knees, as Rivers had often seen him, retching up the last ounce of bile, hardly looked like a human being at all. His body seemed to have become merely the skin-and-bone casing for a tormented alimentary canal. His suffering was without purpose or dignity, and yes, Rivers knew *exactly* what Burns meant when he said it was a joke.

Rivers became aware that he was gripping the edge of the parapet and consciously relaxed his hands. Whenever he spent any time with Burns, he found himself plagued by questions that in Cambridge, in peacetime, he might have wanted to pursue, but which in wartime, in an overcrowded hospital, were no use to him at all. Worse than useless, since they drained him of energy that rightly belonged to his patients. In a way, all this had nothing to do with Burns. The sheer extremity of his suffering set him apart from the rest, but the questions were evoked by almost every case.

He looked down and saw a taxi turn into the drive. Perhaps this was the errant Captain Graves arriving at last? Yes, there was Sassoon, too impatient to wait indoors, running down the steps to meet him.

THREE

Graves, his mouth slightly open, stared up at the massive yellow-grey façade of Craiglockhart. '*My God.*'

Sassoon followed the direction of his gaze. 'That's what I thought.'

Graves picked up his bag and together they went up the steps, through the black and white tiled entrance hall on to the main corridor. Sassoon began to smile. 'Fine prisoner's escort you turned out to be.'

'I know, I'm sorry. God, what a day. Do you know, the train stopped at *every* station?'

'Well, you're here now. Thank God.'

Graves looked sideways at him. 'As bad as that?'

'Hm. So-so.'

'I don't suppose you've seen anybody yet?'

'I've seen Rivers. Which reminds me, he wants to see *you*, but I imagine it'll be all right if you dump your bag first.'

Graves followed Sassoon up the marble staircase to the first floor.

'Here we are.' Sassoon opened a door and stood aside to let Graves enter. 'The guest room. You've even got a lock on your door.'

'You haven't?'

'No. Nor in the bathroom either.'

'Poor old Sass, you'll just have to *fight* the VADs off.' Graves swung his bag on to the nearest chair. 'No, seriously, what's it like?'

'Seriously, it's *awful*. Come on, the sooner you've seen Rivers the sooner we can talk.'

'Sassoon asked me to give you this.'

Rivers took the envelope without comment and placed it unopened on his desk. 'How did you find him?'

The net curtains breathed in the draught from the open window, and a scent of lime trees invaded the room. A sweet smell. Graves, to whom all sweet smells were terrible, wiped the sweat from his upper lip. 'Calmer. I think it's a relief to have things sorted out.'

'I don't know how sorted out they are. You do realize, don't you, that he can walk out of here at any time?'

'He won't do that,' Graves said definitely. 'He'll be all right now. As long as the pacifists leave him alone.'

'I had quite a long talk with him this afternoon, but I don't think

I'm quite clear what happened. I suspect there was a lot going on behind the scenes?'

Graves smiled. 'You could say that.'

'What exactly?'

'Sassoon sent me a copy of his Declaration. I was in a convalescent home on the Isle of Wight at the time –'

'He hadn't talked to you about it?'

'No, I haven't seen him since January. I was absolutely horrified. I could see at once it wouldn't do any good, nobody would follow his example. He'd just destroy himself, for no reason.' He stopped. When he spoke again, his voice was very clear and precise. 'Sassoon's the best platoon commander I've ever known. The men worship him – if he wanted German heads on a platter they'd get them. And *he* loves them. Being separated from them would kill him. And that's exactly what a court-martial would've done.'

'He's separated from them here.'

'Yes, but there's a way back. People can accept a breakdown. There's no way back from being a conchie.'

'So you decided he –'

'Had to be stopped? Yes. I wrote to the CO, asking him to get Siegfried another Board. He'd already skipped one. Then I contacted various people I know and managed to persuade them to treat it as a nervous breakdown. That left Siegfried. I knew it was no use writing. I had to see him, so I got myself passed fit and went back to Litherland. He was in a *shocking* state. He'd just thrown his MC into the Mersey. Did he tell you that?'

Rivers hesitated. 'I believe it was in the Board's report.'

'Anyway, it took a long time, but he saw sense in the end.'

'What made him give in, do you think?'

'He just couldn't go on denying he was ill.'

Rivers didn't reply. The silence deepened, like a fall of snow, accumulating second by second, flake by flake, each flake by itself inconsiderable, until everything is transformed.

'No, it wasn't that.' Graves's knobbly, broken-nosed boxer's face twitched. 'I lied to him.'

Rivers's glasses flashed as he lifted his head. 'Yes, I thought perhaps you had.'

'I swore on the Bible they wouldn't court-martial him, but I didn't know that. I think if he'd held out, they might've done.'

'They might. But you know the advantages of treating this as a nervous breakdown would have been quite apparent to the authorities, even without your pointing them out.'

'The fact remains I lied, and he gave in because he believed the lie. He wouldn't have believed it from anybody else.' He paused. 'Do *you* think I was wrong?'

Rivers said gently, 'I think you did the best you could for your friend. Not the best thing for his *cause*, but then the cause is lost anyway. Did you find the Board difficult to convince?'

'Quite. There was one youngish man who was sympathetic. The other two . . . Well. I got the impression they didn't believe in shell-shock at all. As far as they were concerned, it was just cowardice. I made up my mind right from the start they weren't going to think that. I told them about last year when he took a German trench single-handed and got recommended for the VC. I'd like to see *them* do it. And this April. You know, that bombing expedition of his was fantastic. Everybody I've spoken to who was there thinks he should've got the VC for *that*.' He paused. 'I just wanted them to know what kind of man they were dealing with.' He smiled. 'I kept bursting into tears. I think that helped in a way. I could see them thinking, My God, if this one's fit for duty what *can* the other one be like?'

'And you told them that he had hallucinations?'

'Yes.' Graves looked slightly uncomfortable. 'I had to convince them. There were a lot of things I *didn't* tell them. I didn't tell them he'd threatened to kill Lloyd George.'

'And you persuaded him to say nothing?'

'Yes. The last thing we needed was Siegfried talking sense about the war.'

'*Sense?* You mean you agree with him?'

'Well, yes. In *theory*. In *theory* the war should stop tomorrow, but it won't. It'll go on till there isn't a cat or a dog left to enlist.'

'So you agree with his views, but not his actions? Isn't that rather an artificial distinction?'

'No, I don't think it is. The way I see it, when you put the uniform on, in effect you sign a contract. And you don't back out of a contract merely because you've changed your mind. You can still speak up for your principles, you can argue against the ones you're being made to fight for, but in the end you *do the job*. And I think that way you gain more respect. Siegfried isn't going to change people's minds like this. It may be *in him* to change people's minds about the war, but *this* isn't the way to do it.'

Rivers took his clasped hands away from his mouth. 'I couldn't agree with you more.'

'What's infuriating is that basically *he* knows it better than anybody. He's the one who can communicate with the ordinary soldier. It's just that he got taken over by Bertrand Russell and Ottoline Morrell. You know, I used to admire them. I used to think, well, I don't agree with you, but, on the other hand, I can see it takes *courage* . . .' He shook his head. 'Not any more. I know Russell's over military age, Ottoline's a woman, fair enough, neither of them can understand what he's been through, but they *could* see the state he was in, *and they still went ahead.* They were quite prepared to destroy him for the sake of propagating their views. I don't forgive them for it.' He made a visible effort to calm down. 'Anyway, it's over now. But I must say it gave me great pleasure to write to Russell and tell him Sassoon was on his way here, and he could just *bloody well leave him alone* in future.'

'And what about you?' Rivers asked, after a pause. 'Do you think they'll send you back?'

'No, I don't think so. In fact, the battalion doctor told me if he ever found my lungs in France again, he'd shoot me himself. I'm hoping for Palestine.' A pause. 'I'm glad he's here. At least I can go back to Litherland knowing he's safe.'

'I hope he is.' Rivers stood up. 'And now I think I should let you get back to him. He'll need company on his first evening.'

After Graves had gone, Rivers sat for a while resting his eyes, then opened the envelope Graves had given him. Three sheets of paper. On the top sheet, dated the 22nd April, Sassoon had written in pencil, 'I wrote these in hospital ten days after I was wounded.'

> Groping along the tunnel in the gloom
> He winked his tiny torch with whitening glare,
> And bumped his helmet, sniffing the hateful air.
> Tins, boxes, bottles, shapes too vague to know,
> And once, the foul, hunched mattress from a bed;
> And he exploring, fifty feet below
> The rosy dusk of battle overhead.
> He tripped and clutched the walls; saw someone lie
> Humped and asleep, half-covered with a rug;
> He stooped and gave the sleeper's arm a tug.
> 'I'm looking for headquarters.' No reply.
> 'Wake up, you sod!' (For days *he'd* had no sleep.)

'I want a guide along this cursed place.'
He aimed a kick at the unanswering heap;
And flashed his beam across that livid face
Horribly glaring up, whose eyes still wore
The agony that died ten days before
Whose bloody fingers clutched a hideous wound.
Gasping, he staggered onward till he found
Dawn's ghost that filtered down a shafted stair,
To clammy creatures groping underground,
Hearing the boom of shells with muffled sound.
Then with the sweat of horror in his hair,
He climbed with darkness to the twilight air.

The General

'Good morning, good morning!' the General said
When we met him last week on our way to the line.
Now the soldiers he smiled at are most of 'em dead,
And we're cursing his staff for incompetent swine.
'He's a cheery old card,' muttered Harry to Jack
As they slogged up to Arras with rifle and pack.

. . .

But he did for them both with his plan of attack.

To the Warmongers

I'm back again from hell
With loathsome thoughts to sell;
Secrets of death to tell;
And horrors from the abyss.
Young faces bleared with blood,
Sucked down into the mud,
You shall hear things like this,
Till the tormented slain
Crawl round and once again,
With limbs that twist awry
Moan out their brutish pain,
As the fighters pass them by.

For you our battles shine
With triumph half-divine;
And the glory of the dead
Kindles in each proud eye.
But a curse is on my head,
That shall not be unsaid,
And the wounds in my heart are red,
For I have watched them die.

Rivers knew so little about poetry that he was almost embarrassed at the thought of having to comment on these. But then he reminded himself they'd been given to him as a therapist, not as a literary critic, and from that point of view they were certainly interesting, particularly the last.

Everything about the poem suggested that Sassoon's attitude to his war experience had been the opposite of what one normally encountered. The typical patient, arriving at Craiglockhart, had usually been devoting considerable energy to the task of *forgetting* whatever traumatic events had precipitated his neurosis. Even if the patient recognized that the attempt was hopeless, he had usually been encouraged to persist in it by friends, relatives, even by his previous medical advisers. The horrors he'd experienced, only partially repressed even by day, returned with redoubled force to haunt the nights, giving rise to that most characteristic symptom of war neurosis: the battle nightmare.

Rivers's treatment sometimes consisted simply of encouraging the patient to abandon his hopeless attempt to forget, and advising him instead to spend some part of every day remembering. Neither brooding on the experience, nor trying to pretend it had never happened. Usually, within a week or two of the patient's starting this treatment, the nightmares began to be less frequent and less terrifying.

Sassoon's determination to remember might well account for his early and rapid recovery, though in his case it was motivated less by a desire to save his own sanity than by a determination to convince civilians that the war was mad. Writing the poems had obviously been therapeutic, but then Rivers suspected that writing the Declaration might have been therapeutic too. He thought that Sassoon's poetry and his protest sprang from a single source, and each could be linked to his recovery from that terrible period of nightmares and hallucinations. If that was true, then persuading Sassoon to give in and go back would be a much more complicated and risky business than he had thought, and might well precipitate a relapse.

He sighed and put the poems back in the envelope. Looking at his watch, he saw that it was time to start his rounds. He'd just reached the foot of the main staircase when he saw Captain Campbell, bent double and walking backwards, emerge from the darkened dining room.

'Campbell?'

Campbell spun round. 'Ah, Captain Rivers, just the man.' He came up to Rivers and, speaking in a discreet whisper that was audible the length and breadth of the corridor, as Campbell's discreet whispers tended to be, said, 'That fella they've put in my room.'

'Sassoon. Yes?'

'Don't think he's a German spy, do you?'

Rivers gave the matter careful consideration. 'No, I don't think so. They *never* call themselves "Siegfried".'

Campbell looked astonished. 'No more they do.' He nodded, patted Rivers briskly on the shoulder, and moved off. 'Just thought I'd mention it,' he called back.

'Thank you, Campbell. Much appreciated.'

Rivers stood for a moment at the foot of the stairs, unconsciously shaking his head.

FOUR

'I was walking up the drive at home. My wife was on the lawn having tea with some other ladies, they were all wearing white. As I got closer, my wife stood up and smiled and waved and then her expression changed and all the other ladies began to look at each other. I couldn't understand why, and then I looked down and saw that I was naked.'

'What had you been wearing?'

'Uniform. When I saw how frightened they were, it made *me* frightened. I started to run and I was running through bushes. I was being chased by my father-in-law and two orderlies. Eventually they got me cornered and my father-in-law came towards me, waving a big stick. It had a snake wound round it. He was using it as a kind of flail, and the snake was hissing. I backed away, but they got hold of me and tied me up.'

Rivers detected a slight hesitation. 'What with?'

A pause. In determinedly casual tones Anderson said, 'A pair of lady's corsets. They fastened them round my arms and tied the laces.'

'Like a strait-waistcoat?'

'Yes.'

'Then?'

'Then I was carted off to some kind of carriage. I was thrown inside and the doors banged shut and it was very dark. Like a grave. The first time I looked it was empty, but then the next time you were there. You were wearing a post-mortem apron and gloves.'

It was obvious from his tone that he'd finished. Rivers smiled and said, 'It's a long time since I've worn those.'

'I haven't recently worn corsets.'

'Whose corsets were they?'

'Just corsets. You want me to say my wife's, don't you?'

Rivers was taken back. 'I want you to say –'

'Well, I really don't think they were. I suppose it is *possible* someone might find being locked up in a loony bin a fairly *emasculating* experience?'

'I think most people do.' Though not many said so. 'I want you to say what you think.'

No response.

'You say you woke up vomiting?'

'Yes.'

'I wonder why? I mean I can quite see the sight of me in a post-mortem apron might not be to everybody's taste –'

'I don't know.'

'What was the most frightening thing about the dream?'

'The snake.'

A long silence.

'Do you often dream about snakes?'

'Yes.'

Another long silence. 'Well, go on, then,' Anderson exploded at last. 'That's what you Freudian Johnnies are on about all the time, isn't it? Nudity, snakes, *corsets*. You might at least try to look *grateful*, Rivers. It's a gift.'

'I think if I'd made any association at all with the snake – and after all what possible relevance can my associations have? – it was probably with the one that's crawling up your lapel.'

Anderson looked down at the caduceus badge of the RAMC which he wore on his tunic, and then across at the same badge on Rivers's tunic.

'What the er snake *might* suggest is that medicine is an issue between yourself and your father-in-law?'

'No.'

'Not at all?'

'No.'

Another long silence. Anderson said, 'It depends what you mean by an issue.'

'A subject on which there is habitual disagreement.'

'No. Naturally my time in France has left me with a certain level of distaste for the practice of medicine, but that'll go in time. There's no *issue*. I have a wife and child to support.'

'You're how old?'

'Thirty-six.'

'And your little boy?'

Anderson's expression softened. 'Five.'

'School fees coming up?'

'Yes. I'll be all right once I've had a rest. Basically, I'm paying for last summer. Do you know, at one point we *averaged* ten amputations a day? Every time I was due for leave it was cancelled.' He looked straight at Rivers. 'There's no doubt what the problem is. Tiredness.'

'I still find the vomiting puzzling. Especially since you say you feel no more than a *mild* disinclination for medicine.'

'I didn't say mild, I said temporary.'

'Ah. What in particular do you find difficult?'

'I don't know that there *is* anything *particular*.'

A long silence.

Anderson said, 'I'm going to start timing these silences, Rivers.'

'It's already been done. Some of the younger ones had a sweepstake on it. I'm not supposed to know.'

'Blood.'

'And you attribute this to the ten amputations a day?'

'No, I was all right then. The . . . er . . . problem started later. I wasn't at Étaples when it happened, I'd been moved forward – the 13th CCS. They brought in this lad. He was a Frenchman, he'd escaped from the German lines. Covered in mud. There wasn't an inch of skin showing anywhere. And you know it's not like ordinary mud, it's five, six inches thick. Bleeding. Frantic with pain. No English.' A pause. 'I missed it. I treated the minor wounds and missed the major one.' He gave a short, hissing laugh. 'Not that the minor ones were all that minor. He started to haemorrhage, and . . . there was nothing I could do. I just stood there and watched him bleed to death.' His face twisted. 'It pumped out of him.'

It was a while before either of them stirred. Then Anderson said, 'If you're wondering why that one, I don't know. I've seen many worse deaths.'

'Have you told your family?'

'No. They know I don't like the idea of going back to medicine, but they don't know why.'

'Have you talked to your wife?'

'Now and then. You have to think about the *practicalities*, Rivers. I've devoted all my adult life to medicine. I've no private income to tide me over. And I do have *a wife and a child*.'

'Public health might be a possibility.'

'It doesn't have much . . . *dash* about it, does it?'

'Is that a consideration?'

Anderson hesitated. 'Not with me.'

'Well, we can talk about the practicalities later. You still haven't told me when you said *enough*.'

Anderson smiled. 'You make it sound like a decision. I don't know that lying on the floor in a pool of piss counts as a decision.' He paused. 'The following morning. *On the ward*. I remember them all looking down at me. Awkward situation, really. What do you do when the doctor breaks down?'

At intervals, as Rivers was doing his rounds as orderly officer for the day, he thought about this dream. It was disturbing in many ways. At first he'd been inclined to see the post-mortem apron as expressing no more than a lack of faith in *him*, or, more accurately, in his methods, since obviously any doctor who spends much time so attired is not meeting with uniform success on the wards. This lack of faith he knew to be present. Anderson, in his first interview, had virtually refused treatment, claiming that rest, the endless pursuit of golf balls, was all that he required. He had some knowledge of Freud, though derived mainly from secondary or prejudiced sources, and disliked, or perhaps feared, what he thought he knew. There was no particular reason why Anderson, who was, after all, a surgeon, should be well informed about Freudian therapy, but his misconceptions had resulted in a marked reluctance to reveal his dreams. Yet his dreams could hardly be ignored, if only because they were currently keeping the whole of one floor of the hospital awake. His room-mate, Featherstone, had deteriorated markedly as the result of Anderson's nightly outbursts. Still, that was another problem. As soon as Anderson had revealed that extreme horror of blood, Rivers had begun tentatively to attach another meaning to the post-mortem apron. If Anderson could see no way out of returning to the practice of a profession which must inevitably, even in civilian life, recall the horrors he'd witnessed in France, then perhaps he was desperate enough to have considered suicide? That might account both for the post-mortem apron and for the extreme terror he'd felt on waking. At the moment he didn't know Anderson well enough to be able to say whether suicide was a possibility or not, but it would certainly need to be borne in mind.

The smell of chlorine became stronger as they reached the bottom of the stairs. Sassoon felt Graves hesitate. 'Are you all right?'

'I could do without the smell.'

'Well, let's not bother –'

'No, go on.'

Sassoon pushed the door open. The pool was empty, a green slab between white walls. They began to undress, putting their clothes on one of the benches that lined the end wall.

'What's your room-mate like?' Graves asked.

'All right.'

'Dotty?'

'Not visibly. I gather the subject of German spies is best avoided. Oh, and I've found out why there aren't any locks on the doors. One of them killed himself three weeks ago.'

Graves caught sight of the scar on Sassoon's shoulder and stopped to look at it. It was curiously restful to submit to this scrutiny, which was prolonged, detailed and impersonal, like one small boy examining the scabs on another's knee. 'Oh, *very* neat.'

'Yes, isn't it? The doctors kept telling me how beautiful it was.'

'You were lucky, you know. An inch further down –'

'Not as lucky as you.' Sassoon glanced at the shrapnel wound on Graves's thigh. 'An inch further up –'

'If this is leading up to a joke about ladies' choirs, forget it. I've heard them all.'

Sassoon dived in. A green, silent world, no sound except the bubble of his escaping breath, no feeling, once the shock of cold was over, except the tightening of his chest that at last forced him to the surface, air, noise, light, slopping waves crashing in on him again. He swam to the side and held on. Graves's dark head bobbed purposefully along at the other side of the pool. Sassoon thought, we joke about it, but it happens. There'd been a boy in the hospital, while he was lying there with that neat little hole in his shoulder. The boy – he couldn't have been more than nineteen – had a neat little hole too. Only his was between the legs. The dressings had been terrible to witness, and you had to witness them. No treatment in that overcrowded ward had been private. Twice a day the nurses came in with the creaking trolley, and the boy's eyes followed them up the ward.

Sassoon shut the lid on the memory and dived for Graves's legs. Graves twisted and fought, his head a black rock splintering white foam. 'Lay off,' he gasped at last, pushing Sassoon away. 'Some of us don't have the full complement of lungs.'

The pool was beginning to fill up. After a few more minutes, they climbed out and started to dress. Head muffled in the folds of his shirt, Graves said, 'By the way, I think there's something I ought to tell you. I'm afraid I told Rivers about your plan to assassinate Lloyd George.'

Rivers's round as duty officer ended in the kitchens. Mrs Cooper, her broad arms splashed with fat from giant frying-pans, greeted him with an embattled smile. 'What d' y' think of the beef stew last night, then, sir?'

'I don't believe I've ever tasted anything quite like it.'

Mrs Cooper's smile broadened. 'We do the best we can with the materials available, sir.' Her expression became grim and confiding. 'That beef was *walking*.'

Rivers got to his room a few minutes after ten and found Sassoon waiting, his hair damp, smelling of chlorine. 'I'm sorry I'm late,' Rivers said, unlocking the door. 'I've just been pretending to know something about catering. Come in.' He waved Sassoon to the chair in front of the desk, tossed his cap and cane to one side, and was about to unbuckle his belt when he remembered that the Director of Medical Services was due to visit the hospital some time that day. He sat down behind the desk and drew Sassoon's file towards him. 'Did you sleep well?'

'Very well, thank you.'

'You look rested. I enjoyed meeting Captain Graves.'

'Yes, I gather you found it quite informative.'

'*Ah.*' Rivers paused in the act of opening the file. 'You mean he told me something you'd rather I didn't know?'

'No, not necessarily. Just something I might have preferred to tell you myself.' A moment's silence, then Sassoon burst out, 'What I can't understand is how somebody of Graves's intelligence can can can have such a shaky grasp of of *rhetoric*.'

Rivers smiled. 'You were going to kill Lloyd George rhetorically, were you?'

'I wasn't going to kill him at all. I said I *felt* like killing him, but it was no use, because they'd only shut me up in a lunatic asylum, "like Richard Dadd of glorious memory". There you are, *exact words*.' He looked round the room. 'Though as things have turned out –'

'This is *not* a lunatic asylum. You are *not* locked up.'

'Sorry.'

'What you're really saying is that Graves took you too seriously.'

'It's not just that. It suits him to attribute everything I've done to to to to . . . a state of mental breakdown, because then he doesn't have to ask himself any awkward questions. Like why he agrees with me about the war and does nothing about it.'

Rivers waited a few moments. 'I know Richard Dadd was a painter. What else did he do?'

A short silence. 'He murdered his father.'

Rivers was puzzled by the slight awkwardness. He was used to being adopted as a father figure – he was, after all, thirty years older than the youngest of his patients – but it was rare for it to happen as quickly as this in a man of Sassoon's age. '"Of *glorious* memory"?'

'He . . . er . . . made a list of old men in power who deserved to die, and fortunately – or or otherwise – his father's name headed the list. He carried him for half a mile through Hyde Park and then drowned him in the Serpentine in full view of everybody on the banks. The only reason Graves and I know about him is that we were in trenches with two of his great nephews, Edmund and Julian.' The slight smile faded. 'Now Edmund's dead, and Julian's got a bullet in the throat and can't speak. The other brother was killed too. Gallipoli.'

'Like your brother.'

'Yes.'

'Your father's dead too, isn't he? How old were you when he died?'

'Eight. But I hadn't seen much of him for some time before that. He left home when I was five.'

'Do you remember him?'

'A bit. I remember I used to like being kissed by him because his moustache tickled. My brothers went to the funeral. I didn't – apparently I was too upset. Probably just as well, because they came back terrified. It was a Jewish funeral, you see, and they couldn't understand what was going on. My elder brother said it was two old men in funny hats walking up and down saying jabber-jabber-jabber.'

'You must've felt you'd lost him twice.'

'Yes. We did lose him twice.'

Rivers gazed out of the window. 'What difference would it have made, do you think, if your father had lived?'

A long silence. 'Better education.'

'But you went to Marlborough?'

'Yes, but I was *years* behind everybody else. Mother had this theory we were delicate and our brains shouldn't be taxed. I don't think I ever really caught up. I left Cambridge without taking my degree.'

'And then?'

Sassoon shook his head. 'Nothing much. Hunting, cricket. Writing poems. Not very good poems.'

'Didn't you find it all . . . rather unsatisfying?'

'Yes, but I couldn't seem to see a way out. It was like being three different people, and they all wanted to go different ways.' A slight smile. 'The result was I went nowhere.'

Rivers waited.

'I mean, there was the riding, hunting, cricketing me, and then there was the . . . the other side . . . that was interested in poetry and music, and things like that. And I didn't seem able to . . .' He laced his fingers. 'Knot them together.'

'And the third?'

'I'm sorry?'

'You said three.'

'Did I? I meant two.'

Ah. 'And then the war. You joined up on the first day?'

'Yes, in the ranks. I couldn't wait to get in.'

'Your superior officers wrote glowing reports for the Board. Did you know that?'

A flush of pleasure. 'I think the army's probably the only place I've ever really belonged.'

'And you've cut yourself off from it.'

'Yes, because –'

'I'm not interested in the reasons at the moment. I'm more interested in the result. The effect on you.'

'Isolation, I suppose. I can't talk to anybody.'

'You talk to *me*. Or at least, I think you do.'

'You don't say stupid things.'

Rivers turned his head away. 'I'm pleased about that.'

'Go on, *laugh*. I don't mind.'

'You'd been offered a job in Cambridge, hadn't you? Teaching cadets.'

Sassoon frowned. 'Yes.'

'But you didn't take it?'

'No. It was either prison or France.' He laughed. 'I didn't foresee this.'

Rivers watched him staring round the room. 'You can't bear to be safe, can you?' He waited for a reply. 'Well, you've got twelve weeks of it. *At least.* If you go on refusing to serve, you'll be safe for the rest of the war.'

Two red spots appeared on Sassoon's cheekbones. 'Not *my* choice.'

'I didn't say it was.' Rivers paused. 'You know you reacted then as if I were attacking you, and yet all I did was to point out *the facts*.' He leant forward. 'If you maintain your protest, you can expect to spend the remainder of the war in a state of Complete. Personal. Safety.'

Sassoon shifted in his seat. 'I'm not responsible for other people's decisions.'

'You don't think you might find being safe while other people *die* rather difficult?'

A flash of anger. 'Nobody else in this *stinking* country seems to find it difficult. I expect I'll just learn to live with it. Like everybody else.'

Burns stood at the window of his room. Rain had blurred the landscape, dissolving sky and hills together in a wash of grey. He loathed wet weather because then everybody stayed indoors, sitting around the patients' common room, talking, in strained or facetious tones, about the war the war the war.

A sharper gust of wind blew rain against the glass. Somehow or other he was going to have to get out. It wasn't forbidden, it was even encouraged, though he himself didn't go out much. He got his coat and went downstairs. On the corridor he met one of the nurses from his ward, who looked surprised to see him wearing his coat, but didn't ask where he was going.

At the main gates he stopped. Because he'd been inside so long, the possibilities seemed endless, though they resolved themselves quickly into two. *Into* Edinburgh, or away. And that was no choice at all: he knew he wasn't up to facing traffic.

For the first few stops the bus was crowded. He sat on the bench seat close to the door of the bus. People smelling of wet wool jerked and swayed against him, bumping his knees, and he tensed, not liking the contact or the smell. But then at every stop more and more people got off until he was almost alone, except for an old man and the clippie. The lanes were narrower now; the trees rushed in on either side. A branch rattled along the windows with a sound like machine-gun fire, and he had to bite his lips to stop himself crying out.

He got off at the next stop, and stood, looking up and down a country lane. He didn't know what to do at first, it was so long since he'd been anywhere alone. Raindrops dripped from the trees, big, splashy, persistent drops, finding the warm place between his collar and his neck. He looked up and down the lane again. Somewhere further along, a wood pigeon cooed monotonously. He crossed over and began climbing the hill between the trees.

Up, up, until his way was barred by a fence whose wire twitched in the wind. A tuft of grey wool had caught on one of the barbs. Burns blinked the rain out of his eyes. He pressed two strands of wire apart and eased himself through, catching his sleeve, and breaking into a sweat as he struggled to free it.

Trembling now, he began to scramble along the edge of the ploughed field, slipping and stumbling, his mud-encumbered boots like lead weights pulling on the muscles of his thighs. His body was cold inside the stiff khaki, except for a burning round the knees where the tight cloth chafed the skin.

He was walking up the slope of a hill, tensing himself against the wind that seemed to be trying to scrape him off its side. As he reached the crest, a fiercer gust snatched his breath. After that he kept his head bent, sometimes stopping to draw a deeper breath through the steeple of his cupped hands. Rain beat on to his head, dripping from the peak of his cap, the small bones of nose and jaw had started to sing. He stopped and looked across the field. The distance had vanished in a veil of rain. He didn't know where he was going, or why, but he thought he ought to take shelter, and began to run clumsily along the brow of a hill towards a distant clump of trees. The mud dragged at him, he had to slow to a walk. Every step was a separate effort, hauling his mud-clogged boots out of the sucking earth. His mind was incapable of making comparisons, but his aching thighs remembered, and he listened for the whine of shells.

When at last he reached the trees, he sat down with his back to the nearest, and for a while did nothing at all, not even wipe away the drops of rain that gathered on the tip of his nose and dripped into his open mouth. Then, blinking, he dragged his wet sleeve across his face.

After a while he got to his feet and began stumbling, almost blindly, between the trees, catching his feet in clumps of bracken. Something brushed against his cheek, and he raised his hand to push it away. His fingers touched slime, and he snatched them back. He turned and saw a dead mole, suspended, apparently, in air, its black fur spiked with blood, its small pink hands folded on its chest.

Looking up, he saw that the tree he stood under was laden with dead animals. Bore them like fruit. A whole branch of moles in various stages of decay, a ferret, a weasel, three magpies, a fox, the fox hanging quite close, its lips curled back from bloodied teeth.

He started to run, but the trees were against him. Branches clipped his face, twigs tore at him, roots tripped him. Once he was sent sprawling, though immediately he was up again, and running, his coat a mess of mud and dead leaves.

Out in the field, splashing along the flooded furrows, he heard Rivers's voice, as distinctly as he sometimes heard it in dreams: *If you run now, you'll never stop.*

He turned and went back, though he knew the voice was only a voice in his head, and that the real Rivers might equally well have said: *Get away from here.* He stood again in front of the tree. Now that he was calmer, he remembered that he'd seen trees like this before. The animals were not nailed to it, as they sometimes were, but tied, by wings or paws or tails. He started to release a magpie, his teeth chattering as a wing came away in his hand. Then the other magpies, the fox, the weasel, the ferret and the moles.

When all the corpses were on the ground, he arranged them in a circle round the tree and sat down within it, his back against the trunk. He felt the roughness of the bark against his knobbly spine. He pressed his hands between his knees and looked around the circle of his companions. Now they could dissolve into the earth as they were meant to do. He felt a great urge to lie down beside them, but his clothes separated him. He got up and started to get undressed. When he'd finished, he looked down at himself. His naked body was white as a root. He cupped his genitals in his hands, not because he was ashamed, but because they looked incongruous, they didn't seem to belong with the rest of him. Then he folded his clothes carefully and put them outside the circle. He sat down again with his back to the tree and looked up through the tracery of branches at grey and scudding clouds.

The sky darkened, the air grew colder, but he didn't mind. It didn't occur to him to move. This was the right place. This was where he had wanted to be.

By late afternoon Burns's absence was giving cause for concern. The nurse who'd seen him walk out, wearing his coat, blamed herself for not stopping him, but nobody else was inclined to blame her. The patients, except for one or two who were known to be high suicide risks, were free to come and go as they pleased. Bryce and Rivers consulted together at intervals during the day, trying to decide at what point they should give in and call the police.

Burns came back at six o'clock, walking up the stairs unobserved, trailing mud, twigs and dead leaves. He was too tired to think. His legs ached; he was faint with hunger yet afraid to think of food.

Sister Duffy caught him just as he was opening the door of his room and bore down upon him, scolding and twittering like the small, dusty brown bird she so much resembled. She made him get undressed then and there and seemed to be proposing to towel him down herself, but he vetoed that. She left him alone but came back a few minutes later, laden with hot-water bottles and extra blankets, still inclined to scold, though when she saw how tired he looked, lying back against the pillows, she checked herself and only said ominously that Dr Rivers had been informed and would be up as soon as he was free.

I suppose I'm for it, Burns thought, but couldn't make the thought real. He folded his arms across his face and almost at once began drifting off to sleep. He was back in the wood, outside the circle now, but able to see himself inside it. His skin was tallow-white against the scurfy bark. A shaft of sunlight filtered through leaves, found one of the magpies, and its feathers shone sapphire, emerald, amethyst. There was no reason to go back, he thought. He could stay here for ever.

When he opened his eyes, Rivers was sitting beside the bed. He'd obviously been there some time, his glasses were in his lap, and one hand covered his eyes. The room was quite dark.

Rivers seemed to feel Burns watching him, because after a few moments he looked up and smiled.

'How long have I been asleep?'

'About an hour.'

'I've worried everybody, haven't I?'

'Never mind that. You're back, that's all that matters.'

All the way back to the hospital Burns had kept asking himself why he was going back. Now, waking up to find Rivers sitting by his bed, unaware of being observed, tired and patient, he realized he'd come back for this.

FIVE

Rivers started his night round early. Sister Rogers was in her room, drinking the first of the many cups of coffee that would see her through the night. 'Second-Lieutenant Prior,' she said, as soon as she saw him.

'Yes, I know, and there's nothing I can do about it.' Prior was a new patient, whose nightmares were so bad that his room-mate was getting no sleep. 'Has he spoken to anybody yet?'

'No, and if you speak to him he just stares straight through you.'

It was unlike Sister Rogers to take a dislike to a patient, but there was no mistaking the animosity in her voice. 'All right,' Rivers said, 'let's have a look at him.'

Prior was lying on his bed, reading. He was a thin, fair-haired young man of twenty-two with high cheekbones, a short, blunt nose and a supercilious expression. He looked up as Rivers came in, but didn't close the book.

'Sister tells me you had a bad night?'

Prior produced an elaborate shrug. Out of the corner of his eye Rivers saw Sister Rogers's lips tighten. 'What did you dream about?'

Prior reached for the notepad and pencil he kept beside his bed and scrawled in block capitals, 'I DON'T REMEMBER.'

'Nothing at all?'

Prior hesitated, then wrote, 'NO.'

'Does he talk in his sleep, sister?'

Rivers was looking at Prior as he asked the question, and thought he detected a flicker of uneasiness.

'Nothing you can get hold of.'

Prior's lips curled, but he couldn't hide the relief.

'Could you get me a teaspoon, sister?' Rivers asked.

While she was out of the room, Prior went on staring at Rivers. Rivers, trying to keep the meeting from becoming a confrontation, looked around the room. Sister Rogers came back. 'Thank you. Now I just want to have a look at the back of your throat.'

Again the pad came out. 'THERE'S NOTHING PHYSICALY WRONG.'

'Two l's in "physically", Mr Prior. Open wide.'

Rivers drew the end of the teaspoon, not roughly, but firmly, across the back of Prior's throat. Prior choked, his eyes watered, and he tried to push Rivers's hand away.

'There's no area of analgesia,' Rivers said to Sister Rogers.

Prior snatched up the pad. 'IF THAT MEANS IT HURT YES IT DID.'

'I don't think it *hurt*, did it?' Rivers said. 'It may have been uncomfortable.'

'HOW WOULD YOU KNOW?'

Sister Rogers made a clicking noise with her tongue.

'Do you think you could give us ten minutes alone, sister?'

'Yes, of course, doctor.' She glared at Prior. 'I'll be in my room if you need me.'

After she'd gone, Rivers said, 'Why do you always write in block capitals? Because it's less revealing?'

Prior shook his head. He wrote, 'CLEARER.'

'Depends on your handwriting, doesn't it? I know, if I ever lost *my* voice, I'd have to write in capitals. Nobody can read mine.'

Prior offered the pad. Rivers, feeling like a schoolboy playing noughts and crosses, wrote: 'Your file still hasn't arrived.'

'I SEE WHAT YOU MEAN.'

Rivers said, 'Your file still hasn't arrived.'

Another elaborate shrug.

'Well, I'm afraid it's rather more serious than that. If it doesn't show up soon, we're going to have to try to get a history together – like this. And that's not going to be easy.'

'WHY?'

'Why do we have to do it? Because I need to know what's happened to you.'

'I DON'T REMEMBER.'

'No, not at the moment, perhaps, but the memory will start to come back.'

A long silence. At last Prior scribbled something, then turned over on his side to face the wall. Rivers leant across and picked the pad up. Prior had written: 'NO MORE WORDS.'

'I must say it makes Dottyville almost bearable,' Sassoon said, looking up and down the station platform. 'Knowing you don't have to be vomited over at *every* meal. I'd eat out every night if I could afford it.'

'You'll have to spend *some* time in the place, Sass.' No reply. 'At least you've got Rivers.'

'And at least Rivers doesn't pretend there's anything wrong with my nerves.'

Graves started to speak and checked himself. 'I wish I could say the same about mine.'

'What can I say, Robert? Have my bed. *You* live with a herd of lunatics. I'll go back to Liverpool.'

'I hate it when you talk like that. As if everybody who breaks down is inferior. We've all been' – Graves held up his thumb and forefinger – 'that close.'

'I know how close I've been.' A short silence, then he burst out, 'Don't you see, Robert, that's why I hate the place? I'm frightened.'

'Frightened? *You?* You're not frightened.' He craned round to see Sassoon's expression. 'Are you?'

'Evidently not.'

They stood in silence for a minute.

'You ought to be getting back,' Graves said.

'Yes, I think you're right. I don't want to attract attention to myself.' He held out his hand. 'Well. Give everybody my regards. If they still want them.'

Graves took the hand and pulled him into a bear hug. 'Don't be so bloody stupid, Siegfried. You know they do.'

Alone and shivering on the pavement, Sassoon thought about taking a taxi and decided against it. The walk would do him good, and if he hurried he could probably make it back in time. He threaded his way through the crowds on Princes Street. Now that Robert was gone, he hated everybody, giggling girls, portly middle-aged men, women whose eyes settled on his wound stripe like flies. Only the young soldier home on leave, staggering out of a pub, dazed and vacant-eyed, escaped his disgust.

Once he'd left the city behind, he began to relax and swing along as he might have done in France. He remembered the march to Arras behind a limber whose swaying lantern cast huge shadows of striding legs across a white-washed wall. Then . . . No more walls. Ruined buildings. Shelled roads. 'From sunlight to the sunless land.' And for a second he was back there, Armageddon, Golgotha, there were no words, a place of desolation so complete no imagination could have invented it. He thought of Rivers, and what he'd said that morning about finding safety unbearable. Well, Rivers was wrong, people were more corruptible than that. *He* was more corruptible than that. A few days of safety, and all the clear spirit of the trenches was gone. It was still, after all these weeks, pure joy to go to bed in white sheets and know that he would wake. The road smelled of hot tar, moths flickered between the trees, and when at last, turning up the drive into Craiglockhart, he stopped and threw back his head, the stars burst on his upturned face like spray.

A nightly bath had become essential to Rivers, a ritual that divided his meagre spare time from the demands of the hospital. He was already pulling his tunic off as he crossed the bedroom. Naked, he sat on the edge of the bath, waiting for it to fill. The hot tap was shiny; the cold, misted over, dewed with drops of condensed steam. Absent-mindedly, he played with the drops, making them run together to form larger pools. He was thinking about Prior, and the effect he was having on his room-mate, Robinson, and wondering whether it was worse than the effect Anderson was having on Featherstone. In any event, no single room was available. One solution to the Prior problem was to move Robinson into a room at present shared by two patients, although if the overcrowding were not to prove intolerable, the patients would have to be very carefully selected. He was still running through possible combinations as he bathed.

By his bed was the current issue of *Man*, still in its envelope. He hadn't managed even to glance through it yet. And suddenly he was furious with the hospital, and Prior, and overcrowding and the endless permutations of people sharing that were made necessary by nightmares, sleep-walking, the need of some patients for night-lights and others for absolute darkness.

His irritation, groping for an object, fastened on Sassoon. Sassoon made no secret of his belief that anybody who supported the continuation of the war must be actuated by selfish motives, and yet if Rivers had allowed such motives to dominate, he'd have wanted the war to end tonight. Let the next generation cope with the unresolved problem of German militarism, just get me back to Cambridge and *research*. He flicked through the journal, but he was too tired to concentrate, and, after a few minutes, he switched off the light.

Shortly before dawn he woke. Still dazed from sleep, he put his hand to his left arm, expecting to feel blood. The dry cloth of his pyjama sleeve told him he'd been dreaming. He switched on the lamp and lay for a while, recollecting the details of the dream, then picked up a notepad and pencil from his bedside table and began to write.

I was in my room at St John's, sitting at the table in front of the book case. Head was beside me, his left sleeve rolled up, and his eyes closed. The sleeve was rolled up well above his elbow, so that the full length of the incision was revealed. The scar was purple. The tablecloth was spread with various items of equipment: jugs of water, wisps of cotton wool, bristle brushes, compasses, ice cubes, pins.

My task was to map the area of hypersensitivity to pain on Head's forearm. He sat with his eyes closed and his face turned slightly away. Every time I pricked him he cried out and tried to pull his arm away. I was distressed by this and didn't want to go on, but I knew I had to. Head kept on crying out.

The dream changed and I was drawing a map of the protopathic area directly on to his skin. The pen was as painful as the needle had been. Head opened his eyes and said something I didn't catch. It sounded like, 'Why don't *you* try it?' He was holding an object out towards me. I looked down to see what it was, and saw that my own left arm was bare, though I couldn't recall rolling up my sleeve.

The object in Head's hand was a scalpel. I began to ask him to repeat what he'd said, but before I could get the words out, he'd leant forward and brought the scalpel down my arm, in the region of the elbow. The incision, although about six inches long, was so fine that at first there was no blood. After a second, small beads of blood began to appear, and at that point I woke up.

Rivers started to analyse the dream. The manifest content didn't take long. Except for the cutting of his arm, the dream was an unusually accurate reproduction of events that had actually occurred.

Henry Head had been working for some time on the regeneration of nerves after accidental injury, using as his subjects patients in the public wards of London hospitals, before concluding that, if any further progress was to be made, more rigorously controlled tests would have to be done. Rivers had pointed out that these would have to be carried out on a subject who was himself a trained observer, since an extremely high degree of critical awareness would be needed to exclude preconceptions. Head had volunteered himself as the subject of the proposed experiment, and Rivers had assisted at the operation in which Head's radial nerve had been severed and sutured. Then, together, over a period of five years, they had charted the progress of regeneration.

During the early stage of recovery, when the primitive, protopathic sensibility had been restored, but not yet the finely discriminating epicritic sensibility, many of the experiments had been extremely painful. Protopathic sensibility seemed to have an 'all or nothing' quality. The threshold of sensation was high, but, once crossed, the sensations were both abnormally widely diffused and – to use Head's own word – 'extreme'. At times a pinprick would cause severe and prolonged pain. Rivers had often felt distress at the amount of pain he was causing, but it would not, in life, have occurred to him to stop the experiment for that reason, any more than it would have occurred to Head. In the dream, however, the wish to stop the experiment had been prominent.

The latent content was more difficult. Superficially, the dream seemed to support Freud's contention that all dreams were wish fulfilment. Rivers had wished himself back in Cambridge, doing research, and the dream had fulfilled the wish. But that was to ignore the fact that the dream had not been pleasant. The emphasis in the dream had been on the distress he felt at causing pain, and, on waking, the affect had been one of fear and dread. He didn't believe such a dream could be convincingly explained as wish fulfilment, unless, of course, he wished to torture one of his closest friends. No doubt some of Freud's more doctrinaire supporters would have little difficulty with that idea, particularly since the torture took the form of pricking him, but Rivers couldn't accept it. He was more inclined to seek the meaning of the dream in the conflict his dream self had experienced between the duty to continue the experiment and the reluctance to cause further pain.

Rivers was aware, as a constant background to his work, of a conflict between his belief that the war must be fought to a finish, for the sake of the succeeding generations, and his horror that such events as those which had led to Burns's breakdown should be allowed to continue. This conflict, though a constant feature of his life, would certainly have been strengthened by his conversations with Sassoon. He'd been thinking about Sassoon immediately before he went to sleep. But, on thinking it over, Rivers couldn't see that the dream was a likely dramatization of that conflict. The war was hardly an experiment, and it certainly didn't rest with him to decide whether it continued or not.

Recently almost all his dreams had centred on conflicts arising from his treatment of particular patients. In advising them to remember the traumatic events that had led to their being sent here, he was, in effect, inflicting pain, and doing so in pursuit of a treatment that he knew to be still largely experimental. Only in Burns's case had he found it impossible to go on giving this advice, because the suffering involved in Burns's attempts to remember was so extreme. 'Extreme'. The word Head had used to describe the pain he'd experienced during the protopathic stage of regeneration. Certainly in Burns's case, there was a clear conflict between Rivers's desire to continue using a method of treatment he believed in, but knew to be experimental, and his sense that in this particular instance the pain involved in insisting on the method would be too great.

The dream had not merely posed a problem, it had suggested a solution. 'Why don't you try it?' Henry had said. Rivers felt he'd got there first, that the dream lagged behind his waking practice: he was already experimenting on himself. In leading his patients to understand that breakdown was nothing to be ashamed of, that horror and fear were inevitable responses to the trauma of war and were better acknowledged than suppressed, that feelings of tenderness for other men were natural and right, that tears were an acceptable and helpful part of grieving, he was setting himself against the whole tenor of their upbringing. They'd been trained to identify emotional repression as the essence of manliness. Men who broke down, or cried, or admitted to feeling fear, were sissies, weaklings, failures. Not *men*. And yet he himself was a product of the same system, even perhaps a rather extreme product. Certainly the rigorous repression of emotion and desire had been the constant theme of his adult life. In advising his young patients to abandon the attempt at repression and to let themselves *feel* the pity and terror their war experience inevitably evoked, he was excavating the ground he stood on.

The change he demanded of them – and by implication of himself – was not trivial. Fear, tenderness – these emotions were so despised that they could be admitted into consciousness only at the cost of redefining what it meant to be a man. Not that Rivers's treatment involved any encouragement of weakness or effeminacy. His patients might be encouraged to acknowledge their fears, their horror of the war – but they were still expected to do their duty and return to France. It was Rivers's conviction that those who had learned to know themselves, and to accept their emotions, were less likely to break down again.

In a moment or two an orderly would tap on the door and bring in his tea. He put the notebook and pencil back on the bedside table. Henry would be amused by that dream, he thought. If wish fulfilment had been involved at all, it was surely one of Henry's wishes that had been fulfilled. At the time of the nerve regeneration experiments, they'd done a series of control experiments on the glans penis, and Henry had frequently expressed the desire for a reciprocal application of ice cubes, bristles, near-boiling water and pins.

SIX

Prior sat with his arms folded over his chest and his head turned slightly away. His eyelids looked raw from lack of sleep.

'When did your voice come back?' Rivers asked.

'In the middle of the night. I woke up shouting and suddenly I realized I could talk. It's happened before.'

A Northern accent, not ungrammatical, but with the vowel sounds distinctly flattened, and the faintest trace of sibilance. Hearing Prior's voice for the first time had the curious effect of making him *look* different. Thinner, more defensive. And, at the same time, a lot tougher. A little, spitting, sharp-boned alley cat.

'It comes and goes?'

'Yes.'

'What makes it go?'

Another shrug from the repertoire. 'When I get upset.'

'And coming here upset you?'

'I'd have preferred somewhere further south.'

So would I. 'What did you do before the war?'

'I was a clerk in a shipping office.'

'Did you like it?'

'No. It was *boring*.' He looked down at his hands and immediately up again. 'What did *you* do?'

Rivers hesitated. 'Research. Teaching.'

'Did *you* like it?'

'Yes, very much. Research more than teaching probably, but . . .' He shrugged. 'I enjoy teaching.'

'I noticed. "Two l's in physically, Mr Prior." '

'What an insufferable thing to say.'

'I thought so.'

'I'm sorry.'

Prior didn't know what to say to that. He looked down at his hands and mumbled, 'Yes, well.'

'By the way, your file arrived this morning.'

Prior smiled. 'So you know all about me, then?'

'Oh, I wouldn't say *that*. What *did* become clear is that you had a spell in the 13th Casualty Clearing Station in . . .' He looked at the file again. 'January. Diagnosed neurasthenic.'

Prior hesitated. 'Ye-es.'

'Deep reflexes abnormal.'

'Yes.'

'But on that occasion no trouble with the voice? Fourteen days later you were back in the line. Fully recovered?'

'I'd stopped doing the can-can, if that's what you mean.'

'Were there any remaining symptoms?'

'Headaches.' He watched Rivers make a note. 'It's hardly a reason to stay out of the trenches, is it? "*Not tonight, Wilhelm. I've got a headache*"?'

'It might be. It rather depends how bad they were.' He waited for a reply, but Prior remained obstinately silent. 'You were back in the 13th CCS in April. This time unable to speak.'

'I've told you, I don't remember.'

'So the loss of memory applies to the later part of your service in France, but the early part – the first six months or so – is comparatively clear?'

'Ye-es.'

Rivers sat back in his chair. 'Would you like to tell me something about that early part?'

'No.'

'But you do remember it?'

'Doesn't mean I want to talk about it.' He looked round the room. 'I don't see why it has to *be* like this anyway.'

'Like what?'

'All the questions from *you*, all the answers from *me*. Why can't it be both ways?'

'Look, Mr Prior, if you went to the doctor with bronchitis and he spent half the consultation time telling you about his lumbago, you would not be pleased. Would you?'

'No, but if I went to my doctor *in despair* it might help to know he at least understood the *meaning* of the word.'

'Are you in despair?'

Prior sighed, ostentatiously impatient.

'You know, I talk to a lot of people who *are* in despair or very close to it, and my experience is that they don't *care* what the doctor feels. That's the whole point about despair, isn't it? That you turn in on yourself.'

'Well, all I can say is I'd rather talk to a real person than a strip of empathic wallpaper.'

Rivers smiled. 'I like that.'

Prior glared at him.

'If you feel you can't talk about France, would it help to talk about the nightmares?'

'*No*. I don't think talking *helps*. It just churns things up and makes them seem more real.'

'But they are real.'

A short silence. Rivers closed Prior's file. 'All right. Good morning.'

Prior looked at the clock. 'It's only twenty past ten.'

Rivers spread his hands.

'You can't refuse to talk to me.'

'Prior, there are a hundred and sixty-eight patients in this hospital, all of them wanting to get better, none of them getting the attention he deserves. Good morning.'

Prior started to get up, then sat down again. 'You've no right to say I don't want to get better.'

'I didn't say that.'

'You implied it.'

'All right. *Do* you want to get better?'

'Of course.'

'But you're not prepared to co-operate with the treatment.'

'I don't agree with the treatment.'

Deep breath. 'What methods of treatment do you favour?'

'Dr Sanderson was going to try hypnosis.'

'He doesn't mention it in his report.'

'He was. He told me.'

'How did you feel about that?'

'I thought it was a good idea. I mean *you*'re more or less saying: things are real, you've got to face them, but how *can* I face them when I don't know what they are?'

'That's rather an unusual reaction, you know. Generally, when a doctor suggests hypnosis the patient's quite nervous, because he feels he'll be . . . putting himself in somebody else's power. Actually that's not quite true, but it does tend to be the fear.'

'If it's not true, why don't you use it?'

'I do sometimes. In selected cases. As a last resort. In your case, I'd want to know quite a lot about the part of your war service that you *do* remember.'

'All right. What do you want to know?'

Rivers blinked, surprised by the sudden capitulation. 'Well, anything you want to tell me.'

Silence.

'Perhaps you could start with the day before you went into the CCS for the first time. Do you remember what you were doing that day?'

Prior smiled. 'Standing up to my waist in water in a dugout in the middle of No Man's Land being bombed to buggery.'

'Why?'

'Good question. You should pack this in and join the general staff.'

'If there wasn't a reason, there must at least have been a rationale.'

'There was that, all right.' Prior adopted a strangled version of the public school accent. 'The pride of the British Army requires that absolute dominance must be maintained in No Man's Land at all times.' He dropped the accent. 'Which in *practice* means . . . Dugout in the middle of No Man's Land. Right? Every forty-eight hours two platoons crawl out – night-time, of course – relieve the poor bastards inside, and provide the Germans with another forty-eight hours' target practice. Why it's thought they need all this target practice is beyond me. They seem quite accurate enough as it is.' His expression changed. 'It was flooded. You stand the whole time. Most of the time in pitch darkness because the blast kept blowing the candles out. We were packed in so tight we couldn't move. And they just went all out to get us. One shell after the other. I lost two sentries. Direct hit on the steps. Couldn't find a thing.'

'And you had forty-eight hours of that?'

'Fifty. The relieving officer wasn't in a hurry.'

'And when you came out you went straight to the CCS?'

'I didn't go, I was carried.'

A tap on the door. Rivers called out angrily, 'I'm with a patient.'

A short pause as they listened to footsteps fading down the corridor. Prior said, 'I met the relieving officer.'

'In the clearing station?'

'No, here. He walked past me on the top corridor. Poor bastard left his Lewis guns behind. He was lucky not to be court-martialled.'

'Did you speak?'

'We nodded. Look, *you* might like to think it's one big happy family out there, but it's not. They *despise* each other.'

'You mean you despise yourself.'

Prior looked pointedly across Rivers's shoulder. 'It's eleven o'clock.'

'All right. I'll see you tomorrow.'

'I thought of going into Edinburgh tomorrow.'

Rivers looked up. 'At *nine*.'

'I can guess what Graves said. What a fine upstanding man I was until I fell among pacifists. Isn't that right? Russell used me. Russell wrote the Declaration.'

'No, he didn't say that.'

'Good. Because it isn't true.'

'You don't think you were influenced by Russell?'

'No, not particularly. I think I was influenced by my own experience of the front. I am capable of making up my own mind.'

'Was this the first time you'd encountered pacifism?'

'No. Edward Carpenter, before the war.'

'You read him?'

'Read him. Wrote to him.' He smiled slightly. 'I even made the Great Pilgrimage to Chesterfield.'

'You must've been impressed to do that.'

Sassoon hesitated. 'Yes, I . . .'

Watching him, Rivers perceived that he'd led Sassoon unwittingly on to rather intimate territory. He was looking for a way of redirecting the conversation when Sassoon said, 'I read a book of his. *The Intermediate Sex*. I don't know whether you know it?'

'Yes. I've had patients who swore their entire lives had been changed by it.'

'Mine was. At least I don't know about "changed". "Saved", perhaps.'

'As bad as that?'

'At one point, yes. I'd got myself into quite a state.'

Rivers waited.

'I didn't seem able to feel . . . well. Any of the things you're supposed to feel. It got so bad I used to walk all night sometimes. I used to wait till everybody else was in bed, and then I'd just . . . get out and walk. The book was a life-saver. Because I suddenly saw that . . . I wasn't just a freak. That there was a positive side. Have you read it?'

Rivers clasped his hands behind his head. 'Yes. A long time ago now.'

'What did you think?'

'I found it quite difficult. Obviously you have to admire the man's courage, and the way he's . . . opened up the debate. But I don't know that the concept of an intermediate sex is as helpful as people think it is when they first encounter it. In the end nobody wants to be *neuter*. Anyway, the point is Carpenter's pacifism doesn't seem to have made much impression?'

'I don't know if I was aware of it even. I didn't think much about politics. The next time I encountered pacifism was Robert Ross. I met him, oh, I suppose two years ago. He's totally opposed to the war.'

'And that didn't influence you either?'

'No. Obviously it made things easier at a *personal* level. I mean, frankly, any middle-aged man who Believed in The War would . . .' Sassoon skidded to a halt. 'Present company excepted.'

Rivers bowed.

'I didn't even bother showing him the Declaration. I knew he wouldn't go along with it.'

'Why wouldn't he? Out of concern for you?'

'Ye-es. Yes, that certainly, but . . . Ross was a close friend of Wilde's. I suppose he's learnt to keep his head below the parapet.'

'And you haven't.'

'I don't like holes in the ground.'

Rivers began polishing his glasses on his handkerchief. 'You know, I realize Ross's caution probably seems excessive. To you. But I hope you won't be in too much of a hurry to dismiss it. There's nothing more despicable than using a man's private life to discredit his views.

But it's very frequently done, even by people in my profession. People you might think wouldn't resort to such tactics. I wouldn't like to see it happen to you.'

'I thought discrediting my views was what you were about?'

Rivers smiled wryly. 'Let's just say I'm fussy about the methods.'

Rivers had kept two hours free of appointments in the late afternoon in order to get on with the backlog of reports. He'd been working for half an hour when Miss Crowe tapped on the door. 'Mr Prior says could he have a word?'

Rivers pulled a face. 'I've seen him once today. Does he say what's wrong?'

'No, this is the father.'

'I didn't even know he was coming.'

She started to close the door. 'I'll tell him you're busy, shall I?'

'No, no, I'll see him.'

Mr Prior came in. He was a big, thick-set man with a ruddy complexion, dark hair sleeked back, and a luxuriant, drooping, reddish-brown moustache. 'I'm sorry to drop on you like this,' he said. 'I thought our Billy had told you we were coming.'

'I think he probably mentioned it. If he did, I'm afraid it slipped my mind.'

Mr Prior looked him shrewdly up and down. '*Nah*. Wasn't your mind it slipped.'

'Well, sit down. How did you find him?'

'Difficult to tell when they won't talk, isn't it?'

'Isn't he talking? He was this morning.'

'Well, he's not now.'

'It does come and go.'

'Oh, I'm sure. Comes when it's convenient and goes when it isn't. What's supposed to be the matter?'

'Physically, nothing.' Two l's, Rivers thought. 'I think perhaps there's something he's afraid to talk about, so he solves the problem by making it impossible for himself to speak. This is . . . beneath the surface. He doesn't *know* what he's doing.'

'If he doesn't, it'll be the first time.'

Rivers tried a different tack. 'I believe he volunteered, didn't he? The first week of the war.'

'He did. Against my advice, not that *that's* ever counted for much.'

'You didn't want him to go?'

'No I did not. I told him, time enough to do summat for the Empire when the Empire's done summat for you.'

'It is natural for the young to be idealistic.'

'Ideals had nowt to do with it. He was desperate to get out of his job.'

'I think I remember him saying he didn't like it. He was a clerk in a shipping office.'

'That's right, and getting nowhere. Twenty years wearing the arse of your breeches out and then, if you're a good boy and lick all the right places, you get to be supervisor and then you sit on a bigger stool and watch other people wear their breeches out. Didn't suit our Billy. He's ambitious, you know, you mightn't think it to look at him, but he is. His mam drilled that into him. Schooled him in it. She was *determined* he was going to get on.'

Rather unexpectedly, Rivers found himself wanting to leap to Billy Prior's defence. 'She seems to have succeeded.'

Mr Prior snorted. 'She's made a stool-arsed jack on him, if that's what you mean.'

'You make it sound as if you had no say.'

'I didn't. All the years that lad was growing up there was only one time I put my oar in, and that was when there was this lad at school picking on him. He was forever coming in crying. And one day I thought, well, I've had enough of this. So the next time he come in blubbing I give him a backhander and shoved him out the door. There he was, all tears and snot, yelling his bloody head off. He says, he's waiting for us, our Dad. I says, go on, then. You've got to toughen 'em up, you know, in our neighbourhood. If you lie down there's plenty to walk over you.'

'What happened?'

'Got the shit beat out of him. *And* the next day. *And* the next. *But* – and this is our Billy – when he did finally take a tumble to himself and hit the little sod he didn't just hit him, he half bloody murdered him. I had his father coming round, and all sorts. Not but what *he* got short shrift.'

He seemed to have no feeling for his son at all, except contempt. 'You must be proud of his being an officer?'

'Must I? *I*'m not proud. He should've stuck with his own. Except he can't, can he? That's what she's done to him. He's neither fish nor fowl, and she's too bloody daft to see it. But I tell you one person who *does* see it.' He pointed to the ceiling. 'Oh it's all very lovey-dovey on the surface but underneath he doesn't thank her for it.' He stood up. 'Anyway I'd best be getting back. His nibs'll have a fit, when he knows I've seen you. Wheezing badly, isn't he?' He caught Rivers's expression. 'Oh, I see, he wasn't wheezing either? Not what you could call a successful visit.'

'I'm sure it's done him a lot of good. We often find they don't settle till they've seen their families.'

Mr Prior nodded, accepting the reassurance without believing it. 'Any idea how long he'll be here?'

'Twelve weeks. Initially.'

'Hm. He'd get a damn sight more sympathy from me if he had a bullet up his arse. Anyway . . .' He held out his hand. 'It's been nice meeting you. I don't know when we'll be up again.'

Rivers had completed two reports when Miss Crowe put her head round the door again. '*Mrs* Prior.'

They exchanged glances. Rivers threw down his pen, and said, 'Show her in.'

Mrs Prior was a small upright woman, neatly dressed in a dark suit and mauve blouse. 'I won't stay long,' she said, sitting nervously on the edge of the chair. She was playing with her wedding ring, pulling and pushing it over the swollen knuckle. 'I'd like to apologize for my husband. I thought he was just stepping outside for a smoke, otherwise I'd've stopped him.'

A carefully genteel voice. Fading prettiness. Billy Prior had got his build and features from her rather than the father. 'No, I was pleased to see him. How did you find Billy?'

'Wheezing. I've not seen his chest as tight as that since he was a child.'

'I didn't even know he was asthmatic.'

'No, well, it doesn't bother him much. Usually. As a child it was terrible. I used to have to boil kettles in his room. You know, for the steam?'

'You must be very proud of him.'

Her face softened. 'I am. Because *I* know how hard it's been. I can truthfully say he never sat an exam without he was bad with his asthma.'

'Did he like the shipping office?'

Her mouth shaped itself to say 'yes', then, 'No. It was the same docks as his father and I think that was the mistake. You know, his father was earning more as a ganger than Billy was as a clerk, and I think myself there was a little bit of . . . You see the trouble with my husband, the block had to chip. Do you know what I mean? He's never been able to accept that Billy was different. And I think there might have been a little bit of jealousy as well, because he has, he's had a hard life. I don't deny that. A lot harder than it need have been, because *his* mother sent him to work when he was *ten*. And no need for it either, she had two sons working, but there it is. What can you say? He worships her.' She was silent for a moment, brooding. 'You know sometimes I think the less you do for them, the better you're thought of.'

'Would you say Billy and his father were close?'

'*No!* And yet, you see, the funny thing is our Billy's . . .' She sought for a way of erasing the tell-tale 'our' from the sentence and, not finding one, gave a little deprecatory laugh. 'All for "the common people", as he calls them. I said, "You mean your father?"' She laughed again. 'Oh, no, he didn't mean his father. I said, "But you know nothing about the common people. You've had nothing to do with them." Do you know what he turned round and said? "Whose fault is that?"'

Miss Crowe tapped on the door. 'Your husband says he's going now, Mrs Prior.'

'Yes, well, I'll have to go. You'll take care of him, won't you?'

She was close to tears. Rivers said, 'We'll do our best.'

'I'd be grateful if you wouldn't mention I've been to see you. He's upset enough about his father.'

After she'd gone, Rivers turned to Miss Crowe. 'That was amazing. Do you know, I think they'd have said *anything*?'

'You get married couples like that, sir. One sympathetic word and you're there till midnight. Captain Broadbent's waiting to see you.'

Rivers looked at the pile of papers on his desk and sighed. 'All right, show him in.' The frustration boiled over. 'And do *please try* not to call him "captain". He's no more a captain than I am.'

'You *are* a captain, Captain Rivers.'

Miss Crowe paused at the door to savour the small moment of triumph. Rivers smiled and said, 'All right. But at least try not to *address* him as "captain". It really doesn't help him to have his fantasies confirmed.'

'I'll do my best, sir. Though as long as he's allowed to walk round the hospital with three stars on his sleeve, I don't see that my remembering to call him "mister" is going to make a great deal of difference.' She smiled sweetly and withdrew. A moment later she reappeared. '*Mister* Broadbent, sir.'

'Come in, Mr Broadbent. Sit down.'

It wasn't just the stars. There was also the little matter of the medals, including the Serbian equivalent of the VC awarded to a foreigner for the first and only time in its long and glorious history. And then there were the honorary degrees, though at least he hadn't yet taken to wearing those on his tunic. However, he was doing very good work with the hospital chamber orchestra. 'Well, Broadbent, what can I do for you?'

'I've had some bad news, Dr Rivers,' Broadbent said in his confiding, insinuating way. 'My mother's been taken ill.'

Rivers didn't believe Broadbent's mother was ill. He didn't believe Broadbent had a mother. He thought it entirely possible that Broadbent had been hatched. 'Oh, I *am* sorry.'

'I was hoping for some leave.'

'You'll have to ask the CO about that.'

'I was hoping you might put a word in for me. You see, I don't think Major Bryce *likes* me very much.'

People who'd heard of Broadbent's exploits, but not met him, were apt to picture a rather florid, swashbuckling, larger-than-life figure. In reality, Broadbent was a limp, etiolated youth, with a pallid complexion and a notably damp handshake, whose constant and bizarre infringements of the hospital rules took up far far too much time. He was quite right in thinking Bryce didn't like him.

'It's not a question of liking or not liking,' Rivers said. 'Is your mother very ill?'

'I'm afraid so, Dr Rivers.'

'Then I'm sure Major Bryce will be sympathetic. But it *is his* decision. Not mine.'

'I just thought . . .' Suddenly Broadbent's voice hardened. 'This is *extremely* bad for my nerves. You know what happens.'

'I hope it doesn't happen this time. Because last time, if you remember, you had to be locked up. Why don't you go to see Major Bryce now?'

'Yes, all right.' Broadbent stood up, reluctantly, and spat, '*Thank* you, sir.'

At least he didn't offer to shake hands.

★

After dinner a Charlie Chaplin film was shown in the cinema on the first floor. The whole of the ground floor was deserted. Rivers, taking his completed reports along to the office to be typed, saw that a lamp had been left burning in the patients' common room and went in to switch it off.

Prior was sitting beneath the windows at the far end of the room, looking out over the tennis courts, his face and hands bluish in the dim light. Rivers was tempted to withdraw immediately, but then something about the isolation of the small figure under the huge windows made him pause. 'Don't you want to see the film?'

'I couldn't stand the smoke.'

He was wheezing very badly. Rivers went across to the window and sat beside him. Housemartins were weaving to and fro above the tennis courts, feeding on the myriads of tiny insects that were just visible as a golden haze. He watched them cut, wheel, dive – how skilful they were at avoiding collision – and for a moment, under the spell of the flickering birds, the day's work and responsibility fell away. But he couldn't ignore Prior's breathing, or the whiteness of the knuckles where his left hand gripped the chair. He turned and looked at him, noting the drawn, anxious face. 'It's bad, isn't it?'

'Bit tight.'

Prior was bent forward to help the expansion of his lungs. Looking at him now, Rivers could see the straightness of the shoulders, the surprising breadth of chest in a delicately built man. Once you knew it was obvious. But why nothing on the file?

'I gather you met my father,' Prior gasped. 'Quite a character.'

'He seemed to be a man of strong views.'

Prior's mouth twisted. 'He's a bar-room socialist, if that's what you mean. Beer and revolution go in, *piss* comes out.' He attempted a laugh. 'My mother was quite concerned. "He'll be down there effing and blinding," she said. "Showing us all up."'

'I liked him.'

'Oh, yes, he's very likeable. Outside the house. I've seen him use my mother as a football.' The next breath screeched. 'When I was too little to do anything about it.'

'You know, I think I ought to have a look at that chest.'

Prior managed a ghostly imitation of his usual manner. 'Your room or mine?'

'The sick bay.'

The walk along the corridor to the lift was painfully slow.

'I didn't want you to meet him,' Prior said, as Rivers pressed the button for the second floor.

'No, I know you didn't. I could hardly refuse.'

'I'm not blaming *you*.'

'Is it a question of blame?'

While the nurses made up the bed, Rivers examined Prior. He'd expected Prior to be impossible, but in the event he became strictly impersonal, gazing over Rivers's shoulder as the stethoscope moved across his chest. 'All right, put your jacket on.' Rivers folded the stethoscope. 'I'm surprised you got to France at all with that.'

'They couldn't afford to be fussy.' Prior started the long climb into the bed. 'I won't be moved to another hospital, will I?'

'No, I shouldn't think so. Four doctors, thirty nurses. I think we might manage.'

'Only I don't want to be moved.'

Rivers helped him to pull up the sheets. 'I thought you didn't like it here?'

'Yes, well, you can get used to anything, can't you? Do you think I could have a towel tied to the bed?'

'Yes, of course. Anything you want.'

'Only it helps, you see. Having something to pull on.'

'What was it like in France? The asthma.'

'Better than at home.'

A shout of laughter from below. Charlie Chaplin in full swing. Rivers, following Prior's gaze, saw the single lamp and the deep shadows, and sensed, with a premonitory tightening of his diaphragm, the breath-by-breath agony of the coming night. 'I'll see about the towel,' he said.

He saw Prior settled down for the night. 'I'll be along in the morning,' he said. Then he went to Sister's room next door and left orders he was to be woken at once if Prior got worse.

SEVEN

Sassoon woke to the sound of screams and running footsteps. The screams stopped and then a moment or two later started again. He peered at his watch and made out that it was ten past four.

Because of the rubber underlay, a pool of sweat had gathered in the small of his back. The rubbery smell lingered on his skin, a clinical smell that made his body unfamiliar to him. In the next bed Campbell snored, a cacophony of grunts, snorts and whistles. No screams ever woke *him*. On the other hand he himself never screamed, and Sassoon had been at Craiglockhart long enough now to realize how valuable a room-mate that made him.

Fuliy awake now, he dragged himself to the bottom of the bed, lifted the thin curtain and peered out of the window. Wester Hill, blunt-nosed and brooding, loomed out of the mist. And yesterday, he thought, shivering a little, his statement had been read in the House of Commons. He wondered what would happen next. Whether anything would happen. In any event there was a kind of consolation in knowing it was out of his hands.

He knew he was shivering more with fear than cold, though it was difficult to name the fear. The place, perhaps. The haunted faces, the stammers, the stumbling walks, that indefinable look of being 'mental'. Craiglockhart frightened him more than the front had ever done.

Upstairs whoever-it-was screamed again. He heard women's voices and then, a few minutes afterwards, a man's voice. Rivers, he thought, but he couldn't be sure. Quaking and comfortless, he propped himself up against the iron bedhead and waited for the dawn.

Prior hauled himself further up the bed as Rivers came in. He closed the book he'd been reading and put it down on his bedside table. 'I thought it was you,' he said. 'I can tell your footsteps.'

Rivers got a chair and sat down by the bed. 'Did you manage to get back to sleep?'

'Yes. Did you?'

Silence.

'I wasn't being awkward,' Prior said. 'That was *concern*.'

'I didn't, but it doesn't matter. I don't sleep much after four anyway.' He caught the flicker of interest. How quickly Prior pounced on any item of personal information.

'Thanks for showing up.'

'You hated it.'

Prior looked slightly disconcerted, then smiled. 'I don't suppose anybody'd *choose* to be seen in such a state. I don't really see why they had to call you.'

'They were afraid the fear might bring on another attack. Though in fact you seem to be breathing more easily.'

Prior took a trial deep breath. 'Yes, I think I am. Do you know I detect something in myself. I . . .' He stopped. 'No, I don't think I want to tell you what I detect.'

'Oh, go on. Professional curiosity. I want to see if *I*'ve detected it.'

Prior smiled faintly. 'No, you won't have detected this. I find myself wanting to impress you. Pathetic, isn't it?'

'I don't think it's pathetic. We all care what the people around us think, whether we admit it or not.' He paused. 'Though I'm a bit surprised *my* opinion matters. I mean, to be quite honest, I didn't think you liked me very much.'

'There's a limit to how warm you can feel about wallpaper.'

'Oh, we're back to that again, are we?'

Prior turned away, hunching his shoulders. 'No-o.'

Rivers watched him for a while. 'Why do you think it has to be like that?'

'So that I . . . I'm sorry. So that *the patient* can fantasize freely. So that *the patient* can turn you into whoever he wants you to be. Well, all right. I just think you might consider the possibility that *this* patient might want you to be *you*.'

'All right.'

'All right, what?'

'All right, I'll consider it.'

'I suppose most of them turn you into Daddy, don't they? Well, I'm a bit too old to be sitting on *Daddy*'s knee.'

'Kicking him on the shins every time you meet him isn't generally considered more mature.'

'I *see*. A negative transference. Is *that* what you think we've got?'

'I hope not.' Rivers couldn't altogether conceal his surprise. 'Where did you learn that term?'

'I can *read*.'

'Well, yes, I know, but its –'

'Not popular science? No, but then neither is this.'

He reached for the book beside his bed and held it out to Rivers. Rivers found himself holding a copy of *The Todas*. He stared for a moment at his own name on the spine. He told himself there was no reason why Prior shouldn't read one of his books, or all of them for that matter. There was no rational reason for him to feel uneasy. He handed the book back. 'Wouldn't you prefer something lighter? You are ill, after all.'

Prior leant back against his pillows, his eyes gleaming with amusement. 'Do you know, I *knew* you were going to say that. Now how did I know that?'

'I didn't realize you were interested in anthropology.'

'Why shouldn't I be?'

'No reason.'

Really, Rivers thought, Prior was cuckoo-backed to the point where normal conversation became almost impossible. He was flicking through the book, obviously looking for something in particular. After a minute or so he held it out again, open at the section on sexual morality. 'Do they really go on like that?'

Rivers said, as austerely as he knew how, 'Their sexual lives are conducted along rather different lines from ours.'

'I'll say. They must be bloody knackered. *I* couldn't keep it up, could you?'

'I think my age and your asthma might effectively prevent either of us setting any records.'

'Ah, yes, but I'm only asthmatic *part* of the time.'

'You have to *win*, don't you?'

Prior stared intently at him. 'You know, you do a wonderful imitation of a stuffed shirt. And you're not like that at all, really, are you?'

Rivers took his glasses off and swept his hand across his eyes. *'Mister Prior.'*

'I know, I know, "Tell me about France." All right, what do you want to know? And *please* don't say, "Whatever you want to tell me."'

'All right. How did you fit in?'

Prior's face shut tight. 'You mean, did I encounter any snobbery?'

'Yes.'

'Not more than I have here.'

Their eyes locked. Rivers said, 'But you did encounter it?'

'Yes. It's made perfectly clear when you arrive that some people are more welcome than others. It helps if you've been to the right school. It helps if you hunt, it helps if your shirts are the right colour. Which is a *deep* shade of khaki, by the way.'

In spite of himself Rivers looked down at his shirt.

'Borderline,' said Prior.

'And yours?'

'Not borderline. Nowhere near. Oh, and then there's the seat. *The Seat*. You know, they sent me on a course once. You have to ride round and round this bloody ring with your hands clasped behind your head. No saddle. No stirrups. It was amazing. Do you know, for the first time I realized that somewhere at the back of their . . . *tiny tiny* minds they really do believe the whole thing's going to end in one big glorious *cavalry charge*. "Stormed at with shot and shell,/Boldly they rode and well,/Into the jaws of death,/Into the mouth of hell . . ." And all. That. Rubbish.'

Rivers noticed that Prior's face lit up as he quoted the poem. '*Is* it rubbish?'

'*Yes*. Oh, all right, I was in love with it once. Shall I tell you something about that charge? Just as it was about to start an officer saw three men smoking. He thought that was a bit too casual, so he confiscated their sabres and sent them into the charge unarmed. Two of them were killed. The one who survived was flogged the following day. The military mind doesn't change much, does it? The same mind now orders men to be punished by tying them to a limber.' Prior stretched his arms out. 'Like this. Field punishment No. 1. "Crucifixion." Even at the propaganda level can you imagine anybody being *stupid* enough to order *this*?'

Either the position, or his anger, constricted his breathing. He brought his arms down sharply and rounded his shoulders. Rivers waited for the spasm to pass. 'How was your seat?'

'Sticky. No, that's *good*. It means you don't come off.'

A short silence. Prior said, 'You mustn't make too much of it, you know, the snobbery. I didn't. The only thing that really makes me angry is when people at home say there are no class distinctions at the front. Ball-*ocks*. What you wear, what you eat. Where you sleep. What you carry. The men are pack animals.' He hesitated. 'You know the worst thing? What seemed *to me* the worst thing? I used to go to this café in Amiens and just across the road there was a brothel. The men used to queue out on to the street.' He looked at Rivers. 'They get two minutes.'

'And officers?'

'I don't know. Longer than that.' He looked up. '*I don't pay*.'

Prior was talking so freely Rivers decided to risk applying pressure. 'What were you dreaming about last night?'

'I don't remember.'

Rivers said gently, 'You know, one of the distinguishing characteristics of nightmares is that they are always remembered.'

'Can't've been a nightmare, then, can it?'

'When I arrived you were on the floor over there. Trying to get through the wall.'

'I'm sure it's true, if you say so, but I don't remember. The first thing I remember is you listening to my chest.'

Rivers got up, replaced his chair against the wall and came back to the bed. 'I can't force you to accept treatment if you don't want it. You *do* remember the nightmares. You remember them enough to walk the floor till two or three o'clock every morning rather than go to sleep.'

'I wish the night staff didn't feel obliged to act as *spies*.'

'Now that's just childish, isn't it? You know it's their job.'

Prior refused to look at him.

'All right. I'll see you tomorrow.'

'It isn't fair to say I don't want treatment. I've asked for treatment and you've refused to give it me.'

Rivers looked blank. 'Oh, I see. The hypnosis. I didn't think you were serious.'

'Why shouldn't I be serious? It *is* used to recover lost memory, isn't it?'

'Ye-es.'

'So why won't you do it?'

Rivers started to speak, and stopped.

'I can understand, you know. I'm not stupid.'

'No, I know you're not stupid. It's just that there's . . . there's a certain amount of technical jargon involved. I was just trying to avoid it. Basically, people who've dealt with a horrible experience by splitting it off from the rest of their consciousness sometimes have a general tendency to deal with any kind of unpleasantness in that way, and if they *have*, the tendency is likely to be reinforced by hypnosis. In other words you might be removing one particular symptom – loss of memory – and making the underlying condition worse.'

'But you do do it?'

'If everything else has failed, yes.'

Prior lay back. 'That's all I wanted to know.'

'In your case not everything else *has* failed or even been tried. For example, I'd want to write to your CO. We need a clear picture of the last few days.' Rivers watched Prior's expression carefully, but he was giving nothing away. 'But I'd have to go to the CO with a precise question. You understand that, don't you?'

'*Yes.*'

'There's no point bothering him with a vague inquiry about an unspecified period of time.'

'No, all right.'

'So we still need you to remember as much as possible by conventional means. But we can leave it till you're feeling better.'

'No, I want to get on with it.'

'We'll see how you feel tomorrow.'

After leaving Prior, Rivers walked up the back staircase to the tower and stood for a few moments, his hands on the balustrade, looking out across the hills. Prior worried him. The whole business of the demand for hypnosis worried him. At times he felt almost a sense of foreboding in relation to the case, though he wasn't inclined to give it much credence. In his experience, premonitions of disaster were almost invariably proved false, and the road to Calvary entered on with the very lightest of hearts.

MR MACPHERSON With regard to the case of Second Lieutenant Sassoon, immediately he heard of it, he consulted his military advisers, and in response to their inquiries he received the following telegram: A breach of discipline has been committed, but no disciplinary action has been taken, since Second Lieutenant Sassoon has been reported by the Medical Board as not being responsible for his action, as he was suffering from nervous breakdown. When the military authorities saw the letter referred to, they felt that there must be something wrong with an extremely gallant officer who had done excellent work at the front. He hoped hon. members would hesitate long before they made use of a document written by a young man in such a state of mind, nor did he think their action would be appreciated by the friends of the officer. (*Cheers.*)

Rivers folded *The Times* and smiled. 'Really, Siegfried, what did you expect?'

'I don't know. Meanwhile . . .' Sassoon leant across and pointed to the front page.

Rivers read. '"Platts. Killed in action on the 28th April, dearly loved younger son, etc., aged seventeen years and ten months."' He looked up and found Sassoon watching him.

'He wasn't old enough to *enlist*. And nobody gives a damn.'

'Of course they do.'

'Oh, come on, it doesn't even put them off their sausages! Have you ever sat in a club room and *watched* people read the casualty list?'

'You could say that about the breakfast room here. Sensitivity t-to what's going on in France is not best shown by b-bursting into t-tears over the c-casualty list.' He saw Sassoon noticing the stammer and made an effort to speak more calmly. 'The thing for you to do now is face the fact that you're here, and here for at least another eleven weeks. Have you thought what you're going to do?'

'Not really. I'm still out of breath from getting here. Go for walks. Read.'

'Will you be able to write, do you think?'

'Oh, yes. I'll write if I have to sit on the roof to do it.'

'There's no prospect of a room of your own.'

'No, I know that.'

Rivers chose his words carefully. 'Captain Campbell is an extremely nice man.'

'Yes, I've noticed. What's more, his battle plans are saner than Haig's.'

Rivers ignored that. 'One thing I could do is put you up for my club, the Conservative Club. I don't know whether you'd like that? It'd give you an alternative base at least.'

'I would, very much. Thank you.'

'Though I hope you won't exclude the possibility of making friends here.'

Sassoon looked down at the backs of his hands. 'I thought I might send for my golf clubs. There seem to be one or two keen golfers about.'

'Good idea. I'll see you three times a week. It'd better be evenings rather than mornings, I think – especially if you're going to play golf. Tuesdays, Fridays and Sundays?'

'Fine.' He smiled faintly. 'I've got nothing else on.'

'Eight thirty, shall we say? Immediately after dinner.'

Sassoon nodded. 'It's very kind of you.'

'Oh, I don't know about that.' He closed his appointments book and pulled a sheet of paper towards him. 'Now I need to ask a few questions about your physical health. Childhood illnesses, that sort of thing.'

'All right. Why?'

'For the admission report.'

'Oh, I see.'

'I don't usually include any . . . intimate details.'

'Probably just as well. My intimate details disqualify me from military service.'

Rivers looked up and smiled. 'I know.'

After Sassoon had gone, Rivers got a case sheet from the stack on his side table, paused for a few moments to collect his thoughts, and began to write:

Patient joined ranks of the Sussex Yeomanry on Aug. 3rd, 1914. Three months later he had a bad smash while schooling a horse and was laid up for several months. In May 1915 he received a commission in the Royal Welch Fusiliers. He was in France from Nov. 1915 until Aug. 1916, when he was sent home with trench fever. He had received the Military Cross in June 1916. He was on three months' sick leave and returned to France in Feb. 1917. On April 16th, 1917, he was wounded in the right shoulder and was in the surgical wards of the 4th London for four weeks and then at Lady Brassey's Convalescent Home for three weeks. He then understood that he was to be sent to Cambridge to instruct cadets.

From an early stage of his service in France, he had been horrified by the slaughter and had come to doubt whether the continuance of the War was justifiable. When on sick leave in 1916 he was in communication with Bertrand Russell and other pacifists. He had never previously approved of pacifism and does not think he was influenced by this communication. During his second visit to France, his doubts about the justifiability of the War were accentuated; he became perhaps even more doubtful about the way in which the war was being conducted from a military point of view. When he became fit to return to duty, in July of this year, he felt he was unable to do so, and that it was his duty to make some kind of protest. He drew up a statement which he himself regarded as an act of wilful defiance of military authority (see *The Times*, July 31st, 1917). In consequence of this statement he was ordered to attend a Medical Board at Chester about July 16th, but failed to attend. It was arranged that a second Board should be held at Liverpool on July 20th, which he attended, and he was recommended for admission to Craiglockhart War Hospital for special treatment for three months.

The patient is a healthy looking man of good physique. There are no physical signs of any disorder of the Nervous System. He discusses his recent actions and their motives in a perfectly intelligent and rational way, and there is no evidence of any excitement or depression. He recognizes that his view of warfare is tinged by his feelings about the death of friends and of the men who were under his command in France. At the present time he lays special stress on the hopelessness of any decision in the War as it is now being conducted, but he left out any reference to this aspect of his opinions in the statement which he sent to his Commanding Officer and which was read in the House of Commons. His view differs from that of the ordinary pacifist in that he would no longer object to the continuance of the War if he saw any reasonable prospect of a rapid decision.

He had an attack of double pneumonia when 11 years old, and again at 14. He was at Marlborough College, where he strained his heart at football. He was for four terms at Clare College, Cambridge, where he read first Law and then History, but did not care for either subject. He left Cambridge and spent the following years living in the country, devoting his time chiefly to hunting and cricket. He took no interest in Politics. From boyhood he has written verses at different times, and during his convalescence from his riding accident in 1914 he wrote a poem called 'The Old Hunstman', which has recently been published with other poems under that title.

'I gave Broadbent leave,' Bryce said. 'With some trepidation.'

'Yes, he told me he was going to ask you.'

'You know what he's done? Gone off with his room-mate's new breeches. Marsden's furious.'

Ruggles said, 'You mean this guy's running round the hospital bare-assed frightening the VADs?'

'No, he's wearing his other breeches. And your idea of what might frighten a VAD is –'

'Chivalrous,' said Ruggles.

'Naïve,' said Bryce. 'In the extreme.'

'Why is it always your patients, Rivers?' asked Brock.

The MOs were sitting round a table in Bryce's room over coffee, as they did twice a week after dinner. These gatherings were kept deliberately informal, but they served some of the same purposes as a case conference. Since everybody had now read *The Times* report, Bryce had asked Rivers to say a few words about Sassoon.

Rivers kept it as brief and uncontroversial as possible. While he was speaking, he noticed that Brock was balancing a pencil between the tips of his extremely long bluish fingers. Never a good sign. Rivers liked Brock, but they didn't invariably see eye to eye.

A moment's silence, after Rivers had finished speaking. Then Ruggles asked Bryce if the press had shown any interest. While Bryce was summarizing a conversation he'd had with the *Daily Mail*, Rivers watched Brock, who sat, arms folded across his chest, looking down his long pinched nose at the table. Brock always looked frozen. Even his voice, high, thin and reedy, seemed to echo across arctic wastes. When Bryce had finished, Brock turned to Rivers and said, 'What are you thinking of doing with him?'

'Well, I have been seeing him every day. I'm going to drop that now to three times a week.'

'Isn't that rather a lot? For someone who – according to you – has nothing wrong with him?'

'I shan't be able to persuade him to go back in less than that.'

'Isn't there a case for leaving him alone?'

'No.'

'I mean, simply by *being* here he's discredited. Discredited, disgraced, *apparently* lied to by his best friend? I'd've thought there was a case for letting him be.'

'No, there's no case,' Rivers said. 'He's a mentally and physically healthy man. It's *his* duty to go back, and it's *my* duty to see he does.'

'And you've no doubts about that at all?'

'I don't see the problem. I'm not going to give him electric shocks, or or subcutaneous injections of ether. I'm simply asking him to defend his position. Which he admits was reached largely on emotional grounds.'

'*Grief* at the death of his friends. *Horror* at the slaughter of everybody else's friends. It isn't clear to me why such emotions have to be ignored.'

'I'm not saying they should be ignored. Only that they mustn't be allowed to dominate.'

'The protopathic must know its place?'

Rivers looked taken aback. 'I wouldn't've put it quite like that.'

'Why not? It's your word. And Sassoon does seem to be a remarkably protopathic young man. Doesn't he? I mean from what you say, it's "all or nothing" all the time. Happy warrior one minute. Bitter pacifist the next.'

'Precisely. He's completely inconsistent. And that's all the more reason to get him to *argue* the position –'

'Epicritically.'

'Rationally.'

Brock raised his hands and sat back in his chair. 'I hope you don't mind my playing devil's advocate?'

'Good heavens, no. The whole point of these meetings is to protect the patient.'

Brock smiled, one of his rare, thin, unexpectedly charming smiles. 'Is that what I was doing? I thought I was protecting you.'

Part Two

EIGHT

Prior had lost weight during his time in sick bay. Watching the light fall on to his face, Rivers noticed how sharp the cheekbones had become.

'Do you mind if I smoke?'

'No, go ahead.' Rivers pushed an ashtray across the desk.

The match flared behind Prior's cupped hands. 'First for three weeks,' he said. 'God, I feel dizzy.'

Rivers tried not to say, but said, 'It's not really a good idea with asthma, you know.'

'You think it might shorten my life? Do you know how long the average officer lasts in France?'

'Yes. Three months. You're not in France.'

Prior dragged on the cigarette and, momentarily, closed his eyes. He looked a bit like the boys you saw on street corners in the East End. That same air of knowing the price of everything. Rivers drew the file towards him. 'We left you in billets at Beauvois.'

'Yes. We were there, oh, I think about four days and then we were rushed back into the line. We attacked the morning of the night we moved up.'

'Date?'

'April the 23rd.'

Rivers looked up. It was unusual for Prior to be so accurate.

'St George's Day. The CO toasted him in the mess. I remember because it was so bloody stupid.'

'You were in the casualty clearing station on the . . .' He glanced at the file. '29th. So that leaves us with nine days unaccounted for.'

'Yes, and I'm afraid I can't help you with any of them.'

'Do you remember the attack?'

'Yes. It was exactly like any other attack.'

Rivers waited. Prior looked so hostile that at first Rivers thought he would refuse to go on, but then he raised the cigarette to his lips, and said, '*All right.* Your watch is brought back by a runner, having been synchronized at headquarters.' A long pause. 'You wait, you try to calm down anybody who's obviously shitting himself or on the verge of throwing up. You hope you won't do either of those things yourself. Then you start the count down: ten, nine, eight . . . so on. You blow the whistle. You climb the ladder. Then you double through a gap in the wire, lie flat, wait for everybody else to get out – those that are left, there's already quite a heavy toll – and then you stand up. And you start walking. *Not* at the double. Normal walking speed.' Prior started to smile. 'In a straight line. Across open country. In broad daylight. Towards a line of machine-guns.' He shook his head. 'Oh, and of course you're being shelled all the way.'

'What did you *feel*?'

Prior tapped the ash off his cigarette. 'You always want to know what I *felt*.'

'Well, yes. You're describing this attack as if it were a – a slightly ridiculous event in –'

'Not "slightly". Slightly, I did not say.'

'All right, an *extremely* ridiculous event – in somebody else's life.'

'Perhaps that's how it felt.'

'Was it?' He gave Prior time to answer. 'I think you're capable of a great deal of detachment, but you'd have to be *inhuman* to be as detached as that.'

'All right. It felt . . .' Prior started to smile again. '*Sexy*.'

Rivers raised a hand to his mouth.

'You see?' Prior said, pointing to the hand. 'You ask me how it felt and when I tell you, you don't believe me.'

Rivers lowered his hand. 'I haven't said I don't believe you. I was waiting for you to go on.'

'You know those men who lurk around in bushes waiting to jump out on unsuspecting ladies and – *er-um* – display their equipment? It felt a bit like that. A bit like I *imagine* that feels. I wouldn't like you to think I had any personal experience.'

'And was that your only feeling?'

'Apart from terror, yes.' He looked amused. 'Shall we get back to "inhuman detachment"?'

'If you like.'

Prior laughed. 'I think it suits us *both* better, don't you?'

Rivers let him continue. This had been Prior's attitude throughout the three weeks they'd spent trying to recover his memories of France. He seemed to be saying, 'All right. You can make me dredge up the horrors, you can make me remember the deaths, but you will never make me feel.' Rivers tried to break down the detachment, to get to the emotion, but he knew that, confronted by the same task, he would have tackled it in exactly the same way as Prior.

'You keep up a kind of chanting. "Not so fast. Steady on the left!" Designed to avoid bunching. Whether it works or not depends on the ground. Where we were, it was absolutely pitted with shell-holes and the lines got broken up straight away. I looked back . . .' He stopped, and reached for another cigarette. 'I looked back and the ground was covered with wounded. Lying on top of each other, writhing. Like fish in a pond that's drying out. I wasn't frightened at all. I just felt this . . . amazing burst of exultation. Then I heard a shell coming. And the next thing I knew I was in the air, *fluttering* down . . .' He waved his fingers in a descending arc. 'I know it can't've *been* like that, but that's what I remember. When I came to, I was in a crater with about half a dozen of the men. I couldn't move. I thought at first I was paralysed, but then I managed to move my feet. I told them to get the brandy out of my pocket, and we passed that round. Then a man appeared on the other side of the crater, right at the rim, and, instead of crawling down, he put his hands to his sides, like this, and *slid* down on his bottom. And suddenly everybody burst out laughing.'

'You say "came to"? Do you know how long you were unconscious?'

'No idea.'

'But you *were* able to speak?'

'Yes, I told them to get the brandy.'

'And then?'

'Then we waited till dark and made a dash for the line. They saw us just as we got to our wire. Two men wounded.'

'There was no talk of sending you to a CCS when you got back?'

'No, I was organizing other people there.' He added bitterly, 'There was no talk of sending anybody anywhere. Normally you go back after heavy losses, but we didn't. They just left us there.'

'And you don't remember anything else?'

'No. And *I have tried*.'

'Yes, I'm sure you have.'

A long silence. 'I suppose you haven't heard from the CO?'

'No, I'd tell you if I had.'

Prior sat brooding for a while. 'Well, I suppose we go on waiting.' He leant forward to stub his cigarette out. 'You know, you once told me I had to win.' He shook his head. 'You're the one who has to win.'

'This may come as a shock, Mr Prior, but I had been rather assuming we were on the same side.'

Prior smiled. 'This may come as a shock, Dr Rivers, but I had been *rather assuming* that we were not.'

Silence. Rivers caught and held a sigh. 'That does make the relationship of doctor and patient rather difficult.'

Prior shrugged. Obviously he didn't think that was *his* problem. 'You think you know what happened, don't you?' Rivers said.

'I've told you I don't remember.'

The antagonism was startling. They might've been back at the beginning, when it had been almost impossible to get a civil word out of him. 'I'm sorry, I didn't make myself clear. I wasn't suggesting you knew, only that you might have a *theory*.'

Prior shook his head. 'No. No theory.'

A short, dark-haired man sidled round the door, blinking in the sudden blaze of sunlight. Sassoon, sitting on the bed, looked up from the golf club he'd been cleaning. 'Yes?'

'I've b-brought these.'

A stammer. Not as bad as some, but bad enough. Sassoon exerted himself to be polite. 'What is it? I can't see.'

Books. *His* book. Five copies, no less. 'My God, a reader.'

'I wondered if you'd b-be k-kind enough to s-sign them?'

'Yes, of course.' Sassoon put the golf club down and reached for his pen. He could have dispatched the job in a few moments, but he sensed that his visitor wanted to talk, and he had after all bought *five* copies. Sassoon was curious. 'Why five? Has the War Office put it on a reading list?'

'They're f-for m-my f-family.'

Oh, dear. Sassoon transferred himself from bed to table and opened the first book. 'What name shall I write?'

'Susan Owen. M-y m-mother.'

Sassoon began to write. Paused. 'Are you . . . quite sure your mother *wants* to be told that "Bert's gone syphilitic?" I had trouble getting them to print that.'

'It w-won't c-come as a sh-shock.'

'Won't it?' One could only speculate on the nature of Mrs Owen's previous acquaintance with Bert.

'I t-tell her everything. In m-my l-letters.'

'Good heavens,' Sassoon said lightly, and turned back to the book.

Owen looked down at the back of Sassoon's neck, where a thin line of khaki was just visible beneath the purple silk of his dressing gown. 'Don't *you*?'

Sassoon opened his mouth and shut it again. 'My brother died at Gallipoli,' he said, at last. 'I think my mother has enough on her plate without any searing revelations from me.'

'I s-suppose she m-must b-be c-concerned about your b-being here.'

'Oh, I don't think so. On the contrary. I believe the thought of my insanity is one of her few consolations.' He glanced up, briefly. 'Better *mad* than a pacifist.' When Owen continued to look blank, he added, 'You do know why I'm here?'

'Yes.'

'And what do you think about that?'

'I agreed with every w-word.'

Sassoon smiled. 'So did my friend Graves.' He opened the next book. 'Who's this one for?'

Owen, feeding the names, would have given anything to say one sentence without stammering. No hope of that – he was far too nervous. Everything about Sassoon intimidated him. His status as a published poet, his height, his good looks, the clipped aristocratic voice, sometimes quick, sometimes halting, but always cold, the bored expression, the way he had of not looking at you when you spoke – shyness, perhaps, but it *seemed* like arrogance. Above all, his reputation for courage. Owen had his own reasons for being sensitive about that.

Sassoon reached the last book. Owen felt the meeting begin to slip away from him. Rather desperately, he said, 'I l-liked "The D-Death B-Bed" b-best.' And suddenly he relaxed. It didn't matter what *this* Sassoon thought about him, since the real Sassoon was in the poems. He quoted, from memory, '"He's young; he hated War, how should he die/When cruel old campaigners win safe through?/But death replied: 'I choose him.' So he went." That's beautiful.'

Sassoon paused in his signing. 'Yes, I – I was quite pleased with that.'

'Oh, and "The Redeemer". "He faced me, reeling in his weariness,/Shouldering his load of planks, so hard to bear./I say that He was Christ, who wrought to bless . . ."' He broke off. 'I've been wanting to write that for three years.'

'Perhaps you should be glad you didn't.'

The light faded from Owen's face. 'Sorry?'

'Well, don't you think it's rather easily said? "I say that He was Christ"?'

'You m-mean you d-didn't m-mean it?'

'Oh, I meant it. The book isn't putting one point of view, it's charting the – the *evolution* of a point of view. That's probably the first poem that even attempts to look at the war realistically. And that one doesn't go nearly far enough.' He paused. 'The fact is Christ isn't on record as having lobbed many Mills bombs.'

'No, I s-see what you m-mean. I've been thinking about that quite a b-bit recently.'

Sassoon scarcely heard him. 'I got so sick of it in the end. All those Calvaries at crossroads just sitting there waiting to be turned into symbols. I knew a man once, Potter his name was. You know the miraculous crucifix stories? *"Shells falling all around, but the figure of Our Lord was spared"*? Well, Potter was so infuriated by them he decided to start a one-man campaign. Whenever he saw an undamaged crucifix, he used it for target practice. You could hear him for miles. "ONE, TWO, THREE, FOUR, Bastard on the Cross, FIRE!" There weren't many miraculous crucifixes in Potter's section of the front.' He hesitated. 'But perhaps I shouldn't be saying this? I mean for all I know, you're –'

'I don't know what I am. But I do know I wouldn't want a f-faith that couldn't face the facts.'

Sassoon became aware that Owen was standing at his elbow, almost like a junior officer. 'Why don't you sit down?' he said, waving him towards the bed. 'And tell me your name. I take it this one's for you?'

'Yes. Wilfred. Wilfred Owen.'

Sassoon blew on his signature and closed the book. 'You say you've been thinking about it?'

Owen looked diffident. 'Yes.'

'To any effect? I mean, did you reach any conclusions?'

'Only that if I were going to call myself a Christian, I'd have to call myself a pacifist as well. I don't think it's possible to c-call yourself a C-Christian and . . . and j-just leave out the awkward bits.'

'You'll never make a bishop.'

'No, well, I think I can live with that.'

'And *do* you call yourself a pacifist?'

A long pause. 'No. Do you?'

'No.'

'It's funny, you know, I never thought about it at all in France.'

'No, well, you don't. Too busy, too tired.' Sassoon smiled. 'Too *healthy*.'

'It's not *just* that, though, is it? Sometimes when you're alone, in the trenches, I mean, at night you get the sense of something *ancient*. As if the trenches had always been there. You know one trench we held, it had skulls in the side. You looked back along and . . . Like mushrooms. And do you know, it was actually *easier* to believe they were men from Marlborough's army than to to to think they'd been alive two years ago. It's as if all other wars had somehow . . . distilled themselves into this war, and that makes it something you . . . almost can't challenge. It's like a very deep voice saying, *Run along, little man. Be thankful if you survive*.'

For a moment the nape of Sassoon's neck crawled as it had the first time Campbell talked about German spies; but this was not madness. 'I had a similar experience. Well, I don't know whether it is similar. I was going up with the rations one night and I saw the limbers against the skyline, and the flares going up. What you see every night. Only I seemed to be seeing it from the future. A hundred years from now they'll still be ploughing up skulls. And I seemed to be in that time and looking back. I think I saw our ghosts.'

Silence. They'd gone further than either of them had intended, and for a moment they didn't know how to get back. Gradually, they stirred, they looked round, at sunlight streaming over beds and chairs, at Sassoon's razor glinting on the washstand, its handle smeared with soap. Sassoon looked at his watch. 'I'm going to be late for golf.'

Immediately Owen stood up. 'Well, thanks for these,' he said, taking the books. He laughed. 'Thanks for writing it.'

Sassoon followed him to the door. 'Did you say you wrote?'

'I didn't, but I do.'

'Poetry?'

'Yes. Nothing in print yet. Oh, which reminds me. I'm editor of the *Hydra*. The hospital magazine? I was wondering if you could let us have something. It needn't be –'

'Yes, I'll look something out.' Sassoon opened the door. 'Give me a few days. You could bring your poems.'

This was said with such determined courtesy and such transparent lack of enthusiasm that Owen burst out laughing. 'No, I –'

'No, I mean it.'

'All right.' Owen was still laughing. 'They are quite short.'

'No, well, it doesn't lend itself to epics, does it?'

'Oh, they're not about the war.' He hesitated. 'I don't write about that.'

'Why ever not?'

'I s-suppose I've always thought of p-poetry as the opposite of all that. The ugliness.' Owen was struggling to articulate a point of view he was abandoning even as he spoke. 'S-Something to to t-take refuge in.'

Sassoon nodded. 'Fair enough.' He added mischievously, 'Though it does seem a bit like having a faith that daren't face the facts.' He saw Owen's expression change. 'Look, it doesn't matter what they're about. Bring them anyway.'

'Yes, I will. Thank you.'

Anderson, following Sassoon into the bar of the golf club, knew he owed him an apology. At the seventeenth hole, afraid he was losing, he'd missed a vital shot and in the heat of the moment had not merely sworn at Sassoon, but actually raised the club and threatened to hit him with it. Sassoon had looked startled, even alarmed, but he'd laughed it off. At the eighteenth hole, he'd been careful to ask Anderson's advice about which iron he should use. Now, he turned to Anderson and said, 'Usual?'

Anderson nodded. The trouble was, Anderson thought, it looked so much like bad sportsmanship, whereas in reality the apology was being delayed, not by any unwillingness on his part to admit he was wrong, but by the extent of the horror he felt at his own behaviour. He'd behaved like a spoilt child. *So do something about it,* he told himself. 'Sorry about that,' he said, nodding towards the course.

''S all right.' Sassoon turned from the bar and smiled. 'We all have bad days.'

'Here's your half-crown.'

Sassoon grinned and pocketed it. He was thinking, as he turned back to the bar, that if the club had landed on his head he would have been far more seriously injured than he'd been at Arras. He conjured Rivers up in his mind and asked, *What was that you were saying about 'safety'? Nothing more dangerous than playing golf with lunatics.* 'Lunatic' was a word Sassoon would never have dared use to Rivers's face, so it gave him an additional pleasure to yell it at his image.

They took their drinks, found a quiet corner, and began their usual inquest on the game. Under cover of the familiar chat, Anderson watched Sassoon – a good-looking, rather blank face, big hands curved round his glass – and thought how little he knew about him. Or wanted to know. It was a matter of tacit agreement that they talked about nothing but golf. Anderson had read the Declaration, but he wouldn't have dreamt of discussing Sassoon's attitude to the war, mainly because some return of intimacy would then have been required. He might have had to disclose his own reasons for being at Craiglockhart. His horror of blood. He had a momentary picture of the way Sassoon's head would have looked if he'd hit him, and his hand tightened on the glass. 'You're still not taking your time,' he said. 'You're rushing your shots.'

There were other reasons too why he didn't want to talk about the war. Inevitably such talk would have strengthened his own doubts, and they were bad enough already. He even dreamt about the bloody war, not just nightmares, he was used to those; he'd dreamt he was speaking at a debate on whether it should go on or not. In his dream he'd spoken in favour of continuing to the point of German collapse, but Rivers's analysis had left him in no doubt as to how far his horror at the whole business went. He felt safe with Rivers, because he knew Rivers shared the horror, and shared too the conviction that, in spite of everything, it had to go on.

'I don't know whether to spend that half-crown or frame it,' Sassoon was saying. 'I don't suppose I'll ever win another.'

That was to make Anderson feel better about losing his temper on the course. Sassoon was a pleasant companion, there was no doubt about that. He was friendly, modest. But the Declaration hadn't been modest. What had chiefly struck Anderson about that was its arrogance, its totally outrageous assumption that everybody who disagreed with him was 'callous'. Do you think I'm callous? he wanted to ask. Do you think *Rivers* is callous? But there was no point getting worked up. Rivers would soon sort him out.

'I shan't be seeing you tomorrow, shall I?' Sassoon was saying. 'Your wife's coming up.'

'No, I'm afraid she's had to cancel. So it's business as usual.' He took Sassoon's empty glass and stood up. 'You can *try* to make it five bob, if you like.'

Prior watched the amber lights winking in his beer. He was sitting in the shadowy corner of a pub in some sleazy district of Edinburgh. He didn't know where he was. He'd walked miles that evening, not admitting even to himself what he was looking for, and gradually the winding, insidious streets had led him deeper and deeper into a neighbourhood where washing hung, grey-white, from stacked balconies, and the smell of steak frying reminded him of home.

Remembering the smell, his stomach rumbled. He'd had nothing to eat all evening, except a packet of peanuts. Crumbs of salt still clung to his lips, stinging the cracks where the skin had dried during his asthma attack. It was worth it, though, just to sit quietly, to listen to voices that didn't stammer, to have his eyes freed from the ache of khaki.

No theory. He'd lied to Rivers about that. It was a point of honour with him to lie to Rivers at least once during every meeting. He drained his glass and went out into the night.

A little way down the street was a café. He'd passed it on his way to the pub and been tempted to go in, but the door had opened and the breath of hot, damp, dirty, dishwater-smelling air had decided him against it. Now, though, he was too hungry to care. He went in, noticing how the inner windows dripped from condensation, how the damp air insinuated itself into the spaces between his uniform and his skin. A short silence fell. Nobody in an officer's uniform was likely to be inconspicuous or welcome here. He would eat something, fish and chips, quickly and then go.

A group of women was sitting at the next table. Three of them were young, one older, thirty-five, forty perhaps, with blackened stumps for teeth. As far as he could make out from the conversation her name was Lizzie, and the others were Madge, the blonde, pretty one, Betty, who was dark and thin, and Sarah, who had her back to him. Since they all had a slightly yellow tinge to their skin, he assumed they were munitions workers. Munition*ettes*, as the newspapers liked to call them. Lizzie was keeping the younger girls entertained with a string of stories.

'There's this lass and she's a bit simple and she lived next door to a pro – well you know what a pro is.' Lizzie glanced at him and lowered her voice. 'So she's standing at the door this day, and the pro's coming up the street, you know, *dressed to death*. So she says, "Eeh," she says, "you're always lovely dressed." She says, "You've got beautiful clothes." And she says, "I *love* your hats." So the pro says, "Well, why don't you get yourself down the town like I do?" She says, "If a man winks at you, wink back and go with him and let him have what he wants and charge him 7/6. And go to R&K Modes and get yourself a hat." So the next day the pro's coming up the street again. "Hello." "Hello." She says, "D' y' *get* a hat?" She says, "*Nah*." "Well, did you not do as I telled you?" She says, "Why of course I did." She says, "I went down the town and there was a man winked at us and I winked back. He says, 'Howay over the Moor.'" So she says, "I gans over the Moor with him," she says, "and I let him have what he wanted. He says, 'How much is that?' I says, '7/6.' He says, 'Hadaway and shite,' and when I come back he'd gone."'

The girls shrieked with laughter. He looked at them again. The one called Madge was very pretty, but there was no hope of winkling her out of the group, and he thought he might as well be moving on. As soon as his meal arrived, he began stuffing limp chips and thickly battered fish into his mouth, wiping the grease away on the back of his hand.

'You'll get hiccups.'

He looked up. It was Sarah, the one who'd been sitting with her back to him. 'You'll have to give us a surprise, then, won't you?'

'Drop me key down your back if you like.'

'That's nose bleeds, Sarah,' Betty said.

'She knows what it is,' said Lizzie.

Madge said, 'Hiccups, you're supposed to drink from the other side of the cup.'

She and Prior stared at each other across the table.

'But it's a con, isn't it?' he said. 'You can't do it.'

''Course you can.'

'Go on, then, let's see you.'

She dipped her small, straight nose into her cup, lapped, spluttered and came up laughing and wiping her chin. Betty, obviously jealous, gave her a dig in the ribs. 'Hey up you, you're gonna gerrus slung out.'

The café owner was eyeing them from behind the till, slowly polishing a glass on a distinctly grubby-looking tea towel. The girls went back to their tea, bursting into minor explosions of giggles, their shoulders shaking, while Prior turned back and finished his meal. He was aware of Sarah beside him. She had very heavy, very thick, dark-brown hair, but all over the surface, in a kind of halo, were other hairs, auburn, copper, chestnut. He'd never seen hair like that before. He looked at her, and she turned around and stared at him, a cool, amused stare from greenish eyes. He said, 'Would you like a drink?'

She looked at her cup.

'No, I meant a proper drink.'

'Pubs round here don't let women in.'

'Isn't there a hotel?'

'Well, there's the Cumberland, but . . .'

The other women looked at each other. Lizzie said, 'Howay, lasses, I think our Sarah's clicked.'

The three of them got up, said a good-natured 'goodnight' and tripped out of the café, only bursting into giggles again after they'd reached the pavement.

'Shall we go, then?' said Prior.

Sarah looked at him. 'Aye, all right.'

Outside, she turned to him. 'I still don't know your name.'

'Prior,' he said automatically.

She burst out laughing. 'Don't you lot *have* Christian names?'

'Billy.' He wanted to say, and I'm not 'you lot'.

'Mine's Sarah. Sarah Lumb.' She held out her hand to him in a direct, almost boyish way. It intrigued him, since nothing else about her was boyish.

'Well, Sarah Lumb, lead on.'

Her preferred drink was port and lemon. Prior was startled at the rate she knocked them back. A flush spread across her cheeks in a different place from the rouge, so that she looked as if her face had slid out of focus. She worked in a factory, she said, making detonators. Twelve-hour shifts, six days a week, but she liked the work, she said, and it was well paid. 'Fifty bob a week.'

'I suppose that's something.'

'Too bloody right it is. I was earning ten bob before the war.'

He thought what the detonators she made could do to flesh and bone, and his mind bulged as a memory threatened to surface. 'You're not Scottish, though, are you?'

'No, Geordie. Well, what *you*'d call Geordie.'

'Did your dad come up looking for work?'

'No, they're still down there. I'm in lodgings down the road.'

Ah, he thought.

'"*Ah*," he thinks.' She looked at him, amused and direct. 'I think you're a bad lad.'

'No, I'm not. Nobody bad could be *that* transparent.'

'That's true.'

'Haven't you got a boyfriend?'

'What do you think?'

'I don't think you'd be sitting here if you had.'

'Oh, I might be one of these two-timing lasses, you never know.' She looked down into her glass. 'No, I haven't got one.'

'Why not? Can't all be blind in Scotland.'

'Perhaps I'm not on the market.'

He didn't know what to make of her, but then he was out of touch with women. They seemed to have changed so much during the war, to have expanded in all kinds of ways, whereas men over the same period had shrunk into a smaller and smaller space.

'I did have one,' she said. 'Loos.'

Odd, he thought, getting up and going to the bar to buy more drinks, that one word should be enough. But then why not? Language ran out on you, in the end, the names were left to say it all. Mons, Loos, Ypres, the Somme. Arras. He paid and carried the drinks back to their table. He thought that he didn't want to hear about the boyfriend, and that he was probably going to anyway. He was right there.

'I was in service at the time. It didn't . . .' Her voice became very brisk. 'It didn't seem to sink in. Then his mate came to see me. You weren't supposed to have followers. "Followers" – that's how old-fashioned she was. Especially *soldiers*. "Oh my *deah*." So anyway he come to the front door and . . .' She waved her hand languidly. 'I sent him away. Then I nipped down the basement and let him in the back.' She took a swig of the port. 'It was *our* gas,' she said, red-lidded. 'Did *you* know that?'

'Yes.'

'Our own bloody gas. After he'd gone, you know, I couldn't believe it. I just walked round and round the table and it was like . . . You know when you get a tune stuck in your head? I just kept on thinking, our gas. Anyway after a bit she come downstairs, and she says, "Where's tea?" I says, "Well, you can see for yourself. It's not ready." *We-ell*. First one thing was said and then another and in the end I did, I let her have it. She says, "You'd be making a great mistake to throw this job away, you know, Sarah." I says, "Oh, aye?" She says, "We don't say 'aye', Sarah, we say 'yes'." I says, "All right," I says, "'*yes*'. But 'aye' or 'yes', it's still ten bob a week and you put it where the monkey put the nuts." Same night I was packing me bags. No testimonial. And you know what that would've meant before the war?' She looked him up and down. 'No, I don't suppose you do. Anyway, I turned up at home and me Mam says, "I've no sympathy, our Sarah," she says. "You should have fixed him while you had the chance," she says. "And made sure of the pension. Our Cynthia had her wits about her," she says. "Why couldn't you?" And of course our Cynthia's sat there. Would you believe *in weeds*? I thought, aw to hell with this. Anyway, a couple of days after, I got on talking to Betty – that's the dark girl you saw me with just now – and we decided to give this a go.'

'I'm glad you did.'

She brooded for a while over her empty glass. 'You know, me Mam says there's no such thing as love between men and women. Love for your bairns, yes. Love for a man? *No.*' She turned to him, almost aggressively. 'What do *you* think?'

'I don't know.'

'Well, that makes two of us, then, 'cause I'm buggered if I do.'

'But you loved –'

'Johnny? I can't remember what he looked like. Sometimes his face pops into me mind, like when I'm thinking about something else, but when I *want* to see it, I can't.' She smiled. 'That's the trouble with port and lemon, isn't it? Truth pours out.'

He took the hint and bought another.

By the time they left the pub she'd drunk enough to need his arm.

'Which way's your lodgings?'

She giggled. 'Won't do you any good,' she said. 'My landlady's a dragon. Fifty times worse than me Mam.'

'Shall we go for a walk, then? I don't fancy saying goodnight, just yet, do you?'

'All right.'

They turned away from the lighted pavements, into the darkness of a side street. He put his arm around her, inching his hand further up until his fingers rested against the curve of her breast. She was tall for a woman, and they fitted together, shoulder and hip. He hardly had to shorten his stride. As they walked, she glanced down frequently at her shoes and stockings, admiring herself. He guessed she more usually wore boots.

They came upon a church with a small churchyard around it. Gravestones leant together at angles in the shadow of the trees, like people gossiping. 'Shall we go in there for a bit?'

He opened the gate for her and they went in, into the darkness under the trees, treading on something soft and crunchy. Pine needles, perhaps. At the church door they turned and followed the path round, till they came to a tall, crumbling, ivy-covered wall. There, in the shadows, he pulled her towards him. He got her jacket and blouse unbuttoned and felt for her breast. The nipple hardened against his palm, and he laughed under his breath. She started to say something, but he covered her mouth with his own, he didn't want her to talk, he didn't want her to tell him things. He would have preferred not even to know her name. Just flesh against flesh in the darkness and then nothing.

'I know what *you* want,' she said, pulling away from him.

Instantly he let her go. '*I* know what I want. What's wrong with *that*? I've never forced anybody.' He turned away from her and sat on a tombstone. 'And I don't go on about it either.'

'Then you're a man in a million.'

'I know.'

'Big-headed bugger.'

'Don't I even get a cuddle?' He patted the tombstone. 'No harm in that.'

She came and sat beside him, and after a while he got his arms around her again. But he didn't feel the same way about it. Now, even as he lowered his head to her breast, he was wondering whether he wanted to play this particular game. Whether it was worth it. He tugged gently at her nipple, and felt her thighs loosen. Instantly, his doubts vanished. He pressed her back on to the tombstone and moved on top of her. Cradling her head on his left arm, he began the complicated business of raising her skirts, pulling down her drawers, unbuttoning his breeches, all while trying to maintain their position on a too-short and sloping tombstone. At the last moment she cried 'No-o-o' and shoved him hard off the tombstone into the long grass. He sat for a while, his back against the stone, picking bits of lichen off his tunic. After a while he yawned and said, 'Short-arsed little buggers, the Scots.'

She looked down at the tombstone, which did seem rather small. 'Oh, I don't know. Everybody was shorter in them days.' You could just make out the word 'Beloved', but everything else was covered in lichen or crumbled away. She traced the word with her fingertip. 'I wonder what they think.'

'Down there? Glad to see a bit of life, I should think. Not that they've seen much.'

She didn't reply. He turned to look at her. Her hair had come down, way past her shoulders, he was glad she didn't wear it short, and there was still that amazing contrast of the dark brown velvety mass and its halo of copper wire. He was being stupid. She'd let him have it in the end, and the more he bellyached about it now, the longer he'd have to wait. He said, 'Come on, one kiss, and I'll walk you home.'

'Hm.'

'No, I mean it.'

He gave her a teasingly chaste kiss, making sure he was the first to pull away. Then he helped her dust down her skirt and walked her back to her lodgings. On the way she insisted they stop in the doorway of a shop, and she crammed her hair up into her hat, with the help of the few hairpins she'd managed to retrieve. 'There'd be eyebrows raised if I went in like this.'

'Can I see you again?'

'You know where I live. Or you will do.'

'I don't know your times off.'

'Sunday.'

'I'll come over on Sunday, then, shall I? If I come mid morning, we could have a bite to eat in Edinburgh and then go somewhere on the tram.'

She looked doubtful, but the thought of being collected from her lodgings by an officer was too much for her. 'All right.'

They walked on. She stopped outside the door and raised her face. Oh, no, he thought. No fumbling on doorsteps. He lowered his head until his forehead rested against hers. 'Goodnight, Sarah Lumb.'

'Goodnight, Billy Prior.'

After a few paces he turned and looked back. She was standing on the step, watching him walk away. He raised his hand, and she waved slightly. Then he turned and walked briskly on, looking at his watch and thinking, Christ. Even if he found a taxi *immediately* he still couldn't be back at Craiglockhart before the main doors were locked. Oh well, he thought, I'll just have to face it.

NINE

'Aren't *you* going to start?'

'I imagine Major Bryce has dealt with the matter?'

'You could say. He's confined me to the hospital for a fortnight.'

Rivers made no comment.

'Don't you think that's rather *severe*?'

'It wasn't a simple matter of being late back, was it? Matron says she saw you in town, and you were not wearing your hospital badge.'

'I wasn't wearing the badge because I was looking for a girl. Which – *as you may or may not know* – is not made easier by going around with a badge stuck on your chest saying I AM A LOONY.'

'I gather you also made some rather disrespectful remarks about Matron. Everything from the size of her bosom to the state of her hymen. If you make remarks like that to the CO, what do you *think* is going to happen?'

Prior didn't reply, though a muscle throbbed in his jaw. Rivers looked at the pale, proud, wintry face and thought oh God, it's going to be another one of those.

Prior said, 'Aren't you going to ask me if I got one?'

'One what?'

'Girl. Woman.' When Rivers didn't immediately reply, Prior added, '*Wo-man*?'

'No, I wasn't going to ask.'

'You amaze me. I should've thought that was par for the course.'

Rivers waited.

'*Questions*. On and on and bloody on.'

'Would you like to leave it for today?'

'No.'

'You're sure?'

'Quite sure.'

'All right. We'd got to the time immediately following the April 23rd attack. Have you made any progress beyond that?'

'No.'

'Nothing at all?'

'No.' Prior's hands were gripping the arms of his chair. 'I don't want to talk about this.'

Rivers decided to humour him. 'What do you want to talk about?'

'Something you said earlier on. It's been bothering me ever since. You said officers don't suffer from mutism.'

'It's rare.'

'How many cases?'

'At Craiglockhart? You, and one other. At Maghull, where I was treating private soldiers, it was by far the commonest symptom.'

'Why?'

'I imagine . . . Mutism seems to spring from a conflict between *wanting* to say something, and knowing that if you *do* say it the consequences will be disastrous. So you resolve it by making it physically impossible for yourself to speak. And for the private soldier the consequences of speaking his mind are always going to be far worse than they would be for an officer. What you tend to get in officers is stammering. And it's not just mutism. All the physical symptoms:

paralysis, blindness, deafness. They're all common in private soldiers and rare in officers. It's almost as if for the . . . the labouring classes illness *has* to be physical. They can't take their condition seriously unless there's a physical symptom. And there are other differences as well. Officers' dreams tend to be more elaborate. The men's dreams are much more a matter of simple wish fulfilment. You know, they dream they've been sent back to France, but on the day they arrive peace is declared. That sort of thing.'

'I think I'd rather have their dreams than mine.'

'How do you know?' Rivers said. 'You don't remember your dreams.'

'You still haven't said why.'

'I suppose it's just a matter of officers having a more complex mental life.'

Prior reacted as if he'd been stung. 'Are you serious? You honestly believe that that *gaggle* of noodle-brained half-wits down there has a complex mental life? Oh, *Rivers*.'

'I'm not saying it's *universally* true, only that it's *generally* true. Simply as a result of officers receiving a different and, for the most part, more prolonged education.'

'The public schools.'

'Yes. The public schools.'

Prior raised his head. 'How do I fit into that?'

'We-ell, it's interesting that you were mute and that you're one of the very few people in the hospital who *doesn't* stammer.'

'It's even more interesting that you do.'

Rivers was taken aback. 'That's d-different.'

'How is it different? Other than that you're on that side of the desk?' He saw Rivers hesitate. 'No, I'm not being awkward. I'm genuinely interested.'

'It's usually thought that neurasthenic stammers arise from the same kind of conflict as mutism, a conflict between wanting to speak and knowing that w-what you've got to say is not acceptable. Lifelong stammerers? Well. Nobody really knows. It may even be genetic.'

Prior smiled. 'Now that is lucky, isn't it? Lucky for you, I mean. Because if your stammer *was* the same as theirs – you might actually have to sit down and work out what it is you've spent fifty years trying not to say.'

'Is that the end of my appointment for the day, Mr Prior?'

Prior smiled.

'You know one day you're going to have to accept the fact that you're in this hospital because you're ill. Not me. Not the CO. Not the kitchen porter. *You.*'

After Prior had gone, Rivers sat for a while, half amused, half irritated. Now that his attention had been drawn to his stammer, it would plague him at intervals throughout the day. Bugger Prior, he thought. To be absolutely accurate, b-b-b-bugger Prior.

Prior had left slightly early, so Rivers had a few minutes before his next appointment. He decided to take a turn in the grounds. The grass was silvery with dew – his footsteps showed up dark along the path he'd come – but here and there the ground was beginning to steam. He sat on a bench under the trees, and watched two patients carrying scythes come round the corner of the building and run down the grassy slope that divided the gravel drive from the tennis courts. They looked, Rivers thought, almost comically symbolic: Time and Death invading the Arcadian scene. Nothing symbolic about the scythes, though. The blades over their shoulders glinted a wicked blue-grey. You could only wonder at an administration that confiscated cut-throat razors and then issued the patients with these. They set to work cutting the long grass by the hedges. There was a great deal of laughter and clumsiness at first, and a not a few false starts, before their bodies bent into the rhythm of the task. Moths, disturbed from their daytime sleep, flickered all around them.

One took off his Sam Browne belt and then tunic, shirt and tie, casting them carelessly aside, and then went back to his scything, his dangling braces describing wide arcs around him as he swung the blade. His body was very pale, with a line round the neck, dividing white from reddish brown. The tunic had landed on the hedge, one sleeve raised as if beckoning. The other flung down his scythe and did the same. Work went more quickly now. Soon there was a gratifyingly large area of mown grass for them to look back on. They stood leaning on the scythes, admiring their work, and then one of them dived into the cut grass, winnowing his way through it, obviously excited by it in the way dogs sometimes are. He lay on his back, panting. The other man came across, said, 'Silly bugger,' and started kicking the grass all over him.

Rivers turned and saw Patterson – the Head of Office Administration – making his way at a steady pace down the slope to deliver the inevitable reprimand. King's regulations. No officer must appear in public with any garment missing. Patterson spoke to them, then turned away. Slowly, they reached for their uniforms, pulled khaki shirts and tunics on to sweating bodies, buckled belts. It had to be done, though it seemed to Rivers that the scything went more slowly after that, and there was less laughter, which seemed a pity.

That night Rivers worked late, compiling lists of men to be boarded at the end of August. This was the most difficult task of any month, since it involved deciding which patients were fit to return to duty. In theory, the decision to return a man to service was taken by the Board, but since his recommendations were rarely, if ever, questioned, in practice his report determined the outcome. He was beginning to work on the first of these reports when there was a tap on the door. He called, 'Come in!'

Prior came into the room.

'Good evening,' Rivers said.

'Good evening. I came to say I'm sorry about this morning.'

The day had been so horrific in so many ways – culminating in a three-hour meeting of the hospital management committee – that Rivers had to grope for the memory. He said. 'That's all right.'

'It was stupid. Going on like that.'

'Oh, I don't know. We just caught each other at a bad moment.'

Prior lingered a few feet away from the desk. 'Why don't you sit down?' Rivers said.

'You must be tired.'

'Tired of paperwork.'

Prior's glance took in the list of names. 'The Boards.'

'The Boards.' He glanced at Prior. 'Not you this time.'

'Not enough progress.'

Rivers didn't immediately reply. He was watching Prior, noticing the pallor, the circles round the eyes. He had shadows under the shadows now. 'You have made progress. You've recovered almost all your memory *and* you no longer lose your voice.'

'You must wish I did.'

Rivers smiled. 'Don't exaggerate, Mr Prior. We both know if you *really* wanted to be offensive, you could do a hundred times better than you did this morning.' He waited for a reply. 'Couldn't you?'

Prior produced a curious rippling motion – half shrug, half flounce – and turned away. After a moment he looked sideways at Rivers. 'I did once think of asking you if you ever fucked any of your headhunters.'

'What stopped you?'

'I thought it was your business.'

Rivers pretended to consider the matter. 'That's true.'

'There's no point trying to be offensive, is there, if *that's* the only response you get?'

'You don't really want to be. You've always made a lot of *noise* about stepping over the line, but you've never actually done it.' Rivers smiled. 'Except just now, of course. And that was incredibly indirect.'

A short silence. Prior said, 'I wish I could go out. No, it's all right, I'm not asking. I'm just saying I wish I could. The nightmares get worse when I'm stuck indoors.' He waited. 'This is where you ask about the nightmares and I say I don't remember.'

'I know.'

Prior smiled. 'You never believed me, did you?'

'Should I have done?'

'No.'

'Do you want to talk about them now?'

'I can't. Look, they're just . . .' He laughed. '"*Standard issue battle nightmares. Potty officers for the use of.*" Nothing you won't have heard a hundred times before.'

'Except?'

'Except nothing.'

A long silence.

'Except that *sometimes* they get muddled up with sex. So I wake up, and . . .' He risked a glance at Rivers. When he spoke again, his voice was casual. 'It makes it really quite impossible to *like* oneself. I've actually woken up once or twice and wondered whether there was any point going on.'

And you might well do it, Rivers thought.

'That's why I was so furious when they got you up in the middle of the night.'

Easy to hand out the usual reassurances about the effects on young men of a celibate life, but not particularly helpful. Prior was becoming unmistakably depressed. It was doing him no good to wait for his CO's letter, which might anyway turn out to contain nothing of any great moment. 'We could try hypnosis now, if you liked.'

'Now?'

'Yes, why not? It's the time we're least likely to be interrupted.'

Prior's eyes flickered round the room. He licked his lips. 'It's odd, isn't it? When you said most people were frightened, I didn't believe you.'

'What frightens them,' Rivers said carefully, 'is the belief that they're putting themselves completely in the therapist's power. That he can make them do anything, even things they'd normally consider ridiculous or even immoral. But that isn't true, you remain your*self* throughout. Not that I shall be trying to make you do anything ridiculous or immoral.' He smiled. 'In spite of being the terror of the South Seas.'

Prior laughed, but his face tightened again immediately.

'We can leave it, if you like,' Rivers said gently.

Deep breath. 'No. I can't pester you for it and then turn it down.'

'If it turns out to be . . .' Rivers groped for a sufficiently bland word. '*Distressing,* I'll give you something to make you sleep. I mean, you won't have to face up to the full implications tonight.'

'All right. What do we do?'

'You relax. Sit back in the chair. That's right. Shoulders. Come on, like this. Now your hands. Let the wrists go. Comfortable? I want you to look at this pen. No, don't raise your head. Raise your eyes. That's right. Keep your eyes fixed on the pen. I'm going to count down from ten. By the time I get to zero, you'll be in a light sleep. All right?'

Prior nodded. He looked profoundly sceptical. Like most bloody-minded people he assumed he would be a poor subject for hypnosis. Rivers thought he'd be very easy. 'Ten . . . Nine . . . Eight . . . Seven . . . Your eyelids are heavy now. Don't fight it, let them close. Six . . . Five . . . Four . . . Three . . . Two . . .'

He woke to a dugout smell of wet sandbags and stale farts. He curled his toes inside his wet boots and felt the creak and sag of chicken wire as he turned towards the table. The usual jumble: paper, bottles, mugs, the black-boxed field telephone, a couple of revolvers – all lit by a single candle stuck to the wood in a pool of its own grease. A barely perceptible thinning of the darkness around the gas curtain told him it must be nearly dawn. And sure enough, a few minutes later Sanderson lifted the curtain and shouted, 'Stand-to!' The bulky forms on the other bunks stirred, groaned, groped for revolvers. Soon they were all trying to climb out of the dugout, difficult because rain and recent near-hits had turned the steps into a muddy slide. All along the trench men were crawling out of funk holes. He clumped along the duck-boards to his position, smelling the green, ratty, decomposing smell, stretching the muscles of his face into a smile whenever the men looked up. Then an hour of standing, stiff and shivery, watching dawn grow.

He had first trench watch. He gulped a mug of chlorine-tasting tea, and then started walking along to the outermost position on their left. A smell of bacon frying. In the third fire bay he found Sawdon and Towers crouched over a small fire made out of shredded sandbags and candle ends, coaxing the flames. He stopped to chat for a few minutes, and Towers, blinking under the green mushroom helmet, looked up and offered him tea. A quiet day, he thought, walking on. Not like the last few days, when the bombardment had gone on for seventy hours, and they'd stood-to five times expecting a German counter-attack. Damage from that bombardment was everywhere: crumbling parapets, flooded saps, dugouts with gagged mouths.

He'd gone, perhaps, three fire bays along when he heard the whoop of a shell, and, spinning round, saw the scrawl of dusty brown smoke already drifting away. He thought it'd gone clear over, but then he heard a cry and, feeling sick in his stomach, he ran back. Logan was there already. It must have been Logan's cry he heard, for nothing in that devastation could have had a voice. A conical black hole, still smoking, had been driven into the side of the trench. Of the kettle, the frying-pan, the carefully tended fire, there was no sign, and not much of Sawdon and Towers either, or not much that was recognizable.

There was a pile of sandbags and shovels close by, stacked against the parapet by a returning work party. He reached for a shovel. Logan picked up a sandbag and held it open, and he began shovelling soil, flesh and splinters of blackened bone into the bag. As he shovelled, he retched. He felt something jar against his teeth and saw that Logan was offering him a rum bottle. He forced down bile and rum together. Logan kept his face averted as the shovelling went on. He was swearing under his breath, steadily, blasphemously, obscenely, inventively. Somebody came running. 'Don't stand there gawping, man,' Logan said. 'Go and get some lime.'

They'd almost finished when Prior shifted his position on the duckboards, glanced down, and found himself staring into an eye. Delicately, like somebody selecting a particularly choice morsel from a plate, he put his thumb and forefinger down through the duckboards. His fingers touched the smooth surface and slid before they managed to get a hold. He got it out, transferred it to the palm of his hand, and held it out towards Logan. He could see his hand was shaking, but the shaking didn't seem to be anything to do with him. 'What am I supposed to do with this gob-stopper?' He saw Logan blink and knew he was afraid. At last Logan reached out, grasped his shaking wrist, and tipped the eye into the bag. 'Williams and me'll do the rest, sir. You go on back now.'

He shook his head. They spread the lime together, sprinkling it thickly along the firestep, throwing shovelfuls at a bad patch of wall. When at last they stood back, beating the white dust from the skirts of their tunics, he wanted to say something casual, something that would prove he was all right, but a numbness had spread all over the lower half of his face.

Back in the dugout he watched people's lips move and was filled with admiration for them. There was a sense of joy in watching them, of elation almost. How complex those movements were, how amazing the glimpses of teeth and tongue, the movement of muscles in the jaw. He ran his tongue along the edges of his teeth, curved it back, stroked the ridged palate, flexed his lips, felt the pull of skin and the stretching of muscles in his throat. All present and correct, but how they combined together to make sounds he had no idea.

It was Logan who took him to the casualty clearing station. Normally it would have been his servant, but Logan asked if he could go. They thumped and splodged along cheerfully enough, or at least Prior was cheerful. He felt as if nothing could ever touch him again. When a shell whined across, he didn't flinch, though he knew the Germans had an accurate fix on both communication trenches. They marched from stinking mud to dryish duckboards, and the bare landscape he sensed beyond the tangles of rusty wire gradually changed to fields. Clumps of brilliant yellow cabbage weed, whose smell mimics gas so accurately that men tremble, hung over the final trench.

In the clearing station he sat down, Logan beside him. Lying on the floor was a young man wounded in the back who seemed hardly to know that they were there. From time to time he moaned, 'I'm cold, I'm cold,' but when the doctor came in, he shook his head and said there was nothing he could do. 'There's no need for you to stay,' he said to Logan. 'He'll be all right.' So they shook hands and parted. He sat down on the bench again and tried to think back over the events that had brought him there, but found he could remember very little about them. Two of his men were dead, he remembered that. Nothing else. Like the speechlessness, it seemed natural. He sat on the bench, his clasped hands dangling between his legs, and thought of nothing.

*

Rivers watched the play of emotions on Prior's face as he fitted the recovered memory into his past. He was unprepared for what happened next.

'*Is that all?*' Prior said.

He seemed to be beside himself with rage.

'I don't know about *all*,' Rivers said. 'I'd've thought that was a traumatic experience by any standards.'

Prior almost spat at him. 'It was *nothing*.'

He put his head in his hands, at first, it seemed, in bewilderment, but then after a few moments he began to cry. Rivers waited a while, then walked round the desk and offered his handkerchief. Instead of taking it, Prior seized Rivers by the arms, and began butting him in the chest, hard enough to hurt. This was not an attack, Rivers realized, though it felt like one. It was the closest Prior could come to asking for physical contact. Rivers was reminded of a nanny goat on his brother's farm, being lifted almost off her feet by the suckling kid. Rivers held Prior's shoulders, and after a while the butting stopped. Prior raised his blind and slobbery face. 'Sorry about that.'

'That's all right.' He waited for Prior to wipe his face, then asked, 'What did you think happened?'

'I didn't know.'

'Yes, you did. You *thought* you knew.'

'I knew two of my men had been killed. I thought . . .' He stopped. 'I thought it must've been my fault. We were in the same trenches we'd been in when I first arrived. The line's terrible there. It winds in and out of brick stacks. A lot of the trenches face the wrong way. Even in daylight with a compass and a map you can get lost. At night . . . I'd been there about a week, I suppose, when a man took out patrol to see if a particular dugout was occupied at night. Compasses don't work, there's too much metal about. He'd been crawling round in circles for God knows how long, when he came upon what he thought was a German wiring party. He ordered his men to open fire. Well, all hell was let loose. Then after a while somebody realized there were British voices shouting on both sides. Five men killed. Eleven injured. I looked at his face as he sat in the dugout and he was . . . You could have done *that* and he wouldn't've blinked. Before I'd always thought the worst thing would be if you were wounded and left out there, but when I saw his face I thought, no. This is the worst thing. And then when I couldn't remember anything except that two of my men had been killed, I thought it had to be something like that.' He looked up. 'I couldn't see what else I'd need to forget.'

'Then you must be relieved.'

'Relieved?'

'You did your duty. You've nothing to reproach yourself with. You even finished cleaning the trench.'

'I've cleaned up dozens of trenches. I don't see why that would make me break down.'

'You're thinking of breakdown as a reaction to a single traumatic event, but it's not like that. It's more a matter of . . . *erosion*. Weeks and months of stress in a situation where you can't get away from it.' He smiled. 'I'm sorry to sound so impersonal. I know how you hate being "the patient".'

'I don't mind in the least. I just want to understand why it happened. You see what I find so difficult is . . . I don't think of myself as the kind of person who breaks down. And yet time and time again I'm brought up hard against the fact that I *did*.'

'I don't know that there is "a kind of person who breaks down". I imagine most of us could if the pressure were bad enough. I know I could.'

Prior gazed round the room in mock amazement. 'Did the wallpaper speak?'

Rivers smiled. 'I'll tell them to give you a sleeping tablet.'

At the door Prior turned. 'He had very blue eyes, you know. Towers. We used to call him the Hun.'

After making sure Prior got his sleeping tablet, Rivers went upstairs to his own room and began to undress. He tugged at his tie, and as he did so caught sight of himself in the looking-glass. He pulled down his right lid to reveal a dingy and blood-shot white. *What am I supposed to do with this gob-stopper?* He released the lid. *No need to think about that*. If he went on feeling like this, he'd have to see Bryce and arrange to take some leave. It'd reached the point where he woke up in the morning feeling almost as exhausted as he had done when he went to bed. He sat on the edge of the bath and began to take his boots off. *Ye will surely say unto me this proverb. Physician, heal thyself.* One of his father's favourite texts. Sitting, bored and fidgety, in the family pew, Rivers had never thought it an odd choice, though now he wondered why it cropped up as frequently as it did. Fathers remain opaque to their sons, he thought, largely because the sons find it so hard to believe that there's anything in the father worth seeing. Until he's dead, and it's too late. Mercifully, doctors are also opaque to their patients. Unless the patient happens to be Prior.

Rivers finished undressing and got into the bath. He lay back, eyes closed, feeling the hot water start to unravel the knots in his neck and shoulders. Not that Prior was the only patient to have found him . . . Well. Rather less than opaque. He remembered John Layard, and as always the memory was painful, because his treatment of Layard had ended in failure. He told himself there was no real resemblance between Layard and Prior. What made Prior more difficult was the constant *probing*. Layard had never probed. But then Layard hadn't thought he needed to probe. Layard had thought he knew.

Lying with his eyes closed like this, Rivers could imagine himself back in St John's, hearing Layard's footsteps coming across the court. What was it he'd said? 'I don't see you as a *father*, you know.' Looking up from the rug in front of the fire. Laughing. 'More a sort of . . . *male mother*.' He *was* like Prior. The same immensely shrewd eyes. X-ray eyes. The same outrageous frankness.

Why should he remember that? It was because of that ridiculous image of the nanny goat that had flashed into his mind while Prior was butting him in the stomach. He disliked the term 'male mother'. He thought he could remember disliking it even at the time. He distrusted the implication that nurturing, even when done by a man, remains female, as if the ability were in some way borrowed, or even stolen, from women – a sort of moral equivalent of the *couvade*. If that were true, then there was really very little hope.

He could see why Layard might use the term. Layard's relationship with his father had been difficult, and he was a young man, without any personal experience of fathering. Though fathering, like mothering, takes many forms beyond the biological. Rivers had often been touched by the way in which young men, some of them not yet twenty, spoke about feeling like fathers to their men. Though when you looked at what they *did*. Worrying about socks, boots, blisters, food, hot drinks. And that perpetually harried expression of theirs. Rivers had only ever seen that look in one other place: in the public wards of hospitals, on the faces of women who were bringing up large families on very low incomes, women who, in their early thirties, could easily be taken for fifty or more. It was the look of people who are totally responsible for lives they have no power to save.

One of the paradoxes of the war – one of the many – was that this most brutal of conflicts should set up a relationship between officers and men that was . . . domestic. Caring. As Layard would undoubtedly have said, maternal. And that wasn't the only trick the war had played.

Mobilization. The Great Adventure. They'd been *mobilized* into holes in the ground so constricted they could hardly move. And the Great Adventure – the real life equivalent of all the adventure stories they'd devoured as boys – consisted of crouching in a dugout, waiting to be killed. The war that had promised so much in the way of 'manly' activity had actually delivered 'feminine' passivity, and on a scale that their mothers and sisters had scarcely known. No wonder they broke down.

In bed, he switched off the light and opened the curtains. Rain, silvery in the moonlight, streaked the glass, blurring the vista of tennis courts and trees, gathering, at the lower edge of the pane, into a long puddle that bulged and overflowed. Somebody, on the floor below, screamed. Rivers pulled the curtains to, and settled down to sleep, wishing, not for the first time, that he was young enough for France.

TEN

Sarah watched the grey trickle of tea creep up the sides of her cup. The tea-lady looked at it, doubtfully. 'That strong enough for you, love?'

'It'll do. Long as it's warm and wet.'

'My God,' Betty Hargreave said. 'Virgin's pee. I can't drink that.'

Madge nudged Sarah sharply in the ribs. 'No, well, it wouldn't be very appropriate, would it?'

'Hey up, you'll make us spill it.'

They went to the far end of the top trestle table and squeezed on to the bench. 'Come on, move your bums along,' Madge said. 'Let two little 'uns in.'

Lizzie collected her Woodbines and matches, and shuffled along. 'What happened to your young man, then, Sarah?'

'Didn't bloody show up, did he? I was sat an hour on Sunday all dolled up and nowhere to go.'

'*Aw*,' Lizzie said.

'Probably just as well,' said Madge. 'At least now you know what he was after.'

'I knew what he was after. I just want to know why he's not still after it.'

'Didn't get it, then?' Betty said, bringing her cup to the table.

'No, he bloody did not.'

'He was good-looking, though, wasn't he?' said Madge.

'All right, I suppose.'

Betty laughed. 'Better fish in the sea, eh, Sarah?'

'Aye, and they can stop there 'n' all. Not interested.'

A whoop of incredulity. Sarah buried her nose in her cup and then, as soon as she felt their attention had been withdrawn, looked at the window. You couldn't really see what it was like outside because the glass was frosted, but here and there raindrops clung to the panes, each with its crescent moon of silver. She wished she was outside and could feel the rain on her face. It would have been nice to have gone to the seaside yesterday, she thought. Bugger him, why didn't he show up?

The others were talking about Lizzie's husband, who'd thrown her into a state of shock by announcing, in his last letter, that he was hoping to come home on leave soon.

'I haven't had a wink of sleep since,' said Lizzie.

'You're getting yourself into a state about nothing,' Betty said. 'First of all he mightn't get it, and second, they sometimes only give them a few days. Ten to one, he'll get no further than London.'

'Aye, and he'll be pissed as a newt.'

'Well, better pissed down there than up here.'

'Don't you want to see him?' asked Sarah.

'I do not. I've seen enough of him to last me a lifetime. Aye, I know what you're thinking. You think I'm hard, don't you? Well I *am* hard and so would you be.' Lizzie's yellow face showed two bright spots of colour on the cheekbones. 'Do you know what happened on August 4th 1914?'

Sarah opened her mouth.

'I'll tell you what happened. *Peace* broke out. The only little bit of peace *I*'ve ever had. No, I don't want him back. I don't want him back on leave. I don't want him back when it's over. As far as I'm concerned the Kaiser can keep him.' She lowered her chin, brooding. 'I'll tell you what I'm going to do. I'm going to get meself some false teeth, and I'm going to have a bloody good time.'

'Yes, well, you want to,' said Betty.

'She's been on about them teeth as long as I've known her,' said Madge. 'You want to stop talking about it, and go and do it. You can afford it. All this won't last, you know.' She jerked her thumb at the room full of overall-clad women. 'It's too good to last.'

'It's not the money that bothers me.'

'He'd give you gas,' said Madge. 'You're never going to look anything while you've got them in your mouth. And you're never going to feel right either for the simple reason you're swallowing all the corruption.'

'Yeh, I know. I will go.'

'Time, ladies,' the supervisor said. 'Time.'

'Eeh, it never is,' said Lizzie. 'Do you know, I'm bloody sure they fix that clock!'

'Three hours down,' said Sarah. 'Nine to go.'

All over the room yellow-skinned women were dragging themselves to their feet. As they were going up the stairs, Sarah fell into line beside Betty. Lizzie had nipped into the toilet to finish her cigarette.

'You think she's hard, don't you?' said Betty.

'Well, yes, I do a bit. When you think what he's going through.'

'Yes, well. You know when I was a kid we used to live next door to them, and it was thump thump thump half the bloody night, you'd've thought she was coming through the wall. Oh, and you used to see her in the yard next morning, and her face'd be all swelled up. "I fell over the coal scuttle," she used to say. Well that used to get me Mam. "*He* knocks you about," she says, "and *you* go round apologizing for it," she says. "Where's the justice in that?" And mind you, she was right, you know.'

Willard lay face down on his bed, naked. His thighs and buttocks were trenched with purple scars, some just beginning to silver. These injuries had been sustained when his company was retreating across a graveyard under heavy fire, and several tombstone fragments had become embedded in his flesh. 'You want to try it,' he said. 'Lying two months on your belly in a hospital bed with *Requiescat in Pace* stuck up your arse.'

This remark was ostensibly addressed to the orderly, so Rivers was able to ignore it. 'They've healed well,' he said, moving down the bed.

Willard looked across his shoulder. 'The flesh wounds have. There's still the injury to the spine.'

'Let's have you on your back.'

The orderly came forward to help, but Willard waved him away. His whole upper body was massively powerful, though inevitably running to flab. By heaving and twisting, he could just manage to drag the wasted legs over, though they followed the bulk of his body, passively, like slime trails after a snail. The orderly bent down and straightened his feet.

Rivers waited until Willard was covered up, then nodded to the orderly to leave. After the door had closed, he said, 'There was no injury to the spine.'

Willard lay back against the pillows, his jaw stubbornly set.

'If you believe your spine was damaged, how do you account for the fact that so many doctors have examined you and told you that it isn't?' He watched Willard's face closely. 'Do you think they're all incompetent? *All* of them? Or do you think they're in some kind of conspiracy to convince you you *can* walk when in fact you can't?'

Willard raised himself on to one elbow. It was extraordinary the impression he created, that mixture of immobility and power. Like a bull seal dragging itself across rocks. 'You think I'm malingering.'

'I know you're not.'

'But you've just said I am.'

'No.'

'If there's no injury to the spine, then why can't I walk?'

'I think you know why.'

Willard gave a short, hissing laugh. 'I know what you want me to say. I can't walk because I don't want to go back.' He glared at Rivers. 'Well, I won't say it. It would be tantamount to an admission of cowardice.'

Rivers picked up his cap and cane. 'Not in my book.' He was aware of Willard watching him. 'It's true paralysis occurs because a man wants to save his life. He doesn't want to go forward, and take part in some hopeless attack. *But neither is he prepared to run away*.' He smiled. 'Paralysis is no use to a coward, Mr Willard. A coward needs his legs.'

Willard didn't reply, though Rivers thought he detected a slight relaxation of tension. The bone structure of Willard's face was strong almost to the point of brutality, and his eyes were a curious shade of pale blue. There was a sheen on his hair and skin like the gloss on the coat of an animal. He'd been something of an athlete before the war, though Rivers suspected he had never been remarkable for depth of intelligence. 'Your wife's coming to see you this afternoon, isn't she?'

Willard's eyes went to the photograph on his washstand. 'Yes.'

'Why don't you get dressed? There's no reason for you to be in bed. And if you got dressed you could go out into the grounds. It'd be a lot pleasanter for your wife.'

Willard thought about it, reluctant to concede anything that might suggest his illness was not purely physical. 'Yes, all right.'

'Good. I'll send an orderly in to help you with your boots.'

Sassoon arrived at the Conservative Club about ten minutes early. 'Captain Rivers isn't here yet, sir,' the porter said. 'But if you'd like to wait in the morning room, I'm sure he won't be long. Up the stairs and first right.'

The staircase was of twisting marble, almost too imposing for the size of the hall, like a Roman nose on an unprepossessing face. As Sassoon climbed, he passed portraits of Edinburgh worthies of the past, men with white beards and wing collars, whose gold watch-chains and fobs nestled on swelling abdomens. His first thought on entering the morning room was that somebody with a taste for practical jokes had cut the Edinburgh worthies out of their frames and stuck them in chairs all over the room. Everywhere saurian heads and necks peered out of wing armchairs, looking at the young man in the doorway with the automatic approval his uniform evoked, and then – or was he perhaps being oversensitive? – with a slight ambivalence, a growing doubt, as they worked out what the blue badge on his tunic meant. Perhaps it *was* just oversensitivity, for you saw that same look of mingled admiration and apprehension, wherever you went. Old men were often ambivalent about young men in uniform, and rightly so, when you considered how very ambivalent the young men felt about them.

The chairs, which looked uncomfortable, were very comfortable indeed. Sassoon, glad to be away from the boiled cabbage and custard smells of the Craiglockhart dining room, sank back and closed his eyes. Further along, at a table by the window, two old men were nattering about the war. Both had sons at the front, it seemed, or was it only one? No, the other was trapped in England, apparently, on a training course. He listened to the rumble of their voices and felt a well-practised hatred begin to flow. It needed only a slighting remark about the courage of the German Army to rouse him to real fury, and very soon it came. He was aware of something sexual in this anger. He looked at the cloth straining across their broad backs, at the folds of beef-pink skin that overlapped their collars, and thought, with uncharacteristic crudity, *When did you two last get it up?*

Gordon's death had woken him up, there was no doubt. That moment when he'd come down to breakfast, glanced at the casualty lists and seen Gordon's name had been a turning point of sorts, though he didn't yet know in which direction he would turn. It seemed to him that his first month at Craiglockhart had been spent in a kind of sleep. Too much steam pudding, too much putting little balls into holes. Looking round the room, he knew why he felt sickened by himself, why his fuming against elderly men with sons at the front no longer satisfied him. It was because he'd given in, lapsed, pretended to himself that he was still actively protesting whereas in reality he'd let himself be pacified, sucked into the comforting routine, the uneventfulness of Craiglockhart life. As Rivers had meant him to be.

He got up and began looking at the pictures that lined the walls. The portraits here were not of the professional men and civic dignitaries of the recent past, but of the landed gentry of generations before that, shown, for the most part, either setting off to, or returning from, the hunt. He was obviously not destined to get away from memories of Gordon and hunting today. Walking from picture to picture, he remembered the notebook he'd taken with him into the trenches on his first tour of duty. It had contained nothing but bare details of past hunts, where they'd found, how far he'd run, whether they'd killed. On and on. A terribly meaningless little set of squiggles it would have seemed to anybody else, but for him it had contained the Sussex lanes, the mists, the drizzle, the baying of hounds, clods flying from under the horses' feet, staggering into the house, bones aching, reliving the hunt over dinner, and then, after dinner, shadows on the wall of the old nursery and Gordon's face in the firelight, the scent of logs, the warmth, his whole face feeling numbed and swollen in the heat. His mind switched to his last few hours in France when, already wounded in the shoulder, he'd careered along a German trench, slinging Mills bombs to left and right, shouting, 'View halloa!' *That* was the moment, he thought. That was when the old Sassoon had cracked wide open and something new had stepped out of the shell. *Bless you, my dear,* Eddie Marsh had written, when he told him about it. *Never take it more seriously than that*. But Eddie had missed the point. Hunting had always been serious. Every bit as serious as war.

'Sorry I'm late,' Rivers said, coming up behind him. 'I meant to be here when you arrived.'

'That's all right. These old codgers've been keeping me amused.' He glanced round quickly. 'I mean the ones on the wall.'

'It is rather a geriatric gathering, isn't it?' Rivers sat down. 'Would you like a drink?' He raised his arm and a white-jacketed, elderly waiter came tottering across. 'Gin and tonic for me, I think. What'll you have, Siegfried?'

'The same, please.'

Rivers's inspection of the menu was confined to identifying which particular variety of poached fish was currently on offer. Sassoon gave the matter more thought. Rivers watched him as he pored over the menu and thought how much easier his life would have been if they'd sent Siegfried somewhere else. It wasn't simply the discomfort of having to express views he was no longer sure he held – though, as a scientist, he did find that acutely uncomfortable. No, it was more than that. Every case posed implicit questions about the individual costs of the war, and never more so than in the run up to a round of Medical Boards, when the MOs had to decide which men were fit to return to duty. This would have been easier if he could have believed, as Lewis Yealland, for example, believed, that men who broke down were degenerates whose weakness would have caused them to break down, eventually, even in civilian life, but Rivers could see no evidence of that. The vast majority of his patients had no record of any mental trouble. And as soon as you accepted that the man's breakdown was a consequence of his war experience rather than of his own innate weakness, then inevitably the war became the issue. And the therapy was a test, not only of the genuineness of the individual's symptoms, but also of the validity of the demands the war was making on him. Rivers had survived partly by suppressing his awareness of this. But then along came Sassoon and made the justifiability of the war a matter for constant, open debate, and that suppression was no longer possible. At times it seemed to Rivers that all his other patients were the anvil and that Sassoon was the hammer. Inevitably there were times when he resented this. As a civilian, Rivers's life had consisted of asking questions, and devising methods by which truthful answers could be obtained, but there are limits to how many *fundamental* questions you want to ask in a working day that starts before eight am and doesn't end till midnight. All very well for Sassoon. *He* spent *his* days playing golf.

None of this prevented him from watching Sassoon's continued poring over the menu with affection as well as amusement.

Sassoon looked up. 'Am I taking too long?'

'No, take as long as you like.'

'It's almost pre-war standard, isn't it?'

'I hope you're not going to protest?'

'No. You can rely on me to be inconsistent.'

Rivers was not afraid of Sassoon's noticing any change in *him*. Siegfried's introversion was remarkable, even by the normal standards of unhappy young men. His love for his men cut through that self-absorption, but Rivers sometimes wondered whether anything else did. And yet he had so many good qualities. It was rare to find a man in whom courage was the *dominating* characteristic, as malice or laziness or greed might be the ruling characteristic of lesser men.

The dining room was almost empty. They were shown to a table for two by a window that overlooked the club's small, walled garden. A scent of roses, drenched from the morning's rain, drifted in through the open window.

The waiter was very young, sixteen perhaps. Red hair, big freckles splodged over a pale skin, knobbly, pink-knuckled hand clasping the carving knife. With his other hand he lifted the domed lid from the platter to reveal a joint of very red beef. Sassoon smiled. 'That looks nice.'

The boy carved three slices. As he bent to get the warmed plate from the shelf below, it was possible to see the nape of his neck, defenceless under the stiff collar.

'Is that all right, sir?'

'One more, perhaps?'

The boy was looking at Sassoon with undisguised hero-worship. Not surprisingly, Rivers thought. He's dragging out the weeks in this dreary job waiting for his turn to go out. At least they no longer allowed boys of his age to *lie* their way in. He noticed Sassoon smiling to himself.

'What's amusing you?'

'I was thinking about Campbell. Not *our* Campbell. A *much* less engaging man, and . . . er . . . allegedly sane. He gave lectures – still does, I believe – on "The Spirit of the Bayonet". You know, *"Stick him in the kidneys, it'll go in like a hot knife through butter." "What's the good of six inches of steel sticking out the back of a man's neck? Three inches'll do him. When he croaks, go and find another."* And so on. And you know, the men sit there laughing and cheering and making obscene gestures. *They hate it.*' He smiled. 'I was reminded because that boy was doing so well with the carving knife.'

'Yes, I noticed.'

'Very much the sort of man you'd pick as your servant.'

Rivers said mischievously, 'Not bad-looking either.'

'I'm afraid that has to take second place. You look for skill with the bayonet first because he's always on your left in the attack.'

They ate in silence for a while. Rivers said, 'Have you heard from the friend you were going to write to about Gordon?'

'Yes. It's true apparently, he did die instantly. His father said he had, but they don't always tell parents the truth. I've written too many letters like that myself.'

'It must be some consolation to know he didn't suffer.'

Sassoon's expression hardened. 'I was glad to have it confirmed.' An awkward silence. 'I had some more bad news this morning. Do you remember me talking to you about Julian Dadd? Shot in the throat, two brothers killed? Well, his mental state has worsened apparently. He's in a – what I suppose I ought to call a mental hospital. Given present company. The awful thing is he's got some crazy idea he didn't do well enough. Nobody else thinks so, but apparently there's no arguing with him. He was one of my heroes, you know. I remember looking at him one evening. We'd just come in from inspecting the men's billets – which were lousy as usual, and – he cared. He really cared. And I looked at him and I thought, *I want to be like you.*' He laughed, mocking his hero-worship, but not disowning it. 'Anyway, I suppose I've succeeded, haven't I? Since we're both in the loony-bin.'

The provocation was deliberate. When Rivers didn't rise to it, Sassoon said, 'It makes it quite difficult to go on, you know. When things like this keep happening to people you know and and . . . love. To go on with the protest, I mean.'

Silence.

Sassoon leant forward. '*Wake up*, Rivers. I thought you'd pounce on that.'

'Did you?'

A pause. 'No, I suppose not.'

Rivers dragged his hand down across his eyes. 'I don't feel much like pouncing.'

Rivers left the club an hour later. He'd left Siegfried with Ralph Sampson, the Astronomer Royal of Scotland, whom they'd bumped into after lunch. At first Sassoon had been almost too overawed to speak, but Sampson had soon put paid to that. Rivers had left him chatting away quite happily. Lunch itself had been rather depressing. At one point Siegfried had said, 'I'm beginning to feel used up.' You could understand it. He'd suffered repeated bereavements in the last two years, as first one contemporary then another died. In some ways the experience of these young men paralleled the experience of the very old. They looked back on intense memories and felt lonely because there was nobody left alive who'd been there. That habit of Siegfried's of looking back, the inability to envisage any kind of future, seemed to be getting worse.

Not an easy case, Rivers thought. Not in the usual sense a case at all. He had no idea what the outcome would be, though he thought he could get Siegfried to give in. His love for his men. The need he had to *prove* his courage. By any *rational* standard, he'd already proved it, over and over again, but then the need wasn't altogether rational. Given the strength of that need, it was amazing he'd managed to tolerate being cooped up with 'wash-outs' and 'degenerates' even as long as he had. Putting those forces together and getting him back to France was a task of approximately the same order of difficulty as flicking a stag beetle on to its back. The trouble was Rivers respected Sassoon too much to manipulate him. He had to be *convinced* that going back was the right thing to do.

At the foot of the Craiglockhart drive, Rivers saw Willard and Mrs Willard. For some extraordinary reason Willard had got his wife to push him as far as the gates, despite the downward slope which he must have seen would make the return journey difficult. Now they were marooned.

Rivers greeted Willard, waited for an introduction to his wife, and, when it failed to come, introduced himself. Mrs Willard was extremely young, attractive in the small-breasted, slim-hipped way of modern girls. As they chatted about the deceptive nature of slopes and the awkwardness of wheelchairs, Rivers became aware of Willard's hands clenched on the arms of the chair. He felt Willard's fury at being stranded like this, impotent. Good. The more furious he was the better.

Rivers said to Mrs Willard, 'Here, I'll give you a hand.'

With two of them pushing they made steady progress, though there was one nasty moment near the top, when they struck a muddy patch. But then the wheels bit, and they reached level ground at a cracking pace.

'There you are,' Mrs Willard said, bending over her husband, breathless and laughing. 'Made it.'

Willard's face would have curdled milk.

'Why don't you come in and have a cup of tea?' Rivers suggested.

Mrs Willard looked to her husband for guidance. When none came, she said, 'Yes, that would be lovely.'

'My door's on the left as you go in. I'll just go ahead and arrange things. You'll be all right now?'

'Perfectly, thank you,' said Willard.

Rivers went into the hall, smiling, only to have the smile wiped off his face by the sight of Matron standing immediately inside the entrance. She'd observed the entire incident and evidently disapproved. 'You could have sent an orderly down to push the chair, Captain Rivers.'

Rivers opened his mouth, and shut it again. He reminded himself, not for the first time, that it was absolutely necessary for Matron to win some of their battles.

ELEVEN

Sassoon was trying to decipher a letter from H. G. Wells when Owen knocked on his door.

'As far as I can make out, he says he's coming to see Rivers.'

Owen looked suitably impressed. 'He must be really worried about you.'

'Oh, it's not *me* he wants to talk about, it's his new book.' Sassoon smiled. 'You don't know many writers, do you?'

'Not many.'

And I, Sassoon thought, am showing off. Which at least was better than moaning about Gordon's death to somebody who had more than enough problems of his own. 'I don't suppose he'll come. They all talk about it, but in the end it's just too far. I sometimes wonder whether that's why they put me here. Whether it was a case of being sent to Rivers or just sent as far away as possible.'

'Probably Rivers. He gets all the awkward ones.' Owen stopped in some confusion. 'Not that you're –'

'Oh, I think I count as awkward. By any standard.' He handed a sheet of paper across. 'For the *Hydra*.'

'May I read it?'

'That's the general idea.'

Owen read, folded the paper and nodded.

To forestall possible effusions, Sassoon said quickly, 'I'm not satisfied with the last three lines, but they'll have to do.'

'I tried yesterday, but you were out.'

'I'd be with Rivers.' He smiled. 'Do you ever feel like strangling Brock?'

'No, I get on rather well with him.'

'I *get on* with Rivers. It's just . . . He picked up something I said at lunchtime about not being able to imagine the future. He doesn't often press, but my God when he does . . .'

'Why did he want you to talk about that?'

'Part of the great campaign to get me back to France. He wants me to put the protest in a longer perspective. You know, "What did you do in the Great War, Siegfried?" Well, I spent three very comfortable years in a loony-bin eating steamed pudding and playing golf. While *other people* – some of them rather close friends – got blown to smithereens. He wants me to admit I won't be able to bear it. What's more, he's probably right.'

'Think of the poems you could write.'

'Not war poems.'

Owen's expression darkened. 'There are other subjects.'

'Yes, of course.'

A slightly awkward pause. 'The trouble is he just knows more than I do. You know, he's very good . . . He tries to behave as if we're equal. But in the end he's a Gold Medallist of the Royal Society, and I left Cambridge without taking a degree. And now and again it shows.'

'That doesn't mean he's right.'

'No, but it does make it very difficult for me to keep my end up in a discussion.'

'Did you talk about after the war?'

'No. I can't, I've no plans. Do *you* know what you're going to do?'

'I'm going to keep pigs.'

'Pigs?'

'Yes. People think pigs are dirty, you know, but they're not. They're very clean animals, given half the chance. And it would combine so well with poetry, you see. Actually much better than teaching, because if you're teaching *properly* you're using the same part of your mind. But pig-keeping . . .'

'Perhaps we should go into partnership. It'd shut Rivers up.'

Owen, belatedly aware of being laughed at, blushed and didn't reply.

'No, well, I don't suppose I'd be much use with the pigs, but I may be able to help with the poems.' He nodded at Owen's tunic.

Owen extracted a sheaf of papers. 'I told you they were all short but actually there is one long one. Antaeus and and Hercules.' He handed the papers over. 'Do you know the legend? Antaeus is too strong for Hercules as long as he keeps his feet on mother Earth. But as soon as Hercules lifts him –'

'He's helpless. Yes, it rings a bell.' Sassoon started to read. After a few seconds he looked up. 'Why don't you get yourself a book? There's nothing worse than being watched by the Onlie Begetter.'

'Sorry.' Owen got up and pretended to look at the books on Sassoon's shelf.

At last Sassoon looked up. 'It's very good. Why Antaeus?'

'Oh, it's something Brock's keen on. He thinks we – the patients – are *like* Antaeus in the sense that we've been ungrounded by the war. And the way back to health is to re-establish the link between oneself and the earth, but understanding "earth" to mean society as well as nature. That's why we do surveys and things like that.'

'I thought all the dashing around was to keep your mind off it?'

'No, that's part of the treatment. Ergotherapy.'

'Well, it's an interesting idea. Though I don't know that being stuck in a dugout ever made *me* feel I was losing contact with the earth.'

Owen smiled. 'No, nor me. It does *work*, though.'

Sassoon picked up the next sheet. Craning his neck, Owen could just see the title of the poem. 'That's in your style,' he said.

'Yes. I . . . er . . . *noticed*.'

'No good?'

'Starts and ends well. What happened in the middle?'

'That's quite old, that bit. I wrote that two years ago.'

'They do say if you leave something in a drawer long enough it'll either rot or ripen.'

'The bit at the end . . . About "dirt". Those are the actual words.'

'Yes, and they could do with changing. I've just cut: "You sod" out of a poem. Those were *my* actual words.'

'So it's no good?'

Sassoon hesitated. 'It's not much good *at the moment*. I suppose the thing is, are you interested enough to go on?'

'Ye-es. I have to start somewhere. And I think you're right. It's mad not to write about the war when it's –'

'Such an *experience*.'

They looked at each other and burst out laughing.

'My only doubt is . . . The the *fact* that you admire somebody very much doesn't automatically mean they're a good model. I mean, I admire Wilde, but if I started trying to be witty and elegant and incisive, I'd probably fall flat on my face.'

'Yes, I see that. Well not *that*. I mean I see the point. But I do think I can take something from you.'

'Fair enough.' Sassoon went back to his reading. 'I think you're probably right,' he said, after a while. 'If I do nothing else, I might help you get rid of some of this *mush*.'

'Some of the sonnets are quite early.'

'Puberty?' A long pause. Early sonnets fell like snow. 'Oh, now this is good. "Song of Songs." '

'That's last week.'

'*Is it?* Now you see what I mean about me not being necessarily the right model? *I* couldn't do this. And yet of it's kind it's absolutely perfect.'

Owen sat down. He looked as if his knees had buckled.

'I think that should go in the *Hydra*.'

'No.'

'Why not?'

'a. It's not good enough. b. Editors shouldn't publish their own work.'

'a. I'm a better judge of that than you are. *At the moment*. b. Rubbish. And c.' Sassoon leant across and snatched his own poem back. 'If you don't publish *that*, you can't have this.'

Owen seemed to be contemplating a counter-attack.

'd. I'm bigger than you are.'

'All right, I'll print it.' He took Sassoon's poem back. 'Anonymously.'

'Cheat.' Sassoon was shuffling Owen's papers together. 'Look, why don't you have a go at . . .' He peered at the title. ' "The Dead-Beat"? Work at it till you think you've made some progress, then bring it back and we'll have a go at it together. It's not too traumatic, is it? That memory.'

'Good heavens, no.'

'How long do you spend on it? Not that one, I mean generally?'

'Fifteen minutes.' He saw Sassoon's expression change. 'That's *every day*.'

'Good God, man, that's no use. You've got to sweat your guts out. Look, it's like drill. You don't wait till you *feel* like doing it.'

'Well, it's certainly a new approach to the Muse. "Number from the left! Form fours! Right turn!"'

'It works. I'll see you – shall we say Thursday? After dinner.' He opened the door and stood aside to let Owen past. 'And I shall expect to find *both* poems in the *Hydra*.'

TWELVE

After Prior had been waiting for perhaps five minutes, the lodging house door opened and Sarah stood there. 'You've got a nerve,' she said, beginning to close the door.

Prior put a finger in the crack. 'I'm here now.'

'Which is more than you were last week. Go on, *shift*.'

'I couldn't come last week. I was so late back they kept me in.'

'Bit strict, aren't they? Your *parents*.'

Too late, he remembered the lies he'd told. He pointed to the blue badge on his tunic. 'Not parents. The CO.'

The door stopped shutting.

'I know it sounds stupid, but it *is* the truth.'

'Oh, all right, I believe you.' Her eyes fell on the badge. 'And if you're getting yourself upset about that, don't bother. I knew anyway.'

'How did you know?' What had he been doing? *Drooling?*

'You don't think you're the only one takes it off, do you? They all do. Betty says she had a young man once, she never saw him wearing it. Mind you, knowing Betty, I shouldn't think she saw him wearing much at all.'

By day, the yellowness of her skin astonished him. It said a lot for her that she was still attractive, that she managed to wear it like a rather dashing accessory.

'There is just one thing,' she said, coming out into the porch. 'If I do go out with you, I want one thing clear at the start. I think you must've got a very wrong impression of me the other night. Knocking all that port back.' She raised her eyes to his face. 'I don't usually drink much at all.'

'I know that. You were gone too quick for somebody that was used to it.'

'Right, then. Long as you know. I'll get me jacket.'

He waited, looking up and down the hot street. A trickle of sweat had started in his armpits. From deep inside the house came a woman's voice raised in anger.

'Me landlady,' Sarah said, coming back. 'Belgian, married a Scot, the poor sod. I don't think he knew what he was getting. Still, she only charges a shilling for the laundry, and when you think the sheets come off the bed bright yellow you can't complain about that.'

He felt at home with her, with this precise delineation of the cost of everything, which was not materialistic or grasping, but simply a recognition of the boundaries and limitations of life. 'I thought we'd get out of Edinburgh,' he said. 'It's too hot.'

Most of Edinburgh was using this last weekend in August to escape the city, not deterred by a sallow tinge to the sky that suggested the hot, sticky weather might break into thunder before the day was out. The train was packed, but he managed to get her a seat, and stood near by. She smiled up at him, but in this rackety, sweating box it was impossible to talk. He looked at the other passengers. A trio of girls out on a spree, a young mother with a struggling toddler tugging at her blouse, a middle-aged couple whose bodies sagged together. Something about that stale intimacy sharpened his sense of the strangeness, the separateness of Sarah's body. He was so physically aware of her that when the knee of his breeches brushed against her skirt he felt as if the contact had been skin on skin.

A ganglion of rails, the train juddering over points, and then they were slowing, and people were beginning to stir and clutch bags, and jam the aisles. 'Let's wait,' he said.

Sarah pressed against him, briefly, to let the woman and her child past, and then he sat beside her as the train emptied. After a while she reached down and touched his hand.

They took their time walking to the sea. At first he was disappointed, it was so crowded. Men with trousers rolled up to show knobbly legs, handkerchiefs knotted over sweating scalps, women with skirts tucked up to reveal voluminous bloomers, small children screaming as the damp sand was towelled off their legs. Everywhere people swirling their tongues round ice-cream cones, biting into candy-floss, licking rock, sucking fingers, determined to squeeze the last ounce of pleasure from the day. In his khaki, Prior moved among them like a ghost. Only Sarah connected him to the jostling crowd, and he put his hand around her, clasping her tightly, though at that moment he felt no stirring of desire. He said, 'You wouldn't think there was a war on, would you?'

They walked down to the water's edge. He felt quite callous towards her now, even as he drew her towards him and matched his stride to hers. She belonged with the pleasure-seeking crowds. He both envied and despised her, and was quite coldly determined to *get* her. They owed him something, all of them, and she should pay. He glanced at her. 'Shall we walk along?'

Their linked shadows, dumpy and deformed, stretched across the sand. After a while they came to an outcrop of rock, and, clambering over it, found they'd left the crowded part of the beach behind. Sarah took off her jacket and then, with a great fuss and pleas not to look, her shoes and stockings as well. She paddled at the water's edge, where the waves seethed between her toes.

'I don't suppose you're allowed to take anything off?' she said, looking back at him, teasing.

'Not a thing.'

'Not even your boots?'

'No, but I can wade. I always paddle with me boots on.'

He didn't expect her to understand, or if she did, to admit it, but she turned on him at once. 'Boots have a way of springing a leak.'

'Not mine.'

'Oh, you'd be different, I suppose?'

Until now the air had been so still it scarcely moved against the skin. But now small gusts began to whip up the sand, stinging patches of bare skin. Prior looked back the way they'd come. The sun was past its height. Even the little mounds of worm-casts had each its individual shadow, but what chiefly struck him was the yellowing of the light. It was now positively sulphurous, thick with heat. They seemed to be trapped, fixed, in some element thicker than air. Black figures, like insects, swarmed across the beach, making for the shelter of the town.

Sarah, too, had turned to look back. He said quickly, 'No, don't let's go back. It'll blow over.'

'You think *that's* gunna blow over?'

Reluctantly he said, 'Do you *want* to go back?'

'We'd be drenched before we got there. Anyway, I like storms.'

They stood looking out to sea, while the yellow light deepened. There was no difference now between his skin colour and hers. Suddenly Sarah clutched her head. 'What's happening?'

He could hardly believe what he saw. The coppery wires on the surface of her hair were standing straight up, in a way he had never believed any human hair could do. He pulled his cap off, and winced at the tingling in his scalp.

'What is it?' Sarah said.

'Electricity.'

She burst out laughing.

'No, I mean it.'

Lightning flickered once, illuminating her yellow skin.

'Come on,' Prior said.

He snatched her hand and started to run with her towards the shelter of some bushes. Scrambling up the last slope, he staggered, and would have fallen if he hadn't grabbed a clump of marram grass. He felt a sharp pain, and, bringing his hand up, saw a smear of blood on the palm. Sarah pushed him from behind. They stumbled down the other side of the slope, just as a sudden fierce thickening of rain blinded them, and the first rumblings of thunder came.

A dense thicket of buckthorn offered the only possible shelter. Prior stamped down the nettles and thistles that thronged the gaps, and then held the thorns back for Sarah to crawl inside. He followed her in. They crouched down, the rain scarcely reaching them through the thick roof of thorn, though the wind rocked and beat the bush. Prior looked round. The ground was dry, and very bare, the thorn too thick to allow anything else to grow.

Sarah was feeling her hair. 'Is it all right?'

'It's going down.'

'So's yours.'

He grinned. ''S not surprising. Storm took me mind right off it.'

She laughed, but refused to reply. Prior was remembering childhood games, making dens. An interior like this, so dark, so private, so easily defended, would have been a real find. Mixed with this distinctly childish excitement another excitement was growing. He no longer felt hostile to her, as he'd done back there in the crowd. They seemed to have walked away from all that. It was ages since he'd made love. He felt as he sometimes did coming out of the line, listening to the others talk and sometimes joining in, what they were going to do and how many times they were going to do it, though as far as he knew everybody else's experience was like his own. The first time was almost always a disappointment. Either stuck at half mast or firing before you reached the target. He didn't want to think about Sarah like this.

Sarah rolled over on to her elbow and looked at him. 'This is nice.'

He lay beside her. A few splashes of rain found his upturned face. After a while he touched her hand and felt her fingertips curl round his. Through the thickness in his throat, he said, 'I'm not pushing, but if you wanted to, I'd make sure it was all right.'

After a while he felt her fingers creep across his chest, insinuating themselves between the buttons of his tunic. He kissed her, moving from her lips to her breasts, not looking at her, not opening his eyes, learning her with his tongue, flicking the nipples hard, probing the whorled darkness of her navel, and then on down, down, across the smooth marble of her belly into the coarse and springy turf. His nostrils filled with the scent of rock pools at low tide. He slipped his hands underneath her, and lifted her, until her whole pelvis became a cup from which he drank.

Afterwards they lay in silence, enjoying the peace, until footsteps walking along the coastal path warned them that the storm was over. The buckthorn scattered raindrops over them, as they crawled out on to the grass.

They beat sand and twigs from each other's clothes, then started to walk back along the coastal path.

'What we need is something to warm us up,' Prior said.

'We can't go anywhere looking like this.'

They stopped on the outskirts of the town, and tried more seriously to set themselves to rights. They went to a pub, and leant back against the wooden seat, nudging each other under the table, drunk with their love-making and the storm and the sense of having secrets.

'I can feel your voice through the wood,' Sarah said.

Abruptly, the joy died. Prior became quite suddenly depressed. He pushed his half-finished meal away.

'What is it?'

'Oh, I was remembering a man in my platoon.' He looked at her. 'Do you know, he sent the same letter to his wife every week for two years.'

Sarah felt a chill come over her. She didn't know why she was being told this. 'Why?'

'Why not?'

'How do you know he did?'

'Because I had to censor it. I censored it every week. We read all their letters.'

He could see her not liking this, but she kept her voice light. 'Who reads yours?'

'Nobody.' He looked at her again. 'They rely on our sense of honour. Oh, we're supposed to leave them open so the CO *can* read them if he wants to, but it would be thought *frightfully bad form* if he did.' Prior had slipped into his mock public school voice, very familiar to Rivers.

Sarah took it at face value. 'You lot make me sick,' she said, pushing her own plate away. 'I suppose nobody else's *got* a sense of honour?'

He preferred her like this. On the beach, she was only too clearly beginning to think that something had happened that mattered. He wasn't going to admit that. A few grains of sand in the pubic hair, a mingling of smells. Nothing that a prolonged soak in the tub wouldn't wash away. 'Come on,' he said, putting down a tip. 'We'd better be getting back.'

THIRTEEN

Burns paced up and down the waiting room. Rivers had told him he intended to recommend an unconditional discharge, and though he hadn't actually said the Board would accept the recommendation, this had been very strongly implied. So there was nothing to worry about, though when the orderly came and asked him to step inside, his stomach knotted and his hands started to tremble. The Sam Browne belt, bunching the loose fabric round his waist, made him look rather like a scarecrow tied together with string. He got himself into the room somehow, and managed a salute. He couldn't see their faces to begin with, since they sat with their backs to the tall windows, but after Bryce had told him to sit down, his eyes started to become accustomed to the light.

There was a great deal of light, it seemed to him, floods of silver-grey light filtered through white curtains that stirred in the breeze, and the insistent buzzing of an insect, trapped. He fastened his eyes on Rivers, who managed to smile at him without moving a muscle of his face.

Major Paget, the third, external member of the Board, was obviously startled by Burns's appearance, but he asked a few questions for form's sake. Rivers scarcely listened either to the questions or to the answers. The buzzing continued. He scanned the high windows, trying to locate the insect. The noise was unreasonably disturbing.

Paget said, 'How often do you vomit now?'

Rivers got up and went across to the window. He found a bumble bee, between the curtain and the window, batting itself against the glass, fetched a file from the desk and, using it as a barrier, guided the insect into the open air. He watched it fly away. Directly below him, Anderson and Sassoon were setting off for their daily round of golf. Their voices drifted up to him. Rivers turned back into the room to find everybody, Burns included, staring at him in some surprise. He smiled faintly and went back to his seat.

'This is getting to be a habit, isn't it?'

Prior, hands twined round the iron bars of the bedhead, smiled without opening his eyes. 'Not one I enjoy.'

He hadn't regained the weight he'd lost during his last stay in sick bay. The ribs showed clearly through the stretched skin. 'You were lucky to get back. When did it start?'

'On the train. It was jam-packed. Everybody smoking.'

'Lucky the young woman with you kept her head.'

'Poor Sarah. I don't think she's ever had anybody pass out on her before.'

'You realize you won't have the sick bay to yourself this time?' Rivers indicated the other bed. 'Mr Willard.'

'The legless wonder. Yes, we've met.'

'Don't you have any sympathy for anybody else?'

'Are you suggesting I have any for myself?' He watched Rivers fold the stethoscope. 'You know what you were saying about the greater mental complexity of officers? How long do you think it'll take you to convince that particular specimen of *complexity* that it hasn't actually got a broken spine?'

'How's your voice, Mr Prior?'

Prior took a moment to register the direct hit. 'Fine. Problem over, I think. I miss it. I used to enjoy my little Trappist times.'

'Oh, I can believe that. I've often thought how nice it would be to retreat into total silence now and again.'

'What do you mean "how nice it would be"? You do it all the time.'

'I've arranged for a consultant to come and see you. A Dr Eaglesham. He'll be in some time this week.'

'Why?'

'I need a measurement of your vital capacity.'

'Demonstrations twice nightly.'

'The *other* vital capacity. Try to get some rest now. Sister Duffy tells me you had a bad night.'

Rivers had got to the door before Prior called him back. '*Why* do you need it?'

'This is the second time this has happened in six weeks. I don't think we can let you go in front of a Medical Board without drawing their attention to your *physical* condition.'

'If you're thinking of wangling permanent home service, I don't want it.'

'I'm not thinking of "wangling" anything.' Rivers looked down at Prior and his expression softened. 'Look, if this is what happens when you're exposed to cigarette smoke on a train, how would you cope with gas?'

'Well, *obviously*, I'm affected at lower concentrations than anybody else. But then so what? I can be the battalion canary.' A pause. 'I'm not the only one with asthma.'

'No, I'm sure you're not. I'm *told* there are cases of active TB in the trenches. It doesn't mean it's a good idea.'

'I want to go back.'

A long silence.

'You can't talk to anybody here,' Prior said. 'Everybody's either lost somebody, or knows somebody who has. They don't want the truth. It's like letters of condolence. "Dear Mrs Bloggs, Your son had the side of his head blown off by a shell and took five hours to die. We did manage to give him a decent Christian burial. Unfortunately that particular stretch of ground came under heavy bombardment the day after, so George has been back to see us five or six times since then." They don't want that. They want to be told that George – or Johnny – or whatever his name was, died a quick death and was given a decent send off.' He said deliberately, 'Yesterday, at the seaside, I felt as if I came from another planet.'

'You can talk to people here.'

'It's the last thing this lot want to talk about. The point is, I'm better.'

'That's for the Board to decide.'

'You mean, *you*.'

'No-o. The Board. How are the nights? I mean apart from the asthma? I know last night was bad.'

'I just refuse to play this game. I haven't enough *breath* to answer questions you already know the answers to.'

'What's your *subjective* estimate of your nights?'

'Better.'

'Good. That was Sister Duffy's impression too.'

'Oh *well*, then . . .' Prior glowered. 'There's another reason I want to go back. Rather a nasty, selfish little reason, but since you clearly think I'm a nasty selfish little person that won't come as a surprise. When all this is over, people who didn't go to France, or didn't do well in France – people of my generation, I mean – aren't going to count for anything. This is the Club to end all Clubs.'

'And you want to belong.'

'Yes.'

'You already do.'

'I broke down.'

'And that's why you want to go back? You're ambitious, aren't you?'

Prior didn't answer.

'No reason why you shouldn't be. What do you want to do?'

'Politics.' He started back-tracking immediately. 'Of course, it's probably useless. You can't get anywhere in this shitting country without an Oxford or Cambridge degree.'

'Rubbish.'

'Easily said.'

'Not easily said at all. I didn't go to either.'

Prior looked surprised.

'I got typhoid in my last year at school. We couldn't afford Cambridge without the scholarship. No, you can certainly get on without. And things'll be freer after the war. If only because hundreds of thousands of young men have been thrown into contact with the working classes in a way they've never been before. That has to have some impact.'

'Careful, Rivers. You're beginning to sound like a Bolshevik.'

'I'm just trying to give you some faith in your own abilities. And by the way, I do *not* think you are a nasty selfish little person.'

Prior scowled ferociously, probably to hide his pleasure.

'I'll try to be here when Dr Eaglesham comes. Meanwhile, do you think you could try to get on with Willard?'

Rivers had just started shaving when the VAD banged on his door. She gasped something about 'Captain Anderson' and 'blood', and, dreading what he would find, Rivers hurried downstairs to Anderson's room. He found Anderson huddled in a foetal position, in the corner by the window, teeth chattering, a dark stain spreading across the front of his pyjamas. His room-mate, Featherstone, stood by the washstand, razor in hand, looking at him with more irritation than sympathy.

'What happened?' Rivers asked.

'I don't know, he just started screaming.'

Rivers knelt beside Anderson and quickly checked that he wasn't injured. 'Was he asleep?'

'No, he was waiting for the basin.'

Rivers looked at Featherstone. A thin trickle of blood was dribbling down his wet chin. *Ah.* Rivers stood up, and patted him on the arm. 'Bleed elsewhere, Featherstone, there's a good chap.'

Featherstone – not in the best of tempers – strode out of the room. Rivers went across to the basin, rinsed his flannel out, wiped the bowl, gave the slightly blood-stained towel to the VAD and held the door open for her to leave. 'There,' he said, looking across at Anderson. 'All gone.'

Slowly Anderson relaxed, becoming in the process aware of the stain between his legs. Rivers fetched his dressing gown and threw it across to him. 'You'd better wrap this round you, you'll be chilly once the sweating's stopped.' He went back to the washstand. 'Do you mind if I borrow your flannel?'

He wiped the remaining shaving soap from his face, and checked to see he hadn't cut himself when the VAD banged on his door. That would *not* have been helpful. Out of the corner of his eye he saw Anderson pull the coverlet up to hide the wet patch in the bed. When Rivers next looked round, he was sitting on the bed, swinging his legs and doing his best to look casual. Rivers sat down, far enough away for Anderson not to have to worry about the smell. 'Still as bad as that?'

'I suppose it's as bad as it looks.'

And this was the man who was going to return to medicine. 'You know, we're going to have to start talking about what you realistically want to do.'

'We've been through all that.'

'I can get you a month's extension in October. After that –'

'That's all right. I can't stay here for ever.'

Rivers hesitated. 'Is there any sign of your wife managing to get up?'

Mrs Anderson's visit had been much talked of, but had still not occurred.

'No. It's difficult with a child.'

Others managed. Rivers left Anderson to get dressed and went back to his own room to finish shaving. Now that the surge of excitement had worn off, he felt tired and unwell. Quite unfit for work, though the day would have to be got through somehow.

Willard was his first patient. He was following a regime which involved early-morning exercises in the pool, and was wheeled into the room, wet-haired and smelling of chlorine. He started at once. 'I can't share a room with that man.'

Rivers went on kneading Willard's calf muscles.

'Prior.'

'You're not sharing a room with him, are you? You just happen to be in the sick bay at the same time.'

'In *effect* I'm sharing a room.'

'That feels quite a bit firmer. Does it feel firmer to you?'

Willard felt his calf. 'A bit. He wakes up screaming. It's intolerable.'

'No, well, I don't suppose he likes it much either.'

Willard hesitated. 'It's not just that.' He bent towards Rivers. 'He's one of those.'

Rivers looked and felt stunned. 'I really don't think he is, you know. You mustn't take everything Prior says seriously. He likes to tease.'

'He is. You can always tell.'

'Press against the palm of my hand.'

'I don't suppose you'd consider moving him?'

'No. And again. He's ill, Mr Willard. He *needs* the sick bay. If anybody moves out, it'll be *you*.'

Willard was followed by an unscheduled appointment with Featherstone, also demanding a change of room, though with more reason. Nobody could be expected to share with Anderson, he said. The nightmares and vomiting were too bad, and the loss of sleep was beginning to affect his nerves. All of this was true. Rivers listened and sympathized and promised Featherstone a change of room as soon as the September Boards had introduced some leeway into the system. At the moment the hospital was so crowded there was no hope of a room change for anybody.

Next, Lansdowne, an RAMC captain, whose long-standing claustrophobia had been uncovered by his inability to enter dugouts. A particularly testing session. Lansdowne was always demanding, though Rivers didn't mind that, since he felt he was making progress. Then Fothersgill, Sassoon's new room-mate, a fanatical Theosophist. He spoke throughout in mock medieval English – lots of 'Yea verilys' and 'forsooths' – as if his brief exposure to French horrors had frightened him into a sort of terminal facetiousness. He was forty-three, but with his iron-grey hair, monocle and stiff manners he seemed far older. He didn't take long. Basically, he was suffering from being too old for the war, a complaint with which Rivers had a little more sympathy every day.

Then a meeting of the Hospital Management Committee. Fletcher, one of the two patient representatives, was a highly efficient, conscientious man whose stay in France had ended when he'd developed paranoid delusions that the quartermaster was deliberately and systematically depriving the men of food. This delusion he had now transferred to the hospital steward. The meeting went well enough until the standard of hospital catering came under discussion, and then Fletcher's delusions came to the fore. Tempers became heated, and the meeting closed on an acrimonious note. It was an unfortunate incident, since it would certainly fuel the administration's view that patients should take no part in the running of the hospital. Bryce, supported by Rivers, believed that patient participation was essential, even if this meant that Craiglockhart committee meetings sometimes developed a flavour all of their own.

After lunch, Rivers went along to Bryce's room to discuss Broadbent. Broadbent had been to see his sick mother twice in recent months. Towards the end of the second visit a telegram arrived from Broadbent, saying that his mother had passed on, and asking permission to stay for the funeral. Naturally, permission had been granted. In due course Broadbent came back, wearing a black armband, and – rather less explicably – the red tabs of a staff officer. The red tabs disappeared overnight, but the black armband remained. For some days after that

Broadbent sat around the patients' common room, pink-eyed and sorrowful, being consoled by the VADs. This happy state of affairs came to a close when Mrs Broadbent arrived, demanding to know why she never heard from her son. Broadbent was now upstairs, in a locked room. It was not easy to see how a court-martial could be avoided.

The rest of the afternoon was spent on a succession of young men. Rivers, by now feeling quite ill, was carried through it only by his perception that some at least were showing signs of improvement. One young man in particular, who'd broken down after finding the mutilated body of his friend, had become dramatically better in the last few weeks.

After dinner, Rivers decided to abandon the paperwork he ought to have been doing and have an early night. No bath tonight, he decided, he was too tired. He got between the sheets and stretched out his legs, thinking he'd never been so glad to be in a bed in his life. After a while he pushed the window further open and lay listening to the rain, a soft hushing sound that seemed to fill the room. Soon, still listening, he drifted off to sleep.

He was woken at two am by a pain in his chest. At first he tried to convince himself it was indigestion, but the leaping and pounding of his heart soon suggested other, more worrying possibilities. He pulled himself up, and concentrated on breathing slowly and quietly.

The wind had risen while he was asleep, and rain pelted the glass. All over the hospital, he knew, men would be lying awake, listening to the rain and the wind, thinking of their battalions sinking deeper into the mud. Bad weather was bad for the nerves. Tomorrow would not be an easy day.

An hour later he would have given anything for tomorrow to arrive. He was getting all the familiar symptoms. Sweating, a constant need to urinate, breathlessness, the sense of blood not flowing but squeezing through veins. The slightest movement caused his heart to pound. He was relieved when dawn came and it was possible to summon the orderly.

Bryce arrived shortly afterwards, brisk and sympathetic. He produced a stethoscope, and told Rivers to take his pyjama jacket off. The stethoscope moved across his chest. He sat up, leant forward and felt the same procession of cold rings across his back. 'What do *you* think's wrong?' Bryce asked, putting the stethoscope away.

'War neurosis,' Rivers said promptly. 'I already stammer and I'm starting to twitch.'

Bryce waited for Rivers to settle back against the pillows. 'I suppose we've all got one of those. Your heartbeat's irregular.'

'Psychosomatic.'

'And, as we keep telling the patients, psychosomatic symptoms are REAL. I think you should take some leave.'

Rivers shook his head. 'No, I –'

'That wasn't a suggestion.'

'Oh. I've got the September reports to do. If I do nothing else, I've got to do those.'

Bryce had started to smile. 'There's never going to be a convenient time, is there? Three weeks starting this weekend.'

A mutinous silence.

'That gives you time to do the reports, provided you don't see patients. All right?' Bryce patted the coverlet and stood up. 'I'll tell Miss Crowe to put a notice up.'

Rivers was going on leave. He hadn't been down to dinner for the past few days, but he was there tonight, Sassoon saw, looking rather better than he'd done recently, though still very tired. The MO's table was the noisiest in the room. Even at this distance you could distinguish Brock's high, reedy voice, MacIntyre's broad Glaswegian, Bryce's Edinburgh, Ruggles's American, and Rivers, who, when he got excited in a discussion, as he often did, sounded rather like a soda-water syphon going off. Nobody, listening to him now, would have thought him capable of those endless silences.

Fothersgill, his long nose twitching fastidiously, had started to complain about the soup. 'Nay, verily,' he said. 'A man knoweth not what manner of thing he eateth.' He laughed as he said it, the laugh of a man who takes small discomforts very seriously indeed. Sassoon, marooned between two particularly bad stammerers, felt no need to take part in the conversation. Instead, he twisted round in his seat and looked for Owen, remembering the last poem he'd been shown. '*Out there, we've walked quite friendly up to Death;/Sat down and eaten with him, cool and bland –/Pardoned his spilling mess-tins in our hand . . .*' Precisely, Sassoon thought. And now we complain about the soup. Or rather, *they* do.

After dinner he went straight to Owen's room. 'Do you mind?' he said. 'I'm on the run from Theosophy.'

Owen was already clearing papers from the chair. 'No, come in.'

'I can't stay in the same room with him.'

'You should ask Rivers for a change.'

'Too late. He goes tomorrow. Anyway, I wouldn't want to bother him. Have you got anything for me?'

'This.'

Sassoon took the sheet and read the whole poem through twice, then returned to the first two lines.

> What minute-bells for these who die so fast?
> – Only the monstrous/solemn anger of our guns.

'I thought "passing" bells,' Owen said.

'Hm. Though if you lose "minute" you realize how weak "fast" is. "Only the monstrous anger . . ."'

'"Solemn"?'

'"Only the solemn anger of our guns." Owen, for God's sake, this is War Office propaganda.'

'No, it's not.'

'Read that line.'

Owen read. 'Well, it certainly isn't meant to be.'

'I suppose what you've got to decide is who are "these"? The British dead? Because if they're *British*, then *our* guns is . . .'

Owen shook his head. 'All the dead.'

'Let's start there.' Sassoon crossed out 'our' and pencilled in 'the'. 'You're sure that's what you want? It isn't a minor change.'

'No, I know. If it's "the", it's got to be "monstrous".'

'Agreed.' Sassoon crossed out 'solemn'. 'So:

> What passing-bells for these who die . . . so *fast*?
> – Only the monstrous anger of the guns.

'Well, there's nothing wrong with the second line.'

'"In herds"?'

'Better.'

They worked on the poem for half an hour. The wind had been rising all evening, and the thin curtain billowed in the draught. At one point Sassoon looked up and said, 'What's that noise?'

'The wind.' Owen was trying to find the precise word for the sound of shells, and the wind was a distraction he'd been trying to ignore.

'No, *that*.'

Owen listened. 'I can't hear anything.'

'That tapping.'

Owen listened again. 'No.'

'Must be imagining things.' Sassoon listened again, then said, 'They don't *wail*. They hiss.'

'No, these are going right over.'

'That's right. They hiss.' He looked at Owen. 'I hear hissing.'

'*You* hear tapping.'

The wind went on rising all evening. By the time Sassoon left Owen's room, it was wailing round the building, moaning down chimneys, snapping branches off trees with a crack like rifle fire. All over the decayed hydro, badly fitting windows rattled and thumped, and Sassoon, passing several of his 'fellow breakdowns' in the corridor, thought they looked even more 'mental' than usual.

His own room was empty. He got into bed and lay reading while he waited for Fothersgill to return from his bridge session. As soon as he entered the room, Sassoon rolled over and pretended to be asleep. A tuneless whistling ensued, punctuated by grunts as Fothersgill bent over his shaving mirror and tweezed hairs out of his nostrils.

At last the light was out. Sassoon lay on his back, listening to the roar of wind and rain. Again he heard tapping, a distinct, purposeful sound, quite unlike the random buffeting of the wind. On such a night it was impossible not to think of the battalion. He listened to the surge and rumble of the storm, and his mind filled with memories of his last few weeks in France. He saw his platoon again, and ran through their names – not a particularly difficult feat, since no fewer than eight of them had been called Jones. He recalled his horror at their physique. Many of them were almost incapable of lifting their equipment, let alone of carrying it mile after mile along shelled roads. He'd ended one march pushing two of them in front of him, while a third stumbled along behind, clinging to his belt. None of the three had been more than five feet tall. You put them alongside an officer – almost any officer – and they seemed to be almost a different order of being. And as for their training. One man had arrived in France not knowing how to load a rifle. He saw them now, his little band, sitting on bales of straw in a sun-chinked barn, while he knelt to inspect their raw and blistered feet, and wondered how many of them were still alive.

The windows banged and rattled, and again, in a brief lull, he thought he heard tapping. There were no trees close enough to touch the glass. He supposed there might be rats, but then whoever heard of rats tapping? He tossed and turned, thinking how stupid it was not to be able to sleep here, in safety and comfort, when in France he'd been able to sleep anywhere. If he could sleep on a firestep in drenching rain, surely he could sleep now . . .

He woke to find Orme standing immediately inside the door. He wasn't surprised, he assumed Orme had come to rouse him for his watch. What did surprise him, a little, was that he seemed to be *in bed*. Orme was wearing that very pale coat of his. Once, in 'C' company mess, the CO had said, 'Correct me if I'm wrong, Orme, but I have always assumed that the colour of the British Army uniform is khaki. Not . . . *beige*.' 'Beige' was said in such Lady Bracknellish tones that Sassoon had wanted to laugh. He wanted to laugh now, but his chest muscles didn't seem to work. After a while he remembered that Orme was dead.

This clearly didn't worry Orme, who continued to stand quietly by the door, but Sassoon began to think it ought to worry him. Perhaps if he turned his head it would be all right. He stared at the window's pale square of light, and when he looked back Orme had gone.

Fothersgill was awake. 'Did you see anybody come in?' Sassoon asked.

'No, nobody's been in.' He turned over and within a few minutes was snoring again.

Sassoon waited for the rhythm to be firmly established, then got out of bed and walked across to the window. The storm had blown itself out, though twigs, leaves and even one or two larger branches, scattered across the tennis courts, bore witness to its power. The palms of his hands were sweating and his mouth was dry.

He needed to talk to Rivers, though he'd have to be careful what he said, since Rivers was a thorough-going rationalist who wouldn't take kindly to tales of the supernatural, and might even decide the symptoms of a war neurosis were manifesting themselves at last. Perhaps they were. Perhaps this was the kind of hallucination he'd had in the 4th London, but no, he didn't believe that. His nocturnal visitors *there* had come trailing gore, pointing to amputations and head wounds, rather like the statues of medieval saints pointing to the instruments of their martyrdom. This had been so restrained. Dignified. And it hadn't followed on from a nightmare either. He thought back, wanting to be sure, because he knew this was the first question Rivers would ask. No, no nightmare. Only that tapping at the window before he went to sleep.

He got dressed and sat on the bed. At last eight o'clock came, and the hospital became noisy as the shifts changed. Sassoon ran downstairs.

He felt certain Rivers would go to his office to check the post before he left, and there might just be time for a few words. But when he tapped on the door, a passing orderly said, 'Captain Rivers's gone, sir. He left on the six o'clock train.'

So that was that. Sassoon went slowly upstairs, unable to account for his sense of loss. After all, he'd known Rivers was going. And he was only going for three weeks. Fothersgill was still asleep. Sassoon collected his washbag and went along to the bathroom. He felt almost dazed. As usual he turned to lock the door, and as usual remembered there were no locks. At times like this the lack of privacy was almost intolerable. He filled the basin, and splashed his face and neck. Birds, sounding a little stunned as if they too needed to recover from the night, were beginning, cautiously, to sing. He looked at his face in the glass. In this half-light, against white tiles, it looked scarcely less ghostly than Orme's. A memory tweaked the edges of his mind. Another glass, on the top landing at home, a dark, oval mirror framing the face of a small, pale child. Himself. Five years old, perhaps. Now why did he remember that? Birds had been singing, then, too. Sparrows, twittering in the ivy. A day of shouts and banged doors and tears in rooms he was not allowed to enter. The day his father left home. Or the day he died? No, the day he left. Sassoon smiled, amused at the link he'd discovered, and then stopped smiling. He'd joked once or twice to Rivers about his being his father confessor, but only now, faced with this second abandonment, did he realize how completely Rivers had come to take his father's place. Well, that didn't matter, did it? After all, if it came to substitute fathers, he might do a lot worse. No, it was all right. Slowly, he lathered his face and began to shave.

Part Three

FOURTEEN

'Hymn No. 373.'

With a rustling of paper the maroon-backed hymn books blossomed into white. The congregation struggled to its feet. Children at the front under the watchful eye of Sunday-school teachers, the rest, middle-aged or elderly men, and women. A preliminary wheeze from the organ, then:

> God moves in a mysterious way
> His wonders to perform . . .

Since the Somme, this seemed to have become the nation's most popular hymn. Rivers had lost count of the number of times he'd heard it sung. He lifted his eyes to the flag-draped altar, and then to the east window. A crucifixion. The Virgin and St John on either side, the Holy Ghost descending, God the Father beaming benignly down. Beneath it, and much smaller, Abraham's sacrifice of his son. Behind Abraham was the ram caught in a thicket by his horns and struggling to escape, by far the best thing in the window. You could see the fear. Whereas Abraham, if he regretted having to sacrifice his son at all, was certainly hiding it well and Isaac, bound on a makeshift altar, positively smirked.

Obvious choices for the east window: the two bloody bargains on which a civilization claims to be based. *The* bargain, Rivers thought, looking at Abraham and Isaac. The one on which all patriarchal societies are founded. If you, who are young and strong, will obey me, who am old and weak, even to the extent of being prepared to sacrifice your life, then in the course of time you will peacefully inherit, and be able to exact the same obedience from your sons. Only we're breaking the bargain, Rivers thought. All over northern France, at this very moment, in trenches and dugouts and flooded shell-holes, the inheritors were dying, not one by one, while old men, and women of all ages, gathered together and sang hymns.

Blind unbelief is sure to err,
And scan His works in vain;
He is His own interpreter
And He will make it plain. Amen.

The congregation, having renounced reason, looked rather the happier for it, and sat down to await the sermon. Charles leant towards Rivers and whispered, 'He doesn't usually go on very long.'

That whisper brought back the Sunday mornings of their childhood when they'd drive to church in a pony and trap, and spent the sermon looking up the naughty bits in the Old Testament, a task made easier by the grubby fingerprints of those who had gone before. He remembered Michal's bride-price: an hundred foreskins of the Philistines. As an anthropologist, he still found that fascinating. He remembered the smell of hassocks, and fastened his eyes on the flag-draped altar. They would never come back, those times.

The vicar had reached the top of the pulpit steps. A faint light flashed on his glasses as he made the sign of the cross. 'In the name of the Father and of the Son and of the Holy Ghost . . .'

Charles was busy with a great rehousing of the hens. They were to be transferred from deep litter in the barn to the new coops in Two-acre Field. This was best done after dusk when the hens were drowsy and less likely to rebel. The brothers lingered over tea in the living room, and then went out across the black, sodden, dismal mud of the yard towards the large, low barn. Rivers was wearing a pair of old cord breeches kept up with one of his brother's belts, visible proof that Bertha's strictures on his loss of weight were justified. 'It isn't as if,' she said at every mealtime, piling his plate high, 'you had it to lose.' 'He's all right, Bertha, leave him alone,' Charles always said, though it made no difference. Rivers still staggered away from the table feeling that he'd been force-fed.

Charles carried the hens easily, his arms binding the wings fast to his sides. Rivers, less expert, picked up two birds and set off after him. His fingers dug through the fluffiness into the surprisingly hard quills, and touched clammy flesh. The blood-red combs jiggled as he walked, amber eyes looked up with a kind of bright vacuity. As he tried to nudge the farmyard gate open with his elbow, one of them got its wings free and flapped frantically until he managed to subdue it again. God, I hate hens, he thought.

The chicken farm had been his idea, after Charles came back from the East with malaria. Work in the open air, Rivers had advised. He was paying for it now. As he left the shelter of the hedge and set off across Two-acre Field, a great gust of 'open air' almost lifted him off his feet. He felt responsible for the farm idea, and it wasn't paying. At the moment they were only just breaking even. Mainly it was the effect of the war. Feed was scarce and expensive, male help impossible to get. The last land girl had stayed only long enough to work out the distance to the nearest town, before discovering that some domestic crisis required her immediate return home. But even without the war it might not have been easy. Hens had a curious way of not thriving. They seemed to be subject to a truly phenomenal range of diseases and to take a perverse pleasure in working their way down the list.

It was almost completely dark now, a few faint stars pricking through the clear sky. One hen, weaker than the rest, was being picked on by the others. Its chest was bare of feathers and raw where they'd pecked at it.

'I'll have to get that one out and wring its neck,' Charles said.

'Can't you just isolate her and then put her back in?'

'No. Once they start they never stop.'

They turned and walked back. McTavish, the farm cat, a black, battered tom, met them at the corner of the yard and preceded them across it. A notably morose cat, McTavish, a defect of temperament Rivers attributed to his being perpetually surrounded by forbidden flesh. He was fond of McTavish and slipped him titbits from his plate whenever he thought Bertha wasn't looking.

They moved hens for an hour; slow, tedious work and then, as real darkness set in, went back to the house. Bertha had been baking. An earthenware pot full of bread dough stood by the kitchen range, and the whole firelit room was full of the smell of warm yeast. 'You'll be all right, won't you?' Bertha said, driving a hat pin neatly into her hat, and craning towards the mirror to make sure it was on straight. She and Charles were using Rivers as a chicken-sitter while they enjoyed a rare night out.

'Don't fuss, Bertha,' Charles said.

'There's two loaves in the oven. They'll be done at ten past eight. Turn them out, tap the base. If it sounds hollow, they're done. Do you think you can manage that?'

'He's not a complete idiot, Bertha,' Charles called in from the hall.

Bertha looked doubtful. 'All right, then. Are we off?'

Charles came in wearing his hat and coat.

Rivers said, 'I'll see if I can get those accounts finished, Charles.'

'I wish you would,' Bertha murmured as she went past.

Once they'd gone, Rivers sat in the rocking chair by the fire, and concentrated on not dozing off. He hadn't dared not eat at dinner, and the unaccustomed heavy meal and the firelight were making his eyelids droop. Last spring when he'd been here, boxes of chicks had been put to warm before the fire, and then the room had been full of the pecking and scratching of tiny beaks and feet. He remembered them struggling out of the eggs, how exhausted, wet and miserable they looked, and yet curiously powerful, little Atlases struggling to hold up the world. Now the same chicks were scruffy, bedraggled things running in the coops, and the only sound in the room was the roar of flame.

He stretched out his legs and looked at the account book on the edge of the kitchen table. He had letters he ought to write, the most urgent being one to David Burns, who'd invited him to spend the last few days of his leave at the family's holiday cottage on the Suffolk coast. As far as Rivers could make out, Burns's parents wanted to talk about his future, and although Rivers was not particularly anxious to do this – he found it difficult to envisage any future for Burns – he thought it his duty to accept. And then there was a half-completed letter to Sassoon, but the accounts would have to come first. Ten past eight. He got the loaves from the oven, tipped them out, and tapped the bases. Since he'd never done this before, he had no way of knowing whether this particular sound was 'hollow' or not. He decided they *looked* done, and set them to cool on the tray. Then he fetched the shoe box in which Charles stored his receipts and set to work on finishing the accounts. At intervals as he worked he looked up. The wind which had been blowing a gale all day was beginning to die down. Once he heard an owl hoot from the copse at the other side of Two-acre Field, a cold, shivery sound that made him glad of the fire and the smell of warm bread.

When he'd finished, he took the oil lamp and went along to the front room, intending to have another go at finishing his letter to Siegfried. He put the lamp down on the desk. Ranged at intervals around the walls, big heavy pieces of furniture squatted on their own shadows. Most of them he remembered from his childhood home: Knowles Bank. They were too big to fit into his sisters' cottage, he had no need of them, and so Charles and Bertha had inherited them all. Their presence here in different places, at different angles to the walls and to each other, gave him an odd feeling of slipping back into an out-of-focus version of his childhood.

A cold, unused room. All the farm paperwork was done in the kitchen. He decided to take his letter along and finish it there, but then lingered, fingering the leather of the desk top and looking at the picture that hung above the empty grate. At Knowles Bank it had hung in the same position, above the fireplace, in his father's study. As a picture it could hardly have been more appropriate to his father's dual role as priest and speech therapist, since it showed the Apostles at Pentecost immediately after they had received the gift of tongues. There they sat, each under his own personal flame, rendered in an instant fluent, persuasive and articulate, not merely in their own language but in all known tongues. Rivers remembered the bishop's sermon one Pentecost when he'd explained that the gift of tongues as bestowed upon the Apostles had absolutely nothing to do with 'the gift of tongues' as bestowed regularly every Sunday on uneducated riff-raff in various tin-roofed chapels about the diocese. The gift of Pentecost had made the Apostles *comprehensible* in all known languages. And there they sat still, looking, Rivers couldn't help thinking, most unchristianly smug about it all.

He'd sat with other boys – his father's pupils – underneath that picture for many a long hour, stumbling over the consonants of his own language, remembering to hold down the back of his tongue, project his breath in an even flow, etc., etc. Sometimes his father would walk with him up and down the room, since he believed the measured pace helped to regulate the flow of breath. Rivers hadn't been the star pupil in those classes, not by any means. If anything he'd made rather less progress than the rest, in spite of – or because of? – having his teacher with him all the time. The house was full of stammering boys, any age from ten to nineteen, and at least it meant he was not the only one. It had had another advantage too, he remembered. While the boys were there, the Reverend Charles Dodgson stayed away. Mr Dodgson didn't like boys. As soon as they left at Christmas or in the summer holidays, he arrived, taking lessons every evening after dinner. Rivers, from long exposure to other people's speech impediments, could sum up the main features of a stammer almost as quickly as his father. Dodgson found *m* difficult, and *p* in consonant combinations, particularly in the middle of words, but his arch enemy was hard *c*.

During the day there were boating trips on the river. Dodgson and the four Rivers children, himself, Charles, Ethel and – Dodgson's favourite – Katharine. He'd never enjoyed those trips much, and neither, he thought, had Charles, though probably that was no more than the slight pique of two Victorian schoolboys, finding themselves, for the first time in their lives, not of the preferred sex. Afterwards, during those apparently endless summer evenings, there would be croquet on the lawn, Rivers's father and Dodgson playing, the children watching. There was a photograph of them on the desk, doing just that, he and Charles leaning back against the garden roller, no doubt getting grass stains on their white shirts, the two little girls, his sisters, under the shade of the beech tree. If he tried hard, he could recall the feel of the roller against his shoulder blades, the heat of the sun on the back of his neck.

He had one other memory of Dodgson. One evening he'd crept close to the open window of his father's study, sat down with his back to the wall and listened to the lesson in progress. Why he'd done this he couldn't now remember, except that it hadn't *felt* like eavesdropping, since he knew nothing private was likely to be said. Perhaps he'd just wanted to hear Dodgson put through the same routine he and the other boys were put through. Perhaps he'd wanted to see him cut down to size. Dodgson had just embarked on the sentence about the careful cat catching the mouse – a simple enough tale, but already, in Dodgson's mouth, threatening to become an epic. Rivers listened to his father's advice, the same advice, basically, that *he* got, though conveyed without that peculiar note of fraught patience. He thought suddenly, this is nonsense. It *doesn't* help to remember to keep your tongue down, it doesn't help to think about the flow of breath. So he'd thought, sweeping away his father's life work in a single minute as twelve-year-old boys are apt to do. He'd raised his head very cautiously above the window sill, and seen his father sitting behind the desk – this desk – his back to the window, clean pink neck showing above clean white collar, broad shoulders straining the cloth of his jacket. He stared at the back of his neck, at the neck of the man whom he had, in a way, just killed, and he didn't feel sad or guilty about it at all. He felt glad.

Later that summer he'd given a talk to the speech therapy group on monkeys. *M* was to him what *c* was to Dodgson, but he was interested in monkeys, and still more interested in Darwin's theory of evolution, which by this time had achieved acceptance in some circles. Knowles Bank was not among them. His father had been furious, not because Rivers had stumbled over every single *m* without exception – though indeed he had – but because he'd dared suggest that Genesis was no more than the creation myth of a Bronze Age people. Dinner that night was a strained occasion. Father angry, mother upset, Charles covertly sympathetic, sisters goggle-eyed and making the most of it, Rivers himself outwardly subdued, inwardly triumphant. For the first time in his life, he'd forced his father to listen to what he had to say, and not merely to the way he'd said it.

And yet, Rivers thought, running his hands across the scarred leather of the desk top, the relationship between father and son is never simple, and never over. Death certainly doesn't end it. In the past year he'd thought more about his father than he'd done since he was a child. Only recently it had occurred to him that if some twelve-year-old boy had crept up to his window at Craiglockhart, as he'd done to his father's window at Knowles Bank, he'd have seen a man sitting at a desk with his back to the window, listening to some patient, with a stammer far worse than Dodgson's, try and fail to reach the end of a sentence. Only that boy would not have been his son.

The unfinished letter to Siegfried lay on the desk. He'd got as far as a comment on the weather, and there the letter had ground to a halt. What he did so easily in conversation, always nudging Siegfried gently in the same direction, and yet always avoiding any suggestion of pressure, was a feat he apparently could not perform on paper. Perhaps he was just too tired. He told himself the letter could wait till morning.

He picked up the lamp, pushed aside the heavy dark red curtains and opened the window. A big dizzy moth flew in, with pale wings and a fat, furry body, and began bumping against the ceiling. He leant out of the window, smelling roses he couldn't see. The wind had fallen completely now, giving way to a breathless hush. Faintly, over dark hedges and starlit fields, came the soft thud-thud of the guns. When he'd first arrived, suffering from the usual medley of physical and neurasthenic symptoms – headaches, dry mouth, pounding heart – he'd confused that sound with the throbbing of blood in his head. Then one night, lying sleepless, he'd heard the water jug vibrating in the bowl, and realized what it was that he kept hearing. Siegfried must have heard it in June when he was at home convalescing from his wound.

Perhaps he'd better write tonight after all. He closed the window, and sat down at the desk. The moth's huge shadow, flickering over the walls and ceiling, darkened the page, as, drawing the pad towards him, he tore off the sheet and started again. *My dear Siegfried . . .*

'What draft is this?'

'Lost count,' Owen said. 'You did tell me to sweat my guts out.'

'Did I really? What an inelegant expression. "What passing-bells for these who die as cattle?" I see we got to the slaughterhouse in the end.' Sassoon read through the poem. When he'd finished, he didn't immediately comment.

'It's better, isn't it?'

'Better? It's *transformed.*' He read it again. 'Though when you look at the *sense* . . . You do realize you've completely contradicted yourself, don't you? You start by saying there is no consolation, and then you say there is.'

'Not consolation. Pride in the sacrifice.'

'Isn't that consolation?'

'If it is, it's justifiable. There's a point beyond which –'

'I don't see that.'

'There's a point beyond which you can't press the meaninglessness. Even if the courage is being abused, it's still . . .'

Owen leapt up, went to the drawer of his washstand and produced the typescript Sassoon had lent him. He began leafing quickly but carefully through it. Sassoon, watching, thought, he's getting better. No stammer. Quick, decisive movements. The self-confidence to contradict his hero. And the poem had been a revelation.

'Look, you do exactly the same thing,' Owen said, coming across with the sheet he wanted.

O my brave brown companions, when your souls
Flock silently away, and the eyeless dead
Shame the wild beast of battle on the ridge,
Death will stand grieving in that field of war
Since your unvanquished hardihood is spent.
And through some mooned Valhalla there will pass
Battalions and battalions, scarred from hell;
The unreturning army that was youth;
The legions who have suffered and are dust.

'What's that if not pride in the sacrifice?'

'Grief? All right, point taken. I just don't like the idea of . . . making it out to be less of a horror than it really is.' He looked down at the page. 'I think you should publish this.'

'You mean in the *Hydra*?'

'No, I mean in the *Nation*. Give me a fair copy and I'll see what I can do. You'll need a different title, though. "Anthem for . . ."' He thought for a moment, crossed one word out, substituted another.

'There you are,' he said, handing the page back, smiling. '"Anthem for *Doomed* Youth."'

The main corridor of the hospital stretched the whole length of the building, with wards opening off on either side. From one of these came an unpleasant smell which Madge said was gangrene, though Sarah didn't believe she knew. Ward Fourteen was overcrowded, the beds packed close together, men sitting up and staring with interest at the two girls hesitating just inside the door. Most of them looked reasonably well and cheerful. The trouble was that with their cropped heads and hospital blue uniforms, they also looked exactly alike.

'I won't recognize him,' Madge said in a frantic whisper.

'Go on,' Sarah said, giving her a shove.

They started to walk up the ward. Madge stared from bed to bed with a dazed look. She really mightn't recognize him at this rate, Sarah thought, but then a voice cried, 'Madge!' A dark-haired man with a gingery moustache was sitting up, waving and looking delighted to see her. Madge walked forward cautiously, located the bandaged left arm, checked to see that the swelling beneath the counterpane was the right length and breadth to consist of two legs. He looked all right. He planted a smacking kiss on Madge's lips, and Sarah looked away in embarrassment, only to realize she was herself the object of amused appreciation from all parts of the ward.

'Eh, look, I've brought you these,' Madge said. 'How are you?'

'I'm all right. Went right through,' he said. 'Just here.' He pointed to his biceps. 'No gangrene, no nothing.'

'You were lucky.'

'I'll say. I'm gunna be in here two weeks they reckon, and then I'll have a bit of leave before I go back.'

'This is Sarah,' Madge said.

'Pleased to meet you.'

They shook hands. Madge was now sitting by the bed, beginning, cautiously, to bask in the admiration of her restored lover and to plan what they would do on his leave. After this had been going on for a while, Sarah began to feel distinctly green and hairy. 'I'll just have a walk round the grounds,' she said. 'It's a bit hot in here.'

'Yeh, all right,' Madge said.

'I'll see you at the main entrance, then. Half an hour?'

They hardly noticed her go. None of these men was badly wounded, and several of them whistled and clicked their tongues as she walked past. The whole atmosphere of the ward was happy. The general air of relief at being out of it was what chiefly came across, though she supposed there must be other wards where the wounds were not so slight.

Outside, in the corridor, she looked up and down, realizing she didn't know in which direction the exit lay. She was surrounded by notices directing people to the pharmacy, the path lab, the X-ray department, everywhere except the way out. She tried walking to her left, but her way was blocked by a large notice saying: THEATRES. NO UNAUTHORIZED PERSONNEL BEYOND THIS POINT. She turned right, and shortly afterwards came to a corridor she thought she recognized, and began to walk along it, but the feeling of familiarity soon vanished. The building was enormous, and seemed to have no plan, no structure to it, at all. To add to the sense of unreality most of the notices referred to its civilian use before the war. Maternity, she read, and then the swing doors banged open to reveal beds full of people who were most unlikely ever to give birth.

Obviously she ought to stop and ask somebody, but then everybody seemed to be in such a hurry, and so grim-faced. At last she found a door that led out to the grounds at the back of the hospital, where the tall chimney of an incinerator dribbled brownish-yellow smoke. Here, a huge tent had been erected and this served as another ward. She glanced into the interior, which was golden in the sunlight filtered through the roof, but the atmosphere was close, stifling, a humming darkness in which the clumsiness of bandages and the itch of healing skin must be almost intolerable.

A constant traffic of nurses and orderlies passed between the tent and the main building, and, feeling herself to be in the way, Sarah looked around for somewhere she could find temporary refuge and not bother anybody. There was a conservatory along the side of the hospital, facing east so that at the moment it caught the full warmth of the sun. Shadowy figures sat inside, and the door was open so she thought she might perhaps sit there.

Once across the threshold she became aware of a silence, a silence caused, she suspected, by her entrance. She was still dazzled by the brightness of the light outside and the relative dimness of the interior, and so she had to blink several times before she saw them, a row of figures in wheelchairs, but figures that were no longer the size and shape of adult men. Trouser legs sewn short; empty sleeves pinned to jackets. One man had lost all his limbs, and his face was so drained, so pale, he seemed to have left his blood in France as well. The blue of the hospital uniform looked garish against his skin. They'd been pushed out here to get the sun, but not right outside, and not at the front of the hospital where their mutilations might have been seen by passers-by. They stared at her, but not as the men had stared on the other ward, smiling, trying to catch her eye. This was a totally blank stare. If it contained anything at all, it was fear. Fear of her looking at the empty trouser legs. Fear of her not looking at them. She stood there, unable to go forward, and unable, for a few crucial moments, to turn back, until a nurse bustled up to her and said, 'Who is it you want to see?'

'I'm just waiting for a friend. It's all right, I'll wait outside.'

She backed out, walking away in the sunlight, feeling their eyes on her, thinking that perhaps if she'd been prepared, if she'd managed to smile, to look normal, it might have been better. But no, she thought, there was nothing she could have done that would have made it better. Simply by being there, by being that inconsequential, infinitely powerful creature: *a pretty girl*, she had made everything worse. Her sense of her own helplessness, her being forced to play the role of Medusa when she meant no harm, merged with the anger she was beginning to feel at their being hidden away like that. If the country demanded that price, then it should bloody well be prepared to look at the result. She strode on through the heat, not caring where she was going, furious with herself, the war . . . Everything.

Prior took off his clothes, put on the white hospital gown and sat on the bed to await the arrival of the doctor. This was his second visit. The first time he'd seen Eaglesham, the consultant, a big, kindly, grizzled bear of a man who'd said very little but whom he'd trusted at once. He'd raised his eyebrows when Prior blew into the Vitalograph or whatever the machine was called, but he hadn't said what he thought, and Prior had not wanted to ask. It wasn't going to be Eaglesham today, though. A much younger man with a sallow skin and slick dark hair was popping in and out of the other cubicles. Prior looked down at his thin white legs. He didn't see why he had to take all his clothes off. Were they trying to cater for some unforeseen medical emergency in which his lungs had slipped into his pelvis? He didn't like the way the gown fastened at the back. He didn't mind displaying his wares, if he liked the other person and the time seemed right, but he did like the illusion at least that the act was voluntary. He could hear the doctor's voice in the cubicle next door, talking to a man who couldn't complete a sentence without coughing. At last the curtains were pushed aside and the doctor came in, followed by a nurse, clasping a beige file to her bosom. Prior slipped off the robe and stood up to be examined.

'Second-Lieutenant Prior.'

'Mister' he wanted to say. He said, 'Yes.'

'I see there's some question whether you're fit to go back. I mean apart from the state of your *nerves*.'

Prior said nothing at all.

The doctor waited. 'Well, let's have a look at you.'

He moved the stethoscope all over Prior's chest, pressing so hard that at times the stethoscope left overlapping rings on the skin that flushed and faded to white. He thinks I'm shirking, Prior thought, and the idea made him go cold.

'How *are* your nerves?' the doctor said.

'Better.'

'Shell explosion, was it?'

'Not exactly.'

Not one word of what he'd told Rivers would he repeat to this man.

'Do *you* think you're fit?'

'I'm not a doctor.'

The doctor smiled. Contemptuously, it seemed to Prior. 'Keen to get back, are we?'

Prior closed his eyes. He had a picture of himself driving his knee into the man's groin, and the picture was so vivid that for a moment he thought he might have done it, but then he opened his eyes and there was the sallow face, still smiling. He stared at him.

The doctor nodded, almost as if Prior had replied, and then slowly, to avoid any suggestion of backing off, turned and made a brief note on the file. It's all bluff, Prior thought. It's what Eaglesham says that matters.

He was in a torment as he got back into his uniform, reckoning his chances, despising himself for reckoning them. He didn't thank Rivers for any of this. I haven't lied to any of them, he thought. I haven't made things out to be worse than they really are. He finished lacing his puttees and stood up. The nurse came back with a card. 'If you tell them at the appointments desk, three weeks.'

'Yes, all right. Thank you.'

He took the card, but walking down the long corridor afterwards he was tempted not to make the appointment. In the end he did, then put the card away and strode out into the hospital grounds as fast as he could. He thought he might buy himself something from the barrow at the entrance, fruit or sweets, any little treat that might make him feel better. Less contaminated.

He saw her before she saw him, and called out, 'Sarah.' She turned and smiled. He'd thought about her a lot while he'd been in the sick bay, remembering that time on the beach. Illness, once the worst was over, always made him randy. What he'd forgotten, he thought now, looking at the yellow face beneath the aureole of extraordinary hair, was how much he *liked* her.

'What are *you* doing here?' she asked, obviously delighted.

'Having my chest examined.'

'Are you all right?'

'Fine – thanks to you. What are *you* doing here?'

'I'm with Madge. Her fiancé's been wounded.'

'Is he all right?'

'Yes, I think so.' Her face darkened. 'I've just seen some that aren't all right. There's a sort of conservatory round the back. They're all sat in there. Where the rest of us don't have to see them.'

'Bad?'

She nodded. 'You know I used to wonder how I'd go on if Johnny came back like that. You always tell yourself it'd make no difference. Easy said, isn't it?'

He sensed the anger and responded to it immediately. She might not know much about the war, but what she did know she faced honestly. He admired her for that. 'Look, do you have to wait for Madge?' he asked. 'I mean, how long do you think she'll be?'

'Ages, I should think. She was virtually in bed with him when I left.'

'Well, can't you tell her you're going? She can walk back by herself all right, can't she? It's broad daylight.'

She looked at him consideringly. 'Yes, all right.' She started to move away. 'I won't be a minute.'

Left alone, Prior bought two bunches of chrysanthemums, bronze and white, from the barrow near the entrance. They weren't the flowers he would have chosen, but he wanted to give her something. He stood craning his head for the first sight of her. When she arrived, smiling and out of breath, he handed her the flowers, and then, on a sudden impulse, leant across and kissed her. The flowers, crushed between them, released their bitter, autumnal smell.

*

They were burning leaves on Hampstead Heath where Rivers walked with Ruth Head on the second day of his visit. Acrid smoke drifted across their path and below them London lay in a blue haze. They stopped by one of the ponds, and watched a coot cleave the smooth water. 'You see over there behind those houses?' Ruth said. 'That's the RFC hospital. And then over there – just in that dip there – that's the Big Gun.'

'I'm glad you and Henry don't take refuge in the kitchen every night. Everybody else seems to.'

'Can you imagine Henry cowering under the kitchen table?'

They smiled at each other and walked on.

'Actually the air raids are my guilty secret,' Ruth said.

'You mean you'd rather be under the table?'

'Oh no, quite the opposite. I enjoy them. It's a terrible thing to say, isn't it? All that damage. People killed. And yet every time the siren goes, I feel this immense sense of exhilaration. I'd really like to go out and run about in it.' She laughed, self-deprecatingly. 'I don't of course. But I get this feeling that the . . . the *crust* of everything is starting to crack. Don't you feel that?'

'*Yes*. I'm just not sure we're going to like what's under the crust.'

They started to walk towards Spaniard's Road. Rivers said, 'You know last night I got the distinct impression that Henry was plotting something.'

'About you? If he is, it'll be something to your advantage.'

'You mean you know and you're not going to tell me?'

Ruth laughed. 'That's right.'

By Spaniard's Road, men in blue hospital uniforms sat in wheelchairs, waiting for someone to come and push them away. Ruth was silent for a while after they'd walked past. 'You know there was something I didn't say last night.' She looked up at him. 'I think Sassoon's absolutely right.'

'Oh dear, I was hoping I might be able to introduce you. But if you're going to be a bad moral influence –'

'*Seriously*.'

'All right, seriously. Suppose he *is* right? Does that mean it's a good idea to let him go ahead and destroy himself?'

'Surely it has to be his choice?'

'It *is* his choice.'

Ruth smiled and shook her head.

'Look,' Rivers said, 'I wear the uniform, I take the pay, *I do the job*. I'm not going to apologize for that.'

'I'm not suggesting you should. All the same,' she said, turning to look at him, 'you're tearing yourself in pieces as well as him.'

They walked in silence for a while. Rivers said, 'Is that what Henry thinks?'

Ruth laughed. 'Of course not. You want perception, you go to a novelist, not a psychiatrist.'

'I'm sure you're right.'

'No, you're not. You don't believe a word of it.'

'At any rate, I'm too cowed to disagree.'

That evening, left alone with Henry after dinner, Rivers watched him massage the triangle of skin between the thumb and forefinger of his left hand. 'Does that still bother you?'

'A bit. Cold weather. Do you know, I don't think I'd have the courage to do that now.'

'No, I look back sometimes, and . . . I'm amazed. What are you doing these days?'

'Gross injuries to the spinal cord. We've got a lot of interesting material.' Head's mouth twisted. 'As we call the poor sods.'

Rivers shook his head. He'd seen Head too often on the wards to believe him capable of that particular kind of research-orientated callousness.

'It's an interesting atmosphere,' Head said. 'Dealing with physical trauma and war neurosis in the same hospital. You'd like it.'

'I'm sure I would.' A trace of bitterness. 'I'd like London.'

'There's a job going if you want it.'

'You mean there's a vacancy?'

'No, I mean there's a job *for you* if you want it. I've been asked to sound you out. Psychologist with the Royal Flying Corps. At the Central Hospital, Hampstead.'

'*Ah*. I wondered why Ruth was so keen on the Heath.'

'I imagine you'd find it interesting? Apparently there are some quite striking differences between the rate of breakdown in pilots and in other branches of the service.'

'It sounds marvellous.' He raised his hands and let them drop. 'I just don't see how I can.'

'Why not? You'd be closer to your family, your friends, your research contacts, you'd be able to get back to Cambridge at weekends. And . . . I don't suppose it *matters*, but we'd be able to work together again.'

Rivers buried his face in his hands. 'O-o-o-oh. "Get thee behind me, Satan."'

'I am behind you. I was thinking of giving you a shove.'

'I couldn't leave Bryce.'

Head looked incredulous. 'You mean, your CO?'

'He's in a difficult situation. We're in for a general inspection, and . . . it all goes back a long way. Bryce is determined this time he's not going to play their game. He's not going to parade the patients, or polish the bottoms of the frying-pans, or pretend to be anything other than just an extremely busy, overcrowded and I think bloody good hospital.'

'What do they want?'

'They want a barracks. It's got all the makings of a really nasty confrontation. I think Bryce may have to go.'

'Well, I hate to sound harsh, but wouldn't that rather solve the problem? *Your* problem, I mean.'

'If it happened. Meanwhile, I think I can be . . . of some use to him.'

'When is this inspection?'

'End of the month.'

'We'd need to know about the job . . . Well. Three weeks?'

'I'll think about it.'

'Good. And don't be *too* altruistic, will you? You're isolated up there, it's not good for you.'

'I don't know about isolated. I never have a minute to myself.'

'*Precisely*. Come on, let's find Ruth.'

FIFTEEN

Aldeburgh was the end of the line, but the train, as if reluctant to accept this, produced, as Rivers stepped down on to the platform, an amazing burst of steam. He stood, looking up and down, as the train's hissing subsided into grunts, and the steam cleared. Burns had promised to meet him, but his memory wasn't good, and, faced with the empty platform, Rivers was glad he had the address. But then, just as Rivers was resigning himself to finding the house on his own, Burns appeared, a tall, emaciated figure wearing a coat of stiff herringbone tweed that reached almost to the ground. He'd obviously been running, and was out of breath. 'Hello,' he said. Rivers tried to judge whether Burns looked better or worse. It was hard to tell. His face in the light of the naphtha flares was as expressionless as beaten bronze.

'How are you?' they asked simultaneously, and then laughed.

Rivers decided he should be the one to answer. 'A lot better, thanks.'

'Good,' Burns said. 'It's walking distance,' he added across his shoulder, already striding off. 'We don't need a taxi.'

They came out of the station and began walking downhill, through the quiet cold fringes of the town, past the church, through streets of huddled houses, and out on to the front.

The sea was calm, almost inaudible, a toothless mouth mumbling pebbles in the darkness. Instead of walking along the path, Burns struck out across the shingle and Rivers followed, to where the tide had laid bare a thin strip of sand. The crunch and slither of shingle under their feet blotted out all other sounds. Rivers turned, and saw the bones of Burns's face gleaming in the moonlight. He wondered what he made of the tangles of barbed wire that ran along the beach, with only two narrow channels left for fishing boats and for the lifeboat to come and go. But Burns seemed not to see the wire.

They stood together at the water's edge, two black shadows on the pale shingle, and small waves creamed over at their feet. Then the moon came out from behind a bank of dark cloud, and the fishermen's huts, the boats lined up in two short rows behind the wire, and the heaped nets, cast shadows behind them almost as sharply edged as day.

They returned to the path and began walking along the terrace of houses, which here and there had gaps. Many of the houses were shuttered and had sandbags piled against the front doors. 'The sea's been known to pay visits,' Burns said, following the direction of Rivers's gaze. 'I was here once when it flooded.' Evidently sandbags brought back no other memories.

'This is it,' he said a few minutes later, stopping in front of a tall but extremely narrow house. At this end of the foreshore the sea was much closer, turning and turning in the darkness. Rivers looked out and caught a glint of white. 'What's along there?'

'The marshes. More shingle. I'll show you tomorrow.'

They groped their way into the hall, closing the door carefully behind them before Burns switched on the light. His face, deeply shadowed from the unshaded bulb, peered anxiously at Rivers. 'I expect you'd like to go upstairs,' he said. 'I *think* I've given you a towel . . .' He looked like a child trying to remember what it was that grown-ups said to newly arrived guests. He also looked, for the first time, deranged.

Rivers followed him up the narrow stairs and into a small bedroom. Burns pointed out the bathroom and then went downstairs. Rivers put his bag down, bounced on the bed to test the mattress, and looked round. The walls were covered with paper of an indeterminate and confusing pattern, the background colour faded to the yellow of an old bruise. Everything smelled of the sea, as if the furniture had soaked it in. It reminded him of childhood holidays in Brighton. He splashed his face in the bowl, then, turning off the light, opened the shutters. His room overlooked the sea. The wind was rising, and with each gust the coils of wire twitched as if they were alive.

No sign of Burns's parents. Rivers had mistakenly assumed he was being invited to meet them, since a large part of Burns's letter had dealt with their anxieties about his future. But apparently not. This was probably their room. The house was so narrow there couldn't be more than one, or at the most, two small rooms on each floor.

The evening passed pleasantly enough. No mention of Burns's illness, no mention of the war. These were evidently taboo topics, but they talked about a great range of other things. Whatever else the war had done to Burns, it had certainly deepened his love for his native county. Suffolk flowers, birds, churches, he was knowledgeable about them all. More recently, he'd become interested in the preservation of country crafts. 'Old Clegg', who was apparently something of a local character, had promised to teach him flint-knapping, and he seemed to be looking forward to that. Even before the war he'd been very much a countryman in his interests, rather like Siegfried in a way, though without Siegfried's passion for hunting.

When the conversation turned to other matters, Burns was very much the bright sixth former, idealistic, intolerant, naïve, inclined to offer sweeping generalizations as fact, attractive in the freshness of his vision as such boys often are. Rivers thought how misleading it was to say that the war had 'matured' these young men. It wasn't true of his patients, and it certainly wasn't true of Burns, in whom a prematurely aged man and a fossilized schoolboy seemed to exist side by side. It did give him a curiously ageless quality, but 'maturity' was hardly the word. Still, he was better than he'd been at Craiglockhart, so perhaps his conviction that if he could only get back to Suffolk and forget the war he would be all right had been proved correct. But then why am I here? Rivers thought. Despite Burns's reluctance to mention his illness, Rivers didn't believe he'd been invited to Suffolk to talk about church architecture. But it would be quite wrong to force the pace. Whatever was bothering him, he would raise the matter in his own time.

Rivers woke the following morning to find the beach shrouded in mist. He leant on the window sill, and watched the fishing boats return. The pebbles on the beach were wet, though not from rain or tide. The mist clung to them like sweat, and the air tasted of iron. Everything was so quiet. When a gull flew in from the sea and passed immediately overhead, he heard the creak of its wings.

Burns was already up, in the kitchen by the sound of things, but not, Rivers thought, preparing breakfast. Nothing in the way of dinner or supper had appeared the night before, and Rivers had hesitated, on his first evening, to go into the kitchen and forage for food, though he suspected that might be the only way of getting any.

He washed, dressed, shaved, and went downstairs. By this time the mist on the beach had begun to thin, but it was cold for the time of year, and the sight of a fire in the first floor living room was welcome. He went down a further flight of stairs into the kitchen and found Burns at the kitchen table with a pot of tea.

'There's some cereal,' he said, pointing.

He sounded shy again, though last night he'd begun to talk quite freely by the end of the evening, just as Rivers, caught between the roar of the fire and the roar of the sea, had started nodding off to sleep. 'I'm sorry I had to go to bed so early,' Rivers said, reaching for the cereal packet.

''S all right.' Visibly, he remembered what it was he was supposed to ask next. 'Did you have a good night?'

'Fine.' Rivers bit the reciprocal question back. He'd heard part of Burns's night. Obviously, however hard Burns tried to thrust memories of the war behind him, the nightmare followed.

The doorbell rang, and Burns got up to answer it. 'This is Mrs Burril's day for sorting me out,' he said.

Mrs Burril was a remarkably silent person, but she managed, without words, to make it clear their presence was superfluous.

Burns said, 'I thought we might go for a walk.'

The mist had thinned but not cleared. It moved in slow, cold currents over the marshes, where drainage ditches and sump holes reflected a steely light at the sky. Reeds whispered, with a noise like the palms of hands being rubbed together. It was difficult to breathe, difficult even to move, and they spoke in low voices when they spoke at all.

They walked along a narrow raised path that divided the marshes from the river. Small yachts rode at anchor, the breeze just strong enough to make their rigging rattle, not a loud sound, but persistent and rather disturbing, like an irregular heart beat. Nothing else here could disturb. The estuary lay flat and peaceful under a shrunken, silver sun, and nothing moved, except the reeds, until a flight of ducks whistled past.

Rivers had begun to realize how remarkable the area was. A strip of land, at times no more than a hundred yards wide, divided the estuary from the North Sea. Walking out along this strip, away from the town, into the bleached shingle distances, you became aware of two separate sounds: the roar and suck of waves on shingle, and the lulling sound of the river among its reeds. If you moved to the left, the crunch and chop of boots on shingle cut out the gentler river sounds. If to the right, the tapping of rigging and the lapping of water dominated, though you could still hear that the sea was there.

They turned and looked back at the huddled town. 'You know, I love this place,' Burns said. 'I wouldn't like you to think I'd left London just because of the raids. Actually it wasn't the raids, it was the regular meal-times. You know, everybody sitting down to eat. Waiting for food to be put in front of them. And father going on about the war. He's a great believer in the war, my father.'

'Will they be coming to Suffolk at all?'

'No, I shouldn't think so. They're both very busy in London.' They turned and walked on. 'It's best we don't see too much of each other at the moment. I am not a sight for sore eyes.'

A squat, circular building had begun to loom up out of the mist. It looked rather like a Martello tower, Rivers thought, but he hadn't known they'd been built as far north as this.

'This is the most northerly,' Burns said, slithering down the slope on to the beach. Rivers followed him across the shingle and down into the dank high moat that surrounded the tower. In its shadow, all water sounds, whether hissing waves or lapping water, abruptly ceased. Ferns grew from the high walls of the moat; and the tower, where the look-out turret had crumbled away, was thronged with bindweed, but the overall impression was of a dead place.

The sea must flood the moat at high tide, for all kinds of debris had been washed up and left. Driftwood, the torn-off wing of a gull, bits of blue and green glass. A child would have loved it, picking over these pieces.

'We used to play here,' Burns said. 'Daring each other, you know. Who could go all the way up?'

There was a door, but it had planks nailed across it. Rivers peered through a crack and saw stone steps going down.

'Strictly forbidden. They were always afraid we'd get trapped in the cellars.'

'I suppose they flood, don't they? At high tide?'

'Yes. There's all kinds of stories told about it. People chained up and left to drown. I think we rather liked that. We used to sit down there and pretend we could see ghosts.'

'It feels like a place where people have died. I mean, violent deaths.'

'You feel that, do you? Yes. I expect that's why we liked it. Bloodthirsty little horrors, boys.'

Rivers wasn't sorry when they climbed the bank of shingle and stood on the beach in the strengthening sunlight again.

'Do you feel up to a longish walk?' Burns asked.

'Yes.'

'All right. We can follow that path.'

They walked four or five miles inland, and came out into a wood where great golden tongues of fungus lapped the trees, and a mulch of dead leaves squelched underfoot. Rather to Rivers's surprise they stopped at a pub on the way back, though no food was available. Burns could drink apparently, and did, becoming in the process quite flushed and talkative, though nothing was said about his illness.

They arrived back in the late afternoon with every bone and muscle aching. Mrs Burril had obviously built up the fire before she left, and it was rescuable, just about. Rivers knelt in front of it, sticking strips of cereal packet through the bars, and blowing when he got a flame. 'Have you any newspapers?'

'No,' Burns said.

No, Rivers thought, silly question. Once the fire was burning well, Rivers went out and bought cakes and biscuits for tea, which he served in front of the fire, tucking in himself and not looking to see whether Burns ate or not. He ate, sitting on the hearth rug, his wind-reddened arms clasped about his knees, and the firelight playing on his face.

After the plates were cleared away, Rivers asked if he might work for a couple of hours. He was writing a paper on the Repression of War Experience which he was due to give to the British Medical

Association in December, and he knew, once he got back to Craiglockhart, there would be very little time. He worked at the table in the window, with his back to the room. He began by reading through what he'd written so far on the evil effects that followed from patients trying to suppress their memories of war experience, and was about to start writing when it occurred to him he was in the same room as a man who was doing just that.

Why do I go along with it? he thought. One answer, the easy answer, was that he was no longer Burns's doctor. It was up to Burns now how he chose to manage his illness. But then he'd gone along with the suppression in Craiglockhart too. Whenever he'd tried to apply to Burns the same methods of treatment he used with everybody else, and used, for the most part, successfully, his nerve had failed him. He'd told himself this was because of the peculiar nature of Burns's experience, the utter lack of any redeeming feature the mind could grasp and hold on to while it steadied itself to face the full horror. But was Burns's experience really worse than that of others? Worse than Jenkins's, crawling between the dismembered pieces of his friend's body to collect personal belongings to send back to the family? Worse than Prior's? *What shall I do with this gob-stopper?*

Corpses were everywhere in the trenches. Used to strengthen parapets, to prop up sagging doorways, to fill in gaps in the duckboards. Many of his patients treading on a dead body had been startled by the release of gas. Surely what had happened to Burns was merely an unusually disgusting version of a common experience. And I've let him, Rivers thought – no, that was unfair, that was *completely* unfair – I've let *myself* turn it into . . . some kind of myth. And that was unforgivable. He wasn't dealing with Jonah in the belly of the whale, still less with Christ in the belly of the earth, he was dealing with David Burns, who'd got his head stuck in the belly of a dead German soldier, and somehow had to be helped to live with the memory.

He turned and looked at Burns, who was still sitting on the hearth rug, though now he'd found himself a book and was reading, his tongue protruding slightly between his teeth. As he felt Rivers's gaze, he looked up and smiled. Twenty-two. He should be worrying about the Tripos and screwing up his courage to ask a girl to the May ball. And yet even now Rivers was nervous of raising the subject of his illness. Burns's instinctive reaction had been to get back to this house, to forget. And there had been some improvement under this regime, by day at least, though evidently not by night. If he wants to talk, he'll talk, Rivers thought, and turned back to his paper.

That evening, rather to Rivers's surprise, they went to the pub. He was surprised because he'd been assuming Burns was isolated here, but apparently all the locals knew him. They'd watched him growing up, summer by summer. The family had been staying here when war broke out. Burns had joined up along with most of the local lads. They all remembered him in his uniform, in the first days and weeks of the war, and perhaps that mattered a great deal. In London, Burns said, on his first trip out in civilian clothes, he'd been handed two white feathers.

Here, as soon as they pushed the bar door open, he was hailed by several people, and by one man in particular: 'Old Clegg'. Clegg had rheumy blue eyes, whose overflow had dried to a scurfy crust at his temples; three brown but very strong teeth; unidentifiable stains on his abdomen, and other stains, only too identifiable, further down. His conversation was so encrusted with salty Suffolk sayings that Rivers suspected him of deliberate self-parody. That, or leg-pulling. Once he'd discovered Rivers was interested in folklore, he was well away. Rivers spent a thoroughly enjoyable evening being initiated into the folklore of rural Suffolk. By closing time, he was convinced Clegg was possibly the most unreliable informant he'd ever had. For sheer imaginative flights of fancy none of the Melanesians came anywhere near him. 'That man is a complete fraud,' he said as they left the pub.

But Burns disagreed. 'He's not a fraud, he's a rogue. Anyway as long as he teaches me flint-knapping, I don't care.'

Next morning the weather had changed. At dawn there was a strip of clear blue on the horizon, fading to yellow, but the sky darkened rapidly, until, by mid morning, the clouds humped, liver-coloured, and the sea was dark as iron. The wind had risen during the night, sweeping away the last remnants of mist. At first it came in little gusts, lifting the thin carpet in the hall, swirling dust in corners, then in blasts that made waves on the surface of the estuary, rocking the yachts until the rattle of their rigging became a frenzy, while on the beach great waves swelled like the muscles of an enormous animal, rising to crests that hung and seethed along their full length, before toppling over in thunder and bursts of spray.

Rivers worked on his paper all morning, looking up now and then to find the window mizzled with rain. Burns slept late, having had another bad and very noisy night. He appeared just before noon, pink eyed and twitching, and announced he was going to the White Horse to see Clegg and arrange a definite time for his flint-knapping session. Clegg was proving rather difficult to pin down.

'Git him up agin' a gorse bush, bor,' Rivers said, in a passable imitation of Clegg's voice. 'He ont back away then.'

'That's girls in kissing season, Rivers.'

'Is it? Well, I shouldn't go kissing Clegg. I doubt if flint-knapping's worth it.'

He was immersed in his paper again before Burns left the house.

He came back an hour later, looking rather pleased with himself. 'Thursday.'

'Good.'

'I thought we might go for a walk.'

Rivers looked at the rain-spattered glass.

'It's died down a bit,' Burns said, not altogether convincingly.

'All right, I could do with a break.'

The sea was racing in fast. The fishermen's huts were empty, the boats hauled up high above the last stretch of shingle, with the fishing nets in dark heaps behind them. Either they'd not been out today or they'd turned back early, for Rivers had seen none of them come in. Even the seabirds seemed to be grounded, huddled in the lee of the boats, watching the town with unblinking amber eyes.

Faced with this sea, the land seemed fragile. Was fragile. To the north, cliffs were scoured away, to the south, notice boards were buried up to their necks in shingle. And the little Moot Hall that had once stood at the centre of the town was now on the edge of the sea.

They walked as far as Thorpeness, then turned back, not talking much, since the wind snatched the breath from their mouths. The sea had covered the thin strip of sand, so they had to walk along the steep shelf of shingle, a lopsided business that set the back as well as the legs aching.

It took them two hours, there and back, and Rivers was looking forward to the fire and – if he could contrive it – toasted tea cakes for tea. Breakfast, lunch and dinner, he could do without, but afternoon tea *mattered*. His boot squelched on something soft. Looking down, he saw the place was littered with cods' heads, thirty or more, with blood-stained gills and staring eyes. It gave him no more than a slight *frisson*. Obviously the fishermen gutted their catch and threw the offal away. But Burns had stopped dead in his tracks and was staring at the heads, with his mouth working. As Rivers watched, he jerked his head back, the same movement that had been so common when he first arrived at Craiglockhart.

'It's all right,' he said, when Rivers went back for him. But it was obviously very far from all right.

They got back to the house. Rivers made tea, though Burns didn't manage to eat anything.

After tea they went out and piled sandbags against the doors, struggling with the heavy bags through driving rain and then struggling again to close the storm shutters. The air was full of spray and blown spume.

'We should've done that earlier,' Burns said, wiping the rain from his face and blinking in the firelight. He was very concerned to pretend everything was normal. He sat on the hearth rug, in his favourite position, while the wind buffeted and slogged the house, and talked about his drink with Clegg and various items of local gossip. But he jumped from topic to topic, assuming the connections would be obvious when very often they were not. His mood, once he'd got over the shock of seeing the cods' heads, seemed to be almost elated. He said more than once that he loved storms, and he seemed, at times, to be listening to something other than the roar of wind and sea.

Closing his eyes, Rivers could imagine the town entirely given over to the storm, bobbing on the tide of darkness like a blown eggshell, without substance or power to protect. Burns's conversation became more and more disconnected, the jerking of his head more pronounced. Piling up sandbags, followed by the nearest thing to a bombardment nature could contrive, was not what Rivers would have prescribed. He was prepared to sit up with Burns, if he wanted to stay up, but Burns started talking about bed rather earlier than usual. Probably he took bromides. Rivers would have liked to advise him to stop, since they certainly wouldn't help the nightmares, but he was determined to let Burns be the first to raise the subject of his illness.

The evening ended with nothing to the point having been said. Rivers went to bed and undressed in the darkness, listening to the wind howl, and imagined Burns in the room above, also listening. He read for a while, thinking he might be too tense to go to sleep, but the fresh air and the struggle with the wind along the beach to Thorpeness had tired him out. His eyelids started to droop and he switched off the light. The whole house creaked and groaned, riding the storm like a ship, but he enjoyed that. He'd always found it possible to sleep deeply on board ship, though on land sleep often eluded him.

He was woken by what he immediately took to be the explosion of a bomb. Less than a minute later, while he was still groping for the light switch, he heard a second boom and this time managed to identify it as the sound of a maroon. The lifeboat, no doubt. He was getting out of bed to go to the window when he remembered that he probably ought not to open the shutters, for he could hear from the whistling of wind and lashing of rain that the storm had by no means blown itself out. His heart was pounding, unreasonably, since there was nothing to be afraid of. He supposed it was having come straight from London with its incessant talk of air raids that had made him identify the sound so positively as a bomb.

He lay back and a moment or two later heard footsteps padding past the door of his room. Obviously Burns too had been woken up. Probably he was going downstairs to make himself a cup of tea, perhaps even to sit up the rest of the night.

The more Rivers thought about Burns sitting alone in the kitchen, the more he thought he ought to get up. The sounds of the storm had now been joined by running footsteps. He wouldn't find it easy to sleep again anyway.

The kitchen was empty, and didn't seem to have been disturbed since last night. He told himself that he'd been mistaken, and Burns was still in bed. By now rather anxious, perhaps unreasonably so, he went upstairs and peered into Burns's room. The bedclothes had been pushed back, and the bed was empty.

He had no idea what he should do. For all he knew midnight walks – or rather three am walks – were a habit of Burns's when the nights were particularly bad. Surely he wouldn't go out in this. Rivers heard shouts, followed by more running footsteps. Obviously other people were out in it. Quickly, he returned to his own room, pulled on socks, boots and coat, and went out into the storm.

A small group of figures had gathered round the lifeboat, three of them holding storm lanterns. The overlapping circles of light shone on yellow oilskins glistening with wet, as the men struggled to clear the shingle from the planks that were used to launch the boat. Silver rain slanted down into the lighted area, while beyond, pale banks of shingle faded into the darkness.

A knot of bystanders had gathered by the hut, separate from the labouring figures around the boat. Convinced that Burns must be among them, Rivers ran across to join them, but when he looked from face to face Burns was not there. A woman he thought to be familiar, but couldn't immediately identify, pointed to the marshes south of the town.

As he turned and began walking quickly towards the marshes, he was dimly aware of the boat hitting the sea, and of the waves surging up around her. He left the shelter of the last houses, and the wind, roaring across the marshes, almost knocked him off his feet. He dropped down from the path and walked along beside the river where he was slightly sheltered, though the wind still howled and the yacht rigging thrummed, a sound like no other he had ever heard. He could see fairly clearly most of the time. Once, the moon freed itself from the tatters of black cloud, and then his own shadow and the shadow of the tower were thrown across the gleaming mud.

Looking at the tower, Rivers thought again how squat and unimpressive it was, and yet how menacing. A resemblance that had merely nagged at him before returned to his mind with greater force. This waste of mud, these sump holes reflecting a dim light at the sky, even that tower. It was like France. Like the battlefields. A resemblance greater by night than by day, perhaps, because here, by day, you could see things grow, and there nothing grew.

– They were always afraid we'd get trapped in the cellars.

– I suppose they flood, don't they? At high tide?

Rivers climbed on to the path, trying to work out where the tide was and whether it was rising or falling, but he could hear only the crash of breaking waves and feel the drizzle of blown spume on his face. In spite of his mud-clogged boots and aching thighs, he started to run. As he neared the tower, a stronger blast of wind sent him staggering off the path. He was slithering and floundering through mud, calling Burns's name, though the sound was snatched from his mouth and carried off into the whistling darkness.

He slid down on to the beach. An outgoing wave sucked shingle after it, but the entrance to the moat was clear. He hesitated, peering into the darkness, afraid that an unusually powerful wave might trap him in there. He called '*David*', but he knew he couldn't be heard and would have to go down, into the black darkness, if he were ever to find him.

He groped his way into the moat, steadying himself against the wall. It was so wet, so cold, so evil-smelling, that he thought perhaps the tide had already reached its height and was now falling. At first he could see nothing, but then the moon came out from behind a bank of cloud, and he saw Burns huddled against the moat wall. Rivers called 'David' and realized he was shouting when there was no need. Even the howl of the storm sounded subdued in the shelter of the moat. He touched Burns's arm. He neither moved nor blinked. He was staring up at the tower, which gleamed white, like the bones of a skull.

'Come on, David.'

His body felt like a stone. Rivers got hold of him and held him, coaxing, rocking. He looked up at the tower that loomed squat and menacing above them, and thought, *Nothing justifies this. Nothing nothing nothing.* Burns's body remained rigid in his arms. Rivers was aware that if it came to a fight he might not win. Burns was terribly emaciated, but he was also thirty years younger. His surrender, when it came, was almost shocking. Suddenly his body had the rag-doll floppiness of the newborn. He collapsed against Rivers and started to shake, and from there it was possible to half lead, half push him out of the moat and up on to the relative safety of the path.

At the kitchen table, wrapped in a blanket, Burns said, 'I couldn't seem to get out of the dream. I woke up, I *knew* I was awake, I could move and yet . . . it was still there. My face was dripping. I could taste it.' He tried to laugh. 'And then the bloody maroon went off.'

There were no electric lights. The power lines must be down. They were talking by the light of an oil lamp that smoked and smelled, and left wisps of black smoke like question marks on the air.

'I think we can do without this now,' Rivers said, walking across to the window and pulling the curtains back. He opened the windows and shutters. The storm had almost blown itself out. A weak light seeped into the room, falling on Burns's red eyes and exhausted face.

'Why don't you go to bed? I'll bring you a hot-water bottle if you've got such a thing.'

Rivers saw him settled into bed. Then he went out to the butchers in the High Street, which he'd already noticed was surprisingly well stocked, bought bacon, sausages, kidneys, eggs, took them home and fried them. As he was spooning hot fat over the eggs, he remembered his reaction when he was looking up at the tower. *Nothing can justify this*, he'd thought. *Nothing nothing nothing.* He was rather glad not to be faced with the task of explaining that statement to Siegfried.

He sat down at the table and began to eat. He was still chasing the last dribble of egg yolk with a triangle of toast when Mrs Burril came in. She looked at the plates. 'Cracked, did you?' Two unpacked bags later she added, 'Thought you might.'

'Is the boat back?'

'Not yet. I keep busy.'

Rivers went upstairs to check on Burns and found him still asleep. The room was full of books, stacked up on tables and chairs, spilling over on to the floor. Church architecture, country crafts, ornithology, botany and – a slight surprise – theology. He wondered whether this was an expression of faith, or a quest for faith, or simply an obsession with the absence of God.

One of the reasons the books had to be stacked on tables and chairs was that the bookcase was already full of other books: boys' annuals, the adventure stories of Henty, Scouting for Boys. Games too: Ludo and Snakes and Ladders, a bat for beach cricket, collections of pebbles and shells, a strip of bladderwrack. All these things must have been brought here, or collected here, summer by summer, and then outgrown, but never thrown away, so that the room had become a sort of palimpsest of the young life it contained. He looked at Burns's sleeping face, and then tiptoed downstairs.

The lifeboat came back later that morning. Rivers looked out of the living room window and saw it beached at the water's edge, in that narrow space between the coils of tangled and rusting wire. He went out to watch.

The men were laying down the flat wooden skids over which the boat would be winched slowly back into place. A small group of villagers, mainly relatives of the crew, had gathered and were talking in low voices. The sea was choppy, but with none of the menace of the previous night. A light drizzle had begun to fall, matting the surface hairs on the men's jerseys and woollen caps.

When he got back, he found Burns stirring, though not yet up.

'Are they back?' he asked.

'Yes, they're hauling her up now.'

Burns got out of bed and came across to the window. The drizzle had become a downpour. The lifeboat, now halfway up the beach, was obscured by sheets of smoking rain.

'Be a load off Mrs Burril's mind. She's got two sons in the crew.'

'Yes. She said.'

'You mean she spoke?'

'We had quite a chat. I didn't know the lifeboat was such a family matter.'

'Oh, yes. You see it on the memorial in the church. Not a good idea, really. From the woman's point of view.' A long pause. Then Burns added, 'You get the same thing in a battalion. Brothers joining up together.'

Rivers went very still. This was the first time Burns had volunteered any information at all about France. Even in Craiglockhart, where he couldn't altogether avoid talking about it, the bare facts of his war service had had to be prised out of him.

'You know, you'll be writing letters and suddenly you realize you've written the same name twice.'

Rivers said carefully, 'That must be one of the worst jobs.'

'You get used to it. I did it for eighty per cent of the company once.'

A long silence. Rivers was beginning to think he'd dried up, but then he said, 'That was the day before the Somme. They got out there, and there was this bloody great dyke in the way. You couldn't see it from the trench because there were bramble bushes round it. And it wasn't on the map. Everybody bunched up, trying to get across it. German machine-gunners had a field day. And the few who did manage to get across were cut to pieces on the wire. General came round the following day. He said, "My God, did we really order men to attack across that?" Apparently we were intended to be a diversion from the main action. Further south.'

Slowly, Burns began to talk. He'd been promoted captain at the age of twenty-one, and this promotion coincided with the run-up to the Somme campaign. In addition to all the other strains, he'd been aware of a widespread, though unvoiced, opinion in the company that he was too young for the command, though in length of service he had been senior.

The story was one Rivers was well used to hearing: healthy fear had given way to indifference, and this in turn had given way to a constant, overwhelming fear, and the increasing realization that breakdown was imminent. 'I used to go out on patrol every night,' Burns said. 'You tell yourself you're *setting a good example*, or some such rubbish, but actually it's nothing of the kind. You can't let yourself know you want to be wounded, because officers aren't supposed to think like that. And, you see, next to a battle, a patrol is the best chance of getting a good wound. In the trenches, it's shrapnel or head injuries. On patrol, if you're lucky, it's a nice neat little hole in the arm or leg. I've seen men cry with a wound like that.' He laughed. 'Cry for joy. Anyway, it wasn't my luck. Bullets went round me, I swear they did.' A pause. 'It was going to happen anyway, wasn't it?'

'The breakdown? Oh yes. You mustn't attribute breaking down to that one incident.'

'I went on for three days afterwards.'

'Yes, I know.'

They talked for over an hour. Near the end, after they'd been sitting in silence for a while, Burns said quietly, 'Do you know what Christ died of?'

Rivers looked surprised, but answered readily enough. 'Suffocation. Ultimately the position makes it impossible to go on inflating the lungs. A terrible death.'

'That's what I find so horrifying. Somebody had to *imagine* that death. I mean, just in order to invent it as a method of execution. You know that thing in the Bible? "The imagination of man's heart is evil from his youth"? I used to wonder why pick on that? Why his *imagination*? But it's absolutely right.'

Rivers, going downstairs to make the tea, thought that a curious thing had happened during that conversation. For the first time, Burns had been able to put the decomposing corpse into some kind of perspective. True, he hadn't managed to talk about it, but at least it hadn't prevented him, as it so often had in the past, from talking about other, more bearable aspects of his war experience. Yet, at the same time, Rivers's own sense of the horror of the event seemed actually to have increased. It *was* different in kind from other such experiences, he thought, if only because of the complete disintegration of personality it had produced. He was very fond of Burns, but he could discern in him no trace of the qualities he must have possessed in order to be given that exceptionally early command. Not that one could despair of recovery. Rivers knew only too well how often the early stages of change or cure may mimic deterioration. Cut a chrysalis open, and you will find a rotting caterpillar. What you will never find is that mythical creature, half caterpillar, half butterfly, a fit emblem of the human soul, for those whose cast of mind leads them to seek such emblems. No, the process of transformation consists almost entirely of decay. Burns was young, after all. If today really marked a change, a willingness to face his experiences in France, then his condition might improve. In a few years' time it might even be possible to think of him resuming his education, perhaps pursuing that unexpected interest in theology. Though it was difficult to see him as an undergraduate. He had missed his chance of being ordinary.

SIXTEEN

Rivers arrived back at Craiglockhart in the late afternoon of yet another stormy day. This autumn seemed to have a store of such days, slapping them down remorselessly, one after the other, like a fortune-teller with a deadly pack of cards. The trees had already shed their leaves. They blew across the tennis courts and, when Rivers pushed open the swing doors, accompanied him into the hall.

Where a football match seemed to be in progress. A knot of struggling backs and thighs gradually unravelled, as they became aware of him standing there. On the black and white tiled floor lay a mud-brown, pork-pie hat, evidently belonging to a visitor. Rivers looked round the group and found Sassoon. 'Careful with that hat, Sassoon,' he said, and passed through on his way to his office.

Behind him, a much subdued Sassoon picked up the hat, punched it into some semblance of its former shape, and restored it to the peg. The other footballers slunk away.

Bryce was standing at the window of his room, looking out over the leaf-littered tennis courts. Pausing in the doorway, Rivers thought he looked older, but then he turned, and seemed as full of energy as ever.

'Did you get my letter?' Rivers asked.

'I did.'

'I've said I'll wait and see how things turn out.'

'Take it, for God's sake. It's quite *obvious* how things are going to turn out. I don't expect to be here next month.' He smiled. 'Of course they might appoint *you*.'

Rivers shook his head. 'No, they won't do that. I'm too identified with you.'

'*Will* you take it?'

'I don't know. Probably.'

More than probably, Rivers thought, returning to his own room.

The thought of Craiglockhart without Bryce was intolerable. He sat behind his desk, and looked round the large, overfamiliar room. Whenever he'd come back before, he'd had an almost physical sense of the yoke settling on to his shoulders, beginning to chafe almost before he was into the building. Not this time. He looked at his crowded appointments book and actually managed to feel some affection for it. The offer of a job in London, with its prospect of more frequent contact with other anthropologists, had had the paradoxical effect of making him realize how much he *enjoyed* his work here. It had become of equal importance to him, and he'd begun to think of ways in which the two interests could combine. The condensation and displacement one encountered in the dreams of patients here – might not these mechanisms also be at work in the myth and ritual of primitive people? At any rate it was an idea worth exploring. But these new combinations only occurred because he no longer thought of his work here as an interruption of his 'real' work. Far from it, he thought, spreading his hands across his desk. The work he did in this room was the work he was meant to do, and, as always, this recognition brought peace.

'. . . we actually drove past your place.'

'You should've called in,' Sassoon said. 'Mother wouldn't've stood on ceremony where *you* were concerned. She regards you as the Saviour of the Family Name. From the Disgrace of Pacifism.'

'Prematurely, perhaps?'

No answer.

'Have you been able to think . . . ?'

'I haven't been able to *think* at all. Look, Rivers, I've never asked you for anything. I've never asked or expected to be treated any differently from anybody else.'

'I should hope not,' Rivers said. 'I don't know what the grounds would be.'

Sassoon came to an abrupt halt. 'All right.'

'No, what were you going to say?'

'I was going to point out that the man in my room is driving me stark, staring mad, but it doesn't matter.'

'That could be grounds for a room change. If true. For *you* as for anybody else. What does he do? Does he sleep badly?'

'Snores like a newborn baby, if newborn babies snore.'

'So what *does* he do?'

'Preaches the consolations of Theosophy in his own inimitable brand of pseudo-medieval English.'

'I can see that might be irritating. Give me an example.'

'Friend of mine, Ralph Greaves. He's . . . Is! *Was* a good pianist. He's just had one arm amputated, and the other's almost useless. Do you know what Fothersgill said? "It will assist his spiritual development." '

'Perhaps it would have been wiser not to tell him?'

Silence.

'After all, you must've had some idea of the *kind* of response you were likely to get?'

'I can't keep it in all the time.'

'Look, he's due to be boarded soon. Surely you can put up with the inconvenience for another . . . what, *ten days*?'

'We had a row this morning. I pointed out the casualties for September were 102,000 – *official* figures. He said, "Yes, Sassoon, the Celestial Surgeon is at work upon humanity." '

Rivers sighed. He was thinking that Sassoon's insistence of hammering home the bitter reality was probably not doing Fothersgill much good either. 'What does *he* think about *you*? Do you know?'

'I have a disturbed aura. Apparently.'

'Really?'

'Indigo. I'm glad somebody finds it amusing.'

'I was just thinking how useful it would be. Instant diagnosis.'

'I've woken him up once or twice.'

'Nightmares?'

'Not exactly.'

Sassoon was avoiding his eye, but then he often did at the beginning of interviews. 'Do you want to tell me about it?'

'Oh, it was nothing. I just . . . saw something I couldn't possibly have seen.'

He thinks I'll despise him for being irrational, Rivers thought. 'I did once see . . . well, not see . . . *hear* something I couldn't explain. It was on one of the Solomon Islands. On this particular island, the people believe the souls of the dead go to a bay at the other side – the spirits come up to the house in canoes and carry the dead person's soul away. So you have a kind of wake, and on this particular night we were all crowded together, gathered round the corpse, waiting for the sound of paddles. The whole village was there, all these dark brown intently listening faces. And we listened too and asked questions in whispers.

The atmosphere was unbelievable. And then a moment came when *they* heard the paddles. You saw this expression of mingled joy and grief spread over all their faces, and of course we heard nothing. Until the moment when the spirits were actually in the room, taking the soul away, and then the whole house was suddenly filled with whistling sounds. I could see all the faces. Nobody was making those sounds, and yet we all heard them. You see, the *rational* explanation for that is that we'd allowed ourselves to be dragged into an experience of mass hypnosis, and I don't for a moment deny that that's possible. But what we'd been told to expect was the swish of paddles. Nobody'd said anything about whistling. That doesn't mean that there *isn't* a rational explanation. Only I don't think that particular rational explanation fits all the facts.'

After Rivers had finished there was a pause. Then Sassoon said, with great difficulty, 'What happened to me started with a noise.'

'What sort of noise?'

'Tapping. It started in Owen's room and then when I went back to my own room it started again. Owen didn't hear it. It didn't bother me particularly, I just went off to sleep and . . . when I woke up, somebody was standing just inside the door. I knew who it was. I couldn't see the face, but I recognized his coat.' He paused. 'Orme. Nice lad. Died six months ago.'

'You said "once or twice". The same man?'

'No. Various people.' A long silence. 'I know this must sound like the the kind of thing I was seeing in London, but it isn't. It's . . . nothing like that. In London they were clutching holes in their heads and waving their stumps around. These are . . . very quiet. Very restrained.' He smiled. 'Obviously you get a better class of hallucination round here.'

'What do you feel when you see them?'

Sassoon shrugged. 'I don't feel anything. At the time.'

'You're not frightened?'

'No. That's why I said they weren't nightmares.'

'Afterwards?'

'Guilt.'

'Do they look reproachful?'

Sassoon thought about it. 'No. They just look puzzled. They can't understand why I'm here.'

A long silence. After a while, Sassoon roused himself. 'I wrote about it. I'm sorry, I know you hate this.'

Rivers took the sheet of paper: 'I don't hate it. I just feel inadequate.'

When I'm asleep, dreaming and drowsed and warm,
They come, the homeless ones, the noiseless dead.
While the dim charging breakers of the storm
Rumble and drone and bellow overhead,
Out of the gloom they gather about my bed.
They whisper to my heart; their thoughts are mine.

'Why are you here with all your watches ended?
'From Ypres to Frise we sought you in the line.'
In bitter safety I awake, unfriended;
And while the dawn begins with slashing rain
I think of the Battalion in the mud.
'When are you going back to them again?
'Are they not still your brothers through our blood?'

Sassoon, who'd got up and walked across to the window, turned round when a movement from Rivers seemed to indicate he'd finished. 'It's all right,' he said. 'Don't feel you have to say something.'

But Rivers was not capable of saying anything. He'd taken off his glasses and was dabbing the skin round his eyes. Sassoon didn't know what to do. He pretended to look out of the window again. At last Rivers put his glasses on again and said, 'Does the question have an answer?'

'Oh, yes. I'm going back.'

A long indrawn breath. 'Have you told anybody else yet?'

'No, I wanted you to be the first.'

'Your pacifist friends won't be pleased.'

'No, I know. I'm not looking forward to that.' He was looking at Rivers with an extraordinary mixture of love and hostility. 'You are, though, aren't you? You're pleased.'

'Oh, yes. I'm pleased.'

Part Four

SEVENTEEN

Ada Lumb arrived on the nine o'clock train. Sarah met her at the station, and they spent the morning looking round the shops. Or rather Sarah looked round the shops, while her mother, by a mixture of bullying, wheedling, cajoling, questions, speculations, wild surmises and sudden, bitter silences, extracted the whole story of Sarah's relationship with Billy Prior. By twelve, Sarah was glad to rest her feet, if not her ears, in a café, where they sat at a table for two by the window and ordered ham and chips. The alternative was steak and kidney pie, but Ada was having none of that. 'You can't trust anything with pastry wrapped round it,' she said. 'What they find to put in it, God knows. You've only got to look in the butchers to see there is nowt.'

Sarah was not deceived. She knew once the waitress was out of earshot she was in for a dollop of advice on rather more serious matters. She wiped a hole in the condensation on the window. Outside the people were moving shadows, the pavements of Princes Street jumped and streamed with rain. 'Just in time,' she said.

'I suppose you let him in?'

'*What?*'

'You don't say "what", Sarah. You say "pardon".'

'*What?*'

'I said, I suppose you let him in?'

'Isn't that my business, Mam?'

'Would be if *you* were gunna cope with the consequences.'

'There aren't going to *be* any consequences.'

'You think you know it all, don't you? Well, let me tell you something, something you don't know. In every one of them factories there's a bloke with a pin. Every tenth one gets a pin stuck in it. Not every other one, they know we're not fools. Every tenth.'

'Nice work, if you can get it.'

'Easier than bringing up the kid.' Ada speared a chip. 'The point *is* you gotta put a value on yourself. You don't, they won't. You're never gunna get engaged till you learn to keep your knees together. Yeh, you can laugh, but men don't value what's dished out free.

Mebbe they shouldn't be like that, mebbe they should all be different. But they *are* like that and *your* not gunna change them.'

The waitress came to remove their plates. 'Anything else, madam?'

Ada switched to her genteel voice. 'Yes, we'd like to see the menu, please.' She waited till the waitress had gone, then leant forward to deliver the knock-out blow. 'No man likes to think he's sliding in on another man's leavings.'

Sarah collapsed in giggles. *'Mam.'*

'Aye, well, you can laugh.' She looked round the café, then down at the table, smoothing the white table cloth with brown-spotted hands. 'Nice, isn't it?'

Sarah stopped giggling. 'Yeh, Mam, it's nice.'

'I wish *you* worked somewhere like this.'

'Mam, the wages are rubbish. That girl didn't live at home, she wouldn't eat.'

'She's not bright yellow, though, is she?'

'She not bright anything. She looks anaemic to me.'

'But you meet nice people, Sarah. I mean I know some of the women you work with, and I'm not saying they're not good sorts – some of them – but you got to admit, Sarah, they're *rough*.'

'I'm rough.'

'You could've been a lady's maid if you'd stuck in. That's what gets me about you, you can put it on as well as anybody when you like, but it's too much bloody bother.'

The waitress returned with the menu.

'I don't think I could eat anything else, Mam.'

Ada looked disappointed. 'Aw, go on. It's not often I get a chance to spoil you.'

'All right, then. I'll have the tapioca, please.'

Sarah ate in silence for a while, aware of her mother watching her. At last, she said, 'Trouble is, Mam, the block chipped and you don't like it.'

Ada shook her head. It was true all the same, Sarah thought. Ada, ox-jawed, determined, ruthless, had struggled to bring up her two girls alone, and yet, when it came to *teaching* the girls, she'd tried to encourage all the opposite qualities. Prettiness, pliability – at least the appearance of it – all the arts of pleasing. This was how women got on in the world, and Ada had made sure her daughters knew it. As little girls, Cynthia and Sarah had gone to the tin-roofed chapel at the end of the road, but as soon as their bodices revealed curves rather than straight lines, Ada had called them to her and announced their conversion to Anglo-Catholicism. The Church of St Edmund, King and Martyr, served a very nice neighbourhood. There, Cynthia had obediently ogled the young men in the choir, while Sarah, missing the point completely, had fallen in love with the Virgin Mary. Ada's ambition was to see her daughters go down that aisle in white, on the arm of some young man with a steady income. If, subsequently, early widowhood left them with the income and not the man, then they were indeed blessed. Whether *Ada* was a widow or not, Sarah didn't know. It had never been made clear whether her father had departed this life, the town, or merely his marriage. Certainly black bombazine figured prominently in Ada's wardrobe, but then it was a material that conferred an air of awesome respectability at minimal cost. A dispiriting way to bring girls up, Sarah thought; to make marriage the sole end of female existence, and yet deny that love between men and women was possible. Ada *did* deny it. In *her* world, men loved women as the fox loves the hare. And women loved men as the tapeworm loves the gut. Nor did this view of life generate much sympathy for other women. Ada despised the hares, those who 'got caught'. If a girl came into the shop crying, she might sell her Dr Lawson's Cure, the Sovereign Remedy for Female Blockages and Obstructions (ninepence a bottle, and totally useless), but her sympathy ended there. The business of her life was scratching a living together; her recreation was reading romances, which she devoured three or four at a time, sitting in her rocking chair by the fire, sucking mint humbugs and laughing till her ribs ached.

'How's the tea hut going, Mam?' Sarah asked, pushing her plate away.

'Fine. I'm up there every day now.'

Ada had taken to selling tea to soldiers, young conscripts who did their six weeks' training in one of the local parks before being shipped out to France. The hut, which in peace time had been the boating lake ticket office, she'd turned into a small café.

'How much do you charge?'

'Fivepence.'

'My God.'

Ada shrugged. 'No competition.'

'You're a war profiteer you are, Mam. In a small way.'

'Wouldn't be small if I could get me hands on some money. You could do soup and all sorts, specially with the winter coming on. But it's the same old story. You need money to make money.'

Ada paid the bill, counting out the coppers with those thin, lined hands that Sarah could never see without pain.

'You know Billy?' Sarah asked suddenly.

'No, I don't, Sarah. I've not had the pleasure of an introduction.'

'Well if you'll just listen. If he gets slung out the hospital this time, he'll have a bit of leave, and we thought we might . . . We thought we might drop in on you.'

'Really?'

'Is that all you can say?'

'What am I supposed to say? Look, Sarah, he's an officer. What do you think he wants *you* for?'

'How should I know? Breath of fresh air, perhaps.'

'Bloody gale.'

'If he does come, you will be all right with him, won't you?'

'If he's all right with me, I'll be all right with him.' Ada slipped a penny under the saucer. 'But you're a bloody fool.'

'Why am I?'

'You know why. Next time he starts waving his old doo-lally around, you think about that pin.'

Sassoon arrived late to find Graves sitting by himself in the bar. 'Sorry I'm late.'

'That's all right. Owen was keeping me amused, but then he had to go. Somebody coming to see the printer.'

'Yes, that's right. I'd forgotten that.'

'Good game?'

'Not bad.' Sassoon detected, or thought he detected, a slight chill. 'It's the only thing that keeps me sane.'

'Last time you wrote you were complaining about playing golf with lunatics.'

'Ssh, keep your voice down. One of them's just behind you.'

Graves turned round. 'Seems fairly normal to me.'

'Oh, Anderson's all right. Throws a temper tantrum whenever he looks like losing half a crown.'

'You've been known to do *that* yourself.'

'Only because you were fooling around with a niblick instead of playing properly.' He raised a hand to summon the waiter. 'Have you had time to look at the menu?'

'I've had time to memorize it, Siegfried.'

At the table Graves said, 'What do you find to talk to Owen about?

He says he doesn't play golf. And I don't suppose for a moment he hunts.'

'How acute your social perceptions are, Robert. No, I shouldn't think he'd been on a horse in his life before he joined the army. Poetry, mainly.'

'Oh, he *writes*, does he?'

'No need to say it like that. He's quite good. Matter of fact, I've got one here.' He tapped his breast pocket. 'I'll show you after lunch.'

'He struck me as being a bit shaky.'

'Did he? I don't think he is.'

'I'm just telling you how he struck me.'

'He can't be all that shaky. They're throwing him out at the end of the month. He was probably just overawed at meeting another Published Poet.'

A slight pause.

'Aren't you due to be boarded soon?'

'The end of the month.'

'Have you decided what you're going to do?'

'I've told Rivers I'll go back, *provided* the War Office gives me a written guarantee that I'll be sent back to France.'

'I wouldn't have thought you were in much of a position to *bargain*.'

'Rivers seems to think he can wangle it. He didn't say "wangle" of course.'

'So it's all over? Thank God.'

'I've told him I won't withdraw anything. And I've told him it's got to be France. I'm *not* going to let them put me behind a desk filling in forms for the rest of the war.'

'Yes, I think that's right.'

'Trouble is I don't trust them. Even Rivers. I mean, on the one hand he says there's nothing wrong with me and they'll pass me for general service overseas – there's nothing else they can do – and then in the next breath he tells me I've got a very powerful "anti-war complex". I don't even know what it means.'

'I'll tell you what it means. It means you're *obsessed*. Do you know, you never talk about the future any more? Yes, I know what you're going to say. How can you? Sass, we sat on a hill in France and we talked about the future. We *made plans*. The night before the Somme, we made plans. You couldn't do that now. A few shells, a few corpses, and you've lost heart.'

'How many corpses?'

'The point is . . .'

'The point is 102,000 last month *alone*. You're right, I am obsessed. I never forget it for a second, *and neither should you*. Robert, if you had any *real* courage you wouldn't acquiesce the way you do.'

Graves flushed with anger. 'I'm sorry you think that. I should hate to think I'm a coward. I believe in keeping my word. You agreed to serve, Siegfried. Nobody's asking you to change your opinions, or even to keep quiet about them, but you *agreed to serve*, and if you want the respect of the kind of people you're trying to influence – the Bobbies and the Tommies – you've got to be seen to *keep your word*. They won't understand if you turn round in the middle of the war and say "I'm sorry, I've changed my mind." To them, that's just bad form. They'll say you're not behaving like a gentleman – and that's the worst thing they can say about anybody.'

'Look, Robert, the people who're keeping this war going don't give a damn about the "Bobbies" and the "Tommies". And they don't let "gentlemanly behaviour" stand in the way either when it comes to feathering their own nests.' He made a gesture of despair. 'And as for "bad form" and "gentlemanly behaviour" – that's just suicidal stupidity.'

Over coffee, the conversation changed tack.

'There's something I didn't tell you in June,' Graves said. 'Do you remember Peter?'

'I never met him.'

'No, but you remember him? You remember *about* him? Well, he was arrested. Soliciting outside the local barracks. Actually not very far away from the school.'

'Oh, Robert, I'm sorry. Why didn't you *tell* me?'

'How could I? You were in no state to think about anybody else.'

'This was in July, was it?'

'Same post I got your Declaration in.' Graves smiled. 'It was quite a morning.'

'Yes, I can imagine.'

Graves hesitated. 'It's only fair to tell you that . . . since that happened my affections have been running in more normal channels. I've been writing to a girl called Nancy Nicholson. I really think you'll like her. She's great fun. The . . . the only reason I'm telling you this is . . . I'd hate you to have any misconceptions. About me. I'd hate you to think I was homosexual *even in thought*. Even if it went no further.'

It was difficult to know what to say. 'I'm very pleased for you, Robert. About Miss Nicholson, I mean.'

'Good, that's all right, then.'

'What happened to Peter?'

'You're not going to believe this. They're sending him to Rivers.'

This was a bigger, and nastier, shock than Sassoon knew how to account for. 'Why?'

'What do you mean, "Why?"? To be cured, of course.'

Sassoon smiled faintly. 'Yes. Of course.'

The munitions factory at night looked like hell, Sarah thought, as she toiled down the muddy lane towards it, and saw the red smouldering fires reflected from a bank of low cloud, like an artificial sunset. At the gate she fell in with the other girls all walking in the same direction, all subdued, with that clogged, dull look of people who'd just switched to night shift and hadn't yet managed to adjust.

In the cloakroom, donning ankle-length green overalls, pulling on caps, dragging at a final cigarette, were thirty or forty women. Smells of sweat, lily-of-the-valley, setting lotion. After a while conversations sprang up, the women appeared more normal, even jolly for a time, until the supervisor appeared in the doorway, jabbing her finger at the clock.

'Your mam get off all right, then?' Lizzie asked, as they were walking down the stairs to the basement workroom.

'Got the seven o'clock. She'll be back by midnight, so it's not so bad.'

'How did it go?'

Sarah pulled a face. 'All right. You know, I swore I wasn't gunna tell her about Billy, but she winkled it all out of me.'

'Well, she is your mam. She's bound to be worried.'

'Hm. All I could get out of her was: "What does he see in *you*?" 'S a nice thing to say to your daughter, isn't it? I says, "A breath of fresh air." As far as I can make out they're all disappearing up their own arseholes up there.'

'Long as it's only their own,' Lizzie said.

'They're not all like that,' Sarah said.

'Biggest part are,' said Madge. 'Place I used to work before the war, the son were like that. Oh, and when they found out you should've heard Missus. She *stomped* and she *shrieked*. Chandelier were going like that, I thought bugger were coming down. But you know he had no sisters, so he never met lasses that way. Goes to school, no lasses. Goes to university – no lasses. Time he finally claps eyes on me, it's too late, isn't it? It's *gelled.* And even the ones that aren't like that, they take one look at the Missus and bugger off round the Club.' Madge strutted along the basement corridor with a finger held below her nose, saying in a strangled, public school accent, '"I shall be dining at the Club tonight, m'dear. Don't bother to wait up." Then he staggers in at two o'clock and flops out on bed in dressing room. Beats me how they breed.'

Raucous laughter from the other women as they spilled into the work room and sat down at the benches. The supervisor, a round-faced, bespectacled, crop-haired lady in a severely tailored suit, bore down upon them. 'Do you girls ever intend to start work?'

They watched her walk away. 'Eeh, I hope a man never tries to shove anything up her flue,' Lizzie said. 'Be cruelty to moths.'

Sarah pulled the first belt towards her and started to work. No reason at all why they couldn't talk, since the task here required no concentration. It was intended as a break from the very demanding work on detonators, and from other jobs too, where masks had to be worn. Rather badly fitting masks. On more than one occasion Sarah had pulled hers away from her face and shaken out the yellow dust that had collected inside it. She remembered her mother's strictures on her appearance, the broad hints she'd dropped about handing in her notice and going home to help with the tea hut. But I like it here, Sarah thought. And then she corrected herself. You like it *now* because Billy's here. You mightn't be so keen when he's gone.

She turned, cautiously, to avoid attracting the supervisor's attention, and looked round. The women sat at small tables, each table forming a pool of light under a low-hanging bulb. Apart from the work surfaces, the room was badly lit and so vast that its far end disappeared into shadow. All the women were yellow-skinned, and all, whatever their colouring, had a frizz of ginger hair peeping out from under the green cap. We don't look human, Sarah thought, not knowing whether to be dismayed or amused. They looked like machines, whose sole function was to make other machines.

Sarah's eyes fell on the next table, where the girls were close enough to be identified. After a while she looked puzzled and leant across the table to whisper to Lizzie. 'Where's Betty?'

'You may well ask,' Lizzie said. She sniffed and remained silent, enjoying the moment of power.

'I am asking.'

Lizzie glanced round quickly. 'You know she's missed four times?'

All the girls nodded.

'Tried everything,' Lizzie said. 'She was supping Dr Lawson's Cure as if it was lemonade.'

'It is,' said Sarah.

'Well, she must've got desperate, because she stuck summat up herself to bring it on. You know them wire coat hangers?'

Nods all round.

'One of them. She straightened the curved bit and –'

'We get the picture,' Sarah said.

'Yeh, well it's worse than that. Silly little cow shoved it in her bladder.'

'Aw no.' Madge turned away as if she were going to vomit.

'She was in agony. And you know she kept begging them not to send her to the hospital, because like she knew she hadn't come all right. But anyway the girl she's lodging with got that frightened she went and fetched the landlady. Well of course she took one look. She more or less says, "Sorry, love, you're not dying here." Took her in. And the irony of it is she's still pregnant. She looks awful.'

'You mean you've been to see her?' Sarah asked.

'Why aye. Went last night. You know, her face is all . . .' Lizzie dragged her cheeks down. 'Oh, and she says the doctor didn't half railroad her. She was crying her eyes out, poor lass. He says, "You should be ashamed of yourself," he says. "It's not just an inconvenience you've got in there," he says. "It's a human being."'

Sarah and Madge were eager to know more, but the supervisor had noticed the pause in Lizzie's work and came striding towards them, though when she reached the table she found only silence and bowed heads and feverishly working fingers flicking machine-gun bullets into place inside the glittering belts.

On the night before a Board, Rivers took longer than usual over his rounds, since he knew the patients whose turn it was to be boarded would be feeling particularly tense. He was worried about Pugh, who had somehow managed to convince himself, in spite of repeated reassurances to the contrary, that he was to be sent back to France.

Sassoon, Rivers left till last, and found him lying on the bed in his new room, wrapped in his British warm coat. It was needed. The room was immediately beneath the tower and so cold that, in winter, patients who'd sweated their way through a succession of nightmares often woke to find the bedclothes stiff with frost. Siegfried seemed to like it, though, and at least now he had the privacy he needed to work. Rivers took the only available chair, and stretched out his legs towards the empty grate. 'Well, how do you feel about tomorrow?'

'All right. Still nothing from the War Office?'

'No, I'm afraid not. You'll just have to trust us.'

'*Us?* You're sure you don't mean "them"?'

'You know I'll go on doing anything I can for you.'

'Oh, I know *that*. But the *fact* is once they've got me out of here they can do what they like. Pen-pushing in Bognor, here I come.'

Rivers hesitated. 'You sound rather down.'

'No-o. Missing Robert. Don't know why, we came quite close to quarrelling.'

'About the war?'

'I don't know what about. Except he was in a peculiar mood.' Sassoon stopped, then visibly decided to continue. 'He had a bit of bad news recently.'

Rivers was aware of more going on in this conversation than he could identify. Sassoon had been distinctly reserved with him recently. He'd noticed it yesterday evening particularly, but he'd put it down to pre-Board nerves, and the worry of not hearing from the War Office. 'From France?'

'Oh, no, something quite different. I did *ask* if he'd mind my telling you, so I'm not breaking a confidence. Friend of his – a boy he knew at school and was very fond of – in an entirely honourable, platonic *Robert-like* way – got arrested for soliciting. Outside a barracks, actually not very far away from the school. As far as I can make out, Robert feels . . .' Sassoon came to a halt. '*Well*. Rather as you might feel if you were . . . walking down a pleasant country road and suddenly a precipice opened at your feet. That's how he sees it. Devastated. Because, you see, this . . . this *abominable* thing must've been there all the time, and *he didn't see it*. He's very anxious to make it clear that . . . *he* has no such disgusting feelings himself. We-ell.'

'So you were left feeling . . . ?'

'Like a precipice on a country road.'

'Yes.'

Sassoon looked straight at Rivers. 'Apparently he's being – the boy – sent to some psychiatrist or other.'

'Which school was this?'

'Charterhouse.'

'Ah.' Rivers looked up and found Sassoon's gaze on him.

'To be *cured.*' A slight pause. 'I suppose cured *is* the right word?'

Rivers said cautiously, 'Surely it's better for him to be sent to this psychiatrist than to go to prison?' In spite of himself he started to smile. 'Though I can see *you* might not think so.'

'He wouldn't have got prison!'

'Oh, I think he might. The number of custodial sentences is rising. I think any psychiatrist in London would tell you that.'

Sassoon looked downcast. 'I thought things were getting better.'

'I think they were. Before the war. *Slightly*. But it's not very likely, is it, that any movement towards greater tolerance would persist in wartime? After all, in war, you've got this *enormous* emphasis on love between men – comradeship – and everybody approves. But at the same time there's always this little niggle of anxiety. Is it the right *kind* of love? Well, one of the ways you make sure it's the right kind is to make it crystal clear what the penalties for the other kind are.' He looked at Sassoon. 'One of the reasons I'm so glad you've decided to go back. It's not just police activity. It's the whole atmosphere at the moment. There's an MP called Pemberton Billing. I don't know whether you've heard of him?'

Sassoon shook his head. 'I don't think so.'

'Well, he's going around London claiming to know of the existence of a German *Black Book* containing the names of 47,000 eminent people whose *private lives* make their loyalty to their country suspect.'

'Relax, Rivers. I'm not eminent.'

'No, but you're a friend of Robert Ross, and you've publicly advocated a negotiated peace. That's enough! You're *vulnerable*, Siegfried. There's no point pretending you're not.'

'And what am I supposed to do about it? Toe the line, tailor my opinions –'

'Not your opinions. I think you told me once that Robert Ross opposes the war? *In private*.'

'I wouldn't want to criticize Ross. I think I know him well enough to understand the impact those trials had on him. But what you're really saying is, if I *can't* conform in one area of life, then I *have* to conform in the others. Not just the surface things, *everything*. Even against my conscience. Well, I can't live like that.' He paused, then added, '*Nobody* should live like that.'

'You spend far too much time tilting at windmills, Siegfried. In ways which do *you* a great deal of damage – which I happen to care about – and don't do anybody else any good at all.' He hesitated, then said it anyway. 'It's time you grew up. Started living in the real world.'

EIGHTEEN

Prior was not making a good impression. Getting a few simple facts out of him was like extracting wisdom teeth. At first Rivers thought Prior was simply being awkward – always a fairly safe assumption with Prior – but then he noted the tension in his jaw and realized the extent of the internal conflict that was going on. Prior had said he wanted nothing more than to get back to France as soon as possible, to get away from what he called 'the shame' of home service, and Rivers had no doubt that was true. But it was not the whole truth. He also wanted to save his life, and, in insisting on the importance of the asthmatic attacks, Rivers had, perhaps cruelly, held out the hope that he might be permitted to live. Small wonder, then, that Prior answered questions in monosyllables and finally, when asked whether he felt physically fit for service, said nothing at all, simply stared at Huntley, unable either to claim that he was ill or to deny it. Watching him, Rivers was filled with the most enormous compassion for his dilemma. Poor little blighter, he thought. Poor all of them.

Outside in the waiting room Sassoon looked at his watch. They were running almost an hour late and he wasn't even next. Pugh was next. Pugh was a Welshman with prominent green eyes and the worst twitch Sassoon had ever seen, even in Craiglockhart, that living museum of tics and twitches. Pugh's consisted of a violent sideways movement of the head, accompanied by a sound midway between a gasp and a scream. He did this approximately every thirty-five seconds. Like everybody else in the hospital, Sassoon's reflexes were conditioned by the facts of trench warfare. It was almost impossible for him not to dodge whatever it was Pugh was dodging. Something Owen had told him about Pugh was hovering round the fringes of his mind. Yes, that was it. Some kind of freak accident, a hand grenade bouncing off the wire. Pugh had been picking bits of his platoon off his gas cape for an hour.

Sassoon looked at his watch again. Even allowing for the fact that nobody in their right mind could take long to decide whether Pugh was fit for duty, he couldn't hope to be out of the place before six. He was supposed to have tea with the Sampsons at four thirty. Even if he left now and caught a tram immediately, he still wouldn't be on time. It was too bad. People who were prepared to die had at least the right not to be kept waiting. He closed his eyes again. He was so tired he really thought if it wasn't for Pugh and that dreadful jerking, he might have managed to nod off. He'd hardly slept at all last night.

In his breast pocket was a letter from Joe Cotterill, the Battalion Quartermaster. Sassoon knew it almost off by heart. Joe's journey to Polygon Wood with the rations, the ground as full of holes as a pepperpot lid, nothing but mud and dead trees as far as the eye could see. They'd spent the night in a shell-hole, lost, under heavy fire. Several of the ration party had been killed. But, said Joe, the battalion got their rations. Reading that, Sassoon had wanted to rush back to France at once, but then, right at the end of the letter, Joe had said: *Buck up and get out of there. Go to Parliament. Surely they can't keep you there against your will?* The trouble was, Sassoon thought, sighing and looking at his watch, that Joe's anonymous 'they' was his Rivers.

Thorpe arrived. 'D-d-d-do w-w-w-wwe kn-kn-know w-whwhat's t-t-t-t-taking s-s-so l-l-long?' he asked after a while.

Sassoon shook his head. Pugh shook his head too, though whether in answer to the question it was difficult to tell. And suddenly Sassoon had had enough. 'And I for one don't intend to stay and find out.'

He had a fleeting impression of Thorpe and Pugh with their mouths open, and then he was striding out of the room, down the corridor, through the swing doors and away.

'Pugh next, I think?' said Bryce.

'Hang on, old chap,' Huntley said. 'Got to pump ship.'

The door closed behind him. Bryce said, 'Where do you suppose he finds these nautical expressions?' Receiving no reply, he turned to Rivers.

'Why we had to take an hour over *that* I shall never know.'

'Prior didn't help himself much, did he?'

Rivers didn't answer.

'And at least you got what you wanted. In the end.'

The major came back, buttoning his breeches. 'All right, all right,' he said, as if *he*'d been waiting for *them*. 'Let's get on.'

Pugh was quick and distressing. Since the orderly had gone off to have dinner, Rivers himself went into the waiting room to summon Sassoon. Thorpe was sitting there alone. 'Have you seen Sassoon?'

'He's . . .' Thorpe went into one of his paroxysms. 'G-g-g-g-gone.'

'G-g-?' Deep breath. '*Where* has he gone?'

Thorpe economized with a shrug. Rivers walked along to the patients' common room and looked for Sassoon there, and instead found Prior, sitting at the piano picking out a few notes. Prior looked up. Rivers, thinking it was a long time to wait till the result was officially announced, stuck his thumb in the air and smiled.

'All right, Thorpe,' he said, going back to the ante-room. 'You'd better come in.'

Rivers came out of Thorpe's Board to find Sassoon still missing and Sister Duffy hovering in the corridor, wanting to talk about Prior. 'Crying his eyes out,' she said. 'I thought he'd *got* permanent home service?'

'He did.'

Rivers went up to Prior's room and found him sitting on the bed, not crying now, though rather swollen about the eyes.

'I suppose I'm expected to be grateful?'

'No.'

'Good. Because I'm not.'

Rivers tried to suppress a smile.

'I told you I *didn't want it*.'

'It's not a question of what you *want*, is it? It's a question of whether you're fit.'

'I was all right. It never stopped me doing anything the others did.'

'Now that's not quite true, is it? You told me yourself you were excused running through the gas huts, because on the one occasion you tried it, you collapsed. Your participation in gas-training exercises was restricted to listening to lectures. Wasn't it?'

No response.

'It's all very well to joke about being the battalion canary, but it's true, isn't it? You *would* be overcome by gas at much lower concentrations than most people, and that could be very dangerous. *And not just for you*.'

Prior turned away.

Rivers sighed. 'You realize the other man who got permanent home service is throwing a party tonight?'

'Good for him. I hope it's a good party.'

'Why do you hate it so much?'

Silence. After a while, Prior said, 'I suppose I'm not your patient any more, am I?'

'No.'

'So I don't have to put up with *this*?'

It was on the tip of Rivers's tongue to point out that the relief was mutual, but he looked at the swollen eyes and restrained himself. 'What don't you have to put up with?'

'The blank wall. The silences. The *pretending*.'

'Look. At the moment you hate me because I've been instrumental in getting you something you're ashamed of wanting. I can't do much about the hatred, but I do think you should look at the shame. Because it's not really anything to be ashamed *of*, is it? Wanting to stay alive? You'd be a very strange sort of animal if you didn't.'

Prior shook his head. 'You don't understand.'

'Tell me, then.'

'I'll never know now, will I? About myself . . .'

'But you do know. You were a perfectly satisfactory officer, until –'

'Until the strain got to me and I stopped being *a perfectly satisfactory officer*. Where does that leave me?'

'With the whole of your life ahead of you and other challenges to face.'

'If *you* were a patient here, don't you think you'd feel ashamed?'

'Probably. Because I've been brought up the same way as everybody else. But I hope I'd have the *sense*, or – whatever it is – the *intelligence* to see how unjustified it was.'

Prior was shaking his head. 'Not possible. The hoop's there, you jump through it. If you question it, you've failed. If it's taken away from you, you've failed.'

'No, I don't see that. If it's taken away, it's out of your hands. You didn't *ask* for permanent home service. You were *given* it, on the basis of Eaglesham's report. *Not my report*. There's nothing in your psychological state to prevent your going back.'

Prior didn't answer. Rivers said gently, 'Everybody who survives feels guilty. Don't let it spoil everything.'

'It's not that. Well, partly. It's just that I've never let the asthma stop me. I was *ordered* to stay out of those gas huts, *I* was quite prepared to go through them. Even as a – a child I was *determined* it wasn't going to stop me. I could do anything the others did, and not only that, I could *beat* them. I'm not suggesting this is peculiar to me, I – I think most asthmatics are like that. My mother was always pulling the other way. Trying to keep me in. I shouldn't criticize the poor woman, I think she probably saved my life, but she did *use* it. She wanted me in the house away from all the *nasty rough boys*. And then suddenly here *you* are . . .' He raised his hands. 'Doing exactly the same thing.' He looked at Rivers, a cool, amused, mocking, affectionate, highly intelligent stare. 'Probably why I never wanted you to be *Daddy*. I'd got you lined up for a worse fate.'

Rivers, remembering the nanny goat, smiled. He was rather glad Prior didn't have access to his thoughts.

'Thanks for putting up with me.'

This was muttered so gracelessly Rivers wasn't sure he'd heard correctly.

'I was an absolute pig.'

'Never.'

Prior hesitated. 'Would you mind if I looked you up after the war?'

'*Mind?* I'd be delighted. Though I don't see why you have to wait till after the war. You can always write to me here. If – if I've moved on, they'll know where I am.'

'Thanks. I will write.'

At the door Rivers turned. 'If I don't see you again before you go, good luck.'

It was an effort to talk at dinner, partly tiredness, partly Sassoon's empty place. By now it was clear he'd deliberately skipped the Board. He'd left the Sampsons at six o'clock, but hadn't yet returned to the hospital. It was possible he was having dinner at the Club, putting off the moment when he'd have to face Rivers, but he was impetuous enough, and perhaps desperate enough, to take the train for London and launch himself into some further crackpot scheme to stop the war. Rivers knew the full extent of the dilemma that would face him if Sassoon *had* deserted and *did* make another public protest. He would be asked to take part in declaring him insane; they would never court-martial him. Not now. The casualty lists were too terrible to admit of any public debate on the continuation of the war.

Rivers roused himself to take part in the conversation to find Major Huntley riding one of his hobby horses again. Racial degeneration, this time. The falling birth rate. The need to keep up what he called 'the supply of heroes'. Did Rivers know that private soldiers were on average *five inches* shorter than their officers? And yet it was often the better type of woman who chose to limit the size of her family, while her feckless sisters bred the Empire to destruction. Rivers listened as politely as he could to the major's theories on how the women of Britain might be brought back to a proper sense of their duties, but it was a relief when dinner was over, and he could plead pressure of work and escape to his own room.

He'd left a message with Sister Duffy that Sassoon was to be sent to him as soon as he got back, no matter how late that might be. It was very late indeed. He came in, looking penitent and sheepish.

Rivers said, 'Sit down.'

Sassoon sat, folded his large hands in his lap, and waited. His demeanour was very much that of a keen, and basically decent, head boy who knows he's let the headmaster down rather badly, and is probably in for 'a bit of a wigging', but expects it to be all right in the end. Nothing could have been more calculated to drive Rivers to fury. 'I'm sure you have a perfectly satisfactory explanation.'

'I was late for tea with Sampson.'

Rivers closed his eyes. 'That's it?'

'Yes.'

'It would have been quite impossible for you to *telephone* Sampson, and *tell* him that you were going to be late?'

'It didn't seem . . . courteous. It –'

'And what about the courtesy due to Major Bryce? Major Huntley? Don't you think you at least owed them an *explanation* before you walked out?'

Silence.

'Why, Siegfried?'

'I couldn't face it.'

'Now that *does* surprise me. Juvenile behaviour I might have expected from you, but never cowardice.'

'I'm not offering excuses.'

'You're not offering anything. Certainly not *reasons*.'

'I'm not sure there are any. I was fed up with being kept waiting. I thought if I was going to *die*, at least other people could make the effort to be on time. It was . . .' A deep breath. 'Petulance.'

'So you can't suggest a reason?'

'I've told you, there aren't any.'

'I don't believe you.'

'Look, I'll apologize. I'll *grovel* if you like.'

'I'm not interested in your grovelling. I'd rather you told the truth.'

Sassoon wriggled in his chair. 'All right. I've had this idea floating around in my mind, for . . . oh, for five or six weeks. I thought if I could get myself passed fit and then go to London, I could see somebody like . . . Charles Mercier.'

'*Dr* Mercier?'

'Yes.'

'Why on earth would you want to see him?'

'For a second opinion. He's all right, isn't he?'

'Oh, yes, you couldn't do better. Except that . . . if you'd just been passed fit by the Board – why would you need to see Mercier?'

'So they couldn't say I'd had a relapse, if I went on with the protest.'

Rivers sat back in his chair. 'Oh, I see.'

Silence.

'And had you definitely decided to do that?'

'I hadn't definitely decided anything. If you want the *reason* I walked out, that's probably it. It suddenly struck me that in a few hours' time I'd be packing and I had no idea where I was going. And then at the back of my mind there was the idea that if I went to Mercier I'd be . . .'

Rivers waited.

'Doing the dirty on you.'

'You could've had a second opinion at any time. I'd no idea you wanted it. People whose psychiatrists tell them they're completely sane don't usually ask for second opinions.'

'That *is* what they'd do, though, isn't it? Say I'd had a relapse?'

'Yes. Probably. I take it you've definitely decided not to go back?'

'No, I want to go back.'

Rivers slumped in his chair. 'Thank God. I don't pretend to understand, but thank God.' After a while he added, 'You know the real irony in all this? This morning I had a letter from the War Office. Not exactly an undertaking to send you back, but . . . signs of progress.'

'And now I've gone and ruined it all by having tea with an astronomer.'

'Oh, I don't suppose you have. I'll write to them tonight.'

Sassoon looked at the clock.

'Well, we don't want him hearing it from Huntley, do we? By the way, late as it is, I think Major Bryce would still like to see you.'

Sassoon took the hint and stood up. 'What do you think he'll do?'

'No idea. *Roast* you, I hope.'

NINETEEN

Prior had never broken into a house before. Not that he was exactly breaking into this one, he reminded himself, though it felt like it, standing cold and shivering in the back yard, in a recess between what must be, he supposed, the coalhouse and the shithouse. He wrapped his coat more tightly round him and craned his neck to see the sky. Light cloud, no moon, stars pricking through, a snap of frost.

He was waiting for the signal of the lamp at Sarah's window, but she was a long time coming, and there was a chill inside him that had nothing to do with the cold. The darkness, the nervousness, the repeated unnecessary swallowing . . . He was back in France, waiting to go out on patrol.

He remembered the *feel* of No Man's Land, the vast, unimaginable space. By day, seen through a periscope, this immensity shrank to a small, pock-marked stretch of ground, snarled with wire. You never got used to the discrepancy. Part of its power to compel the imagination lay precisely in that. It was the difference between *seeing* a mouth ulcer and probing it with your tongue. He told himself he was never going back, he was free, but the word 'free' rang hollow. *Hurry up, Sarah,* he thought.

He was beginning to wonder whether she'd met her landlady on the stairs, when a light appeared at the window. Immediately, he started to climb, clambering from the rusting washer on to the sloping roof of the scullery. Nothing difficult about the climb, the only hazard was the poor state of the tiles. He shuffled along, trying not to make too much noise, though if they did hear they'd probably think it was a cat.

Sarah's room was on the first floor. As he reached the main wall, he stood up, cautiously, and hooked his fingertips into the crack between two bricks. Sarah's window was perhaps three feet away, but there was a convenient drainpipe. He swung his left foot out, got a toe-hold on the drainpipe – fortunately in a better state of repair than the roof – and launched himself at the dark hole. He landed safely, though not quietly, colliding with Sarah, who'd come back to see why he was taking so long. They froze, listening for any response. When none came, they looked at each other, and smiled.

Sarah was carrying an oil lamp. She set it down on the table by the bed, and went to draw the curtains. He was glad to have the night shut out, with its memories of fear and worried sentries whispering. She turned back into the room.

They looked at each other, not finding anything to say. The bed, though only a single, seemed very big. Their imminent nakedness made them shy of each other. In all the weeks of love-making, they'd never once been able to undress. Prior was touched by Sarah's shyness, and a little ashamed of his own.

With an air of unconcern, he started to look round the room. Apart from the bed, there was a bedside table, a chair, a chest of drawers, and a washbasin, squeezed into the corner beside the window. A camisole hung from the back of the chair, and a pair of stays lay on the floor beside it. Sarah, seeing the direction of his gaze, kicked them under the chair.

'It's all right,' he said. 'I'm not tidy.'

The sound of his voice released them from nervousness. Prior sat on the bed, and patted it for her to come and sit beside him.

'We'd better not talk much,' she said. 'I told them I'd be late back, but if they hear voices they'll all be in.'

He couldn't have talked much anyway; his breath caught in his throat. They stared at each other. He reached up and unpinned her hair, shaking it out at the sides of her head. Then they lay down side by side, still gazing at each other. At this distance, her eyes merged into a single eye, fringed by lashes like prehistoric vegetation, a mysterious, scarcely human pool. They lay like that for ten or fifteen minutes, neither of them wanting to hurry, amazed at the time that lay ahead.

After a while Prior rolled over on to his back and looked at the photograph on the bedside table, moving the lamp so he could see better. A wedding group. Cynthia's wedding, he thought, and that rather fat, pasty-faced soldier, smiling sheepishly at the centre of the group, must now be dead. People in group photographs look either idiotic or insane, their faces frozen in anticipation of the flash. Not Sarah's mother. Even in sepia, her eyes jetted sparks. And that *jaw*. It would've been remarkable on a man. 'Your mother looks like my doctor,' he said. He looked at the photograph again. 'She's not smiling much, is she?'

'She was smiling at the memorial service.' She looked at the photograph. 'I love her, you know.'

'Of cou . . .' He stopped. Why 'of course'? He didn't love his father.

'I'm glad you're not going back.'

Without warning, Prior saw again the shovel, the sack, the scattered lime. The eyeball lay in the palm of his hand. 'Yes,' he said.

She would never know, because he would never tell her. Somehow if she'd known the worst parts, she couldn't have gone on being a haven for him. He was groping for an idea that he couldn't quite grasp. Men said they didn't tell their women about France because they didn't want to worry them. But it was more than that. He needed her ignorance to hide in. Yet, at the same time, he wanted to know and be known as deeply as possible. And the two desires were irreconcilable.

'Do you think your mam'll like me?'

They'd arranged to spend part of his leave together.

'Not as much as she would if you were going back.'

'Tell her about me lungs. That'll cheer her up.' He felt he knew Ada already.

Sarah rolled over and started to undress him. He pretended to struggle, but she pushed him back on to the bed, and he lay there, shaking with laughter, as she got into a tangle over his puttees. At last she gave up, rested her head on his knees, giggling. 'They're like *stays*.'

'Don't tell the War Office. You'll have a lot of worried men.'

They stopped laughing and looked at each other.

'I love you,' he said.

'Oh, there's no need to say *that*.'

'Yes, there is. It's true.'

She took her time thinking about it. At last she said on an indrawn breath, '*Good*. I love you too.'

Owen and Sassoon sat in a corner of the lounge at the Conservative Club. They had the room to themselves, except for one other member, and he was half hidden behind the *Scotsman*. After the waiter had served the brandies and departed, Sassoon produced a book from his pocket. 'I'd like to read you something. Do you mind?'

'No, go ahead. Anybody I know?'

'Alymer Strong. Given to me by the author. He brought me a copy of Lady Margaret's book and – er – happened to mention he wrote himself. Like a fool, I made encouraging noises.'

'Not *always* disastrous. Why am I being read it?'

'You'll see. There's a sort of dedication. In one of the poems.'

> Siegfried, thy fathers warr'd
> With many a kestrel, mimicking the dove.

Owen looked blank. 'What does it mean?'

'What a philistine question. I hope this isn't the future pig-keeper speaking. I believe it to be a reference to the persecution of the Jews.'

'But you're not a Jew.'

'I am, actually. Or rather my "fathers" were.'

'I didn't know that.' Owen contemplated the fact through a haze of burgundy. 'That's why you're called Siegfried?'

'No-o, I'm called Siegfried because my mother liked Wagner. And the only thing I have in common with orthodox Jews is that I do profoundly thank God I was born a man and not a woman. If I were a woman, I'd be called Brünnhilde.'

'This is our last evening and I feel as if I've just met you.'

'You know all the important things.'

They looked at each other. Then a rustling of the *Scotsman*'s pages returned their attention to the book. Sassoon began reading extracts, and Owen, who was drunk and afraid of becoming too serious, laughed till he choked. Sassoon had begun by declaiming the verse solemnly, but when he came to:

> Can it be I have become
> This gourd, this gothic vaccu-um?

he burst out laughing. 'Oh, I love that. *You* might like this better.'

> What cassock'd misanthrope,
> Hawking peace-canticles for glory-gain,
> Hymns from his rostrum'd height th' epopt of Hate?

'The *what* of hate?'

'E*popt*.'

'No such word.'

'There is, you know. It's the heroic form of epogee.'

'Can I see?' Owen read the poem. 'This man's against the war.'

'Oh, yes.' Sassoon's lips twitched. 'And particularly devastated by the role the Christian Church is playing in it. The parallels are worrying, Owen.'

'I'm worried.' He made to hand the book back. 'It's incredible, isn't it?'

'No, look inside.'

Owen looked at the flyleaf and read: *Owen. From S.S. Edinburgh.*

Oct. 26th 1917. Underneath Sassoon had written:

When Captain Cook first sniffed the wattle,
And Love columbus'd Aristotle.

'That's absolutely typical,' Owen said.

'It does rather encapsulate his style, doesn't it?'

'You know what I mean. The only *slightly* demonstrative thing you've ever done and you do it in a way which makes it impossible to take seriously.'

'Do you think it's a good idea to be serious tonight?'

'For God's sake, I'm only going to Scarborough. *You'll* be in France before I will.'

'I hope so.'

'No news from the War Office?'

'No. And Rivers dropped a bombshell this morning. He's leaving.'

'Is he?'

'I don't look forward to Craiglockhart without either of you. I did mention you to Rivers, you know.'

'What did he say?'

'That you were an extremely gallant and conscientious young officer . . .'

'*Oooh.*'

'"*Oooh*". Who needed no one to teach him his duty. *Unlike* dot dot dot. And there were no grounds at all that he could see for keeping you at the hospital a moment longer. I think he was a bit put out about being asked to overrule Brock.'

'I'm not surprised. You shouldn't have done it. Look, I could do a lot with another month. I *hate* leaving. But the fact is I'd be taking up a bed some other poor blighter needs far more than I do.'

'As I shall be doing.'

'I didn't mean that.'

'No, but it's true.' He glanced at his watch. 'I'd better be off. Under the new regime I believe the penalty for staying out late is public crucifixion.'

In the hall Sassoon produced an envelope from his breast pocket. 'This is a letter of introduction to Robert Ross. It's sealed because there's something else inside, but that doesn't mean you can't read it.'

Owen tried to think of something to say and failed.

'Take care.'

'And you.'

Sassoon patted him on the shoulder, and was gone. Nothing else, not even 'goodbye'. Perhaps it was better that way, Owen thought, going back to the lounge. Better for Siegfried, anyway. Their empty brandy glasses stood together on the table, in the pool of light cast by the standard lamp, but the unseen listener had gone. The *Scotsman*, neatly folded, lay on a table by the door.

Owen sat down, got out the letter of introduction, but didn't immediately open it. The ticking of the clock was very loud in the empty room. He lay back in the chair and closed his eyes. He was afraid to measure his sense of loss.

TWENTY

Rivers was due to leave Craiglockhart on 14 November, having fulfilled his promise to Bryce to see the new CO in. He was leaving in what he considered a totally undeserved blaze of glory. Willard was walking at last. Rivers could understand the VADs, the orderlies, the secretaries and the kitchen staff regarding this 'cure' as a great medical feat, but it was a little dismaying to find that even some of the senior nursing staff seemed to agree.

Willard himself was exasperating. All Rivers's efforts to inculcate insight into his condition, to enable him to understand *why* he'd been in the wheelchair and how the same outcome might be avoided in future, were met with a stare of glassy-eyed, quivering respect. Whenever Rivers came anywhere near him, Willard positively leapt to the salute. He *knew* his spinal cord had been broken. He *knew* Rivers had reconnected the severed ends. Needless to say the other MOs were unimpressed. Indeed, after observing Rivers acknowledge one particularly sizzling salute, Brock was heard to murmur: '*And for my next trick I shall walk on water.*'

The last evening round was distressing both for Rivers and the patients. He left Sassoon till last and then, remembering that he'd spent the day with Lady Ottoline Morrell and had, presumably, been exposed to a great dose of pacifist propaganda, went along to his room.

Sassoon was sitting on the floor, hands clasped around his knees, staring into the fire.

'How was Lady Ottoline?' Rivers said, taking the only chair. 'In full cry?'

'Not really. The war was hardly mentioned.'

'Oh?'

'No, we talked about Carpenter mainly. Homosexuality. Or rather I talked. She listened.'

Poor Lady Ottoline. 'The war didn't come up at all?'

'Not today. Last night it did. I think we both knew there was no point going over that again. Do you know what she asked me? Did I realize that going back would involve killing Germans?' He brought his anger under control. 'Pacifists can be amazingly brutal.'

That brief flash of anger was the only emotion Sassoon had shown since skipping the Board. He seemed at times to be almost unaware of his surroundings, as if he could get through this interim period between one Board and the next only by shutting down all awareness of where he was or what was happening. And yet he was writing, and he seemed to think he was writing well. All the anger and grief now went into the poetry. He'd given up hope of influencing events. Or perhaps he'd just given up hope. At the back of Rivers's mind was the fear that Craiglockhart had done to Sassoon what the Somme and Arras had failed to do. And if that were so, he couldn't escape responsibility.

Sassoon roused himself. 'You're off first thing, aren't you?'

'Yes. The six o'clock.'

'So this is goodbye, then.'

'Only for a fortnight. I'll be back for the Board. Meanwhile . . .' He stood up. 'Keep your head down?'

Rivers stayed overnight with the Heads and then moved into his new lodgings in Holford Road, a short walk from the RFC hospital. The floor below was occupied by a family of Belgian refugees whose demands for better food and apparent indifference to rationing irritated the landlady, Mrs Irving, beyond measure. She was inclined to stop Rivers on the stairs and complain about them at considerable length. The other lodgers were apparently more easily satisfied, and gave no grounds for complaint.

The nights were disturbed by air raids, though less by German action than by the guns on the Heath that boomed out with a sound like bombs falling. Everybody congregated in the basement during these raids, the Belgian refugees, Mrs Irving, her unmarried daughter who worked at the hospital, all the other lodgers, and the two young girls who lived in the attics and between them did the whole work of the house. As far as he could make out, they sat around, or under, the table, venturing out to the kitchen to make endless cups of cocoa. He was invited to join these parties, but always declined, saying that the air raids didn't bother him much and he needed his sleep.

He managed to sleep through some of the raids, but on other nights, the guns made sleep impossible. He was not particularly well, but he didn't want to take more sick leave, and he had no routine leave due to him. He spent a lot of the time with the Heads, who turned up one night and swept him off to the theatre to see the Russian ballet. They came out, still dazed with swirling light and colour, to find another raid in progress. In Leicester Square they stopped and looked up at the sky, and there was a Zeppelin floating like a strange, silver fish. Rumour had it they were piloted by women. It seemed incredible to Rivers that anybody should believe this, but he soon discovered that most people did. Mrs Irving knew it for a fact.

As soon as he started work at the hospital he became busy and, as Head had predicted, fascinated by the differences in severity of breakdown between the different branches of the RFC. Pilots, though they did indeed break down, did so less frequently and usually less severely than the men who manned observation balloons. They, floating helplessly above the battlefields, unable either to avoid attack or to defend themselves effectively against it, showed the highest incidence of breakdown of any service. Even including infantry officers. This reinforced Rivers's view that it was prolonged strain, immobility and helplessness that did the damage, and not the sudden shocks or bizarre horrors that the patients themselves were inclined to point to as the explanation for their condition. That would help to account for the greater prevalence of anxiety neuroses and hysterical disorders in women in peacetime, since their relatively more confined lives gave them fewer opportunities of reacting to stress in active and constructive ways. Any explanation of war neurosis must account for the fact that this apparently intensely masculine life of war and danger and hardship produced in men the same disorders that women suffered from in peace.

So he had plenty to think about, and before long it was clear he would have plenty to do. Many of his old Craiglockhart patients who were living in London or the south of England had already written to ask if they could come to see him. That, by itself, would supply him with a great deal of work.

He was due back at Craiglockhart on the 25th of November. On the

24th he'd accepted an invitation to visit Queen Square. The invitation had been issued several times before and he'd always found a reason for refusing, but now that he was one of the small number of physicians in London dealing with the psycho-neuroses of war, he judged it rather more expedient than pleasant that he should accept. And so, at half past nine on the 24th November, he walked up the steps of the National Hospital. His night had been even more disturbed by the guns than usual, and he was feeling distinctly unwell. If he'd been able to cancel or postpone this visit without giving offence, he would certainly have done so. He gave his name to the receptionist. Dr Yealland was expecting him, she said. Go up.

He took the lift to the third floor. He pushed through the swing doors on to a long, empty, shining corridor, which, as he began to walk down it, seemed to elongate. He began to be afraid he was really ill. This deserted corridor in a hospital he knew to be overcrowded had something eerie about it. Uncanny. Almost the feeling his patients described, talking about their experience of the front, of No Man's Land, that landscape apparently devoid of life that actually contained millions of men.

The swing doors at the far end of the corridor flapped open. At first Rivers was pleased, expecting to be received by some bustling nurse or VAD, but instead a creature – it hardly resembled a man – crawled through the door and began moving towards him. The figure made remarkably rapid progress for somebody so bent, so apparently deformed. His head was twisted to one side, and drawn back, the spine bent so that the chest was parallel with the legs, which themselves were bent at the knees. In addition one arm, the left, was pulled away from the body and contracted. The right hand clung to the rail, not sliding along it, but brought forward step by step, making repeated slapping sounds on the wood.

As they converged, the man turned his head, insofar as he was able to turn it, and stared up at Rivers. Probably this was dictated by no more than the curiosity patients always feel at the appearance of a doctor on wards where nothing else ever happens, but it seemed to Rivers that his expression was both sombre and malevolent. He had to drag his own gaze away. At that moment a VAD came out of a side ward and said in that bracingly jolly way of theirs, 'Nearly ten o'clock. Let's have you in bed.'

The morning round. Rivers wondered if he was in for that.

He was. Yealland came out of his room, flanked by two junior doctors, shook hands briskly and said that he thought the best general introduction was perhaps simply a ward round.

The party consisted of Yealland, the two junior doctors who were being put through their paces, a ward sister, who made no contribution and was invited to make none, and a couple of orderlies who hovered in the background in case they were required to lift. Yealland was an impressive figure. In conversation he did not merely meet your eye, but stared so intently that you felt your skull had become transparent. His speech was extremely precise. Something in this steady, unrelenting projection of authority made Rivers want to laugh, but he didn't think he'd have wanted to laugh if he'd been a junior doctor or a patient.

They did the post-treatment ward first. The bulk of the conversation was between Yealland and the two junior doctors, with occasional asides to Rivers. Contact with patients was restricted to a brisk, cheerful, authoritative greeting. No questions were asked about their psychological state. Many of them, Rivers thought, showed signs of depression, but in every case the removal of the physical symptom was described as a cure. Most of these patients would be out within a week, Yealland said. Rivers asked questions about the relapse rate, the suicide rate, and received the expected reply. Nobody knew.

The admissions ward was next. An immensely long ward, lined with white-covered beds packed close together. On both sides windows reached from floor to ceiling, and the room was flooded with cold northern light. The patients, many displaying bizarre contractures of their limbs, sat, if they were capable of sitting, upright in their beds, as near to attention as they could get. Rivers's corridor acquaintance was just inside the room, lying face down on his bed, buttocks in the air, presumably the only position he was capable of maintaining. It couldn't be said he added to the desired impression of tidiness, but the nurses had done their best. The little procession came to a halt by his bed.

Yealland's previous performance had been perfunctory. Rivers suspected he lost interest in the patients once the miracle had been worked. Now, though, he turned to Rivers with real zest. 'This one's fairly typical,' he said, and nodded to the ginger-haired doctor.

A shell had exploded close to the patient, who had been buried up to the neck and had remained in that position for some time under continued heavy fire. For two or three days after being dug out he'd been dazed, though he did have a vague recollection of the explosion. Six weeks later he'd been sent to England, to a hospital in Eastbourne where he'd been treated with physical exercises. During this time the abnormal flexure of the spine had grown worse.

The sheets were pulled back. It was not possible to bend the trunk passively, the doctor said, demonstrating. The patient couldn't eat from a table and, as they could all see, he couldn't lie straight in bed. He complained of considerable pain in the head, which was worse at night. And when he woke up there were coloured lights dancing in front of his eyes. Some right hemianalgesia was present. There was tenderness – probing – from the sixth dorsal spine down to the lumbar region. Free, but not excessive, perspiration of the feet. A mark made on the sole of the foot lasted an abnormally long time.

'*And?*' Yealland said.

The young man looked frightened, a fear Rivers remembered only too clearly. The missing fact came to him just in time. 'No sign of organic disease,' he finished triumphantly.

'Good. So at least we may be encouraged to believe the patient is in the right hospital?'

'Yes, sir.'

Yealland walked to the head of the bed. 'You will receive treatment this afternoon,' he said. 'I shall begin by making your back straight. This will be done by the application of electricity to your spine and back. You have power to raise your head, indeed you can even extend it. I am sure you understand the pain is due to the position you assume. The muscles are in too great a stretch and there is no relief, because even when you rest the same position is maintained. The electricity may be strong, but it will be the means of restoring your lost powers – the power to straighten your back.'

It was extraordinary. If Yealland had appeared authoritative before, it was nothing compared with the almost God-like tone he now assumed. The patient was looking distinctly alarmed. 'Will it hurt?' he asked.

Yealland said: 'I realize you did not intend to ask that question and so I will overlook it. I am sure you understand the principles of the treatment, which are . . .' He paused, as if expecting the patient to supply them. 'Attention, first and foremost; tongue, last and least; questions, never. I shall see you this afternoon.'

And so on round the ward. Yealland stopped in some triumph by the last bed. 'Now this *is* interesting.'

Rivers had been aware of this patient ever since they entered the ward. He sat up very straight in bed, and followed their progress with an air of brooding antagonism.

'Callan,' Yealland said. 'Mons, the Marne, Aisne, first and second Ypres, Hill 60, Neuve-Chapelle, Loos, Armentières, the Somme and Arras.' He looked at Callan. 'Have I missed any?'

Callan obviously heard the question, but made no response. His eyes flicked from Yealland to Rivers, whom he looked up and down dispassionately. Yealland leant closer to Rivers and murmured, 'Very negative attitude.' He nodded to the junior doctor to begin.

Callan had broken down in April. He'd been employed behind the lines on transport at the time, perhaps because his nervous state was already giving cause for concern. While feeding the horses, he had suddenly fallen down, and had remained unconscious for a period of five hours. When he came round, he was shaking all over and was unable to speak. He hadn't spoken at all since then. He attributed his loss of speech to heatstroke.

'Methods of treatment?' Yealland asked.

The patient had been strapped to a chair for periods of twenty minutes at a time, and very strong electric current applied to his neck and throat. Hot plates had been applied repeatedly to the back of the throat, and lighted cigarettes to the tongue.

'I'm sorry?' Rivers said. 'What was that?'

'Lighted cigarettes to the tongue. Sir.'

'None of it persevered with,' Yealland said. 'It's the worst possible basis for treatment because the electricity's been tried and he knows – or thinks he knows – that it doesn't work.' He walked to the head of the bed. 'Do you wish to be cured? Nod if you do.'

Callan smiled.

'You appear to me to be very indifferent to your condition, but indifference will not do in such times as these. I have seen many patients suffering from similar conditions, and not a few in whom the disorder has existed for a much longer time. It has been my experience with these cases to find two kinds of patients, those who want to recover and those who do not want to recover. I understand your condition thoroughly and it makes no difference to me which group you belong to. You must recover your speech at once.'

As they were leaving the ward, Yealland drew him aside. 'Do you have time to witness a treatment?'

'Yes. I'd very much like to.' Apart from anything else he was curious to know how strong 'strong' was when describing an electric current.

It was a matter on which published papers were apt to be reticent. 'Would it be possible for me to see the man we've just left?'

'Yes. Though it won't be quick. And I can't interrupt the treatment.'

'That's all right. I've no afternoon appointments. I'd like to see *him* because of the the previous *failed* treatments.'

'Oh, quite right. *He's* the interesting one. The others are just routine.'

They were walking down to the MOs' dining room for lunch.

'You do only one session?' Rivers asked.

'Yes. The patient has to know when he enters the electrical room that there's no way out except by a full recovery.' Yealland hesitated. 'I normally do treatments alone.'

'I'll be as unobtrusive as I can.'

Yealland nodded. 'Good. The last thing these patients need is a sympathetic audience.'

TWENTY-ONE

After lunch they went straight to the electrical room. Rivers sat on a hard chair in the corner, prepared to stay as long as necessary. The only other furniture was a small desk under the tall window, with a stack of buff-coloured files on it, the battery and the patient's chair, rather like a dentist's chair, except for the straps on the arms and around the foot rest. Yealland, who'd been emptying his bladder in preparation for a long session, came in, rubbing his hands. He nodded cheerfully to Rivers, but didn't speak. Then, rather to Rivers's surprise, he began pulling down the blinds. The blinds were the thick, efficient blinds of wartime, and after he'd finished not a chink of light from the dank, November day could get into the room. Rivers now expected him to turn on the overhead lights, but he didn't. Instead, he left the room in darkness, except for a small circle of light round the battery. This light was reflected off his white coat and up on to his face.

Callan was brought in. He looked indifferent, or defiant, though once he was settled in the chair his eyes shifted from side to side in a way that suggested fear.

'I am going to lock the door,' Yealland said. He returned to stand before the patient, ostentatiously dropping the key into his top pocket. 'You must talk before you leave me.'

All very well, Rivers thought. But Yealland had locked himself in as well as the patient. There could be no backing down.

Yealland put the pad electrode on the lumbar spines and began attaching the long pharyngeal electrode. 'You will not leave me,' he said, 'until you are talking as well as you ever did. No, not a minute before.'

The straps on the chair were left unfastened. Yealland inserted a tongue depressor. Callan neither co-operated nor struggled, but simply sat with his mouth wide open and his head thrown back. Then the electrode was applied to the back of his throat. He was thrown back with such force that the leads were ripped out of the battery. Yealland removed the electrode. 'Remember you must behave as becomes the hero I expect you to be,' Yealland said. 'A man who has been through so many battles should have a better control of himself.' He fastened the straps round Callan's wrists and feet. 'Remember *you must talk before you leave me*.'

Callan was white and shaking, but it was impossible to tell how much pain he was in, since obviously he could no more scream than he could speak. Yealland applied the electrode again, continuously, but evidently with a weaker current since Callan was not thrown back. 'Nod to me when you are ready to attempt to speak.'

It took an hour. Rivers during all that time scarcely moved. His empathy with the man in the chair kept him still, since Callan himself never moved, except once to flex the fingers of his strapped hands. At last he nodded. Immediately the electrode was removed, and after a great deal of effort Callan managed to say 'ah' in a sort of breathy whisper.

Yealland said, 'Do you realize that there is already an improvement? Do you appreciate that a result has already been achieved? Small as it may seem to you, if you will consider rationally for yourself, you will believe me when I tell you that you will be talking before long.'

The electrode was applied again. Yealland started going through the sounds of the alphabet: ah, bah, cah, dah, etc., encouraging Callan to repeat the sounds after him, though only 'ah' was repeated. Whenever Callan said 'ah' on request, the electrode was momentarily removed. Whenever he substituted 'ah' for other sounds, the current was reapplied.

They had now been in the room an hour and a half. Callan was obviously exhausted. Despite the almost continuous application of the electric current he was actually beginning to drop off to sleep. Yealland evidently sensed he was losing his patient's attention and unstrapped him. 'Walk up and down,' he said.

Callan did as he was bid, and Yealland walked beside him, encouraging him to repeat the sounds of the alphabet, though, again, only 'ah' was produced and that in a hoarse whisper, very far back in the throat. Callan stumbled as he walked, and Yealland supported him. Up and down they went, up and down, in and out of the circle of light around the battery.

Rebellion came at last. Callan wrenched his arm out of Yealland's grasp and ran to the door. Evidently he'd forgotten it was locked, though he remembered at once and turned on Yealland.

Yealland said, 'Such an idea as leaving me now is most ridiculous. You cannot leave the room. The door is locked and the key is in my pocket. You will leave me when you are cured, remember, not before. I have no doubt you are tired and discouraged, but that is not my fault; the reason is that you do not understand your condition as I do, and the time you have already spent with me is not long in comparison with the time I am prepared to stay with you. Do you understand me?'

Callan looked at Yealland. For a second the thought of striking him was clearly visible, but then Callan seemed to admit defeat. He pointed to the battery and then to his mouth, miming: *Get on with it*.

'No,' Yealland said. 'The time for more electrical treatment has not yet come; if it had, I should give it to you. Suggestions are not wanted from you; they are not needed. When the time comes for more electricity, you will be given it whether you want it or not.' He paused. Then added with great emphasis: '*You must speak, but I shall not listen to anything you have to say.*'

They walked up and down again, Callan still repeating 'ah', but making no other sound. The 'ah' was produced by an almost superhuman effort, the muscles of the neck in spasm, the head raised in a series of jerks. Even the torso and the arms were involved in the immense effort of pushing this sound across his lips. Rivers had to stop himself trying to make the sound for him. He was himself very tense; all the worst memories of his stammer came crowding into his mind.

Yealland said, 'You are now ready for the next stage of treatment, which consists of the administration of strong shocks to the *outside* of the neck. These will be transmitted to your voice box and you will soon be able to say anything you like in a whisper.'

Callan was again placed in the chair and again strapped in. The key electrode was applied in short bursts to his neck in the region of the larynx, Yealland repeating 'ah, bah, cah, dah', etc. in time with the shocks. On the third repetition of the alphabet, Callan suddenly said 'ba'. Instead of attempting the next sound, he went on repeating 'ba', not loudly, but venomously. 'Bah, bah', and then, unmistakably 'Baaaa! Baaaaa! Baaaaaa!'

Yealland actually looked gratified. He said, 'Are you not glad you have made such progress?'

Callan started to cry. For a while there was no other sound in the room than his sobbing. Then he wiped his eyes on the back of his hand and mimed a request for water.

'Yes, you will have water soon. Just as soon as you can utter a word.'

Callan pushed Yealland aside and ran to the door, rattling the handle, beating on the wood with his clenched fists. Rivers couldn't bear to go on watching. He looked down at the backs of his clasped hands.

Yealland said, 'You will leave this room when you are speaking normally. I know you do not want the treatment suspended now you are making such progress. You are a noble fellow and these ideas which come into your mind and make you want to leave me do not represent your true self. I know you are anxious to be cured and are happy to have recovered to such an extent; now you are tired and cannot think properly, but you must make every effort to think in the manner characteristic of your true self: *a hero of Mons*.'

Perhaps Callan remembered, as Yealland apparently did not, that Mons had been a defeat. At any rate he went back to the chair.

'You must utter a sound,' Yealland said. 'I do not care what the nature of the sound is. You will understand me when I say I shall be able to train any sound into the production of *vowel* sounds, then into *letter* sounds, and finally into *words* and *sentences*. Utter a sound when you take a deep breath, and as soon as I touch your throat.'

Callan, although he appeared to be co-operating, could make no expiratory sound.

Yealland appeared to lose patience. He clamped his hands down on to Callan's wrists and said, 'This has gone on long enough. I may have to use a stronger current. I do not want to hurt you, but if necessary I must.'

Rivers couldn't tell whether the anger was acted or real, but there was no doubt about the strength of the current being applied to the neck in shock after shock. But it worked. Soon Callan was repeating 'ah' at a normal pitch, then other sounds, then words. At this point Yealland stopped the use of electricity, and Callan sagged forward in the chair. He looked as if he were going to fall, but the straps held him in place. 'Go on repeating the days,' Yealland said.

'S-s-s-sunday. M-m-m-m-m-monday. T-t-t-tuesday . . .'

Saturday came at last.

Yealland said, 'Remember there is no way out, except by the return of your proper voice and by that door. I have one key, *you* have the other. When you can talk properly, I shall open the door and you can go back to the ward.'

And so it went on, through the alphabet, the days of the week, the months of the year – the shocks sometimes mild, sometimes extremely strong – until he was speaking normally. As soon as he could say words clearly at a normal pitch, he developed a spasm or tremor – not unlike paralysis agitans – in his left arm. Yealland applied a roller electrode to the arm. The tremor then reappeared in the right arm, then the left leg, and finally the right leg, each appearance being treated with the application of the electrode. Finally the cure was pronounced complete. Callan was permitted to stand up. 'Are you not pleased to be cured?' Yealland asked.

Callan smiled.

'I do not like your smile,' Yealland said. 'I find it most objectionable. Sit down.'

Callan sat.

'This will not take a moment,' Yealland said. 'Smile.'

Callan smiled and the key electrode was applied to the side of his mouth. When he was finally permitted to stand up again, he no longer smiled.

'Are you not pleased to be cured?' Yealland repeated.

'Yes, sir.'

'Nothing else?'

A fractional hesitation. Then Callan realized what was required and came smartly to the salute. 'Thank you, sir.'

TWENTY-TWO

That evening after dinner Rivers tried to work on a paper he was due to give to the Royal Society of Medicine in December. As he read through what he'd written, he became aware that he was being haunted by images. The man in the corridor at Queen Square, Yealland's hands, Callan's open mouth, the two figures, doctor and patient, walking up and down, in and out of the circle of light round the battery. It was unusual for Rivers to visualize as intensely as this, indeed to visualize at all, but then the whole experience, from beginning to end, had had something . . . hallucinatory about it.

Rivers left the typewriter and went to sit in his armchair by the fire. As soon as he abandoned the attempt to concentrate on the paper, he knew he was ill. He was sweating, his heart pounded, pulses all over his body throbbed, and he felt again that extraordinary sensation of blood squeezing through his veins. He thought he might have a slight temperature, but he never, as a matter of principle, took his own temperature or measured his pulse. There were depths of neuroticism to which he was not prepared to sink.

His confrontation with Yealland had exhausted him, for, however polite they had each been to each other, it *had* been a confrontation. He was too tired to go on working, but he knew if he went to bed in this state he wouldn't sleep, even if there was no disturbance from the guns. He decided to take a turn on the Heath, fetched his greatcoat from the peg and crept downstairs. Mrs Irving was a pleasant enough woman, but she was also a very lonely woman, and inclined to air her grievances about the excessive demands of Belgian refugees. He reached the bottom of the stairs, listened a moment, then quietly let himself out of the house.

He felt his way along the dark street. Shuttered windows, like blind eyes, watched from either side. It was something new this darkness, like the deep darkness of the countryside. Even on the Heath, where normally London was spread out before you in a blaze of light, there was only darkness, and again darkness. Starlight lay on the pond, waking a dull gleam, like metal. Nothing else. He started to walk round the edge, trying to empty his mind of Queen Square, but the images floated before him like specks in the eye. Again and again he saw Callan's face, heard his voice repeating simple words, a grotesque parody of Adam naming created things. He felt pursued. There they were, the two of them, Yealland and his patient, walking up and down inside his head. Uninvited. If this was what habitual visualizers experienced, he could only say he found it most unpleasant.

He stopped and looked at the pond. He was aware of rustling, dragging footsteps. Somebody bumped into him and muttered something, but he moved away. By the time he got back to his lodgings he felt much better, well enough to greet Mrs Irving in the hall and compliment her on a more than adequate dinner.

Back in his own rooms he went straight to bed. The sheets felt cold, so cold he again wondered if he was running a temperature, but at least the palpitations and the breathlessness had gone. He thought he might manage to sleep if the Zeppelins and the guns allowed it, and indeed he did fall asleep almost as soon as he turned off the light.

He was walking down the corridor at Queen Square, an immensely long corridor which elongated as he walked along it, like a strip of elastic at full stretch. The swing doors at the far end opened and shut, flap-flapping an unnaturally long time, like the wings of an ominous bird. Clinging to the rail, the deformed man watched him approach. The eyes swivelled to follow him. The mouth opened and out of it came the words: *I am making this protest on behalf of my fellow-soldiers because I believe the war is being deliberately prolonged by those who have the power to end it.*

The words echoed along the white corridor. Abruptly the dream changed. He was in the electrical room, a pharyngeal electrode in his hand, a man's open mouth in front of him. He saw the moist, pink interior, the delicately quivering uvula, the yellowish, grainy surface of the tongue, and the tonsils, like great swollen, blue-purple eggs. He slipped the tongue depressor in, and tried to apply the electrode, but the electrode, for some reason, wouldn't fit. He tried to force it. The man struggled and bucked beneath him, and, looking down, he saw that the object he was holding was a horse's bit. He'd already done a lot of damage. The corners of the man's mouth were raw, flecked with blood and foam, but still he went on, trying to force the bit into the mouth, until a cry from the patient woke him. He sat up, heart pounding, and realized he had himself cried out. For a second the dream was so real that he went on seeing the chair, the battery, the tortured mouth. Then, nothing. Gradually, his heart beat returned to normal, though when he got out of bed and went across to sit by the window the small effort made it pound again.

No raid tonight. It was ironic that on this one quiet night he should have woken himself up with a nightmare. As with all nightmares, the horror lingered. He was still inclined to accuse himself. That, he thought – self-reproach – had been the dominant affect. At first he was inclined to connect it with the quasi-sexual imagery of the dream, for the dream action had been both an accurate representation of Yealland's treatment and uncomfortably like an oral rape. He didn't feel, however, that the underlying conflict had been sexual.

The manifest content came from his visit to Queen Square, and was present with relatively little transformation. There was no doubt that the visit had been rife with opportunities for conflict. From the beginning he'd felt a tension between, on the one hand, his sympathy for the patients, his doubts about the quality of the treatment they were receiving, and on the other, the social and professional demands on him to be reasonably polite. As the day had gone on, this conflict had certainly deepened. Over lunch Yealland had told him about an officer patient of his who stammered badly, and whom Yealland had cured in – as usual – one session. Rivers – to his own amusement and exasperation – had responded to the story by beginning to stammer rather badly. And whenever he'd hesitated over a word, he'd sensed Yealland calculating the voltage. All nonsense of course. He'd been more amused by the situation than anything else, but nevertheless the worsening of his stammer did point to an underlying conflict that might well find expression in a dream.

The man in the corridor with the spinal contracture seemed to represent Sassoon, since he'd quoted the Declaration, though it was difficult to imagine anybody more physically unlike Sassoon than that deformed, pseudo-dwarf. And the expression of antagonism – that certainly didn't correspond with anything in the real Sassoon's attitude towards him. But then there was no reason why it should. The dream action is the creation of the dreamer. The mood of this dream, a mood so powerful he could still not shake it off, was one of the most painful self-accusation. The man's expression need reflect no more than *his* feeling that Sassoon, perhaps, had grounds for antagonism.

He hadn't been able to see the face of the second patient, and had no clear sense of who it was. The obvious candidate was Callan, since it was Callan he'd watched being treated. And Callan had been working with horses when he became mute, which might account for the bit. And yet he was fairly certain the dream patient had not been Callan.

On the wards he'd been struck by a slight facial resemblance between Callan and Prior, who had also been mute when he arrived at Craiglockhart. He remembered an incident shortly after Prior's arrival when he'd dragged a teaspoon across the back of his throat, hoping that the choking reflex would trigger the return of speech. This did sometimes happen. He'd seen more than one patient recover his voice in that way. But he'd tried it while in a state of acute irritation with Prior, and the choking had occasioned a momentary spasm of satisfaction. Very slight, but enough to make him feel, in retrospect, discontented with his own behaviour. Mute patients *did* arouse exasperation, particularly, as with both Prior and Callan, when their satisfaction with their condition was hardly at all disguised. Perhaps the dream patient was a composite figure, part Callan, part Prior, the combination suggested by his application of a teaspoon to Prior's throat and Yealland's application of an electrode to Callan's.

But there was no comparison in the amount of pain inflicted. On the face of it he seemed to be congratulating himself on dealing with patients more humanely than Yealland, but then why the mood of self-accusation? In the dream he stood in Yealland's place. The dream seemed to be saying, in dream language, don't flatter yourself. There *is* no distinction.

A horse's bit. Not an electrode, not a teaspoon. A bit. An instrument of control. Obviously he and Yealland were both in the business of controlling people. Each of them fitted young men back into the role of warrior, a role they had – however unconsciously – rejected. He'd found himself wondering once or twice recently what possible meaning the restoration of mental health could have in relation to his work. Normally a cure implies that the patient will no longer engage in behaviour that is clearly self-destructive. But in present circumstances, recovery meant the resumption of activities that were not merely self-destructive but positively suicidal. But then in a war nobody is a free agent. He and Yealland were both *locked in*, every bit as much as their patients were.

Bits. The scold's bridle used to silence recalcitrant women in the Middle Ages. More recently, on American slaves. And yet on the ward, listening to the list of Callan's battles, he'd felt that nothing Callan could say could have been more powerful than his silence. Later, in the electrical room, as Callan began slowly to repeat the alphabet, walking up and down with Yealland, in and out of the circle of light, Rivers had felt that he was witnessing the *silencing* of a human being. Indeed, Yealland had come very close to saying just that. 'You must speak, but I shall not listen to anything you have to say.'

Silencing, then. The task of silencing somebody, with himself in Yealland's place and an unidentified patient in the chair. It was possible to escape still, to pretend the dream accusation was general. Just as Yealland silenced the unconscious protest of *his* patients by removing the paralysis, the deafness, the blindness, the muteness that stood between them and the war, so, in an infinitely more gentle way, *he* silenced *his* patients; for the stammerings, the nightmares, the tremors, the memory lapses, of officers were just as much unwitting protest as the grosser maladies of the men.

But he didn't believe in the general accusation. He didn't believe this was what the dream was saying. Dreams were detailed, concrete, specific: the voice of the protopathic heard at last, as one by one the higher centres of the brain closed down. And he knew who the patient in the chair was. Not Callan, not Prior. Only one man was being silenced in the way the dream indicated. He told himself that the accusation was unjust. It was Sassoon's decision to abandon the protest, not his. But that didn't work. He knew the extent of his own influence.

He went on sitting by the window as dawn grew over the Heath, and felt that he was having to appeal against conviction in a courtroom where he himself had been both judge and jury.

TWENTY-THREE

Head's room was very quiet. The tall windows that overlooked the square were shrouded in white net. Outside was a day of moving clouds and fitful sunlight, and whenever the sun shone, the naked branches of plane trees patterned the floor. So Head's patients must sit, hour after hour, with those bright, rather prominent eyes fixed on them, while elsewhere in the house doors banged and a telephone started to ring. But there the normality of the 'consultation' ended, for Head would never, not even under the most extreme provocation, have told a *patient* that he was talking a load of self-indulgent rubbish. Rivers opened his mouth to protest and was waved into silence.

'All right,' Head swept on. 'He's muddle-headed, immature, liable to fits of enthusiasm, inconsistent. All of that. But . . . *And* he virtually had no father *and* he's put you in his father's place. *But*, he's also' – ticking off on his fingers – 'brave, capable of resisting any amount of pressure – the mere fact he protested at all in the present climate tells us that – and above all – no, let me finish – he has *integrity*. Everything you've told me about him suggests he was always going to go back, as soon as he knew the protest was useless, simply because there's no way he can *honourably* stay in Craiglockhart taking up a bed he doesn't need.'

Rivers smiled. 'What are friends for if not letting you off the hook?'

'Well, let me get you off the other hook while I'm about it. You and Yealland doing *essentially the same thing*. Good God, man, if you really believe that it's the first sign of dementia. I can't imagine anybody less like Yealland – methods, attitudes, values – everything. The whole attitude to the patient. And in spite of all this *self-laceration*, I can't help thinking you know that. Who would you rather be sent to if you were the patient?'

'You.'

Head smiled. 'No. I don't say I do a bad job, but I'm not as good with these particular patients as you are.'

'I suppose I'm worried about him.'

'Yes. Well . . .'

'I think what bothers me more than anything else is this total inability to think about after the war. You see, I think he's made up his mind to get killed.'

'All the more reason for you to get it clear whose decision it was that he went back.' A pause. 'You know after dinner the other night Ruth was saying how much she thought you'd changed.'

Rivers was looking out of the window.

'Do you think you have?'

'I'm probably the last person to know. I can't imagine going back to the same way of life. But . . .' He raised his hands. 'I've been there before. And . . .' A little, self-deprecating laugh. 'Nothing happened.'

'When was this?'

'After my second trip to the Solomons.'

Head waited.

'I don't know whether you've ever had the . . . the experience of having your life changed by a quite trivial incident. You know, nothing dramatic like the death of a parent, or the birth of a child. Something *so* trivial you almost can't see *why* it had the effect it had. It happened to me on that trip. I was on the *Southern Cross* – that's the mission boat – and there was a group of islanders there – recent converts. You can always tell if they're recent, because the women still have bare breasts. And I thought I'd go through my usual routine, so I started asking questions. The first question was, what would you do with it if you earned or found a guinea? Would you share it, and if so who would you share it *with*? It gets their attention because to them it's a lot of money, and you can uncover all kinds of things about kinship structure and economic arrangements, and so on. Anyway at the end of this – we were all sitting cross-legged on the deck, miles from anywhere – they decided they'd turn the tables on me, and ask me the same questions. Starting with: What would *I* do with a guinea? Who would I share it with? I explained I was unmarried and that I wouldn't necessarily feel obliged to share it with anybody. They were *incredulous*. How could anybody live *like that*? And so it went on, question after question. And it was one of those situations, you know, where one person starts laughing and everybody joins in and in the end the laughter just feeds off itself. They were rolling round the deck by the time I'd finished. And suddenly I realized that *anything* I told them would have got the same response. I could've talked about sex, repression, guilt, fear – the whole sorry caboodle – and it would've got exactly the same response. They wouldn't've felt a twinge of disgust or disapproval or . . . sympathy or anything, because it would all have been *too bizarre*. And I suddenly saw that their reactions to my society were neither more nor less valid than mine to theirs. And do you know that was a moment of the most *amazing* freedom. I lay back and I closed my eyes and I felt as if a ton weight had been lifted.'

'*Sexual* freedom?'

'That too. But it was it was more than that. It was . . . the *Great White God* de-throned, I suppose. Because we did, we quite unselfconsciously *assumed* we were the measure of all things. That was how we approached them. And suddenly I saw not only that we weren't the measure of all things, but that *there was no measure*.'

'And yet you say nothing changed?'

'Nothing changed *in England*. And I don't know why. I think partly just the sheer force of other people's expectations. *You* know you're walking around with a mask on, and you desperately want to take it off and you can't because everybody else thinks it's your face.'

'And now?'

'I don't know. I think perhaps the patients've . . . have done for me what I couldn't do for myself.' He smiled. 'You see healing *does* go on, even if not in the expected direction.'

Rivers's return to Craiglockhart on this occasion was quieter than any previous return had been. There were no boisterous young men playing football with a visitor's hat; indeed, the whole building seemed quieter, though Brock, whom Rivers sat next to at dinner, said that the change in regime had not been as striking as had been intended. The wearing of Sam Browne belts was strictly enjoined and offenders relentlessly pursued, but, aside from that, the attempt to run a psychiatric hospital on parade ground lines had been briefly and vociferously tried, then rapidly and quietly abandoned.

After dinner Rivers set out to see the patients who were due to be Boarded the following day. Anderson had at last received a visit from his wife, though it didn't seem to have cheered him up much. The conflict between himself and his family, as to whether he should return to medicine or not, was deepening as the time came for him to leave Craiglockhart. The nightmares were still very bad, but in any case the haemophobia alone prevented any hospital service whether in Britain or France. Rivers hoped that he would be given a desk job in London, which would also enable Rivers to go on seeing him. At the same time he was a little doubtful even about that. Anderson had moved from a position of being sceptical and even uncooperative to a state of deep attachment, in which there was a danger of dependency. He left Anderson's room shaking his head.

Sassoon was sitting by the fire in almost the same position he'd been in when Rivers left.

'What have you been doing with yourself?' Rivers asked.

'Trying to keep my head down.'

'Successfully?'

'I think so.'

'Have you managed to write?'

'Finished the book. It's called *Counter-Attack*.'

'Very appropriate.'

'You shall have the first copy.'

Rivers looked round the room, which seemed cold and bleak in spite of the small fire. 'Do you hear from Owen at all?'

'Constantly. He . . . er . . . writes distinctly effusive letters. You know . . .' He hesitated. 'I knew about the hero-worship, but I'm beginning to think it was rather more than that.'

Rivers watched the firelight flicker on Sassoon's hair and face. He said, 'It happens.'

'I just hope I was kind enough.'

'I'm sure you were.'

'I don't suppose you've heard from the War Office?'

'On the contrary. I had dinner with Hope the other night, and I have an *informal* assurance that no obstacles will be put in your way. It's not a guarantee, but it's the best I can do.'

Sassoon took a deep breath. 'All right. Back to the sausage machine.'

'It doesn't mean you don't have to be careful with the Board.'

Sassoon smiled. 'I shall say as little as possible.'

The Board was chaired by the new CO, Colonel Balfour Graham. The previous evening Rivers and Brock had discussed the likely effects of this on the conduct of the Board, but had not been able to reach any firm conclusion. Balfour Graham hadn't had time to get to know most of the patients. Either he'd be content simply to move things along as smoothly as possible or, at worst, he might feel obliged to assert his authority by asking both patient and MO more questions than was usual. The third member of the Board was Major Huntley, still – if his conversation over breakfast was anything to go by – obsessed by rose growing and racial degeneracy.

Anderson came first. Balfour Graham expressed some surprise that Rivers was not recommending a general discharge.

'He still wants to serve his country,' Rivers said. 'And there's absolutely no reason why he shouldn't be able to do so. In an administrative capacity. I rather think he may be given a desk job in the War Office.'

'Are we doing the War Office or the patient a favour?' Balfour Graham asked.

'He's an able man. It might be quite good for them to have somebody with extensive experience of France.'

'Lord, *yes*,' said Huntley.

'It merely occurred to me that it might be convenient for Anderson to be able to postpone the moment when he has to face the prospect of civilian medicine.'

'That too,' said Rivers.

The actual interview with Anderson was reasonably quick. Indeed, the whole morning went quickly. They stopped for lunch – over which Rivers professed great interest in mildew and blackspot – and then sat down rather wearily but on time for the next ten. Rivers hardly knew at this stage whether he felt reassured or not. Balfour Graham was quick, courteous, efficient – and shrewd. Huntley's interventions, though rare, were rather unpredictable, and seemed to depend entirely on whether he liked the patient. He took to Willard at once, and was scandalized when Rivers made some comment deploring Willard's lack of insight. 'What's he want insight for? He's supposed to be killing the buggers, Rivers, not psychoanalysing them.'

Sassoon was last but one. 'A *slightly* unusual case,' Rivers began, dismissively. 'In the sense that I'm recommending him for general service overseas.'

'More than *slightly* unusual, surely?' Balfour Graham asked with a faint smile. 'I don't think it's ever been done before. Has it?'

'I couldn't make any other recommendation. He's completely fit, mentally and physically, he *wants* to go back to France, and . . . I have been given an assurance by the War Office that no obstacles will be placed in his way.'

'Why should they be?' asked Huntley.

Balfour Graham said, 'This is the young man who believes the war is being fought for the wrong reasons, and that we should explore Germany's offer of a negotiated peace. Do you think –'

'Those *were* his views,' Rivers said, 'while he was still suffering from exhaustion and the after-effects of a shoulder wound. Fortunately a brother officer intervened and he was sent here. Really no more was required than a brief period of rest and reflection. He now feels very strongly that it's his duty to go back.'

'He was dealt with very leniently, it seems to me,' Huntley said.

'He has a good record. MC. Recommended for the DSO.'

'Ah,' Huntley said.

'I do see what you mean by unusual,' Balfour Graham said.

'The point is he *wants* to go back.'

'Right, let's see him.'

Sassoon came in and saluted. Rivers watched the other two. Balfour Graham acknowledged the salute pleasantly enough. Major Huntley positively beamed. Rivers took Sassoon through the recent past, framing his questions to require no more than a simple yes or no. Sassoon's manner was excellent. Exactly the right mixture of confidence and deference. Rivers turned to Balfour Graham.

Balfour Graham was shuffling about among his papers. Suddenly, he looked up. 'No nightmares?'

'No, sir.'

Sassoon's expression didn't change, but Rivers sensed he was lying.

'Never?'

'Not since I left the 4th London, sir.'

'That was in . . . April?'

'Yes, sir.'

Balfour Graham looked at Rivers. Rivers looked at the ceiling.

'Major Huntley?'

Major Huntley leaned forward. 'Rivers tells us you've changed your mind about the war. Is that right?'

A startled glance. 'No, sir.'

Balfour Graham and Huntley looked at each other.

'You *haven't* changed your views?' Balfour Graham asked.

'No, sir.' Sassoon's gaze was fixed unwaveringly on Rivers. 'I believe exactly what I believed in July. Only if possible more strongly.'

A tense silence.

'I see,' Balfour Graham said.

'Wasn't there something in *The Times*?' Huntley asked. 'I seem to . . .'

He reached across for the file. Rivers leant forward, pinning it to the table with his elbow. 'But you do now feel quite certain it's your duty to go back?'

'Yes, sir.'

'And you have no doubts about that?'

'None whatsoever.'

'*Well*,' Balfour Graham said as the door closed behind Sassoon, 'I suppose you are sure about this, Rivers? He's not going to go back and foment rebellion in the ranks?'

'No, he won't do that. He won't do anything to lower the morale of his men.'

'I hope you're right. He was lying about the nightmares, you know.'

'Yes, I gathered that.'

'I suppose he thinks that might be a reason for keeping him here. The point is do *we* see a reason for keeping him here? Huntley?'

Major Huntley seemed to return from a great distance. 'Spanish Jews.'

Balfour Graham looked blank.

'Father's side. Spanish Jews.'

'You know the family?' Rivers asked.

'Good lord, yes. Mother was a Thornycroft.' He shook his head. '*Ah well.* Hybrid vigour.'

Rivers was across the rose garden several paces ahead of Balfour Graham. 'So you think he's fit?'

''*Course he's fit.* Good God, man, how often do you see a physique like that, even in the so-called upper classes?'

They were back to eugenics again, but for once Rivers had no desire to interrupt.

After dinner Sassoon came to say goodbye. He'd been told the result of the Board and had spent the intervening time packing. Rivers hadn't expected him to linger. Apart from Owen, he'd made no friends at Craiglockhart, not even Anderson, though they'd spent a large part of every day together. And he'd never bothered to disguise his hatred of the place.

'What are you going to do?' Rivers asked.

'Oh, I'll have a couple of days in London, then go home, I suppose.'

'Time for a consultation with Dr Mercier? No, I mean it.'

'I know you mean it. You old fox. Then Garsington, try to explain myself to the pacifists.' He pulled a face. 'I don't look forward to that.'

'Blame me. They will.'

'I shall do no such thing.'

'It's a possible way of telling the story, you know.'

'Yes, I know. But it's not the way I'd tell it. Was it difficult, the Board?'

'No, surprisingly easy. Major Huntley thinks you have a great future as a rose bush. Hybrid vigour.'

'Ah, I see. Dad's lot.'

'I must say the sheer *force* of your refusal to recant came as rather a shock.'

Sassoon looked away. 'I couldn't lie.'

'You managed all right about the nightmares.'

Silence.

'How long has that been going on?'

'Since you left. I'll be all right once I'm out of this place.'

Sassoon didn't want to talk about the nightmares. He was feeling distinctly cheerful. Exactly the same feeling he had had on board ship going to France, watching England slide away into the mist. No doubts, no scruples, no agonizing, just a straightforward, headlong retreat towards the front.

Rivers seemed to read his thoughts. 'Don't take unnecessary risks.'

'No, of course not,' Sassoon said. Though he thought he might.

He stood up, visibly anxious to be off. Rivers followed him to the door and then out into the entrance hall. Balfour Graham and Huntley were there, deep in conversation. It was going to be a very public farewell.

'I'll keep in touch,' Sassoon said.

'Yes. Try and see me before you leave England.'

They shook hands. Then Sassoon, glancing sideways at the colonel and the major, smiled a distinctly conspiratorial smile and came smartly to the salute. 'Thank you, sir.'

For a moment, it was Callan standing there. Then the electrical room at Queen Square faded, and Rivers was back at Craiglockhart, on the black and white tiled floor, alone.

He returned to his desk, and drew a stack of files towards him. He was writing brief notes on the patients who'd been Boarded that day, but this he could do almost automatically. His thoughts wandered as he wrote. He wasted no time wondering how he would feel if Siegfried were to be maimed or killed, because this was a possibility with any patient who returned to France. He'd faced that already, many times. If anything, he was amused by the irony of the situation, that he, who was in the business of changing people, should himself have been changed and by somebody who was clearly unaware of having done it.

It was a far deeper change, though, than merely coming to believe that a negotiated peace might be possible, and desirable. That at least it ought to be explored. He remembered telling Head how he had tried to change his life when he came back from Melanesia for the second time and how that attempt had failed. He'd gone on being reticent, introverted, reclusive. Of course it had been a very introverted, self-conscious attempt, and perhaps that was why it hadn't worked. Here in this building, where he had no time to be introverted or self-conscious, where he hardly had a moment to himself at all, the changes had taken place without his knowing. That was not Siegfried. That was all of them. Burns and Prior and Pugh and a hundred others. As a young man he'd been both by temperament and conviction deeply conservative, and not merely in politics. Now, in middle age, the sheer extent of the *mess* seemed to be forcing him into conflict with the authorities over a very wide range of issues . . . medical, military. Whatever. A society that devours its own young deserves no automatic or unquestioning allegiance. Perhaps the rebellion of the old might count for rather more than the rebellion of the young. Certainly poor Siegfried's rebellion hadn't counted for much, though he reminded himself that he couldn't *know* that. It had been a completely honest action and such actions are seeds carried on the wind. Nobody can tell where, or in what circumstances, they will bear fruit.

How on earth was Siegfried going to manage in France? His opposition to the war had not changed. If anything it had hardened. And to go back to fight, believing as he did, would be to encounter internal divisions far deeper than anything he'd experienced before. Siegfried's 'solution' was to tell himself that he was going back only to look after some men, but that formula would not survive the realities of France. However devoted to his men's welfare a platoon commander might be, in the end he is there to kill, and to train other people to kill. Poetry and pacifism are a strange preparation for that role. Though Siegfried had performed it before, and with conspicuous success. But then his hatred of the war had not been as fully fledged, as articulate, as it was now.

It was a dilemma with one very obvious way out. Rivers knew, though he had never voiced his knowledge, that Sassoon was going back with the intention of being killed. Partly, no doubt, this was youthful self-dramatization. *I'll show them. They'll be sorry.* But underneath that, Rivers felt there was a genuine and very deep desire for death.

And if death were to be denied? Then he might well break down. A real breakdown, this time.

Rivers saw that he had reached Sassoon's file. He read through the admission report and the notes that followed it. There was nothing more he wanted to say that he could say. He drew the final page towards him and wrote: *Nov. 26, 1917. Discharged to duty.*

AUTHOR'S NOTE

Fact and fiction are so interwoven in this book that it may help the reader to know what is historical and what is not. Siegfried Sassoon (1886–1967) did, in July 1917, protest against the continuation of the war. Robert Graves persuaded him to attend a Medical Board and he was sent to Craiglockhart War Hospital, where he came under the care of Dr W. H. R. Rivers, FRS (1864–1922), the distinguished neurologist and social anthropologist, who then held the rank of captain in the RAMC. During Sassoon's stay he formed a friendship with one of Dr Brock's patients, Wilfred Owen (1893–1918), though it is probably fair to say that this friendship played a more central role in Owen's life, then and later, than it did in Sassoon's.

Rivers's methods of treating his patients are described in 'The Repression of War Experience' (*Lancet,* 2 Feb. 1918) and in his posthumously published book *Conflict and Dream* (London, Kegan Paul, 1923), in which Sassoon makes a brief appearance as 'Patient B'.

Dr Lewis Yealland's rather different methods of treating his patients are described in detail in his book: *Hysterical Disorders of Warfare* (London, Macmillan, 1918).

There is an interesting discussion of Rivers's pre-war work with Henry Head on nerve regeneration, and the concept of protopathic and epicritic innervation which evolved from it, in 'The Dog Beneath the Skin' by Jonathan Miller (*Listener,* 20 July 1972).

The amendments suggested by Sassoon to the early draft of 'Anthem for Doomed Youth' appear in Sassoon's handwriting on the MSS. See *Wilfred Owen: The Complete Poems and Fragments,* Vol. II, edited by Jon Stallworthy (Chatto & Windus, The Hogarth Press and Oxford University Press, 1983). Two modern texts which contain stimulating discussions of 'shell-shock' are *No Man's Land: Combat and Identity in World War I* by Eric Leed (Cambridge University Press, 1979) and *The Female Malady* by Elaine Showalter (Virago Press, 1987).

Julian Dadd, whose psychiatric illness caused Sassoon some concern during his stay at Craiglockhart, subsequently went on to make a complete recovery.

I'm grateful for help received from the staff of the following libraries: Sheffield Public Library, Newcastle University Medical Library, Cambridge University Library, Napier Polytechnic Library, Edinburgh (formerly Craiglockhart War Hospital), The Oxford University English Faculty Library, the Imperial War Museum, and St John's College, Cambridge, where the Deputy Librarian M. Pratt did much to make my visit interesting and enjoyable.

THE EYE IN THE DOOR

It was on the moral side, and in my own person, that I learned to recognize the thorough and primitive duality of man; I saw that, of the two natures that contended in the field of my consciousness, even if I could rightly be said to be either, it was only because I was radically both . . .

The Strange Case of Dr Jekyll and Mr Hyde

– R. L. Stevenson

Part One

ONE

In formal beds beside the Serpentine, early tulips stood in tight-lipped rows. Billy Prior spent several moments setting up an enfilade, then, releasing his companion's arm, seized an imaginary machine-gun and blasted the heads off the whole bloody lot of them.

Myra stared in amazement. 'You barmy bugger.'

He shook his head sadly. 'Five months in a loony bin last year.'

'Go on.'

She didn't believe him, of course. Smiling, he came back and offered her his arm. They had been wandering along beside the lake for an hour, but now the afternoon was waning. A coppery light, more like autumn than spring, slanted across the grass, turning the thorned twigs of rose bushes into strips of live electric filament that glowed, reddish, in the dusk.

Prior, always self-conscious, was aware of approving glances following them as they passed. They made a romantic picture, he supposed. The girl, young and pretty, clinging to the arm of a man in uniform, a man, moreover, wearing a greatcoat so grotesquely stained and battered it had obviously seen a good deal of active service. As indeed it had, and was about to see more, if only he could persuade the silly bitch to lie on it.

'You're cold,' he said tenderly, unbuttoning the greatcoat. 'Put your hand in here. You know, we'd be warmer under the trees. We'd be out of the wind.'

She paused, doubtfully, for by the lake it was still light, whereas the avenue of trees he was pointing to smoked darkness. 'All right,' she said at last.

They set off across the grass, their shadows stretching ahead of them, black, attenuated figures that reached the trees and began to climb before they were anywhere near. In the darkness they leant against the trunk of one of the trees and started to kiss. After a while she moaned, and her thighs slackened, and he pressed her back against the fissured bark. His open greatcoat shielded them both. Her hands slid round him, underneath his tunic, and grasped his buttocks, pulling him hard against her. She was tugging at his waistband and buttons and he helped her unfasten them, giving her free play with his cock and balls. His hands were slowly inching up her skirt. Already he'd found the place where the rough stockings gave way to smooth skin. 'Shall we lie down?'

Her hands came up to form a barrier. 'What, in this?'

'You'll be warm enough.'

'I bloody won't. I'm nithered now.' To emphasize the point she pressed her hands into her armpits and rocked herself.

'All right,' he said, his voice hardening. 'Let's go back to the flat.' He'd wanted to avoid doing that, because he knew his landlady would be in, and watching.

She didn't look at him. 'No, I think I'd better be getting back.'

'I'll take you.'

'No, I'd rather say goodbye here, if you don't mind. Me mother-in-law lives five doors down.'

'You were keen enough the other night.'

Myra smiled placatingly. 'Look, I had a woman come nosying round. The voluntary police, you know? They can come into your house, or anything, they don't have to ask. And this one's a right old cow. I knew her before the war. She was all for women's rights. I says, "What about my rights? Aren't I a woman?" But there's no point arguing with 'em. They can get your money stopped. And anyway it isn't right, is it? With Eddie at the Front?'

Prior said in a clipped, authoritative voice, 'He was at the Front on Friday night.' He heard the note of self-righteousness, and saw himself, fumbling with the fly buttons of middle-class morality. Good God, *no*. He'd rather tie a knot in it than have to live with that image. 'Come on,' he said. 'I'll walk you to the station.'

He strode towards Lancaster Gate, not caring if she followed or not. She came trotting breathlessly along beside him. 'We can still be friends, can't we?'

He felt her gaze on his face.

'Can't we?'

He stopped and turned to face her. 'Myra, you're the sort of girl who ends up in a ditch with her stockings round her neck.'

He walked on more slowly. After a while, her hand came creeping through his arm, and, after a moment's hesitation, he left it there.

'Have you got a girl?' she said.

A brief struggle. 'Yes.'

She nodded, satisfied. 'Thought you had. Lying little git, aren't you? Friday night, you said you hadn't.'

'We both said a bellyful on Friday night.'

At the underground station he bought her ticket, and she reached up and kissed his cheek as if nothing had happened. Well, he thought, nothing had happened. On the other side of the barrier she turned, and looked as if she might be regretting the evening they'd planned, but then she gave a little wave, stepped out on to the moving staircase and was carried smoothly away.

Outside the station he hesitated. The rest of the evening stretched in front of him and he didn't know what to do. He thought about going for a drink, but rejected the idea. If he started drinking as early as this and in this mood, he'd end up drunk, and he couldn't afford to do that; he had to be clear-headed for the prison tomorrow. He drifted aimlessly along.

It was just beginning to be busy, people hurrying to restaurants and bars, doing their best to forget the shortages, the skimped clothes, the grey bread. All winter, it seemed to Prior, an increasingly frenetic quality had been creeping into London life. Easily justified, of course. Soldiers home on leave had to be given a good time; they mustn't be allowed to remember what they were going back to, and this gave everybody else a magnificent excuse for never thinking about it at all.

Though this week it had been difficult to avoid thinking. Haig's April 13th Order of the Day had appeared in full in every newspaper. He knew it off by heart. Everybody did.

There is no other course open to us but to fight it out. Every position must be held to the last man: there must be no retirement. With our backs to the wall, and believing in the justice of our cause, each one of us must fight on to the end.

Whatever effect the Order had on the morale of the army, it had produced panic among civilians. Some women, apparently, were planning in all seriousness how they should kill themselves and their children when the Germans arrived. Those atrocity stories from the first months of the war had done the trick. Rather too well. Nuns with their breasts cut off. Priests hung upside-down and used as clappers to ring their own bells. Not that there hadn't been atrocities, but prisoners of war were always the main victims, and the guilt was more evenly distributed than the press liked to think.

There were times – and tonight was one of them – when Prior was made physically sick by the sight and sound and smell of civilians. He remembered the stench that comes off a battalion of men marching back from the line, the thick yellow stench, and he thought how preferable it was to this. He knew he had to get off the streets, away from the chattering crowds and the whiffs of perfume that assaulted his nostrils whenever a woman walked past.

Back in the park, under the trees, he began to relax. Perhaps it was his own need that coloured his perceptions, but it seemed to him that the park on this spring evening was alive with desire. Silhouetted against the sunset, a soldier and his girl meandered along, leaning against each other so heavily that if either had withdrawn the other would have fallen. It made him think of himself and Sarah on the beach in Scotland, and he turned away sharply. No point thinking about that. It would be six weeks at least before he could hope to see her again. Further along towards Marble Arch the figures were solitary. Army boots tramped and slurred along the paths or, in the deepest shadow, jetted sparks.

He sat on a bench and lit a cigarette, still trying to decide what to do with the stump of his evening. He needed sex, and he needed it badly. Tossing off was no use, because . . . because it was no use. Prostitutes were out because he didn't pay. He remembered telling Rivers, who'd been his doctor at Craiglockhart War Hospital, the 'loony bin' where he'd spent five months of the previous year, about a brothel in Amiens, how the men, the private soldiers, queued out on to the pavement and were allowed two minutes each. 'How long do officers get?' Rivers had asked. 'I don't know,' Prior had said. 'Longer than that.' And then, spitting the words, *'I don't pay.'* No doubt Rivers had thought it rather silly, a young man's ridiculous pride in his sexual prowess, his ability to 'get it' free. But it was nothing to do with that. Prior didn't pay because once, some years ago, he had been paid, and he knew exactly how the payer looks to the one he's paying.

'Got a light?'

Automatically, Prior began tapping his pockets. At first he hardly registered the existence of the speaker, except as an unwelcome interruption to his thoughts, but then, as he produced the matches, some unconsciously registered nervousness in the other man's voice made him look up. He had been going to offer the box, but now he changed his mind, took out a match and struck it himself. The rasp and flare sounded very loud. He cupped his hands to shield the flame, and held it out as the other bent towards it. An officer's peaked cap, dark eyes, a thin moustache defining a full mouth, the face rounded, though not fat. Prior was sure he knew him, though he couldn't remember where he'd seen him before. When the cigarette was lit, he didn't immediately move off, but sat further along the bench, looking vaguely around him, the rather prominent Adam's apple jerking in his throat. His left leg was stretched out awkwardly in front of him, presumably the explanation of the wound stripe on his sleeve.

Prior could see the problem. This wasn't exactly the right area, though it bordered upon it, and his own behaviour, though interesting, had not been definitely inviting. He was tempted to tease. Instead he moved closer and said, 'Have you anywhere to go?'

'Yes.' The man looked up. 'It's not far.'

The square contained tall, narrow, dark houses, ranged round a fenced-off lawn with spindly trees. The lawn and the surrounding flowerbeds were rank with weeds. Further along, on the right, a bomb had knocked out three houses and partially demolished a fourth, leaving a huge gap. They walked along, not talking much. As they approached the gap, the pavement became gritty beneath their feet, pallid with the white dust that flowed so copiously from stricken houses and never seemed to clear, no matter how carefully the ruin was fenced off. Prior was aware of a distinct sideways pull towards the breach. He'd felt this before, walking past other bombed sites. He had no idea whether this sideways tug was felt by everybody, or whether it was peculiar to him, some affinity with places where the established order has been violently assailed.

They stopped in front of No. 27. The windows were shuttered. A cat, hunched and defensive, crouched on the basement steps, growling over something it had found.

Prior's companion was having trouble with the lock. 'Part of the damage,' he said over his shoulder, pulling a face. He jabbed the door with his shoulder, then seized the knob and pulled it towards him. 'It works if you pull, I keep forgetting that.'

'Not *too* often, I hope,' said Prior.

His companion turned and smiled, and for a moment there was a renewed pull of sexual tension between them. He took off his cap and greatcoat, and held out his hand for Prior's. 'The family's in the country. I'm staying at my club.' He hesitated. 'I suppose I'd better introduce myself. Charles Manning.'

'Billy Prior.'

Covertly, they examined each other. Manning had a very round head, emphasized by thick, sleek dark hair which he wore brushed back with no parting. His eyes were alert. He resembled some kind of animal, Prior thought, an otter perhaps. Manning saw a thin, fair-haired man, twenty-three or four, with a blunt-nosed, high-cheekboned face and a general air of picking his way delicately through life. Manning pushed open a door on the left, and a breath of dead air came into the hall. 'Why don't you go in? I won't be a minute.'

Prior entered. Tall windows shuttered, furniture shrouded in white sheets. A heavy smell of soot from the empty grate. Everything was under dust-sheets except the tall mirror that reflected, through the open door, the mirror in the hall. Prior found himself staring down a long corridor of Priors, some with their backs to him, none more obviously real than the rest. He moved away.

'Would you like a drink?' Manning asked from the door.

'Yes, please.'

'Whisky all right?'

'Fine.'

Alone, Prior walked across to the grand piano, lifted the edge of the dust-sheet and found himself looking at a photograph of a woman with two small boys, one of them clutching a sailing boat to his chest.

When Manning came back, carrying a whisky bottle, a jug and two glasses, Prior was staring at a crack above the door. 'That looks a bit ominous,' he said.

'Yes, doesn't it? I don't know what I'm supposed to do about it, really. One can't get workmen, so I just come in and look at it now and then.' He held up the jug. 'Water?'

'Just a dash.'

They moved across to the fireside chairs. Manning pulled off the sheets, and Prior settled back against the stiff brocade. It didn't give at all, but held him tensely upright. They started making the sort of conversation they might have made if they'd been introduced in the mess. Prior watched Manning carefully, noting the MC ribbon, the wound stripe, the twitches, the signs of tension, the occasional stammer. He was in a state, though it was difficult to tell how much of his nervousness was due to the situation. Which *was* dragging on a bit. If this went on they'd demolish the whole bloody bottle and still be swopping regimental chit-chat at midnight. All very nice, Prior thought, but not what I came for. He noticed that Manning's eyes, though they roamed all over the place, always returned to the stars on

Prior's sleeve. *Well, you knew I was an officer,* he said silently. He was beginning to suspect Manning might be one of those who cannot – simply cannot – let go sexually with a social equal. Prior sighed, and stood up. 'Do you mind if I take this off?' he said. 'I'm quite warm.'

He wasn't warm. In fact, to coin a phrase, he was bloody nithered. However. He took off his tie, tunic and shirt, and threw them over the back of a chair. Manning said nothing, simply watched. Prior ran his fingers through his cropped hair till it stood up in spikes, lit a cigarette, rolled it in a particular way along his bottom lip, and smiled. He'd transformed himself into the sort of working-class boy Manning would think it was all right to fuck. A sort of seminal spittoon. And it worked. Manning's eyes grew dark as his pupils flared. Bending over him, Prior put his hand between his legs, thinking he'd probably never felt a spurt of purer class antagonism than he felt at that moment. He roughened his accent. 'A' right?'

'Yes. Let's go upstairs.'

Prior followed him. On the first floor a door stood open, leading into a large bedroom with a double bed. Manning pulled the door shut. Prior smiled faintly. 'E would not take Oi into the bed where 'e 'ad deflowered 'is broide. Instead 'e went up and up and bloody up. To what were obviously the *servants'* quarters. Manning pushed open a door at the end of the corridor, handed Prior the lamp and said, 'I won't be a minute.'

Prior went in. A double bed with a brass bedstead almost filled the tiny room. He sat on the edge and bounced up and down. It was quite possibly the noisiest bed he'd ever encountered. Thank God the house was empty. Apart from the bed there was a washstand with a jug and bowl, a table with a looking-glass, and a small closet curtained off. He got up and pulled the curtain back. Two housemaids' uniforms hung there, looking almost like the maids themselves, the sleeves and caps had been so neatly arranged. A smell came from the closet: lavender and sweat, a sad smell. Prior's mother had started her life in service in just such a house as this. He looked round the room, the freezing little box of a room, with its view of roofs, and, on a sudden impulse, got one of the uniforms out and buried his face in the armpit, inhaling the smell of sweat. This impulse had nothing to do with sex, though it came from a layer of personality every bit as deep. Manning came back into the room just as Prior raised his head. Seeing Prior with the uniform held against him, Manning looked, it had to be said, daunted. Prior smiled, and put the uniform back on the peg.

Manning set a small jar down on the table by the bed. The click of glass on wood brought them into a closer, tenser relationship than anything they'd so far managed to achieve. Prior finished undressing and lay down on the bed. Manning's leg was bad. Very bad. Prior leant forward to examine the knee, and for a moment they might have been boys in the playground again, examining each other's scabs.

'It looks as if you're out of it.'

'Probably. The tendons've shortened, you see. They think I've got about as much movement as I'm going to get. But then who knows? The way things are going, is anybody out of it?'

Prior straightened up, and, since he was in the neighbourhood, began to rub his face across the hair in Manning's groin. Manning's cock stirred and rose and Prior took it into his mouth, but even then, for a long time, he simply played, flicking his tongue round and round the glistening dome. Manning's thighs tautened. After a while his hand came up and caressed Prior's cropped hair, his thumb massaging the nape of his neck. Prior raised his head and saw that Manning looked nervous, rightly, since in this situation it was a gesture of tenderness that would precipitate violence, if anything did. And Manning was in no state to cope with that. He went back to his sucking, clasping Manning's buttocks in his two hands and moving his mouth rapidly up and down the shaft. Manning pushed him gently away and got into bed. They lay stretched out for a moment side by side. Prior rolled on to his elbow and started to stroke Manning's chest, belly and thighs. He was thinking how impossible it is to sum up sex in terms of who stuffs what into where. This movement of his hand had in it lust; resentment, of Manning's use of the room among other things; sympathy, for the wound; envy, because Manning was *honourably* out of it . . . And a growing awareness that while he had been looking at Manning, Manning had also been looking at him. Prior's expression hardened. He thought, Well, at least I don't twitch as much as you do. The stroking hand stopped at Manning's waist, and he tried to turn him over, but Manning resisted. 'No,' he said. 'Like this.'

Athletic sod. Prior unscrewed the jar, greased his cock with a mixture of vaseline and spit, and wiped the residue on Manning's arse. He guided Manning's legs up his chest, being exceedingly careful not to jerk the knee. He was too eager, and the position was hopeless for control, he was fighting himself before he'd got an inch in, and then Manning yelped and tried to pull away. Prior started to withdraw, then suddenly realized that Manning needed to be hurt. 'Keep still,' he said, and went on fucking. It was a dangerous game. Prior was capable of real sadism, and knew it, and the knee was only a inch or so away from his hand. He came quickly, with deep shuddering groans, a feeling of being pulled out of himself that started in his throat. Carefully, he lowered Manning's legs and sucked him off. He was so primed he was clutching Prior's head and gasping almost before he'd started. 'I needed that,' he said, when it was over. 'I needed a good fucking.'

You all do, Prior thought. Manning went to the bathroom. Prior reached out and turned the looking-glass towards him. Into this glass they had looked, half past five every morning, winter and summer, yawning, bleary-eyed, checking to see their caps were on straight and their hair tucked away. He remembered his mother telling him that, in the house where she'd worked, if a maid met a member of the family in the corridor she had to stand with her face turned to the wall.

Manning came back carrying the whisky bottle and glasses. He was limping badly. Despite Prior's efforts the position couldn't have done the knee any good.

'Where d'you get it?' Prior asked, nodding at the wound.

'Passchendaele.'

'Oh, yes. Your lot were in the assault on the ridge?'

'That's right.' Manning poured the whisky and sat at the end of the bed, propping himself up against the bedstead, and stretching his left leg out in front of him. 'Great fun.'

Prior said, 'I've just had a Board.' He didn't want to talk about his condition, but he was incapable of leaving the subject alone. Manning's silence on the subject, when a question would have been so much more natural, had begun to irritate him.

'What did they say?' Manning asked.

'They haven't said anything yet. I'm supposed to be Permanent Home Service, but with things the way they are . . .'

Manning hesitated, then asked, 'It *is* neurasthenia, isn't it?'

No, Prior wanted to say, it's raging homicidal mania, with a particular predilection for dismembering toffee-nosed gits with wonky knees. 'No, it's asthma,' he said. 'I *was* neurasthenic, but then I had two asthmatic attacks in the hospital, so that confused things a bit.'

'Which hospital were you in?'

'Craiglockhart. It's up in –'

'Ah, then you know Rivers.'

Prior stared. 'He was my doctor. Still is. He's . . . he's in London now.'

'Yes, I know.'

It was Prior's turn not to ask the obvious question.

'Are you still on sick leave?' Manning asked, after a pause.

'No, I'm at the Ministry of Munitions. In the . . .' He looked at Manning. 'And *that*'s where I've seen you. I *knew* I had.'

Manning smiled, but he was very obviously not pleased. 'Just as well I didn't call myself "Smith". I thought about it.'

'If you're going to do that I'd remove the letters from the hall table first. They aren't addressed to "Smith".' Prior looked down into his glass, and gave up the struggle. 'How do you know Rivers?'

Manning smiled. 'He's my doctor, too.'

'Shell-shock?'

'No. Not exactly. I . . . er . . . I was picked up by the police. About two months ago. Not quite caught in the act, but . . . The young man disappeared as soon as we got to the police station. Anyway.'

'What happened?'

'Oh, we all sat around. Nobody did anything unpleasant. I sent for my solicitor, and eventually he arrived, and they let me go. Wound helped. Medal helped.' He looked directly at Prior. '*Connections* helped. You mustn't despise me too easily, you know. I'm not a fool. And then I went home and waited. My solicitor seemed to think if it went to court I'd get two years, but they probably wouldn't give me hard labour because of the leg.'

'That's big of them.'

'Yes. Isn't it? Then somebody said the thing to do was to go to a psychologist and get treatment and and . . . and that would help. So I went to Dr Head, who has quite a reputation in this field – I was actually told in so many words "Henry Head can cure sodomites" – and he said he couldn't do me, he was snowed under, and he recommended Rivers. So I went to him, and he said he'd take me on.'

'Do you *want* to be cured?'

'No.'

'What does he do?'

'Talks. Or rather, *I* talk. He listens.'

'About sex?'

'No, not very often. The war, mainly. You see that's where the confusion comes in because he took one look at me and decided I was neurasthenic. I mean, I can see his point. I was in quite a state when I came out of hospital. A lot worse than I realized at the time. One night at dinner I just picked up a vase and smashed it against the wall. It was quite a large party, about twelve people, and there was this awful . . . silence. And I couldn't explain why I'd done it. Except the vase was hideous. But then my wife said, "So is your Aunt Dorothea. Where is that sort of thinking going to lead?"' He smiled. 'I can't talk to anybody else, so I talk to him.'

Prior put his hand on Manning's arm. 'Are you going to be all right? I mean, are they going to leave you alone?'

'I don't know. I think if they were going to bring charges they'd've brought them by now.' His voice deepened. '"*At that moment there was a knock on the door . . .*"'

Prior was thinking. 'All the same, it's rather convenient, isn't it? That you're neurasthenic?'

'Not particularly.'

'I meant for Rivers. He doesn't have to talk abou –'

'I don't know what Rivers thinks. Anyway, it's the war I need to talk about. And even with him, you know, there are some things I couldn't –'

'You will.'

They lay and looked at each other. Manning said, 'You were going to say which part of the ministry –'

'Yes, so I was. Intelligence.'

'With Major Lode?'

'Yes. With Major Lode. And you?'

'I'm on the fifth floor.'

Evidently the location was the answer. Manning turned and threw his arm across Prior's chest. 'Do you fancy a bit of turn and turn about? Or don't you do that?'

Prior smiled. 'I do anything.'

TWO

Charles Manning left the Ministry of Munitions two hours earlier than usual and went to his house, where he'd arranged to meet a builder who'd promised to repair the bomb damage. It was mid-afternoon. A surprisingly sticky day for spring, warm and damp. When the sun shone, as it did fitfully, emerging from banks of black cloud, the young leaves on the trees glowed a vivid, almost virulent green.

He was walking abstractedly past the bombed site, when the crunch of grit and the smell of charred brick made him pause, and peer through a gap in the fence. The demolished houses had left an outline of themselves on either side of the gap, like after-images on the retina. He saw the looped and trellised bedroom wallpaper that once only the family and its servants would have seen, exposed now to wind and rain and the gaze of casual passers-by. Nothing moved in that wilderness, but, somewhere out of sight, dust leaked steadily from the unstaunchable wound.

Suddenly a cat appeared, a skinny cat, one of the abandoned pets that hung around the square. It began picking its way among the rubble, sharply black and sleek, a silhouette at once angular and sinuous. It stopped, and Manning was aware of baleful yellow eyes turned in his direction, of a cleft pink nose raised to sift the air. Then it continued on its way, the soft pads of its feet finding spaces between shards of glittering glass. Manning watched till it was out of sight. Then, thinking he must get a move on, he swung his stiff leg up the steps to his house and inserted his key in the lock, remembering, with a faint smile, that he must *pull* and not push.

There was an envelope in the post-box. He took it out and carried it through into the drawing-room, his eyes gradually becoming accustomed to the darkness. A heavy smell of soot. There must have been another fall: chimney-sweeping was another job one couldn't get done. He looked down at the envelope. Typewritten. Tradesman, probably. His family and friends all knew he was staying at his club. He put the letter down on the dust-sheet that covered the sofa and walked to the other end of the room, where he opened the shutters, letting in a flood of sickly yellow light.

He went to look at the crack above the door. Is it a load-bearing wall? the builder had asked. Manning thumped with his clenched fist. It didn't sound hollow or feel flimsy, but then these houses were very solidly built. He crossed to the front wall, banged again and thought perhaps he *could* detect a difference. Not much in it, though. He went back to the crack and noticed that the whole surround of the door had been loosened. In fact the more closely one examined it the worse it appeared. That looks ominous, Prior had said, smiling slightly. Odd lad. Even as he felt himself begin to stir at the recollection of the evening, Manning's mind was at work, categorizing. At first, noting Prior's flattened vowels, he'd thought, oh yes. Temporary gentleman. A nasty, snobbish little phrase, but everybody used it, though obviously one tried not to use it in connection with people one liked. But the amazing thing was how persistent one's awareness of class distinction was. The mind seemed capable of making these minute social assessments in almost any circumstances. He remembered the Somme, how the Northumberlands and Durhams had lain, where the machine-guns had caught them, in neat swathes, like harvested wheat. Later that night, crashing along a trench in pitch-blackness, trying desperately to work out where the frontage he was responsible for ended, he'd stumbled into a Northumberlands' officer, very obviously shaken by the carnage inflicted on his battalion. And who could blame him? God knows how many they'd lost. Manning, sympathizing, steadying, well aware that his own nerves had not yet been tested, had none the less found time to notice that the Northumberlands' officer dropped his aitches. He'd been jarred by it. Horrified by the reaction, but jarred nevertheless. And the odd thing was he knew if the man had been a private, he would not have been jarred, he would have handled the situation much better.

As the evening with Prior had gone on, the description 'temporary gentleman' had come to seem less and less appropriate. It suggested one of those dreadful people – well, they *were* dreadful – who aped their betters, anxious to get everything 'right', and became, in the process, pallid, morally etiolated and thoroughly nauseating. Prior was saved from that not because he didn't imitate – he did – but because he wasn't anxious. Once or twice one might almost have thought one detected a glint of amusement. A hint of parody, even. All the same, the basic truth was the man was neither fish nor fowl nor good red herring. *Socially*. Sexually too, of course, though this was a less comfortable reflection. He had a girl in the north, he said, but then they all said that. Manning had suggested they should meet again, and Prior had agreed, but politely, without much enthusiasm. Probably he wouldn't come, and probably it would be just as well. His working at the Ministry brought the whole thing rather too close to . . . well. Too close.

Manning looked at his watch. Ten minutes before the builder was due. He walked across to the piano, lifted the dust-sheet and brought out the photograph of Jane and the boys. Taken last summer. What a little podge Robert had been. Still was. He'd always be a round-cheeked, nondescript sort of child. He was clutching the boat as if he suspected somebody was planning to take it away from him. No doubt James had been. He's like me, Manning thought, looking at Robert.

He felt an almost painful love for his elder son, and sometimes he heard himself speaking too sharply to the boy, but it was only because he could see so much of himself. He knew the areas of vulnerability, and that made him afraid, because in the end one cannot protect one's children. Everybody – Robert too, probably, that was the sad thing – assumed James was his favourite. It wasn't true. His love for James was an altogether sunnier, less complicated emotion. He had more *fun* with James, because he could see James was resilient. He had his mother's dark, clearly defined brows, her cheekbones, her jaw, the same amused, direct look. The photograph didn't do her justice; somehow the sunlight had bleached the strength out of her face. Probably she looked prettier because of it, but she also looked a good deal less like Jane. 'It was *hideous*.' The vase he'd thrown at the wall. 'So is your Aunt Dorothea. Where is that sort of thinking going to lead?' Typical Jane. It sounded unsympathetic, but it wasn't. Not really. She was a woman who could have faced any amount of physical danger without flinching, but the shadows in the mind terrified her.

Manning moved across to the fireplace. On the way he noticed the letter and picked it up again, wondering once more who would have written to this address. There were no outstanding bills. Everybody knew he was at the club. He began to open it, thinking he should probably ask the builder to do something about the dent in the wall where the vase had struck. Inside the envelope, instead of the expected sheet of paper, was a newspaper cutting. He turned it the right way up and read:

THE CULT OF THE CLITORIS

To be a member of Maud Allen's private performance in Oscar Wilde's *Salome* one has to apply to a Miss Valetta, of 9 Duke Street, Adelphi, WC. If Scotland Yard were to seize the list of these members I have no doubt they would secure the names of several thousand of the first 47,000.

He'd seen the paragraph before. It had been reproduced – usually without the heading – in several respectable newspapers, though it had originated in the *Vigilante*, Pemberton Billing's dreadful rag. Maud Allan – they hadn't even spelt her name right – was sueing Pemberton Billing for libel. A grave mistake, in Manning's view, because once in the witness-box Pemberton Billing could accuse anybody with complete impunity. He would be immune from prosecution. The people he named would not. Of course you could see it from Maud Allan's point of view. She would be ruined if she didn't sue. She was probably ruined anyway.

The question was, why had it been sent to him, and by whom? The postmark told him nothing useful. There was no covering letter. Manning dropped the cutting on the sofa, then picked it up again, holding the flimsy yellowing page between his thumb and forefinger. He wiped his upper lip on the back of his hand. Then he turned to the mirror as if to consult himself and, because he'd left the drawing-room door open, found himself looking into a labyrinth of repeated figures. His name was on that list. He was going to *Salome*, and not simply as an ordinary member of the public, but in the company of Robert Ross who, as Oscar Wilde's literary executor, had authorized the performance.

Immediately he began to ask himself whether there was an honourable way out, but then he thought, no, that's no use. To back out now would simply reveal the extent of his fear to to to . . . to whoever was watching. For obviously somebody was. Somebody had known to send the cutting here.

Prior worked in the Intelligence Unit with Major Lode. Perhaps that had something to do with it? He didn't know. He didn't know anything, that was the devil of it.

The bell rang. Still holding the page, Manning went to the door. A thin, spry, greying man, with rheumy blue eyes and 'a top o' the morning to you, sorr' expression, stood on the step.

'Captain Manning?' He took off his cap. 'O'Brien, sir. I've come about the repairs.'

Manning became aware that he was gaping. He swallowed, pushed the cutting into his tunic pocket, and said, 'Yes, of course. Come in.'

He showed O'Brien the crack in the wall, feeling almost too dazed to follow what he was saying. He made himself concentrate. It was a load-bearing wall.

'How long do you think it'll take?'

O'Brien pursed his lips. 'Three days. *Normally*. Trouble is, you see, sir, you can't get the lads. Williams now.' O'Brien shook his head sadly. 'Good worker in his day. The nipper. Willing lad. Not forward for his age. Samuels.' O'Brien tapped his chest. 'Dust gets on his lungs.'

'How long?'

'Fortnight? Three weeks?'

'When can you start?'

'Any time, sir. Would Monday suit you?'

It had to be said O'Brien was a man who inspired instant mistrust. I hope I'm doing the right thing, Manning thought, showing him to the door. He went back to look at the crack again. In the course of exploring its load-bearing properties O'Brien had dislodged a great quantity of plaster. Manning looked down at the grey dust. He was beginning to suspect O'Brien's real talent might be for demolition. Oh, what does it matter, he thought. His fingers closed round the cutting and he brought it out again. He'd remembered that, a couple of months ago, when the article about the Black Book and the 47,000 had first appeared, Robert Ross had been sent a copy. Just like this. Anonymously. No covering letter. He walked to the window and looked into the garden. There was a curious tension about this yellow light, as if there might be thunder in the offing. And the bushes – all overgrown, there'd been no proper pruning done for years – were motionless, except for the very tips of their branches that twitched ominously, like cats' tails. A few drops of rain began to fall, splashing on to the dusty terrace. A memory struggled to surface. Of sitting somewhere in the dust and rain beginning to fall. Drops had splashed on to his face and hands and he'd started to cry, but tentatively, not sure if this was the right response. And then a nursery maid came running and swept him up.

He'd ask Ross tonight whether he'd received a cutting, or knew of anybody else who had. Not that it would be reassuring. Ross was a dangerous person to know, and would become more dangerous as the hysteria over the Pemberton Billing case mounted. The prudent thing would be to drop him altogether. Somehow, articulating this clearly for the first time helped enormously. Of course he wasn't going to drop Ross. Of course he was going to *Salome*. It was a question of courage in the end.

Why to the house? Anybody who knew him well enough to know his name would be on the list of subscribers must also know he was staying at his club. But then perhaps they also knew he visited the house regularly, to check that everything was all right, and . . . other things.

He mustn't fall into the trap of overestimating what they knew. At the moment he was doing their job for them.

Opening the letter like this in his own home was in some ways a worse experience than opening it at the club would have been. His damaged house leaked memories of Jane and the children, and of himself too, as he had been before the war, memories so vivid in comparison with his present depleted self that he found himself moving between pieces of shrouded furniture like his own ghost.

There was nothing to be gained by brooding like this. He made sure the fallen plaster was caught on the dust-sheet and had not seeped underneath to be trodden into the carpet, shuttered the windows, replaced the photograph beneath the dust-sheet, and let himself out.

Rain was falling. As he left the square and started to walk briskly down the Bayswater Road, reflections of buildings and shadows of people shone fuzzily in the pavements, as if another city lay trapped beneath the patina of water and grease. He kept his head down, thinking he would go to see Ross tonight, and remembering too that he was due to see Rivers next week. He passed the Lancaster Gate underground with its breath of warm air, and walked on.

In Oxford Street a horse had fallen between the shafts of a van and was struggling feebly to get to its feet. The usual knot of bystanders had gathered. He was going to be *all right*. He was . . .

Suddenly, the full force of the intrusion into his home struck at him, and he was cowering on the pavement of Oxford Street as if a seventy-hour bombardment were going on. He pretended to look in a shop window, but he didn't see anything. The sensation was extraordinary, one of the worst attacks he'd ever had. Like being naked, high up on a ledge, somewhere, in full light, with beneath him only jeering voices and millions of eyes.

THREE

Prior sat in the visitors' waiting-room at Aylesbury Prison, right foot resting on his left knee, hands clasping his ankle, and stared around him. The shabbiness of this room was in marked contrast to the brutal but impressive blood-and-bandages façade of the prison, though the shabbiness too was designed to intimidate. Everything – the chipped green paint, the scuffed no-colour floor, the nailed-down chairs – implied that those who visited criminals were probably criminals themselves. A notice on the wall informed them of the conditions under which they might be searched.

Prior looked down at his greatcoat and flicked away an imaginary speck of dust. This was not the battered and stained garment that Myra had so foolishly refused to lie on, but an altogether superior version which had cost two months' salary. In these circumstances, it was worth every penny.

The door opened and the wardress came in. With very slightly exaggerated courtesy, Prior rose to his feet. Sad but true, that nothing puts a woman in her place more effectively than a chivalrous gesture performed in a certain manner.

'Yes, well, it does seem to be in order,' she said.

He nodded. 'Good.'

'If you'd like to come this way.'

He reached the door first and held it open. He wasn't inclined to waste sympathy on her, this middle-aged, doughy-skinned woman. She had her own power, after all, more absolute than any *he* possessed. If she were humiliated now, no doubt some clapped-out old whore would be made to pay.

He followed her down the corridor and out into the yard.

'That's the women's block,' she said, pointing.

A gloomy, massive building. Six rows of windows, small and close together, like little piggy eyes. Prior looked at the yard. 'But surely the men can see the women when they exercise?'

'Oh, no,' she said. 'They can't see out of the windows. They're too high up for that.'

He asked her one or two questions about the way the prison was run, how the shift system worked, whether transport to the prison was provided. It had occurred to him that it might not be some anonymous whore who paid for his victory, but the woman he had come to see, and he was anxious to avoid that. 'Shift working must be quite difficult,' he said. 'Particularly for women.'

They stood in the cold yard while he got the story of her ailing mother. Then he held the door of the women's block open for her, and this time she blushed instead of bridling, since the gesture was being offered in a different spirit. Or she thought it was.

Another corridor. 'I know this is terribly irregular,' he said. 'A man seeing a female prisoner alone. But you do understand, don't you? It *is* a matter of *security* . . .'

'Oh, yes, yes. The only reason I questioned it was her being confined to the cell. We know all about security. We've had a leader of the Irish rebellion in *here*.' An internal struggle, then she burst out, 'She was a *countess*.'

Her face lit up with all the awe and deference of which the English working class is capable. Oh dear oh dear.

'Roper's a different kettle of fish,' she went on. 'Common as muck.'

They went through another set of doors and into a large hall. Prior would have liked some warning of this. He'd expected another corridor, another room. Instead he found himself standing at the bottom of what felt like a pit. The high walls were ringed with three tiers of iron landings, studded by iron doors, linked by iron staircases. In the centre of the pit sat a wardress who, simply by looking up, could observe every door. Prior's escort went across and spoke to her colleague.

Prior looked around him, wondering what sort of women needed to be kept in a place like this. Prostitutes, thieves, girls who 'overlaid' their babies, abortionists who stuck their knitting needles into something vital – did they really need to be here? A bell rang. Behind him the doors opened and a dozen or so women trudged into the room, diverging into two lines as they reached the stairs to the first landing. They wore identical grey smocks that covered them from neck to ankle and blended with the iron grey of the landings, so that the women looked like columns of moving metal. Evidently they were not allowed to speak, and for a while there was no sound except for the clatter of their boots on the stairs, and a chorus of coughs.

Then a youngish woman turned her head and noticed him. Instantly, a stir of excitement ran along the lines, like the rise of hair along a dog's spine. They broke ranks and came crowding to the railings, shouting down comments on what they could see, and speculations on the size of what they couldn't. Somebody suggested he might like to settle the matter by getting it out. Then a short square-headed woman jostled her way to the front and lifted her smock to her shoulders, high enough for it to become apparent that His Majesty's bounty did not extend to the provision of knickers. She jabbed her finger repeatedly towards the mound of thinning hair. Then a whistle blew, wardresses came running, and the women were hustled back into line. The tramp of feet started again, and soon the landings were empty and silent, except for the banging of doors and the rattle of keys in locks. The entire incident had taken less than three minutes.

Prior's wardress came back. 'That's a relief,' he said. 'I was beginning to feel like a pork chop in a famine.'

This did not go down well. 'Roper's on the top landing,' she said.

Their boots clanged on the stairs. Looking down now at the empty landings, Prior was puzzled by a sense of familiarity that he couldn't place. Then he remembered. It was like the trenches. No Man's Land seen through a periscope, an apparently empty landscape which in fact held thousands of men. That misleading emptiness had always struck him as uncanny. Even now, as he tramped along the third landing, he felt the prickle of hair in the nape of his neck.

The wardress stopped outside No. 39. She bent and peered through the peephole before unlocking the door. 'Here you are,' she said. 'I'm afraid I'll have to lock you in. When you're finished just bang on the door. I'll be along at the end. Good loud bang, mind.' She hesitated. 'She's been on hunger strike. You'll find her quite weak.'

He followed the wardress into the room. It seemed very dark, though a small, high, barred window set into the far wall let in a shaft of light. The reflection of the bars was black on the floor, then suddenly faded, as a wisp of cloud drifted across the sun. As his eyes became accustomed to the dark, he saw a grey figure huddled on the plank bed, one skinny arm thrown across its face. Apart from the bed, the only other furnishing was a bucket, smelling powerfully of urine and faeces.

'Roper?'

The figure on the bed neither moved nor spoke.

'This is Lieutenant Prior. He's come to talk to you.'

Still no response. For a moment he thought she was dead, and he'd arrived too late. He said, 'I'm from the Ministry of Munitions.'

Her face remained hidden. 'Then you'd better bugger off back there, then, hadn't you?'

The wardress clicked her tongue. 'I'll leave you to it,' she said. She glanced round the bare cell. 'Do you want a chair?'

'No, I can manage.'

'He'll not be stopping long enough to need a chair.'

The door banged shut. He listened for the sound of retreating footsteps. He walked closer to the bed. 'You know, if you co-operate, there could be a chance of remission.'

Silence.

'That's if you give us the information we need.'

Her eyes stayed shut. 'I've told *you* once already. Bugger off back to London you greasy, arse-licking little sod.'

At last he heard the clump of boots on the landing. 'Prison hasn't done much for your language has it, Beattie?'

Her eyes opened. He moved so that the light from the window fell directly on to his face.

'Billy?'

He went closer. She looked him up and down, even touched his sleeve, while a whole army of conflicting emotions fought for possession of her face. She settled for the simplest. Hatred of the uniform. 'Your dad must be turning in his grave.'

'Well, I expect he would be if he was *in* it. He isn't, he's alive and kicking. My mother, mainly.' She'd never liked him to talk about his father's treatment of his mother. Now, with that remark, they were back in Tite Street, in the room behind the shop, beef stew and dumplings simmering on the stove, Hettie peering into the mirror above the mantelpiece, tweaking curls on to her forehead. Before the sense of intimacy could be lost, he went and sat on the end of her bed, and she shifted a little to make room for him. 'You'll never guess what *I*'ve just seen,' he said in the same gossipy tone, and lifted an imaginary smock above his head.

Her face lit up with amusement. 'Mad Mary,' she said. 'Eeh, dear me, everybody sees that, chaplain, governor. I says, "Put it away, Mary, it's going bald." But you can't reason with her, she's away to the woods is that one, but you'd be surprised how many are. There's women in here should *never*'ve been sent to prison. They need help. Hey, and we've had a countess, an Irish rebel, I met her in the yard. She says, "You're the woman who tried to kill Lloyd George. Let me shake your hand." I says, "Well, it's very kind of you, love, but I didn't."'

'Didn't you?'

''Course I bloody didn't.' She stared at him. 'Did I try to kill Lloyd George by sticking a curare-tipped blowdart in his arse? No. I. did. not. Now if you're asking, "Suppose you *had* a curare-tipped blowdart and Lloyd George's arse was just here, would you stick it in?" 'course I bloody would, because there'll be no peace while that bugger's in power.'

Prior shook his head. 'You can't fasten it on to *one* person like that.'

'Can't you? *I* can.'

'I don't see how you can derive that from a Marxist analysis.'

'Bugger Marxist analysis, I hate the sod.'

He waited. 'Enough to kill him?'

'Yes, enough to kill him! And I wouldn't feel guilty about it either. Any more than he feels guilty about the millions and millions of young lives he's chucked away.' She fell back, her mouth working. 'I'm not your milk-and-water, creeping Jesus sort of pacifist.'

'It might've been better if you hadn't said all that in court.'

'I told the *truth* in court. The truth, the whole truth, and nothing but the truth.' She laughed. 'Bloody fatal, that was. Do you know, Billy, I've seen the time I could con anybody into anything, when I was a young woman. Now they ask me a simple question and the truth pours out.' She shook her head. 'It's mixing with bloody Quakers, that's what's done it. Good Christian company's been the ruin of me.'

'So you didn't plan to kill him?'

'The poison was for the dogs.'

She hitched herself up the bed and propped her head against the wall. It was possible in this position to see how emaciated she was, how waxy her skin. Her hair, which had been brown the last time he saw her, was now almost entirely white. Thin strands escaped from the bun at the back of her head and straggled about her neck. He started to speak, but she interrupted him. 'What are you here for, Billy?'

'To help you.'

She smiled. 'So what was all that about information?'

'I had to say that. She was listening.'

'But you *are* from the Ministry of Munitions?'

''Course I am. How do you think I got in? Doesn't mean I'm here for information, does it?' He leant forward. 'Think about it, Beattie. What information have you *got*?'

She bridled. 'You'd be surprised. People coming in and out.' Then she pulled a face. 'Actually, there's not that many politicals in here. They're all on about their fannies. You lose patience.'

'I want you to tell me what happened.'

'You mean you don't know?'

'I haven't got a transcript of the trial.'

'Haven't you? You do surprise me. Why don't you go and talk to Spragge?'

'I will. I want your version first, because I haven't heard your version.' He waited. 'Look, Beattie, whatever damage was done was done at the trial. I'm not asking you to name any names that didn't come out then.'

She brooded for a moment. 'You know Tommy Blenkinsop's dead?'

'Tommy –'

'The deserter I had stopping with me. Hettie had gone away to live, you know, she was teaching over at Middleton, so I had this spare room, and I said I'd put Tommy up. Eeh, poor little Tommy, eleven kids, and do you know to look at him you wouldn't've thought he had a fuck in him? He says to me, "You know, Beattie, I only joined up for a bit of peace." Poor lad. Anyway, that night we were sat over the fire, Tommy and me, and there was this knock on the door, and I says to Tommy, "You go on upstairs, love." I answered it and there was . . .' She sighed, looking into the distance. 'Spragge. Rain pouring off him, it was a terrible night. And he said he had a letter from Mac, so of course I asked him to come in. I've had time to think since then. It was *Mac* he was after. *He* was the big fish, we just got caught in the net. And the letter was genuine enough, he'd took Mac in as well as me, so he must've been convincing, mustn't he? Anyway, he explained he was on his way to Liverpool, and he says, "Can you put me up?" and I says, "Well, no, not really." And then I thought, we-ell, and I says, "Unless you don't mind sharing a bed," and I told him about Tommy. "Is he of the homogenic persuasion?" he says. Well, I just looked at him. I says, "No, I shouldn't think so, he's got eleven kids, do you want the bed or not?" So he decided he was stopping and we sat down round the table, and after a while he notices the photograph of our William on the mantelpiece. I don't know whether he knew about our William, I think he must've done, though, because he kept bringing the conversation round, and saying what a fine lad he was and all that. And you know I was worried sick about our William, because I knew what was going on, you see, he'd managed to get a letter smuggled out.'

'What *was* going on?'

'Well. You see, William didn't get exemption. He . . . Partly he was unlucky with the Board, but you know they don't like *moral* objectors anyway. If you're religious – doesn't matter how batty it is – you can say you've got the Holy Spirit in a jamjar on the mantelpiece – that's all right, that's *fine*. If you say, "I think it's morally wrong for young men to be sent out to slaughter each other," God help you. The Chairman of the Board actually said to our William, "You can't be a *conscientious* objector because you don't believe in God, and people who don't believe in God don't have consciences." That was the level of it. Anyway, if you're refused exemption you get handed over to the army. The military police show up and take you off to the barracks and you get given your first order, generally, "Get stripped off and put the uniform on." And of course the lads refuse, and then it's the detention centre. Our William was sent to Wandsworth, and it was really tough. He was stripped and put in a cell with a stone floor and no glass in the window – this is *January*, mind – and then, he says, they just put a uniform beside you and they wait to see how long it'll take you to give in. Of course I was worried sick, I thought he was going to get pneumonia, but actually he said in his letter it wasn't the cold that bothered him, it was being *watched* all the time. The eye in the door.' She laughed. 'I didn't know what he meant.'

She looked past Prior's shoulder, and he turned to follow her gaze. He found himself looking at an elaborately painted eye. The peephole formed the pupil, but around this someone had taken the time and trouble to paint a veined iris, an eyewhite, eyelashes and a lid. This eye, where no eye should have been, was deeply disturbing to Prior. For a moment he was back in France, looking at Towers's eyeball in the palm of his hand. He blinked the image away. 'That's horrible,' he said, turning back to Beattie.

''S not so bad long as it stays in the door.' She tapped the side of her head. 'You start worrying when it gets in here.'

'Anyway, go on. He was talking about William.'

'Yes, he kept bringing the conversation round, and of course I was worried, and out it all came. It wasn't just our William that was bothering me, it was all of them.'

'All the conchies?'

'You know I don't mean that.'

No, he thought. She was one of those who felt every death. She'd never learnt to read the casualty lists over breakfast and then go off and have a perfectly pleasant day, as the vast majority of civilians did. If she had learnt to do that, she mightn't have been here. 'Go on,' he said.

'He could see I was getting upset and he says, "Why don't we have a drink?" Well, money was a bit tight, you know, with feeding Tommy as well, but he says, "Don't you worry, love, this one's on me." And he went into the scullery and came back with two bloody great big jugs, and off he went. Eeh, special brew. Well, you know me, Billy, two glasses of that, he was me long-lost brother, and I did, I *talked*, I played me mouth. I cussed Lloyd George, I cussed the King, I don't know what bugger I didn't cuss, but I was *lonely*, Billy. I'd had nobody to talk to except Tommy for months, and *he* was no company, poor little bugger, his nerves were gone. And of course at the trial it all got twisted. He said I kept dropping hints Lloyd George was going to die. I can remember exactly what I said. I says, "That bloody, buggering bastard Lloyd George, he's got a head on him like a forty-shilling pisspot, but you mark my words he'll come to rue." There. That was it. That was *the death threat*.' She shook her head. 'It was nowt of the sort. Anyway we were half way down the second jug – or I was – and he says, "Can I trust you?" I says, "Well, you're in a pretty pickle if you can't." And then he starts telling me about this detention centre where the regime was very bad. Worse than Wandsworth. And you know all the stuff he was telling me was stuff *I'd* told *him*, about being naked in the cells and all that, but I was too daft to see it. And then he says, him and some of his mates had found a way to get the lads out. They had a contact inside the centre, one of the guards it was supposed to be. But, he says, the problem was the dogs. They had these dogs patrolling the perimeter fence. I says, "Well, *poison*." He says, well, yes, but there was a problem about that. It had to look like an outside job because of the guard. You see, they didn't want the detention centre to twig about *him*. So I says, "Curare."'

'Fired through the fence in a blowdart?'

'Yes.'

'Fired *at the dogs*?'

'Yes.'

'Of course,' Prior said, 'you do realize, don't you, a lot of people wouldn't know about curare?'

For the first time she looked uneasy. 'Yes, well, I read about it in a book on South America, and then I happened to mention it to Alf – our Winnie's husband – and he says, "Oh, yes, we've got some of that in the lab." That's the only way I knew about it.'

'No previous thoughts of killing Lloyd George? They said at the trial you'd plotted to kill him before, when you were in the suffragettes.'

'The suffragettes *never* threatened human life. That was a point of honour: property, not life. It just shows Spragge's ignorance, does that. Couldn't even think up a convincing lie.'

'He seems to have convinced the jury.'

'You know what was going on there as well as I do. You put a pacifist – any pacifist – in the dock – could be Jesus Christ – and the biggest rogue unhung in the witness-box, and who do you think they're gunna believe?'

'What did he say when you mentioned curare?'

'He says, yes, but how on earth was he going to get his hands on that? I says I knew where to get it, but it was too risky. And then he says if I helped him, he'd help me. He'd get little Tommy across to Ireland, and that clinched it for me, because you know Tommy was getting really weird. I mean, to be honest, I thought if I didn't get him out I was gunna have a loony on me hands, like Lily Braithwaite's husband. You know what a state *he* was in when he come back.'

'So you agreed to get the curare?'

'Yes, he give me an address and told me to write to him when I got it. I wrote to our Winnie's Alf, and he mentioned dogs in his letter back to me, but that letter was never produced, I think it slipped down a crack in the pavement. And Alf said, yes, he'd get it. He works in a big medical laboratory, and he had to sign for the poison. But he wasn't worried, see, because the dogs'd be dying at the other end of the country and nobody would make the connection. But can you imagine him signing his name like that if he'd thought it was for Lloyd George?'

'Then what?'

'I waited. The post seemed to take such a long time, but of course unbeknownst to us all the letters were being opened. The parcel was opened. And then when it was finally delivered the police were on the doorstep in a matter of minutes. And I was charged with conspiracy to murder Lloyd George, *and others*. That's the other thing they dropped. It wasn't just Lloyd George they were on about. To begin with it was *hundreds* of people I was supposed to be plotting to kill. And, of course, all I could say was, "The poison was for the dogs," but I couldn't prove it, it was Spragge's word against mine, and *he* was working for the bloody Ministry of Munitions. Oh, and the trial. You know he read all the letters out in court?'

'Smith did?'

'Yeh, Smith. The Attorney-General. Oh, I was honoured, they wheeled out all the big guns. And he read me letters out in court, about Winnie's period being late and all that. And you know he read the words the way I'd wrote them. Just to get a laugh out of me, because I can't spell, I never have been able to. But I wonder how good *his* spelling'd be, if he'd left school when he was eight?'

'He shouldn't've done that.'

'I was fair game. Language too. He couldn't get over the language, this dreadful, coarse, lewd, vulgar, low woman who kept using all these words his dear little wifie didn't even know. *I'll bet*.'

Prior sat back against the wall. He was finding the eye in the door difficult to cope with. Facing it was intolerable, because you could never be sure if there were a human eye at the centre of the painted eye. Sitting with his back to it was worse, since there's nothing more alarming than being watched from behind. And when he sat sideways, he had the irritating impression of somebody perpetually trying to attract his attention. It tired him, and if it tired *him* after less than an hour, what must it have done to Beattie, who'd had to endure it for over a year? He noticed that the latrine bucket had been placed where it could be seen from the door. 'Why's the bucket there?' he asked.

'Because some poor bloody cow drowned herself in her own piss.'

'My God.' He stared at her. 'You're not as bad as that, are you?'

'No, I keep going. Trouble is, you're punished if you go on hunger strike, so I can't have any visitors. I haven't seen our Hettie for . . . oh, I don't know, it must be two months.'

'I'll see what I can do.'

'That's what Spragge said. When I told him about not being able to get Tommy across to Ireland, he says, "I'll see what I can do."'

'The difference is I'm not asking for anything back.'

She touched his sleeve. 'We were close once, Billy. You were like a son to me.' She waited. 'I'm not going to ask whose side you're on because you mightn't tell me the truth, and if you did, I wouldn't believe you. But just tell me this. Do you *know* whose side you're on?'

He looked at her and smiled, but didn't reply.

FOUR

The Ministry of Munitions was housed in the Hotel Metropole. The reception desk, now guarded by armed police, had once been manned by smooth-faced young men, trained not to look surprised when the sixth couple in succession turned out to be called Smith, or when prosperous-looking gentlemen, entertaining their curiously unprosperous-looking nephews, requested a double room. No such innocent frolics now, Prior thought, crossing the foyer. Goodness how the moral tone had declined.

On the third floor he tapped on Major Lode's door. Lode looked up from the file he was reading, dabbing, as he always did when confronted by a new situation, at the outer corners of his large, silky, red-gold moustache. In defiance of biology, Prior saw this moustache as a *feminine* adornment: perhaps because it seemed to require so much protection from the outside world.

'How did it go?' Lode asked.

'Quite well, I think. She was . . . fairly hostile to begin with, but I think towards the end she was starting to open up.'

'Did you mention MacDowell?'

'Only in passing. I thought it better not to . . . focus on him.'

'Hmm, yes, quite right. So what's the next step?'

'I'd like to see Hettie Roper. The younger daughter. You remember she was walking out with MacDowell?'

Lode smiled. 'Walking out? Yes. I was just thinking, what a quaint expression. But I thought that was over? That's what she told the police.'

'I don't believe it. They were too close.'

'Yes, well, do what you need to do. Good.'

And now, Prior thought, closing the door quietly behind him, you can fumigate your fucking office. 'What a quaint expression.' *I could buy and sell you*, he told the closed door. Lode had *no idea*. He'd spent his entire adult life – boyhood too, for that matter – in uniformed, disciplined, hierarchical institutions, and he simply couldn't conceive of the possibility that other people might function differently. It was all a great big chessboard to him. This rag-bag collection of Quakers, socialists, anarchists, suffragettes, syndicalists, Seventh Day Adventists and God knows who else was merely an elaborate disguise, behind which lurked the real anti-war movement, a secret, disciplined, highly efficient organization dedicated to the overthrow of the state as surely and simply as Lode was dedicated to its preservation. And on the other side of the board, at the head of the opposing army, elusive, tenacious, dangerous: the Black King himself, Patrick MacDowell. It wasn't complete nonsense, of course. Mac was certainly a more effective opponent of the war than most, if only because he was not in love with suffering. Poor Mac, he'd had enough of that by the time he was ten.

Prior walked down the corridor to his own room, tiny in comparison with Lode's, hardly more than a cupboard. Evidently, in pre-war days this room had been reserved for those obliged to sin on a budget. He felt dirty, physically dirty, after the long train journey, and when he looked into the small glass above the washbasin he saw that his face was covered in smuts. He washed as much of himself as he could reach without undressing, and then began searching through the filing cabinet. He'd made a list of a number of files that contained reports from Lionel Spragge, and it took him only a few moments to gather them together and dump them on his desk. He had an hour to read through them before Spragge arrived. Spragge had been reluctant to come to the Ministry at all, suggesting they should meet outside, at some pub or other, but Prior had wanted this first meeting to be on his own ground.

He'd read the reports several times already, so it was merely a matter of refreshing his memory. When he came to Beattie's file, to Spragge's reports on the Roper affair and then to his deposition, he read more slowly. After a while he looked up, puzzled by the sense of something unfamiliar in the room. He stared round him, but could see nothing different, and then he realized that the change was in himself. He had not been angry until now.

LIONEL ARTHUR MORTIMER SPRAGGE
on his oath saith as follows:

2 February 1917. I am employed at the Ministry of Munitions. I entered the employ of the Ministry on 1 July 1916. I have been engaged making certain inquiries concerning various organizations amongst others the Independent Labour Party and the No Conscription fellowship. I reported to Major Lode. He was the officer from whom I chiefly got my directions.

Between October and December 1916 I was sent to Liverpool to make inquiries concerning one Patrick MacDowell. He had been the leading organizer of the Sheffield strike in the Munitions factories. I told MacDowell I wanted to go to the Manchester area. MacDowell gave me a letter to give to Mrs Beatrice Roper. On the night of I think the 23rd December I went to Mrs Roper's shop, at 11 Tite Street, Salford, and gave her the letter. After reading the letter Mrs Roper agreed that I could stay with her and we shook hands very heartily indeed. She sat at one end of the table, and I sat next to her. There was another man staying in the house at the time who was introduced to me as Tommy Blenkinsop, a deserter. He did not come downstairs until later. Mrs Roper asked me about myself. I told her I had been refused exemption and that I had been on the run since September as a moral objector. I told her about being locked up in a detention centre and I think I told her something of the treatment I had received there. At that she said, 'That is just like my William,' and she got up and fetched a photograph from the dresser. It was a small photograph of her son, William Roper. As she was showing me the photograph she told me that before the war she had been active in the suffragettes and that she had burnt down a church. I think her exact words were, 'You know about St Michael's? We were nearly copped, but we bloody well did it.' She laughed and said, 'You should have seen the flames go up.' She then said, 'And that was not all we did.' She told me she had been party to a plan to kill Mr Lloyd George, by inserting a curare-tipped nail through the sole of his boot in such a way that it would pierce the skin when he put his weight on the foot, causing instant lassitude followed by seizures. They had been planning to do this on the Isle of Wight where Mr Lloyd George was staying at that time. There was a waiter in his hotel sympathetic to the suffragette cause. I do not recollect the name of the hotel, or of the waiter. I asked her why the attempt had not succeeded. She replied, 'The bloody, shitting, buggering old sod pissed off to France, didn't he?' Mrs Roper's language was fairly good most of the time but when she spoke of Mr Lloyd George she used bad language. I then made diligent inquiries as to the nature of Mrs Roper's attitude to Mr Lloyd George. She several times expressed the opinion that he ought to be killed. I then asked her whether there was anybody else who ought to be killed and she replied, 'Yes, the other George, that poncing old git in the Palace, he'd not be missed.'

I then asked her whether this was all talk or whether some plan was afoot. She replied, 'Can I trust you?' I think I said something to the effect that she was in a pretty pickle if she could not. She then said that she knew where to get curare and that Walton Heath Golf-course would be a good place to get Mr Lloyd George with an air-gun. She said she knew three good lads in London who would do the job. She then asked me if I wanted to be in on it and I considered it my duty to reply in the affirmative in order to procure further information. I passed that night at Mrs Roper's house, and the following morning I reported back to Major Lode's department in code.

Spragge was a big, fleshy, floridly handsome man, with thick brows and startling blue-green eyes that slanted down at the outer corners. His neck and jowls had thickened, and rose from his broad shoulders in a single column. Hair sprouted from his ears, his nostrils, the cuffs of his shirt. He was as unmistakably and crudely potent as a goat. Beattie would have gone for him, Prior thought, as he stood up to shake hands. He wondered how he knew that, and why he should mind as much as he did.

'I asked you to come in,' Prior said, after Spragge had settled into his chair, 'because we're thinking of employing you again.' He watched the flare of hope. Spragge was less well turned out than he appeared to be at first sight. His suit was shiny with wear, his shirt cuffs frayed. 'You'll have gathered from the papers there's a lot of unrest in the munitions industry at the moment. Particularly in the north, where you spent a good deal of time, didn't you? In '16.'

'Yes, I –'

'With MacDowell. Who'd just come out of a detention centre, I believe?'

'Yes, he's a deserter. Conchie. You should see the size of him, for God's sake. Built like a brick shithouse. See some of the scraggy little buggers that get sent to France.' Spragge was looking distinctly nervous. 'I don't think I could approach him again. I mean, he knows me.'

'He knows you from the Roper case, doesn't he?'

'Before that.'

'You might be able to give advice, though. Obviously we'd need to keep you away from the areas you were working in before.'

Spragge looked relieved.

'You met MacDowell in the summer of '16? In Sheffield?'

'Yes, I was making inquiries into the shop stewards' movement.'

Prior made a show of consulting his notes. 'You stayed with Edward Carpenter?'

'I did.' Spragge leant forward, his florid face shining with sweat, and said in a sinister whisper, 'Carpenter is of the homogenic persuasion.'

'So I believe.' That phrase again. It had stuck in Beattie's memory, and no wonder. It was transparently obvious that Spragge's natural turn of phrase would have been something like 'fucking brown 'atter'. 'Of the homogenic persuasion' was Major Lode. Who had once told Prior in, of all places, the Café Royal, 'This country is being brought to its knees. *Not* by Germany' – here he'd thumped the table so hard that plates and cutlery had leapt into the air – 'NOT BY GERMANY, but by an unholy alliance of socialists, sodomites and shop stewards.' Prior had felt scarcely able to comment, never having been a shop steward. 'Do you think that's relevant?'

'It was relevant to *me*. There was no lock on the door.'

'He *is* eighty, isn't he?' said Prior.

Spragge shifted inside his jacket. 'A vigorous eighty.'

'You went to a meeting, next day? Addressed by Carpenter.'

'I went with Carpenter.'

'And in the course of his speech he quoted a number of . . . well, what would you call them? Songs? Poems? In praise of homogenic love.'

'He did. In public.'

'Well, it was a public meeting, wasn't it? And then after the meeting you went into a smaller room, and there you were introduced to a number of people, including the author of these songs?'

'Yes.'

'Walt Whitman.'

'Yes.'

'Walt Whitman is an American poet.' Prior waited for Spragge's mouth to open. 'A *dead* American poet.'

'He didn't look well.'

'1819 to 1892.'

Spragge jerked his head. 'Yeh, well, it's the money, innit?'

'Is it?'

'I'll say it is. Two pound ten a week I was promised. Mind you, he says the information's got to be good and you've got to keep it coming.' Spragge sat back and snorted. 'Didn't matter how good it was, I never had two pound ten in my hand, not regular, just like that. Bonuses, yes. But what use are dribs and drabs like that to me? I'm a family man.'

'You got bonuses, did you?'

'Now and then.'

'That would be if you turned up something special?'

Spragge hesitated. 'Yes.'

'How big a bonus did you get for Beattie Roper?'

Spragge hesitated again, then clearly decided he had nothing to lose. 'Not big enough.'

'But you got one?'

'Yes.'

'All in one go?'

'Half on arrest, half on conviction.'

'You got a *bonus* if she was *convicted*?'

'Look, I know what you're after. You're saying I lied under oath. Well, I didn't. Do you think I'm gunna risk – what is it, five years – for a measly fifty quid? 'Course I'm bloody not. I'd have to be mad, wouldn't I?'

'Or in debt.'

Spragge blinked. 'Just because I lied about Walt Whitman doesn't mean I was lying all the time. That was the first report I wrote, I was desperate to get enough in.'

'You never talked about dogs to Mrs Roper?'

Spragge made an impatient gesture. 'What dogs? There weren't any fucking dogs. They're not *used* in detention centres. You might not know that, but she does. She's talked to men who've been in every detention centre in England. She *knows* there aren't any dogs.' He stared at Prior. 'Have you been talking to her?'

'I've interviewed her, yes.'

Spragge snorted. 'Well, all I can say is the old bitch's got you properly conned.'

'I haven't said I *believed* her.'

'She was *convicted*. It doesn't matter what you believe.'

'It matters a great deal, from the point of view of your job prospects.' Prior gave this time to sink in. 'The letter that came with the poison. From Mrs Roper's son-in-law.' He drew the file towards him. '"If you get close enough to the poor brutes, I pity them. Dead in twenty seconds."'

'All that proves is that the *son-in-law* thought it was for the dogs. Well, she'd have to tell him something, wouldn't she?'

'You still say she plotted to kill Lloyd George?'

'Yes.'

'And that the suggestion came from her, and not from you?'

'*Yes*. She didn't need any bloody encouragement!'

'Even to the details? Even to suggesting Walton Heath Golf-course as a good place to do it?'

'That's right.'

'How would she know that? She's spent her entire life in the back streets of Salford, how would *she* know where Lloyd George plays golf?'

Spragge shrugged. 'Read it in the paper? I don't suppose it's a state secret.' He leant forward. 'You know, you want to be careful. If you're saying I acted as an *agent provocateur* – and that *is* what you're saying, isn't it? – then you're also saying that Major Lode *employed* an *agent provocateur*. Either knowingly, in which case he's a rogue, or unknowingly, in which case he's a fool. Either way, it's not gunna do *his* career much good, is it? You watch yourself. You might find out it's your head on the chopping-block.'

Prior spread his hands. 'Who's talking about chopping-blocks? I'm interviewing a new agent – new to *me*. And I've made it clear – at least I *hope* I've made it clear – that any little flight of fancy – Walt Whitman rising from the dead – and I'll be on to it. If there *aren't* any flights of fancy, well then . . . no need to worry.' With the air of a man getting to the real purpose of the meeting at last, Prior drew another file towards him. 'Now tell me what you know about MacDowell.'

After he'd finished milking Spragge of information, all of which he knew already, and had sent him home to await the summons, Prior sat motionless for a while, his chin propped on his hands.

'The poison was for the dogs.'

'There weren't any fucking dogs. You might not know that, but she does.'

Was it possible Beattie had tried to reach out from her corner shop in Tite Street and kill the Prime Minister? The Beattie he'd known before the war would not have done that, but then that Beattie had been rooted in a communal life. Oh, she'd been considered odd – any woman in Tite Street who worked for the suffragettes was odd. But she hadn't been isolated. That came with the war.

Shortly after the outbreak of war, Miss Burton's little dog had gone missing. Miss Burton was a spinster who haunted the parish church, arranged flowers, sorted jumble, cherished a hopeless love for the vicar – how hopeless probably only Prior knew. He'd been at home at the time, waiting for orders to join his regiment, and he'd helped her search for the dog. They found it tied by a wire to the railway fence, in a buzzing cloud of black flies, disembowelled. It was a dachshund. One of the enemy.

In that climate Beattie had found the courage to be a pacifist. People stopped going to the shop. If it hadn't been for the allotment, the family would have starved. So many bricks came through the window they gave up having it mended and lived behind boards. Shit – canine and human – regularly plopped through the letter-box on to the carpet. In that isolation, in that semi-darkness, Beattie had sheltered deserters and later, after the passing of the Conscription Act, conscientious objectors who'd been refused exemption. Until one day, carrying a letter from Mac, Spragge had knocked on her door and uncovered a plot to assassinate the Prime Minister. Or so he said.

Could she have plotted to kill Lloyd George? Prior thought he understood how the powerless might begin to fancy themselves omnipotent. The badges of hopeless drudgery, the brush and the cooking-pot, become the flying broomstick and the cauldron, *and not only in the minds of the persecutors.* At first there would be only wild and flailing words, prophecies that Lloyd George would come to a dreadful end and then, nudged along by Spragge – because whatever Beattie's part in this, Spragge had not been innocent – the sudden determination to act out the fantasy: to destroy the man she blamed for prolonging the war and causing millions of deaths.

Lode would have had no difficulty in believing Spragge. The poison plot fitted in very neatly with his preconceptions about the anti-war movement. Not much grasp of reality in all this, Prior thought, on either side. He was used to thinking of politics in terms of conflicting interests, but what seemed to have happened here was less a conflict of interests than a disastrous meshing together of fantasies.

He began putting away the files. It was a situation where you had to hang on to the few certainties, and he was certain that Spragge had lied under oath, and since Spragge had been the only witness, this of itself meant the conviction was unsafe.

He locked the filing cabinet and the door of his room, and walked along to the end of the corridor. The lift was stuck on the fifth floor. He decided not to wait and ran downstairs, coming out on to the mezzanine landing where he paused and looked down into the foyer, as he often did, liking to imagine the hotel as it must have been before the war, before this drabness of black and khaki set in.

The shape of a head caught his attention. *Charles Manning*, waiting for the lift, and with him – good God – Winston Churchill and Edward Marsh. Prior watched. Manning, though obviously junior, seemed perfectly at ease in their company. Certainly he was not merely dancing attendance; there was a good deal of shared laughter, and, as they moved into the lift, Marsh's hand rested briefly on his shoulder. Well, well, well, Prior thought, continuing on his way downstairs. 'Connections' indeed!

Prior lived in a seedy basement flat in Bayswater. He could have afforded better, but he preferred to spend his money on properly tailored uniforms, and these did not come cheap. His bedroom had french windows that opened on to a small high-walled yard, so dark that he had never been tempted to sit out, though his landlady had made an effort. The walls were painted cream to a height of about ten feet, and there were a number of thin, straggly plants dying in a great variety of containers.

The room was small and L-shaped. His bed lay along the upright of the L, facing the window, with a desk and hard chair at the foot. The baseline of the L contained a wardrobe, with an oval mirror set into the door. There was space for nothing else.

The bathroom was next door. He had a tepid bath, and then, wrapped in his dressing-gown, lay on the bed and lit a cigarette. He was too tired to think constructively, and yet his mind whirred on. This was the frame of mind that led to a bad night, and it irritated him, almost to the point of tears, that he could do nothing about it.

He thought of Beattie in her cell. Eighteen months since Lionel Spragge knocked on her door. Eighteen months ago he'd been in

France. Eighteen months ago William Roper had been in Wandsworth Detention Centre. An image of William began to form in Prior's mind, tiny but powerful, like the initial letter of a gospel. William, naked in his cell, watched constantly through the eye in the door, and beside him, on the stone floor, the uniform he'd refused to put on. A small, high, barred window, lit with a bluish glow from the snow outside.

He found himself resenting the power of this image. The claim it made on his sympathy. Deliberately, he entered the cell and then let himself drift out of the window, between the bars, into the falling snow. He was in France now, lying out in the open with his platoon. The trenches had been blown flat, there was no shelter from the icy wind, no hope of getting the wounded back. And no water, because the water in the water-bottles had frozen. Once a hawk flew over, its shadow black against the snow. The only movement, the only life, in a landscape dead as the moon. Hour after hour of silence, and the snow falling. Then, abruptly, Sanderson's convulsed and screaming face, as they cut the puttees away from his frost-bitten legs.

This was no use. Prior sat up and started reading *The Times*, but the print blurred and Beattie's face took its place, the white hair straggling round her neck. He closed his eyes. The bell of the shop in Tite Street rang as he pushed the door open. How old? Four? Five? A smell of cat pee and tarred string from the bundles of firewood in the corner. Beattie's cat had never been able to resist marking those bundles. Mrs Thorpe plonked their Alfie on the counter while she paid her bill. Alfie swung his short legs in their sturdy boots, puffing away at a fag end, though he was only three. Between drags, he sucked his mother's breast, puffing and sucking alternately, peering round the white curve at Prior, who was a Big Boy and therefore an object of interest and suspicion. It was late in the afternoon. Mrs Thorpe would be far gone. Jugs of best bitter were her favourite, chased down by sips of something medicinal that she kept in a flask fastened to her thigh with a home-made elastic garter. Whisky for the heart, brandy for the lungs, gin for the bladder. Alfie, guzzling away at his mother's milk, looked contented, and well he might, since it could hardly have been less than 70 proof.

The past is a palimpsest, Prior thought. Early memories are always obscured by accumulations of later knowledge. He made himself walk to the counter again, this time remembering nothing but the moment, push his sweaty coin across the cool marble, and ask, 'What can I have for a ha'penny?'

There was a white apron round Beattie's waist with two pockets, stained black from the coins inside them. These coins smelled very strong when she emptied them on to the table to count them, a dark, dank, heavy smell.

'What can I have for a ha'penny?'

Beattie's voice, patient as if she hadn't said all this a million times before, reeled off the list: aniseed ball, sherbet delight, liquorice stick, a packet of thousand-and-ones, and finally – his favourite because it lasted so long – a gob-stopper.

Towers's eye lay in the palm of his hand. 'What am I supposed to do with this gob-stopper?' Logan's hand reached out, grasped his shaking wrist, and tipped the eye into the bag.

Don't think about it, he told himself. It was too late in the day to risk thinking about that.

He had no memory of Beattie's face. She'd been an object then, a mountain, the side of a house, vast, taken for granted, not a person to whom you could attach adjectives. Though he could attach them readily enough now: lively, opinionated, intelligent, uneducated, foul-mouthed, impulsive, generous, quick-tempered, kind. Prior's mother, his gentle and, it had to be said, *genteel* mother, hated Beattie Roper, though, when his mother became ill with suspected tuberculosis, it was to Beattie he'd been sent. That must have been his father's decision.

For almost a year, when he was five or six years old, he'd lived with Beattie and played with her two daughters, Winnie, who was now in Leeds Prison, and Hettie, who'd been charged with conspiracy to murder, but acquitted. He'd been the baby, when they played houses; the customer, when they played shops; the pupil, when they played schools; the patient, when they played nurses; and all these roles had been extremely boring, except, now and then, the role of patient.

They'd played under the big table in the kitchen, because its green tasselled cloth hanging down all round them made a separate world. Particularly on wash days, when the house was invaded by smells of soda, Dolly Blue and wet wool, and the wind blew grit in from the yard, the table was their refuge. Between the green tassels they looked out at adult boots coming and going, and felt a pleasant sense of power.

Mr Carker's boots. Mr Carker was secretary of the Independent Labour Party, and sometimes he and Beattie sat together at the table, discussing politics. These discussions had been, in every sense, above Prior's head, though he remembered one remark of Mr Carker's to the effect that the suffragettes simply exploited working-class women like Beattie. 'It's all very well, talking about sisterhood, but when *they* go home at night and drop their knickers, it's somebody else's job to pick them up.'

Probably it was the reference to dropping knickers that had made that particular remark stick in his mind. Perhaps it excited Mr Carker too, for shortly afterwards his boot crept along the floor and brushed against Beattie's foot. She moved her foot. The boot followed, accompanied this time by a hand on her knee, a hand that just lifted the green tassels. Prior looked round and saw Hettie's stricken face. It was a house with no father, and all the children, but particularly Hettie, were passionate in defence of their mother. For the first time in his life, perhaps, Prior was aware of another's pain. Stealthily, he reached out and tied Mr Carker's boot laces together, so that when, finally, he got up to go, he tripped and measured his full length on the floor.

The disciplining of children must have been the only subject on which Beattie held no advanced views. She'd hauled him out of his hiding place, tipped him over her knee and tanned his arse; and he'd clenched his teeth, divided between a blaze of joy that he was suffering for Hettie's sake, and regret that the suffering should not have taken a more dignified form.

Major Lode, interviewing him for his present post, had leant across the table and said, 'You see, you *know* these people, don't you?'

Prior took a last drag of his cigarette, leant over the edge of the bed and stubbed it out in the ashtray. *Yes.*

He drew the curtains and got inside the sheets. He was afraid to go to sleep, but he had learnt, from long experience, that to keep himself awake at night only to fall asleep shortly before dawn made for the worst nightmares of all. He lay and stared at the ceiling, unblinking, until his eyelids prickled, then rolled over on to his side and brought his knees up to his chin.

He was back in the winter landscape, with a sound like wind blowing, only it was not the wind, but the sound of emptiness. A hawk flew over and he watched its shadow on the snow. They were marching back. His boot went through thin ice into freezing mud. The ice meshed out round his foot, white opaque lines radiating out so that he stood at the centre of a frozen web.

The cold half woke him. He found his leg outside the covers and brought it back inside, but now his whole body was cold. He was lying naked on a stone floor. Because his sleep was light, he knew he was dreaming, and he knew also that he had to wake up before something worse happened. He turned and saw the eye watching him, an eye not painted but very much alive. The white glittered in the moonlight. The same noise of emptiness he'd heard in France had followed him into the cell. He stared at the eye, and then, by a supreme effort of will, forced himself to sit up.

Sweating and clammy, he reached down for his cigarettes, and remembered he'd left them on the desk. He got up and felt his way along, not wanting to switch on the light because the horror of the nightmare was heavy on him, and he was afraid of what the glare might reveal. He was standing by the desk, in the half-darkness, dabbing his hands among his papers, searching for the cigarette packet, when he heard a chuckle and spun round. The eye was watching him from the door. He shrank back against the table, his hands groping behind him for the paper-knife. His fingers closed round the hilt and he sprang at the door, stabbing the eye again and again, his naked body spattered with blood and some thick whitish fluid that did not drip but clung to his belly, and quickly chilled. Then, exhausted, he slipped to the floor and lay there, sobbing, and the sound of his sobbing woke him up.

At first he simply stared at the door. Only when he was sure there was no eye did he start to relax and take in the strangeness of his position. The fingertips of his right hand patted the cold oilcloth, as if by touching it he could make it turn into a mattress and sheets. No, he was out of bed, lying on the floor. Nightmare, he thought, drawing a deep breath. He started to pull himself up, feeling a wetness in his groin, and, as he did so, his splayed fingers touched the knife. So that had been real. With a spasm of revulsion, he struck out at it and sent it skittering across the floor.

FIVE

The aerodrome consisted of two runways and a straggle of low buildings set in one corner of a field.

Rivers and Dundas got out of the car and stood looking at the sky: clear, except for one bank of dark cloud away on the horizon.

'Good weather for it, anyway,' Dundas said.

It was possible to tell he was frightened, but only because Rivers had been observing him closely for weeks. Dundas suffered from abnormal reactions in the air. Where healthy pilots experienced no sensation at all, Dundas reported feeling his head squashed into his body, or a loss of movement in his legs. He suffered from nausea. More seriously still, he had more than once experienced the preliminary stages of a faint. After every physiological test possible had proved negative, he had been handed over to Rivers for psychological observation. Unfortunately, Rivers was making no progress. Dundas seemed to be exactly the sort of cheerful, likable, slightly irresponsible young man he'd grown accustomed to dealing with in the Royal Flying Corps. Apart from flying, his main interests were amateur dramatics, music and girls, not necessarily in that order. He appeared, in fact, to be entirely normal. Until he got into an aeroplane. And they were here to do just that.

'We seem to have arrived a bit early,' Dundas said. 'Would you like a cup of tea?'

The canteen was empty, except for a group of young fliers gathered round a table in the far corner, most of them in their twenties, one ginger-haired lad noticeably younger. Dundas went off to get the tea, and Rivers sat down at a table whose entire surface was covered with interlocking rings of tea stains. The young men were reading newspapers, chatting in a desultory fashion about the events of the day: the massive German advance, Maud Allan's libel action against Pemberton Billing, the cult of the clitoris. A dark-haired young man held up a photograph of Maud Allan. 'If she ever fancies anything bigger she's welcome to knock on my door.'

'She'd not notice the difference,' somebody said.

A good-natured scuffle. Then a new voice: 'Did you hear the one about Lord Albemarle? Went into the Turf, and said . . .' A desiccated, aristocratic bleat. '"Keep reading in the papers about this Greek chap, Clitoris. Anybody know who he is?"' They all laughed, the younger lad with braying anguish; it was immediately clear his confusion at least equalled Lord Albemarle's.

Dundas came back with the tea and two very greasy doughnuts.

'Not for me, thank you,' Rivers said, patting his stomach. 'I have to be careful.'

Dundas nodded uncomprehendingly. Obviously duodenal ulcers and having to be careful were a million miles away from his experience.

He ate both doughnuts with every sign of relish. Rivers sipped his tea and tried not to think that if Dundas's medical records were anything to go by (my God, they'd better be!) he could expect to see the doughnuts again before long.

They didn't talk much. Dundas was too tense, and Rivers respected his need for silence. When they'd finished, they walked across to the hangars together. Dundas disappeared inside the first hangar for a moment and came back carrying flying helmets, jackets and gauntlets. Rivers put a jacket on and followed Dundas across to the aeroplane.

'Here she is,' Dundas said, patting the fuselage. 'Terrible old bucket. Can't think why they've given us this one.'

Because it's the one they can best afford to lose, Rivers thought. He'd intended this reflection as a small private joke, but instead it brought him face to face with his own fear.

'Right,' Dundas said. 'If you'd like to hop in.'

Rivers climbed into the observer's seat and fastened the harness. Dundas bent over him to check the buckles. A faint smile acknowledged the reversal of the usual caring role. 'All right?' he said.

'Fine.'

'You've done a lot of flying, haven't you?'

'I don't know about a lot. Some.'

'But you've done spins and loops and things?'

'Yes.'

Dundas smiled. 'That's all right, then.'

Something about Dundas's smile held Rivers's attention. Suddenly, he felt certain Dundas was withholding something, even perhaps concealing it. Not malingering. In fact, rather the reverse. He thought Dundas might be minimizing his symptoms. It wasn't a good moment for that particular perception to strike.

Dundas pulled his helmet on, climbed in, exchanged a whole series of shouts and waves with the mechanics. The engine stuttered, began to roar, and then they were taxiing away from the hangar.

Rivers looked round him, at hedgerows thick with blossom, a sky tumultuous with rising larks; then he snapped his goggles into place, and the splendour contracted to a muddy pond.

He was now definitely afraid. The situation might almost be regarded as a small experiment, with himself as the subject. The healthy reaction to fear in a normal human being is the undertaking of some manipulative activity designed to avoid or neutralize the danger. Provided such activity is available, the individual ought to be unaware of feeling fear. But no such activity was available. Like every other man who sits in the observer's seat, he was entirely dependent on his pilot. And what a pilot. He had long believed that the essential factor in the production of war neurosis among the two most vulnerable groups, observers and trench soldiers, was the peculiarly passive, dependent and immobile nature of their experience. It isn't often that a hypothesis conceived in the scientist's cortex is confirmed by his gut, but his gut certainly seemed to be doing its best to prove this one. He bit his lips to control the pain and concentrated hard on the back of Dundas's head, at the wisps of reddish-gold hair escaping from beneath the helmet, the pink neck, the edge of white scarf, the brown leather of his flying jacket, scuffed and scarred with wear.

'ALL RIGHT?' Dundas yelled.

They had reached their take-off position. The engine raced. Rivers felt himself pushed hard back against the vibrating seat. The plane lifted, bumped, lifted again, and then climbed steeply away from the huddle of buildings.

He looked over the side, shielding his mouth from the wind. The countryside stretched below them, grey striations of lanes and roads, the glitter of a pond, great golden swathes of laburnum, a line of hedgerow white with blossom, blue smoke from a bonfire drifting across a field of green wheat.

A movement from Dundas brought him back to the task in hand. Dundas was making a spinning movement with his hand. The comforting roar of the engine faltered, then became an infuriated mosquito whine as the plane started to spin. Dundas's eyes were fixed on his instruments. Rivers watched the sun revolve in a great spiral round the falling plane. Abruptly, the sun vanished, and the green fields rushed up to meet them. Dundas pulled on the stick, but something was wrong. The horizon was tilted. Rivers leant forward and tilted his hand to the left. Slowly the horizon straightened.

Dundas had lost his sense of the horizontal. Already.

'HOW WAS IT?' Rivers yelled.

Dundas waved his hand in an incomprehensible gesture, then put one hand on top of his head and pressed repeatedly, indicating he'd felt his head being squashed into his body. He made the spinning movement again. Rivers shook his head and made a looping movement. After a moment's hesitation, Dundas's thumb went up.

The plane banked steeply as Dundas turned and made for the city. He was not meant to do this, and Rivers guessed he was trying to make the flight last as long as possible. In a short time he saw beneath him the sulphurous haze of London. This was the view seen by the German pilots as they came in on moonlit bombing raids, following the silver thread of the Thames, counting bridges, watching for the bulge of the Isle of Dogs.

Rivers tapped Dundas on the shoulder. Dundas turned round and nodded. So much of his face was hidden by the goggles it was impossible to read his expression. Rivers sat back and again concentrated on his own sensations. After the fifth loop he began to feel he was loose in his seat, a reaction he remembered from other flights and knew to be a frequent, though not universal, reaction of healthy fliers. They again came out with one wing down. Dundas leant over the side and retched, but didn't vomit. Rivers jerked his thumb at the ground, but Dundas ignored him.

With no idea at all now which manoeuvre to expect, Rivers sat back and tried to relax as the plane climbed. The vast blue haze of London fell away beneath the left wing-tip. Higher and colder. Wisps of cloud hid the sun; columns of shadows flitted rapidly across the city. Rivers felt calm, suddenly. There were worse ways to die, and he'd seen most of them.

Again the engine faltered, giving way to the mosquito whine as the plane began to fall. Dundas came out of the spin, white, giddy, confused and clearly finding it difficult to focus on his instruments. Rivers could see him peering at them. He yelled, 'DOWN!' and jerked his finger at the ground. Dundas leant out of the plane and was sick.

They had a bumpy landing, though not worse than many others Rivers had experienced. After the plane had taxied to a halt, Dundas stayed in his seat for a few moments before jumping down. He staggered slightly and held on to the wing. Rivers climbed down and immediately went up to him.

'I'm all right,' Dundas said, letting go of the wing.

Two mechanics were walking towards the plane. Dundas turned to them and made some comment on the flight. The three went into a huddle, and Rivers walked to one side. Dundas was smiling and talking cheerfully, but then Dundas was a very good actor.

When he came across to join Rivers, he said, 'Sorry about that.'

'Shall we go and sit down?'

Dundas looked towards the canteen, but shook his head. 'I think I'd just as soon get back, if you don't mind.'

Rivers's legs were trembling as they walked back to the car. He was angry with himself for getting into such a state – angry, ashamed and inclined to pretend he'd been less frightened than he knew he had been. He observed this reaction, thinking he was in the state of fatigue and illness that favours the development of an anxiety neurosis, and behaving in the way most likely to bring it about. He was doing exactly what he told his patients not to do: repressing the awareness of fear.

In the car going back to the hospital, Dundas examined his reactions minutely. During the first spin, in addition to the squashed head feeling, he'd felt sick. 'Not so much sick. More a sort of bulge in my throat. And then during the loop I felt really sick. And faint. The sky went dark.'

'And in the last spin?'

'That was terrible. I felt really confused.'

After leaving Dundas in the hospital entrance hall, Rivers went into his room and threw his cap and cane on to the chair. Henry Head came in a moment later. 'How was he?'

'Bad.'

'Sick?'

'And faint.'

'Are you all right?'

'No, I seem to be suffering from terminal stiff upper lip. You know the way I go on about not repressing fear? What did I do?' He spread his hands.

'It's the Public School Factor, Will. We're all too well trained.'

'It's the Silly Old Fool Factor. Too many young men around.'

Head smiled. 'No, well, I know what you mean. One doesn't want to seem *totally* decrepit.'

'I had this sudden sense that Dundas was hiding something. And that didn't –'

'He is.'

Rivers looked surprised.

'He's got a bottle of Bumstead's Gleet Cure in his locker.'

'Has he?'

'Sister Mitchell noticed it. Syphilis wouldn't make him go faint, mind.'

'Lying awake worrying about it might.' Rivers sat in silence for a moment. 'Well. Redirects the investigation a bit, doesn't it?'

'Makes it a helluva lot simpler.' Head dropped into a sergeant-major's baritone. '"Show us yer knob, lad." Are you coming to dinner?'

'Yes, and then I must dash. I'm supposed to be seeing somebody at eight.'

Rivers had the top floor of a large house near Hampstead Heath. The house was within a hundred yards of the great gun, and there were times when its proximity showed in every line of his face.

Prior arrived exactly on time, and was about to ring the bell when he saw Rivers walking rapidly up the hill.

'Have you rung?' Rivers asked, getting out his key.

'No, I saw you coming.'

Rivers opened the door and stood aside to let Prior in. Mrs Irving, Rivers's landlady, was hovering in the hall, wanting to complain about the Belgian refugees on the second floor whose failure to understand the extent of the food shortages was making her life a misery. When that subject was exhausted, there were the raids to be discussed. Wasn't it scandalous they'd been kept awake all night and not a word about it in *The Times*? Then there was her daughter, who'd been summoned back from France, ostensibly because her mother was ill, in fact because she was incapable of sorting out her servant problems. Girls kept leaving her employ on the flimsy excuse that they could earn five times as much in the munition factories. There was no accounting for modern girls, she said. And Frances was so *moody*.

At last Mrs Irving was called away, by Frances presumably, at any rate by a young woman with braided hair who gave Rivers a cool, amused, sympathetic smile before she closed the door of the drawing-room.

'I hope she's letting you live rent free,' Prior said.

They walked up the stairs together. Rivers paused on the second floor to look down into the garden. The laburnum, he said, was particularly fine. Prior didn't believe in this sudden interest in horticulture. The pause was to give him time to get his breath back. His chest was tighter than it had been on his last visit, and Rivers would have noticed that. Damn Rivers, he thought, knowing the response was utterly unfair. Whenever he needed Rivers he became angry with him, often to the point where he couldn't talk about what was worrying him. He mustn't let that happen tonight.

Normally Prior took a long time to get started, but this evening he was no sooner settled in his chair than he launched into an account of his visit to Mrs Roper. What emerged most vividly was the eye in the door. He reverted to this again and again, how elaborately painted it had been, even to the veins in the iris, how the latrine bucket had been placed within sight of it, how it was never possible to tell whether a human eye was looking through the painted one or not. It was clear from Prior's expression, from his whole demeanour, that he was seeing the eye as he spoke. Rivers was always sensitive to the signs of intense visualization in other people, since this was a capacity in which he himself was markedly deficient, a state of affairs which had once seemed simple and now seemed very complicated indeed. He switched his attention firmly back to Prior, asked a few questions about his previous relationship with Mrs Roper, then listened intently to his account of the nightmare. 'Whose eye was it?' he asked, when Prior had finished.

Prior shrugged. '*I* don't know. How should I know?'

'It's your dream.'

Prior drew a deep breath, reluctant to delve into a memory that could still make his stomach heave. 'I suppose Towers is the obvious connection.'

'Had you been thinking about that?'

'I remembered it when I was in the cell with Beattie. I . . . I actually saw it for a moment. Then later I remembered I used to go and buy gob-stoppers from Beattie's shop.' He paused. 'I don't know whether you remember, but when I picked up Towers's eye, I said, "What shall I do with this gob-stopper?"'

'I remember.'

A long silence.

Rivers said slowly, 'When one eye reminded you of the other, was that just the obvious connection? I mean, because they were both eyes?'

Prior produced one of his elaborate shrugs. 'I suppose so.'

Silence.

'I don't know. It *was* in the prison, but later . . . I don't know. I knew I was going to have a bad night. You you you just get to know the the feeling. I felt sorry for Beattie. And then I started thinking about William – that's the son – and . . . you know, naked in his cell, stone floor, snow outside . . .' He shook his head. 'It was . . . quite powerful, and I . . . I *think* I resented that. I resented having my sympathies manipulated. Because it's nothing, is it?' A burst of anger. '*I lost three men with frost-bite*. And so I started thinking about that, about those men and . . . It was a way of saying, "All right, William, your bum's numb. Tough luck." Though that's irrelevant, of course.' He smiled wryly. 'It isn't a suffering competition.'

'And then you thought about Towers?'

'Yes. But not in the same way as . . . as as the other men, I mean, I wasn't focusing on the horror of it. It was . . . I don't know.' He held out his hand to Rivers, palm upwards. 'A sort of talisman. Do you know what I mean? If *that* happens to you . . .' The outstretched hand started to shake. 'There's no possible room for doubt where your loyalties are.'

Prior looked down at his shaking hand, and seemed to become aware of it for the first time. He swallowed. 'Sorry, will you excuse me a moment?'

He crashed out of the room. Doors opened and closed as he tried to locate the bathroom. Rivers got up to help, then heard retching, followed by a gush of water, followed by more retching. Prior wouldn't want to be seen in that condition. He sat down again.

It was obviously his day to cope with people being sick.

He rested his chin on his clasped hands, and waited. It had taken two months' hard work at Craiglockhart to get Prior to the point where he remembered picking up Towers's eye, and even then he'd had to resort to hypnosis, something he always did with great reluctance. Prior had arrived at the hospital mute, rebellious, possibly the least co-operative patient Rivers had ever encountered, and with a very marked tendency to probe. To insist on a two-way relationship. He had accused Rivers of being merely 'a strip of empathic wallpaper' and asked him what the hell use he thought that was. Later this had became something of a joke between them, but the probing went on, combined with a sort of jeering flirtatiousness that had been surprisingly difficult to handle.

Prior's nightmares had been dreadful. He'd always insisted he couldn't remember them, though this had been obviously untrue. Eventually, he'd told Rivers in a tone of icy self-disgust that his dreams of mutilation and slaughter were accompanied by seminal emissions.

Prior came back into the room.'Sorry about that,' he said casually, settling back into his chair.

He hadn't reached the bathroom in time. The front of his tunic was wet where he'd had to sponge it down. He noticed Rivers noticing the stain, and his face tightened. He's going to make me pay for seeing that, Rivers thought. No point questioning the logic of it. That was Prior. 'Would you like a break?' Rivers asked, trying to relieve the tension.

Prior nodded.

'Let's go by the fire.'

They left the desk and settled themselves in armchairs. Rivers took off his glasses and swept a hand down across his eyes.

'Tired?'

'Slightly. As Mrs Irving was saying, we had our own personal air-raid last night. I suppose somebody panics and starts firing.'

A pause while they stared into the fire. Prior said, 'I bumped into a patient of yours the other night. Charles Manning.'

Rivers had started to clean his glasses. 'I umm –'

'Can't talk about another patient. No, of course you can't. *He* talked, though. You know, when he mentioned your name I thought "war neurosis" – well, he does tend to twitch a bit, doesn't he? – but no, apparently not. Met a handsome soldier. Nasty policeman's hand on shoulder. What do you know, suddenly he requires treatment. What was the . . .? Henry Head, that was it. "Henry Head can cure sodomites." So off he goes to Head, who says, "Sorry, like to help. Snowed under." With sodomites, presumably. The mind does rather boggle doesn't it? "Why don't you try Rivers?"' Prior waited. When there was no response he went on, 'Manning was surprisingly open about his little tastes. Cameronians with sweaty feet, apparently. Touching, isn't it, how some people develop a real devotion to the Highland regiments? I wonder, Rivers . . .' Prior was making little smacking movements with his lips, a don worrying away at some particularly recondite problem. 'How would you set about "curing" somebody of fancying Cameronians with sweaty feet?'

Rivers said coldly, 'I should apply carbolic soap to the feet.'

'Really? A leap ahead of Dr Freud there, I think.'

Rivers leant forward. '*Stop this.* Dr Head is "snowed under" by young men who've had large parts of their brains shot away. In a rational society, a man who spent his days like that wouldn't have to spend his evenings, his own time, remember, with men who could perfectly well be left to get on with their own lives in their own way. The fact that he's prepared to do it is a tribute to Head.'

'He's a friend of yours?'

'Yes.'

'I suppose he could refuse to take them?' Prior said.

'No, he can't do that. Two years' hard labour, remember?'

A short silence. 'I'm sorry.'

Rivers spread his hands.

But Prior wouldn't let go. 'All the same there must *be* times when one patient actually does *need* to talk about another. I mean, it must be obvious the conversation about the Cameronians could *only* have taken place in bed?'

'The thought had occurred.'

'Well, suppose I need to talk about it? Suppose I'm racked with guilt?'

'Are you?'

'The point is –' Abruptly, Prior gave up. 'No. I don't seem to feel sexual guilt, you know. At all, really. About anything.'

Not true, Rivers thought. Prior had felt enormous guilt about the nocturnal emissions that accompanied his nightmares. Guilt about an involuntary action.

'I used to,' Prior said.

'When was that?'

'When I was twelve. Where we lived there was a young man who used to be wheeled around on a trolley. I don't know what was wrong with him, tuberculosis of the spine, something like that, something terrible. And the trolley creaked, so you could always hear it coming. And he was pointed out to us as an illustration of what happened if you indulged in self-abuse.'

'Who told you that?'

'Scoutmaster. Mr Hailes. He actually said what came out was spinal fluid. And of course you've only got a limited supply of that, and mine was going down pretty fast. I used to lie awake and try not to do it, and I'd get more and more frightened. Unfortunately, there was only one thing that took my mind off the fear. So I did it again. And all the time this creaking trolley was getting nearer and nearer. And we'd been told the first signs of collapse were pallor and shadows under the eyes. And I used to get out of bed in the morning and look in the mirror, and what do you know? Pallor. Shadows under the eyes.' He laughed. 'It's funny now, but at one time I actually thought about suicide.'

'What got you out of it?'

Prior smiled. 'Not what. Who. Paddy MacDowell.'

'The man who organized the Sheffield strike?'

The smile broadened. 'Yes, at a later stage. He was otherwise engaged at the time. "Bashing his bishop." That's what we used to call it. Mac's bishop got bashed oftener than anybody else's. He used to more or less pull it out and do it in public – and he was taller and stronger than any of us. So that planted the first seed of doubt. And then Hailes said the way to purity was to keep a glass of cold water by your bed, and then when temptation struck, you could plunge "the Inflamed Organ" – he always called it that – into the water. Well, I relayed this to Mac. Mac was *common*, he didn't go to Scouts – and he said, "But if it's stiff how do you get it into the glass without spilling the water?" And I suddenly had this picture of poor bloody Hailes standing there with his limp "organ" in a glass of water and I just knew he was talking rubbish. Poor little sod, he must've forgotten what an erection looked like. Anyway, after that I gave up on guilt. I think I got through a lifetime's supply in six months.'

'Was it a close friendship? With MacDowell?'

'You mean, did we –'

'*No*, I –'

'Yes, it was close. We were that age, I suppose.'

Prior was looking much more relaxed. 'Do you want to go on?' Rivers asked.

A slight hesitation. 'No, but I think I'd better.' For a while he didn't speak, then, measuring the words with movements of his steepled fingertips, he said, 'Dreams are attempts to resolve conflict. Right? Well, I can't see any conflict in this one.'

'You stabbed somebody in the eye.'

'Rivers. It was a *door*.'

'The *eye* was alive.'

'Yes.'

'So why do you say there was no conflict?'

'Because I was so identified with William or Beattie or . . . I don't know. William, probably, because I was naked. And I was attacking what seemed to me the most awful feature of their situation, which is the eye. The constant surveillance. So I don't see that there's any conflict. I mean it might be very inconvenient in real life but in the dream there was no doubt whose side I was on. Theirs.'

Rivers waited. When it was clear Prior could offer nothing more he said, 'You say the worst feature of their situation is the eye?'

'Yes.'

'The constantly being spied on?'

'Yes.'

Rivers asked gently, 'In that meeting with Mrs Roper, who was the spy?'

'I –' Prior's mouth twisted. 'I was.'

Another pause. Rivers prompted. 'So?'

'So,' Prior said in a disgusted singsong, jabbing with his index finger, '"eye" was stabbing myself in the "I". And God knows one wouldn't want a reputation for puns like that!'

A pause. Rivers asked, 'What do you think about that? Does it seem . . .'

'It's possible, I suppose. I hate what I do. And I suppose I probably felt I was in a false position. Well, obviously I did, I'd have to be mad not to.'

'I want you to do something for me,' Rivers said. 'I want you to write down any dreams you have that are as . . . as bad as this one. Just record them. Don't try to interpret. And send them to me. I'll be seeing you again on –'

'No, I'm sorry, I can't. It'll have to be the following week. If that's all right? I'm going to see Hettie Roper.'

'Back to Salford? Where will you be staying?'

'At home.' He pulled a face. 'Yes, I know. How can I stay anywhere else?'

Rivers nodded. He was remembering a visit of Prior's parents to Craiglockhart. In one afternoon they'd undone every slight sign of progress and precipitated an asthmatic attack. 'Does your father know what you're doing? I mean, does he know what the job involves?'

'My God, I hope not.' Prior shifted restlessly. 'This is a dirty little war, Rivers. I can honestly say I'd rather be in France.'

'Yes. I'm sure you would.'

Prior gave him a sharp look. 'You're worried, aren't you? Why? Because I'm going home?'

'No, not particularly.'

'Oh, I *see*. Yes. It was a suicide dream.' His expression changed. 'You needn't worry. If anybody comes a cropper over this one, *it will not be me*.'

He looked quite different, suddenly: keen, alert, cold, observant, detached, manipulative, ruthless. Rivers realized he was seeing, probably for the first time, Prior's public face. At Craiglockhart he'd been aggressive and manipulative, but always from a position of comparative helplessness. At times he'd reminded Rivers of a toddler clinging to his father's sleeve in order to be able to deliver a harder kick on his shins. Now, briefly, he glimpsed the Prior other people saw: the Lodes, the Ropers, the Spragges, and it came as a shock. Prior was formidable.

SIX

Against a yellow backcloth a woman draped in brilliant green veils writhed and twisted. She looked like an exotic lizard or a poisonous snake. That, apparently, had been Wilde's intention. Robert Ross had been telling them about it before the performance, recalling a day in Paris, Wilde darting across the boulevards to look in shop windows, asking, 'What about that?' or 'Or perhaps she should be naked except for the jewels?' Yellow and green was *his* colour scheme, though Wilde could not have foreseen what, for Charles Manning, was its most disturbing feature: that the yellow was the exact shade of munition girls' skins. Others wouldn't notice that, of course. It only struck *him* because one of his duties at the Ministry was to serve as the military member on a committee set up to inspect the health and safety standards of munitions factories. One saw row after row of such girls, yellow-skinned, strands of ginger hair escaping from under their green caps, faces half hidden by respirators.

Ross had been quite interesting on Wilde's plans for *Salome*, rather more interesting than the performance so far. The most startling piece of information was that Wilde himself had once played Salome, which did rather boggle the imagination, since in photographs he looked far from sylph-like, even by the normal standards of prosperous middle-aged men. Manning directed his attention back to the stage. Since he'd made the effort to attend – and it had *been* an effort, he was feeling very far from well – he ought at least to give the play a chance, particularly since it had obviously meant a great deal to Wilde. Iokanaan's head had been brought in on a charger and Salome was kneeling, hands outstretched towards it. Manning felt an unexpected spasm of revulsion, not because the head was horrifying, but because it wasn't. Another thing Wilde couldn't have foreseen: people in the audience for whom severed heads were not necessarily made of papier mâché.

Salome began to fondle the head. *'Ah! thou wouldst not suffer me to kiss thy mouth, Iokanaan. Well! I will kiss it now. I will bite it with my teeth as one bites a ripe fruit. Yes, I will kiss thy mouth, Iokanaan. I said it: did I not say it? I said it. Ah! I will kiss it now.'*

Manning was bored. If he were honest all this meant nothing to him. He could see what Wilde was doing. He was attempting to convey the sense of a great passion constricted, poisoned, denied legitimate outlets, but none the less forced to the surface, expressed as destruction and cruelty because it could not be expressed as love. It was not that he thought the theme trivial or unworthy or out of date – certainly not that – but the language was impossible for him. France had made it impossible.

He'd only to think for a second of the stinking yellow mud of the salient, that porridge in which the lumps were human bodies, or parts of them, for an impassable barrier to come between his mind and these words.

A line of men in gas masks clumps along the duckboards. Ahead of the marching column what looks like a lump of mud sticks to the edge of the track. Closer, it turns out to be a hand. Clumping feet. His own breathing harsh inside the respirator, and then wriggling worm-like across the mud, a voice, sly, insinuating, confidential: 'Where's Scudder? Where's Scudder? Where's –'

On stage another question was being asked: *'But wherefore dost thou not look at me, Iokanaan? Thine eyes that were so terrible, so full of rage and scorn, are shut now. Wherefore are they shut?'*

He's dead, for Christ's sake, Manning thought. His knee had gone into spasm, and he was in acute pain. He glanced sideways at Ross, whose gaze was fixed on the stage, registering every nuance of the performance. He looked ill. Even in this golden reflected light, he looked ill. Oh, God, Manning thought, I wish this was over.

At last Herod cried, *Kill that woman!* and the soldiers rushed towards Salome, daughter of Herodias, and crushed her beneath their shields.

A moment's silence, then the applause burst out and Maud Allan, impersonal beneath the heavy make-up, was curtsying, blowing kisses, smiling, the severed head dangling from one small white hand.

Ross was surrounded as soon as the lights went up. Manning pushed through and shook hands with him, added his murmur to the general buzz of congratulation, then pointed to his knee, and to the back of the auditorium. Ross nodded. 'But you will come backstage?'

Pushing against the crowd to get to the top exit, Manning realized how painful his leg was. He opened the door marked FIRE EXIT and went through. A stone corridor, dimly lit, stretched ahead of him, with none of the gilt and plush of the rest of the theatre. The men's lavatory was at the end of the corridor, down a short flight of stairs. He peed, and then lingered over the business of washing his hands, wanting to postpone the moment when he would have to go backstage and swap the usual chit-chat. He would much rather have gone home. He was sleeping in his own house again, making the need to keep an eye on the builders his excuse, though he was glad of the chance to get away from the club. That silly incident, the newspaper clipping sent to his house, had disturbed him, simply because it could have been sent by *anybody*. He no longer felt he could trust people, members of his club, people he worked with. Even tonight his unwillingness to attend had not been primarily from fear of being seen with Ross – though that *was* a factor – so much as from simple reluctance to mix. Perhaps he was becoming too much of a recluse. Rivers certainly seemed to think he was.

He looked into the mirror. The overhead light cast deep shadows across his face.

Clumping feet. His own breathing harsh inside the respirator, and then wriggling worm-like across the mud, a voice, sly, insinuating, confidential:

'What did you think of it?'

A man had come out of one of the cubicles and was staring at him in the mirror. His sudden silent appearance startled Manning. 'Not for me, I'm afraid,' Manning said, starting to dry his hands. 'What did you think?'

The man, who had not moved, said abruptly, 'I thought it was the mutterings of a child with a grotesquely enlarged and diseased clitoris.'

'Did you? I just thought it had dated rather badly.'

'No,' the man said, as if his opinion were the only one that could carry weight. 'It isn't dated. In fact, in terms of what they're trying to do, it's an extremely clever choice.'

Manning looked into the mirror, determined not to be thrown by this ludicrous and yet curiously menacing figure. 'You think enlarged clitorises are a modern problem, do you?'

'All the discontents of modern women can be cured by clitoridectomy.'

'It's a bit more complicated than that, surely.'

It was as if he hadn't spoken. The man came closer until his face was beside Manning's in the glass. 'There are women in this city whose clitorises are so grotesquely enlarged, so horribly inflamed, they can be satisfied ONLY BY BULL ELEPHANTS.'

Silence. Manning couldn't think of anything to say.

'Didn't I see you in the box with Robert Ross?'

Manning turned to face him. Looking him straight in the eye and loading every word with significance, he said, 'I am from the Ministry of Munitions.' He touched the side of his nose, raised a cautionary finger and departed.

Walking along the corridor, he was surprised to find himself trembling. The man was a complete lunatic. One didn't have to be Rivers to diagnose that, and yet he had been, in a rather horrible way, impressive.

In the crush of Maud Allan's dressing-room, he accepted a glass of wine and edged his way towards Ross. 'I've just met the most extraordinary man in the downstairs lavatory.'

'Hmm.'

'No, not "hmm." Mad. He went on and on about diseased clitorises.'

'It'll be Captain Spencer. Grein said he'd seen him.'

'Who is he?' Manning asked.

'The source of all the trouble, my dear. He's the man who saw the Black Book. Who *knows the names*.'

'But he's mad.'

'That won't stop them believing him. The fact is . . .' Ross looked around cautiously. 'She shouldn't have sued. I know I'm the *last* person to say that, but –'

'What else could she have done?'

Ross shook his head. 'Once they're in court they can name *anybody*.'

'Are they leaving you alone?'

'No. I have a police officer more or less permanently stationed in the drawing-room. I'd offer the poor man a bed if I didn't think it would be misinterpreted.'

When they left, twenty minutes later, Manning noticed Captain Spencer standing under a street lamp on the other side of the road, watching. Manning reached out to touch Ross's sleeve, then thought better of it, and let his hand drop.

SEVEN

On the train to Manchester, Prior read the Roper correspondence.

Dear Winnie,
Don't worry about me pet I am orlrite Hettie come home for Xmas and we had a good time even little Tommy purked up a bit and you no what he's like you notice this new year there wasnt the same nonsense talked as there was last I think last year knocked the stuffing out of a lot of people except that bloody buggering Welsh windbag he dont change his tune much the poor lads

Hettie made me go to the sales with her cos she new I wanted a blowse there was a nice black one *no trimings* but Hettie says aw Mam your making yourself an old woman anyway you no Hettie I come away with a navy blue with a little yellow rose on it I think it looks orlrite cant take it back if it dont with it being in the sale we bumped into Mrs Warner you no her from the suffragettes and of corse she asked after you but she was only standoffish you could see her wanting to get away she says she thort to much was made of Xmas and turcy was a very dry meat I says well Ive never tasted it so I wouldnt no You no what Ronnie Carker used to say dont you theyre only mecking use of you, Beattie when *they* go home at night they dont even have to pick their nickers up mind you if Ronnie was there they wouldnt need to take them of either

As regards your late visitor you want to remember youve had a lot of worry with Alfs Mam being bad and then thier Ivy being so funny but whatever you do dont let it go past the fortnite YOU COME HOME otherwise youll end up with some bloody mucky cow with a neck you can plant taties in women like that do *no end of damidge* Ive seen bits of young lasses dragging themselves round years after

Did Alf get the letter I sent it on thursday but the post is very slow isnt it I spose its the backlog from Xmas if he did get it ask him to send me the stuff as soon as poss if he didn't tell him not to worry Ill rite again I want it for a man who stopped here just before Xmas he needs it to do somethink a bit risky *but only for him* he doesnt no anythink about you and Alf so theres no danger of you getting dragged in Anyway wil close now hoping this finds you as it leaves me

Buckets of love
Mam

Dear Mam,
School again, dunno who's more fed up, me or the kids. The hall roof sprang a leak during the holidays. No hope of getting it mended, of course, and it was blowing a gale today. Absolutely streaming down the panes and no lights on and Weddell rabbiting on about the Empire and how we must all tighten our belts and brace ourselves, though you don't see *him* bracing himself much, and he couldn't tighten his belt not with that belly on him. I just kept praying one of the drops from the ceiling was going to land on his bald pate, but no luck. And all the kids coughing like mad. One starts off and then they all start. So we got 'Our glorious Empire . . .' *cough cough*. 'We must fight to the last man.' *cough cough* 'Our valiant lads . . .' *cough cough*. Oh, and he's worked out how many old boys are in the trenches. Quite a lot, which surprised me, I'd've thought they all had rickets. There's rickets in my class. You know that very domed forehead they get? Once you know to look out for that you realize how much of it there is. And then we have to listen to all this puke about what we're fighting for. Still, it's better than it was before Christmas. I really did think I was going to throw up then. Peace on earth to men of goodwill, and how we were all showing goodwill by blowing up the Jerries and saving gallant little Belgium. I tried to tell Standard Six what gallant little Belgium got up to in the Congo, but he soon put a stop to that. I told him I was only doing it to compare a *bad* colonial regime with the splendid record of our glorious Empire, but I don't think he believed me. He doesn't trust me further than he could throw me and that wouldn't be far. He's put me on teaching the little ones this term and I don't think that's a coincidence either.

8's been in touch. You know I've been worried sick about him ever since he got nabbed, but he says it's not too bad. One of the lads had a beard and they shaved him with a cut-throat razor. He ended up pretty cut about, but it's surprising what they can find to laugh at. He says he hasn't seen our William but of course he wouldn't with him being in solitary. It might be the last we hear, though, Mam, because he says the guard who smuggles the letters out is being moved.

One thing I have found out – from 10, you won't know him – is the state of things in Étaples. That's the big camp where they all get sent to train and he says he's never seen anything like it. He says they treat the conscripts like shit. Men tied to posts for the least little thing with their arms above their heads. Doesn't *sound* much, does it, but he says it's agony. He says as sure as anything there's going to be a blow up there. I hope so, I *do* hope so. A few officers shot by their own men, that's all it'll take, just the one little spark, and it'll spread like wildfire. I *know* it will.

Haven't heard anything from Mac. I try to keep busy, I'm running round like scalded cat half the time because I daren't let myself think. The little ones are nice, though. Nobody's got to them yet. I thought of a new nursery rhyme the other day.

Georgie Georgie, pudding and pie
Perhaps the girls'll make him cry

Let's keep our fingers crossed, eh?

You want to stock up on food, Mam. I know it's difficult when you've got Tommy to feed, but if you get the chance put a few tins by. If it ever comes to coupons, conchies' families'll be at the back of the queue, *if they get any at all*.

Don't worry about me, I'm all right. You think about yourself for a change,

Lots of love,
Hettie

P.S. If that bloody Mac doesn't write soon I'll bash his bloody head in.

Dear Ma,
Find the stuff you asked for enclosed. Tell your friend to follow the directions *exactly*. You will think me a softie I expect but I feel sorry for the dogs. If you get close enough to the poor brutes, I pity them. Dead in twenty seconds. Anyway, good luck. Reckon we'll have peace by *next* Christmas? Here's hoping,

Alf

P.S. Winnie says to say she came all right.

My darling Hettie,
You'll be wondering why you haven't heard sooner. Well, there's been all hell let loose. Do you remember that lad with the hump on his back? Would insist on going in front of the tribunal instead of getting out of it on health grounds, which he certainly would have done. I've been trying to get him a passage to Ireland and eventually succeeded, but he was picked up just as he was getting on to the boat. The hump gave him away. We'd tried everything to hide it. Charlie suggested putting a dress on him and trying to make him look like a pregnant woman walking backwards, but I don't know how you do that. Anyway, he's back in Wandsworth, where they're doing their best to flatten it for him no doubt. But it's a nuisance because it means *we* have to lie low and that means everybody else has had their trips to the Emerald Isle postponed. It clogs the entire system up, and I lose patience, I'm afraid. I *know* individuals matter, but getting six or seven men across to Ireland isn't going to stop the war. There's only one way do that, and we both know what it is.

I'm staying with Charlie Greaves's mother. DON'T WRITE. I know you know the address, but the trouble is you're not the only one who knows it. *All incoming post is opened*. I don't want you in this any deeper than you are already. And I'm *not* treating you like 'the little woman'. There's got to be people they *don't* know about, otherwise there's no safe houses, and no network to pass people on. Speaking of which, I sent a lad to your Mam just before Christmas. Did you happen to bump into him? I wondered afterwards if I'd done the right thing. Not that I've any doubts about him, he's a good lad, keen as mustard, but he does get carried away. I don't suppose it matters, but if you write to your Mam you might mention it, though I suppose he'll have moved on by now. How is she, by the way? I wish we could get Tommy out of there. He's not doing her any good at all.

I'm writing this in bed, which is a big brass one, masses of room, and bouncy. It's tippling down outside and the wind's blowing, and I'd give anything to have you in here with me. *Soon*.

All my love,
Mac

It seemed strange to Prior to be reading his friends' private letters, though these had all – with the exception of Alf's letter and its inconvenient mention of dogs – been read aloud at the Old Bailey. Even Hettie's little nursery rhyme had boomed around No. 1 Court, as the

Attorney-General argued it implied her involvement in the conspiracy. No, there was no privacy left in these letters; he was not violating anything that mattered. And yet, as the train thundered into a tunnel and the carriage filled with the acrid smell of smoke, Prior turned to face his doubled reflection in the window and thought he didn't like himself very much. It was the last letter he minded: the gentleness of Mac's love for Hettie exposed, first in open court and now again to him.

They'd found that letter in the pocket of Hettie's skirt when they went to the school to arrest her.

EIGHT

Harry Prior was getting ready to go out. A clean shirt had been put to air on the clothes-horse in front of the fire, darkening and chilling the room. Billy Prior and his mother sat at the table, she with her apron on, he in shirt and braces, unable either to continue their interrupted conversation or to talk to Harry. He bent over the sink, lathering his face, blathering and spluttering, sticking his index fingers into his ears and waggling them. Then, after rinsing the soap off, he placed one forefinger over each nostril in turn and slung great gobs of green snot into the sink.

Prior, his elbow touching his mother's side, felt her quiver fastidiously. He laced his fingers round the hot cup of tea and raised it to his lips, dipping his short nose delicately as he drank. How many times as a child had he watched this tense, unnecessary scene, sharing his mother's disgust as he would have shared her fear of lightning. Now, as a man, in this over-familiar room – the tiles worn down by his footsteps, the table polished by his elbows – he thought he could see the conflict more even-handedly than he had seen it then. It takes a great deal of aggression to quiver fastidiously for twenty-eight years.

He thought, now, he could recognize his mother's contribution to the shared tragedy. He saw how the wincing sensitivity of her response was actually feeding this brutal performance. He recalled her gentle, genteel, whining, reproachful voice going on and on, long after his father's stumbling footsteps had jerked him into wakefulness; how he had sat on the stairs and strained to hear, until his muscles ached with the tension, waiting for her to say the one thing *he* would not be able to bear. And then the scuffle of running steps, a stifled cry, and he would be half way downstairs, listening to see if it was just a single slap, the back of his father's hand sending his mother staggering against the wall, or whether it was one of the bad times. She never had the sense to *shut up*.

But then, he thought, his face shielded by the rim of his cup, one might equally say she had never been coward enough to refrain from speaking her mind for fear of the consequences. It would be very easy, under the pretext of 'even-handedness', to slip too far the other way and blame the violence in the home not on his brutality, but on her failure to manage it.

As a child, Prior remembered beating his clenched fist against the palm of the other hand, over and over again, saying, with every smack of flesh on flesh, PIG PIG PIG PIG. Obviously, his present attempt to understand his parents' marriage was more mature, more adult, more perceptive, more sensitive, more insightful, more almost anything you cared to mention, than PIG PIG PIG PIG, but it didn't content him, because it was also a lie: a way of claiming to be 'above the battle'. And he was not above it: he was its product. *He* and *she* – elemental forces, almost devoid of personal characteristics – clawed each other in every cell of his body, and would do so until he died. 'They fight and fight and never rest on the Marches of my breast,' he thought, and I'm fucking fed up with it.

His father had got his jacket and cap on now, and stood ready to go out, looking at them with a hard, dry, stretched-elastic smile, the two of them together, as they had always been, waiting for him to go. 'I'll see you, then,' he said.

There was no question, as in the majority of households there would have been, of father and son going for a drink together.

'When will you be back?' his mother asked, as she had always done.

'Elevenish. Don't wait up.'

She always waited up. Oh, she would have said there was the fire to damp down, tomorrow's bait to be got ready, the table to be laid, the kettle to be filled, but all these tasks could have been done earlier. Prior, once more lowering his eyes to the cup, tried not to ask himself how many violent scenes might have been avoided if his mother had simply taken his father at his word and gone to bed. Hundreds? Or none? The man who spoke so softly and considerately now might well have dragged her out of bed to wait on him, when he staggered in from the pub with ten or eleven pints on board.

Leave it, he told himself. *Leave it.*

After his father had gone, Prior and his mother went on sitting at the table while they finished drinking their tea. She never mentioned France or Craiglockhart. She seemed to want to ignore everything that had happened to him since he left home. This was both an irritation and a relief. He asked after boys he'd known at school. This one was dead, that one wounded, Eddie Wilson had deserted. He remembered Eddie, didn't he? There were deserters in the paper every week, she said. The policeman who found Eddie Wilson hiding in his mother's coal-hole had been awarded a prize of five shillings.

'There was a letter in the paper the other week,' she said. 'From Father Mackenzie. You remember him, don't you?'

She found last week's paper and handed it to him. He read the letter, first silently and then aloud, in a wickedly accurate imitation of Father Mackenzie's liturgical flutings. '"There may be some among you, who, by reason of your wilful and culpable neglect of the Laws of Physical development, are not fit to serve your country, but –" Oh, for Christ's sake!' He thew the paper down. '*Some among them* carry their wilful and culpable neglect to the point of getting rickets. If he's physically well developed it's because his mother could afford to shove good food in his gob four times a day.' And goodness wasn't he well developed, Prior thought, remembering Father Mackenzie in his socks.

'He just thinks a lot of people are shirking, Billy. You've got to admit he's got a point.'

'Do you know the height requirement for the Bantam regiments? *Five feet.* And do you know how many men from round here *fail that*?'

'Billy, sometimes you sound exactly like your father.'

He picked up the paper and pretended to read.

'There's a lot of talk about a strike at the munition works. Your father's all for it. Well, *he* would be, wouldn't he?'

'What's it about?'

'I don't know.' She groped for an unfamiliar word. 'Dilution?'

'Sounds right.'

'Well, you can imagine your dad. "Bits of lasses earning more than I do." "You mark my words," he says, "after the war they'll bring in unskilled labour. The missus'll be going to work, and the man'll be sat at home minding the bairn. It's the end of craftsmanship. This war's the Trojan horse, only they're all too so-and-soing daft to see it."'

Typical, Prior thought. However determined his father might be to raise the status of the working class as a whole, he was still more determined to maintain distinctions within it.

'Oh, and he doesn't like false teeth. That's another thing,' his mother went on. 'Mrs Thorpe's got them, you know. "Mutton dressed up as lamb," he says. The way he goes on about her teeth you'd think she'd bit him. And then there's Mrs Riley's dustbin. *Lobster* tins, would you believe. "They were glad of a bit of bread and scrape before the war."'

'He's got a funny idea of socialism.'

She shrugged. 'I wouldn't know. Things like women's rights, he was never in favour of that.'

'*No.*'

'I remember him going on at Beattie Roper about that.'

A pause. 'I went to see Beattie.'

She looked stunned. 'In prison?'

'Yes.'

'You've no call to go getting yourself mixed up in that.'

Faced with this sudden blaze of anger, he said, 'I have to. It's my job.'

'Oh.' She nodded, only half believing him.

'How's Hettie?'

His mother froze. 'I wouldn't know. I never see her.'

There had been a time, when he was seventeen, when he and Hettie Roper had been 'walking out', and, for once, the 'quaint expression' had been painfully accurate. 'Walking' was exactly what they did. And talking too, of course: passionate, heated talk, about socialism and women's rights, spiritualism, Edward Carpenter's ideas on male comradeship, whether there could be such a thing as free love. He remembered one day on the beach at Formby, sitting in the dunes as the sky darkened, and the sun hung low over the sea. All day he had been wanting to touch her, and had not dared do it. The sun lingered, tense and swollen, then spilled itself on to the water. 'Come on,' he said, picking up his jacket. 'We'd better be getting back.'

That night, as on so many other nights, his mother had been waiting up for him. A book was open on her knee, but she hadn't bothered to light the gas. And then the questions started. He realized then that she hated Hettie Roper. He didn't know why.

'Does she still run the shop?' he asked.

'No point. Nobody'd buy anything off her if she did.'

'Does she work?'

'Not that I know of.'

'So how does she live?'

A shrug. 'She's still got the allotment.'

'I thought I'd pop round and see her.'

Silence.

Reminding himself he was no longer seventeen, Prior stood up and put his cup on the draining-board. 'I won't be long.'

Before the war, women used to sit on their steps in the warm evenings until after dark, postponing the moment when the raging bedbug must be faced, and taking pleasure in the only social contact they could enjoy without fear of condemnation. A woman seen chatting to her neighbours during the day quickly felt the weight of public disapproval. 'Eeh, look at that Mrs Thorpe. Eleven kids. You'd think she could find herself summat to do, wouldn't you?' Now, looking up and down the street, Prior saw deserted doorsteps. Women were out and about, but walking purposefully, as if they had somewhere to go.

He supposed it was Mrs Thorpe's name that came particularly to mind because she'd been one of the worst offenders, with her lard-white breasts the size of footballs, and Georgie or Alfie or Bobby worrying away at them, breaking off now and then for a drag on a tab end. Or perhaps, subconsciously, he'd already identified her, for there she was, coming towards him, divested of the clogs and shawl he'd always seen her in and wearing not merely a coat and hat but flesh-coloured stockings *and shoes*. It was scarcely possible the attractive woman with her should be Mrs Riley, but he didn't know who else it could be.

They greeted him with cries of delight, hugging, kissing, standing back, flashing their incredible smiles. There was a saying round here: for every child born a tooth lost, and certainly, before the war, Mrs Thorpe and Mrs Riley had advertised their fecundity every time they opened their mouths. Now, in place of gaps and blackened stumps was this even, flashing whiteness. 'What white teeth you have, Grandma,' he said.

'All the better to eat you with,' said Mrs Riley. 'And who are *you* calling Grandma?'

Mrs Thorpe asked, 'How long have you got, love?' And then,

before he had time to answer, 'Eeh, aren't we awful, always asking that?'

'Two days.'

'Well, make the most of it. Don't do anything we wouldn't do, mind.'

He smiled. 'How much scope does that give me?'

'Fair bit, these days,' said Mrs Riley.

He remembered, suddenly, that he'd sucked the breasts of both these women. His mother had been very ill for two months after his birth, and he'd been fed on tins of condensed milk from the corner shop, the same milk adults used in their tea. Babies in these streets were regularly fed on it. Babies fed on it regularly died. Then Mrs Thorpe and Mrs Riley had appeared, at that time, he supposed, lively young girls each with her own first baby at her breast. They had taken it in turns to feed him and, in so doing, had probably saved his life. He had known this a long time, but somehow, when Mrs Thorpe and Mrs Riley had been shapeless bundles in shawls, it had not *registered*. Now, though not easily discomforted, he felt himself start to blush.

'Look at that,' said Mrs Riley. 'He's courting, I can always tell.'

'*Are* you courting?' Mrs Thorpe asked.

'Yes. Her name's Sarah. Sarah Lumb.'

'Good strong name that,' said Mrs Riley.

'She's a good strong lass.'

'Mebbe has need to be,' said Mrs Riley, looking him up and down, speculatively. 'Do y' fancy a drink?'

'No, I'd like to, but I've got to see somebody.'

'Well, if you change your mind we'll be in the Rose and Crown.'

And off they went, cackling delightedly, two married women going out for a drink together. Unheard of. And in his father's pub too. No wonder the old bugger thought Armageddon had arrived.

Prior walked on, noticing everywhere the signs of a new prosperity. Meat might be scarce, bread might be grey, but the area was booming for all that. Part of him was pleased, delighted even. 'Bits of lasses earning more than I do'? *Good*. Lobster tins in Mrs Riley's dustbin? *Good*. He would have given anything to have been simply, unequivocally, unambiguously pleased. But he passed too many houses with black-edged cards in the window, and to every name on the cards he could put a face. It seemed to him the streets were full of ghosts, grey, famished, unappeasable ghosts, jostling on the pavements, waiting outside homes that had prospered in their absence. He imagined a fire blazing up, a window shaking its frame, a door gliding open, and then somebody saying, 'Wind's getting up. Do you feel the draught?' and shutting the door fast.

The glow he'd felt in talking to Mrs Thorpe and Mrs Riley faded. He slipped down the back alley between Marsh Street and Gladstone Terrace, making for Tite Street and Beattie Roper's shop, a journey he must have taken thousands of times as a child, a boy, a young man, but now he moved silently across the cobbles, feeling almost invisible. He was no more part of the life around him than one of those returning ghosts.

He came out at the top of Hope Street and started to walk down it. Hope Street ran parallel with the canal and was known, predictably, as No-Hope Street, because of the alacrity with which its inhabitants transferred themselves from one to the other. At least before the war they did. Suicides were rare now. The war had cheered everybody up.

Half way down, on the corner of Hope Street and Tite Street, was Beattie's shop, its windows boarded up. He knocked loudly on the door.

'You'll not get an answer there, love,' a woman said, passing by. He waited until she'd turned the corner, then knelt and peered through the letter-box. The counters were cleared, the floor swept clean. He called, 'Hettie. It's me, Billy.' The door into the living-room stood open. He felt her listening. 'Hettie, it's me.'

She came at last, kneeling on her side of the door to check he was alone. There was a great rattling of bolts and chains, and she stood there, a thin, dark, intense woman, older than he remembered. No longer pretty.

'Billy.'

'I've been to see your mother.'

'Yes. She wrote.'

A long hesitation, which told him immediately what he wanted to know. He took off his cap and stepped forward. Almost simultaneously, she stood aside and said, 'Come in.'

The living-room was empty. Both doors, one to the scullery, the other to the stairs, were closed. He looked round the room, taking his time. A fire blazed in the grate. The kettle stood on the hob beside it. The table, with its green cloth, still took up most of the space, six empty chairs ranged neatly round it. Hettie followed his gaze, and he could see how changes she'd become accustomed to – the empty chairs

– became strange again, and unbearable as she saw them through his eyes. 'Oh, Billy,' she said, and then she was in his arms and crying.

He cuddled her, lifting her off her feet, rocking her from side to side. Only when the sobs subsided did he loosen his grip, and let her slide to the ground. Her spread fingers encountered belt, buckles, buttons, tabs, stars: the whole hated paraphernalia. He said quickly, 'I see you've still got Tibbs.'

A fat tabby cat lay coiled on the rug, the pale underside of his chin exposed. Ghost smells of cat pee and creosote drifted in from the shop.

'Yes,' she said, laughing and sniffing. 'Pees on everything now.'

Her laughter acknowledged the fund of shared memories. Thank God, Prior thought, pulling out a chair and sitting down.

She fetched the tea-pot and started making tea. 'How's me mam? She *says* she's all right.'

'Thin. But she's eating. She's come off the strike.'

'Hmm. How long for? I tell her she shouldn't do it, but she says, "How else can I convince them?"'

'Have you been to see her?'

'I'm going next week. I gather we've got you to thank for that?'

'I put in a word.'

She poured the tea. 'How come you're in a position to put in a word?'

'Got a job in the Ministry, that's all. They're not sending me back 'cause of the asthma.'

'But what do you do?'

He laughed. 'Exactly what I did before the war. Push pieces of paper across a desk. But I managed to get me hands on your mam's file – via a young lady in the filing department – and then I thought I'd go and see her.'

'And you just *bluffed* your way in?'

'Well, not exactly, I had Ministry of Munitions headed notepaper. That gets you anywhere.'

'Huh! I wish *we* had some.'

She believed him. Just as once her mother had believed Spragge. She was sitting at the head of the table, in her mother's chair, no doubt because that made her mother's absence seem less glaring, and he was sitting, almost certainly, where Spragge had sat. He looked across to the dresser, and there sure enough was the photograph of William.

Hettie saw him looking at it, and reached behind her. 'I don't think you've seen this one, have you?' she said, and handed it across.

William was leaning against a stone wall, his arms loosely folded, and he was smiling, though the smile had become strained as the photographer fiddled with his camera. He was wearing bicycle clips. A pencilled date on the back said 'May 1913'. Prior thought he knew the place, they'd gone there together, the three of them. Behind the wall, not visible in the photograph, a steep bank shelved away, covered with brambles and bracken, full of rabbits whose shiny round droppings lay everywhere.

'Why does it look so long ago?' he said, holding the photograph out in front of him. Without conscious duplicity (though not without awareness), he was groping for the tone of their pre-war friendship.

She laughed, a harsh yelp that didn't sound like Hettie.

'No, but it does, doesn't it?' he persisted. 'I mean, it *looks* longer than it is. You know, I was thinking about that on the way over. About . . .' He took a deep breath. 'You know if you were writing about something like . . . oh, I don't know, enclosures, or the coming of the railways, you wouldn't have people standing round saying . . . ' He put a theatrical hand to his brow. '"Oh, dear me, we *are* living through a period of terribly rapid social change, aren't we?" Because nobody'd believe people would be so . . . *aware*. But here we are, living through just such a period, and everybody's bloody well aware of it. I've heard nothing else since I came home. Not the words, of course, but the *awareness*. And I just wondered whether there aren't periods when people *do* become aware of what's happening, and they look back on their previous unconscious selves and it seems like decades ago. Another life.'

'Yes, I think you're right.' She thought for a moment. 'I went to London a couple of months ago, to see one of the few suffragette friends who still wants to know me. And we were sitting in her house, and there was a raid, and we actually heard shrapnel falling on the trees, and do you know it sounded exactly like rain. And she was . . . *full of herself*. Short hair, breeches, driving an ambulance, all things she'd never've been allowed to do in a million years. And suddenly she grabbed hold of me and she said, "Hettie, for women, this is the first day in the history of the world."'

'And the last for a lot of men.'

Her face darkened. 'Don't beat *me* over the head with that, Billy. *I*'m the pacifist, remember.'

'At least you've got the vote.'

'No, I haven't. I'm not thirty. Mam hasn't, she's in prison. Winnie hasn't, same reason. William hasn't, he's had his vote taken away 'cause he's a conchie. So as far as votes go this family's one *down* on before the war.'

'Where is William?' Prior said, looking at the photograph again.

'Dartmoor. He took the Home Office scheme. He's doing "useful work unconnected with the war".' She snorted. 'Breaking stones.'

'I'm surprised he took it.'

'You wouldn't be if you saw him. He's that thin, you wouldn't know him.'

'I had Mike Riordan in my platoon. You remember Mike? I didn't know *him* either. Only in his case it was the face that was missing.'

'It isn't a competition, Billy.'

'No. You're right.'

She touched his sleeve. 'I wish we were on the same side.'

'Well, as far as your mam's concerned we are. You surely don't think I'm on Spragge's side?'

Her expression changed. 'Oh, that man. Do you know, I met him once, just for a couple minutes, and I *knew* there was something wrong with him.'

'You didn't know about the poison?'

'No, she kept all that from me. I wish she hadn't, I'd've told her she was daft to trust him. And that smirking bastard at the Old Bailey. It was awful, Billy. You're stood in that dock and you *feel* guilty, even though you know you haven't done it. For months afterwards I felt people could look straight through me.' She stopped. 'Here, drink your tea. It'll get cold.'

'How are you managing?'

'I survive. Your dad brings me a bit of meat now and then. Don't look so surprised, Billy.' A pause. 'I tell you who's been good. Mrs Riley. Every time she bakes she brings something round. You know mebbe just half a dozen rock buns, but every bit helps. I've nothing to thank the others for, except a few bricks through the window. What gets me you know is the way they used to cut me mam dead in the street, they'd just look through her. But let them be in trouble, or their daughters be in trouble, and there they were, banging on the back door. I says, "You're a fool, Mam. Why should you risk prison for them?" But it was, "Oh, well, she had to have instruments last time," or "Poor bairn, she's only seventeen." And she'd do it for them. And it all came out at the trial. You know, killing a baby when its mother's two months gone, that's a terrible crime. But wait twenty years and blow the same kid's head off, that's all right.'

Prior winced, thinking how strange it was that such words should come so easily from her mouth, that she should have so little conception of what memories they conjured up for him.

'What about Mac? Do you ever see him?'

Her face became guarded. 'No.'

'Never?'

'You know bloody well, Billy, he wouldn't dare come here.'

Prior sat back in his chair. 'I know he couldn't stay away.' He waited. 'I thought I heard somebody just now.'

Her eyes went to the scullery door.

'Walking up and down.'

'It's a restless house. You've got to remember me mam held seances here. In this room.'

'You don't believe in that.'

'I know me mam wasn't a fraud. *Something* happened. Whether it was just the force of people's need or not, I don't know, but there used to be nights when this table was shaking. It changes a place. I sit here on me own some nights and I hear footsteps going round and round the table.'

He had a dreadfully clear perception of what her life must be like, alone in this house, with the empty chairs and the boarded-up windows. It didn't surprise him that she heard footsteps going round the table.

'Talking of Mac,' he said, and felt her stiffen. 'I thought I'd go round and see his mam. I don't suppose he still sees her, does he?'

'That's a good idea, Billy. I'd willingly go, but I doubt if she'd thank me for it. In fact, I doubt if she'd invite me in.'

'No, she's a great patriot, Lizzie.' He was smiling to himself. 'You know the last time I was home I bumped into her. Well.' He laughed. 'Fell over her. You know the alley behind the Rose and Crown? "Just resting," she says. I got her on her feet and she took one look at the uniform and she says, "Thank God for an honest man." And out it all came. Apparently on the day war broke out she did seven men for free because they'd just come back from the recruiting office. *They said.* "And do you know," she says. "Five of them were still walking round in civvies a year after." She says she had a go at Wally Smith about it. And he says, "Well they wouldn't let me in because of me teeth." And Lizzie says, "What the fuck do they want you to do? *Bite the buggers?*"'

Hettie was looking very uncomfortable. Since she was far from prudish he could only suppose the story of Lizzie and her August 4th burst of generosity was likely to be painful to the person on the other side of the scullery door. He thought of saying, 'Oh, come on, Mac, stop arsing about,' but he didn't dare risk it. Better make his plea first, then leave them alone to talk about it.

'I'd like to see Mac, Hettie.'

'So would I,' she flashed. 'Fat chance.'

'No, I mean I really do need to see him. If I'm going to do anything for your mam, I've got to talk to him first. He –'

'He didn't know anything about it.'

'No, but he knew Spragge. Spragge was with him the night before he came here. He gave Spragge the address.'

'Do you think he doesn't know that? Spragge took in an awful lot of people, Billy. He had *letters*.'

'I know. I'm not . . . I'm not *blaming* Mac. I just want to talk to him. He might remember something that would help. You see, if we could prove Spragge acted as an *agent provocateur* with somebody else – or even tried to – that would help to discredit his evidence in your mam's case.'

She glanced at the scullery door. 'I know somebody who bumps into Mac now and then. I'll see if I can get a message through.'

'That's all I ask.' He stood up. 'And now I'd better be off.'

She didn't try to detain him. At the door he paused and said loudly, 'I thought I'd go for a walk by the cattle pens. I thought I'd go there now.'

She looked up at him. 'Goodnight, Billy.'

NINE

It was not quite dusk when Prior reached the cattle pens, empty at this time of the week and therefore unguarded. Mac, if he came at all, would wait till dark, so there was time to kill. He lit a cigarette and strolled up and down, remembering the taste of his first cigarette – given to him by Mac – and the valiant efforts he'd made not to be sick.

He stood for a while, his hands gripping the cold metal of one of the pens. He was recalling a time when he'd been ill – one of the many –

and he'd gone out and wandered the streets, not well enough yet to go back to school but bored with being in the house. It had been a hot day, and he was muffled up, a prickly scarf round his neck, a poultice bound to his chest. The heat beat up into his face from the pavements as he dragged himself along, stick-thin, white, bed-bound legs moving in front of him, the smell of Wintergreen rising into his nostrils. The name made him think of pine trees, snow-covered hills and the way the sheets felt when you thrust your hot legs into a cool part, away from the sticky damp.

He heard their hoofs before he saw them and, like everybody else, stopped to watch as the main street filled with cattle being driven to the slaughterhouse. A smell of hot shit. Dust rising all round, getting into his lungs, making him cough and bring up sticky green phlegm. He backed away from the noise and commotion, ran up a back alley between the high dark walls, then realized that, as in a nightmare, a cow was following him, with slithering feet and staring eyes, and men chasing after her. More men came running from the other end of the alley. They cornered her, closing in from both sides, and the terrified animal slipped in her own green shit and fell, and they threw heavy black nets around her and dragged her back to the herd, while all along the alley housewives whose clean washing had been swept aside erupted from their backyards, shouting and waving their arms.

At the moment the nets landed Prior had looked across the heaving backs and seen a boy, about his own age, standing pressed back against the wall, his white, still face half hidden by a mass of cottery black hair. Mac.

The sight of the cow in the net stayed with him. Many a night he dreamt about her and woke to lie staring into the swirling darkness. Sometimes when he woke it was already light, and then, afraid to go back to sleep, he would creep downstairs, open the door quietly and slip out into the empty, dawn-smelling streets. The only other person about at that hour was the knocker-up, an old woman with bent back and wisps of white hair escaping from a black woollen shawl, who went from house to house, tapping on the upper windows with her long pole, waiting for the drowsy or bad-tempered answer, and moving on. Drifting along behind her, he'd found his way to the cattle pens, and to the deepest friendship of his childhood.

He left the pens now and walked into the high shed, which was as vast as a cathedral, and echoing. He walked up and down, dwarfed by the height, imagining the place as it used to be and presumably still was, if you came at the right time of week. He remembered the rattle of rain on the corrugated iron roof, imagined it pouring down as it had on the night he first stayed here with Mac. He looked round, and the empty stalls filled with terrified cattle, huge shadows of tossing horns leapt across the ceiling as the guards moved up and down with lanterns, checking that the overcrowded animals were not suffocating to death. If they suffocated before they could be slaughtered, their meat was unfit for human consumption, though it found its way on to the market as 'braxy', in shops patronized only by the very poor. There was no profit to be had from braxy, so if an animal was distressed and appeared to be near death the guards would rouse the slaughterman to come and dispatch it. These guards were supposed to be on duty all night, but since they'd been away for long stretches on the drovers' road they naturally wanted to sleep with their wives or girlfriends, and that was where Mac came in. The job was subcontracted to him at a penny a night, and he was good at it. He could calm a cow, even a cow who'd already scented blood, to the point where she would yield milk into a lemonade bottle. Prior could almost see him now, wedged into a wall of sweating flesh, slithering on the green shit that always had about it the smell of terror, coaxing, whispering, stroking, burrowing his head into the cow's side, and then coming back in triumph with the warm milk. They'd swigged it from the bottle, sitting side by side on the bales of straw that stood in one corner of the shed, and then, slowly and luxuriously, like businessmen savouring particularly fine cigars, they smoked the tab ends Mac had picked up from the streets.

Prior wandered across to the bales of straw and sat down, his cigarette a small planet shining in the darkness, for the night was closing in fast. He could just see the nail in the wall which had always been their target in peeing competitions, and from the nail he moved in imagination to the school playground. He had a lot of playground memories of Mac, and classroom memories too, though few of these were happy. Mac was dirty and his hair was lousy. He wore men's shoes, and a jacket whose sleeves came to the tips of his fingers, and he was always being beaten. As children do, Prior supposed, he'd started by assuming that Mac was beaten more often than anybody else because he was naughtier than anybody else. He was inclined to believe now that the *only* valuable part of his education at that abysmal school had been learning that this was not true. Lizzie's profession was well known. On the one occasion she'd come to school, her speech had been slurred and she'd raised her voice in the corridor; they'd all watched her through the classroom windows, every varied pitch of her indignation expressed in the jiggling of the feather on her hat. No doubt she'd come down to protest because they'd beaten Mac too hard. If so, the visit did no good: he was beaten again as soon as she left. Prior remembered those beatings. He remembered the painful pressure of emotions he'd felt: fear, pity, anger, excitement, pleasure. He wondered now whether the pleasure could possibly have been as sexual as he remembered it. Probably not.

After one such occasion Prior had sat with his back to the railings that divided the boys' playground from the girls', munching a sandwich and watching Mac. Mac was running up and down the playground with Joe Smailes on his back, staggering beneath the weight, his grubby hands with their scabbed knuckles clasping Joe Smailes's podgy pink thighs. Mac was a bread horse: he gave other boys rides on his back in exchange for the crust from their bread or the core of their apple. Lizzie had not been poor, as the neighbourhood understood poverty, but she was too disorganized by drink to provide regular meals. What disturbed Prior this time, what ensured that his eyes never left Mac's face as he staggered up and down, was the knowledge that he'd deserved a beating every bit as much as Mac, but because *he* was clean, tidy, well turned out, likely to win a scholarship and bring desperately needed credit to the school, he'd been spared. He bit into his second sandwich, thought, munched, choked. Suddenly he ran across the playground, thrust what was left of the sandwich into Mac's hands, burst into tears, and ran away.

Who needed Marx when they had Tite Street Board School, Prior thought, stubbing out his cigarette carefully between strips of golden straw. Still absorbed in memories of the past, he got to his feet and started to walk up and down. The moon had risen; its light was bright enough to cast his shadow across the floor. His first awareness of Mac was of a shadow growing beside his own, then the touch of a hand on his shoulder, and a light amused voice asking, 'Am I to understand you've been up my mother?'

Prior turned. 'What makes you say that?'

'All that stuff about "Thank God for an honest man", I don't know what else it could mean.'

'Now would *I* do that?'

'I don't know. Before the war you'd've fucked a cow in a field if you could've found one to stand still for you.'

And the bull. 'Mac, I swear –'

'Aw, forget it. If I was sensitive about that I'd've croaked years ago.' Mac was smiling. This was almost, but not quite, a joke.

Prior said, 'Shall we sit down?'

They sat on bales of straw a few feet apart, united and divided by the rush of memory. They could see clearly enough, by moonlight and the intermittent glow of cigarettes, to be able to judge each other's expression.

'It *was* you in the kitchen, then,' Prior said. 'I thought it was.'

'Why, who'd you think it might be?'

Prior hesitated. 'I was afraid it might be some poor frightened little sod of a deserter, I was afraid he'd –'

'What would you have done?'

'Turned him in.'

Mac looked at him curiously. 'Even though he's "a poor frightened little sod"?'

'*Yes*. What about the poor frightened little sods who *don't* desert?'

'Well, at least we know where we stand.'

'I don't want to start by telling you a pack of lies.'

Mac laughed. 'You told Hettie a few. That girl in the filing department, the one who got you the files, my God, Billy, you must be ringing *her* bell.'

'Say it, Mac.'

'All right, I'll say it. It strikes me you'd be a bloody good recruit, *for them*. You with your commission and your posh accent, and your . . .' With a kind of mock delicacy, Mac touched his own chest. '*Low* friends. Officers' mess one night, back streets of Salford the next. Equally at home or . . .' He smiled, relishing the intimacy of his capacity to wound. 'Equally *not* at home, in both.'

'Whereas *you* of course are firmly embedded in the bosom of a loving proletariat? Well, let me tell you, Mac, the part of the proletariat I've been fighting with – the vast majority – they'd string *you* up from the nearest fucking lamp-post and not think twice about it. And as for your striking munition workers . . .' Prior swept the shed with a burst of machine-gun fire.

There was a moment's shocked silence, as if the childish gesture had indeed produced carnage.

'And don't think they wouldn't do it, they would. *I know them*.'

Mac said, 'I'm surprised you feel *quite* so much pleasure at the idea of the workers shooting each other.'

'No pleasure, Mac. Just facing reality.' Prior produced a flask from his tunic pocket and handed it over. 'Here, wash it down.'

Mac unscrewed the cap, drank, blinked as his eyes watered, then passed the flask back, its neck unwiped. After a moment's hesitation Prior drank, thinking, as he did so, that the sacramental gesture was hollow. Milk in unwiped lemonade bottles was a lifetime away.

'You still haven't explained,' Mac said.

'About the files? I work in the Intelligence Unit.'

Mac made a slight, involuntary movement.

'They'd've been here by now.'

Mac smiled. 'Must be quite nice, really. A foot on each side of the fence. Long as you don't mind what it's doing to your balls.'

'They're all right, Mac. Worry about your own.'

'Oh, I *see*. I wondered when that was coming. *Men* fight, is that it?'

'No. I can see it takes courage to be a pacifist. At least, I suppose it does. You see, my trouble is I don't know what courage means. The only time I've ever done anything even slightly brave, I couldn't remember a bloody thing about it. Bit like those men who bash the wife's head in with a poker. "Everything went black, m'lud."'

Mac nodded. 'Well, since you're being honest, I think a load of fucking rubbish's talked about how much courage it takes to be a pacifist. When I was deported from the Clyde, they came for me in the middle of the night. One minute I was dreaming about a blonde with lovely big tits and the next minute I was looking up at six policemen with lovely big truncheons. Anyway, they got me off to the station and they started pushing me around, one to the other, you know, flat-of-the-hand stuff, and they were all grinning, sort of *nervous* grins, and I knew what was coming, I knew they were working themselves up. It's surprising how much working up the average man needs before he'll do anything *really* violent. Well, you'd know all about that.'

'Yes,' Prior said expressionlessly.

'I was shitting meself. And then I thought, well. They're not going to blind you. They're not going to shove dirty great pieces of hot metal in your spine, they're not going to blow the top of your head off, they're not going to amputate your arms and legs without an anaesthetic, so what the fuck are you worried about? If you were in France you'd be facing all that. And of course there's always the unanswered question. *Could* you face it? Could you *pass the test*? But where I think we differ, Billy, is that *you* think that's a Very Important Question, and I think it's fucking trivial.'

Prior glanced sideways at him. 'No, you don't.'

'All right, I don't.'

'You could always say you're showing *moral* courage.'

'No such thing. It's a bit like medieval trial-by-combat, you know. In the end moral and political truths have to be proved *on the body*, because this mass of nerve and muscle and blood is what we are.'

'That's a very dangerous idea. It comes quite close to saying that the willingness to suffer proves the rightness of the belief. But it *doesn't*. The most it can ever prove is the believer's sincerity. And not always that. Some people just like suffering.'

Mac was looking round the shed. He said, 'I don't think I do,' but he seemed to have tired of the argument, or perhaps the whisky had begun to soften his mood. 'I often think about those days.'

Prior waited. 'You *can* trust me, you know.'

'I trusted Spragge.'

'You didn't have pissing competitions with Spragge.'

'Oh, that's it, is it? *Piss* brothers?'

Prior laughed. 'Something like that.'

A long silence. 'What do you want?'

'I want you to tell me about Spragge.'

Mac gave a choking laugh. 'He's your fucking employee.'

'Not any more. The trial blew his cover.'

'Good.'

'He was with you, wasn't he, the night before?'

'I sent him there.'

Mac must find that almost intolerable, Prior thought. His debt to the Ropers was total. Without Beattie, he'd've been a scabby, lousy, neglected kid, barely able to read and write, fit only for the drovers' road and the slaughterhouse. Beattie had taken him in. By the age of thirteen he'd been living more with her than with his own mother. As soon as the older boys in the street gang stopped speculating about sex and started climbing Lizzie's stairs in search of more concrete information, Mac had found his own home unbearable. He'd disappeared altogether for a time, going up the drovers' road one summer, returning, older, harder, the first traces of cynicism and deadness round his mouth and eyes. Then Beattie took charge. 'What the hell's the matter with you?' she asked. 'You can read, can't you? Just 'cos the teachers think you're stupid, doesn't mean you are. Some of *them* aren't too bright. Here, read this. No, go on, *read it*. I want to know what you think.'

'He was after *you*, wasn't he?' Prior asked.

'Yes.'

'Do *you* think she meant to kill Lloyd George?'

'Nah. You know Beattie. She finds a spider in the sink, she gets a bit of newspaper and puts it in the yard.'

'Hmm. I just wonder what she'd do if she found Lloyd George in the sink.'

'Run the fucking taps.'

They looked at each other and burst out laughing.

'Look, if there *was* anything, the idea came from Spragge. And I think helping people escape from a detention centre sounds about right. And Spragge had tried it on before.'

'Who with?'

'Charlie Greaves, Joe Haswell. He offered them explosives to blow up a munitions factory. Said he knew where he could get some. Well, for God's sake. They're not exactly lying around, are they? As soon as they said no, he started backing off. Pretended he hadn't meant it.'

'And you still sent him to Beattie?'

'This is *hindsight*, man. It sticks in my mind *now* because of what happened. At the time I just thought, oh God, another mad bugger.'

'Could you get them to write it down? With dates, if possible.'

'I don't even know where they are.'

'It's for Beattie, Mac.'

Mac let out a sharp breath. 'What do you want it for?'

'To discredit Spragge, of course.'

'They won't reopen the case.'

'Not publicly. But they might let her out. Quietly. She's going to die in there, Mac. She won't last anywhere near ten years.'

A dragging silence.

'I'm not asking them to incriminate themselves. All they have to do is say "He offered us explosives and we refused."'

'And you think they're going to be believed?'

'I think there's a better chance than you might think. There's a lot of questions being asked about the way spies are used in munition factories. Some of them are better at starting strikes than you are, Mac.'

'All right.' Mac stood up. 'It'll take a few weeks.'

'As long as that?'

'I've told you. I don't know where they are.'

'Where can I contact you?'

Mac laughed. 'You fucking can't. Here, give me your address.'

Prior took the notepad and pencil, and scribbled. 'All right?'

'*Don't* write to Hettie. The post's opened. And one more thing.' Mac came very close, resting his hands heavily on Prior's shoulders. 'If this is a trap, Billy, you're dead. I'm not a fucking Quaker, remember.'

For a moment the pressure on his shoulders increased, then Mac turned and strode away.

Prior decided to take the short-cut home across the brick fields. This patch of waste land always reminded him of France. Sump holes reflected a dull gleam at the sky, tall grasses bent to the wind, pieces of scrap metal rusted, rubbish stank, a rusting iron bedstead upreared itself, a jagged black shape that, outlined against the horizon, would have served as a landmark on patrol.

One of the ways in which he felt different from his brother officers, one of the many, was that *their* England was a pastoral place: fields, streams, wooded valleys, medieval churches surrounded by ancient elms. They couldn't grasp that for him, and for the vast majority of the men, the Front, with its mechanization, its reduction of the individual to a cog in a machine, its blasted landscape, was not a contrast with the life they'd known at home, in Birmingham or Manchester or Glasgow or the Welsh pit villages, but a nightmarish culmination. 'Equally not at home in either,' Mac had said. He was right.

Prior lingered a while, listening to the night noises, remembering the evenings in his childhood when he'd sat on the stairs, unable to sleep, until his father had come in and gone to bed, and he knew his mother was safe. Engines rumbled, coughed, whistled, hissed. Trucks shunted along, bumpers clanged together. A few streets away a drunk started singing: 'There's an old mill by the stream, Nelly Dean.'

He ought to be getting back. He'd already been away much longer than he'd meant. He began walking rapidly across the brick fields. One moment he was striding confidently along and the next he was falling, sliding rather, down a steep slope into pitch-black. He lay on his back at the muddy bottom of the hole and saw the tall weeds wave against the sky. He wasn't hurt, but the breath had been knocked out of him. Gradually, his heart stopped thumping. The stars looked brighter down here, just as they did in a trench. He reached out for something to hold on to, and his groping fingers encountered a sort of ledge. He patted along it and then froze. It was a firestep. It couldn't be, but it was. Disorientated and afraid, he felt further and encountered a hole, and then another beside it, and another: funk holes, scooped out of the clay. *He was in a trench.* Even as his mind staggered, he was groping for an explanation. Boys played here. Street gangs. They must have been digging for months to get as deep as this. But then probably the trench was years old, as old as the real trenches, perhaps. He clambered out, over what he suspected was No Man's Land, and there, sure enough, were the enemy lines.

Smiling to himself, unwilling to admit how deeply the bizarre incident had shocked him, he walked on, more cautiously now, and reached the railings at the far side. He was trembling. He had to hold on to the railings to steady himself.

The shock made him rebellious. He decided he wouldn't go straight home after all. Witnessing these nasty little rows between his parents did them no good, and him a great deal of harm. The time had come to call a halt. He would go to the pub. Which pub? His way home took him past the Rose and Crown, whose brass door flashed to and fro, letting out great belches of warm beery air. He would go there. He would do what other men do who come home on leave. Get drunk and forget.

He was greeted by a fug of human warmth, so hot he felt the skin on his nose tingle as the pores opened. He stood looking round at the flushed and noisy faces, and in the far corner spotted Mrs Thorpe and Mrs Riley with a great gaggle of other women. He decided he ought to stand them a drink. After all, they'd stood him many a drink in their day. A cry of recognition greeted him as he approached, and the whole boozy crowd of them opened up and took him in.

Two hours later Harry Prior was stumbling home, gazing in bleary appreciation at the full moon, riding high and magnificent in the clear sky. He paused on the bridge that spanned the canal to take a quick leak and admire the view. The moon was reflected in the water. He looked down at it, as a jet of hot piss hit the wall and trickled satisfyingly between the cobbles, and wondered why it should be bobbling up and down. He checked to see the real moon was behaving itself, then peered more closely at its reflection.

It wasn't the bloody moon at all, it was an arse. My God, the lad was going at it. Harry had half a mind to cheer him on, but then he thought, no, better not. A person might very easily be mistaken for a peeping Tom. He leant further over, pressing himself against the rough granite, wishing he could see more. All he could see of the woman was knees. Who the bloody hell wants to watch a male arse bobbing up and down? Bloody golf-balls. Still, it didn't half give you ideas. Bugger all doing at home, knees glued together. He rubbed himself against the wall for comfort, then wandered disconsolately on.

'There's somebody on the bridge.'

Prior turned, but he couldn't see anything. He listened to the fading footsteps. 'They're going.'

She'd gone tense and braced herself against him. He'd have to start from the beginning. He kissed her mouth, her nose, her hair, and then, lowering his head in pure delight, feeling every taboo in the whole fucking country crash round his ears, he sucked Mrs Riley's breasts.

Part Two

TEN

Prior returned to London to find the city sweltering in sticky, humid, thundery heat. Major Lode was more difficult than ever, and not merely because of the weather. An attempt was under way to centralize the intelligence services under the control of the War Office, and Lode was fighting for the survival of the unit. The change was being pushed through at an exalted level and very little filtered down to Prior, but he observed Lode daily becoming fiercer, the blue eyes more vulnerable, the moustache in ever greater need of protective dabbings and strokings, as his empire collapsed around him. The files, 'the brain cells of the unit' Lode proclaimed (God help it, thought Prior), were to be transferred to the War Office. The task of 'tidying them up' before they were transferred was allotted to Prior. At first he took this to be merely a routine clerical task, perhaps designed to keep him out of trouble, but it quickly became clear that Lode wanted 'sensitive material' referred to him. In other words, evidence for the worst of the unit's cock-ups was to be removed. The job, though huge – the files numbered more than eight hundred – suited Prior very well, since it solved what had hitherto been his main problem: how to get enough access to past files to compile a dossier on Spragge.

He was busy and, within reason, happy, though he did not feel particularly well. Then, four days after his return, something disturbing happened.

He'd gone out to lunch in a nearby pub, bought himself a pint of beer and opened *The Times*, as he always did, at the casualty lists. The name leapt out at him.

Hore, Captain James Frederick. Killed in action on the 5th April, dearly beloved younger son . . .

Jimmy Hore. They'd met on a riding course, trotting round a ring with their stirrups crossed in front of them, their hands clasped behind their heads. Acquiring the correct seat. The seat of gentlemen. Prior, who'd already experienced the realities of trench warfare, had been angry and amused, though he kept both reactions to himself, since he was convinced nobody else could appreciate the idiocy of the situation as he did. Certainly not this blank-faced moron trotting towards him, but then, as they trotted past each other, he caught Jimmy's eye and realized his face wasn't blank at all, but rigid with suppressed laughter. That glance of shared amusement had been too much for Jimmy, who burst out laughing and fell off his horse.

Prior looked round the pub. Prosperous-looking men in pin-striped suits jostled at the bar, chinking coins, bestowing well-oiled smiles on the pretty, chestnut-haired barmaid. And Jimmy was dead. All the poor little bugger had ever wanted to do was get married to . . . whatever her name was. And work in a bank. Prior would have liked nothing better, at that moment, than for a tank to come crashing through the doors and crush everybody, the way they sometimes crushed the wounded who couldn't get off the track in time. The violence of his imaginings – he saw severed limbs, heard screams – terrified him.

He couldn't eat. He would just drink up and go. But when he lifted his glass, his attention was caught by the amber lights winking in the beer. Sunlight, shining through the glass, cast a ring of shimmering gold on the surface of the table that danced when his hand moved. He started to play with it, moving his hand to and fro.

He was back at his desk. No interval. One second he was in the pub, the next sitting behind his desk. He looked across at the closed door. Blinked. Thought, I must've gone to sleep. He felt relaxed, but without the clogged feeling that follows midday sleep. He'd been reading *The Times . . . Jimmy Hore was dead.* He couldn't remember leaving the pub. He must have walked all the way back in a complete dream. He looked at his watch, and his brain struggled to make sense of the position of the hands. Ten past four.

Three hours had passed since he broke for lunch, and of that he could account for perhaps twenty to twenty-five minutes. The rest was blank.

He made himself work until six. After all, in France he'd done paperwork on a table that kept jumping several feet into the air. He could surely manage to ignore a little disturbance like this. Though, as file after file passed across his desk, he was aware, somewhere on the fringes of his consciousness, that it was not 'a little disturbance'. Something catastrophic had happened.

Shortly after six he thought he recognized voices, and went out of his room and a little way along the corridor. Major Lode and Lionel

Spragge were deep in conversation by the lifts. It was not possible to hear what they were saying, but he noticed that Lode shook Spragge's hand warmly as the lift arrived. Prior slipped back into his room, but left the door open.

He was ready to produce some small query that would bring Lode into his room, but in the event he didn't need to. Lode stood in the doorway, grinning. 'Just seen Spragge,' he said in his clipped, staccato voice. 'What have you been doing to him?'

'Me? Nothing.'

'Says you offered him a job.'

'I didn't offer him anything. Wishful thinking, I'm afraid.'

'Well, he certainly seems to *think* you did. I had to tell him there was nothing doing. Nap*poo*.' Lode looked at him for a moment, then said in a menacing, nannyish singsong, 'He's got it *in* for *you*.'

Bastard, Prior thought, as Lode closed the door behind him. It's not my fault your frigging unit's being closed down.

Towards six it began to thunder, a desultory grumble on the horizon, though the sun still shone. Prior worked for a further half hour, then gave up. He'd been having bad headaches ever since he got back to London and blamed them on the weather, though in fact he knew they'd started after his fall into the children's trench. He would go somewhere fairly reasonable to eat. Cosset himself.

A sudden downpour began just as he reached the main steps. He looked up, trying to judge how long it would last. A white sun shone through a thin layer of cloud, but there were darker clouds massing over Nelson's Column. He went back upstairs to fetch his greatcoat. As he passed Lode's room, he heard an unfamiliar voice say, 'Do you think he believed it?'

Lode replied, 'Oh, I think so. I don't see why he shouldn't.'

Prior went along to his own room, shrugged himself into the heavy greatcoat, and walked back to the lift. For once it arrived immediately in a great clanking of cables and gates. He told himself there was no reason to connect the overheard conversation with himself, but he found it difficult not to. The atmosphere in the unit was rather like that. Plots and counterplots, many of them seemingly pointless. So far he'd managed to hold himself aloof.

The underground was crowded. Currents of hot, dead air moved across his face as he waited on the edge of the platform. He couldn't carry his greatcoat – that was forbidden – and the sweat streamed down his sides. He found himself wondering whether this reaction was not excessive, whether he was not really ill. A subterranean rumbling, and the train erupted from the tunnel. He found himself a seat near the door and glanced at the girl beside him. Her hair was limp, her neck had a creased, swollen whiteness, and yet she was attractive in her rumpled skirt and white blouse. He glanced at her neckline, at the shadow between her breasts, then forced himself to look away. He found that rumpled look in women amazingly attractive.

He ate at a small café not far from Marble Arch. It wasn't as pleasant as it had looked from the outside: the walls had faded to a sallow beige, the windows streamed with condensation, blasts of steamy air belched from the swing doors into the kitchen as waitresses banged in and out. After his meal he lit a cigarette, drank two cups of hot, sweet, orange-coloured tea and persuaded himself he felt better.

A twisting flight of stairs led down to his basement flat. The dustbins from all the apartments in the house were kept in the small forecourt outside his living-room window. The smell of rotting cabbage lingered. At night there were rustlings that he tried to convince himself were cats. He put his key in the lock and walked in. The hall was dark, but not cool. He threw his briefcase and coat down on to a chair, then, pulling his tie off, went along the corridor to the bathroom, ran a cold bath and nerved himself to get in. His skin under the water looked bloated, and there were lines of silver bubbles trapped in his pubic hair. He ran his fingers through, releasing them, then clasped the edges of the bath and lowered his head beneath the water.

He got out, wrapped himself in a towel, opened the french windows into the small yard and lay down on the bed. Despite the open windows there was no decrease in stuffiness. The only way you could get a movement of air through the place was to have the french windows *and* the front door open. But then you let the smell of cabbage in as well.

His head was aching. He turned and looked at the photograph of Sarah by his bed. She was sitting on the bottom step of some kind of monument, younger, plump, though not fat, with her hair dressed low so that it almost covered her forehead. She was pretty, but he thought she looked more ordinary than she did now, when her cheekbones had become more prominent, and she wore her hair back from the high rounded forehead. Her smile was different too. In the photograph it looked friendly, confiding, almost puppyish. Now, though still warm, it always kept something back. She was coming to see him sometime in the next few weeks, or at least it seemed *almost* certain that she was.

He was afraid to count on it. He was afraid to picture her in the flat, because he knew that if he did the emptiness when her imagined presence failed him would be intolerable.

What he needed was to get out. These days he tried to circumvent the nightmares by going for a long walk early in the evening and then having three very large whiskies before bed. He'd reluctantly come to the conclusion that Rivers was right: sleeping draughts stopped working after the first few weeks, and when they stopped the nightmares returned with redoubled force. At least with the walk and the whisky he could count on a few good hours before they started.

Walking the city streets on a hot evening, he seemed to feel the pavements and the blank, white terraces breathe the day's stored heat into his face. His favourite walks were in Hyde Park. He liked the dusty gloom beneath the trees, the glint of the Serpentine in the distance. Close to, by the water's edge, there was even the whisper of a breeze. He stopped and watched some children paddling, three little girls with their dresses tucked into their drawers, then switched his attention to two much bigger girls, who came strolling along, arm in arm, but they read the hunger in his eyes too clearly and hurried past, giggling.

He felt restless, and, for once, the restlessness had nothing to do with sex. He had a definite and very strange sensation of wanting to *be* somewhere, a specific place, and of not knowing what that place was. He began to stroll towards the Achilles Monument. This was a frequent objective on his evening walks, for no particular reason except that its heroic grandeur both attracted and repelled him. It seemed to embody the same unreflecting admiration of courage that he found in 'The Charge of the Light Brigade', a poem that had meant a great deal to him as a boy, and still did, though what it meant had become considerably more complex. He stared up at the stupendous lunging figure, with its raised sword and shield, and thought, not for the first time, that he was looking at the representation of an ideal that no longer had validity.

Feeling dissatisfied, as if he'd expected the walk to end in something more than this routine encounter with Achilles, he turned to go, and noticed a man staring at him from under the shadow of the trees. We-ell. Young men who linger in the park at dusk can expect to be stared at. Deliberately, he quickened his pace, but then the back of his neck began to prickle, and a second later he heard his name called.

Lionel Spragge came lumbering up to him, out of breath and plaintive. 'Where are you going?' he demanded.

'Home.'

At that moment a gang of young people, five or six abreast, came charging along the path, arms linked, broke round Spragge like a river round a stone, and swept on. Two more boys, running to catch up, elbowed him out of the way. Under cover of this disturbance, Prior walked away.

'Hey, hang on.' Spragge came puffing up behind him. 'You can't just go walking off like that.'

'Why not?'

Spragge tapped his watch. 'Achilles. Nine o'clock.'

'Well?'

Spragge looked genuinely bewildered. 'Why make the appointment if you don't want to talk?'

Prior was beginning to feel frightened. 'I came out for a walk.'

'You came to see me.'

'Did I? I don't think so.'

'You *know* you did.' He stared at Prior. 'Well, if this doesn't take the biscuit. You said, "I can't talk now. Statue of Achilles, nine o'clock." What's the point of denying it? I mean what *is* the *point*?'

Spragge stank. His shirt was dirty, there was three days' growth of stubble on his chin, he'd been drinking, his eyes were bloodshot, *but the bewilderment was genuine.*

Prior said, 'Well, I'm here now anyway. What do you want?'

'If you hadn't turned up I'd've come to your house.'

'You don't know where I live.'

'I do. I followed you home.'

Prior laughed. A bark of astonishment.

'I was behind you on the platform. I sat three seats away from you on the train.' Spragge waggled his finger at his temple. 'You want to watch that. First step to the loony bin.'

'Piss off.'

Spragge caught his arm. 'Don't you want to know what I've got to say?'

'Not particularly.'

'Yes, you do,' Spragge said confidingly, leaning close, breathing into his face. 'Come on. Sit down.'

They found a place. At the other end of the bench an elderly woman sat, feeding a squirrel on nuts. Prior watched the animal's tiny black hands turning the nut delicately from side to side. 'Make it quick, will you?'

'I've remembered where I saw you.'

'Have you?'

'Meeting in Liverpool. You were speaking for the war, your father was speaking against.'

'Get to the point.'

'Oh, I know a lot about you. It's amazing what you can find out when you try, and finding out things was my job, wasn't it? When I had a job.'

'You didn't find things out,' Prior said crisply. 'You made them up.'

'You and the Ropers. You were like this.' Spragge jabbed his crossed fingers into Prior's face. 'Thick as thieves. *And* MacDowell.'

'That's why I got the job.'

'Oh, yeh, chuck me out and push you in.'

'I came a year after you left.'

'You told me I'd got a job.'

'No, I didn't.'

'Yes, you did. I went straight back home and told the wife. And then when I didn't hear anything I went to see Lode, and he threw me out. Bloody laughed at me.' Spragge turned his downwards-slanting turquoise eyes on Prior. 'You were just pumping me. Trying to make out I put the old cunt up to it.'

Prior got up. 'Wash your mouth out.'

'I thought that'd get you. You and her, you were –'

Prior crossed his fingers. 'Like this?'

Spragge stared at him, a vein standing out at his temple, like a worm under the clammy skin. 'People don't change.'

'No, I agree, they don't. I was a socialist then, I'm a socialist now. As far as the war goes, I don't have to prove my patriotism to *you*. I didn't offer you a job. I'm sorry if you told your wife I did, but that's your responsibility, not mine. Now bugger off and leave me alone.'

Prior walked away. He was aware of Spragge shouting, but was too angry to hear what he said. He thought Spragge might follow him, and that if he did there would be a fight. Spragge was taller, but older and flabbier. And he didn't care anyway. He wanted a fight. Spragge's face floated in front of him: the slightly bulbous nose, the sheen of sweat, the enlarged pores around the nostrils, the tufts of grey hair protruding from them. He'd never experienced such intense awareness of another person's body before, except in sex. What he felt was not simple dislike, but an intimate, obsessive, deeply *physical* hatred.

Back in the flat he rinsed his face in cold water and, trembling slightly, lay down on the bed. He plumped the pillows up behind him and groped in the pocket of his tunic for a cigarette. Weren't any. Then he remembered he'd been wearing his greatcoat. He got up, checked the pockets and found a packet of cigars. He didn't smoke cigars. But he must have bought them, and either smoked or offered them to somebody else, because there were two missing from the pack. Just as he must have arranged to meet Spragge. Spragge wouldn't have lied about that. It was too blatant, too easily discounted. No, he'd made the appointment all right. God knows when, or why.

He got up from the bed, feeling the palms of his hands sticky. He went to the front door and locked it, then stood with his back to it, looking down the dark corridor to the half-open door of his bedroom, feeling a momentary relief at being locked in, though he quickly realized this was nonsense. Whatever it was he needed to be afraid of, it was on this side of the door.

ELEVEN

After a pause, Rivers asked, 'Have there been any further episodes since then?'

'Yes, but I don't think any of them involved other people. I don't *think* they did.' Prior's mouth twisted. 'How would I know?'

'Nobody's said anything?'

'No.'

'How many?'

'Seven.'

'As many as *that*?'

Prior looked away.

'How long do they last?'

'Longest, three hours. Shortest . . . I don't know. Twenty minutes? The long ones are frightening because you don't know what you've done . . .' He attempted a laugh. 'You just know you've had plenty of time to do it.'

'I don't think you should assume you've done anything wrong.'

'Don't you? Well, if it's so bloody good, why do I need to forget it?'

Rivers waited a while. 'What do you think you might have done?'

'I don't know, do I? Nipped across to Whitechapel and ripped up a few prostitutes.'

Silence.

'Look,' Prior said, with the air of one attempting to engage the village idiot in rational discourse, 'you know as well as I do that that . . .' He flung himself back in his chair. 'I'm not going to do this, I just refuse.'

Rivers waited.

Still not looking at him, Prior said, or rather chanted, 'I have certain impulses which I do not give way to except in strict moderation and at *the other person's* request. At least, in *this* state I don't. I'm simply pointing out that in the the the the *other* state I might not be so *fucking* scrupulous. And don't look at me like that.'

'I'm sorry.'

'You think this is a load of self-dramatizing rubbish, don't you?'

Rivers said carefully, 'I think you've been alone with the problem too long.'

'There's nothing ridiculous in anything I've said.'

Rivers looked at the pale, proud, wintry face and caught a sigh. 'I certainly wouldn't call it ridiculous.'

'The fact is I don't know and neither do you, so you're in no position to pontificate.'

Silence. Rivers said, 'How are the nightmares?'

'Bad. Oh, I had one you'll like. I was was walking along a path in a kind of desert and straight ahead of me was an eyeball. Not this size.' Prior's cheeks twitched like boiling porridge. 'Huge. And alive. And it was directly in front of me and I knew this time it was going to get me.' He smiled. 'Do whatever it is eyeballs do. Fortunately, there was a river running along beside the path, so I leapt into the river and I was all right.' He gazed straight at Rivers. 'But then I suppose all your patients jump into fucking rivers sooner or later, don't they?'

The antagonism was startling. They might have been back at Craiglockhart, at the beginning of Prior's treatment. 'How did you feel about being in the river?'

'Fine. It sang to me, a sort of lullaby, it kept telling me I was going to be all right and I *was* all right – as long as I stayed in the river.'

'You didn't feel you wanted to get out?'

'In the dream? No. Now, YES.'

Rivers spread his hands. 'Your coming here is entirely voluntary.'

'With *that* degree of dependency? Of course it's not fucking voluntary.' He started to say something else and bit it back. 'I'm sorry.'

'Don't be, there's no need.' Suddenly Rivers leant across the desk. 'I'm not here to be liked.'

'I *am* sorry,' Prior said, his face and voice hardening. 'I thought I was supposed to be accepting my emotions? Well, my emotion is that I'm sorry.'

'In that case I accept your apology.'

A pause. 'Do you know what I do when I come round from one of these spells? I look at my hands because I half expect to see them covered in hair.'

Rivers made no comment.

'You've read Jekyll and Hyde?'

'Yes.' Rivers had been waiting for the reference. Patients who suffered from fugue states invariably referred to the dissociated state – jocularly, but not without fear – as 'Hyde'. 'In real life, you know, the fugue state is – well, I was going to say "never", but, in fact, there is one case – is almost never the darker side of the personality. Usually it's no more than a difference in mood.'

'But we don't *know*. You see, the conversation I'm trying not to have is the one where I point out that you could find out in five minutes flat and you say, "Yes, I know, but I won't do it."'

Silence.

'Well?'

'I'm sorry, I thought you said you didn't want that conversation.'

'You know, for somebody who isn't here to be liked you have the most wonderful manner. You used hypnosis at Craiglockhart.'

'Yes, but in that case we could check the memory. You see, one of the things people who believe in . . . the extensive use of hypnosis claim – well, they don't even claim it, they assume it – is that memories recovered in that way are genuine memories. But they're very often not. They can be fantasies, or they can be responses to suggestions from the therapist. Because one's constantly making suggestions, and the ones you're not aware of making – not conscious of – are by far the most powerful. And that's dangerous because most therapists are interested in dissociated states and so they – unconsciously of course – encourage the patient further down that path. And one can't avoid doing it. Even if one excludes everything else, there's still the enlargement of the pupils of the eyes.'

Prior leant forward and peered. 'Yours are enlarged.'

Rivers took a deep breath. 'You can get your memory back by the same methods we used at Craiglockhart. You were very good at it.'

'Is that why you do this?' Prior swept his hand down across his eyes.

Rivers smiled. 'No, of course not, it's just a habit. Eye-strain. Now can we –'

'No, that's not true. If it was eye-strain, you'd do it at random and you don't. You do it when . . . when something touches a nerve. Or or . . . It *is* a way of hiding your feelings. You've just said it yourself, the eyes are the one part you can't turn into wallpaper – and so you cover them up.'

Rivers found this disconcerting. He tried to go on with what he'd been going to say, and realized he'd lost the train of thought. After so many hours of probing, manipulating, speculating, provoking, teasing, Prior had finally – and almost casually – succeeded. He couldn't ignore this; it had to be dealt with. 'I think . . . if as you say it *isn't* random – and I don't *know* because it's not something I'm aware of – it's probably something to do with not wanting to see the patient. For me the patient's expressions and gestures aren't much use, because I have no visual memory, so I think perhaps I stop myself seeing him as a way of concentrating on what he's saying. All right? Now perhaps we can –'

'No visual memory at all?'

'None at all.'

'I don't see how you think.'

'Well, I suspect you're a very visual person. Could we –'

'Have you always been like this?'

Rivers thought, *all right*. He stood up and indicated to Prior that they should exchange seats. Prior looked surprised and even uneasy, but quickly recovered and sat down in Rivers's chair with considerable aplomb. Rivers saw him look round the study, taking in his changed perspective on the room. 'Isn't this against the rules?' he asked.

'I can't think of a single rule we're not breaking.'

'Can't you?' Prior said, smiling his delicate smile. 'I can.'

'I'm going to show you how boring this job is. When I was five . . .'

Prior shifted his position, leant forward, rested his chin on his clasped hands, and said, in meltingly empathic tones, 'Yes? Go on.'

Rivers was not in fact breaking the rules. He intended to do no more than offer Prior an illustration from his own experience that he'd already used several times in public lectures, but he hadn't reckoned on doing it while confronted by a caricature of himself. 'One of the expressions of having no visual memory is that I can't remember the interior of any building I've ever been in. I can't remember this house when I'm not in it. I can't remember Craiglockhart, though I lived there for over a year. I can't remember St John's, though I've lived there twenty years, but there is one interior I *do* remember and that's a house in Brighton I lived in till I was five. I can remember *part* of that. The basement kitchen, the drawing-room, the dining-room, my father's study, but I can't remember anything at all about upstairs. And I've come to believe – I won't go into the reasons – that something happened to me on the top floor that was so terrible that I simply had to forget it. And in order to ensure that I forgot I suppressed not just the *one* memory, but the capacity to remember things visually at all.' Rivers paused, and waited for a response.

'You were raped,' Prior said. 'Or beaten.'

Rivers's face went stiff with shock. 'I really don't think I was.'

'No, well, you wouldn't, would you? The whole point is it's too terrible to contemplate.'

Rivers said something he knew he'd regret, but he had to say it. 'This was my father's vicarage.'

'I was raped in a vicarage once.'

It was on the tip of Rivers's tongue to say that no doubt Prior had been 'raped' in any number of places, but he managed to restrain himself. 'When I said terrible I meant to a child of that age. I was five remember. Things happen to children which are an enormous shock to the child, but which wouldn't seem terrible or or or even particularly important to an adult.'

'And equally things happen to children which are genuinely terrible. And would be recognized as terrible by *anybody* at *any* age.'

'Yes, of course. How old were you?'

'Eleven. I wasn't meaning myself.'

'You don't classify that as "terrible"?'

'*No*. I was receiving extra tuition.' He gave a yelping laugh. 'God, was I receiving extra tuition. From the parish priest, Father Mackenzie. My mother offered him a shilling a week – more than she could afford – but he said, "Don't worry, my good woman, I have seldom seen a more promising boy."' He added irritably, 'Don't look so shocked, Rivers.'

'I am shocked.'

'Then you shouldn't be. He got paid in kind, that's all.' Suddenly

Prior leant forward and grasped Rivers's knee, digging his fingers in round the kneecap. 'Everything has to be paid for, doesn't it?' He grasped the knee harder. *'Doesn't it?'*

'No.'

Prior let go. 'This terrible-in-big-black-inverted-commas thing that happened to you, what do *you* think it was?'

'I don't know. Dressing-gown on the back of a door?'

'As bad as *that*? Oh, my God.'

Rivers pressed on in defiance of Prior's smile. 'I had a patient once who became claustrophobic as the result of being accidentally locked in a corridor with a fierce dog. Or it seemed fierce to him. In that –'

'Oh, I see. Even the bloody dog wasn't *really* fierce.'

'In that case his parents didn't even know it had happened.'

'You say you were five when this . . . non-event didn't happen?'

'Yes.'

'How old were you when you started to stammer?'

'Fi-ive.'

Prior leant back in Rivers's chair and smiled. *'Big dog.'*

'I didn't mean to imply there was –'

'For God's *sake*. Whatever it was, you *blinded* yourself so you wouldn't have to go on seeing it.'

'I wouldn't put it as dramatically as that.'

'You destroyed your visual memory. You put your mind's eye *out*. Is that what happened, or isn't it?'

Rivers struggled with himself. Then said simply, 'Yes.'

'Do you ever think you're on the verge of remembering?'

'Sometimes.'

'And what do you feel?'

'Fear.' He smiled. 'Because the child's emotions are still attached to the memory.'

'We're back to the dressing-gown.'

'Yes. Yes. I'm afraid we are, because I do sincerely believe it may be as simple as that.'

'Then one can only applaud,' Prior said, and did. Three loud claps.

'You know . . .' Rivers hesitated and started again. 'You must be wary of filling the gaps in your memory with . . . with monsters. I think we all tend to do it. As soon as we're left with a blank, we start projecting our worst fears on to it. It's a bit like the guide for medieval map-makers, isn't it? *Where unknown, there place monsters*. But I do think you should try not to do it, because what you're really doing is subjecting yourself to a constant stream of suggestion of of a very negative kind.'

'All right. I'll try not to. I'll substitute the Rivers guide to map-making: *Where unknown, there place dressing-gowns*. Or just possibly, *dogs*. Here, have your chair back.' Prior settled himself back into the patient's chair, murmuring, 'Do you know, Rivers, you're as neurotic as I am? And that's saying quite a lot.'

Rivers rested his chin on his hands. 'How do you feel about that?'

'Oh, my God, we *are* back to normal. You mean, "Do I feel a nasty, mean-spirited sense of triumph?" No. I'm mean-spirited enough, I'm just not stupid enough.' Prior brooded a moment. 'There's one thing wrong with the Rivers guide to map-making. Suppose there really are monsters?'

'I think if there are, we'll meet them soon enough.'

Prior looked straight at Rivers. 'I'm frightened.'

'I know.'

When Prior finally left – it had been a long, exhausting session – Rivers switched off the desk lamp, went to sit in his armchair by the fire, and indulged in some concentrated, unobserved eye-rubbing. *Did* he do it 'when something touched a nerve'? It was possible, he supposed. If there was a pattern, Prior would certainly have spotted it. On the other hand, Prior was equally capable of making the whole thing up.

He didn't regret the decision to give Prior what he'd always claimed he wanted – to change places – because in the process he'd discovered an aspect of Prior that mightn't have been uncovered in any other way. Not so much the 'extra tuition' – though that was interesting, particularly in view of Prior's habit of aggressive flirtation – as the assumption that Rivers's loss of visual memory must have some totally traumatic explanation. That had revealed more about Prior than he was aware of.

Though Prior had been a formidable interrogator. *Whatever it was, you blinded yourself so you wouldn't have to go on seeing it . . . You put your mind's eye out*. Simply by being rougher than any professional colleague would ever have been, Prior had brought him face to face with the full extent of his loss. People tended to assume he didn't know what he'd lost, but that wasn't true. He did know, or glimpsed at least. Once, in the Torres Straits, he'd attended a court held by the British official in collaboration with the native chiefs, and an old woman had given evidence about a dispute in which she was involved. As she spoke, she'd glanced from side to side, clearly reliving every detail of the events she was describing, and very obviously *seeing* people who were not present in court. And he had looked at her, this scrawny, half-naked, elderly, illiterate woman, and he had envied her. No doubt he'd encountered Europeans who had visual memories of equal power, but his own deficiency had never before been brought home to him with such force.

It *was* a loss, and he had long been aware of it, though he had been slow to connect it with the Brighton house experience. Slower still to recognize that the impact of the experience had gone beyond the loss of visual memory and had occasioned a deep split between the rational, analytical cast of his mind and his emotions. It was easy to overstate this: he had, after all, been subject to a form of education which is designed to inculcate precisely such a split, but he thought the division went deeper in him than it did in most men. It was almost as if the experience – whatever it was – had triggered an attempt at dissociation of personality, though, mercifully, not a successful one. Still, he had been, throughout most of his life, a deeply divided man, and though he would once have said that this division exercised little, if any, influence on his thinking, he had come to believe it had determined the direction of his research.

Many years after that initial unremembered experience, he and Henry Head had conducted an experiment together. The nerve supplying Head's left forearm had been severed and sutured, and then over a period of five years they had traced the progress of regeneration. This had taken place in two phases. The first was characterized by a high threshold of sensation, though when the sensation was finally evoked it was, to use Head's own word, 'extreme'. In addition to this all-or-nothing quality, the sensation was difficult to localize. Sitting blindfold at the table, Head had been unable to locate the stimulus that was causing him such severe pain. This primitive form of innervation they called the protopathic. The second phase of regeneration – which they called the epicritic – followed some months later, and was characterized by the ability to make graduated responses and to locate the source of a stimulus precisely. As the epicritic level of innervation was restored, the lower, or protopathic, level was partially integrated with it and partially suppressed, so that the epicritic system carried out two functions: one, to help the organism adapt to its environment by supplying it with accurate information; the other, to suppress the protopathic, to keep the animal within leashed. Inevitably, as time went on, both words had acquired broader meanings, so that 'epicritic' came to stand for everything rational, ordered, cerebral, objective, while 'protopathic' referred to the emotional, the sensual, the chaotic, the primitive. In this way the experiment both reflected Rivers's internal divisions and supplied him with a vocabulary in which to express them. He might almost have said with Henry Jekyll, *It was on the moral side, and in my own person, that I learned to recognize the thorough and primitive duality of man; I saw that, of the two natures that contended in the field of my consciousness, even if I could rightly be said to be either, it was only because I was radically both . . .*

It was odd how the term 'Jekyll and Hyde' had passed into the language, so that even people who had never read Stevenson's story used the names as a shorthand for internal divisions. Prior spoke of looking at his hands to make sure they had not been transformed into the hairy hands of Hyde, and he was not alone in that. Every patient Rivers had ever had who suffered from a fugue state sooner or later referred to that state as 'Hyde', and generally this was a plea for reassurance. In a hospital setting, where the fugue state could be observed, such reassurance was easily given, but it was less easy to reassure Prior. Partly because the fugue state *couldn't* be observed, but also because Prior's sense of the darker side of his personality was unusually strong. He might talk about being incapable of sexual guilt, but, Rivers thought, he was deeply ashamed of his sadistic impulses, even frightened of them. He believed there were monsters on his map, and who was to say he was wrong?

There was one genuinely disturbing feature of the case: that odd business of making an appointment in the fugue state and keeping it in the normal state. It suggested the fugue state was capable of influencing Prior's behaviour even when it was not present, in other words, that it was functioning as a co-consciousness. Not that a dual personality need develop even from that. He intended to make sure it didn't. There would be no hypnosis, no artificial creation of dissociated states for experimental purposes, no encouraging Prior to think of the fugue state as an alternative self. Even so. It had to be remembered Prior was no mere bundle of symptoms, but an extremely complex personality with his own views on his condition. And his imagination was already at work, doing everything it could to transform the fugue state into a malignant double. He believed in the monsters – and whatever Rivers might decide to do, or refrain from doing – Prior's belief in them would inevitably give them power.

TWELVE

'Now I want you to draw me an elephant,' Head said.

His voice distorted, as if he were blowing bubbles in soapy water, Lucas replied, 'Yeth ah seen dom. Up. Uvver end.'

He took the notepad and pencil, and began to draw. Rivers was sitting beside Head, but neither of them spoke since Lucas's concentration must not be disturbed. They had been doing the tests for half an hour and Lucas was already tired. His tongue protruded between his teeth, giving him the look of a small boy learning to read, except that, in Lucas's case, the protrusion was permanent.

Rivers noticed Head looking at the shrapnel wound on Lucas's shaved scalp, and knew he was thinking about the technical problems of duplicating this on the skull of the cadaver he'd been working on that morning. It was an interesting technique, Rivers thought. Head measured the dimensions of the wound on the living patient, then traced the outline on to the skull of a cadaver, drilled holes at regular intervals around the outline, and introduced a blue dye into the holes. The entire skull cap could then be lifted off and the brain structures underlying the dyed area dissected and identified. In this way the area of brain death could be correlated precisely with the nature of the patient's language defects.

A laborious business, made more so by the need to duplicate the wounds of *two* patients on every cadaver. One of the more surprising consequences of the war was a shortage of suitable male corpses.

Rivers lifted his hands to his chin, smelling the medical school smell of human fat and formaldehyde, only partially masked by carbolic soap. He watched Head's expression as he looked at Lucas's shaved scalp, and realized it differed hardly at all from his expression that morning as he'd bent over the cadaver. For the moment, Lucas had become simply a technical problem. Then Lucas looked up from his task, and instantly Head's face flashed open in his transforming smile. A murmur of encouragement, and Lucas returned to his drawing. Head's face, looking at the ridged purple scar on the shaved head, again became remote, withdrawn. His empathy, his strong sense of the humanity he shared with his patients, was again suspended. A necessary suspension, without which the practice of medical research, and indeed of medicine itself, would hardly be possible, but none the less identifiably the same suspension the soldier must achieve in order to kill. The end was different, but the psychological mechanism employed to achieve it was essentially the same. What Head was doing, Rivers thought, was in some ways a benign, epicritic form of the morbid dissociation that had begun to afflict Prior. Head's dissociation was healthy because the researcher and the physician each had instant access to the experience of the other, and both had access to Head's experience in all other areas of his life. Prior's was pathological because areas of his conscious experience had become inaccessible to memory. What was interesting was why Head's dissociation didn't lead to the kind of split that had taken place in Prior. Rivers shifted his position, and sighed. One began by finding mental illness mystifying, and ended by being still more mystified by health.

Lucas had finished. Head leant across the desk and took the drawing from him. 'Hmm,' he said, looking at the remarkably cow-like creature in front of him. A long pause. 'What's an elephant got in front?'

Again the blurting voice, always on the verge of becoming a wail. 'He got a big' – Lucas's good hand waved up and down – 'straight about a yard long.'

'Do you know what it's called?'

'Same what you. Drive. Water with.'

'Has he got a *trunk*?'

Lucas wriggled in his wheelchair and laughed. 'He lost it.'

He reached for his drawing, wanting to correct it, but Head slipped it quickly into the file. 'Sums now.'

They went quickly through a range of simple sums. Lucas, whose ability to understand numbers was unimpaired, got them predictably right. It was Head's custom to alternate tasks the patient found difficult or impossible with others that he could perform successfully. The next task – designed to discover whether Lucas's understanding of 'right' and 'left' was impaired – involved his attempting to imitate movements of Head's arms, first in a mirror and then facing him across the desk.

Rivers watched Head raise his left hand – 'professional in shape and size; . . . large, firm, white and comely' – and thought he probably knew that hand better than any part of his own body. He'd experimented on it for five years, after all, and even now could have traced on to the skin the outline of the remaining area of protopathic innervation – for the process of regeneration is never complete. A triangle of skin between the thumb and forefinger retained the primitive, all-or-nothing responses and remained abnormally sensitive to changes in temperature. Sometimes, on a cold day, he would notice Head shielding this triangle of skin beneath his other hand.

For a while, after the tests were complete, Head chatted to Lucas about the results. It was Head's particular gift to be able to involve his patients in the study of their own condition. Lucas's face, as Head outlined the extent of his impairments, was alight with what one could only call clinical interest. When, finally, an orderly appeared and wheeled him out of the room, he was smiling.

'He has . . . improved,' Head said. 'Slightly.' He brushed his thinning hair back from his forehead and for a moment looked utterly bleak. 'Tea?'

'I wouldn't mind a glass of milk.'

'Milk?'

Rivers patted his midriff. 'Keeps the ulcers quiet.'

'Why, are they protesting?'

'God, how I hate psychologists.'

Head laughed. 'I'll get you the milk.'

Rivers glanced at *The Times* while he waited. In the Pemberton Billing trial they'd reached the medical evidence – such as it was. As Head came back into the room, Rivers read aloud: '"Asked what should be done with such people. Dr Serrel Cooke replied, 'They are monsters. They should be locked up.'" The voice of psychological medicine.'

Head handed him a cup. 'Put it down, Rivers.'

Rivers folded the paper. 'I keep trying to tell myself it's funny.'

'Well, it is, a lot of it. It was hilarious when that woman told the Judge his name was in the Black Book.' He waited for a reply. 'Anyway, when do you want to see Lucas? Tomorrow?'

'Oh, I think we give the poor little blighter a rest, don't we? Monday?'

They talked for a while about Lucas, then drifted into a rambling conversation about the use of pacifist orderlies. The hospital contained a great many paralysed patients in a building not designed to accommodate them. There were only two lifts. The nurses and the existing orderlies – men who were either disabled or above military age – did their best, but the lives of patients were inevitably more restricted than they need have been. What was desperately required was young male muscle, and this the pacifist orderlies – recruited under the Home Office scheme – supplied. But they also aroused hostility in the staff obliged to work with them. It had now reached a point where it was doubtful whether the hospital could go on using them. The irrationality of getting rid of much needed labour exasperated Rivers, and he had spoken out against it at the last meeting of the hospital management committee, rather too forcefully, perhaps, or at least Head seemed to think so. 'I'm not g-going b-back on it,' he said. 'I've spent m-most of my l-life t-t-toning down what I w-wanted to s-say. I'm not d-doing it any more.'

Head looked at him. 'What happened to the gently flowing Rivers we all used to know and love?'

'Went AWOL in Scotland. Never been seen since.'

'Yes.'

'Yes what?'

'Yes, that was my impression.'

The lift door was about to close. Rivers broke into a run, and Wantage, one of the non-pacifist orderlies, clanged the gate open again. 'There you are, sir,' he said, stepping back. 'Room for a thin one.'

He was returning a man in a wheelchair to the ward. Rivers squeezed in beside the wheelchair and pressed the button for the top floor.

Wantage was the most popular of the orderlies, partly because his built-up boot supplied an instant explanation for why he wasn't in France. He was a fat, jolly man with a limitless capacity for hate. He hated skivers, he hated shirkers, he hated conchies, he hated the Huns, he hated the Kaiser. He loved the war. He had the gentlest hands in the hospital. He would have given anything to be able to go and fight. Whenever Rivers saw him lurching along behind a wheelchair, he was reminded of the crippled boy in the Pied Piper story, left behind when the other children went into the mountain.

At the second floor the lift stopped and a young nurse got in. Viggors, the patient in the wheelchair, spoke to her, blushing slightly – she was evidently a great favourite – and then sat, slumped to one side, his eyes level with her waist, gazing covertly at her breasts. Wantage chattered on. On the third floor the lift stopped again and Wantage pushed the wheelchair out.

Rivers was left wishing he hadn't seen that look. Every day in this hospital one was brutally reminded that the worst tragedies of the war were not marked by little white crosses.

For safety reasons – *his* patients were mobile and could use the fire escapes – both his wards were on the top floor. The hospital had been built as a children's hospital; the top floor had been the nursery and the walls were decorated with Baa-baa Black Sheep, Little Bo Peep, Red Riding Hood, Humpty-Dumpty. The windows were barred. On his arrival Rivers had asked for these bars to be removed, but the War Office refused to pay for any alterations beyond the absolute minimum: the provision of adult-size baths and lavatories. *Not* washbasins. Lawrence was there now, shaving in a basin that barely reached his knees. The eye, deprived of normal perspective, saw him as a giant. No amount of experience seemed to correct the initial impression.

Rivers collected his overnight key from sister and walked along the corridor to his own room. The room was vast, with a huge bay window overlooking Vincent Square. He went through into the adjoining room and asked his secretary to send Captain Manning in.

Manning had been admitted because the anxiety attacks he'd suffered ever since his return from France had become more severe, partly as a result of his obsession with the Pemberton Billing affair. Rivers would have liked to tell him to ignore the trial for the farrago of muck-raking nonsense it was, but that was not possible. Manning had been sent a newspaper cutting about Maud Allan and the 'cult of the clitoris'. More recently he'd received a copy of the 47,000 article. Manning was being targeted, presumably by someone who knew he was a homosexual, and he could hardly be expected to ignore that.

'Have you been waiting long?' Rivers asked.

'Couple of minutes.'

Manning looked tired. No doubt last night had been spent dreading coming into hospital. 'How are you settling in?'

'All right. I've been given a room to myself. I didn't expect that.'

'Have you brought the article with you?' Rivers asked.

Manning handed it over. It was not, as Rivers had been assuming, a newspaper cutting, but a specially produced copy, printed on to thick card. At the top – typewritten – was the message: *In the hope that this will awaken your conscience.*

'Did you read it at the time?' Manning asked. 'When it first came out?'

'No.' Rivers smiled faintly. 'A pleasure postponed.'

AS I SEE IT – THE FIRST 47,000

Harlots on the Wall

There have been given many reasons why England is prevented from putting her full strength into the War. On several occasions in the columns of the *Imperialist* I have suggested that Germany is making use of subtle but successful means to nullify our effort. Hope of profit cannot be the only reason for our betrayal. All nations have their Harlots on the Wall, but these are discovered in the first assault and the necessary action is taken. It is in the citadel that the true danger lies. Corruption and blackmail being the work of menials is cheaper than bribery. Moreover, fear of exposure entraps and makes slaves of men whom money could never buy. There is all the more reason, as I see it, to suppose that the Germans, with their usual efficiency, are making use of the most productive and cheapest methods.

Often in this column I have hinted at the possession of knowledge which tends to substantiate this view. Within the past few days the most extraordinary facts have been placed before me which co-ordinate with my past information.

Spreading Debauchery

There exists in the *cabinet noir* of a certain German Prince a book compiled by the Secret Service from the reports of German agents who have infested this country for the past twenty years, agents so vile and spreading debauchery of such a lasciviousness as only German minds could conceive and only German bodies execute.

Sodom and Lesbia

The officer who discovered this book while on special service briefly outlined for me its stupefying contents. In the beginning of the book is a precis of general instructions regarding the propagation of evils which all decent men thought had perished in Sodom and Lesbia. The blasphemous compilers even speak of the Groves and High Places mentioned in the Bible. The most insidious arguments are outlined for the use of the German agent in his revolting work. Then more than a thousand pages are filled with the names mentioned by German agents in their reports. There are the names of 47,000 English men and women.

It is a most catholic miscellany. The names of privy councillors, youths of the chorus, wives of Cabinet Ministers, dancing girls, even Cabinet Ministers themselves, while diplomats, poets, bankers, editors, newspaper proprietors and members of His Majesty's household follow each other with no order of precedence.

As an example of the thoroughness with which the German agent works, lists of public houses and bars were given which had been successfully demoralized. These could then be depended upon to spread vice with the help of only one fixed agent. To secure those whose social standing would suffer from frequenting public places, comfortable flats were taken and furnished in an erotic manner. Paphian photographs were distributed, while equivocal pamphlets were printed as the anonymous work of well-known writers.

The Navy in Danger

No one in the social scale was exempted from contamination by this perfect system. Agents were specially enlisted in the navy, particularly in the engine-rooms. These had their special instructions. Incestuous bars were established in Portsmouth and Chatham. In these meeting places the stamina of British sailors was undermined. More dangerous still, German agents, under the guise of indecent liaison, could obtain information as to the disposition of the fleet.

Even the loiterer in the streets was not immune. Meretricious agents of the Kaiser were stationed at such points as Marble Arch and Hyde Park Corner. In this black book of sin details were given of the unnatural defloration of children who were drawn to the parks by the summer evening concerts.

The World of High Politics

Impure as were all these things, the great danger was seen in the reports of those agents who had obtained *entrée* to the world of high politics. Wives of men in supreme position were entangled. In Lesbian ecstasy the most sacred secrets of State were betrayed. The sexual peculiarities of members of the peerage were used as a leverage to open fruitful fields for espionage.

In the glossary of this book is a list of expressions supposed to be used among themselves by the soul-sick victims of this nauseating disease so skilfully spread by Potsdam.

Lives are in Jeopardy

In his official reports the German agent is not an idle boaster. The thought that 47,000 English men and women are held in enemy bondage through fear calls all clean spirits to mortal combat. There are three million men in France whose lives are in jeopardy, and whose bravery is of no avail because of the lack of moral courage in 47,000 of their countrymen, and numbering among their ranks, as they do, men and women in whose hands the destiny of this Empire rests.

As I see it, a carefully cultivated introduction of practices which hint at the extermination of the race is to be the means by which the German is to prevent us avenging those mounds of lime and mud which once were Britons.

The Fall of Rome
When in time I grasped the perfection of this demoniacal plan, it seemed to me that all the horrors of shells and gas and pestilence introduced by the Germans in their open warfare would have but a fraction of the effect in exterminating the manhood of Britain as the plan by which they have already destroyed the first 47,000.

As I have already said in these columns, it is a terrible thought to contemplate that the British Empire should fall as fell the great Empire of Rome, and the victor now, as then, should be the Hun.

The story of the contents of this book has opened my eyes, and the matter must not rest.

Rivers threw the page down. 'If only *German* minds can conceive of this lasciviousness and only *German* bodies execute it, how on earth do the 47,000 manage to do it?' He took off his glasses and swept his hand down across his eyes. 'Sorry, I'm being donnish.' He looked at Manning, noting the lines of strain around his eyes, the coarse tremor as he raised the cigarette to his mouth. For somebody like Manning, profoundly committed to living a double life, the revelation that both sides of his life were visible to unknown eyes must be like having the door to the innermost part of one's identity smashed open. 'Has anybody else been sent this?'

'Ross. One or two others.'

'Friends of Ross?'

'Yes.'

'Ross is a . . . quite a dangerous man to know.'

'What can I do, Rivers? It's not a recent friendship.'

Rivers sighed. 'I don't think you can do anything.'

Manning sat brooding. 'I think it would help if I felt I could understand it. I mean, I can see the war's going pretty badly and there are always going to be people who want scapegoats instead of *reasons*, but . . . Why this? I can *see* why people with German names get beaten up . . . or or interned. And conchies. I don't approve, but I can understand it. I don't understand this.'

'I'm not sure I do. I *think* it's the result of certain impulses rising to the surface in wartime, and having to be very formally disowned. Homosexuality, for instance. In war there's this enormous glorification of love between men, and yet at the same time it arouses anxiety. Is it the right kind of love? Well, one way to make sure it's the right kind is to make public disapproval of the other thing crystal clear. And then there's pleasure in killing –'

Manning looked shocked. 'I don't know that –'

'No, I meant civilians. Vicarious, but real nevertheless. And in the process sadistic impulses are aroused that would normally be repressed, and that also causes anxiety. So to put on a play by a *known* homosexual in which a woman kisses a man's severed head . . .'

'I talked about the trial to Jane. I said I thought the real target was Ross, and one or two others, and she said of course I did. Seeing – what was it? "Seeing his own sex as peripheral to the point at issue was a feat of mental agility of which no man is capable."'

'I look forward to meeting Mrs Manning one day.'

'She says the the . . . *sentimentality* about the role women are playing – doing their bit and all that – really masks a kind of deep-rooted fear that they're getting out of line. She thinks pillorying Maud Allan is actually a way of teaching them a lesson. Not just lesbians. *All* women. Just as Salome is presented as a strong woman by Wilde, and yet at the same time she has to be killed. I mean it is quite striking at the end when all the men fall on her and kill her.'

'What do you think about that?'

'I think it's a bit naïve. I think it ignores Wilde's identification with Salome. He isn't saying women like this have to be destroyed. He's saying people like me have to be destroyed. And how right he was. *Is*.'

This was all very well, Rivers thought, but Manning was ill, and it was not literary discussion that was going to cure him.

'Do you think Spencer's mad?' Manning asked abruptly.

'On the basis of his evidence, yes. Though whether he'll be recognized as mad . . .'

'It's an odd contrast with Sassoon, isn't it?'

Rivers looked surprised.

'Spencer being fêted like this. Sassoon says something perfectly sensible about the war, and he's packed off to a mental hospital.'

Of course, Rivers thought, all the members of Robert Ross's circle would know the story of Sassoon's protest against the war, and the part he'd played in persuading Sassoon to go back.

Manning said, 'I suppose I shouldn't mention him?'

'Why not?'

'Because he's a patient.'

'He's somebody we both know.'

'Only he's been on my mind lately. I was wondering if they'd have the nerve to send this to *him*. Or to anybody out there.'

'I think the sort of mind that produces this can't conceive of the possibility that any of "the 47,000" might be in France.'

So far Manning had found it impossible to talk about the war. Manning himself would have denied this. He would have said they talked about it all the time: strategy, tactics, war aims, the curiously inadequate response of civilian writers, the poems of Sassoon and Graves. Suddenly, Rivers thought he saw a way of beginning, very gently, to force the issue. 'Are you familiar with the strict Freudian view of war neurosis?' he asked. Manning, he knew, had read a certain amount of Freud.

'I didn't know there was one.'

'Oh, yes. Basically, they believe the experience of an all-male environment, with a high level of emotional intensity, together with the experience of battle, arouses homosexual and sadistic impulses that are normally repressed. In vulnerable men – obviously those in whom the repressed desires are particularly strong – this leads to breakdown.'

'Is that what *you* believe?'

Rivers shook his head. 'I want to know what *you* think.'

'I don't know what makes other people break down. I don't think sex had much to do with *my* breakdown.' A slight smile. 'But then I'm not a repressed homosexual.'

Rivers smiled back. 'But you must have a . . . an instinctive reaction, that it's *possible*, or it's obvious nonsense, or –'

'I'm just trying to think. Do you know Sassoon's poem "The Kiss"?'

'The one about the bayonet. Yes.'

'I think that's the strongest poem he's ever written. You know, I've never served with him so I don't know this from personal experience, but I've talked a lot to Robert Graves and he says the extent to which Sassoon contrives to be two totally different people at the Front is absolutely amazing. You know he's a tremendously successful and *bloodthirsty* platoon commander, and yet at the same time, back in billets, out comes the notebook. Another anti-war poem. And the poem uses the experience of the platoon commander, but it never uses any of his attitudes. And yet for once, in that *one* poem, he gets both versions of himself in.'

Yes, Rivers thought. 'Yes,' he said. 'I see that.'

'And of course it's crawling with sexual ambiguities. But then I think it's too easy to see that as a matter of personal . . . I don't know what. The fact is the *army*'s attitude to the bayonet is pretty bloody ambiguous. You read the training manuals and they're all going on about importance of close combat. Fair enough, but you get the impression there's a value in it which is independent of whether it gains the objective or not. It's proper war. *Manly* war. Not all this nonsense about machine-guns and shrapnel. And it's reflected in the training. I mean, it's one long stream of sexual innuendo. *Stick him in the gooleys. No more little fritzes.* If Sassoon had used language like that, he'd never have been published.' Manning stopped abruptly. 'You know I think I've lost the thread. No, that's it, I was trying . . . I was trying to be honest and think whether I hated bayonet practice more because . . . because the body that the sack represents is one that I . . . come on, Rivers. Nice psychological term?'

'Love.'

'I don't know what the answer is. I don't *think* so. We *all* hate it. I've no way of knowing whether I hate it more, because we don't talk about it. It's just a bloody awful job, and we get on and do it. I mean, you split enormous parts of yourself off, anyway.'

'Is that what you did?'

'I suppose so.' For a moment it seemed he was about to go on, then he shook his head.

When he was sure there'd be no more, Rivers said, 'You know we are going to have to talk about the war, Charles.'

'I do talk about it.'

Silence.

'I just don't see what good it would do to churn everything up. I know what the theory is.' He looked down at his hands. 'My son Robert, when he was little . . . he used to enjoy being bathed. And then quite suddenly he turned against it. He used to go stiff and scream blue murder every time his nurse tried to put him in. And it turned out he'd been watching the water go down the plug-hole and he obviously thought he might go down with it. Everybody told him not to be stupid.' Manning smiled. 'I must say it struck me as an *eminently* reasonable fear.'

Rivers smiled. 'I won't let you go down the plug-hole.'

At dinner the talk was all of the Pemberton Billing trial. Everybody was depressed by the medical evidence, since this was the first time psychologists had been invited to pronounce in court on such a subject.

'What do we get?' somebody asked. 'Serrel Cooke rambling on about monsters and hereditary degeneracy. The man's a joke.'

If he is, I've lost my sense of humour, Rivers thought.

After dinner he was glad to escape from the hospital and go for a stroll round the square. London had become a depressing place. Every placard, every newsboy's cry, every headline focused on the trial. Lord Alfred Douglas was in the witness-box now, apparently blaming England's poor showing in the war on the plays of Oscar Wilde. Any serious consideration of the terrible state of affairs in France was pushed into second place by the orgy of irrational prejudice that was taking place at the Old Bailey. Manning was quite right of course, people didn't want reasons, they wanted scapegoats. You saw it in the hospital too, where hostility to the pacifist orderlies mounted as the news from France grew worse, but there was some element of logic in that. Men were being whipped back into line. Into *the* Line. Unless he were suffering from the complaint Jane Manning had diagnosed, of being incapable of seeing his own sex as peripheral to anything. But no, he thought Manning was right. Maud Allan was in the firing line almost by accident. The real targets were men who couldn't or wouldn't conform.

Rivers's thoughts turned to Sassoon. Manning's experience clearly showed that every member of Robert Ross's circle was at risk, liable to the same treatment as Ross himself. It didn't help that Ross was opposed to the war, though he had not approved of Sassoon's protest, arguing – quite rightly in Rivers's opinion – that it would destroy Sassoon without having any impact on the course of events. Ross's own method of opposition, according to Manning, was to show photographs of mutilated corpses to any civilian who might benefit from the shock. Rivers was glad Sassoon was well away from Ross, and the trial.

Once, at Craiglockhart, he'd tried to warn Sassoon of the danger. As long ago as last November he'd told him about the *cabinet noir*, the Black Book, the 47,000 names of eminent men and women whose double lives left them open to German blackmail.

– Relax, Rivers. I'm not eminent.

– No, but you're a friend of Robert Ross, and you've publicly advocated a negotiated peace. That's enough! You're vulnerable, Siegfried. There's no point pretending you're not.

– And what am I supposed to do about it? Toe the line, tailor my opinions . . . But what you're really saying is, if I can't conform in one area of life, then I have to conform in the others. Not just the surface things, everything. Even against my conscience. Well, I can't live like that. Nobody should live like that.

It had been pleasant talking to Manning about Siegfried. Apart from Robert Graves, whom Rivers saw occasionally, Manning was the only acquaintance they had in common.

The square was deserted. On nights of the full moon people hurried back to the safety of their cellars. Rivers's footsteps seemed to follow him, echoing along the empty pavement. The moon had drifted clear from the last gauzy wrack of cloud, and his shadow stretched ahead of him, the edges almost as sharp as they would have been by day.

So calm, so clear a night. We're in for it, he thought. That was one thing he'd never had to cope with at Craiglockhart: bombs falling within earshot of patients who jumped out of their skins if a teaspoon rattled in a saucer. He turned and began to walk rapidly towards the dark and shuttered building.

THIRTEEN

Head is the one awake inside the sleeping hospital. Masked and gowned, a single light burning above his head, he stands beside a dissecting table on which a man lies, face upwards, naked, reeking of formaldehyde. The genitals are shrivelled, the skin the dingy gold of old paper. Head finishes drawing an outline on the shaven head, says, 'Right then,' and extends his gloved hand for the drill. But something's wrong. Even as the drill whirs, the golden-skinned man stirs. Rivers tries to say, 'Don't, he's alive,' but Head can't, or won't, hear him. A squeak of bone, a mouth stretched wide, and then a hand grasps Head's hand at the wrist, and the cadaver in all its naked, half-flayed horror rises from the table and pushes him back.

The corridor outside Rivers's room is empty, elongated, the floor polished and gleaming. Then the doors at the end flap open with a noise like the beating of wings and the cadaver bounds through, pads from door to door, sniffs, tries to locate him more by smell than sight. At last it finds the right door, advances on the bed, bends over him, thrusts its anatomical drawing of a face into his, as he struggles to wake up and remember where he is.

Christ. He lay back, aware of sweat on his chest and in his groin. He was in a hospital bed, too high, too narrow, the mattress covered with rubber that creaked as he moved. He could see that ruin of a face bending over him. In these moments between sleep and waking, he was able to do – briefly – what other people take for granted: see things that were not there.

Quickly, before the moment passed, he began to dissect the images of which the dream was composed. The dissecting-room in the dream had not been the room at the Anatomical Institute where he'd watched Head at work that morning, but the anatomy theatre at Bart's, where he had trained.

The whole emotional impression left by the dream was one of . . . He lay, eyes closed in the darkness, sifting impressions. Contamination. To imagine Head, the gentlest of men, drilling the skull of a conscious human being was a sort of betrayal. The link with Head's carrying out the tests on Lucas was obvious. Rivers had thought, as he watched Head looking at Lucas, that the same suspension of empathy that was so necessary a part of the physician's task was also, in other contexts, the root of all monstrosity. Not merely the soldier, but the torturer also, practises the same suspension.

The dream was about dissociation. Like most of his dreams these days, a dream about work. He never seemed to dream about sex any more, though before the war sexual conflicts had been a frequent subject of dreams. A cynic might have said he was too exhausted. He thought it was probably more complicated, and more interesting, than that, but he had little time for introspection. Certainly no time for it now. He sat up and flapped his pyjama jacket to make the sweat evaporate, then lay back and tried to compose himself for sleep. He never slept well on the nights he stayed at the hospital, partly because of the uncomfortable bed, partly because the expectation of being woken kept his sleep light.

He was just beginning to drift off when the whistles blew.

By the time the orderly knocked on his door, he was out of bed and fastening his dressing-gown. He followed the man along the corridor to the main ward where Sister Walters greeted him. She was a thin, long-nosed Geordie with a sallow skin and a vein of class-hatred that reminded him of Prior. Oddly enough, it seemed to be directed entirely at her own sex. She hated the VADs, most of whom were girls of good family 'doing their bit' with – it had to be admitted – varying degrees of seriousness.. She loved her officer patients – my boys, she called them – but the VADs, girls from a similar social background after all, she hated. One night last December, as the guns thudded and the ground shook beneath the direct hit on Vauxhall Bridge, they'd sat drinking cocoa together, and the barriers of rank had come down, enough at least for her to say bitterly, 'They make me sick, the way they go on. "Oooh! Look at me! I'm dusting!" "I'm sweeping a floor." Do you know, when I was training we got eight quid *a year*. That was for a seventy-hour week, and you got your breakages stopped off that.'

Cocoa was being made now and carried round on trays. Rivers went from bed to bed of the main ward. Most of the men were reasonably calm, though jerks and twitches were worse than normal. In the single rooms, where the more seriously disturbed patients were, the signs of distress were pitiful. These were men who had joked their way through bombardments that rattled the tea-cups in Kent, now totally unmanned. Weston had wet himself. He stood in the middle of his room, sobbing, while a nurse knelt in front of him and coaxed him to step out of the circle of sodden cloth. Rivers took over from her, got Weston into clean pyjamas and back into bed. He stayed with him till he was calm, then handed over to an orderly and went in search of Sister Walters.

She handed him his cocoa. 'Captain Manning's smoking. Do you think you could –'

'Yes, of course.'

At Craiglockhart the corridors had reeked of cigarettes, and there the staff had contrived not to notice. Here, with two wards full of paralysed patients, the no-smoking rule had to be enforced. Rivers tapped once and walked in.

Manning was sitting up in bed. 'Hello,' he said, sounding surprised.

'I'm afraid I've got to ask you to put that out. Two lifts. Twenty wheelchairs.'

'Yes, certainly.' Manning stubbed his cigarette out. 'Stupid of me. I didn't know you did nights.'

'Only at full moons.'

'I thought that theory of mental illness had been exploded.'

Rivers smiled. 'You know what I mean.'

'Sister Walters says they got Vauxhall Bridge twice. Is that right?'

'Yes. Though we don't need to worry when they hit it. Only when they miss.'

'Reminds me of last Christmas. Do you remember that raid? I was staying with Ross, Sassoon was there as well, and it was very funny because it was the first raid I'd experienced, and I was all set to be the cool, collected veteran, calming down the poor nervous civilians. I was a complete bloody wreck. Ross's housekeeper was better than me. Sassoon was the same. In fact I remember him saying, "All that fuss about whether I should go back or not. I won't be any bloody good when I do." '

A ragged sound of singing. 'Listen,' Manning said. He began to sing with them, almost under his breath.

Bombed last night
And bombed the night before
Gunna get bombed tonight
If we never get bombed any more.
When we're bombed we're scared as we can be . . .

'First time I've heard that outside France.' A pause. 'You know, I've been thinking about what you said . . . about remembering and trying to talk about it.'

Rivers propped his chin on his hands and said, 'Go on.' Even as he spoke, he recalled Prior's wickedly accurate imitation of this position. *Damn* Prior.

'You know these attacks I have? Well, they tend to start with a sort of waking dream. It's nothing very much actually, it's not horrifying, it's just a line of men marching along duckboards wearing gas masks and capes. Everything's a sort of greenish-yellow, the colour it is when you look through the visor. The usual . . . porridge.' He swallowed. 'If a man slips off the duckboard it's not always possible to get him out and sometimes he just sinks. The packs are so heavy, you see, and the mud's fifteen feet deep. It's not like ordinary mud. It's like a bog, it . . . sucks. They're supposed to hold on to the pack of the man in front.'

'And you say this . . . dream triggers the attack?'

'I don't know. I suppose so.'

'What in particular?'

Manning tried to answer and then shook his head.

'If you had to pick out the worst thing, what would it be?'

'There's a hand coming out of the mud. It's holding the duckboard and . . . nothing else. Everything else is underneath.'

A short silence.

'Oh, and there's a voice.' Manning reached for his cigarettes and then remembered he couldn't smoke. 'It's not coming *from* anybody. It's just . . . there.'

Rivers waited. 'What does it say?'

'"Where's Scudder?"' Manning smiled. 'It's a rather nasty, *knowing* little voice. "Where's Scudder? Where's Scudder?"'

'Do you answer?'

Manning shook his head. 'No point. It knows the answer.'

Silence, except for the sound of singing, fading now, and then, in the distance, the thudding of the guns.

Rivers said, 'You know, if we went down to my room you could smoke.'

Manning looked surprised. *'Now?'*

'Why not? Unless you think you can get back to sleep?'

Manning didn't answer that. There was no need.

'There,' Rivers said, putting an ashtray at Manning's elbow. The lamp created a circle of light around the desk, a world.

'You don't, do you?' Manning said, lighting up.

'A cigar now and then.'

Manning inhaled deeply, his eyes closed. 'One of the reasons I don't talk about it,' he said, smiling, 'apart from cowardice, is that it seems so futile.'

'Because it's impossible to make people understand?'

'Yes. Even a comparatively small thing. The feeling you get when you go into the Salient, especially if you've been there before and you know what you're facing. You really do say goodbye to everything. You just put one foot in front of another, one step, then the next, then the next.'

Rivers waited.

'It's . . . ungraspable,' Manning said at last. 'I don't mean *you* can't grasp it because you haven't been there. I mean, *I* can't grasp it and I *have* been there. I can't get my mind round it.'

'You were going to tell me about Scudder.'

'Was I?'

Their eyes met.

Manning smiled. 'Yes, I suppose I was. He was a man in my company. You know, the whole thing's based on the idea that if you've got the right number of arms and legs and you're not actually mentally defective you can be turned into a soldier. Well, Scudder was the walking proof that it isn't true. He was hopeless. He knew he was. The night before we were due to move up, he got drunk. Well, a lot of them got drunk, but he was . . . legless. He didn't turn up for parade, and so he was court-martialled. I went to see him the night before. He was being held in a barn, and we sat on a bale of straw and talked. It turned out he'd been treated for shell shock the previous year. With electric shocks. I didn't know they did that.'

'Oh, yes,' Rivers said. 'They do.'

'He was at Messines when the mines went up. Apparently he used to dream about mines and blood. And he used to jerk his head and make stupid noises. That's what the doctor called them. *Stupid noises*. Anyway it worked, after a fashion. The electric shocks. The night after he had the treatment he didn't dream about mines. He dreamt he was back in the trenches having electric shock treatment. I stayed with him a couple of hours, I suppose.' Manning smiled faintly. 'He was a most unfortunate-looking youth. I mention that in case there's a doctrinaire Freudian lurking under your desk.'

Rivers pretended to look. 'No-o. There isn't one behind it either.'

Manning laughed. 'The thing was he was extremely bright. And I don't know whether it was snobbery or . . . or what it was, but I'd been assuming he wasn't. Actually I don't think it was snobbery, it was just he was so bloody *bad* at everything. You couldn't believe there was an intelligent mind behind all those . . . cock-ups. But there was.' His expression became momentarily remote. 'After that, I noticed him more. I thought –'

'What did he get?'

'At the court martial? Two hours' field punishment a day. When everybody else was resting – uh! – he'd be cleaning limbers, that sort of thing. I used to stop and have a word with him. I don't think it helped because it took him away from the other men, and in the end it's the other men who keep you going.'

'Go on. You say you thought –'

'I thought he was clumsy. And then after this talk I watched him, I watched him at bayonet practice, running in and lunging and . . . *missing*. You know, the thing's this big, and he was missing it. And suddenly I realized it was nothing to do with clumsiness. He couldn't switch off. He couldn't . . . turn off the part of himself that minded. I'm quite certain when he finally got the bayonet in, he saw it bleed. And that's the opposite of what should be happening. You know I saw men once . . . in close combat, as the manuals say, and one man was reciting the instructions. *Lunge*, one, two: *twist*, one, two, *out*, one, two . . . Literally, killing by numbers. And that's the way it has to be. If a man's properly trained he'll function on the day almost like an automaton. And Scudder was the opposite of that. Somehow the whole thing had gone into reverse. I think probably because of the breakdown, because I can see the same sort of thing happening to me. Like red – the colour red – whatever it is, even if it's a flower or a book – it's always blood.'

Rivers had gone very still. He waited.

'When I was out there, I could be in blood up to the elbows, it didn't bother me. It's almost as if instead of normal feelings being cut off, there aren't any divisions left at all. Everything washes into everything else. I don't know if that makes sense.'

'Very much so.'

A pause. 'Anyway, we moved forward. It was raining. I don't know why I bother to say that. It was always raining. The heavens had opened. And we were told to report to *the graveyard*.' Manning laughed, a genuine full-blooded laugh. 'I thought, my God somebody's developed a sense of humour. But it was absolutely true. We were *billeted* in the graveyard. And it was extraordinary. All the tombs had been damaged by shells and you could see through into the vaults, and this was in an area where there were corpses everywhere. The whole business of collecting and burying the dead had broken down. Wherever you looked there were bodies or parts of bodies, and yet some of the younger ones – Scudder was one – were fascinated by these vaults. You'd come across them lying on their stomachs trying to see through the holes, because the vaults were flooded, and the coffins were floating around. It was almost as if these people were *really* dead, and the corpses by the road weren't. Any more than we were really alive.

'We were shelled that night. Three men wounded. I was organizing stretcher-bearers – not easy, as you can imagine – and I'd just finished when Hines walked up and said, "Scudder's gone." He'd just got up and walked away. The other men thought he'd gone to the latrine, but then he didn't come back. We got together a search-party. I thought he might have fallen into one of the vaults, and we crawled round calling his name, and all the time I knew he hadn't. I decided to go after him. I know, not what a company commander ought to have done, but I had a very good second in command and I knew he couldn't have got far. You see, everything was coming forward for the attack, and the road was absolutely choked. I hoped I could get to him before the military police picked him up. He'd have been shot. We were far enough forward for it to count as desertion in the face of the enemy. I was struggling and floundering along, and it really was almost impossible, and then I saw him. He hadn't got very far. When I caught up with him, he didn't even look at me. Just went on walking. And I walked beside him and tried to talk to him, and he obviously wasn't listening. So I just pushed him off the road, and we slithered down and stopped on the rim of a crater. There's always gas lingering on the water. When you get close your eyes sting. He was blue. And I tried to talk to him. He said, "This is mad." And I said, "Yes, I know, but we've all got to do it." In the end I simply named people. Men in his platoon. And I said, "*They*'ve got to do it. You'll only make it harder for them." In the end he just got up and followed me, like a little lamb.'

Manning stirred and reached for another cigarette. 'We went forward almost as soon as we got back. The orders were full of words like "trenches" and "attacking positions". There weren't any trenches. The attacking position was a line of sticks tied with bits of white ribbon. We were late arriving, and it was getting light. If we hadn't been late, we'd've crawled straight past them in the dark. The "line" was a row of shell-craters, filled with this terrible sucking mud. And you just crouched beneath the rim, and . . . waited. We advanced. No close work, but machine-guns directly ahead up the slope. A *lot* of casualties. *A lot*, and no hope of getting them back. It was taking the stretcher-bearers a couple of hours to go a hundred yards. So there we were, crouched in another row of shell-holes exactly like the first. And all hell was let loose. As soon as it died down a bit, I tried to crawl from one hole to another. It took me an hour to crawl between two holes. And in the other hole I found four men, none of them wounded, and I thought, thank God, and then suddenly one of them said, "Where's Scudder?" Well, there was nothing I could do about it. I couldn't move, the shelling was so heavy. And then there was a lull, and we heard a cry. It seemed to be coming from a crater slightly further back, not far, and we crawled along and found him.

'He'd either slipped or been blown down the slope. Blown, I suspect, because he'd got quite a way in. He was already up to his chest. We tried to get him out, but even forming a line and holding out a rifle we couldn't reach him. He could just get the tips of his fingers on the butt, but his hands were slippery with mud and they kept sliding off. I could see if we went on trying somebody else was going to slip in. And Scudder was panicking and . . . *pleading* with us to do something. I have never seen anything like his face. And it went *on* and *on*. He was slipping away all the time, but *slowly*. I knew what I had to do. I got the men lined up and told him we were going to try again, and while he was looking at the others I crawled round the other side, and fired.' Manning closed his eyes. 'I missed. And that was terrible, because then he knew what was happening. I fired again, and this time I didn't miss.

'We spent the rest of the night there, in that hole. It was very odd. You know, I don't think any of the men would have said, "You did the wrong thing. You should have let him die slowly." And yet nobody wanted to talk to me. They kept their distance.'

A long silence. 'His mother wrote to me in hospital. To thank me. Apparently Scudder had written to her and told her I'd been kind to him.'

Rivers said firmly, 'You were.'

Manning looked at him and then quickly away. 'We were relieved the following night. I reported back to Battalion HQ and they expressed extreme displeasure. Apparently we'd been a bulge in the line. We'd been sitting in the wrong shell-holes. They were having dinner, veal and ham pie and red wine, and suddenly I realized they weren't even going to offer us a fucking drink. I had Hines with me, he was dead on his feet. So I leant across the table, took two glasses, gave one to Hines and said, "Gentlemen, the King." And of course they all had to struggle to their feet.' He laughed. 'And then we got the hell out of it before they could work out how to put an officer on a charge for proposing the loyal toast. We staggered down that road giggling like a pair of schoolboys. We were still laughing when the shell got us. I got this. Poor old Hines . . . I crawled across to him. And he looked straight at me and said, "I'm all right, Mum." And died.'

Rivers stirred. He was about to speak when he heard bugles in the streets. 'Let's have the curtains open, shall we?' he said.

He pulled the heavy curtains back, and grey dawn light flooded into the room. Manning flinched. He got up and joined Rivers by the window, and was just in time to see a taxi drive along the other side of the square. Rivers opened the windows, and the sound of birdsong filled the room.

'You know,' Manning said, 'when Ross told me they sounded the all-clear by driving boy scouts with bugles round the streets in taxis, I didn't believe him.'

They watched the taxi leave the square. Manning said, 'I used to find a certain kind of *Englishness* engaging. I don't any more.'

FOURTEEN

Sarah was coming. The thought buoyed Prior up as he walked along the Bayswater Road to the underground station. Only when he was on the train, staring sightlessly at his reflection in the black glass, did his thoughts turn to Spragge. He hadn't seen him face to face since that evening in the park, but he'd suspected more than once that Spragge was following him. Possibly it was just nerves. His nerves *were* bad, and the intolerable sticky heat didn't help. The gaps in his memory were increasing both in length and frequency, and they terrified him.

Like the undiscovered territory on medieval maps, Rivers said. *Where unknown, there place monsters.* But a better analogy, because closer to his own experience, was No Man's Land. He remembered looking down a lane in France. The lane had a bend in it, and what was beyond the bend was hidden by a tall hedge. Beyond that was No Man's Land. Beyond that again, the German lines. Full of men like himself. Men who ate, slept, shat, blew on their fingers to ease the pain of cold, moved the candle closer, strained their eyes to read again letters they already had by heart. He knew that, they all knew it. Only it was impossible to believe, because the lane led to a country where you couldn't go, and this prohibition alone meant that everything beyond that point was threatening. Uncanny.

Something about the lifeless air of the underground encouraged morbid thoughts. Above ground, in the relatively cool, coke-smelling air of King's Cross, he felt more cheerful. Please God, he thought, no gaps while Sarah's here.

He waited by the barrier, sick with excitement. The train slid to a halt, grunted, wheezed, belched, subsided into a series of disgruntled mutters, and then all along its length doors swung open, and people started to get out. The sheer excitement of knowing he was going to see her stopped him seeing her, and for one terrifying moment all the women on the platform were Sarah. Then his mind cleared, and there was only one woman, walking straight towards him.

He caught her in his arms and swung her off her feet. When, finally, he set her down they stared at each other. He noticed the yellow skin, the dark shadows round her eyes, the fringe of ginger hair which was not her own colour, but some effect of the chemicals she worked with.

'Well?' she said.

'You look beautiful. But then you always do.'

He took her bag and steered her towards the taxi rank.

'Can't we go on the underground?' she said, pulling back.

He looked surprised.

'I've never been on it.'

Her face lit up as she stepped out on to the descending staircase. She was too excited to talk until they were on the train, and had stopped at several stations, and the first novelty of hurtling in a lighted capsule through dark tunnels had worn off. Then she turned to him and said, 'You look a bit tired. Are you all right?'

'It's the heat,' he said. 'I haven't been sleeping well.'

'You will tonight.'

He smiled. 'I was hoping not to sleep at all tonight.'

But that was too direct. She smiled but looked away.

'How's your mother?'

'The same. The shop's not doing too well. No demand for second-hand stuff these days.'

'What about Dr Lawson's Cure for Female Blockages and Obstructions? I bet she's doing a roaring trade in that.'

'Geraway, man. It's all sixpenny ticklers these days.'

'Is it?' Prior asked innocently.

She smiled and eventually laughed.

'How was your trip home?' she asked after a while.

'Not bad. I met a few old friends.'

'Did you tell your mam about me?'

He hesitated.

'You didn't,' she said.

'I prepared the ground.'

'*Billy*. You think she won't like me, don't you?'

He knew she wouldn't. He had a very clear idea of the sort of girl his mother wanted him to marry. One of those green-skinned, titless girls who wore white lawn blouses and remembered their handkerchiefs. The Ministry was full of them. The extraordinary thing was he *did* find them attractive, though not in a way he liked. They woke his demons up, just as surely as making love to Sarah put them to sleep. 'It's not that,' he said.

'Isn't it?' She smiled, and he realized she simply didn't care. 'What about your dad?'

'I don't tell him anything.'

'Do you think *he*'d like me?'

He'd never thought about it. As soon as he considered it, he knew his father *would* like her, and she'd like him. She wouldn't *approve* of the old sod, but she'd get on all right with him. Instantly the idea of taking her home became even less attractive. 'There's plenty of time,' he said.

Leading her down the steps to the basement he was ashamed of the overflowing bins and the smell, but he needn't have worried. Sarah was delighted with the flat. He realized, as he took her from room to room, that it could have been twice as dark, twice as stuffy, and she would still have been pleased with it. For two days and nights this would be their home, and that was all that mattered.

She ended the tour sitting on the single bed in his room, unselfconsciously bouncing up and down to test the mattress. Then she looked up and found him watching her, and her face was suffused with a blush that banished the yellow from her skin. His breath caught in his throat, and he swallowed hard. 'If you'd like to get washed or or bathed, it's next door.'

'Yes, I –'

'I'll get a towel.'

Prior wished sometimes he didn't *know* what it was like to be groped, to be pounced on before you're ready. As he pulled a towel out of the airing cupboard, he heard the bathroom door open and then felt her arms come round him and clasp his chest. She pressed her face between his shoulders, her mouth against his spine. 'Can you feel this?' she asked. And she began to groan, deep noises, making his spine and the hollows of his chest vibrate with her breath. He pushed her gently away. 'You must be tired,' he said.

She giggled, and he felt her laughter in his bones. 'Not *too* tired.'

They did have a bath, eventually. Afterwards, lying on the bed, she traced his ribs with the tips of her fingers, propped up on one elbow, her hair screening them both. 'You know the part of men I like best?' she said, moving her finger down.

'Men?' Cupping his hands around his mouth, he called into the passage, 'Ge-orge? Albert? Are you there?'

She smiled, but persisted. 'This part.' Her finger slid into the hollow beneath his ribs and down across his belly.

'There?'

'Yes.'

'Uh? Uh?' he said, thrusting his hips upward.

'Oh, *that*.'

'"*That*"!' He struggled to sit up, only to subside as she slid down the bed and took his flaccid penis into her mouth.

She looked up and smiled. 'He's nice too.'

'He's a bloody disgrace at the moment. Look at him.'

'You can't expect miracles.'

He closed his eyes. 'Go on doing that you might just get one.'

Hanging over her, watching the stretched mouth, the slit eyes, the head thrown back until it seemed her spine must crack, he remembered other faces. The dying looked like that.

'What shall we do?' he asked. 'Are you hungry?'

'Not really.'

'We could go to Oxford Street. Look round the shops.'

'Don't sound so enthusiastic.'

'Or Kew.'

'What do *you* want to do?'

'Kew, I think. The weather can't last and we can do indoor things tomorrow.'

'More? You'll wear me out.'

'*Other* things.'

'Oh.'

Once in the gardens they wandered aimlessly, more interested in each other than in the plants. As the afternoon wore on, the heat thickened until there was a brassy glare in the sky, as if a furnace door had opened. Still they walked, each adjusting to the other's stride, hardly aware when their linked shadow faded from the grass.

Drops of rain striking their faces startled them out of their absorption. They looked around, dazed. The rain began to beat down, lashing their heads and shoulders. In less time than seemed possible, Sarah's hair was hanging in dark, reddish-brown strands and the sleeves of her blouse had become transparent. Prior looked for shelter, but could see only some trees. They made for those and stood under them, but there was little protection. Rain streaked the trunks and splashed through the leaves on to the backs of their necks.

Sarah was beginning to shiver with cold. Prior didn't know where they were. He could see a little mock Grecian temple on a grassy mound, but that was open to the wind. From his previous visits he remembered the Palm House, which was certainly warm. That would be the best place if he could manage to locate it. He worked out where the main gate was, and thought he could remember that you turned left. 'I think we should make a run for it,' he said. 'This isn't going to go over.'

They ran, heads bent, Prior with his arm round Sarah, splashing through puddles. Rivulets of mud, washed out of flowerbeds, ran down the paths. Sarah refused the offer of his tunic and strode through it all, drenched, skirt caught between her legs, blouse transparent, hair stringy, skin glowing, with a stride that would have covered mountains. She had decided to *enjoy* it, she said.

The lake was a confusion of exploding circles and bubbles, too turbulent to reflect the inky sky. They ran the last few yards and entered the Palm House. Prior felt a rippling effect on his face and neck and then, immediately, an uncomfortable wave of damp heat. He began to cough. Sarah turned to him. 'Isn't this bad for your chest?'

'No,' he said, straightening up. 'In fact it's ideal.'

The aisles were crowded, so much so it was difficult to move. Thick green foliage surrounded them, and towered to the dazzling glass roof above their heads. Smells of wet earth, of leaves dripping moisture, a constant trickle of water, and somewhere a trapped blackbird singing. But as they moved deeper into the crush, it was the smell of people that took over: damp cloth, wet hair, steamy skin.

Prior took Sarah's arm and pointed to the gangway above. 'Come on, it'll be less crowded.'

He had a dim feeling there might also be more air up there, for in spite of what he'd said to Sarah he was finding the atmosphere oppressive. Sarah followed slowly, wanting to look at the plants. She tugged at his arm and pointed to a flower that had the most incredibly pink penile-looking stamens. 'Isn't he beautiful?'

'I thought you were a rib-cage girl?'

'Not ribs. The –'

He laughed and pulled her to him. They were standing at the bottom of the spiral staircase. She slid her hand between his legs and rubbed. 'I could be converted.'

He pressed her more closely against him, his mouth buried in her wet hair, looking over her head, focusing on nothing. Suddenly his eye registered a familiar shape. The green blur cleared, and he found himself gazing, through the branches of some tall plant with holes in its leaves, into the face of Lionel Spragge. There could be no mistake. They stared at each other through the foliage, no more than four or five feet apart. Then Spragge turned and pushed into the crowd, which swallowed him.

Sarah looked up. 'What's the matter?'

'Let's go upstairs.'

He took her hand and pulled her towards the staircase. At every turn he looked down through the green leaves of the canopy at the heads and shoulders below, until eventually they ceased to look like individual people. As they climbed higher, the sound of rain on the glass roof grew louder. The windows were misted up, and a steamy, diffuse, white light spread over everything. He looked down on to the gleaming canopy of leaves. And then at the aisles, searching for Spragge's broad shoulders and square head. He thought he saw him several times as he and Sarah walked round the gangway, but could never be sure. At first Sarah exclaimed over the different shapes and patterns of the leaves, which were indeed beautiful, as he acknowledged after a cursory glance. Then, gradually, sensing his withdrawal, she fell silent.

I should have spoken to him, Prior thought, though he couldn't imagine what he would have said. But somehow the not speaking seemed in retrospect to give the encounter a hallucinatory quality. He looked down again, and now he would have been relieved to see Spragge's square head moving below.

He felt Sarah watching him and made an effort to behave more normally, rubbing condensation from the glass, trying to see out. 'You know, I think we might just as well make a dash for it.'

He had begun to feel exposed, here above the leaves, with the white light flooding over everything. Down there in the crowd, Spragge had only to look up through a gap in the foliage and there he was, floodlit under the white light of the dome.

'Yes, all right,' Sarah said.

She sounded puzzled, but ready to go along with whatever he suggested. But she was no fool, his Sarah. He was going to have to tell her something.

Others had also decided to make a dash for it. A group of women with heavy drenched skirts were running stiff-legged towards the main gate.

'Can you run?' he asked.

A glint of amusement. 'Can *you*?'

Good question. By the time they reached the underground station, he was more out of breath than her. He remembered, as he pressed his hand to his side, Spragge saying, 'I was behind you on the platform.' Suddenly he didn't want the underground. He didn't want to be shut in. 'Look, I've got a better idea,' he said. 'Why don't we go on the river? If we get off at Westminster Bridge we could see the Abbey.'

The boat was already moored when they reached the landing stage, and beginning to be crowded. At the last moment, as the engine began to throb, a crowd of people swept on board, including what looked like a girls' school party. Prior stood up and gave one of the teachers his seat. 'I'll get you a cup of tea,' he whispered to Sarah and went to the bar.

As he stood waiting his turn, the roar increased, the river churned, and they began moving out into midstream. He got the tea, took it back to Sarah, and tried to drink his own, but found it too difficult to keep his feet on the tilting deck, so he moved away from her and went to stand in the doorway that connected the covered deck with the open benches in the stern. Even these were full, and in fact the rain had almost stopped. A white sun could be glimpsed now and then through a hazy veil of cloud.

On the front bench a group of elderly cockney men were making the best of a bad job, laughing and joking at everything. A little way behind, on the end of the third bench, sat a man with unusually broad shoulders. He looked like Spragge, but it was difficult to tell because he was wearing a hat and facing away from Prior. Prior craned to see the side of his face. It *was* Spragge. Had to be. And yet he wasn't sure. There was something odd about the way the man didn't turn, didn't move. Edging along the railing towards him, Prior became aware of a slowness in his movements, as if he were wading through glue. He saw himself, in his mind's eye, go up to the man, tap him on the shoulder, wait for him to turn, and the face that turned towards him . . . was his own. He sat down, his eyes level with the railings from which a row of glittering raindrops hung. He reached out his hand and, with the tip of his forefinger, destroyed them one by one. The wet, running uncomfortably under his shirt cuff, brought him back to himself. He looked again. It might or might not be Spragge, but it certainly looked nothing like *him*. The whole powerful, brutal bulk of the head and shoulders was as different from his own slight build as any two physiques could be, and yet again, as he got up and began to move forward, he felt he was looking at the back of his own head. He breathed deeply, gazing through the rails at the brown, swollen, sinuous river, making himself follow individual twigs and leaves as they were borne along, noticing how the different currents of water, as they met and parted, rippled like muscles under skin. They were approaching another bridge. He steadied himself, walked up to the man and tapped him on the shoulder.

Spragge's face was a relief. So much so that it took several seconds for the anger to surface. 'What the hell are you doing here?'

'Going back to London. What are *you* doing?'

He sounded genuinely surprised, but Prior had caught the hiccup of laughter in his voice. Spragge had spoken more loudly than he needed, playing to the small audience of cockneys, and to the larger audience on the benches behind.

Prior lowered his voice. 'Are you following me?'

'*Following* you?' Again very loud. 'Now why should I do that?'

He sounded like a bottom-of-the-bill music-hall actor conveying injured innocence. The impression was not of somebody who'd decided to act as one possible response to a situation, but of somebody who couldn't *not* act. You had the feeling he would act in front of the bathroom mirror. That if ever you succeeded in ripping the mask off there would be no face behind it. Prior felt a wave of revulsion. 'If you're following me,' he said, 'I'll –'

'Yes, what will you do?' Spragge waited, as if the question genuinely interested him. 'Call the police? Have me arrested? It's not against the law to go to Kew.' He smiled. 'Nice girl,' he said, nodding towards the prow. And then he cupped his hands against his chest.

'If you go anywhere near her, I'll break your fucking neck.'

Spragge laughed, jowls shaking. He put his hand on Prior's chest and slapped it, genially. 'That's all right,' he said. Then he sat down again and looked out over the river, with no more than a sideways glance at the cockneys, and a faint smile.

In something not moving, something too steady for a boat. Hands, mottled purple and green, moved along polished wood. Then he was back, staring up at a window made of chips of purple and green light. He looked for Sarah and couldn't see her. In a panic he leapt up and began searching the Abbey, thrusting tourists aside, trailing hostile stares.

He found her at last, standing by the effigy of an eighteenth-century bishop, running her hand over the smooth marble. A shaft of sunlight had found the auburn lights in her hair.

She looked up as he arrived, breathless. 'You back now?'

The question was so apposite it silenced him. For a moment he thought, *she knows*. And immediately rejected the idea. Of course she didn't know.

They went home by taxi. Prior thought about Spragge, because he was afraid of thinking about anything else. What angered him was the thought that Spragge might have seen that little act of intimacy in the Palm House when Sarah had moved closer and rubbed his cock through the hard cloth of his breeches. A *good* moment. In all that press of wet, sweating, steamy-skinned people, they'd been alone, and then Spragge's face peering through the leaves. *Had* he seen? He must have. Prior was aware of feeling an almost excessive sense of exposure, of violation even, as if he'd been seen, arse upwards, in the act itself.

The taxi jolted and swayed. A memory started to surface that seemed to have nothing to do with the afternoon's events. He was ill with asthma, walking with his father's hand. Where could they have been going? His father had never taken him anywhere, he'd been too ashamed of the little runt that had mysteriously sprung from his loins. Perhaps his mother had been ill. Yes, that was it.

They'd sat on a bench somewhere, and a woman brought him lemonade. *Real* lemonade, his father had said proudly – but why proudly? – not that gassy bottled stuff. There had been lime jelly too, with jelly babies suspended in it. While he was picking at it, his father and the woman went upstairs. He could hear voices from the open window above his head. *The boy, Harry*. Then his father's voice, thick and hurried. *He's all right. Wraps himself round that lot he won't have much to grumble about.*

'Wrapping himself round that lot' had not been easy. He loved jelly, but hated jelly babies, mainly because of the way people ate them, nibbling at their feet, then at their faces, then boldly biting off the head and turning the headless body round to display the shiny open wound. He contemplated eating his way round them, freeing them from their quivering prison, but he knew he couldn't do that. The jelly had been specially made – it wasn't grown-up food – and his father would be angry. So, one by one, he had forced them down, swallowing them whole, his eyes fixed on the trees so he wouldn't have to think about what he was doing. Even so, he'd gagged once or twice, his eyes had watered, while upstairs the thick whispers came and went and the bed springs creaked.

On the way home his father had said, casually, 'Better not tell your mam.' And then he'd sat him astride his shoulders and carried him all the whole way home, all the way up the street with everybody looking, his meaty hands clasped round his son's thin white thighs. For once he'd ridden home in triumph. And he hadn't told his mam, though he'd stood by her sick bed and listened to his father describe a visit to the park. He'd been invited to join the great conspiracy and even at the age of five he knew the value of it. He wasn't going to jeopardize future outings by telling her anything.

That night he'd woken up, hot and sticky, knowing he was going to be sick. He started to cry and after a long time his father came in, blundering round and stubbing his toes before he found the light. He looked up at him, the huge man, looming over the bed. Then, slowly, erupting from his mouth, the jelly babies returned – intact, or very nearly so – while his father stood and gaped.

It must have been quite a sight, Prior thought, helping Sarah out of the cab and turning to pay the driver. Like watching a sea-horse give birth.

Once inside the flat he lit the gas fire and made two mugs of strong sweet tea, while Sarah went to take off her wet clothes. She came back wearing his dressing-gown, shivering from the cold. He sat her down between his knees and towelled her hair.

'You know you were saying about the bit you liked best? For me it's your hair,' he said, feeling his tongue thick and unwieldy, getting in the way of his teeth. 'It was the first thing I noticed. The different colours.'

'You told me,' she said, twisting round. 'And you needn't make it sound so romantic. You were wondering which colour was down there. Weren't you?'

He smiled. 'Yes.'

They sat sipping their tea. She said, 'Well, are you going to tell me?'

'Yes.' He picked up two handfuls of hair and tugged on them. 'But it's worse than you think. I need *you* to tell *me* what happened.'

'When?'

'On the boat.'

Her eyes widened, but she didn't argue. 'You gave your seat to that woman and got a cup of tea and then you went and stood over by the bar. I didn't see what happened then, I was looking at the bank. Then the sun came out and some of the girls went out on deck and this woman thought she ought to go and keep an eye on them. So next time you came back there was a seat next to me. I asked you which bridge we were going under and you didn't answer. I could see you were in one of your moods. So I left you to it. Then when we got out, that man in the Palm House was waiting at the top of the steps. He said something about me – I honestly didn't hear what it was – and you hit him. He came back at you, and you lifted your cane and you were obviously going to brain him, so he backed off. He went across the bridge, and you got hold of me and dragged me into the Abbey. I kept saying, "What's the matter?" I couldn't get an answer, so I thought, sod it. And I went off and looked at things on me own.' She waited. 'Are you telling me you don't remember all that?'

'I remember the first bit.'

'You don't remember hitting him?'

'No.'

'Who is he?'

'Doesn't matter.'

'It does bloody matter.'

'It's got nothing to do with you.'

Her face froze.

As she pulled away, he said, 'No, look, I didn't mean it like that.' He buried his head in his hands. 'I'll tell you all about him if you like, but that's not the bit that matters. What matters is that I can't remember.'

'It's happened before?'

'It's been happening for oh . . . two months.'

He could see her mind busily at work, trying to minimize the significance. 'But you lost your memory once before, didn't you? I mean, when you came back from France you said you couldn't remember anything.' She switched to a tone of condemnation. 'You've let yourself get run down, that's what you've done.'

'Look, I need you to tell me about it.' He tried to sound light-hearted. 'You're the first person who's met him.'

'Don't you mean "me"? Well, it *is* you, isn't it?'

Prior shook his head. 'You don't understand.' He leapt up and took a piece of paper out of the top drawer of the sideboard. 'Look.'

Sarah looked down and read: *Why don't you leave my fucking cigars alone?*

'I found some cigars in my pocket. I threw them away.'

'But it's your writing.'

'YES. How can I say "I" about that?'

Sarah was thinking. 'When I said it was you, I didn't just mean . . .

the obvious. I meant I . . . I meant I recognized you in that mood. Do you remember the first time we went out together? That day on the beach.'

'Yes, of –'

'Well, you were like that then. Hating everybody. You were all right on the train, but once we were on the beach, I don't know what happened, you just went right away from me and I couldn't reach you. I could feel the hatred coming off you. It was like anybody who hadn't been to France was *rubbish*. Well, you were like that on the boat. And there's no talking to you when you're in that mood. You just despise everybody.' She hesitated. 'Including me.'

'It's not a mood, Sarah. People remember moods.'

In bed that night, coiled round her, he kissed all along her spine, gently, so as not to wake her, his lips moving from one vertebra to the next.

Stepping stones to sanity.

But the day after tomorrow, she would be gone.

FIFTEEN

Sarah left early on the Monday morning. They clung together by the barrier at King's Cross, breathing in coke fumes, and did not say goodbye.

He worked late, putting off the moment when he'd have to face the empty flat. On his way home he kept telling himself it wouldn't be too bad, or at least it wouldn't be as bad as he expected.

It was worse.

He wandered from room to room, searching for traces of her, trying to convince himself a dent in the sofa cushion was where her head had rested. He sat down and put his own head there, but this simply provided a more painful vantage point from which to survey the emptiness of the room.

It'll get better, he told himself.

It didn't.

*

He took to walking the streets at night in an effort to get tired enough to sleep. London by night fascinated him. He walked along the pavements, looking at place-names: Marble Arch, Piccadilly, Charing Cross, Tottenham Court Road. All these places had trenches named after them. And, gradually, as he walked through the streets of the night city, that other city, the unimaginable labyrinth, grew around him, its sandbag walls bleached pale in the light of a flare, until some chance happening, a piece of paper blown across the pavement, a girl's laugh, brought him back to a knowledge of where he was.

He got a letter from Sarah and put it on the mantelpiece, under a small china figure of a windblown girl walking a dog, where he would see it as soon as he came through the door.

Often, on his night-time walks, he thought about Spragge, and the more he thought the more puzzled he became. The man's whole sweaty, rumpled, drink-sodden appearance suggested a down-and-out, a man blundering through life, and yet the effort required to watch the flat and follow him all the way to Kew revealed a considerable degree of persistence. It didn't make sense.

One obvious explanation was that he was working for Lode, but Prior distrusted the idea. The atmosphere in the Intelligence Unit was such that baseless suspicions were mistaken for reality at every turn. It was like a trick picture he'd seen once, in which staircases appeared to lead between the various floors of a building. Only very gradually did he realize that the perspective made no sense, that the elaborate staircases connected nothing with nothing.

His landlady, Mrs Rollaston, turned up on the doorstep, cradling her bosom in her arms as women do when they feel threatened. 'I thought you'd like to know there's somebody coming to do the bins. I know I said Monday, but I just couldn't get anybody.'

She was obviously *continuing* a conversation.

Prior nodded, and smiled.

He could recall no occasion on which he'd spoken to Mrs Rollaston about the bins.

He needed to see Spragge, but the address on the file, as he discovered standing on a gritty, windswept pavement in Whitechapel, was out of date. The bloodless girl who peered up at him from the basement, a grizzling baby in her arms, said she'd lived there a year and no, she didn't know where the previous tenant had gone. The landlady might, though.

The landlady, traced to the snug bar of the local pub, confirmed the name had been Spragge. She didn't know where he was now. Did *he* know this was the very pub Mary Kelly had been drinking in the night the Ripper killed her? She'd known Mary Kelly as well as she knew her own sister, heart in one place, liver in another, intestines draped all over the floor, *in that very chair* –

He bought her a port and lemon and left her to her memories. Odd, he thought, that the fascination with the Ripper and his miserable *five* victims should persist, when half of Europe was at it.

He was losing more time. Not in huge chunks, but frequently, perhaps four or five times a day. In the evenings, unless he was seeing Rivers, he stayed at home. He knew the flat was bad for him, both physically and mentally, but he was afraid to venture out because it seemed to give *him* more scope. Nonsense, of course. *He* could and did go out, though sometimes the only sign was the smell of fresh air on Prior's skin.

One morning Lode sent for him.

'I just thought I'd share the good news,' Lode said. 'Since there isn't much of it these days. They've caught MacDowell.'

Prior was knocked sick by the shock, but he managed to keep his face expressionless. 'Oh? When?'

'A few days ago. In Liverpool. Charles Greaves's house. They got Greaves too.'

'Hmm. Well, that *is* progress.'

'Good news, isn't it?'

Prior nodded.

'You know,' Lode said, watching him narrowly, 'I used to think I understood you. I used to think I had you taped.' He waited. 'Ah, well. Back to work.'

Prior wondered why Lode's endless patting and petting of his moustache should ever have struck him as a sign of vulnerability. It didn't seem so now.

The nights were bad. He was still taking sleeping draughts, sometimes repeating the dose when the first one failed to work. Rivers strenuously advised him against it, but he ignored the advice. He had to sleep.

That evening, fast asleep after the second draught, he was awakened by a knocking on the door. The bromide clung to him like glue. Even when he managed to get out of bed, he felt physically sick. For a moment, as he pulled on his breeches and shirt, he thought he might actually be sick. The knocking went on, then stopped.

Presumably whoever it was had got tired and gone away. Prior was about to fall back into bed when he remembered he'd left the door open. Of all the bloody stupid things to do. But it was the only way of getting some air into the place.

It was no use, he'd have to go and close it.

The passage was full of the smell of rotting cabbage. The area round the bins had not been cleaned, in spite of Mrs Rollaston's promise. Prior stumbled along, hitching up his braces as he went.

The door was open. He looked out. The sky was not the normal blue of a summer evening, but brownish, like caught butter. He went back inside and closed the door.

He was walking past the door of the living-room when he heard a movement.

Slowly, he pushed the half-open door wide. Spragge was sitting, stolidly, in the armchair, thick fingers relaxed on his splayed thighs. He looked up with a sheepish, rather silly expression on his face. Sheepish, but obstinate. 'Well?' he said. 'What do you want to see me about?'

'Do you always walk into people's houses uninvited?'

'I thought I heard you say come in.' He didn't bother to make the lie convincing. 'I knew you must be in because the door was open. You want to watch that. You could get burgled.' A glance round the room pointed out that there was nothing worth taking.

Prior was angry. Not because Spragge had walked in uninvited; it was deeper, less rational than that. He was angry because of the way Spragge's fingers curled on his thighs, innocent-looking fingers, the waxy pink of very cheap sausages.

'I'll get up and knock again if you like,' Spragge said, pulling a comical face.

'It doesn't matter,' Prior said, sitting down. 'What do you want?'

'What do *you* want?'

Prior looked blank.

'You're the one who's been chasing me.'

Spragge was drunk. Oh, he hid it well. There was just the merest hint of over-precision in his speech, a kind of truculence bubbling beneath the surface.

'What about a drink?' Prior suggested.

'Yeh, all right.'

Prior needed time to think, to work out how he was going to approach Spragge. He went into the kitchen where he kept the whisky. The trouble was he detested Spragge to the point where the necessary manipulation became distasteful. You didn't *manipulate* people like Spragge. You squashed them.

He poured a jug of water and, in the sudden silence after he'd turned off the tap, heard a movement, furtive, it seemed to him, in the next room. Rapidly, he crossed to the door.

Spragge was removing Sarah's letter from underneath the ornament on the mantelpiece. No, not removing it. *Putting it back*.

'Have you read that?' Prior burst into the room. He was remembering how explicit Sarah's references to their love-making had been. 'Have you read it?'

Spragge swallowed hard. 'It's the job.'

'You shouldn't've done that.'

'Aw, for God's sake,' Spragge said. 'Do you think she'd mind? I saw her in the Palm House, she virtually had your dick out.'

Prior grasped Spragge lightly by the forearms and butted him in the face, his head coming into satisfying, cartilage-crunching contact with Spragge's nose. Spragge tried to pull away, then slumped forward, spouting blood, snorting, putting up an ineffectual shaking hand to stop the flow.

Prior tried to make him stand up, like a child trying to make a toy work. Spragge staggered backwards and fell against the standard lamp, which crashed over and landed on top of him. He lay there, holding his spread fingers over his shattered nose, trying to speak, and gurgling instead.

Disgusted, with himself as much as Spragge, Prior went into the kitchen, wrung out a tea-towel in cold water, came back, and handed it to Spragge. 'Here, put this over it.'

Wincing, tears streaming down his face, Spragge dabbed at his face with the wet cloth. 'Broken,' he managed to say. He gestured vaguely at the towel, which was drenched in blood. Prior took it away and brought another. He looked at the roll of fat above Spragge's trousers and contemplated landing a boot in his kidneys. But you couldn't, the man was pathetic. He threw the tea-towel at Spragge and sat down in the nearest chair, shaking with rage, unappeased. He wanted to *fight*. Instead of that he was farting about with tea-towels like Florence fucking Nightingale.

After a while Spragge started to cry. Prior stared at him with awed disgust and thought, my God, I'm not taking this. 'Come on,' he said, grabbing Spragge by the sleeve. *'Out.'*

'Can't walk.'

'I'll get you a taxi.'

Prior struggled into his boots and puttees, then returned to the living-room and dragged Spragge to his feet. Spragge lurched and stumbled to the door, half of his own volition, half dragged there by Prior. *Bastard*, Prior thought, pushing him up the steps, but the anger was ebbing now, leaving him lonely.

They staggered down the street, Spragge leaning heavily on Prior. Like two drunks. 'Do you realize how much trouble I'd get into if I was seen like this?' Prior asked.

The first two taxis went past. Spragge's face, in the brown air, looked dingy, but less obviously bloody than it had in the flat. He stood, swaying slightly, apart from the noise and heat, the passing crowds, the sweaty faces. He was visibly nursing his bitterness, carrying it around with him like a too full cup. 'Lode offered me a passage to South Africa. Did you know that? All expenses paid.'

'Will you go?'

'Might.' He looked round him, and the bitterness spilled. 'Fuck all here.'

Prior remembered there were things he needed to know. 'Did Lode tell you to follow me?'

'Yes.'

'Were you following me when I went to see Hettie Roper?'

'No, not there.'

Either Spragge was a better actor than he'd so far appeared, or he was telling the truth. Spragge started waving and shouting 'Taxi!'

It pulled up a few paces further on. 'I'll need money,' he said.

Prior dug in his breeches pockets. 'Here, take this.'

Spragge bent down and said, 'Marble Arch.' He wasn't going to give an address while Prior was within hearing.

'You must have been following me,' Prior said. 'It was you who told the police where to find MacDowell.'

Spragge looked up from the dim interior. 'Not me, guv.' His tone was ironical, indifferent. 'Lode says it was you.'

SIXTEEN

In the Empire Hospital Charles Manning surveyed the chess-board and gently, with the tip of his forefinger, knocked over the black king.

'You win,' he said. 'Again.'

Lucas grinned, and then pointed over Manning's shoulder to the figure of a man in army uniform, standing just inside the entrance to the ward.

Manning stood up. For a second there might have been a flicker of fear. Fear was too strong a word, perhaps, but Manning certainly wasn't at ease though he gave the usual, expensively acquired imitation of it, coming towards Prior, offering his hand. 'Well,' he said. 'This *is* a surprise.'

'How are you?'

'Getting better. Let's go along to my room.'

Manning chatted easily as they walked along the corridor. 'Remarkable chap, that. Do you know, he can't remember the names of any of the pieces? But, my God, he knows how to play.'

Manning's room was pleasant, with a bowl of roses on the bedside table, and a bright, yellow and red covered book lying face down on the bed.

'A name you'll know,' Manning said, picking it up.

Prior read the title, *Counter-Attack*, and the name, Siegfried Sassoon.

'You must've been at Craiglockhart at the same time,' Manning said.

'Ye-es. Though I don't know how much of a bond that is. Frankly.' Prior closed the book and put it on the bedside table beside a photograph of Manning's wife and children, the same photograph that had been on the grand piano at his house. 'He *hated* the place.'

'Did he?'

'Oh, yes, he made that perfectly clear. *And* the people. Nervous wrecks, lead-swingers and degenerates.'

'Well,' Manning said, waving Prior to a chair, 'as one nervous, lead-swinging degenerate to another . . . how are you?'

'All right, I think. The Intelligence Unit's being closed down, so I don't quite know what's going to happen.'

Manning smiled. 'I suppose you want to stay in the Ministry?'

'Not particularly.'

'Oh? Well, that might be a bit more difficult. I've got a friend at the War Office – Charles Moncrieff – I don't know whether you know him? Anyway, one of his jobs is to select instructors for cadet battalions. I suppose that might be a possibility?'

Prior leant forward. 'Hang on a minute. I didn't come here to brown-nose you *or* your fucking friend at the War Office. What I was going to say – if you wouldn't mind *listening* – is that I want to talk to you about something.'

'What?'

'Who. A woman called Mrs Roper. Beattie Roper.'

Manning was looking puzzled. '*The* Mrs Roper? Poison-plot Roper?'

'Yes.' Prior got a file out of his briefcase. 'Except she didn't do it.'

Manning took the file from him. 'You want me to read it?'

'I've summarized it. It'll only take you a few minutes.'

Manning read with total concentration. When he finished he looked up. 'Can I keep this?'

'Yes, I've got a copy. I've got copies of the documents as well.'

'You mean you've made personal copies of Ministry files?' Manning pursed his lips. 'You certainly don't play by the rules, do you?'

'Neither do you.'

'We're in the same boat there, aren't we?' A hardening of tone. 'I would have thought we were in *exactly* the same boat.'

The merest hint of a glance at the photograph. 'Not quite.'

Manning got up and walked across to the window. For a while he said nothing. Then he turned and said, 'Why? Why on earth couldn't you just come in and say, "Look, I'm worried about this. Will you read the report?" *All right*, you've got the opening to do so because of . . . There was no need for anything like that.'

Prior had a sudden chilling perception that Manning was right. 'Rubbish. Beattie Roper's a working-class woman from the back streets of Salford. You don't give a fuck about her. I don't mean you personally – *though that's true too* – I mean your class.'

Manning was looking interested now rather than angry. 'You really do think class determines everything, don't you?'

'Whether people are taken seriously or not? Yes.'

'But it's not a question of individuals, is it? All right, I don't know anything about women in the back streets of Salford. I don't pretend to. I don't want to. It doesn't mean I want to see them sent to prison on perjured evidence. Or anybody else for that matter.'

'Look, can we skip the moral outrage? When I came in here, you assumed I was after a cushy job. I didn't even get the first bloody sentence out. Are you seriously saying you would have made that assumption about a person of your own class?'

'Yes.'

'I don't believe you.'

'No, I would.'

'You get dozens of them, I suppose, begging for safe jobs?'

'Yes,' Manning said bleakly.

Prior looked at him. 'Golly. What fun.'

'Not really.'

They sat in silence, each registering the change in atmosphere, neither of them sure what it meant. 'You're right,' Manning said at last. 'It was an insulting assumption to make. I'm sorry.'

At that moment the door opened and Rivers came in.

'Charles, I – ' He stopped abruptly when he saw Prior. 'Hello. I'm sorry, I didn't realize you had a visitor.' He smiled at Prior. 'I hope you're not tiring my patient?'

'He's wearing me out,' Prior snapped.

'What did you want to see me about?' Manning asked.

Rivers said, 'Nothing that can't wait.'

He went out and left them alone.

There was a short silence. 'I'm sorry too,' Prior said. 'You're right, of course. Class prejudice isn't any more admirable for being directed upwards.' Just more fucking justified. 'Do you think I should show that to her MP?'

'Oh, God, no, don't do that. Once they've denied it in the House, it'll be set in concrete. No, I'll have a word with Eddie Marsh. Only don't expect too much. I mean, it's perfectly clear even from your report she was sheltering deserters. *That's* two years' hard labour. She's only done one.'

'She wasn't charged with that.'

Manning said, 'They're not going to let her out yet.'

'So what will they do?'

'Wait till the war's over. Let her go quietly.'

Prior shook his head. 'She won't last that long.'

That night, at nine o'clock, Prior went out for a drink. He came to himself in the small hours of the morning, fumbling to get his key into the lock. He had no recollection of the intervening five hours.

Rivers rubbed the corners of his eyes with an audible squidge. 'That's the longest, isn't it?'

'Yes. Just.'

'Any clues? I mean, had you been drinking?'

'Like a fish. I've still got the headache.'

Rivers replaced his glasses.

'One of the . . . how shall I put it?' Prior breathed deeply. '*Inconveniences* of my present position is that I do tend to end up with somebody else's hangover. Really rather frequently.'

'Not "somebody else's".'

Prior looked away. 'You've no idea how disgusting it is to examine one's own underpants for signs of "recent activity".'

Rivers looked down at the backs of his hands. 'I'm going to say something you probably won't like.'

The telephone began to ring in the next room.

Prior smiled. 'And I'm going to have to wait for it too.'

The call was from Captain Harris, telephoning to arrange the details of a flight they were to make tomorrow. Rivers jotted the time down, and took a few moments to collect his thoughts before returning to Prior.

Prior was standing by the mantelpiece, looking through a stack of field postcards. Well, that was all right, Rivers thought, closing the door. Field postcards contained *no* information about the sender except the fact that he was alive. Or had been at the time it was posted. 'His book's out, you know?' Prior said, holding a postcard up. 'Manning's got a copy.'

'Yes.'

Rivers sat down and waited for Prior to join him.

'I suppose this is the real challenge,' Prior said. 'For you. The ones who go back. They must be the ones you ask the questions about. I mean obviously all this face your emotions, own up to fear, let yourself feel grief . . . works wonders. *Here*.' Prior came closer. Bent over him. 'But what about *there*? Do you think it helps *there*? Or do they just go mad quicker?'

'Nobody's ever done a follow-up. Electric shock treatment has a very high relapse rate. What mine is, I just don't know. Obviously the patients who stay in touch are a self-selected group, and such evidence as they provide is anecdotal, and therefore almost useless.'

'My God, Rivers. You're a cold bugger.'

'You asked me a scientific question. You got a scientific answer.'

Prior sat down. 'Well dodged.'

Rivers took his glasses off. 'I'm really not trying to dodge anything. What I was going to say is I think perhaps you should think about coming into hospital. The –'

'No. You can't order me to.'

'No, that's true. I hoped you trusted me enough to take my advice.'

Prior shook his head. 'I just can't face it.'

Rivers nodded. 'Then we'll have to manage outside. Will you at least take some sick leave?'

Another jerk of the head. 'Not yet.'

Prior avoided thinking about the interview with Beattie Roper till he was crossing the prison yard. She'd been on hunger strike again, the wardress said, jangling her keys. And she'd had flu. No resistance. In sick bay all last week. He'd find her weak. The prison doctor had wanted to force-feed her, but the Home Office in its wisdom had decided that such methods were not to be used.

She was thinner than he remembered.

He stood just inside the door. She was lying on the bed, the light from the barred window casting a shadow across her face. The wardress stood against the wall, by the closed door.

'I need to see her alone.'

He expected an argument, but the wardress withdrew immediately.

'The voice of authority, Billy.'

Mucus clung to the corners of her lips when she spoke, as if her mouth were seldom opened.

He moved closer to the bed. 'I hear you've been ill.'

'Flu. Everybody's had it.'

He remained standing, as if he needed her permission to sit. She nodded towards the chair.

'I've been doing what I can,' he said. 'I'm afraid it doesn't amount to much. I was hoping Mac might be able to help, but –'

A chest movement that might have been a laugh. 'Not where he is. You know where they've sent him, don't you? Wandsworth.'

'You see, you did shelter deserters. They think you'd do it again.'

She hoisted herself up the bed. 'Bloody right 'n' all. I might look like a bloody scarecrow but *in here*' – she tapped the side of her head – 'I'm the same.'

Outside the door the wardress coughed.

'You remember a lad called Brightmore?'

'No.'

'Go on, you do.'

He didn't, but he nodded.

'Lovely lad. They sent him to Cleethorpes. Twelve months' detention. 'Course he went on refusing to obey orders so he got twenty-eight days solitary and what they did they dug a hole, and it was flooded at the bottom and they put him in that. Couldn't sit down, couldn't lie down. Nothing to look at but clay walls. Somebody come to the top of the pit and told him his pals had been shipped off to France and shot, and if he didn't toe the line the same thing'd happen to him. He thought his mind was going to give way. Then it started pissing down and the hole flooded and the soldiers who were guarding him were that sorry for him they took him out and let him sleep in a tent. They didn't half cop it when the CO found out. Next day he was back in the pit. If one of them soldiers hadn't given him a cigarette packet to write on, he'd've died in there. As it was they got a letter smuggled out –'

'And the officers who did it were court-martialled. Beattie, there's a million men in France up to their *dicks* in water. Who's going to get court-martialled for that?'

'Every bloody general in France if I had my way. You're not the only one who cares about them lads, what do you think this is about if it's not about *them*?' A pause. 'What I was *trying* to say was compared with a hole in the ground this is a fucking palace. And I'm lucky to be here.'

He looked at her, seeing her heart beat visibly under the thin shift. 'Have you seen Hettie?'

'Twice. Fact, she's due today. I gather we've got you to thank for that?'

'It's nothing.'

'No, it's not nothing, Billy. It's a helluva lot.' She hesitated. 'One thing I should tell you – I'm not saying *I* believe it, mind – our Hettie thinks it was a bit too much of a coincidence Mac getting picked up the way he was. She . . .' Beattie shook her head. 'She thinks you told them where to go.'

'That's not true.'

'No, I know it's not. It's all right, son, I'll talk to her.'

He put his hand on her bare arm and felt the bone. 'I've got to go,' he said.

He went to the door and knocked. 'I'll see you again,' he said, turning back to her.

She looked at him, but didn't answer.

Following the wardress across the yard, he was hardly aware of the massive walls with their rows of barred windows. He didn't see Hettie coming towards him, carrying a string bag, accompanied by another wardress, until they were almost level. Then he called her name and, reluctantly, she stopped.

The wardresses stood and watched.

Hettie came towards him. 'I'm surprised you've got the nerve to show your face.'

In spite of the words he bent towards her, expecting a greeting. She spat in his face.

The wardress grasped her arm. Wiping his cheek, slowly, not taking his eyes off Hettie, he said, 'It's all right. Let her go.'

Each with an escort, they moved off in opposite directions, toiling across the vast expanse of asphalt like beetles. Hettie turned before the building swallowed her and, in a voice that cracked with despair, she shouted, 'You bastard. *What about Mac?*'

Outside, Prior stared up at the building as the blood-and-bandages façade darkened in the light drizzle. Hettie's spit seemed to burn his skin. He raised his hand and wiped his cheek again, then turned and began walking rapidly towards the station. A refrain beat in his head. With every scuff and slurry of his boots on the gravel, he heard: the bastards have won. The bastards have won. The bastards . . .

Part Three

SEVENTEEN

Rivers had cleared the afternoon to finish a report on military training for the Medical Research Council. For days now he'd had infantry-training manuals piled up on his desk, and he spent the first hour immersed in them, before going back to the last sentence he'd written.

Many of those who pass unscathed through modern warfare do so because of the sluggishness of their imaginations, but if imagination is active and powerful, it is probably far better to allow it to play around the trials and dangers of warfare than to carry out a prolonged system of repression . . .

A tap on the door. Captain Bolden had attacked a nurse. Rivers did a disguised run along the corridor, saw the lift was in the basement and took the stairs three at a time. He found a group of nurses and two orderlies clustered round Bolden's door. Apparently he was refusing to let them in. From a babble of indignant chatter he managed to extract the information that Bolden had thrown a knife at Nurse Pratt. Not a very sharp knife, and it hadn't hit her, but still a knife. Nurse Pratt was one of the oldest and most experienced nurses on the ward. Unfortunately her experience had been gained on the locked wards of large Victorian lunatic asylums, where in any altercation between a member of staff and a patient the patient was automatically and indisputably wrong. One could see it so clearly from both points of view. Bolden resorted to violence quickly and easily, but then he had spent the past four years being trained to do exactly that. Nurse Pratt was being asked, for the first time in a working life of thirty years, to handle patients who were as accustomed to giving orders as to taking them.

Rivers handed his stick to an orderly and tapped on the door. 'Can I come in?'

A grunt, not definitely discouraging. Rivers opened the door and walked in. Bolden was standing by the window, still angry, sheepish, ashamed. Rivers, who was taller than Bolden, sat down, allowing Bolden to tower over him. Bolden was a very frightened man. 'Now then. What is it this time?'

'I told her the beef was inedible. She said I should think myself lucky to have it.'

'So you threw a knife?'

'I missed, didn't I?'

They talked for half an hour. Then Rivers stood up to go.

'I'll tell her I'm sorry,' Bolden said.

'Well, that would be a start. As long as you don't get irritated by her response.'

'I do try,' Bolden said, glowering at him.

'I know you do. And you're right about the beef. I couldn't eat it either.'

Rivers had a word with Sister Walters, hoping she could persuade Nurse Pratt to receive the apology graciously, and then thought he might as well have a word with Manning, since he was on the ward anyway. He set off towards Manning's room, then checked, remembering Manning was more likely to be on the neurological ward where he had struck up a firm friendship with Lucas and a couple of other chess fanatics. Manning was making good progress. He was almost ready to go home.

They *were* playing chess. Entirely silent and absorbed. He was standing beside them before they looked up.

Now that the discharge from Lucas's wound had stopped, his hair was growing back, and it covered the white scalp in a dark fuzz. Rather touching. He looked like some kind of incongruous, ungainly chick. 'How's it going?' Rivers asked, directing the question at Manning.

'I'm being trounced,' Manning said cheerfully. '19–17 in his favour.'

Lucas pointed to the board. '*20*–17,' he gurgled and grinned.

He certainly knew his numbers, Rivers thought, smiling as he walked away. In an unscreened bed further down the ward one of the pacifist orderlies was cleaning up an incontinent patient. Viggors's legs circled continuously in an involuntary stepping movement, and it really needed two people to change him, one to clean him up, the other to hold his legs. He was getting liquid excrement on his heels, and spreading it all over the bottom sheet. Martin, the orderly, was red-faced and flustered, Viggors white with rage and shame.

Rivers stopped by the bed. 'Have you heard of screens?' he asked.

Martin looked up. 'Wantage said he was going to get them.'

Wantage was lounging in the doorway of the staff-room, smoking a cigarette, clearly in no hurry to rescue a conchie orderly from an impossible position. His eyes widened. 'I was just –'

'I know exactly what you're doing. Screens round that bed. *Now*. And get in there and help.' He called over his shoulder as he walked off. 'And put that cigarette out.'

Rivers was still shaking with anger when he got back to his desk. He made himself concentrate on the uncompleted sentence.

. . . if imagination is active and powerful, it is probably far better to allow it to play around the trials and dangers of warfare than to carry out a prolonged system of repression by which morbid energy may be stored so as to form a kind of dump ready to explode on the occurrence of some mental shock or bodily illness.

Exploding ammunition dumps had become a cliché, he supposed. Still, Bolden did a very good imitation of one. He wasn't doing too badly himself.

A tap on the door. *'No,'* Rivers said. 'Whatever it is, *no*.'

Miss Rogers smiled. 'There was a telephone call, while you were up on the ward. About a Captain Sassoon.'

Rivers was on his feet. 'What about him?'

'He's in the American Red Cross Hospital at Lancaster Gate with a head wound, they said. Would you go and see him?'

'How bad is it?'

'I don't know. They didn't say.'

In the taxi going to Lancaster Gate, Rivers's own words ran round and round in his head. *If imagination is active and powerful, it is probably far better to allow it to play around* . . . He looked out of the window, shaking his head as if to clear it. It wasn't even as if the advice were appropriate. He didn't need imagination, for Christ's sake. He was a neurologist. He knew exactly what shrapnel and bullets do to the brain.

The ward was a large room with ornate plasterwork, and tall windows opening on a view of Hyde Park. Two of the beds were empty. The others contained lightly wounded men, all looking reasonably cheerful. On a table in the centre of the ward a gramophone was playing a popular love song. *You made me love you*.

A nurse came bustling up to him. 'Who were you –'

'Captain Sassoon.'

'He's been moved to a single room. Didn't they tell you? Another two floors, I'm afraid, but I don't think he's allowed . . .' Her eye fell on his RAMC badges. 'Are you Dr Rivers?'

'Yes.'

'I think Dr Saunders is expecting you.'

Dr Saunders was waiting outside the door of his room, a small man with pouched cheeks, receding ginger hair and blue eyes ten years younger than the rest of his face. 'They sent you to the main ward,' he said, shaking hands.

Rivers followed him into the room. 'How bad is he?'

'The *wound* – not bad at all. In fact, I can show you.' He took an X-ray from a file on his desk and held it to the light. Sassoon's skull stared out at them. 'You see?' Saunders pointed to the intact bone. 'The bullet went right across there.' He indicated the place on his own head. 'What he's got is a rather neat parting in the scalp.'

Rivers breathed out. 'Lucky man,' he said, as lightly as he could.

'I don't think *he* thinks so.'

They sat at opposite sides of the desk. 'I got a rather garbled message, I'm afraid,' Rivers said. 'I wasn't clear whether *you*'d asked me to see him or – '

'It was me. I saw your name on the file and I thought since you'd dealt with him before you might not mind seeing him again.' Saunders hesitated. 'I gather he was quite an unusual patient.'

Rivers looked down at his own signature at the end of the Craiglockhart report. 'He'd protested against the war. It was . . .' He took a deep breath. 'Convenient to say he'd broken down.'

'Convenient for whom?'

'The War Office. His friends. Ultimately for Sassoon.'

'And you persuaded him to go back?'

'He decided to go back. What's wrong?'

'He's . . . He was all right when he arrived. Seemed to be. Then he had about eight visitors all at his bed at the one time. The hospital rules say *two*. But the nurse on duty was very young and apparently she felt she couldn't ask them to leave. She won't make *that* mistake again. Anyway, by the time they finally did leave he was in a terrible state. Very upset. And then he had a bad night – everybody had a bad night – and we decided to try a single room and no visitors.'

'Is he depressed?'

'No. Rather the reverse. Excitable. Can't stop talking. And now he's got nobody to talk *to*.'

Rivers smiled. 'Perhaps I'd better go along and provide an audience.'

Deep-carpeted corridors, gilt-framed pictures on the wall. He followed

Saunders, remembering the corridors of Craiglockhart. Dark, draughty, smelling of cigarettes. But this was oppressive too, in its airless, cushioned luxury. He looked out of a window into a deep dark well between two buildings. A pigeon stood on a window-sill, one cracked pink foot curled round the edge of the abyss.

Saunders said, 'He seems to have a good patch in the afternoon. He might be asleep.' He opened the door softly and they went in.

Sassoon was asleep, his face pale and drawn beneath the cap of bandages. 'Shall I –' Saunders whispered, pointing to Sassoon.

'No, leave him. I'll wait.'

'I'll leave you to it, then,' Saunders said, and withdrew.

Rivers sat down by the bed. There was another bed in the room, but it was not made up. Flowers, fruit, chocolate, books were piled up on the bedside table. He did not intend to wake Siegfried, but gradually some recollection of whispered voices began to disturb the shuttered face. Siegfried moistened his lips and a second later opened his eyes. He focused them on Rivers, and for a moment there was joy, followed immediately by fear. He stretched out his hand and touched Rivers's sleeve. He's making sure I'm real, Rivers thought. A rather revealing gesture.

The hand slid down and touched the back of his hand. Siegfried swallowed, and started to sit up. 'I'm glad to see you,' he said, offering his hand. 'I thought for a mo –' He checked himself. 'They won't let you stay,' he said, smiling apologetically. 'I'm not allowed to see anybody.'

'No, it's all right. They know I'm here.'

'I suppose it's because you're a doctor,' Siegfried said, settling back. 'They wouldn't let Lady Ottoline in, I heard Mrs Fisher talking to her in the corridor.'

His manner *was* different, Rivers thought. Talkative, restless, rapid speech, and he was looking directly at Rivers, something he almost never did, particularly at the beginning of a meeting. But he seemed perfectly rational, and the changes were within normal bounds. 'Why won't they let you see anybody?'

'It's because of Sunday, everybody came, Robert Ross, Meicklejon, Sitwell, oh God, Eddie Marsh, and they were all talking about the book and I got excited and –' He raised his hands to his forehead. 'FIZZLE. POP. I had a bad night, kept everybody awake, and they put me in here.'

'How was *last* night?'

Siegfried pulled a face. 'Bad. I keep thinking how big it is, the *war*, and how impossible it is to write about, and how useless it is to get angry, that's such a trivial reaction, it doesn't, it just doesn't do any sort of justice to the to the to the tragedy, you know you spend your entire life out there obsessed with this tiny little sector of the Front, I mean *thirty yards* of sandbags, that's the war, you've no conception of anything else, and now I think I can see all of it, vast armies, flares going up, *millions* of people, *millions, millions*.'

Rivers waited. 'You say you see it?'

'Oh, yes, it just unfolds.' A circling movement of his arms. 'And it's marvellous in a way, but it's terrible too and I get so frightened because you'd have to be Tolstoy.' He gripped Rivers's hand. 'I've got to see Ross, I don't care about the others, but you've got to make them let me see him, he looks awful, that *bloody bloody bloody* trial. Do you know Lord Alfred Douglas called him "the leader of all the sodomites in London"? Only he said it in the witness-box, so Robbie can't sue.'

'Just as well, perhaps.'

'*And* he's been asked to resign from all his committees, I mean he offered, but it was accepted with alacrity. *I've got to see him*. Apart from anything else he brings me the reviews.'

'They're good, aren't they? I've been looking out for them.'

'*Most* of them.'

Rivers smiled. 'You can't write a controversial book *and* expect universal praise, Siegfried.'

'Can't I?'

They laughed, and for a moment everything seemed normal. Then Siegfried's face darkened. 'Do you know we actually sat in dug-outs in France and talked about that trial? The papers were full of it, I think it was the one thing that could have made me *glad* I was out there, I mean, for God's sake, the Germans on the Marne, five thousand prisoners taken and all you read in the papers is who's going to bed with whom and are they being blackmailed? *God*.'

'I'll see what I can do about Ross.'

'Do you think they'll listen to you?'

Rivers hesitated. 'I think they might.' Obviously Siegfried didn't know he'd been called in professionally. 'How's the head?'

A spasm of contempt. 'It's a scratch. I should never've let them send me back, do you know that's the last thing I said to my servant, "I'm coming back." "Back in three weeks," I yelled at him as I was being driven away. And then I let myself be corrupted.'

'*Corrupted?* That's a harsh word, isn't it?'

'I should've refused to come back.'

'Siegfried, nobody would have listened to you if you had. Head injuries have to be taken seriously.'

'But don't you see, the timing was perfect? Did you see my poem in the *Nation*? "I Stood with the Dead". Well, there you are. Or there I was rather, perched on the top-most bough, carolling away. BANG! Oops! Sorry. Missed.'

'I'm glad it did.'

A bleak sideways glance from Siegfried. 'I'm not.'

Silence.

'I feel amputated. I don't belong here. I keep looking at all this . . .' The waving hand took in fruit, flowers, chocolates. 'I just wish I could parcel it up and send it out to them. I did manage to send them a gramophone. Then I got . . . ill.'

'You know, what I don't understand,' Rivers said, 'is how you could possibly have been wounded there.'

'I was in No Man's Land.'

'No, I meant *under the helmet*.'

'I'd taken it off.' An awkward pause. 'We'd been out to lob some hand-grenades at a machine-gun, two of us, they were getting cheeky, you see, they'd brought it too far forward, and so we . . .' He smiled faintly. 'Re-established dominance. Anyway, we threw the grenades, I don't think we hit anybody – by which I mean there were no screams – and then we set off back and by this time it was getting light, and I was so *happy*.' His face blazed with exultation. 'Oh, God, Rivers, you wouldn't *believe* how happy. And I stood up and took the helmet off, and I turned to look at the German lines. And that's when the bullet got me.'

Rivers was so angry he knew he had to get away. He walked across to the window and stared, unseeing, at the road, the railings, the distant glitter of the Serpentine under the summer sun. He had been lying to himself, he thought, pretending this was merely one more crisis in a busy working day. This anger stripped all pretence away from him. '*Why?*' he said, turning back to Siegfried.

'I wanted to see them.'

'You mean you wanted to get killed.'

'No.'

'You stand up in the middle of No Man's Land, in the morning, the sun rising, you take off your helmet, you turn to face the German lines, and you tell me you weren't trying to get killed.'

Siegfried shook his head. 'I've told you, I was happy.'

Rivers took a deep breath. He walked back to the bed, schooling himself to a display of professional gentleness. 'You were happy?'

'Yes, I was happy most of the time, I suppose mainly because I've succeeded in cutting off the part of me that hates it.' A faint smile. 'Except when writing poems for the *Nation*. I was . . . There's a book you ought to read. I'll try to dig it out, it says something to the effect that a man who makes up his mind to die takes leave of a good many things, and is, in some sense, *dead already*. Well, I had made up my mind to die. What other solution was there for me? But making up your mind to die isn't the same as trying to get killed. Not that it made much difference.' He touched the bandage tentatively. 'I must say, I thought the standard of British sniping was higher than this.'

'*British* sniping?'

'Yes, didn't they tell you? My own NCO. Mistook me for the German army, rushed out into No Man's Land shouting, "Come on, you fuckers," and shot me.' He laughed. 'God, I've never seen a man look so horrified.'

Rivers sat down by the bed. 'You'll never be closer.'

'I've *been* closer. Shell landed a foot away. Literally. Didn't explode.' Siegfried twitched suddenly, a movement Rivers had seen many thousands of times in other patients, too often surely for it to be shocking.

'You can't get shell-shock, can you?' Siegfried asked. 'From a shell that doesn't explode?'

Rivers looked down at his hands. 'I think that one probably did a fair amount of damage.'

Siegfried looked towards the window. 'You know, they're going on a raid soon, Jowett, five or six of the others, *my* men, Rivers, *my men*, men *I* trained and I'm not going to be there when they come back.'

'They're not *your* men now, Siegfried. They're somebody else's men. You've got to let go.'

'I can't.'

EIGHTEEN

Rivers had been invited to dinner with the Heads, and arrived to find the Haddons and Grafton Elliot Smith already there. No opportunity for private conversation with Henry or Ruth presented itself until the end of the evening, when Rivers contrived that he should be the last to leave. It was not unusual after a dinner with the Heads for him to stay behind enjoying their particular brand of unmalicious gossip, well aware that his own foibles and frailties would be dissected as soon as he left, and sure enough of their love for him not to mind.

Not that he was inclined to gossip tonight. As soon as they were alone, he told them about Siegfried, clarifying his own perception of the situation as he spoke.

'Excited, you say?' Henry asked.

'Yes.'

'Manic?'

'Oh, no, nowhere near. Though there was a hint of . . . elation, I suppose, once or twice, particularly when he was talking about his feelings immediately before he was wounded. And the afternoons *are* his best time. Apparently the nights are bad. I've promised I'll go back. In fact, I ought to be going.' He stood up. 'I'm not *worried*. He'll be all right.'

'Does he regret going back?' Ruth asked.

'I don't know,' Rivers said. 'I haven't asked.'

After seeing Rivers off, Head came back into the living-room to find Ruth gazing reflectively into the fire.

'No, well, he wouldn't, would he?' she said, looking up.

'He might think there wasn't much point,' Henry said, sitting down on the other side of the fire.

A long, companionable silence. They were too replete with company and conversation to want to talk much, too comfortable to make the move for bed.

'He came to see me last year, you know,' Henry said. 'Almost a sort of consultation. He got himself into quite a state over Sassoon.'

'Yes, I know. I didn't realize he'd talked to you about it.'

Head hesitated. 'I think he suddenly realized he was using . . . his professional skills, if you like, to defuse a situation that wasn't . . . *medical*. There's really nothing else you can do if you're a doctor in the army in wartime. There's always the possibility of conflict between what the army needs and what the patient needs, but with Sassoon it was . . . very sharp. I told him basically not to be silly.'

Ruth gave a surprised laugh. 'Poor Will.'

'No, I meant it.'

'I'm sure you did, but you wouldn't have said it to a patient.'

'I told him Sassoon was capable of making up his own mind, and that his influence probably wasn't as great as he thought it was. I thought he was being . . . I don't know. Not vain –'

'Over-scrupulous?'

'Frankly, I thought he was being neurotic. But I've seen him with a lot of patients since then, and I'm not so sure. You know how you get out of date with people if you haven't seen them for a while? I think I was out of date. Something happened to him in Scotland. Somehow or other he acquired this enormous power over young men, people generally perhaps, but particularly young men. It really is amazing, they'll do anything for him. Even get better.'

'Even go back to France?'

'Yes, I think so.'

Ruth shrugged slightly. 'I don't see the change. But then I suspect he's always shown a slightly different side to me anyway.' She smiled. 'I'm very fond of him, but –'

'He is of you.'

'I sometimes wonder why we even *like* each other, you know. When you think how it started. You going to Cambridge every weekend so he could stick pins in your arm. I never had a weekend with you the whole of the first year we were married.'

'It wasn't as bad as that. Anyway, you got on all right.'

'Do you think he still thinks Sassoon went back because of him?'

Head hesitated. 'I think he knows the extent of his influence.'

'Hmm,' Ruth said. 'Do you think he's in love with him?'

'He's a patient.'

Ruth smiled and shook her head. 'That's not an answer.'

Head looked at her. 'Yes, it is. It has to be.'

Siegfried was sitting up in bed, pyjama jacket off, face and chest gleaming with sweat. 'Is it hot, Rivers?' he asked, as if their conversation had never been interrupted. 'Or is it just me?'

'Warm.'

'I'm *boiling*. I've been sitting here simmering like a kettle.'

Rivers sat down beside the bed.

'I've been writing to Graves. In verse. Do you want to read it?'

Rivers took the notepad and found himself reading an account of his visit that afternoon. The pain was so intense that for a moment he had to keep quite still. 'Is that how you see me?' he said at last. 'Somebody who's going to make you go back to France till you break down altogether?'

'Yes,' Sassoon said cheerfully. 'But that's all right, I want you to. You're my external conscience, Rivers, my father confessor. You can't let me down now, you've *got* to make me go back.'

Rivers read the poem again. 'You shouldn't send this.'

'Why not? It took me ages. Oh, I know what it is, you don't think I should say all that about the lovely soldier lads. Well, they are lovely. You think Graves is going to be shocked. Frankly, Rivers, I don't care; shocking Graves is one of my few remaining pleasures. I wrote to him – not to shock him – just an ordinary letter, only I made the mistake of talking with enthusiasm about training in one paragraph, and in the next paragraph I said what a bloody awful business the war was, and what do I get back? A lecture on consistency, oh, and some very pathetic reproaches about not terrifying your friends by pretending to be mad, I thought that was particularly rich. I've done *one* totally consistent, totally *sane* thing in my life, and that was to protest against the war. And who stopped me?'

Graves, Rivers thought. But not only Graves. It was true, he saw it now, perhaps more clearly than he had at the time, that whatever the *public* meaning of Siegfried's protest, its private meaning was derived from a striving for consistency, for singleness of being in a man whose internal divisions had been dangerously deepened by the war.

'You mustn't blame Graves. He did what –'

'I don't blame him, I'm just not prepared to be lectured by him. I survive out there by being two people, sometimes I even manage to be both of them in one evening. You know, I'll be sitting with Stiffy and Jowett – *Jowett is beautiful* – and I'll start talking about wanting to go and fight, and I'll get them all fired up and banging the table and saying, yes, enough of training, time to get stuck in to the real thing. And then I leave them and go to my room and think how young they are. Nineteen, Rivers. *Nineteen*. And they've no bloody idea. Oh, God, I hope they live.'

Suddenly, he started to cry. Wiping the back of his hand across his mouth, he sniffed and said, 'Sorry.'

'That's all right.'

'You know what finally put the kibosh on my Jekyll and Hyde performance, no, listen, this is funny. I got a new second in command. Pinto. Absolute jewel. But the first time I met him he was reading *Counter-Attack*, and he looked up and said, "Are you the same Sassoon?" My God, Rivers, what a bloody question. But of course I said, "Yes." What else could I say? And yet do you know I think that's when things started to unravel.' A marked change in tone. 'It was when I faced up to how bloody stupid it was.'

Rivers looked puzzled. 'What was?'

'My pathetic little formula for getting myself back to France.' He adopted a mincing, effeminate tone. '"I'm not going back to kill people. I'm only going back to look after some men."' His own voice. 'Why didn't you kick me in the head, Rivers? Why didn't you put me out of my misery?'

Rivers made himself answer. 'Because I was afraid if you started thinking about that, you wouldn't go back at all.'

He might as well not have spoken. 'You've only got to read the training manual. "A commander must demand the impossible and not think of sparing his men. Those who fall out must be left behind and must no more stop the pursuit than casualties stopped the assault." That's it. Expendable, interchangeable units. That's what I went back to "*look after*".' A pause. 'All I wanted was to see them through their first tour of duty and I couldn't even do that.'

'Pinto's there,' Rivers said tentatively.

'Oh, yes, and he's good. He's really good.'

Siegfried's face and neck were running with sweat. 'Shall I open the window?' Rivers asked.

'Please. They keep shutting it, I don't know why.'

Rivers went to open the window. Behind him, Siegfried said, 'I'm sorry you don't like my lovely soldier lads.'

'I didn't say I didn't *like* them. I said you shouldn't *send* them.'

'There was one in particular.'

'Jowett,' said Rivers.

'I wrote a poem about Jowett. Not that he'll ever know. He was asleep. He looked as if he were dead.' A silence. 'It's odd, isn't it, how one can feel fatherly towards somebody, I mean, *genuinely* fatherly, not exploiting the situation or even being tempted to, and yet there's this other current. And I don't think one invalidates the other. I think it's perfectly possible for them both to be genuine.'

'Yes,' said Rivers, with the merest hint of dryness, 'I imagine so.' He came back to the bed. 'You say things "started to unravel"?'

'Yes, because I'd always coped with the situation by blocking out the killing side, cutting it off, and then suddenly one's brought face to face with the fact that, no, actually there's only one person there and that person is a potential killer of Huns. That's what our CO used to call us. It had a very strange effect. I mean, I went out on patrol, that sort of thing, but I've always done that, I've never been able to sit in a trench, it's not courage, I just can't do it, but this time it was different because I wasn't going out to kill or even to test my nerve, though that did come into it. *I just wanted to see*. I wanted to see the other side. I used to spend a lot of time looking through the periscope. It was a cornfield. Farmland. Sometimes you'd see a column of smoke coming up from the German lines, but quite often you'd see nothing.' A pause, then he said casually, 'I went across once. Dropped down into the trench and walked along, and there were four Germans standing by a machine-gun. One of them turned round and saw me.'

'What happened?'

'Nothing. We just looked at each other. Then he decided he ought to tell his friends. And I decided it was time to leave.'

A tense silence.

'I suppose I should have killed him,' Siegfried said.

'He should certainly have killed you.'

'He had the excuse of surprise. You know, Rivers, it's no good encouraging people to know themselves and . . . face up to their emotions, because out there they're better off not having any. If people are going to have to kill, they need to be brought up to expect to have to do it. They need to be trained *not to care* because if you don't . . .' Siegfried gripped Rivers's hand so tightly that his face clenched with the effort of concealing his pain. 'It's too cruel.'

Rivers had been with Siegfried for over an hour and so far nothing had been said that might not equally well have been dealt with at some more convenient time of day. But now, his excitement began to increase, words tripped him up, his mind stumbled along in the wake of his ideas, trying desperately to catch up. He spoke of the vastness of the war, of the impossibility of one mind encompassing it all. Again and again he spoke of the need to train boys to kill; from earliest childhood, he said, they must be taught to expect nothing else and they must never never be allowed to question what lies ahead. All this was mixed in with his anxieties about the raid Jowett and the others were going on. He spoke so vividly and with so much detail that at times he clearly believed himself to be in France.

There was no point arguing with any of this. It took Rivers three hours to calm him down and get him to sleep. Even after his breathing had become steady, Rivers went on sitting by the bed, afraid to move in case the withdrawal of his hand should cause him to wake. Long hairs on the back of Siegfried's forearm caught the light. Rivers looked at them, too exhausted to think clearly, remembering the experiments he and Head had done on the pilomotor reflex. Head's hairs had become erect every time he read a particular poem. The holy shiver, as the Germans call it. For Head it was awakened by poetry; for Rivers, more than once, it had been the beauty of a scientific hypothesis, one that brought into unexpected harmony a whole range of disparate facts. What had intrigued Rivers most was that human beings should respond to the highest mental and spiritual achievements of their culture with the same reflex that raises the hairs on a dog's back. The epicritic grounded in the protopathic, the ultimate expression of the unity we persist in regarding as the condition of perfect health. Though why we think of it like that, God knows, since most of us survive by cultivating internal divisions.

Siegfried was now deeply asleep. Cautiously, Rivers withdrew his hand, flexing the fingers. It had grown colder and Siegfried had fallen asleep outside the covers. Rivers went to shut the window, and stood for a moment attempting to arrange the story he'd been told into a coherent pattern, but that wasn't possible, though the outline was clear enough. Siegfried had always coped with the war by being two people: the anti-war poet and pacifist; the bloodthirsty, efficient company commander. The dissociation couldn't be called pathological, since experience gained in one state was available to the other. Not just *available*: it was the serving officer's experience that furnished the raw material, the ammunition, if you liked, for the poems. More importantly, and perhaps more ambiguously, that experience of bloodshed supplied the moral authority for the pacifist's protest: a *soldier's* declaration. No wonder Pinto's innocent question had precipitated something of a crisis.

Though he would have broken down anyway this time, Rivers thought. He had gone back hating the war, turning his face away from the reality of killing and maiming, and as soon as that reality was borne in upon him, he had found the situation unbearable. All of which might have been foreseen. Had been foreseen.

Night had turned the window into a black mirror. His face floated there, and behind it, Siegfried and the rumpled bed. If Siegfried's attempt at dissociation had failed, so had his own. He was finding it difficult to be both involved and objective, to turn steadily on Siegfried both sides of medicine's split face. But that was *his* problem. Siegfried need never be aware of it.

It was still dark. A light wind stirred the black trees in the park. He took his boots off and climbed on to the other bed, not expecting to be able to sleep, but thinking that at least he might rest. He closed his eyes. At first his thoughts whirred on, almost as active as Siegfried's and not much more coherent. For some reason the situation reminded him of sleeping on board the deck of a tramp steamer travelling between the islands of Melanesia. There, one slept in a covered cabin on deck, on a bench that left vertical stripes down one's back, surrounded by fellow passengers, and what a motley assemblage they were. He remembered a particular voyage when one of his companions had been a young Anglican priest, so determined to observe holy modesty in these difficult conditions that he'd washed the lower part of his body underneath the skirt of his cassock, while Rivers stripped off and had buckets of water thrown over him by the sailors who came up to swab the deck.

His other companion on that trip had been a trader who rejoiced in the name of Seamus O'Dowd, though he had no trace of an Irish accent. O'Dowd drank. In the smoky saloon after dinner, belching gin and dental decay into Rivers's face, he had boasted of his exploits as a blackbirder, for he'd started life kidnapping natives to work on the Queensland plantations. Now he simply cheated them. His most recent coup had been to convince them that the great Queen (nobody in the Condominion dared tell the natives Victoria was dead) found their genitals disgusting, and could not sleep easy in her bed at Windsor until they were covered by the long johns that Seamus had inadvertently bought as part of a job lot while even more drunk than usual.

They wore them on their heads, Rivers remembered. It had been a feature of the island in that first autumn of the war, naked young men wearing long johns elaborately folded on their heads. They looked beautiful. Meanwhile, in England, other young men had been rushing to don a less flattering garb.

Drifting between sleep and waking, Rivers remembered the smells of oil and copra, the cacophony of snores and whistles from the sleepers crammed into the small cabin on deck, the vibration of the engine that seemed to get into one's teeth, the strange, brilliant, ferocious southern stars. He couldn't for the life of him think what was producing this flood of nostalgia. Perhaps it was his own experience of duality that formed the link, for certainly in the years before the war he had experienced a splitting of personality as profound as any suffered by Siegfried. It had been not merely a matter of living two different lives, divided between the dons of Cambridge and the missionaries and headhunters of Melanesia, but of being a different person in the two places. It was his Melanesian self he preferred, but his attempts to integrate that self into his way of life in England had produced nothing but frustration and misery. Perhaps, contrary to what was usually supposed, duality was the stable state; the attempt at integration, dangerous. Certainly Siegfried had found it so.

He raised himself on his elbow and looked at Siegfried, who was sleeping with his face turned to the window. Perhaps the burst of nostalgia was caused by nothing more mysterious than this: the attempt to sleep in a room where another person's breathing was audible. Sleeping in the same room as another person belonged with his Melanesian self. In England it simply didn't happen. But it was restful, the rise and fall of breath, like the wash of waves round the prow of the boat, and gradually, as the light thinned, he drifted off to sleep.

He woke to find Siegfried kneeling by his bed. The window was open, the curtains lifting in the breeze. A trickle of bird-song came into the room.

In a half-embarrassed way, Siegfried said, 'I seem to have talked an awful lot of rubbish last night.' He looked cold and exhausted, but calm. 'I suppose I had a fever?'

Rivers didn't reply.

'Anyway, I'm all right now.' Diffidently, he touched Rivers's sleeve. 'I don't know what I'd do without you.'

NINETEEN

A week later Rivers was sitting in his armchair in front of the fire, feeling physically tired in an almost sensuous way. This was a rare feeling with him, since most days produced a grating emotional exhaustion which was certainly not conducive to sleep. But he had been flying, which always tired him out physically, and he'd seen Siegfried a lot calmer and happier than he had recently been, though still very far from well.

Prior was the mystery. Prior had missed an appointment, something he'd never done before, and Rivers wasn't sure what he should do about it. There was little he *could* do except drop Prior a line expressing his continued willingness to help, but there had been some suggestion that Prior worried about the degree of his dependence. If he had decided to break off the association there was nothing Rivers could – or should – do about it. He wouldn't come now. He was over two hours late.

Rivers was just thinking he really must make the effort to do something when there was a tap on the door, and the maid came in. 'There's a Mr Prior to see you,' she said, sounding doubtful, for it was very late. 'Shall I tell him –'

'No, no. Ask him to come up.'

He felt very unfit to cope with this, whatever it was, but he buttoned his tunic and looked vaguely around for his boots. Prior seemed to be climbing the stairs very quickly, an easy, light tread quite unlike his usual step. His asthma had been very bad on his last visit. He had paused several times on the final flight of stairs and even then had entered the room almost too breathless to speak. The maid must have misheard the name, that or –

Prior came into the room, pausing just inside the door to look round.

'Are you all right?' Rivers asked.

'Yes. Fine.' He looked at the clock and seemed to become aware that the lateness of the hour required some explanation. 'I had to see you.'

Rivers waved him to a chair and went to close the door.

'Well,' he said, when Prior was settled. 'Your chest's a lot better.'

Prior breathed in. Testing. He looked hard at Rivers and nodded.

'You were going to go to the prison last time we spoke,' Rivers said. 'To see Mrs Roper. Did you go?'

Prior was shaking his head, though not, Rivers thought, in answer to the question. At last he said, in a markedly sibilant voice, 'I didn't think you would have *pretended*.'

'Pretended what?' Rivers asked. He waited, then prompted gently, 'What am I pretending?'

'That we've met before.'

Momentarily, Rivers closed his eyes. When he opened them again Prior was grinning. 'I thought of saying, "Dr Rivers, I presume?"'

'If we haven't met before, how did you know me?'

'I sit in.' Prior spread his hands. '*I sit in.* Well, let's face it, there's not a lot of choice, is there? I don't know how you put up with him. *I* couldn't. Are you *sure* it's a good idea to let him get away with it?'

'With what?'

'With being so cheeky.'

'The sick have a certain licence,' Rivers said dryly.

'Oh, and he *is* sick, isn't he?' Prior said earnestly, leaning forward. 'Do you know, I honestly believe he's getting *worse*?'

A long silence. Rivers clasped his hands under his chin. 'Do you think you could manage to say "I"?'

''Fraid not. No.'

The antagonism was unmistakable. Rivers was aware of having seen Prior in this mood before, in the early weeks at Craiglockhart. Exactly this. The same incongruous mixture of effeminacy and menace.

'You know, it's really quite simple,' Prior went on. 'Either we can sit here and have a totally barren argument about which pronouns we're going to use, or we can talk. I think it's more important to talk.'

'I agree.'

'Good. Do you mind if I smoke?'

'I never do mind, do I?'

Prior was patting his tunic pockets. 'I'll *kill* him,' he said smiling. 'Ah, no, it's all right.' He held up a packet of cigars. 'I've got him trained. He used to throw them away.'

'What would you like to talk about?'

A broad smile. 'I thought *you* might have some ideas.'

'You say you "sit in". Does that mean you know everything he knows?'

'Yes. But he doesn't know anything I know. Only it's . . . it's not quite as neat as that. Sometimes I see things he can't see, even when he's there.'

'Things he doesn't notice?'

'Doesn't want to notice. Like for example he hates Spragge. I mean, he has perfectly good reasons for *disliking* him, but what he feels goes a long way beyond that. And he knows that, and he doesn't know why, even though it's staring him in the face. Literally. Spragge's like his father.'

'Like his own – like Spragge's father?'

'No. Well, he may be. How would *I* know? Like *Billy's* father. I mean, it's a really striking resemblance, and he just doesn't see it.' Prior paused, puzzled by some quality in Rivers's silence. 'You see what I mean?'

'*His* father?'

'Yes.'

'Are you really saying he's not *your* father?'

'Of course he isn't. How could he be?'

'How could he not be? In the end one body begets another.'

Prior's expression hardened. 'I was born two years ago. In a shell-hole in France. I have no father.'

Rivers felt he needed time to think. A week would have been about right. He said, 'I met Mr Prior at Craiglockhart.'

'Yes, I know.'

'He mentioned hitting Billy. Was that a frequent occurrence?'

'No. Oddly enough.'

'How do you know?'

'I've told you. I know everything he knows.'

'So you have access to his memories?'

'Yes.'

'And you also have your own memories.'

'That's right.'

'Why "oddly"?'

A blank look.

'You said it was odd his father didn't beat him.'

'Just because when you look at the relationship you think there must have been something like that. But there wasn't. Once his parents were having a row and he went downstairs and tried to get between them, and his father picked him up and threw him on the sofa. Only, being a bit the worse for wear, he missed the sofa and hit the wall.' Prior laughed. 'He never went down again.'

'So he just used to lie in bed and listen.'

'No, he used to get up and sit on the stairs.'

'What was he feeling?'

'I'm not good on feelings, Rivers. You'd better ask him.'

'Does that mean you don't know what he was feeling?'

'Angry. He used to do this.' Prior banged his clenched fist against the palm of the other hand. 'PIG PIG PIG PIG. And then he'd get frightened, I suppose he was frightened that if he got too angry he'd go downstairs. So he fixed his eyes on the barometer and blotted everything out.'

'Then what happened?'

'Nothing. He wasn't there.'

'Who was there?'

Prior shrugged his shoulders. 'I don't know. Somebody who didn't care.'

'Not you?'

'No, I *told* you –'

'You were born in a shell-hole.' A pause. 'Can you tell me about it?'

An elaborate shrug. 'There isn't much to tell. He was wounded. Not badly, but it hurt. He knew he had to go on. And he couldn't. So I came.'

Again that elusive impression of childishness. 'Why were *you* able to go on when he couldn't?'

'I'm better at it.'

'Better at . . .?'

'Fighting.'

'*Why* are you better?'

'Oh, for God's sake –'

'No, it *isn't* a stupid question. You're not taller, you're not stronger, you're not faster . . . you're not better trained. How could you be? So why are you better?'

'I'm not frightened.'

'Everybody's frightened sometimes.'

'I'm not. And I don't feel pain.'

'I see. So you didn't feel the wound?'

'No.' Prior looked at Rivers, narrowing his eyes. 'You don't believe a bloody word of this, do you?'

Rivers couldn't bring himself to reply.

'Look.' Prior drew strongly on his cigar, until the tip glowed red, then, almost casually, stubbed it out in the palm of his left hand. He leant towards Rivers, smiling. 'This isn't acting, Rivers. Watch the pupils,' he said, pulling down the lid of one eye.

The room filled with the smell of burning skin.

'And now you can have your little blue-eyed boy back.'

A withdrawn, almost drugged look, like extreme shock or the beginning of orgasm. Then, abruptly, the features convulsed with pain, and Prior, teeth chattering uncontrollably, raised his shaking hand and rocked it against his chest.

*

'I haven't got any pain-killers,' Rivers said. 'You'd better drink this.'

Prior took the brandy and held out his other hand for Rivers to complete the dressing. 'Aren't you going to tell me what happened?' he said.

'You burnt yourself.'

'Why?'

Rivers sighed. 'It was a dramatic gesture that went wrong.'

He'd decided not to tell Prior about the loss of normal sensation. It was a common symptom of hysterical disorders, but knowledge of it would only serve to reinforce Prior's belief that the alternating state of consciousness was a monster with whom he could have nothing in common.

'What was he like?' Prior asked.

'What were you like? Bloody-minded.'

'Violent?'

'Well, yes. *Obviously*,' Rivers said, indicating the burn.

'No, I meant –'

'Did you take a swing at me? No.' Rivers smiled. 'Sorry.'

'You make it sound as if it's something I *want*.'

Rivers was thinking deeply. 'I think that's true,' he said, knotting the ends of the bandage.

'*No*. Why should I want it? It's creating bloody havoc.'

'You know, Billy, the really interesting thing about tonight is that you turned up *in the other state*. I mean that while in the other state you still wanted to keep the appointment.'

'What did you call me?'

'Billy. Do you mind? I – '

'No, it's just that it's the first time. Did you know that? Sassoon was Siegfried. Anderson was Ralph. I noticed the other day you called Manning Charles. I was always "Prior". In moments of exasperation I was *Mister* Prior.'

'I'm sorry, I –' Oh, God, Rivers thought. Prior was incapable of interpreting that as anything other than snobbery. And perhaps it had been. Partly. Though it had been more to do with his habit of sneering suggestiveness. 'I'd no idea you minded.'

'No, well, you're not very perceptive, are you? Anyway, it doesn't matter.' He stood up. 'I'd better be off.'

'You can't go now, the trains have stopped. And, in any case, you're in no state to be on your own. You'd better sleep here.'

Prior hesitated. 'All right.'

'I'll make up the bed.'

Rivers saw Prior settled for the night, then went to his own room, telling himself it would be fatal, at this late hour, to attempt any assessment of Prior's situation. That must wait till morning. But the effort of *not* thinking about Prior proved almost equally disastrous, for he drifted off into a half-dreaming state, the only condition, apart from feverish illness, in which he had normal powers of visualization. He tossed and turned, scarcely aware of his surroundings, while persistent images floated before him. France. Craters, a waste of mud, splintered trees. Once he woke and lay looking into the darkness, faintly amused that his identification with his patients should have reached the point where he dreamt *their* dreams rather than his own. He heard the church bell chime three, and then sank back into his half-sleep. This was a dreadful place. Nothing human could live here. Nothing human did. He was entirely alone, until, with a puckering of the surface, a belch of foul vapours, the mud began to move, to gather itself together, to rise and stand before him in the shape of a man. A man who turned and began striding towards England. He tried to call out, no, not that way, and the movement of his lips half woke him. But he sank down again, and again the mud gathered itself into the shape of a man, faster and faster until it seemed the whole night was full of such creatures, creatures composed of Flanders mud and nothing else, moving their grotesque limbs in the direction of home.

Sunlight was streaming into the room. Rivers lay thinking about the dream, then switched his thoughts to yesterday evening. In the fugue state (though it was more than that) Prior had claimed to feel no pain and no fear, to have been born in a shell-hole, to have no father. Presumably *no* relationships that pre-dated that abnormal birth.

To feel no pain and no fear in a situation that seemed to call for both was not impossible, or even abnormal. He'd been in such a state himself, once, while on his way to the Torres Straits, suffering from severe sunburn, severe enough to have burnt the skin on his legs black. He'd lain on the deck of a ketch, rolling from side to side as waves broke across the ship, in constant pain from the salt water that soaked into his burns, vomiting helplessly, unable to stand or even sit up. Then the ketch had dragged her anchor and they'd been in imminent danger of shipwreck, and for the whole of that time he'd moved freely, he hadn't vomited, he'd felt no pain and no fear. He had simply performed coolly and calmly the actions needed to avert danger, as they all had. After they'd landed, his legs had hurt like hell and he'd once more been unable to walk. He'd been carried up from the beach on a litter, and had spent the first few days seeing patients from his sick bed, shuffling from the patient to the dispensing cupboard and back again on his bottom. He smiled to himself, thinking Prior would like that story. Physician, heal thyself.

Other people had had similar experiences. Men had escaped from danger before now by running on broken legs. But Prior had created a state whose freedom from fear and pain was persistent, encapsulated, inaccessible to normal consciousness. Almost as if his mind had created a warrior double, a creature formed out of Flanders clay, as his dream had suggested. And he had brought it home with him.

Rivers, thinking over the previous evening, found that he retained one very powerful impression. In Prior's speech and behaviour there had been a persistent element of childishness. He'd said, *He was wounded. Not badly, but it hurt. He knew he had to go on. And he couldn't. So I came.* So I came. The simplicity of it. As if one were talking to a child who still believed in magic. And on the stairs. *What happened then? Nothing. He wasn't there.* It was like a toddler who believes himself to be invisible because he's closed his eyes. And that extraordinary claim: *I have no father.* Surely behind the adult voice, there was another, shrill, defiant, saying, *He's not my Dad*? At any rate it was a starting-point. He could think of no other.

Rivers had not thought Prior would appear for breakfast, but no sooner had he sat down himself than the door opened and Prior came in, looking dejected, and in obvious pain. 'How did you sleep?' Rivers asked.

'All right. Well, I got a couple of hours.'

'I've asked the girl to bring us some more.'

'It doesn't matter, I'm not hungry.'

'Well, at least have some coffee. You ought to have something.'

'Yes, thanks, but then I must be going.'

'I'd rather you stayed. For a few days. Until things are easier.'

'I wouldn't dream of imposing on you.'

'You wouldn't be "imposing".'

'All right,' Prior said at last. 'Thank you.'

The maid arrived with a second tray. Rivers was amused to see Prior devour the food with single-minded concentration, while he sipped milky coffee and read *The Times*. 'I've got an hour before I need go to the hospital,' he said, when Prior had finished. 'Do you feel well enough?'

When they were settled in chairs beside the desk, Rivers said, 'I'd like to go back quite a long way.'

Prior nodded. He looked too exhausted to be doing this.

'Do you remember the house you lived in when you were five?'

A faint smile. 'Yes.'

'Do you remember the top of the stairs?'

'Yes. It's no great feat, Rivers. Most people can.'

Rivers smiled. 'I walked into that one, didn't I? Do you remember what was there?'

'Bedrooms.'

'No, I mean on the landing.'

'Nothing, there wasn't . . . No, the barometer. That's right. The needle always pointed to stormy. I didn't think that was funny at the time.'

'Do you remember anything else about it?'

'No.'

'What did you do when your father came in drunk?'

'Put my head under the bedclothes.'

'Nothing else?'

'I went down once. He threw me against the wall.'

'Were you badly hurt?'

'Bruised. He was devastated. He cried.'

'And you never went down again?'

'No. I used to sit on the landing, going PIG PIG PIG PIG.' He made as if to pound his fist against the other palm, then remembered the burn.

'Where were you exactly? Leaning over the banisters?'

'No, I used to sit on the top step. If they started shouting I'd shuffle a bit further down.'

'And where was the barometer in relation to you?'

'On my left. I hope this is leading somewhere, Rivers.'

'I think it is.'

'It was a bit like a teddy-bear, I suppose. I mean it was a sort of companion.'

'Can you imagine yourself back there?'

'I've said I –'

'No, take your time.'

'All right.' Prior closed his eyes, then opened them again, looking puzzled.

'Yes?'

'Nothing. It used to catch the light. There was a street lamp . . .' He gestured vaguely over his shoulder. 'This is going to sound absolutely mad. I used to go into the shine on the glass.'

A long silence.

'When it got too bad. And I didn't want to be there.'

'Then what happened? Did you go back to bed?'

'I must've done, mustn't I? Look, if you're saying this dates back to then, you're wrong. The gaps started in France, they got better at Craiglockhart, they started again a few months ago. It's nothing to do with bloody barometers.'

Silence.

'Say something, Rivers.'

'I think it has. I think when you were quite small you discovered a way of dealing with a very unpleasant situation. I think you found out how to put yourself into a kind of trance. A dissociated state. And then in France, under that *intolerable* pressure, you rediscovered it.'

Prior shook his head. 'You're saying it isn't something that happens. It's something I do.'

'Not deliberately.' He waited. 'Look, you know the sort of thing that happens. People lose their tempers, they burst into tears, they have nightmares. They behave like children, in many respects. All I'm suggesting is that you rediscovered a method of coping that served you well as a child. But which is –'

'I went into the shine on the glass.'

Rivers looked puzzled. 'Yes, you said.'

'No, in the pub, the first time it happened. The first time in England. I was watching the sunlight on a glass of beer.' He thought for a moment. 'And I was very angry because Jimmy was dead, and . . . everybody was enjoying themselves. I started to imagine what it would be like if a tank came in and crushed them. And I suppose I got frightened. It was so vivid, you see. Almost as if it had happened.' A long pause. 'You say it's self-hypnosis.'

'I think it must be. Something like that.'

'So if I could do it and tell myself to remember in theory that would fill in the gaps. All the gaps, because I'd bring all the memories back with me.'

'I don't know if that's the right thing to do.'

'But in theory it would work.'

'If you could become sufficiently aware of the process, yes.'

Prior was lost in thought. '*Is* it just remembering?'

'I don't think I know what you mean.'

'If I remember is that enough to heal the split?'

'No, I don't think so. I think there has to be a moment of . . . recognition. Acceptance. There has to be a moment when you look in the mirror and say, yes, this too is myself.'

'That could be difficult.'

'Why should it be?'

Prior's lips twisted. 'I find some parts of me pretty bloody unacceptable even at the best of times.'

The sadism again. 'There was nothing I saw or heard last night that would lead me to believe anything . . . terrible might be happening.'

'Perhaps you're just not his type.'

'"*Mister* Prior."'

A reluctant smile. 'All right.'

Rivers stood up. 'I think we've got as far as we can for the moment. *Don't* spend the day brooding, will you? And don't get depressed. We've made a lot of progress. It'll do you much more good to have a break. Here, you'll need this.' Rivers went to his desk, opened the top drawer, and took out a key. 'I'll tell the servants to expect you.'

TWENTY

Prior woke with a cry and lay in the darkness, sweating, disorientated, unable to understand why the grey square of window was on his right, instead of opposite his bed as it should have been. He'd been with Rivers for over a fortnight and yet he still had these moments when he woke and couldn't remember where he was. Footsteps came padding to his door.

'Are you all right?' Rivers's voice.

'Come in.' Prior put the lamp on. 'I'm sorry I woke you.'

'You cried out. I couldn't think what it was.'

'Yes, I know, I'm sorry.'

They looked at each other. Prior smiled. 'Shades of Craiglockhart.'

'Yes,' Rivers said. 'We've done this often enough.'

'You were on duty then. Go on, get back to bed. You need the rest.'

'Will you be able to get back to sleep?'

'Oh, yes, I'll be all right.' He looked at Rivers's exhausted face. 'And *you* certainly should. Go on, go back to bed.'

The dream had been about Mac, Prior thought, as the door closed behind Rivers. He couldn't remember it clearly, only that it had been full of struggling animals and the smell of blood. Rivers seemed to think it was a good sign that his nightmares had moved away from the war, back into his childhood, but they were no less horrifying, and in any case they were still about the war, he knew they were. Rivers made him talk endlessly about his childhood, particularly his early childhood, the rows between his parents, his own fear, the evenings he'd spent at the top of the stairs, listening, words and blows burnt into him till he could bear it no longer, and decided not to be there. He could still not remember what happened in the childhood gaps, though now he remembered that there had been gaps, though only when he was quite small. Once, in sheer exasperation, he'd asked Rivers how he was getting on with his own gap, the darkness at the top of his own stairs, but Rivers had simply smiled and pressed on. One always thought of Rivers as a *gentle* man, but Prior sometimes wondered why one did. Relentless might have been a better word.

The nightmares, though, were not about the rows between his parents. The nightmares were about Mac. And that was strange because most of his memories of Mac were pleasant.

An expanse of gritty asphalt. A low building with wire cages over the windows. Smells of custard and sweaty socks. The singing lesson, Monday morning, straight after Assembly, with Horton prowling up and down the aisles, swishing his cane against his trouser leg, listening for wrong notes. His taste had run to sentimental ballads, 'The Lost Chord' a firm favourite. This was the time Mr Hailes was inculcating a terror of masturbation, with his lectures on Inflamed Organs and the exhaustion which followed from playing with them. Horton sat down at the piano and sang in his manly baritone:

I was seated one day at the organ
Weary and ill at ease.

Prior gave an incredulous yelp of laughter, one or two of the others sniggered, Mac guffawed. The piano faltered into silence. Horton stood up, summoned Mac to the front of the room and invited him to share the joke. 'Well?' said Horton. 'I'm sure we could all do with being amused.'

'I don't think you'd think it was funny, sir.'

Mac was savagely caned. Prior was let off. Horton had heard Prior laugh too, he was sure of it, but Prior, thanks to his mother's scrimping and saving, was always well turned out. Shirts ironed, shoes polished, he looked like the sort of boy who might get a scholarship, as indeed he did, thanks partly to Father Mackenzie's more robust approach to organ playing. *Bastard*, Prior thought, as Horton's arm swung.

Years later, after witnessing the brutalities of trench warfare, he still thought: *Bastard*.

At the time he had been determined on revenge. Angrier on Mac's behalf than he would ever have been on his own.

Horton was a man of regular habits. Precisely twenty minutes before the bell rang for the end of the dinner break, he could be seen trekking across the playground to the masters' lavatory. Not for him the newspaper the boys had to make do with. Bulging from one side of his jacket, like a single tit, was a roll of toilet-paper. He marched across the yard with precise military tread, almost unnoticed by the shouting and running boys. Humour in the playground was decidedly scatological, but Horton's clockwork shitting was too old a joke to laugh at.

One dinnertime, posting Mac where he could see the main entrance to the school, Prior went in on a recce. Next day he and Mac slipped into the lavatory and locked the door of one of the cubicles. Prior lit a match, applied it to the wick of a candle, shielded the flame with both hands until it burned brightly, and fixed it in its own wax to a square of plywood.

Prompt to the minute, Mr Horton entered. He was puzzled by the locked cubicle. 'Mr Barnes?'

Prior produced a baritone grunt of immense effort and Horton said no more. Not even that constipated grunt tempted them to giggle. Horton's beatings were no laughing matter. They waited in silence, feeling the rise and fall of each other's breath. Then, slowly, Prior lowered the candle into the water that ran beneath the lavatory seat. It was one long seat, really, though the cubicles divided it. The candle flickered briefly, but then the flame rose up again and burnt steadily. Prior urged it along the dark water, and it bobbed along, going much faster than he'd thought it would. Mac was already unbolting the door. They ran across the playground, to where a game of High

Cockalorum was in progress (by arrangement) and hurled themselves on top of the heap of struggling boys.

Behind them, candle flame met arse. A howl of pain and incredulity, and Horton appeared, gazing wildly round him. No use him looking for signs of guilt. He inspired such terror that guilt was written plain on every one of the two hundred faces that turned towards him. In any case there was dignity to be considered. He limped across the playground and no more was heard.

Once he was safely out of sight, Prior and Mac went quietly round the corner to the forbidden area by the pile of coke and there they danced a solemn and entirely silent dance of triumph.

And why am I bothering to recall such an incident in so much detail, Prior asked himself. Because every memory of friendship I come up with is a shield against Hettie's spit in my face, a way of saying of course I couldn't have done it. What surprised him now was how *innocent* he'd felt when Beattie first mentioned Hettie's belief that he'd betrayed Mac. 'I didn't do it,' he'd said automatically, with total assurance, for all the world as if he could answer for every minute of his waking life. Only on the train coming back to London had he forced himself to accept that it was *possible* he'd betrayed Mac. Or at any rate that it was impossible for him to deny it.

Since then he'd gained one fact from Rivers that filled him with fear. He now knew that in the fugue state he'd denied that his father was his father. If he was prepared to deny that – a simple biological fact after all – what chance did pre-war friendships have? Rivers had hesitated visibly when telling him what his other state had said, and yet Prior's reaction to it had been more complicated than simple rejection or denial. To say that one had been born in a shell-hole is to say something absurdly self-dramatizing. Even by my standards, Prior thought wryly. Yet if you asked anybody who'd fought in France whether he thought he was the same person he'd been before the war, the person his family still remembered, the overwhelming majority – no, not even that, *all of them, all of them* would say no. It was merely a matter of degree. And one did feel at times very powerfully that the only loyalties that actually mattered were loyalties forged there. Picard clay was a powerful glue. Might it not, applied to pre-war friendships with conscientious objectors, be an equally powerful solvent?

Not in *this* state, he reminded himself. In *this* state he'd risked court martial for Beattie's sake, copying out documents that incriminated Spragge. But then Beattie was a woman, and couldn't fight. His other self might be less tolerant of healthy strapping young men spending the war years trying to disrupt the supply of ammunition on which other lives depended.

But *Mac*, he thought. Mac.

He did eventually drift off to sleep, and woke three hours later, to find the room full of sunshine. He peered sleepily at his watch, then reached for his dressing-gown. Rivers, already shaved and fully dressed, was sitting over the remains of breakfast. 'It seemed better to let you sleep,' he said. 'I'm afraid the coffee's cold.'

'Did you get back to sleep?'

'Yes.'

Lying hound, thought Prior. He drank the cold coffee as he shaved and dressed. Rivers was waiting by the desk. For a moment Prior felt rebellious, but then he looked at Rivers and saw how tired he was and thought, my God, if he can manage it, I can. He sat down, and the familiar position, the light falling on to Rivers's face, made him aware that he'd taken a decision. 'I'm going to see Mac,' he said.

Silence. 'I think the reason I'm not making any progress is that . . . there's a there's th-there's *oh, for Christ's sake*.' He threw back his head. 'There's a barrier, and I think it's something to do with him.'

'Finding out one fact about your behaviour over the past few weeks isn't going to change anything.'

'I think it might.'

Another long silence. Rivers shifted his position, 'Yes, I do see that.'

'And although I see the point, I mean, I see how important it is to get to the root of it, I do need to be functioning *now*. Somehow going over what happened with my parents just makes me feel like a sort of lifelong hopeless neurotic. It makes me feel I'll never be able to *do* anything.'

'Oh, I shouldn't worry about that,' Rivers said. 'Half the world's work's done by hopeless neurotics.'

This was accompanied by an involuntary glance at his desk. Prior laughed aloud. 'Would you like me to help you with any of it?'

Rivers smiled. 'I was thinking of Darwin.'

'Like hell. Why don't you let me do that?' Prior asked, pointing to a stack of papers on the desk. 'You're just typing it out, aren't you? You're not altering it.'

'It's very kind of you, but you couldn't read the writing. That's why I have to type it. My secretary can't read it either.'

'Let's have a look. Do you mind?' Prior picked up a sheet of paper.

'Rivers, do you realize this is the graphic equivalent of a stammer? I mean, whatever it is you couldn't say, you certainly didn't intend to write it. '

Rivers pointed his index finger. 'You're getting better.'

Prior smiled. Without apparent effort, he read a sentence aloud: *Thus, a frequent factor in the production of war neurosis is the necessity of restraint of the expression of dislike or disrespect for those of superior rank.* 'There's no hope for me, then, is there? I wonder why you bother.' He pushed Rivers gently off the chair. 'Go on, you get on with something else.'

Rivers shook his head. 'Do you know, nobody's ever done that before.'

'I'm good at breaking codes.'

'Is that a boast?'

'No. Pure terror.'

As Rivers turned the corner, he saw a man leaving Sassoon's room. They met face to face in the narrow corridor, and stopped.

'Dr Rivers?'

'Yes.'

'Robert Ross.'

They shook hands. After a few pleasantries about the weather, Ross said, 'I don't know whether Siegfried's talked about the future at all?'

'I believe he has various plans. Obviously he's in no state to do anything very much at the moment.'

'Gosse has some idea he could be useful in war propaganda, you know. Apparently Siegfried told him his only qualification for the job was that he'd been wounded in the head.'

They laughed, united by their shared affection for Siegfried, then said goodbye. Rivers was left with the impression that Ross had wanted to tell him something, but had thought better of it.

Siegfried was sitting up in bed, a notepad on his knees. 'Was that you talking to Ross?'

'Yes.'

'He looks ill, doesn't he?'

He looked worse than 'ill'. He looked as if he were dying. 'It's difficult to tell when you don't know the person.'

'I shan't be seeing him next week. He's off to the country.'

Rivers sat down by the bed.

'I've been trying to write to Owen,' Sassoon said. 'You remember

Owen? Little chap. Used to be in the breakfast-room selling the *Hydra*.'

'Yes, I remember. Brock's patient.'

'Well, he sent me a poem and I praised it to to the skies and now it's been passed round . . .' Siegfried pulled a face. 'Nobody else likes it. And now I look at it again *I*'m not sure either. The fact is . . .' he said, putting the pad on his bedside table, 'my judgement's gone. And not just for Owen's work. I thought *I*'d done one or two good things, but when I look at them again they're rubbish. In fact, I don't think I've done anything good since I left Craiglockhart.'

Rivers said carefully, 'You think that at the moment because you're depressed. Give yourself a rest.'

'Am I depressed?'

'You know you are.'

'I don't know what point there is in it anyway. What's an anti-war poet except a poet who's dependent on war? I thought a lot of things were simple, Rivers, and . . .' A pause. 'Eddie Marsh came to see me. He thinks he can find me a job at the Ministry of Munitions.'

'What do you think about that?'

'I don't know.'

Rivers nodded. 'Well, you've got plenty of time.'

'I don't even know whether I'm going back to France. Am I?'

'I shall do everything I can to prevent it. I don't think anybody expects you to go back this time.'

'I never regretted going back, you know. Not once.' He sat up suddenly, clasping his arms round his knees. 'You know what I'd really like to do? Go to Sheffield and work in a factory.'

'In a factory?'

'Yes, why not? I don't want to spend the rest of my life wrapped up in the sort of cocoon I was in before the war. I want to find out about ordinary people. Workers.'

'Why Sheffield?'

'Because it's close to Edward Carpenter.'

Silence.

'Why not?' Siegfried demanded. '*Why not?* I did everything anybody wanted me to do. Everything *you* wanted me to do. I gave in, I went back. Now why can't I do something that's right for *me*?'

'Because you're still in the army.'

'But you say yourself nobody expects –'

'That's a very different matter from a General Discharge. I see no grounds for that.'

'Does it rest with you?'

'Yes.' Rivers got up and walked to the window. He had hoped this time to be able to use his skills unambiguously for Siegfried's benefit. Instead, he was faced with the task of putting obstacles in the way of yet another hare-brained scheme, because this was another protest, smaller, more private, less hopeful, than his public declaration had been, but still a protest.

Behind him Siegfried said, 'There was a great jamboree in the park yesterday. Bands playing.'

Rivers turned to look at him. 'Of course, I was forgetting. August 4th.'

'They were unveiling some sort of shrine to the dead. Or giving thanks for the war, I'm not sure which. There's a Committee for War Memorials. One of the committees Robbie had to resign from. Can't have the Glorious Dead commemorated by a sodomite. Even if some of the Glorious Dead *were* sodomites.'

'You're very bitter.'

'And you're right, it's no good. You can *ride* anger.' Siegfried raised his hands in a horseman's gesture, forefingers splayed to take the reins. 'I don't know what you do with bitterness. Nothing, probably.'

Rivers caught and held a sigh. 'There's something I want to say. In my own defence, I suppose. If *at any time* you'd said to me, "I am a pacifist. I believe it's always and in all circumstances wrong to kill", I . . . I wouldn't have agreed with you, I'd've made you argue the case every step of the way, but in the end I'd've done everything in my power to help you get out of the army.'

'You don't need a defence. I told you, I never regretted going back.'

'But then you have to face the fact that you're *still* a soldier.' Rivers opened his mouth, looked down at Siegfried, and shut it again. 'You know, you really oughtn't to be lying in bed on a day like this. Why don't you get dressed? We could go out.'

Siegfried looked at his tunic, hanging on the back of the door. 'No, thanks, I'd rather not.'

'You haven't been dressed since you arrived.'

'I can't be bothered to dazzle the VADs.'

'*Dazzle?* Isn't that a bit conceited?'

'*Fact*, Rivers.' Siegfried smiled. 'One of life's minor ironies.'

Rivers walked across the room, took Siegfried's tunic from the peg and threw it on to the bed. 'Come on, Siegfried. Put it on. You can't spend the rest of your life in pyjamas.'

'I can't spend the rest of my life in that either.'

'No, but you have to spend the rest of the war in it.'

For a moment it looked as if Siegfried would refuse. Then, slowly, he pushed back the covers and got out of bed. He looked terrible. White. Twitching. Exhausted.

'We needn't go far,' Rivers said.

Slowly, Sassoon started to put on the uniform.

It was easier for Prior to arrange a visit to Mac than he had expected. He still had Ministry of Munitions headed notepaper, having taken a pile with him when he cleared his desk. But probably even without it, the uniform, the wound stripe, the earnestly expressed wish to save an old friend from the shame of pacifism, would have been enough to get him an interview.

Mac was sitting on his plank bed, his head in his hands.

Prior said, 'Hello, Mac.'

The hands came down. Mac looked . . . as people do look who've had repeated disagreements with detention camp guards.

'On your feet,' the guard said.

'No,' Prior said sharply. 'Leave us.'

The man looked startled, but obeyed. It was a relief when the door clanged shut behind him. Prior had been dreading a situation where Mac refused to salute him, and the guards spent the next half hour bouncing his head off the wall.

'Well,' Prior said.

No chair. No glass in the window. A smell of stale urine from the bucket, placed where it could be seen from the door. And behind him . . . yes, of course. The eye.

'I didn't expect to see *you*,' Mac said. Neither his voice nor his manner was friendly, but he showed no obvious rancour. Perhaps, like a soldier, he'd become accustomed to the giving and receiving of hard, impersonal knocks. There was no room for emotion in this.

'At least they've given you a blanket.'

Mac was naked underneath the blanket and the cell was cold even in summer.

'For your visit. It goes when you go.'

Prior sat down at the foot of the plank bed and looked around him.

'One of the main weapons, that,' said Mac conversationally. 'Marching you about the place naked. Especially since they don't give you any paper to wipe yourself with and the food in here's enough to give a brass monkey the shits.' He waited. 'The arsehole plays a major part in breaking people down, did you know that?'

'You look as if they've worked you over.'

'*Work?* Pleasure. One of them . . .' Mac raised his forearm. 'Hang your towel on it.'

'Is that over now?'

'The beatings? They're over when I give in.'

A uniform was lying, neatly folded, on the end of the bed.

'Can I ask you something, Billy? Do you talk about the war in the trenches? I don't mean day-to-day stuff, pass the ammunition, all that, I mean, "Why are we fighting?" "What is it all for?"'

'No. We're 'ere because we're 'ere.'

'Same in here.'

Prior looked puzzled. 'There's nobody to talk *to*.'

Mac smiled. 'Morse code on the pipes. I take it I can rely on you not to tell the CO?'

'Of course.'

'"Of course", Billy?'

'It wasn't me.'

Mac smiled and shook his head. 'Why come here if you're going to say that? Why come at all? I don't know. Do you just want to see what you've done?'

Prior opened his mouth for a second denial, and closed it again. 'I've got something for you,' he said, digging into his tunic pocket and bringing out two bars of chocolate. He watched Mac's pupils flare, then go dead. 'Yes, I know. It's contaminated. I've touched it.' He held the chocolate out, using his body to screen Mac from the eye. 'But you have to survive.'

Mac aligned himself exactly with Prior so that he could take the chocolate without being seen. 'That's true.'

'You'd better eat it. They'll search you.'

'They won't. That would mean doubting your integrity. An officer and a gentleman, no less. All the same I think I will have some.' He slit the paper with his fingernail, broke off a piece and started to eat. The movements of his mouth and throat were awkward. Hunger had turned eating into an act as private as bishop-bashing. Prior tried to look away, but there was nothing to look at. His eyes could only wander round the cell and return to Mac.

'Nine steps that way. Seven this. I do a lot of walking.'

'How long are you in for?'

'Solitary? Ninety days. If I reoffend – which *is* my intention – back in. Another ninety.'

Prior looked down at his hands. 'And no letters?'

'No.'

Mac managed a smile between mouthfuls. 'Why did you come, Billy?'

'To find out what you thought.'

'About you? What a self-centred little shit you are.'

'Yes.'

'I didn't believe it. The sergeant in Liverpool told me it was you, I mean, he mentioned your name. He was standing on my scrotum at the time, so, as you can imagine, it had a certain ring to it. I still didn't believe it, but the more I thought about it the more I thought, yes.' Mac was speaking intently, and yet almost indifferently, as if he didn't care whether Prior listened or not. Perhaps speaking at all was merely a way of salving his pride, of distracting Prior's attention while the all-important business of devouring the chocolate went on. 'And then I thought, he told you. Do you remember in the cattle shed I asked you what you'd have done if you'd found a deserter in Hettie's scullery and you said, "I'd turn him in. What else could I do?" And then I remembered a story I heard, about a man who found a snake half dead and nursed it back to life. He fed it, took care of it. And then he let it go. And the next time they met it bit him. And this was a very poisonous snake, he . . . knew he was going to die. And with his last gasp, he said, "But why? I saved you, I fed you, I nursed you. Why did you bite me?" And the snake said, "But you knew I was a snake."'

A long silence. Prior moved at last. 'It's a good story.'

'It's a fucking marvellous story. Only . . .'

Prior waited. 'Only what?'

'Now shall I be greedy, and eat it all?'

'Make sure of it. I would.'

'I probably hate you a lot less than you think. Not that I'd say we were bosom pals exactly, in fact if I meet you after the war I'll probably try to kill you . . .' He smiled and shook his head. 'Was it all a lie about wanting to help Beattie?'

'No, it was all true.'

'You know what I'd like? I'd like you to look me straight in the eye, put on that phoney public school accent of yours, and say, yes I told the police where to find you, and I'm not ashamed of that. It was my duty.'

'I can't.'

Mac was watching him intently. 'Then I don't understand. I thought you'd finally worked out whose side you were on.'

'There was never any doubt about that,' Prior said, raising his sleeve. 'People who wear this. More or less with pride.' He stood up. 'I shan't say I'm sorry.'

Mac looked up at him. 'Don't. Chocolate's too precious to bring back.'

Prior knocked, and waited impatiently for the guard to appear. He realized the painted eye must be looking straight at his belt buckle. Surreptitiously, he put his finger into the hole until it touched cool glass. Towers's eye, he remembered, lying in the palm of his hand, had been warm.

The guard appeared and, with one backward glance, he followed him along the iron landing and down the stairs. He had the rest of the day to get through before he could talk to Rivers, but he was glad of that. It was right that the first confusion and pain should be borne alone. He did not doubt for a moment that Mac's story was true – Mac had no reason to lie. Though he still had no memory of doing it, he had betrayed Mac.

He remembered an occasion when he'd held out a shaking hand to Rivers, stuttering something totally incoherent about Towers's eye, how the memory of holding it in his hand had become a talisman, a reminder of where the deepest loyalties lie. That was still true. And yet he could not justify what he had done to Mac. Even if his other self hated Mac for refusing to fight, for trying to bring the munitions factories to a halt, it remained true that in arranging to meet Mac he had in effect offered him a safe conduct – for Beattie's sake. Even leaving aside the childhood friendship, there had been a personal undertaking given in the present, trusted in the present, betrayed in the present. He could not, whether to satisfy Mac or console himself, say, 'I did my duty.' What had happened was altogether darker, more complex than that.

Drill was going on in the yard outside. Familiar shouts, the slurrying and stamping of boots, lines of regimented bodies moving as one. In the front rank a conchie was being 'persuaded' to take part. That is, he was being manhandled first into one position, then another. 'Marking time' consisted of being kicked on the ankles by the guards on either side. No attempt was made to hide what was happening. Presumably it was taken for granted that an officer would approve.

Prior watched for a while, then turned away.

TWENTY-ONE

A freshening breeze, blowing across the Serpentine, fumbled the roses, loosening red and yellow petals that lay on the dry soil or drifted across the paths. Rivers and Sassoon had been wandering along beside the lake for no more than fifteen minutes, but already Sassoon looked tired.

'I've been very good,' he said. 'The last few days. Out of bed and dressed before breakfast.'

'Good.'

Glutinous yellow sunlight, slanting between the trees, cast their shadows across the water.

'Do you remember me telling you about Richard Dadd?' Siegfried asked suddenly. 'Drowning his father in the Serpentine?'

'Yes,' Rivers said, and waited for more. When Siegfried didn't speak, he asked, 'Should I be hanging on to a tree?'

Siegfried smiled. 'No, not you.'

The deck-chairs beside the lake were empty, bellying in the wind, but on a sunny sheltered bank soldiers home on leave sat or lay entwined with their girls, the girls' summer dresses bright splashes against the khaki of their uniforms. A woman in a black uniform appeared on the ridge and began to make her way diagonally down the slope. As she advanced, a black beetle toiling across the grass, the lovers drew apart, and a girl close to the path tugged anxiously at the hem of her skirt.

'I've even been to the common room,' Siegfried said. 'You know what the topic of conversation was? The changes you notice when you're home on leave and whether any of them are for the better. And somebody said, yes, every time you came home women's skirts were shorter. I'm afraid it's not much consolation to *me*.'

Rivers caught a sigh. Depression and bitterness had become Siegfried's settled state. If he seemed better than he had when he first arrived, it was mainly because depression – provided it hasn't reached the point of stupor – is more easily disguised than elation. He was actually very ill indeed.

'I must say I'll be glad to be out of London,' Siegfried went on. 'Have you heard any more about this convalescent home?'

'Oh, yes. They can take you.'

'It's . . . I'm sorry, I've forgotten where you said it was.'

'Coldstream. Near Berwick-on-Tweed.'

'Is that anywhere near Scarborough? It's just Owen's stationed in Scarborough.'

'Well, it's not *near*, but you could probably get there and back in a day.' Rivers hesitated. 'There is one thing I think you . . . might not like. There has to be a Medical Board first.'

'Yes.'

Siegfried sounded puzzled. This wasn't the first time he'd been in hospital: riding accident during training, trench fever, wounded, 'shell-shocked' at Craiglockhart, wounded again. He knew the routine backwards.

'At Craiglockhart,' Rivers said.

A stunned silence. '*No*. Why Craiglockhart?'

'Because you're my patient. Because I want to be on the Board.'

Siegfried couldn't take it in. 'I can't go back there.'

'I'm afraid you've got to. It's only for a few days, Siegfried.'

Siegfried shook his head. 'I can't. You don't know what you're asking.'

There was an empty bench a few yards further on. Rivers sat down and indicated that Siegfried should join him. 'Tell me, then.'

A silence during which Sassoon struggled visibly with himself.

'Why can't you?' Rivers prompted gently.

'Because it would mean admitting I'm one of them.'

Rivers felt a flare of anger, but brought it quickly under control. 'One of whom?'

Siegfried was silent. At last he said, 'You know what I mean.'

'Yes, I'm afraid I do. One of the degenerates, the loonies, the lead-swingers, the cowards.' He waited for a response, but Siegfried had turned his head away. 'You know, Siegfried, sometimes I . . . reproach myself with having exercised too great an influence on you. At a time when you were vulnerable and . . . perhaps needed to be left alone to come to your own decision in your way.' Rivers shook his head. 'Well, I shan't be doing *that* again. If you still think like that I haven't influenced you at all. I haven't managed to convey a single bloody thing. Not a bloody thing.' He looked out over the lake. The wind blew a dark ripple across the surface like goose pimples spreading across skin. 'Perhaps we'd better be getting back.'

'Not yet.'

'You have to go back to Craiglockhart. I'm sorry, I'll make it as short as I can, but you have to go.'

Siegfried nodded. He was sitting with his big hands clasped between his knees. 'All right. But you do see what I'm trying to say? I *know* you find it offensive, but . . . It's not just admitting I'm one of them *now*, it's admitting I always was. Don't you see?'

'Yes, and it's nonsense. One day I'm going to give you a copy of your admission report. "No physical or mental signs of any nervous disorder." If you're tormenting yourself with the idea that your protest was some kind of symptom, well, for God's sake, stop. It wasn't. It was an entirely valid, sane response to the situation we're all in.' He paused. '*Wrong*, of course.'

'When I was in France I used to think of it as breakdown. It was easier than –'

'Than remembering what you believed?'

'Yes.' Siegfried looked down at his hands. 'Now I just feel as if a trap's been sprung.' A slight laugh. 'Not by you, I don't mean by you. But it has, hasn't it? It's absolutely *full circle*. *Literally* back to the beginning. Only worse, because now I belong there.'

'Three days. I promise.'

Siegfried got up. 'All right.'

Rivers remained seated for a moment. He wanted to say, if there *is* a trap, I'm in it too, but he couldn't. 'Come on,' he said, standing up. 'Let's go back.'

The bomb site had been tidied up, Prior saw. Rubble cleared away, the pavements swept clean of white dust, the houses on either side of the gap shored up. A cold wind whistled through the gap, disturbing the trees, whipping up litter into whirlpools that ran along the gutters. The sun blazed in the windows of the houses opposite the gap, turning the far side of the square into a wall of fire.

Prior was early for his appointment and dawdled along, noticing what on his previous visit, walking with Charles Manning through the spring dark, he had not noticed: that many of the elegant houses had dingy basements, like white teeth yellow round the gums.

He pressed the bell of Manning's house and turned slightly away, expecting to have to wait, but the door was opened almost immediately and by Manning himself, so quickly indeed that he must have been hovering in the hall. He might have appeared anxious, but his smile, his whole bearing, gave the impression of impulsive informality.

'It's all right, I've got it,' he said to somebody over his shoulder, and stood aside to let Prior in. 'I'm glad you could come. I thought of waiting till we were both back at work, but –'

'I'm not going back,' Prior said quickly.

'Ah.'

The living-room door stood open. No dust-sheets now.

'Oh, yes, come and see,' Manning said, noticing the direction of his glance.

They went in. A smell of furniture polish and roses.

'You found a builder, then,' Prior said, looking up at the door.

'Yes. I must say he didn't inspire a lot of confidence, but he seems to have done all right. As far as one can tell.' Manning patted the wall. 'I've got a sneaking suspicion the wallpaper might be holding the plaster up.'

They found themselves staring rather too long at the place where the crack had been, and glanced at each other, momentarily at a loss. 'Come and sit down,' Manning said.

A bowl of red and yellow roses stood in the fireplace where before there had been scrumpled newspaper dusted with soot. No mirror either – that had been moved. The whole room had been redecorated. So much was changed that the unyielding brocade of the sofa came as a shock. Prior flexed his shoulders, remembering. It was almost as if the body had an alternative store of memory in the nerve endings, for the sensation of being held stiffly erect induced a state of sensual awareness. He looked at Manning, and knew that he too was remembering.

'Would you like a drink?'

Manning went across to the sideboard. Prior, noticing a book lying face down on the floor near an armchair, reached across and picked it up. *Rex v. Pemberton Billing*. It was a complete transcript of the trial. What an extraordinary thing for Manning to be reading. Manning came back with the drinks. 'Is it good?' Prior asked, holding up the book.

'Fascinating,' Manning said. 'I realized while I was reading it wh-wh-what's actually h-happening. It's just that people are saturated with tragedy, they simply can't respond any more. So they've decided to play the rest of the war as farce.'

'I can't say I'd be prepared to fork out good money for this.'

'I didn't,' Manning said, sitting down. 'It was sent to me. By "a well-wisher".'

Prior raised his eyebrows. 'Really?'

'Oh, yes. I've had several little . . . communications.'

'Captain Spencer came to see us, you know.'

'"Us"?'

'The Intelligence Unit. I think somebody must have told him the first question he'd be asked in court was whether he'd informed the appropriate authorities when he discovered the Great Conspiracy. So he was scurrying round London informing them.' Prior laughed.

'Did he mention any names?'

'Good Lord, yes.' Prior looked up and caught a fleeting expression of anxiety. 'Not you.'

'No, I didn't think that, I'm not important enough. Robert Ross?'

'Well, yes.'

Manning nodded. 'You say you're not going back?'

'There's nothing to go back *to*. I went in to check my pigeonhole and . . . it was like the *Marie Celeste*. Files gone. Lode gone.'

'He's . . .'

'Teaching cadets. In Wales. No doubt that pleases him.'

'Why, is he Welsh?'

'I was being sarcastic. I shouldn't think it pleases him in the least. Spragge. I don't know whether you –'

'The informer?'

'That's right. He's gone – or going, I'm not sure which – to South Africa. *All expenses paid*.'

Manning hesitated. 'I . . . don't think you should feel *nothing* useful came out of that. I showed Eddie Marsh your report and . . . he was rather impressed actually. As I was. He thought it was . . . very cogently argued. Very effective.'

'It may have been cogently argued. It certainly wasn't *effective*. She's still in prison.'

Manning smiled. 'The point is –'

The french windows were thrown open, and a chubby-cheeked child peered, blinking, into the dark interior. 'Daddy?'

'Not now, Robert,' Manning said, turning round. 'Ask Elsie.'

Manning's face softened as he watched the child close the door carefully behind him. His delight in his house and family was so obvious it seemed churlish to wonder if he ever regretted the empty rooms of early spring, the smells of soot and fallen plaster, the footsteps that had followed him upstairs to the maids' bedroom.

'The point is that being able to organize an array of complicated facts and present them succinctly is quite a rare ability. And just the sort of thing we're looking for in my line of work.'

'Which is . . .'

'Health and safety. To cut a long story short, I'm offering you a job.'

'Ah.'

'I think you might find it worth while. Since it's basically protecting the interests of the workers.'

Prior was in no hurry to reply. He had resigned himself, not entirely with reluctance, to going back to Scarborough, to resuming the boring, comfortless life of an army camp in England. At the same time he knew Manning's offer was one for which a great many men would have given an arm or a leg, and not merely in the meaningless way that expression was normally used. 'Is Rivers behind this?'

'No.'

Prior wasn't sure he believed him. 'I'm very grateful, Charles – don't think I don't appreciate it – but I'm afraid I can't accept.'

'Why not?'

'Sarah – that's my girlfriend – she's in the north. I'd be able to see quite a lot of her if I was in Scarborough. And that's a big factor. And . . . I'm not sure how much I want a cushy job.'

Manning hesitated. 'It does have one very big advantage. It's most unlikely you'd be sent back to France. Though I suppose that's not very likely anyway.'

'Oh, I don't know.'

'What rating are you?'

'A4.'

'That's a long way from the top.'

'With a Board in two weeks' time.'

'Rivers wouldn't let it happen.'

'Rivers has nothing to do with it. I was given my original rating on the basis of my asthma.'

'But he'd write to the Board if you asked him.'

'I know. In fact I think Rivers could be quite eloquent on the subject of my unfitness for France. The point is, he won't be asked.'

'How are you really?'

'A lot better.'

Manning toyed with his glass. 'What was the trouble exactly?'

Prior smiled, remained silent just long enough for Manning to feel embarrassed by the intrusiveness of the question, then answered it. 'Memory lapses. Black-outs, I suppose. They do seem to be over.'

'Do you know what you did during them?'

'Yes.' Prior smiled again. 'Nothing I don't have a tendency to do.'

Manning became aware that he was looking almost indecently curious, and quickly corrected his expression.

'How about you?' Prior said.

'Mending. It was much harder *work* than I thought it would be.'

'Rivers? Oh, yes.'

'I mean, he's an absolute slave-driver. And you can't grumble because you know he's driving himself even harder.'

A glance of amusement and shared affection. Then Manning said, 'You sound almost as if you want to go back.'

'Yes, I suppose I do, in a way. It's odd, isn't it? In spite of everything – I mean in spite of Not Believing in the War and Not Having Faith in Our Generals and all that, it still seems the only *clean* place to be.'

'Yes. My God, *yes*.'

They stared at each other, aware of a depth of understanding that the surface facts of their relationship scarcely accounted for.

'Not an option for me, I'm afraid,' Manning added, stretching out his leg. 'But I do know what you mean.'

'Do you think we're mad?'

'Both been in the loony bin.'

'You'd better not let Rivers hear you calling it that.'

'I wouldn't dare. The offer's open for the next few days, you know,' Manning said, putting down his glass. 'I shan't be seeing Marsh till –'

Prior smiled and shook his head. 'No. Thank you, but no.'

'You don't think you might regret it?'

Prior laughed. 'Charles, if I get sent back – if, if, if, if – I shall sit in a dug-out and look back to this afternoon, and I shall think, "You *bloody* fool."'

'Well,' Manning said, standing up. 'I tried.'

In the hall a maid came forward carrying Prior's cap and cane. Prior glanced at her: she was sallow-skinned, middle aged, about as old as his mother, he supposed. He stared at her uniform, remembering how he'd pressed his face into the armpits, smelling the careworn, sad smell.

Manning was saying something, but he didn't hear what it was. He turned to him and said, 'Now I come to think of it, Spencer *did* mention other names.'

Manning said smoothly, 'Thank you, Alice. I'll see Mr Prior out.'

'Winston Churchill and Edward Marsh.'

Manning gave an astonished yelp. *'Churchill?'*

'Yes.'

'Then he *is* mad.'

'Yes, that's what I thought.' Prior walked to the door, then stopped. 'He said Churchill and Marsh spent an entire afternoon beating each other's buttocks with a plaited birch.'

'Yes.'

'What do you mean "yes"?'

'Churchill was Home Secretary at the time.'

'Oh, well, that explains everything.'

'It was a new kind of birch.' Manning looked impatient. 'I don't know the details, there'd been some sort of controversy about it. I think people were saying it was cruel. So *naturally* they –'

'Tried it out on each other.'

'Yes.' Manning's expression hardened. 'They were doing their duty.'

'What conclusion did they reach?'

'I think they both thought they'd had worse beatings at school.'

Prior nodded, glanced round to make sure they were unobserved, then took hold of Manning's pudgy cheeks and chucked them. 'There'll always be an England,' he told him and ran, laughing, down the steps.

AUTHOR'S NOTE

The reader may find it useful to have a brief outline of the historical events that occurred in 1917–1918 on which this novel is based.

Beattie Roper's story is loosely based on the 'poison plot' of 1917. Alice Wheeldon, a second-hand clothes dealer living in the back streets of Derby, was accused and convicted of having conspired to murder Lloyd George, Arthur Henderson and other persons by poisoning. The poison, in the case of Lloyd George, was to be administered by a curare-tipped blowdart. The trial depositions are in the Public Record Office, Chancery Lane, and provide a fascinating insight into the lives of absolutist pacifists on the run, and the Ministry of Munitions agents who spied on them. Mrs Wheeldon was convicted on the unsupported evidence of such informers and sentenced to ten years' hard labour, despite her insistence that the poison she had procured was intended for the guard dogs at a detention centre. After the war she was released, but, weakened by prison diet, hard labour and repeated hunger strikes, died in 1919.

Friends of Alice Wheeldon by Sheila Rowbotham (Pluto Press, 1986) contains a useful essay: 'Rebel Networks in the First World War'.

In January 1918 the *Imperialist* (later the *Vigilante*), a newspaper owned and edited by the MP Noel Pemberton Billing, carried an article entitled 'The First 47,000'. It purported to be written by Pemberton Billing himself, but in fact the author was a Captain Harold Spencer, who claimed that he had been a British Intelligence agent at the time when he saw and read the Black Book in the *cabinet noir* of 'a certain German Prince'.

In April this article was followed by a short paragraph entitled 'The Cult of the Clitoris', again purporting to be written by Pemberton Billing, and again written by Harold Spencer. This suggested that the list of subscribers to a private performance of Oscar Wilde's *Salome* might contain many names of the 47,000. Maud Allan, who was to dance the part of Salome, sued Pemberton Billing for libel, since the paragraph clearly implied she was a lesbian.

The trial was presided over by Lord Justice Darling. Pemberton

Billing defended himself. Having been identified early in the proceedings as one of the 47,000, Darling lost control of the court.

The star defence witness was Harold Spencer. In addition to giving free rein to his obsession with women who had hypertrophied and diseased clitorises and therefore could be satisfied only by bull elephants, Spencer alleged that many members of the Asquith War Cabinet had been in the pay of the Germans, that Maud Allan was Asquith's wife's lover and a German agent, that many high-ranking officers in the British army were Germans, and that persons who had the courage and patriotism to point these facts out were marooned on desert islands where they had to subsist on iron rations from submarines.

Lord Alfred Douglas, another defence witness, seized the opportunity of pursuing his personal dispute with Robert Ross, Oscar Wilde's devoted friend and literary executor, identifying him as 'the leader of all the sodomites in London'.

After six days of chaos in the courtroom and hysteria in the newspapers, Pemberton Billing won the case and was carried shoulder-high through the cheering crowds that had gathered outside the Old Bailey.

Later that year Harold Spencer was certified insane.

Robert Ross died of heart failure, on 5 October, aged forty-nine.

Pemberton Billing went on to have a distinguished parliamentary career.

In 1917 Siegfried Sassoon (1886–1967), after protesting against the war, had been persuaded by his friend Robert Graves to accept a Medical Board, which decided that he was suffering from a mental breakdown and that he should be sent to Craiglockhart War Hospital, Edinburgh. There he came under the care of Dr W. H. R. Rivers, FRS (1864–1922), the distinguished neurologist and social anthropologist. At Craiglockhart, Sassoon reached the conclusion that, although his views on the war had not changed, it was nevertheless his duty to return to active service, where he could at least share the suffering of his men.

After a period in Palestine he returned to France on 9 May 1918. On 13 July, returning late from a patrol, he was wounded in the scalp by a rifle shot from one of his own NCOs; he was then sent back to England, to the American Women's Red Cross Hospital at Lancaster Gate. The fact that he was ill enough for Rivers to have found it necessary to sit up with him is recalled in a letter from Katharine Rivers to Ruth Head (unpublished letters of the Rivers family, Imperial War Museum).

Winston Churchill's and Edward Marsh's devotion to duty while at the Home Office is mentioned in *Edward Marsh, Patron of the Arts: A Biography* by Christopher Hassall (Longmans, 1959).

THE GHOST ROAD

Now all roads lead to France
And heavy is the tread
Of the living; but the dead
Returning lightly dance

'Roads', Edward Thomas

Part One

ONE

In deck-chairs all along the front the bald pink knees of Bradford businessmen nuzzled the sun.

Billy Prior leant on the sea-wall. Ten or twelve feet below him a family was gathering its things together for the trek back to boarding-house or railway station. A fat, middle-aged woman, swollen feet bulging over lace-up shoes, a man with a lobster-coloured tonsure – my God, he'd be regretting it tomorrow – and a small child, a boy, being towelled dry by a young woman. His little tassel wobbled as he stood, square-mouthed with pain, howling, 'Ma-a-am.' Wet sand was the problem. It always was, Prior remembered. However carefully you tiptoed back from that final paddle, your legs got coated all over again, and the towel always hurt.

The child wriggled and his mother slapped him hard, leaving red prints on his chubby buttocks. He stopped screaming, gulped with shock, then settled down to a persistent grizzle. The older woman protested, 'Hey, our Louie, there's no need for that.' She grabbed the towel. 'C'mon, give it here, you've no bloody patience, you.'

The girl – but she was not a girl, she was a woman of twenty-five or twenty-six, perhaps – retreated, resentful but also relieved. You could see her problem. Married, but the war, whether by widowing her or simply by taking her husband away, had reduced her to a position of tutelage in her mother's house, and then what was the point? Hot spunk trickling down the thigh, the months of heaviness, the child born on a gush of blood – if all that didn't entitle you to the status and independence of a woman, what did? Oh, and she'd be frustrated too. Her old single bed back, or perhaps a double bed with the child, listening to snores and creaks and farts from her parents' bed on the other side of the wall.

She was scrabbling in her handbag, dislodging bus tickets, comb, purse, producing, finally, a packet of Woodbines. She let the cigarette dangle wetly from her lower lip while she groped for the matches. Her lips were plump, a pale salmon pink at the centre, darkening to brownish red at the edges. She glanced up, caught him looking at her, and flushed, not with pleasure – his lust was too blatant to be flattering – but drawn by it, nevertheless, into the memory of her unencumbered girlhood.

Her mother was helping the little boy step into his drawers, his hand a dimpled starfish on her broad shoulder. The flare of the match caught her attention. 'For God's sake, Louie,' she snapped. 'If you could only see how common you look . . .'

Louie's gaze hadn't moved. Her mother turned and squinted up into the sun, seeing the characteristic silhouette that said 'officer'. 'Look for the thin knees,' German snipers were told, but where they saw prey this woman saw a predator. If he'd been a private she'd have asked him what the bloody hell he thought he was gawping at. As it was, she said, 'Nice weather we're having, sir.'

Prior smiled, amused, recognizing his mother's speech, the accent of working-class gentility. 'Let's hope it lasts.'

He touched his cap and withdrew, thinking, as he strolled off, that the girl was neither a widow nor married. The way the mother's voice had cracked with panic over that word 'common' said it all. Louie's knees were by no means glued together, even after the child. And her mother was absolutely right, with that fag stuck in her mouth she did look common. Gloriously, devastatingly, *fuckably* common.

He ought to be getting back to barracks. He had his medical in less than an hour, and it certainly wouldn't do to arrive gasping. He had no business to be drifting along the front looking at girls. But he looked anyway, hoarding golden fuzz on a bare arm, the bluish shadow between breasts thrust together by stays, breathing in lavender sharpened by sweat.

The blare of music inside the fairground drew him to stand in the entrance. So far today the only young men he'd seen had been in uniform, but here were men as young as himself in civilian dress. Munitions workers. One of them was chatting to a young girl with bright yellow skin. He felt the automatic flow of bile begin and turned away, forcing himself to contemplate the bald grass. A child, holding a stick of candy-floss, turned to watch him, attracted to the man who stood so still among all the swirl and dazzle. He caught her looking at him and smiled, remembering the soft cotton-wool sweetness of candy-floss that turned to clag on the roof of your mouth. She bridled and turned away, clutching her mother's skirt. Very wise.

As he walked on, his smile faded. *He* could have been a munitions worker, he thought. Kept out of danger. Lined his pockets. His father would have wangled him a place in a nice safe reserved occupation, and would not have despised him for it either, unlike many fathers. The weedy little runt would at least have been behaving like a *sensible* weedy little runt, refusing to fight in 'the bosses' war'. But he'd never seriously considered doing that.

Why not? he wondered now. Because I don't want to be one of *them*, he thought, remembering a munitions worker's hand patting a girl's bottom as he helped her into the swing-boat. Not duty, not patriotism, not fear of what other people would think, certainly not that. No, a kind of . . . fastidiousness. Once, as a small boy, he'd slipped chewed-up pieces of fatty mutton into the pocket of his trousers, because he couldn't bring himself to swallow them, and his father, when the crime came to light, had said, in tones of ringing disgust, 'That bairn's too fussy to live.' Too fussy to live, Prior thought. There you are, nowhere near France and an epitaph already. The thought cheered him up enormously.

By now he was walking up the hill towards the barracks, a chest-tightening climb, but he was managing it well. His asthma was good at the moment, better than it had been for months. All the same it might be as well to sit quietly somewhere for a few minutes before he went into the examination room. In the end all he could do was to turn up in a reasonable state, and answer the questions honestly (or at least tell no lies that were likely to be found out). The decision would be taken by other people. It always was.

Though he had managed to take *one* decision himself.

His thoughts shifted to Charles Manning and the last evening they'd spent together in London.

– *Have you stopped to think what's going to happen if you're not sent back?* Manning had asked. *Six months, at least six months, probably to the end of the war, making sure new recruits wash between their toes.*

– *Might have its moments.*

– *Doing a hundred and one completely routine jobs, each of which could be done equally well by somebody else. You'd be much better working at the Ministry. I can't promise to keep the job open.*

– *No, thank you, Charles.*

No, thank you. He was passing the Clarence Gardens Hotel where he'd been stationed briefly last winter before the summons to London came. Plenty of routine jobs there. He and Owen, his fellow nut-case, had arrived on the same day, neither of them welcomed by the CO. They'd been assigned to 'light duties'. Prior became an administrative dogsbody, sorting out the battalion's chaotic filing system. Owen fared yet worse, chivvying the charladies, ordering vegetables, peering into lavatory bowls in search of unmilitary stains. Mitchell had given them hell. Prior got him in the mornings when he was *totally* vile, Owen in the evenings when brandy had mellowed him slightly.

– *What do you expect?* Prior said, when Owen complained. *He's lost two sons. And who shows up instead of them? Couple of twitching Nancy boys from a loony-bin in Scotland.*

Silence from Owen.

– *That's what he thinks, you know.*

As he reached the entrance to the barracks, a squad of men in singlets and shorts, returning from a cross-country run, overtook him and he stood back to let them pass. Bare thighs streaked with mud, steam rising from sweaty chests, glazed eyes, slack mouths, and as they pounded and panted past, he recognized Owen at the head of the column, turning to wave.

'Good heavens,' Mather said, as Prior pulled off his shirt. 'You haven't been getting much outdoor exercise, have you?'

'I've been working at the Ministry of Munitions.'

Mather was middle aged, furrow-cheeked, sandy-haired, shrewd.

'All right, drop your drawers. Bend over.'

They always went for the arse, Prior thought, doing as he was told. An army marches on its stomach, and hobbles on its haemorrhoids. He felt gloved fingers on his buttocks, separating them, and thought, Better men than you have paid for this.

'I see you've got asthma.'

There? 'Yes, sir.'

'Turn round.'

Another unduly intimate gesture.

'Cough'

Prior cleared his throat.

'I said, *cough*.' The fingers jabbed. 'And again.' The hand changed sides. 'Again.'

Prior was aware of wheezing as he caught his breath.

'How long?'

Prior looked blank, then stammered. 'S-six months, sir.'

'Six months? But it says –'

'I mean, the doctor told my mother I had it when I was six months old, sir.'

'Ah.' Mather turned over a page of the file. 'That makes more sense.'

'Apparently I couldn't tolerate milk.'

Mather looked up. 'Awkward little bugger, weren't you? Well, we'd better have a listen.' He reached for his stethoscope and came towards Prior. 'What were you doing at the Ministry of Munitions?'

'Intelligence, sir.'

'Oooh, *very* impressive. Catch anybody?'

Prior looked bleakly ahead of him. 'Yes.'

'Patrol here caught a German spy on the cliffs.' Mather snorted, fitting the stethoscope. 'Tickled a local yokel with their bayonets more like.'

Prior started to say something, but Mather was listening to his chest. After a few minutes, he straightened up. 'Yes, you have got a bit of a wheeze.' His attention was caught by the scar on Prior's elbow. He turned the arm towards him.

'The Somme,' Prior said.

'Must've hurt.'

'The expression "funny bone" didn't seem appropriate at the time.'

Mather went back to the desk, sat down. 'Now let's see if I've got this straight. You were invalided home with shell-shock. That right? April last year?'

'Yes, sir.'

'And you were sent first to Netley and then to Craiglockhart War Hospital, where you remained till . . . November.' He looked up. 'I suppose you get a lot of dipsomania, in places like that? *Alcohol*, man,' he explained, as Prior continued to look blank.

'Didn't see any, sir. If I had I'd certainly have drunk it.'

'So what *were* your symptoms?'

'I was mute, sir. Some people found it an improvement on the basic model.'

But Mather was reading, not listening. 'W. H. R. Rivers,' he said. 'I knew him. He was two years ahead of me at Bart's. Paralytic stammer.'

Prior looked puzzled. 'No.'

'Ah? Got his own voice back too. He must be good.' He tapped a sheet of paper. 'The discharge report says asthma.'

'I had two attacks while I was there.'

'Hm.' Mather smiled. 'Any problems with the nerves now?'

'No.'

'Appetite?'

'I could eat more than I get.'

'So could we all, laddie. Sleeping all right?'

'Not last night. Bloody tent leaks.'

'Generally?'

'I sleep all right.'

Mather sat back in his chair. 'How did you get in?'

'Through the flap.'

Mather's forefinger shot up. 'Watch it, *laddie*. How did you get into the *army*?'

A brief struggle with temptation, ending as Prior's struggles with temptation usually did. 'I lied to the doctor, Doctor.'

Surprisingly, Mather laughed, a short bark.

'Everybody lied,' Prior said.

'So they did, I remember it well. I saw men who'd climbed out of the window of the workhouse infirmary to come and enlist. Syphilis, epilepsy, tuberculosis, rickets. One lad – little squeaky voice, not a hair on his chin, fourteen, if that – looked me straight in the eye and swore on his mother's life he was nineteen.' Mather smiled, revealing brown teeth. 'Not one of them got past me.'

Oh fuck.

'Gas training,' Mather said.

Silence.

'Well?'

'*Terribly* good idea,' Prior said earnestly.

'Did you go through the huts?'

'No.'

'You must be affected at very low concentrations?'

'I was known as the battalion canary, sir. Partly that. Partly my pleasant, cheerful personality.'

Mather looked at him. 'Get dressed.'

'The point is I managed perfectly well *for three years*. I didn't *once* report sick with asthma *or* the effects of gas.'

'Yes, laddie.' Mather looked unexpectedly compassionate. 'And it might be said you've done your bit.'

A twitch of the pale, proud face. 'Not by me.'

'And the asthma never played you up in France?'

'Never.'

'Two attacks in Craiglockhart. None in France. I wonder why?'

'Open-air life suited my chest, sir.'

'We're not running a sanatorium, laddie. Go on, get dressed. Then you go left along the corridor, turn left at the end, and you'll see a row of chairs. Wait there.'

Mather went into the adjoining room and started on his next victim. Prior dressed, pausing to wipe the sweat off his upper lip. Like going over the top, he thought. No, it wasn't. Nothing was like that. Civilians seemed to use that expression all the time now. I went a bit over the top last night, they said, meaning they'd had a second glass of port. Prior peered into the small looking-glass behind the wash-basin, checking the knot in his tie. If they didn't send him back he was going to be awfully lonely, marooned among civilians with their glib talk. His reflection jeered, *Lonely? You? Oh, c'mon, duckie. You can always split in two*. At least the Board didn't know about *that*. Or rather they didn't, provided Rivers hadn't written to them. A *paralytic* stammer. Not just any old stammer. Paralytic. Interesting, Prior thought, letting himself out of the room.

The place smelled like a barracks. Well, it was a barracks, but the Clarence Gardens Hotel, after months of army use, had not smelled anything like this. His nose twitched, identifying armpits, feet, socks, oil, boot-polish, carbolic soap, the last blown in bubbles between the raw fingers of a boy scrubbing the floor. Rear-end like a truck and a face to match, but Prior produced a charming smile, nevertheless, because he owed it to himself, and strode on, leaving a trail of muddy footprints across the wet floor.

One man waiting. Owen.

'The O's and the P's again,' Owen said, picking up a pile of *John Bulls* from the vacant chair and dumping them on the floor. They'd last waited together like this at Craiglockhart, at their final board.

Prior jerked his head at the door. 'Who's in?'

'Nesbit. He's been in thirty minutes.'

'What's taking so long?'

Owen hesitated, then mouthed, 'Clap.'

Well, Prior thought, that was one way of getting out of it. And then he thought, You uncharitable bastard, how do you know he got it deliberately? And then he thought, Well, I *am* an uncharitable bastard.

'I won't take long,' Owen said. 'I'm GS already.'

'Then why are you here?'

'Irregular heartbeat. I added my name to the draft, but when I had the final medical they promptly took it off again.'

'You added your name to the draft? Sure it's your *heart* that's wrong?'

Owen laughed, and looked away. 'I'd just heard Sassoon was wounded. It seemed the only thing to do.'

Yes, Prior thought, it would. He remembered them at Craiglockhart: the incongruous pair, Sassoon so tall, Owen so short, the love Owen hadn't been able, or hadn't bothered, to disguise.

'*Also*,' Owen said, 'I was getting pretty tired of being regarded as "a twitching Nancy boy from a loony-bin in Scotland".'

Prior smiled. 'I applied it to myself as well.'

Owen had cut himself shaving, he noticed. Blood in shiny brown flakes filled the crease between cheek and earlobe.

'Do you think you'll be all right this time?'

Owen said cheerfully, 'Oh, yes, I should think so. I've been doing a lot of running.'

'I saw.'

The door opened. Nesbit came out, looking distinctly pale.

Owen stood up. 'Do they want me in?'

'I don't know.'

Owen sat down again. 'Worse than the dentist, isn't it?' he said, forcing a laugh.

A few minutes later he was called in. Prior sat listening to the murmur of voices, thinking what bloody awful luck it was to have got Mather. Some MOs would send a corpse back if you propped one up in front of them, particularly now when every man was needed for the latest in a long line of 'one last pushes'. Abruptly, before he was ready, the door opened and Owen came out. Owen started to speak and then, realizing the Board's secretary had followed him, raised a thumb instead. From which Prior concluded that Owen's chances of ending the year deaf, blind, dumb, paralysed, doubly incontinent, insane, brain damaged or – if he were lucky – just plain dead had enormously increased. We're all mad here, he thought, following the secretary into the room, saluting, sitting down in the solitary chair facing the long table, meeting every eye confidently but not *too* confidently. And really, amidst the general insanity, was it fair to penalize a man merely because in conditions of extreme stress he tended to develop two separate personalities? You *could* argue the army was getting a bargain.

After the first few questions he began to relax. They were concentrating on his asthma and the risks of exposure to gas, and to those questions he had one totally convincing answer: he had been out to France three times and on none of these occasions had he been invalided back to base or home to England because of asthma. Trench fever, yes; wound, yes; shell-shock, yes. Asthma, *no*.

When the last question had been asked and answered, Mitchell drew the papers together in front of him, and patted them into shape. Prior watched the big white hands with their sprinkling of age spots and the shadowing of hair at the sides.

'Right,' Mitchell said at last. 'I think that's all . . .'

The pause was so long Prior began to wonder whether he would ever speak again.

'Your asthma's worse than you're letting on, isn't it?' He tapped the discharge report. 'According to this anyway.'

'It *was* bad at Craiglockhart, sir. But I can honestly say it was worse there than it ever was in France.'

'Well,' Mitchell said. 'Results posted this afternoon.' He smiled briskly. 'You won't have long to wait.'

TWO

Crude copies of Tenniel's drawings from *Alice in Wonderland* decorated one end of Ward Seven, for in peacetime this had been a children's hospital. Alice, tiny enough to swim in a sea of her own tears; Alice, unfolding like a telescope till she was nine feet tall; Alice, grown so large her arm protruded from the window; and, most strikingly, Alice with the serpent's neck, undulating above the trees.

Behind Rivers, a creaking trolley passed from bed to bed: the patients' breakfast dishes were being cleared away.

'Come on, Captain McBride, drink up,' Sister Roberts said, crackling past. 'We've not got all day, you know.'

This was said loudly, for *his* benefit. He'd arrived on the ward too early, before they were ready for him.

'You knew him, didn't you?' Elliot Smith said, coming up to him, looking over his shoulder.

Rivers looked puzzled.

'Lewis Carroll.'

'Oh, yes. Yes.'

'What was he like?'

Rivers spread his hands.

'Did you like him?'

'I think I wanted him very much to like me. And he didn't.' A slight smile. 'I'm probably the last person to ask about him.'

Elliot Smith pointed to the snake-neck. 'That's interesting, isn't it?'

'Ready now, Captain Rivers,' Sister Roberts said. They watched her march off.

'"*Captain,*"' Elliot Smith murmured.

'I'm in the dog house,' Rivers said. 'I only get "Dr" when she approves of me.'

Behind the screens Ian Moffet lay naked from the waist down. He looked defiant, nervous, full of fragile, ungrounded pride. His skin had a greenish pallor, though that might merely be the reflection of light from the green screens that surrounded his bed, creating a world, a rock pool full of secret life. Rivers pushed one screen back so that light from the window flooded in. Now Moffet's legs, stretched out on the counterpane, were the dense grey-white of big, cheap cod. Muscles flabby but not wasted, as they would have been in a case of spinal injury, though he'd been unable to walk for more than three months, an unusually long time for hysterical paralysis to persist.

The history was, in one sense, simple. Moffet had fallen down in a 'fainting fit' while on his way to the Front, shortly after hearing the guns for the first time. When he recovered consciousness he could not move his legs.

'It was ridiculous to *expect* me to go to the Front,' he'd said in their first interview. 'I can't stand noise. I've never been able to stay in the same room as a champagne cork popping.'

You poor blighter, Rivers had thought, startled out of compassion. More than any other patient Moffet brought the words 'Pull yourself together, man' to the brink of his lips.

'Why didn't you apply for exemption?' he'd asked instead.

Moffet had looked at him as if he'd just been accused of eating peas from a knife. 'One is not a pacifist.'

He'd tried everything with Moffet. No, he hadn't. He'd not, for example, tried attaching electrodes to Moffet's legs and throwing the switch, as Dr Yealland would certainly have done by now. He'd not held tubes of radium against his skin till it burnt. He'd not given him subcutaneous injections of ether. All these things were being done to get men back to the Front or keep them there. He'd not even hypnotized him. What he'd actually tried was reason. He didn't *like* what he was going to do now, but it had become apparent that, until Moffet's reliance on the physical symptom was broken, no more rational approach stood any chance of working.

'You understand what I'm going to do?' he asked.

'I *know* what you're going to do.'

Rivers smiled. 'Tell me, then.'

'Well, as far as I can make out, you . . . er . . . intend to draw . . .' Minute muscles twitched round Moffet's nose and lips, giving him the look of a supercilious rabbit. '*Stocking tops?* On my legs, here.' With delicately pointed fingers he traced two lines across the tops of his thighs. 'And then, gradually, day by day, you propose to . . . um . . . *lower* the stockings, and as the stockings are *unrolled*, so to speak, the . . . er . . . paralysis will . . .' A positive orgy of twitching. 'Retreat.'

'That's right.'

Moffet's voice drooled contempt. 'And you have no doubt this procedure will work?'

Rivers looked into the pupils of his eyes so intently that for a moment he registered no colour except black. 'None whatsoever.'

Moffet stared at him, then turned away.

'Shall we get started?' Rivers lifted Moffet's left leg and began to draw a thick black line on to his skin, two inches below the fold of the groin.

'I hope that's not indelible.'

'Of course it's not. I'm going to have to wash it off in the morning.'

Rivers looked at the length of Moffet's legs and tried to calculate how long it was going to take him to reach the toes. Two weeks? And that would have to include Sundays, which put paid to his plans for a weekend in Ramsgate with his sisters. Katharine was far from well; in fact she was virtually bedridden and for much the same reasons as Moffet. Rivers frowned with concentration as he carried the pencil line under the thigh. Moffet's flabby skin kept snagging the pencil point.

Elliot Smith's comment on the serpent: 'That's interesting.' It was no more than he'd thought himself. Evidently snakes had lost the right to be simply snakes. Dodgson had hated them, a quite exceptionally intense hatred, and the woods round Knowles Bank were full of them, particularly in spring when you regularly stumbled across knots of adders, as many as thirty or forty sometimes, drowsy from their winter sleep. They'd gone for a walk once, the whole family, Ethel and Katharine holding Dodgson's hands, himself and Charles trailing behind, imitating his rather prissy, constipated-hen walk, though careful not to let their father catch them at it. They rounded a bend, Dodgson and the girls leading, and there, right in the centre of the path, was a snake. Zigzag markings, black on yellow, orange eyes, forked tongue flickering out of that wide, cynical (anthropomorphic rubbish) mouth. Dodgson went white. He sat down, collapsed rather, on a tree stump and the girls fanned him with their hats, while father caught the snake in a cleft stick and threw it far away, a black *s* against the sky unravelling as it fell.

Later he went back to look for it, spending an hour searching through the flamy bracken, but only found a cast-off skin draped over a stone, transparent, the brilliant markings faded, the ghost of a snake.

Why was the devil shown in the form of a snake? he asked his father, because it was the only question he knew how to ask.

Later there'd been other questions, other ways of finding answers. Once, while he was home for the weekend, Katharine sat on an adder, and ran home screaming. He'd gone straight out and killed it, or so he thought, intending to dissect it at Bart's. Finding the family in the drawing-room, he'd tipped the snake out on to the hearthrug to show them, and found himself confronted by an adder that was very far from dead. The girls screamed and hid behind the sofa, while he and his father and Charles trampled it to death.

How do you think about an incident like that *now*? he wondered, beginning the second circle. Probably every generation thinks the world of its youth has been changed past recognition, but he thought for his generation – Moffet's too, of course – the task of making meaningful connections was quite unusually difficult. A good deal of innocence had been lost in recent years. Not all of it on battlefields.

He lowered Moffet's leg and walked round the bed. From here he could see, through a gap in the screens, the drawings of Alice. Suddenly, with Moffet's paralysed leg clamped to his side as he closed the circle, Rivers saw the drawings not as an irrelevance, left over from the days when this had been a children's ward, but as cruelly, savagely appropriate. All those bodily transformations causing all those problems. *But they solved them too*. Alice in Hysterialand.

'There,' he said, putting the leg down. 'Now can you prop yourself up a bit?'

Moffet raised himself on to his elbows and looked down at his legs. 'Quite apart from anything else,' he said, enunciating each word distinctly, 'it looks bloody obscene.'

Rivers looked down. 'Ye-es,' he agreed. 'But it won't when we get below the knee. And *tomorrow* the sensation in this area' – he measured it out with his forefingers – 'will be normal.'

Their eyes met. Moffet would have liked to deny it was possible, but his gaze shifted. He'd already begun to invest the circles with power.

Rivers touched his shoulder. 'See you tomorrow morning,' he said.

Quickly, he ran downstairs and plunged into the warren of corridors, wondering if he'd have time to read the files on the new patients before the first of them arrived for his appointment. He glanced at his watch, and something about the action tweaked his memory. Now that *would* be 'interesting', he thought. An innocent young boy becomes aware that he is the object of an adult's abnormal affection. Put bluntly, the Rev. Charles Do-do-do-do-Dodgson can't keep his hands off him, *but* – thanks to that gentleman's formidable conscience – nothing untoward occurs. The years pass, puberty arrives, friendship fades. In the adult life of that child no abnormality appears, except perhaps for a certain difficulty in integrating the sexual drive with the rest of the personality (What do you mean 'perhaps'? he asked himself), until, in middle age, the patient begins to suffer from the delusion that he is turning into an extremely large, eccentrically dressed white rabbit, forever running down corridors consulting its watch. What a case history. Pity it didn't happen, he thought, pushing the door of his consulting-room open, it would account for quite a lot.

He thought, sometimes, he understood Katharine's childhood better than his own.

Cheshire Cat! Cheshire Cat! he and Charles had chanted as she sat enthroned in Dodgson's lap, grinning from ear to ear. The nickname, so casually bestowed, had lasted all her childhood, and his only consolation was she hadn't minded it a bit. Poor Kath, she'd had little enough to smile about since.

Files, he told himself. He took them out of his briefcase and started to read. Geoffrey Wansbeck, twenty-two years old. Wansbeck had – well, *murdered*, he supposed the word would have to be – a German prisoner, for no better reason (Wansbeck said) than that he was feeling tired and irritable and resented having to escort the man back from the line. For . . . eight months – in fact, nearer ten – he'd experienced no remorse, but then, while in hospital recovering from a minor wound, he'd started to suffer from hypnagogic hallucinations in which he would wake suddenly to find the dead German standing by his bed.

Always, accompanying the visual hallucination, would be the reek of decomposition. After a few weeks the olfactory hallucination began to occur independently, only now the smell seemed to emanate from Wansbeck himself. He was convinced others could smell it and, no matter how often he was reassured, avoided close contact with other people as much as he could.

Hmm. Rivers took off his glasses and rubbed his eyes, swinging his chair round to face the window. He'd had a bad night and was finding it difficult to concentrate. Late August sunlight, the colour of cider, streamed into the room, and he was suddenly seized by sadness, a banal, calendar-dictated sadness, for the past summer and all the summers that were past.

At dinner one evening Mr Dodgson had leant across to mother and said, 'I l-l-l-love all ch-ch-ch-ch-'

'Train won't start,' Charles had whispered.

'Children, M-Mrs R-Rivers, as l-l-l-long as they're g-g-g-girls.'

He had looked down the table at the two boys, and it had seemed to Rivers that the sheer force of his animosity had loosened his tongue.

'*Boys are a mistake*.'

Charles hadn't minded that Mr Dodgson disliked them, but *he* had. Mr Dodgson was the first adult he'd met who stammered as badly as he did himself, and the rejection hurt.

'Are w-we a m-m-m-m-mistake?' he'd asked his mother at bedtime. 'W-why are w-we?'

'Of course you're not a mistake,' his mother had said, smoothing the hair back from his forehead.

'So w-why d-d-does h-he s-say w-w-w-w-we are?'

'I expect he just likes girls more than boys.'

'B–b-b-b-but w-w-why d-d-does he?'

Wansbeck's eyes were inflamed, whether from crying or because of his cold was difficult to tell.

Rivers waited for the latest paroxysm of coughing to pass. 'You know we don't *have* to do this now. I can equally well see you when you're feeling better.'

Wansbeck wiped his raw nose on the back of his hand. 'No, I'd rather get it over with.' He shifted in his seat, flicking his tongue over cracked lips, and gazed fretfully round the room. 'Do you think we could have the window open?'

Rivers looked surprised – in spite of the sunshine, the wind was bitingly cold – but he got up and opened the window, realizing, as he did so, that Wansbeck's request was prompted by his fear of the smell. The breeze sucked the net curtains through the gap. Rivers went back to his chair and waited.

'I used a bayonet I found on a corpse. We were going through a wood, and there'd been a lot of heavy fighting. I remember the man I took it from, he'd died with an expression of absolute agony on his face. Big man, very dark, lot of blood round his nose, black, covered with flies, a sort of . . . buzzing moustache. I remember him better than the man I killed. He was walking ahead of me, I couldn't do it in his back, so I shouted at him to turn round. He knew straight away. I stuck it in, and he screamed, and . . . I pulled it out, and stuck it in. And again. And again. He was on the ground and it was easier. He kept saying, "*Bitte, Bitte,*" and putting his hands . . .' Wansbeck raised his own, palms outwards. 'The odd thing was I heard it in English. Bitter, bitter. I knew the word, but I didn't register what it meant.'

'Would it have made a difference?'

A puckering of the lips.

'What were you thinking about immediately before you picked up the bayonet?'

'Nothing.'

'Nothing at all?'

'I just wanted to go to sleep, and this bastard was stopping me.'

'How long had you been in the line?'

'Twelve days.' Wansbeck shook his head. 'Not good enough.'

'What isn't good enough?'

'That. As an excuse.'

'Reasons aren't excuses.'

'No?'

Rivers was thinking deeply. 'What do you think I can do to help?'

'Nothing. With respect.'

'Oh, damn that.'

Wansbeck smiled. 'As you say.' He held his handkerchief to his mouth as another fit of coughing seized him. 'I'll try not to give you this at least.'

Wansbeck was a man of exceptionally good physique, tall, broad-shouldered, deep-chested. Rivers, estimating height, weight, muscular tone, noting the tremor of the huge hands, a slight twitch of the left eyelid, was aware, at a different level, of the pathos of a strong body broken – though he didn't know why the word 'broken' should occur to him, since, objectively speaking, Wansbeck's physical suffering amounted to nothing more than a bad cold. He'd made a good recovery from his wound.

'When did you first notice the smell?'

'In the hospital. Look, everybody goes on about the smell. I *know* there isn't one.' A faint smile. 'It's just I can still smell it.'

'When was the first time?'

'I was in a side ward. Three beds. One man quite bad, he'd got a piece of shrapnel stuck in his back. He was called Jessop, not that it matters. The other was a slight arm wound, and he was obviously getting better and I realized there was a chance I'd be left alone with Jessop. The one who couldn't move. And I started to worry about it, because he was helpless and I knew if I wanted to kill him I could.'

'Did you dislike him at all? Jessop.'

'Not in the least. No.'

'So it was just the fact that he was helpless?'

Wansbeck thought a moment. 'Yes.'

'*Were* you left alone with him?'

'Yes.'

'What happened?'

A sound midway between a snort and a laugh. 'It was a long night.'

'Did you want to kill him?'

'Yes –'

'No, *think*. Did you *want* to kill him or were you *afraid* of wanting to kill him?'

Silence. 'I don't know. What difference does it make?'

'Enormous.'

'Afraid. I *think*. After that I asked if I could go on to the main ward. And to answer your question, the first time I noticed the smell was the following morning.' A long silence, during which he started to speak several times before eventually saying, 'You know when I told the doctor about not wanting to be left alone with Jessop, he said, "How long have you suffered from homosexual impulses?"' A quick, casual glance, but Wansbeck couldn't disguise his anger. 'I didn't want to to to *fuck* him, I wanted to *kill* him.'

'Does it still bother you to be alone with people?'

Wansbeck glanced round the room. 'I avoid it when I can.'

They exchanged smiles. Wansbeck put his hand up and stroked his neck.

'Is your throat bothering you?'

'Bit sore.'

Rivers went round the desk and felt his glands. Wansbeck stared past him with a strained look. Evidently the smell was particularly bad. 'Yes, they are a bit swollen.' He touched Wansbeck's forehead, then checked his pulse. 'I think you'd be better off in bed.'

Wansbeck nodded. 'You know, I can tell the smell isn't real, because I can still smell it. I'm too bunged up to smell anything else.'

Rivers smiled. He was starting to like Wansbeck. 'Tell Sister Roberts I've told you to go to bed, and would she take your temperature, please. I'll be up to see you later.'

At the door Wansbeck turned. 'Thank you for what you *didn't* say.'

'And what's that?'

'"It was only a boche – if it was up to me I'd give you a medal. Nobody's going to *hang* you for it."'

'You mean other people *have* said that?'

'Oh, yes. It never seems to occur to them that punishment might be a relief.'

Rivers looked hard at him. 'Self-administered?'

'No.'

A fractional hesitation?

'Go to bed,' Rivers said. 'I'll be up in a minute.'

After Wansbeck had gone, Rivers went to close the window, and stood for a moment watching boys playing in the square. High sharp cries, like seagulls.

'Are w-we a m-m-m-m-mistake? W-why are w-we?'

'Of course you're not a mistake,' his mother had said, smoothing the hair back from his forehead.

'So w-why d-d-does h-he s-say w-w-w-w-we are?'

'I expect he just likes girls more than boys.'

'B–b-b-b-but w-w-why d-d-does he?'

Rivers smiled. I know, he thought, I know. Questions, questions.

'Boys are rough and noisy. And they fight.'

'B-b-but you h-h-have to to to f-f-f-ight, s-s-sometimes.'

Yes.

THREE

Prior dawdled along, scuffing the sleeve of his tunic along the sea-wall, looking out over the pale, level, filthy sands to where the waves turned. Silence was a relief after the jabber of tongues in the mess: who was going out with the next draft, who was up for promotion, who had been recommended for an MC. The eyes that slid to your chest and then to your left sleeve. The cards, the gossip, the triviality, the muck-raking, the rubbish – he'd be glad to be shot of it all.

He was going back to France. He'd spent the evening writing to people: Sarah, his mother, Charles Manning, Rivers. And the last letter had reminded him of Craiglockhart, so that now he drifted along, remembering the light flashing on Rivers's glasses, and the everlasting *pok-pok* from the tennis courts that somehow wove itself into the pattern of their speech and silence, as Rivers extracted his memories of France from him, one by one, like a dentist pulling teeth.

He wondered what Rivers would think of his going back. Not much.

The beach was dark below him. They were all gone, the munitions workers and their girls, the war profiteers with stubby fingers turning the pages of *John Bull*. German boats came in close sometimes. 'Not close enough,' Owen had said, as they'd waited for the draft list to go up on the wall. And he'd laughed, with that slightly alarmed look he sometimes had.

A friendly, lolling, dog-on-its-back sort of sea. You could swim in that and not feel cold. He started to wander along with no idea of where his feet were taking him or why. After a few minutes he rounded the headland and looked along the half-circle of South Bay at the opposite cliffs, surmounted by their white Georgian terraces. Some of his brother officers were up there now, living it up at the most expensive of the town's oyster bars. He'd been there himself two nights ago, but tonight he didn't fancy it.

Closer at hand were souvenir shops, coconut-shies, swing-boats, funny hats, the crack of rifle fire, screams of terror from the haunted house where cardboard skeletons leapt out of the cupboards with green electric light bulbs flashing in the sockets of their skulls. If they'd seen . . . *Oh, leave it, leave it.*

Behind him, along the road that led to the barracks, were prim boarding-houses with thick lace curtains that screened out the vulgarity of day-trippers. You couldn't go for a walk anywhere in Scarborough without seeing the English class system laid out before you in all its full, intricate horror.

He heard a gasp of pain beside him, and a hand clutched his sleeve. A red-haired woman, flashily dressed and alone. 'Sorry, love, it's these shoes.' She smiled brightly at him. 'I keep going over on the heel.'

She rested her arms beside his on the railings, her right elbow lightly touching his sleeve.

'No, thanks.'

'Why, you been offered summat?'

She muttered on. It had come to summat if a decent woman couldn't have a rest without being . . . *pestered.* And who did he think he was anyway? Couple of bits of gold braid, they think their shit smells of violets –

'I don't pay.'

A whoop of laughter. 'Well, you're certainly not getting it free.'

He smiled, allowing a note of pathos to creep into his voice. 'I'm going back to France next week.'

'Aw, piss off.'

For a moment he hoped she might take her own advice, but she didn't. They stood side by side, almost touching, but he was miles away, remembering Lizzie MacDowell and the first day of the war. 'Long Liz' they called her, for, among the girls who worked Commercial Road, most of them reared in the workhouse, Lizzie's height – a full five feet no less – made her a giant. She was his best friend's mother, a fact not at the forefront of his mind when he met her in a back alley on his way home from the pub and told her he'd enlisted.

– *Good lad!* she'd said.

Lizzie was a great enthusiast for the Empire. And somehow or other he'd gone home with her, stumbling up the passage and into the back bedroom, until finally, in a film of cooling sweat, they'd lain together on the sagging bed, while the bedbugs feasted and a smell of urine rose from the chamberpot underneath. She'd told him about her regulars. One man came every month, turned a chair upside-down and shoved each one of the four legs in turn up his arse. Didn't want her to do anything, she said. Just watch.

– Well, you know what a worry-guts I am. I keep thinking what'll I do if he gets stuck?

– Saw the bloody leg off.

– Do you mind, that's the only decent chair I've got.

'What's so funny?'

'Just thinking about an old friend.'

Money had not changed hands on that occasion. He'd been Lizzie's patriotic gesture: one of seven. Poor Lizzie, she'd been very disillusioned when five of the seven turned out not to have enlisted at all.

'Do you fancy a bit of company, then?'

He looked at her. 'You don't give up, do you?' And then suddenly the shrieks, the rattle of rifle fire, pub doors belching smells of warm beer were intolerable. Anything not to have to go on being the oil bead on this filthy water. 'All right.'

She was telling the truth about her shoes. If she hadn't clung to his arm she'd have fallen over more than once as they climbed the steep steps to the quieter streets behind the foreshore.

'What do they call you?' she asked, breathing port into his face.

'Billy. You?'

'Elinor.'

I'll bet, he thought. 'D' y' get "Nellie"?'

'Sometimes,' she said, her voice pinched with dignity. 'It's just round the corner here.' Perhaps she sensed he was having second thoughts for her arm tightened. ''S not far.'

They went up a flight of steps to the door. As she fumbled with the key he looked round, and almost stumbled over a cluster of unwashed milk bottles, furred green.

'*Mind,*' she said. 'You'll have everybody out.'

The hall dark, smelling of drains and mice. A face – no more than a slit of sallow skin and one eye – peered through a crack in the door on his left.

'You'll have to be quiet,' Nellie whispered, and then, catching sight of the face just as the door closed, yelled, 'There's some right nosy bastards round here.'

They walked up the stairs, arms round each other's waists, shoulders and hips bumping in the narrow space, catching the breath of each other's laughter, until her tipsiness communicated itself to him and all doubt and reluctance dissolved away.

She unlocked the door. A naked overhead bulb revealed a tousled bed, a chair piled high with camisoles and stays, a wash-stand and – surprisingly businesslike, this – a clean towel and a bar of yellow soap.

'You won't mind having a little wash.'

He didn't *mind*. He was buggered if he'd rely on it, though.

'Do you know,' she said, unbuttoning her blouse, 'I had one poor lad the other week washed his *hands*?'

Prior tugged at his tie, looking around for somewhere to put his clothes, and noticed a chair by the fireplace. Rather a grand fireplace, with a garland of flowers and fruit carved into the mantel, but boarded up now, of course, and a gas fire set into it. He was pulling his half-unbuttoned tunic over his head when he noticed a smell of gas. Faint but unmistakable. Tented in dark khaki, he fought back the rush of panic, sweat streaming down his sides, not the gradual sweat of exercise but a sudden drench, rank, slippery, hot, then immediately cold. He freed himself from the tunic and went to open the window, looking out over sharp-angled, moonlit roofs to the sea. He told himself there was no reason to be afraid, but he was afraid. All the usual reactions: dry mouth, wet armpits, skipping heart, the bulge in the throat that makes you cough. Tight scrotum, shrivelled cock. Jesus Christ, he was going to have to put a johnny on that, talk about a kid in its father's overcoat. He heard his own voice, awkward, sounding younger than he felt. 'I'm afraid this isn't going to work.'

'Aw, don't say that, love, it'll be al –'

Phoney warmth. She was used to pumping up limp pricks.

'No, it won't.'

He came back into the room and looked at her. Her hair had fallen across her shoulders, not in a cloudy mass but in distinct coils, precise crescents, like you see on the floor of a barber's shop. He picked up one of the coils and wound it round his fingers. Red stripes marked the places where the bones of her stays bit into the skin. Catching the direction of his glance, she rubbed ineffectually at them. He wasn't behaving as clients generally behaved, and any departure from the usual run of things made her nervous. Two people's fear in the room now. But her gaze remained steady, surprisingly steady, when you thought that only five minutes ago she'd been too tipsy to walk straight. *Now* . . . well, she'd had a few, but she certainly wasn't drunk. Perhaps she needed the mask of drunkenness more than she needed drink.

'Have I got a spot on the end of me conk or what?'

'No,' he said stupidly.

They stared at each other.

'Wouldn't hurt to lie down,' she said.

He finished undressing, reached out and tentatively took the weight of her breasts in his hands. So far, he realized, he hadn't had the shopping list, the awful litany that started whenever you met a woman's eyes in Covent Garden or the Strand. '. . . and five bob extra to suck me tits.'

'Two quid,' she said, reading his thoughts. 'On the table there.'

He got into bed, telling himself the cold damp patch under his left buttock was imagination. He put his hand down. It wasn't. Dotted here and there on the sheet were tiny coils of pubic hair. He wondered whose spunk he was lying in, whether he knew him, how carefully she'd washed afterwards. He groped around in his mind for the appropriate feeling of disgust, and found excitement instead, no, more than that, the sober certainty of power.

All the men who'd passed through, through Scarborough, through her, on their way to the Front . . . And how many of them dead? As she squatted over the bowl to wash – a token affair, he was glad to see – he felt them gathering in the hall, thronging the narrow stair, pressing against the door. Halted on the threshold only by the glare of light.

'Can we have that out?' he said. 'It's in my eyes.'

And now they were free to enter. Waiting, though, till the springs creaked and sagged beneath her weight. His hands were their hands, their famished eyes were his. Pupils strained wide in starlight fastened on a creamy belly and a smudge of dark hair. He stroked and murmured and her fingers closed round him. 'There you are, you see. I told you it'd be all right.'

He fucked her slowly. After a while her hands came round and grasped his arse, nails digging in, though whether this was a pretence to hurry things along or a genuine flicker of response he couldn't tell. He was aware of their weight on him, his arms were braced to carry it . . .

And then something went wrong. He looked down at the shuttered face and recognized the look, recognized it not with his eyes but with the muscles of his own face, for he too had lain like this, waiting for it to be over. A full year of fucking, before he managed to come, on the narrow monastic bed, a crucifix above it, on the far wall – he would never forget it – a picture of St Lawrence roasting on his grid. The first time Father Mackenzie knelt, holding him round the waist, crying, *We really touched bottom that time, didn't we?* One way of putting it, but *we*? What the fuck did he mean by *we*? Later – though not much later, he'd been a forward child – he'd begun to charge, not so much resorting to prostitution as inventing it, for he knew of nobody else who got money that way. First Father Mackenzie. Then others.

The only way not to be her was to hate her. Narrowing his eyes, he blurred her features, ran them together into the face they pinned to the revolver targets. A snarling, baby-eating boche. But they didn't want that, the men who used his eyes and hands as theirs. He felt them withdraw, like a wave falling back.

All right, then, for *me*. He lowered his forehead on to hers, knowing without having to be told that she wouldn't let him kiss her. She wriggled beneath him, and he lifted his weight. Slowly and deliberately, she put her index finger deep into her mouth, and brought it out with a startling *pop*, and then – he had time to guess what she intended – scratched the small of his back delicately so that he shivered and thrust deeper, and rammed the finger hard up his arse. *Ah*, he cried, more with shock than pleasure, but already he was bursting, spilling, falling towards her, gasping for breath, laughing, gasping again, tears stinging his eyes as he rolled off her and lay still. Hoist on his own petard. That had always been one of *his* tricks to speed the unreasonably lingering guest.

She got up immediately and squatted over the bowl. He took the hint and started to dress, sniffing round the fireplace as he buttoned his tunic.

'What's the marra with *you*?'

'I thought I could smell gas.'

'Oh that, yeh, you probably can. Tap leaks. I'm tired of telling her.'

He wouldn't do this again, he decided, buckling his belt. It might work for some men, but . . . not for him. For him, it was all slip and slither, running across shingle. He hadn't been sure at the end who was fucking who. Even the excitement he'd felt at the idea of sliding in on another man's spunk was ambiguous, to say the least. Not that he minded ambiguity – he couldn't have lived at all if he'd minded *that* – but this was the kind of ambiguity people hide behind. And he was too proud to hide.

On his way back to the barracks he forgot her. A few hundred yards from the gate he drew level with a group of officers. Most had paced themselves well, and were now rather more sober than they'd been when he bumped into them earlier in the evening. But Dalrymple was in a desperate state, striding along with the exalted, visionary look of somebody whose sole aim in life is to get to the lavatory in time.

'Will he be all right?' Prior asked.

'We'll get him there,' said Bainbrigge.

As they entered the barracks gates, thunder rumbled on the horizon;

the clouds were briefly lit by lightning. Prior waited till the crowd cleared before going across to the main building to get washed, thinking, as he stripped off and splashed cold water over his chest and groin, that a deserted wash-room at night, all white tiles and naked lights, is the most convincing portrayal of hell the human mind can devise. He peered into the brown-spotted glass, remembering the moment when Nellie's face had dissolved into the face of the boche target.

– *What's the worst thing you could have done?* Rivers asked.

A phoney question. Rivers didn't believe in the worst things. He thought Prior was being histrionic. And perhaps I was, Prior thought, staring into the glass at the row of empty cubicles behind him, feeling 'the worst things' crowd in behind him, jostling for the privilege of breathing down his neck. He'd even, coming to himself at four or five o'clock in the morning with no idea of how the night had been spent, thought it possible he might have killed somebody. And yet, why should that be 'the worst thing'? His reflection stared back at him, hollow-eyed. Murder was only killing in the wrong place.

The wind was rising as he hurried across the gritty tarmac to his tent. Bent double, he braced himself to face the smell of armpits and socks, heavy on the day's stored heat, for though they left the flaps open, nothing could prevent the tents becoming ovens in hot weather. He took a deep breath, as deep as he could manage, and crawled into the stinking dark.

A voice said, 'Hello.'

Of course. Hallet. The past week he'd had the tent to himself, because Hallet had been away on a bombing course in Ripon.

'Can you see all right?'

The beam of a torch illuminated yellow grass littered with cigarette butts.

'I can manage, thanks.'

Blinking to reaccustom himself to the blackness, Prior wriggled into his sleeping-bag.

'You're just back from London, aren't you?'

He resigned himself to having to talk. 'Yes. Week ago.'

A flicker of lightning found the whites of Hallet's eyes. 'Have you been boarded yet?'

'Out next draft. You?'

'Next draft.'

Voice casual, but the mouth dry.

'First time?' Prior asked.

'Yes, as a matter of fact it is.'

Now that Prior was accustomed to the gloom he could see Hallet clearly: olive-skinned, almost Mediterranean-looking, a nice crooked mouth with prominent front teeth that he was evidently self-conscious about, for he kept pulling his upper lip down to hide them. Quite fetching. Not that in these circumstances Prior ever permitted himself to be fetched.

'I'm really rather looking forward to it.'

The words hung on the air, obviously requiring an answer of some kind, but then what could one say? He was scared shitless, he was *right* to be scared shitless, and any 'reassuring' remark risked drawing attention to one or other of these unfortunate facts.

'Some of the men in my platoon have been out three times,' Hallet said. 'I think that's the only thing that bothers me, really. How the hell do you lead men who know more than you do?'

'You pray for a good sergeant. A really good sergeant tells you what orders to give him, doesn't let anybody else see him doing it, and doesn't let himself know he's doing it.'

'How many times have you – ?'

'This'll be the fourth. Wound, shell-shock, trench fever. Not in that order.'

Hallet was lying on his back, hands clasped behind his head, nothing much visible from Prior's angle except his chin. How appallingly random it all was. If Hallet's father had got a gleam in his eye two years later than he did, Hallet wouldn't be here. He might even have missed the war altogether, perhaps spent the rest of his life goaded by the irrational shame of having escaped. 'Cowed subjection to the ghosts of friends who died.' That was it exactly, couldn't be better put. Ghosts everywhere. Even the living were only ghosts in the making. You learned to ration your commitment to them. This moment in this tent already had the quality of *remembered* experience. Or perhaps he was simply getting old. But then, after all, in trench time he *was* old. A generation lasted six months, less than that on the Somme, barely twelve weeks. He was this boy's great-grandfather.

He looked at Hallet again, at the warm column of his neck, and tried to think of something to say, something light-hearted and easy, but could think of nothing. He stared instead at the stained canvas, lit by flickers of summer lightning, and noticed that the largest stain looked like a map of Africa.

FOUR

Two black lines circled Moffet's legs immediately above the knee.

'Close your eyes,' Rivers said. 'I want you to tell me exactly what you feel.'

'Pinprick.'

'How many?'

The pins touched again.

'Two.'

Again.

'One.'

Again.

'Two.' Moffett sounded bored. 'Two. Two.' A pause. 'Not sure.'

'All right. You can open your eyes now.'

He hadn't lied once. He'd lain with closed eyes, a fluttering visible beneath the thin lids, and Rivers had read in every line and fold of his face the temptation to lie, and yet the progression of yeses and noes had been totally accurate. True, he couldn't have hoped to lie convincingly, or not for long, but it was interesting that he hadn't tried. This was pure hysteria, uncontaminated by malingering.

'Rivers, do you ever think you were born into the wrong century?'

Rivers looked surprised. 'Survived into, perhaps.'

'It's just this reminds me of seventeenth-century witch-finders, you know? They used to stick pins in people too.'

'I expect they were looking for the same thing. Areas of abnormal sensation.'

'Do you think they found them?'

Rivers lifted Moffet's left leg and began to draw a line three inches lower than the line he'd drawn yesterday morning. 'I don't see why not. Some witches were probably hysterics. At least a lot of the reported phenomena suggest that.'

'And the witch-*finders*?'

'I don't know. Simpler. Nastier.'

'I don't like that word. Applied to this.'

'Hysteria?' He could quite see that 'shell-shock', useless and inaccurate though the term was, might appeal to Moffet rather more. It did at least sound appropriately male. 'I don't think anybody likes it. The trouble is nobody likes the alternatives either.'

'It derives,' Moffet continued, hardening his voice, 'from the Greek *hysterā*. The womb.'

'Yes,' Rivers said dryly. 'I know.'

The problem with Moffet was that he was too intelligent to be satisfied with such a crude solution as paralysis. Hysterical symptoms of this gross kind – paralysis, deafness, blindness, muteness – occurred quite frequently in the immediate aftermath of trauma but they normally lingered only in those who were either uneducated or frankly stupid. Moffet was neither.

And whether this rather dramatic form of treatment was helping . . . Oh, it would get rid of the paralysis, but was there not the possibility that it might also reinforce a belief in magical solutions? Rivers sighed and walked round the bed. All his instincts were against it, but he knew it would get Moffet on his feet again. A witch-doctor could do this, he thought, beginning to draw, and probably better than I can. Come to think of it, there was *one* person who'd have done it brilliantly . . .

In Melanesia he'd quickly formed the habit of accompanying Njiru on his rounds. They would set off together, always in single file, because the path winding through thick bush was too narrow for them to walk abreast.

Seen from the rear, the extent of Njiru's spinal curvature was dreadfully apparent. Rivers wondered how such deformities were explained – which spirit inflicted them, and why? Sweat stung his bitten eyelids – he kept having to wipe his forearm across his face. Mainly the heat, but partly also anxiety. It was a bit like your first day at a new school, he thought, knowing you've *got* to get things right and that your chances of getting them right are infinitesimal because you know *nothing*. Only at school, provided you start at the same time as everybody else, you can solve the problem by fading into the group, darting about with all the other little grey minnows, safety in the shoal, but here he was alone, except for Hocart, and Hocart had been running a fever ever since they arrived, and today had chosen to stay behind in their tent.

At the village he crawled into a hut and squatted on the earth floor, watching and listening, while Njiru attended to his patient. An old woman, evidently a regular to judge by the way she and Njiru laughed and joked together. She was introduced as Namboko Taru, though 'Namboko', which he at first took to be a name, turned out to be a title: 'widow'. The same word also meant 'widower', but was not used as a title when applied to men. Two more disconnected facts to add to his discouragingly small heap.

Namboko Taru lay down, pushing the strip of brown bark cloth she wore down far enough to expose her belly. Njiru poured coconut oil on to her abdomen and began a massage, while Rivers tried to find out what was wrong. Constipation, it appeared. Was it, he wanted to ask, in view of her age, chronic constipation, or had there been a recent change in bowel habit? And was it simply constipation, or was there alternating diarrhoea? But his attempts to convey 'alternating diarrhoea' in a mixture of pidgin and mime threatened to bring the proceedings to a halt entirely, and he gave up, while Namboko Taru wiped tears of laughter from her cheeks. He might not be contributing to the cure but he was certainly taking her mind off the condition.

Meanwhile the movements of Njiru's hands began to focus on a region below and to the left of the navel. He was chanting under his breath, swaying backwards and forwards, scooping the slack flesh together between the heel of his palms, like a woman gathering dough. The constant low murmur and the rhythmic movement were hypnotic. Suddenly, with a barking cry, Njiru seemed to catch something, shielded it in his cupped hands while he crawled to the door, and then threw it as far as he could into the bush. A brief conversation between doctor and patient, then Namboko Taru fastened her cloth and went into the bush, from whence, ten minutes later, a far happier woman emerged.

Meanwhile Rivers and Njiru talked. Namboko Taru's complaint belonged to a group of illnesses called *tagosoro*, which were inflicted by the spirit called Mateana. This particular condition – *nggasin* – was caused by an octopus that had taken up residence in the lower intestine, from where its tentacles might spread until they reached the throat. At this point the disease would prove fatal. As so often happened, one could detect behind the native belief the shadowy outline of a disease only too familiar to western medicine, though perhaps this was not a helpful way of looking at it. Namboko Taru believed she was cured. And certainly as a treatment for simple constipation the massage could hardly have been bettered, and had not differed in any essential respect from western massage, until very near the end.

Rivers pointed to himself and then to the coconut oil. Njiru nodded, poured oil into his palms and began the massage, chanting, rocking . . . Once again that curious hypnotic effect, a sense of being totally focused on, totally cared for. Njiru was a good doctor, however many octopi he located in the colon. The fingers probed deeper, the chanting quickened, the movements of the hands neared a climax, and then – nothing. Njiru sat back, smiling, terminating the physical contact as tactfully as he'd initiated it.

Rivers sketched the movement Njiru hadn't made. 'You no throw . . . *nggasin*?'

A gleam of irony. 'You no got *nggasin*.'

But *you* have, Rivers thought, sponging yesterday's black lines off Moffet's legs.

'And tomorrow,' he said authoritatively, measuring with his forefingers, 'this area will be normal.'

Moffet glared at him. 'You are consciously and deliberately destroying my self-respect.'

'I think you'll find that starts to come back once you're on your feet.'

Sister Carmichael was hovering on the other side of the screens, waiting to snatch the trolley from him. She was shocked by his insistence on doing everything himself, including the washing off of the previous lines. Consultants do not wash patients. *Nurses* wash patients. She would have been only marginally more distressed if she'd come on to the ward and found him mopping the floor. What he could not get across to her was that the rules of medicine are one thing, the rules of ritual drama quite another.

Wansbeck had had a bad night, she said, once the trolley had been snatched away. Temperature of 103, and he kept trying to open the window.

'All right, I'll see him next.'

The nurses had just finished sponging Wansbeck down, and he lay half naked, his skin a curdled bluish white against the snowy white of the sheets. As Rivers watched a shiver ran along his arms and chest, roughening and darkening the skin. They finished drying him, covered him up, and he was free to talk, though too weak to manage more than a few words.

Rivers was beginning to feel concerned about Wansbeck. Spanish influenza was quite unusually virulent and he had it badly, and yet he seemed indifferent to the outcome. Rivers grasped him firmly round the wrist. 'You know you've got to fight this.'

Probably 'fight' was the only word he understood. 'Done enough of that,' he muttered, and turned away.

*

In Westminster the leaves were already beginning to turn. Not to the brilliant reds and golds of the countryside, but a shabby tarnished yellow. In another few weeks they would start to fall. The worst thing about London was that summer ended so soon.

'You know, sometimes,' Rivers said carefully, his glasses flashing as he turned back from the window, 'it helps just to go back and try to to to to . . . gather things together. So. Let's see if I've got this right. You were in hospital after a riding accident –'

'Yes, that's right. I didn't notice the mare –'

'*Yes.* And while you were there, one of the nurses cut your penis off and put it in a jar of formaldehyde in the basement.'

Telford shook his head. 'I didn't say for for . . .'

'Formaldehyde. No, I know you didn't. They don't use pickling vinegar.'

'Ah, well, you see, you'd know that.'

A deep breath. 'Why do you think she did that?'

Telford shrugged. 'Dunno.'

'But you must have *wondered*. I mean it was quite an astonishing thing to do, wasn't it?'

'Wasn't for me to ask questions.' Telford leant forward, delivering what he obviously thought was the *coup de grâce*. 'You wouldn't want me teaching you *your* job, would you?'

At the moment he'd have welcomed assistance from any quarter. 'Didn't the doctor say anything?'

'Not a dicky bird.'

'Telford.' Rivers clasped his hands. 'What do you pee out of?'

'M'cock, you stupid bugger, what do you pee out of?'

Rivers concentrated on straightening his blotter. 'I wonder if it would help if we talked a little about women?'

It might have done. He was never to know. A few minutes later Telford said, 'I can't say I care for the tone of this conversation, Rivers. It may have escaped your notice, but we're not in a barracks.' He stood up. 'God knows, the last thing I want to do is pull rank, but I'd be grateful if you'd address me as *Major* Telford in future.'

He went out, slamming the door.

Moffet lay back, eyes closed, grinding, '*Yes, yes, yes, yes,*' as the pin pricked his skin.

The usual routine, and yet something was different. The air of indifference had gone. Deliberately, Rivers let the pin stray across the line on to skin that should still have been numb.

'*Yes, yes, yes.*'

The pin stopped. Moffet opened his eyes and smiled wearily. 'You can go all the way down if you like.' He closed his eyes again. Rivers moved the pin down the leg at intervals of two inches. 'Yes. Yes. Yes. Yes.' Wearily now, each 'yes' coming precisely at the moment the pin touched the skin. Over the shin, across the arch of the foot, down to the tip of the big toe. 'YES.'

Moffet had yelled the word. Through the gap in the screens, Rivers saw the other patients turn and stare at the shrouded bed. He put the pin down. 'Well.'

He wasn't particularly surprised: the removal of hysterical paralysis was often – one might almost say generally – as dramatic as the onset. Moffet lay still, his face sallow against the whiteness of the pillow, making no attempt to hide his depression, and indeed why should he? His sole defence against the unbearable had been taken away and nothing put in its place.

'When did this happen?'

'First thing.'

'Have you tried to walk?'

'Not yet.'

'Do you want to?'

'Seems the logical next step. So to speak.'

'Can you swing yourself round? Sit on the side.'

Rivers knelt and began massaging Moffet's calves, chafing the slack flesh between his hands.

'I suppose I'm expected to be grateful.'

'No.' He stood up. 'All right, shall we try? Put your hands on my shoulders.'

Moffet levered himself off the edge of the bed.

'How does it feel?'

'Don't know. Weird.'

'Do you want to try a few steps?' Awkwardly, like untalented dancers, they shuffled across the floor, the curtains ballooning out around them. Rivers put his hands up and loosened Moffet's grip. 'No, you're all right, I've got you.' Two steps, then Moffet fell forward into his arms. Rivers lowered him back on to the bed. 'I think that's probably enough for now.'

Moffet collapsed against the pillows.

'It's important to keep at it, but I wouldn't try it just yet without an orderly.' He hesitated. 'You know we're going to have to talk about *why* this happened.'

He waited, but Moffet remained stubbornly silent.

'I'll be along again later.'

Later that afternoon, Major Telford – as he must now remember to call him – sidled up and tapped him discreetly on the shoulder. 'Yes, Major Telford, what is it?'

A conspiratorial whisper. 'Spot of bother in the latrines.'

Rivers followed him into the wash-room, wondering which bit of Telford's anatomy had dropped off now.

Telford pointed to the bathroom. 'Chap's been in there ages.'

'Yes, but –'

'Keeps groaning. Well, he did – stopped now.'

Rivers rattled the handle. 'Hello?'

'Tried that, it's locked.'

It couldn't be – there weren't any locks. Rivers lay down and looked under the door. A lot of water had slopped on to the floor, he could see an arm drooping over the edge of the bath – a puffy, white arm with blood oozing from the wrist. A chair had been wedged under the door handle. He tried pushing it, but it was no use. He stood up and kicked. The door was hardly thicker than cardboard – the bathrooms were mere cubicles put in cheaply when the War Office adapted the hospital for military use – and the second kick broke the hinges. He burst into the room, startled by his own face in the looking-glass. Moffet lay in the bath, pink water lapping the shining belly as it rose and fell. Breathing anyway. His head had slipped to one side, but his nostrils were clear of the water. A whisky bottle skittered across the floor as Rivers knelt by the bath. Cuts on both wrists, superficial on the right – deep on the left. Loss of blood probably fairly heavy, but you can never bloody well tell in water. He pushed Moffet's eyelids up, smelled his breath, felt for the pulse . . .

'Dead, is he?' Telford asked cheerfully.

Dead drunk. 'I think he'll be all right.'

Lack of space was the problem. Barely enough room to squeeze between the wash-basin and the bath at knee height. He had to bend from the waist to get his hands round Moffet's chest and then his fingertips slipped on the cold, plump skin. Telford stood, looking on.

'Get his legs.'

They heaved, but without co-ordination, Rivers finally managing to haul the shoulders out of the water just as Telford grew tired of waiting and dropped the legs back in. They were gasping for breath, shoulders bumping in the confined space.

'All right, together,' Rivers said. 'One, two . . .'

Moffet came clear, only to fall back with a splash, a great plume of water flying up and drenching them both.

'I'll try to get m'leg under him,' Telford said.

They lifted again, and Telford stepped into the water so that Moffet was balanced across his thigh, Rivers supporting the head and shoulders. They froze like that, an improbable and vaguely obscene *pietà*. 'All right?' Rivers asked.

'Right, I've got him.'

They collapsed in a heap on the floor, blood from Moffet's left wrist flowing more copiously now, bright, distinct drops splashing on to the mottled tiles. Rivers dragged a clean towel off the rail and pressed it hard against the deepest cut. 'There, you take over,' he said. 'I'll get Sister Roberts. Just press now, no need for anything else. *No tourniquets.*'

'Shouldn't dream of it,' Telford said, fluffing his shoulders.

Rivers intercepted Sister Roberts on her way down the ward. 'Moffet,' he said, pointing behind him. 'He's slashed his wrists. We need a wheelchair.'

He returned to find Telford entertaining the now semi-conscious Moffet with a story about an inexperienced groom who'd applied a tourniquet to the leg of his favourite hunter. 'Gangrene set in, would you believe? We had to shoot the poor sod.' Telford looked down at the fluttering lids. 'And it was only a graze.'

Moffet flapped like a landed fish, moaned, vomited yellow bile. Rivers tapped his cheek. 'Have you taken anything?'

Sister Roberts came creaking to the door with a wheelchair. Telford looked up at her, horrified, whipped a flannel off the side of the bath and draped it over Moffet's genitals.

'For God's sake, man,' Rivers snapped. 'She's a *nurse*.' Though with Telford's history it probably wasn't Sister Roberts's modesty he thought he was protecting. 'If you could get us a couple of blankets,' he said, twisting in the narrow space.

Moffet's head lolled to one side as they hauled him into the chair and wrapped blankets round him, though Rivers was beginning to suspect he was less drowsy than he seemed.

'Well,' he said, straightening up. 'I think I can manage now, Major Telford. Thank you, you've been a great help.'

'That's all right.' He looked down at Moffet and sniffed. 'Helps break up the afternoon. Anyway, what's all this Major nonsense?' he demanded, punching Rivers playfully in the biceps. 'Don't be such a stuffed shirt, man.'

And off he went, whistling 'A Bachelor Gay Am I'.

They wheeled Moffet into a side ward, since nothing is worse for morale on a 'shell-shock' ward than a suicide attempt. Except a successful suicide of course. He remembered the man at Craiglockhart who'd succeeded in hanging himself. Quite apart from his own tragedy he'd undone weeks of careful work on other people.

The deepest gash required stitching. Rivers set to work immediately, and was rather surprised to find Moffet stoical. He watched the needle dip in and out, only licking his lips once towards the end.

'There,' Rivers said. 'All done.'

Moffet rolled his head restlessly. 'I didn't make a very good job of it, did I?'

'Not many people do. The only person I've ever known to succeed by that method was a surgeon – he virtually severed his left hand.' He got up and stretched his legs, pressing a hand hard into the small of his back. 'How much whisky did you have?'

'Half a bottle. Bit more perhaps.'

No point talking to him, then.

'Where did you get it?'

'My mother. Does it matter?'

'And the razor?'

Moffet looked puzzled. 'Mine.'

'All right. You try to get some sleep.'

'Will you have to tell the police?'

'No.' Rivers looked down at him. 'You're a soldier. You're under military discipline.'

He found Sister Roberts waiting for him. 'I'm afraid we can't let this go,' he said. 'The lockers are supposed to be searched regularly.'

'I'll ask Miss Banbury. She was the last person to do it.'

She was also Sister Roberts's *bête noire*, for no better reason than that she was well-meaning, clumsy, enthusiastic, unqualified and upper class.

'His mother gave him the whisky.'

'Can't say I'm surprised. Silly woman.'

Sister Roberts, as he knew from numerous air-raid conversations of the previous winter, was the eldest girl in a family of eleven. She'd clawed her way out of the Gateshead slums and therefore felt obliged to believe in the corrosive effects on the human psyche of good food, good housing and good education.

'Telford was a bit of a revelation, wasn't he?' she said. 'Surprisingly cool.'

'Oh, Telford's fine. Until he opened his big mouth nobody noticed he was mad.' He added, not entirely as an afterthought, 'He works at the War Office.'

Outside in the corridor he met Wansbeck, now much better though surely not well enough to be up and about.

'How do you feel?' Rivers asked.

'Bit weak. Throat's still sore, but I'm not coughing as much.'

'You'd be better off in bed. Go on, back with you.'

As the doors banged shut behind Wansbeck, Rivers became aware of an insistent clicking. Nothing to account for it. The long corridor stretched ahead, empty, its grey, palely shining floor faintly marked with the shadows of the window frames. Click, click, click. And then he realized the sound was being caused by the bobbles on the end of the blind strings, tapping against each other in the slight breeze. But identifying the sound didn't seem to lessen its potency. It was almost the sound of a yacht's rigging, but the memory went deeper than that.

He had reached the lift before he managed to dredge it up. That day Njiru took him to see the skull houses at Pa Na Gundu, they'd walked for miles in sweltering heat, scarcely a breath of wind, and no sound except the buzzing of flies. Then, abruptly, they came out into a clearing, sharp blades of sunlight slanting down between the trees, and ahead of them, rising up the slope, six or seven skull houses, their gratings ornamented with strings of dangling shells. The feeling of being watched that skulls always gave you. Dazzled by the sudden light, he followed Njiru up the slope, towards a knot of shadows, and then one of the shadows moved, resolving itself into the shape of Nareti, the blind mortuary priest who squatted there, all pointed knees and elbows, snail trails of pus running from the corners of his eyes.

The furthest of the skull houses was being repaired, and its occupants had been taken out and arranged on the ground so that at first sight the clearing seemed to be cobbled with skulls. He'd hung back, not sure how close he was permitted to approach, and at that moment a sudden fierce gust of wind shook the trees and all the strings of votary shells rattled and clicked together.

The lift doors clanged open in his face, startling him back into the present day.

FIVE

Ada Lumb always wore black, less in mourning for her husband – if she'd ever had one – than because black enabled an air of awesome respectability to be maintained at minimal cost.

Respectability was Ada's god. She'd arrived in this neighbourhood eighteen years before, recently widowed, or so she claimed, with two pretty, immaculately dressed little girls in tow. The house had belonged to a man called Dirty Dick, who rambled and muttered and frightened children on street corners. Yellowing newspapers were stacked high in every room. Within a few weeks Ada had the house painted, doorstep scrubbed, range black-leaded, net curtains up at every window. At a safe distance from the house, she bought a lock-up shop, selling boiled boots, second-hand clothes and – below the counter – a great variety of patent medicines designed to procure abortion or cure clap. Pennyroyal Syrup, Dr Lawson's Cure for Female Blockages and Obstructions, Dr Morse's Invigorating Cordial, Curtis's Manhood, Sir Samuel Hannay's Specific, Bumstead's Gleet Cure, The Unfortunate's Friend, and Davy's Lac-Elephantis, a foul-smelling suspension of chalk and God knows what, which claimed to be the medicated milk of elephants.

But on Sundays she locked up the shop and entertained the Vicar, the Rev. Arthur Lindsey, in a room which might have been designed as a stage set for the purpose. Dark oak furniture, plants with thick, durable, rubbery leaves – Ada had no patience with flowers, always drooping and dying – and, prominently displayed on a side table, the family Bible, open at a particularly fortifying text. In this setting Ada poured tea into china cups, dabbed her rat trap of a mouth with a starched napkin and engaged in light, or, in deference to the Sabbath, improving conversation on the topics of the day.

Billy Prior sat at the other end of the table, a concession to his new status as future son-in-law. No more material concessions had been forthcoming: he and Sarah had not been left alone together for a second. Though Ada was gratified by the engagement. She believed in marriage, the more strongly, Prior suspected, for never having sampled it herself. *You don't know that*, he reminded himself. But then he looked round the room and thought, *Yes, I do*. Photographs of Sarah and Cynthia stood on the sideboard, but none of the grandparents, none of their father. No portrait of Ada-the-blushing-bride. And the fortifying text she'd selected for display was the chapter of the Book of Job in which Eliphaz the Temanite visits his friend and seeks to console him for the plague of boils which covers his skin from crown to sole by pointing out that he had it coming. One thing Ada *did* have was a sense of humour. Oh, and an eye for male flesh. Yesterday he'd helped her hang curtains, and her gaze on his groin as she handed the curtains up had been so frankly appraising he'd almost blushed. *You might fool Lindsey*, he thought, *but you don't fool me*.

He made an effort to attend to the conversation. They were talking about the granting of the vote to women of thirty and over, an act of which Ada strongly disapproved. It had pleased Almighty God, she said, to create the one sex visibly and unmistakably superior to the other, and that was all there was to be said in the matter. From the way Lindsey simpered and giggled, one could only assume he thought he knew which sex was meant. He was one of those Anglo-Catholic young men who waft about in a positive miasma of stale incense and seminal fluid. Prior knew the type – biblically as well.

Sarah touched the teapot, and stood up. 'I think this could do with freshening. Billy?'

'Does it take two of you, Sarah?'

'I need Billy to open the door, Mother.'

In the kitchen she burst out, 'Honestly, what century does she think she's living in?'

Prior shrugged. From the kitchen window Melbourne Terrace sloped steeply down, a shoal of red-grey roofs half hidden in swathes of mist and rain. He wondered whether Ada had taken this house for the view, for the sweep of cobbled road, the rows and rows of smoking chimney-stacks, was as dramatic in its way as a mountain range, and, for Ada, rather more significant. For there, below her, was the life she'd saved her daughters from: scabby-mouthed children, women with black eyes, bedbugs, street fights, marriage lines pasted to the inside of the front window to humiliate neighbours who had none of their own to display. He could quite see how the vote might seem irrelevant to a woman engaged in such a battle.

Sarah came across and joined him by the window, putting her arms round his chest from behind and resting her face against his shoulder. 'I hope it's nicer tomorrow. You haven't had much luck with the weather, have you?'

Wasn't all he hadn't had. He turned to face her. 'When are we going to get some time alone?'

'I don't know.' She shook her head. 'I'll work something out.'

'Look, you could pretend to go to work, and –'

'I can't *pretend* to go to work, Billy. We need the money. Come on, she'll be wondering where we are.'

Prior found a plate of lardy cake thrust into his hand, and followed her back into the front room.

They found Lindsey confiding his ideas for next week's sermon – he was attracted to the idea of sacrifice, he said. Are you indeed? thought Prior, plonking the plate down. Cynthia, not long widowed, was hanging on every word, probably on her mother's instructions: she was by far the more biddable of the two girls. Sitting down, Prior nudged Lindsey's foot under the table and was delighted to see a faint blush begin around the dog collar and work its way upwards. A sidelong, flickering glance, a brushing and shying away of eyes, and . . . *You're wasting your lardy cake on that one, Ma,* Prior told his future mother-in-law silently, folding his arms.

After Lindsey had gone, Ada changed into her weekday dress and settled down with a bag of humbugs and a novel. She sat close to the fire, raising her skirt high enough to reveal elastic garters and an expanse of white thigh. As her skirt warmed through, a faint scent of urine rose from it, for Ada, as he knew from Sarah, followed the old custom and when taken short in the street straddled her legs like a mare and pissed in the gutter. His being allowed to witness these intimacies was another concession to the ring on Sarah's finger.

The young people gathered round the piano, and, after the requisite number of hymns had been thumped and bellowed through, passed on to sentimental favourites from before the war.

'You'll know this one, Ma,' Prior said, drawing out the vowel sounds, ogling her over his shoulder. Rather to his surprise, she sang with him.

For her beauty was sold,
For an old man's gold,
She's just a bird in a gilded cage!

'By heck, it was never my luck,' Ada said, going back to her book.

Prior glanced at his watch. 'Do you fancy a turn round the block?' he asked Sarah, closing the piano lid.

'Yes.' A quick glance at Cynthia.

'I'm too tired,' said Cynthia.

'You're never thinking of walking in this?' Ada said. 'Listen at it. It's blowing a gale.'

It was too.

'Anyway it's work tomorrow, our Sarah,' Ada said, closing her book. 'I think we'd all be better for an early night. Are you comfortable on that sofa, Billy?'

'Fine, thank you.' Except there's this ruddy great pole sticking into the cushions.

'You might try lying on your back.'

They'd have burnt her in the Middle Ages. Sarah brought down blankets and pillows from her bedroom, and, watched by Ada from the foot of the stairs, kissed him chastely goodnight.

It's my embarkation leave, he wanted to howl. We're engaged.

The door closed behind her. He wasn't ready for bed – or rather he wasn't ready for bed *alone*. He took off his tunic and boots, wandered round the room, looked at photographs, finally threw himself on to the sofa and picked up Ada's discarded novel.

Ada had a great stock of books. A few romances, which she read with every appearance of enjoyment, gurgles of laughter erupting from the black bombazine like a hot spring from volcanic earth. But she preferred penny dreadfuls, which she read propped up against the milk bottle as she prepared the evening meal. Fingerprints, translucent with butter, encrusted with batter, sticky with jam, edged every page. Bloody thumbprints led up to one particularly gory murder. All the books had murders in them, all carried out by women. Aristocratic ladies ranged abroad, pushing their husbands into rivers, off balconies, over cliffs, under trains or, in the case of the more domestically inclined, feminine type of woman, remained at home and jalloped them to death. Only the final pages were free of cooking stains, and for a long time this puzzled him, until he realized that, in the final chapter, the adulterous murderesses were caught and punished. Ada had no truck with that. *Her* heroines got away with it.

The clock ticked loudly, as it had done all last night, a malevolent tick that kept him awake. He picked it up, intending to put it in the kitchen, but it stopped at once and only resumed its ticking when he replaced it on the mantel shelf. For Christ's sake, he thought, even the bloody clock's trained to keep its knees together.

He could hear the girls getting undressed in the room overhead: the thump of shoes being kicked off, snatches of conversation, giggles, almost – he convinced himself – the sigh of petticoats dropping to the floor. Sarah's momentary nakedness, before the white shroud of night-dress came down. He got up and went to the piano, stroking the keys, singing under his breath.

Far, far from Wipers
I long to be,
Where German snipers
Can't get at me.

Damp is my dug-out,
Cold are my feet
Waiting for Whizzbangs
To put me to sleep.

The door opened. He turned and saw Sarah, a white column of night-gown, a thick plait hanging down over her left shoulder.

'I'm sorry,' he said, closing the piano. 'Have I been making too much noise?'

'No, I just wanted to see you.'

Incredibly, impossibly, the sound of girlish whispering and giggling continued overhead.

'Cynthia,' Sarah said, closing the door. 'She's pretending I'm still there.'

She knelt on the hearthrug, and began feeding the few remaining sticks of wood into the fire. Then, carefully, so as not to douse the flames, she dropped shiny nuggets of coal into the fiery caverns the dying fire had made. A hiss, for the coal was damp after recent rain, and, for a moment, the glow on her face and hair darkened, then blazed up again.

'We seem to keep missing each other,' she said.

'You mean we're kept apart.'

That amazing hair, he thought. Even now, when it was all brushed and tamed for bed, he could see five or six different shades of copper, auburn, bronze, even a strand of pure gold that looked as if it must belong to somebody else.

She turned to look at him. 'It's her house, Billy.'

'Have I said anything?'

The firelight, gilding her face, disguised the munitions-factory yellow of her skin.

'We could get married by special licence,' he said. 'At least I suppose we could, I don't know how long it takes.'

'No, we couldn't.'

No, he thought, because after the war things'll be different, I could be getting on in the world, I might not want to be saddled with a wife from Beale Street. I have to be protected from myself. Sarah had a great sense of honour. About as much use to a woman as a jock-strap, he'd have thought, but there it was, Sarah was saddled with it. 'I love you, Sarah Lumb.'

'I love you, Billy Prior.'

She leant back, and he unbuttoned her night-dress, pushing it off her shoulders so that the side of one heavy breast was etched in trembling gold. He slid to the floor beside her and took her in his arms, feeling her tense against him. 'It's all right, it's all right.'

And all he wanted, at that moment, was to hide his face between her breasts and shut out the relentless ticking of the clock. But a voice above shouted, 'Sarah? Cynthia? Time you were asleep.'

'I'll have to go.'

'All right.'

But his hands refused to loosen their grip, and she had to pull herself away.

'Look, tomorrow night she goes to the spuggies. I'll tell her I've got a headache, and see if I can stay here.'

Next morning, after they'd all gone to work, he went upstairs to Sarah's room, exhausted after another bad night measured by the chiming of the clock. He needed to lie in the bed where Sarah slept, to wrap himself in these stained sheets, for even in this fanatically clean household the girls' skins sloughed off, staining the sheets yellow, and no amount of washing would get the stains out. He didn't mind. He would lie happily here, in the trough made by her body during the night, smelling the faint smell of lavender and soap.

On the bedside table was a photograph of himself, taken when he was first commissioned. Unformed schoolboy face. Had he ever been as young as that? Undressed and in bed, he squinted at the half-drawn curtains, wondering if it was worth the effort of getting up to close them. No, he decided, he would simply turn his back to the light.

He turned over, and for a second closed his eyes, his brain not immediately interpreting what in that brief glance he had seen. Then he sat up. On the dresser stood a photograph of a young man in uniform, a private's uniform. Not Cynthia's husband – he knew his face from wedding groups. He got out of bed and went to look. Johnny, of course. Who else? Sarah's first fiancé.

The usual inanely smiling face half whited out by the sun. Behind him, a few feet of unbombed France. And why should he begrudge this? *Because I thought I'd taken his place.* He hadn't even thought it, he'd just assumed it. She'd talked only once about Johnny and then she'd been drunk on the port he'd been plying her with to get her knickers off. Loos. That was it. Gas blown back over the British lines. He peered again at the unknown face. The whiting out seemed almost to be an unintended symbol of the oblivion into which we all go. Last night, he'd wondered what colour Sarah's skin had been under the jaundice produced by the chemicals she worked with. This man had known. He'd known *this* Sarah – picking up a snapshot – this happy, slightly plump, hoydenish girl struggling to keep her skirts down on the boat-swing. What you noticed in Sarah now was the high rounded forehead, the prominent cheekbones, the bright, cool amused gaze. Always the sense of something being held back. He'd been looking all along at a face scoured out by grief, and he'd never known it till now.

'Nice walk in the fresh air,' Ada said, spearing black felt with a hat-pin. 'Just the thing for a headache.'

'I won't be in the fresh air, Mam. That room gets awfully stuffy, you know.'

Ada bent down, thrusting her face into her daughter's. 'Sarah, go and get your coat.'

Sarah looked at Billy and shrugged slightly.

'I'll come too,' he said, standing up.

'Are you sure?' Ada asked. 'The spuggies aren't everybody's cup of tea.'

'Wouldn't miss it for the world.'

They walked down the street together, Ada leading the way, sweeping along in her black skirt, for in the matter of skirt length she made no concessions to the present day. She glided along as if on invisible casters.

'I suppose she does know contacting the dead's a heresy?' Billy asked. 'The Vicar wouldn't like it.'

'Oh, she doesn't believe in it. She only goes for the night out.'

The meeting was held above a shop that sold surgical appliances, a range of products whose advertising is necessarily discreet. The window, lined with red and green crêpe paper left over from Christmas, contained nothing but a picture of a white-haired man swinging his granddaughter above his head.

They went up a narrow staircase into a tiny room. A piano, a table with a vase of flowers, five or six rows of chairs, net curtains whose shadows tattooed skin. They couldn't find four seats together and so Prior found himself sitting behind Sarah.

'How's your headache, Sarah?' Ada asked.

'Bit better, thank you, Mam.'

How's your ballsache, Billy? Bloody awful, thank you, Ma.

A man walked up and stood on the rostrum, looking carefully round the room. Counting the penny contributions to tea and biscuits? Assessing the general level of credulity? Or was he perhaps not a rogue at all but simply mad? No, not mad. A small, self-satisfied man with brown teeth.

Prior followed his gaze round the room, as the blinds were drawn down, shutting out the sun. Women, mostly in black, a scattering of men, all middle aged or older, except one, whose hands and face twitched uncontrollably. Too many widows. Too many mothers looking for contact with lost sons – and this was an area where they'd all joined up together. Whole streets of them, going off in a day. And this man, smoothing down his thin hair, announcing the number of the hymn, had known them all – birthmarks, nicknames, funny little habits – he knew exactly what every woman in this room wanted to hear. Fraud, Prior thought, and that he deceived himself made it no better.

> Angels of Jesus, Angels of Light
> Singing to we-elcome the pilgrims of the night.

They sat down with the usual coughs, chair scrapings, tummy rumbles, and he stood in front of them, establishing the silence, deepening it.

At last he was ready. Their loved ones were with them, he said, they were present in this room. The messages started coming. First a description, then a flicker of the eyes in the direction of the woman whose husband or son he had been describing, then the message. Anodyne messages. They were having a whale of a time, it seemed, on the other side, beyond this vale of tears, singing hymns, rejoicing in the Lamb, casting down their golden crowns around the glassy sea. Ah, yes, Prior wanted to ask, but how's the fucking?

Then, without warning, the twitching man stood up and started to speak. Not words. A gurgling rush of sound like the overflow of a drainpipe, and yet with inflections, pauses, emphases, everything that speech contains except meaning. People turned towards him, watching the sounds jerk out of him, as he stood with thrown-back head and glazed eyes. The man on the rostrum was wearing a forced, sickly smile. One hysteric upstaged by another. I'd take the pair of you on, Prior thought.

He touched Sarah's shoulder. 'I can't stand any more of this. I'll wait outside.'

He ran downstairs, then crossed the street and slipped into the alley opposite, positioning himself midway between two stinking midden holes. He lit a cigarette and thought *glossolalia.* 'A spiritual gift of no intrinsic significance, unless the man possessing it can interpret what he receives in a way that tends to the edification of the faithful.' Father Mackenzie, preparing him for Confirmation, when he was . . . eleven years old? Twelve? What a teacher the man was – in or out of his cassock.

From his vantage point, watching like a stranger, he saw Sarah come out and look up and down the empty road.

'Sarah.'

She ran across, face pale beneath the munitions-factory yellow. 'What happened?'

'Nothing. I couldn't stand it, that's all.' A pause. 'We have to die, we don't have to worship it.'

They stood together, looking up and down the street, which was dotted here and there with puddles of recent rain. Fitful gleams of sunlight.

'I'm not going back in.'

'No.'

She waited, still worried.

'We could go back home,' she said.

'Have you got a key?'

'Yes.'

They stared at each other.

'Come on,' he said, grabbing her arm.

They ran along the shining street, splashing through puddles, Sarah's hair coming loose in a cascade of pins, then down an alley where white sheets bellied and snapped, shirt-sleeves caught them, wet cotton stung their faces and necks. They arrived at the door red-faced, Sarah's hair hanging in rat's-tails down her back.

She rattled the key in the lock, while he stood looking back the way they'd come, half expecting to see Ada hurtling towards them on her Widow-of-Windsor casters. They half fell into the passage, and he ran towards the stairs. '*No*,' she said. *No*, he thought. The front room, then. He made to pull the curtains across. 'No, don't do that, they'll think somebody's dead. Behind the sofa.' He was already on his knees in front of her, his hands under her skirt, groping for the waistband of her drawers, pulling them down, casting them aside, he didn't care where they fell. At the last moment he thought, This isn't going to work. They'd had to leave the front door open – it would be impossible to explain why it was locked – but the thought of Ada Lumb looking down at your bare arse was enough to give a brass monkey the wilts.

'Careful,' Sarah said, as he went in.

But he's always careful, always prepared – though never prepared for the surge of joy he feels now. He's like some aquatic animal, an otter, returning to its burrow, greeting its mate nose to nose, curling up, safe, warm, dark, wet. His mind shrinks to a point that listens for footsteps, but his cock swells, huge and blind, filling the world. His thrusts deepen and quicken, but then he forces himself to pull back, to keep them shallow, a butterfly fluttering that he knows she likes. Her hands come up and grasp his buttocks – always a moment of danger – and for a while he has to stop altogether, hanging there, mouth open. Then, cautiously, he starts again. Cords stand out in her neck, her belly tightens, the fingers clutching his arse are claws now. She groans, and he feels the movement of muscles in her belly. Another groan, a cry, and now it's impossible to stop, every thrust as irresistible as the next breath to a drowning man. She raises her legs higher, inviting him deeper, and he tries not to hear the desperation in her gasps, the disappointment in her final cry, as he spills himself into her.

'Yes?' he gasps, as soon as he can speak.

'No.'

Oh God. He drives himself on, thrusting away in a frictionless frenzy, his knob a point of fire, feeling her teeter teeter on the brink, and then at last at last tip over, fall, clutching and throbbing round his shrinking cock till he cries out in pain. Oh, but she's there, she's laughing, he hears her laughter deep in his chest.

Only his groin's wet, too wet. He lifted himself off her and looked down. Spunk, beaten stiff as egg-white, streaked their hair, flecks of foam on a horse's muzzle, spume blown back from the breaking wave, but to him it meant one thing. The johnny – unfortunate word in the circumstances – was still inside Sarah. He hooked it out, and they stared at it.

Sarah felt inside. 'I think I'm all right,' she said. 'It's all outside.'

No oiled casters, but a firm tread approached the house. He flung the rubber into the fire, a million or so Billies and Sarahs perishing in a gasp of flame. Small bloody comfort if another million were still inside her. She pulled her skirts down and sat, sweating and desperate, in her mother's chair. He was about to sit down himself when he caught sight of her drawers thrown across the family Bible, one raised leg drawing a decent veil over Job and his boils. He snatched them up and stuffed them down the neck of his tunic, which left him no time for his flies. He picked up the Bible and sat with it in his lap.

'Well,' Ada said. 'What happened to you?'

Sarah said, 'Billy started thinking about a friend of his, Mam.'

Prior sat with his head on one hand, a passable imitation of David mourning Jonathan.

Ada sniffed. 'I see you've not thought to put the kettle on, our Sarah. It's a true saying in this life, if you want anything doing do it yourself.'

She went into the kitchen. Cynthia, glancing timidly from one to the other, sat down on the edge of the sofa. Billy pulled Sarah's drawers out of his tunic and threw them across to her. Cynthia squealed, bunching her clothes between her legs like a little girl afraid of wetting herself. Sarah calmly stood up and put the drawers on, while Prior fumbled with buttons beneath the Bible.

Ada came back into the room. 'You missed a good show,' she said. 'Mrs Roper had to be carried out. Still, no doubt you've been better employed.' She indicated the Bible.

'I was just trying to find the bit about the war-horse to show Sarah. But it's all right, I know it off by heart.' He looked straight at Ada. '*He paweth in the valley and rejoiceth in his strength: he goeth on to meet the armed men. He mocketh at fear, and is not affrighted; neither turneth he back from the sword. He saith among the trumpets, Ha, ha; and he smelleth the battle afar off, the thunder of the captains, and the shouting.*'

He got up and replaced the Bible, aware of three faces gawping at him. An odd moment. 'And now if you don't mind,' he said, 'I think I'd like to lie down.'

Sarah was allowed to go to the railway station with him unaccompanied. They stood on the empty platform, exhausted mentally and physically, obliged to cherish these last moments together, both secretly, guiltily wanting it to be over.

He picked up her hand and kissed the ring. 'Don't worry, Sarah.'

'I'm not worried.' She smiled. 'This time next year.'

He hadn't thought about the actual marriage at all, once she'd made it clear she didn't want a quick wedding. Next year was a lifetime away. Perhaps even a bit more. He watched a pigeon walk along the edge of the platform, raw feet clicking on the concrete. 'Come on,' he said. 'Let's walk along.'

They stopped under the shelter of the roof, for there was a fine rain blowing. White northern light filtered through sooty glass. Sarah's face pinched with cold.

'Write as soon as you get there,' she said.

'I'll write from London. I'll write on the train if you like.'

She smiled and shook her head. 'I'm glad you told your mam anyway.'

'She was delighted.'

She was horrified.

– Marrying a factory girl not that it matters of course as long as you're happy but I'd've thought you could have done a bit better for yourself than that.

His father was incredulous.

– Married? You?

– Oscar Wilde was married, Dad, Prior had not been able to resist saying.

But then his father had come to the station to see him off – first time in four years – *and* he'd to get out of bed to do it, because he was on nights, *and* he was wearing his Sunday suit, *and* he'd shaved, *and* he was sober. Jesus Christ, Prior had thought, all we need is the wreath.

A small hard pellet of dismay lodged in his throat. Premonition? *No-o*, nothing so portentous. A slight sense of pushing his luck, perhaps. This was the fourth time, and four was one too many.

'I expect they'll invite you over.'

Sarah smiled. 'I think I'll wait till you get back.'

He glanced covertly at his watch. Where was the bloody train? And then he saw it, in the distance, crawling doubtfully along, trailing its plume of steam. No sound yet, though as he stepped closer to the edge of the platform he felt or sensed a vibration in the rails. He turned to face Sarah, blocking her view of the train.

She was looking up at the rafters. 'Have you seen them?'

He followed her gaze and saw that every rafter was lined with pigeons. 'The warmth, I suppose,' he said vaguely.

The roar of the approaching train startled the birds. They rose as one, streaming out from under the glass roof in a great flapping and beating of wings, wheeling, banking, swooping, turning, a black wave against the smoke-filled sky. Prior and Sarah watched, open-mouthed, drunk on the sight of so much freedom, their linked hands slackening, able, finally, to think of nothing, as the train steamed in.

SIX

After tea he took Kath's photograph album up to her room. He usually brought snapshots of family and friends with him on these visits, because he knew how much pleasure they gave her. She was sitting up in bed, faded brown hair tied back by a blue ribbon, a pink bed jacket draped around her shoulders. Blue and pink: the colours of the nursery. He took the tray off her lap and gave her the album and the photographs.

She seized on a group of staff at the Empire Hospital. 'You've got your usual I-don't-want-to-be-photographed expression,' she said, holding it up to the light.

'Well, I didn't.'

She was already busy pasting glue on to the back. 'Is it true the natives think the camera steals their souls?'

'Some of them. The sensible ones.'

She pressed her handkerchief carefully around the edges of the photograph, catching the seepage of glue. 'It's a good one of Dr Head.'

'Oh, Henry isn't worried, he hasn't got a soul.'

'*Will.*'

He looked at the tray. 'You haven't eaten much.'

'I'm glad Ethel's having a break. It's been a shocking year.'

Ramsgate had been bombed heavily, a great many civilians, mainly women and children, killed. As a result Kath's health, which had long given cause for concern, had dramatically deteriorated. Ethel, who'd looked after their father in his old age, and then after this invalid younger sister, had begun to show signs of strain herself, and the brothers had decided something must be done. A holiday was out of the question, ruled out by Ethel herself – she could not and would not go – but she *had* agreed to stay with friends for a long weekend.

'I think that's the car now,' Rivers said. 'I'd better get the suitcase down.'

He found Ethel in the hall, pinning on her hat.

'Now,' she said, unable to let go, 'you've got the telephone number?'

'Yes.'

'You're sure you've got it?'

'Yes.' He pushed her gently towards the door.

'No, *listen*, Will. If you're worried, don't hesitate, call the doctor.'

'Ethel, I *am* a doctor.'

'No, I mean a *proper* doctor.'

He was still smiling as he went back upstairs.

'Is she gone?'

'Yes, I had to push her out of the door, but she's gone. Have you finished sticking them in?'

He took the album from her and began turning the pages, pausing at a photograph of himself and the other members of the Torres Straits expedition. Barefoot, bare-armed, bearded, sun-tanned, wearing a collection of spectacularly villainous hats, they looked for all the world like a low-budget production of *The Pirates of Penzance*. The flower of British anthropology, he thought, God help us. He turned a few more pages, stopping at a snapshot from his days in Heidelberg. What on earth made him think those side whiskers were a good idea?

'I knew you'd stop there,' Katharine said. 'It's her, isn't it? The stout one.'

'Alma? Of course it isn't.' His sisters had teased him mercilessly at the time, because he'd happened to be standing next to Alma in a snapshot. 'Anyway, she wasn't stout, she was . . . comfortable.'

'She was stout. We really did think you were going to marry her, you know. She was the only woman we ever saw you with.'

'That's not true either. Remember all the young ladies mother used to invite to tea?'

'I remember you sloping off upstairs to get away from them. You were just like Mr Dodgson. He used to do that.'

Kath sometimes combined with childlike innocence a child's sharpness of perception.

'*Like Dodgson?* God forbid.'

'You didn't like him, did you?'

He hesitated. 'No.'

'You were jealous. You and Charles.'

'Yes, I think we were. Ah, *this* is the girl I'm looking for,' he said, holding up a photograph of a little girl in a white dress. Even in faded sepia it was possible to tell what an exceptionally beautiful child she'd been.

Light from the standard lamp fell on the side of Dodgson's face as he opened the book.

'S-shouldn't we wait f-for K-K-K-Kath?' he asked, the name clotting on his tongue.

Sitting on the sofa beside Charles, Will thought, That's because it's the same sound as hard *c*. *C* was Dodgson's worst consonant. *F* and *m* were his.

'No, I think we should start,' his father said. 'It's not fair to keep everybody waiting, just because Kath's late.'

'She'll be here soon,' Mother said. 'Her stomach's a good clock.'

'Aren't you w-w-w-w-w-woorr . . .?'

'Not really. She knows she mustn't leave the grounds.'

Will intercepted a glance between his parents. Mother shouldn't have completed Mr Dodgson's sentence for him like that. You were supposed to let people flounder, no matter how long it took.

Mr Dodgson stammered less when he read. And why was that? Because he knew the words so well he didn't have to think about them? Or because, although his voice was loud, he was really just reading to Ethel, who sat curled up in the crook of his arm, where she could see the pictures? He never stammered much when he was talking to the girls. Or was it because these were *his* words, and he was determined to get them out, no matter what? It certainly wasn't because he was thinking about the movements of his tongue, which was what father said you should do.

'The rabbit hole,' Mr Dodgson read, or rather recited, for he was not looking at the page but at the top of Ethel's head, 'went straight on like a tunnel for some way, and then dipped suddenly down, so suddenly that Alice had not a moment to think about stopping herself before she found herself falling down a very deep –'

Kath burst in, hot, dirty, dishevelled, trailing her hat by its long blue ribbon, raspberry stains round her mouth, grubby hands streaked with cuckoo spit. She went straight to Mr Dodgson and gave him a bunch of flowers whose stalks had wilted in the heat and flopped over the back of her hand.

He took them from her and sat looking stupid, not knowing where to put them, when his attention was caught. 'Look,' he said, 'you've g-g-got a l-l-l-ladybird in your h-hair.'

Kath stood, breathing through her mouth with concentration, as he teased the strands of hair apart and persuaded the insect on to the tip of his finger. He showed it to her, then carefully stood up, meaning to carry it to the window, but the scarlet shards parted, the black wings spread, and the insect sailed out, a dark speck on the blue air.

Dodgson sat down, drew Katharine on to his lap, folded his other arm round Ethel again, and picked up the book.

'– *well*,' he said, and everybody laughed.

'Do you remember how he hated snakes?' Kath said, leaning back against the pillows with the sunlight on her greying hair.

'Yes, I remember.'

He was thinking that the whole course of Kath's life had been constriction into a smaller and smaller space. As children they'd both had a hundred acres of safe woods and fields to roam in, but from that point on *his* life had expanded: medical school, round the world as a ship's doctor, Germany, the Torres Straits, India, Australia, the Solomon Islands, the New Hebrides. And over the same period the little girl who'd rambled all day through woods and fields had become the younger of the two Miss Rivers, scrutinized by her father's parishioners, the slightest breach of decorum noted, and then, after father's retirement, a small house in Ramsgate, deteriorating health, confinement to the house, then to the bedroom, then to the bed. And yet she was no more intrinsically neurasthenic than he was himself. But a good mind must have something to feed on, and hers, deprived of other nourishment, had fed on itself.

He said slowly, 'I think what I remember most is endless croquet.'

Oh God, he remembered, hours and hours of it, a vast red sun hanging above the trees, Dodgson's body forming a hoop round Kath's, his hands enclosing hers, the click of mallets on balls, and mother's voice drifting across the lawn asking how much longer were they going to be? It was time for Kath to come in. 'Mathematical croquet,' Rivers said. 'Nobody could win.'

'I used to win.'

'He helped you cheat.'

'Yes.' A faint smile. 'I know he did.'

Once, on the river, Dodgson had tried to pin up Kath's skirts so she could paddle. He'd done it often enough before, indeed he carried safety-pins in his lapels specifically for the purpose, but this time she'd pushed him away. Some intensity in his gaze? Some quality in his touch? Their mother had spoken sharply to her, but Dodgson had said, 'No, leave her alone.'

'It's a pity we lost his letters,' Rivers said.

'Oh, and the drawings. There was a whole crate of things went missing. I'm sure that painting of Uncle Will went at the same time –'

'I don't remember that.'

'Yes, you do.'

'Where was it?'

'At the top of the stairs. You couldn't put it in the drawing-room, it was too horrible.'

'What was it of?'

'Uncle William having his leg cut off. And there was somebody waiting with a sort of cauldron full of hot tar ready to pour it over the stump.'

'Are you sure?'

'You didn't like it. When we all went downstairs in the morning I used to see you not looking at it. You were like this.' She turned her head to one side.

'Well, you have surprised me.'

A modestly triumphant smile. 'I remember more than you do.'

Though, even as she spoke, he had a faint, very faint, recollection of Father lifting him up to look at something. A curious exposed feeling at the nape of his neck. 'Father tried very hard with Charles and me. Didn't he?'

'You more than Charles.'

'Ah, well, yes, I was the guinea-pig, wasn't I? The first child always is.' A greater bitterness in his voice than he knew how to account for.

He brushed it aside. 'I'll make us some cocoa, shall I? And then I think you should try and get some sleep.'

– Do you remember how he hated snakes?
– Yes, I remember.

That's the trouble, Rivers thought, taking off his shirt in the spare bedroom that had once been his father's study, I remember her childhood better than my own. Though another person's life, observed from outside, always has a shape and definition that one's own life lacks.

It was odd he couldn't remember that picture, when Kath, ten years younger, remembered it so clearly. He'd certainly have been shown it, many many times. He was named after William Rivers of the *Victory*, who, as a young midshipman, had shot the man who shot Lord Nelson. That was the family legend anyway. And the great man, dying, had not indulged in any effete nonsense about kissing Hardy, nor had he entrusted Lady Hamilton to the conscience of a grateful nation. *No*, his last words had been, 'Look after young Will Rivers for me.' And young Will Rivers had needed looking after. He'd been wounded in the mouth and leg, and the leg had had to be amputated. Without an anaesthetic, since there were no anaesthetics, except rum. And then hot tar to cauterize the spurting stump. My God, it was a wonder any of them survived. And throughout the ordeal – family legend again – he had not once cried out. He'd survived, married, had children, become Warden of Greenwich Hospital. There was a portrait bust of him there, in the Painted Hall.

Now *that* he did remember being taken to see. Was that the occasion on which his father had lifted him up to look? No, he'd have been eight or nine.

And then he remembered. Quite casually, a bubble breaking on the surface. He'd had his hair cut, he'd just been breeched, yes, that was it, his neck felt funny, and so did his legs. And he was crying. Yes, it was all coming back. He'd embarrassed his father in the barber's shop by howling his head off. Bits of him were being cut off, bits of him were dropping on to the floor. His father shushed him, and when that didn't work, slapped his leg. He gasped with shock, filled his lungs with air, and howled louder. So being shown the picture was a lesson? You don't behave like *that*, you behave like *this*. '*He* didn't cry,' his father had said, holding him up. '*He didn't make a sound.*'

And I've been stammering ever since, Rivers thought, inclined to see the funny side. Though what had it meant – Trafalgar, the Napoleonic wars – to a four-year-old for whom a summer's day was endless? Nothing, it could have meant nothing. Or, worse, it had meant something fearfully simple. The same name, the slapped leg, being told not to cry. Had he perhaps looked at the picture and concluded that this was what happened to you if your name was William Rivers?

He'd avoided looking at it, Kath said, even turning his head away so that he could not glimpse it by mistake as he went past. Had he also deliberately suppressed the visual image of it, making it impossible for himself to see it in his mind's eye? Prior, told that Rivers attributed his almost total lack of visual memory to an event in his childhood that he had succeeded in forgetting, had said brutally, 'You were raped or beaten . . . Whatever it was, you put your mind's eye out rather than have to go on seeing it. Is that what happened, or isn't it?' Yes, Rivers had been obliged to admit, though he'd argued very strongly for a less dramatic interpretation of events. It could have been something quite trivial, he'd said, though terrifying to a child. Something as simple as the fearsome shadow of a dressing-gown on the back of the nursery door. Small children are not like adults, he'd insisted. What terrifies them may seem trivial to us.

Was this *the* suppressed memory? He didn't know. Was it trivial? Well, yes, in a way, compared with Prior's lurid imaginings. A smack on the leg, a lesson in manliness from an over-conscientious but loving father. It's a long way from sadistic beatings or sexual assault. And yet it wasn't as trivial as it seemed at first. That silence – for him now that was the centre of the picture – not the blood, not the knife, but that resolutely clenched mouth. Every day of his working life he looked at twitching mouths that had once been clenched. Go on, he said, though rarely in so many words, cry. It's all right to grieve. Breakdown's nothing to be ashamed of – the pressures were intolerable. But, also, stop crying. Get up on your feet. Walk. He both distrusted that silence and endorsed it, as he was bound to do, he thought, being his father's son.

He went to Greenwich by train, visited the portrait bust in the Painted Hall, then continued his journey by steamer, arriving at Westminster steps in the late afternoon. The underground was crowded, he couldn't find a taxi, and by the time he turned the corner of Holford Road Prior was already there, standing on the steps. 'Have you knocked?' Rivers asked.

'No, I saw you coming. Been at the hospital?'

'No, I've just got back from Ramsgate.' He fitted his key into the lock. 'Now if we tiptoe across the hall . . .'

Prior smiled, having encountered Rivers's landlady many times in the past.

'All clear,' Rivers said.

They walked upstairs side by side, Rivers noticing how easily Prior was breathing. Sometimes, during the past summer, he'd listened to Prior's step on these stairs and counted the pauses. He'd never gone out on to the top landing to greet Prior as he did with all his other patients because he knew how intolerable he would find it to be seen fighting for breath. But now his chest was remarkably clear, a reflection perhaps of the satisfaction he felt at going back to France. Rivers opened the door of his rooms, and stood aside to let Prior enter.

Somehow or other he had to prevent this meeting becoming a confrontation, as consultations with Prior still tended to do. Prior would enjoy the skirmish at the time – there was nothing he liked better – but he'd regret it later. 'Well, sit yourself down,' Rivers said, taking Prior's coat and pointing to a chair by the fire. 'How are you?'

'Quite well. Chest works. Tongue works.'

'Nightmares?'

'Hmm . . . a few. I had one where the faces on the revolver targets – you know, horrible snarling baby-eating boche – turned into the faces of people I love. But only after I'd pulled the trigger, so there was nothing I could do about it. 'Fraid I killed you every time.'

'Ah, so it isn't a *bad* nightmare, then?'

They smiled at each other. Rivers thought Prior was entirely unaware of what he'd said, though that was always a dangerous assumption to make about Prior. Perhaps because he'd recently been thinking about his own father Rivers was more than usually aware of the strong father–son element in his relationship with Prior. He had no son; Prior utterly rejected his natural father. 'Oh, by the way, congratulations on your engagement.'

Hmm, Prior thought. Charles Manning's congratulations had also been brief, though in his case the brevity might be excused, since he'd had to take Prior's cock out of his mouth to be able to say anything at all. 'Thank you.'

'Have you fixed a date?'

'Next August. We met in August, we got engaged in August, so . . .'

'And when do you leave for France?'

'Tonight. I'm glad to be going.'

'Yes.'

Prior smiled. 'Do *you* think I'm ready to go back?'

A slight hesitation. 'I think I'd be happier if you did another twelve weeks' home service. Which would still,' he persisted across Prior's interruptions, 'get you back to France by the end of November.'

'Why?'

'You know why. Two months ago you were having memory lapses. Rather bad ones actually. Anyway this is purely hypothetical. Wasn't my decision –'

Prior leant forward. 'I was afraid you'd write.'

'It never occurred to me anybody would think of sending you back.'

'I think the MO was against it. Well, that was my impression anyway. How would I know? As for the Board, well, they wanted to send me back. I wanted to go.'

'What did they ask you about? Nerves?'

'No, not mentioned. They don't believe in shell-shock. You'd be surprised how many army Medical Boards don't.'

Rivers snorted. 'Oh, I don't think I would. Anyway, you're going back. You've got what you wanted.'

'At the moment I can't wait to see the back of England.'

'Any particular reason?'

'It's nothing really. I just had my fur rubbed up the wrong way.' He hesitated. 'Manning took me to meet Robert Ross. I don't know whether you've met him? Through Sassoon?'

'Briefly.'

'I liked him, he was charming – I wasn't equally keen on some of his friends.'

Rivers waited.

'One in particular. Apparently he'd been stood up by his boyfriend – he'd been expecting an amorous weekend – and the poor chap had decided it wasn't worth the train fare from Leeds. And this man – Birtwhistle, his name is – was saying, "Of course one can't rely on them. Their values are totally different from ours. They're a different species, really. The WCs." Smirk, smirk.'

Rivers looked puzzled.

'Working classes. Water-closets. The men who're getting their ballocks shot off so he can go on being the lily on the dung heap. God, they make me sick.'

'I'm sure you more than held your own.'

'No, I didn't, that's what bothers me. It all got tangled up with being a guest and being polite. To Ross, of course, not him. Anyway I decided to give this prat a run for his money so we adjourned upstairs afterwards.'

'You and Manning?'

'No, me and Birtwhistle. Birtwhistle and I.'

'It doesn't sound much like a punishment.'

'Oh, it was. Nothing like *sexual* humiliation, Rivers. Nobody ever forgets that.'

Rivers looked into the trustless eyes, and thought, My God, I wouldn't want to cross you. Though he had crossed him many times, in the course of therapy, *and* refused more than one invitation to 'adjourn upstairs'.

'I just wish your last evening had been pleasanter.'

Prior shrugged. 'It was all right. It just . . . he happens to represent everything in England that *isn't* worth fighting for. Which made him a rather bracing companion.' He glanced at his watch. 'I'd better be going. I'm catching the midnight train.'

Rivers hesitated. 'Please don't think because I *personally* would have recommended another three months in England that I don't have every confidence in your ability to . . . to . . .'

'Do my duty to King and country.'

'Yes.'

'Rivers, you don't think I should be going back at all.'

Rivers hesitated. 'The Board at Craiglockhart recommended permanent home service and that wasn't because of your nerves, it was on the basis of your asthma alone. I haven't seen anything to make me change my mind.'

Prior looked at him, smiled, and slapped him on both arms. 'I've got to go.'

Rivers said slowly, as he went to get Prior's coat, 'Do you remember saying something to me once about the the the ones who go back b-being the *real* test cases? From the point of view of finding out whether a particular therapy works?'

'Yes, I remember.' Another smile. 'I was getting at you.'

'You always were. Well, it just occurs to me you're actually rather better equipped than most people to observe that process. I think you have great powers of detachment.'

'"Cold-blooded little bastard,"' Prior translated, then thought for a moment. 'You're giving me a football to kick across, aren't you? You remember that story? The Suffolk's kicking a football across No Man's Land when the whistles blew on the Somme? Bloody mad.'

'No, the battle was mad. The football was sane. Whoever ordered them to do that was a very good psychologist.'

'*Ah!*'

'But I know what you mean. It's become the kind of incident one can't take seriously any more. Only I'm not sure that's right, you see. I suppose what one *should* be asking is whether an ideal becomes invalid because the people who hold it are betrayed.'

'If holding it makes them into naïve idiots, *yes*.'

'Were they?'

'If they were, I can't talk. I'm going back.'

Rivers smiled. 'So you don't want my football?'

'On the contrary, I think it's a brilliant idea. I'll send you the half-time score.'

Rivers handed him his greatcoat, examining it first. 'I'm impressed.'

'So you should be at the price.' Prior started to put it on. 'Do you know you can get these with scarlet silk linings?'

'Army greatcoats?'

'Yes. Saw one in the Café Royal. On the back of one of my old intelligence colleagues. Quite a startling effect when he crossed his legs, *subtle*, you know, like a baboon's bottom. Apparently he's supposed to sit there and "attract the attention of anti-war elements".'

'Was he?'

'He was attracting attention. I don't know what their views on the war were. Another thing that made me glad to be getting out of it.' He held out his hand. 'Don't come down.'

Rivers took him at his word, but went through to the bedroom window and looked out, lifting the curtain an inch to one side. Miss Irving's voice, a laughing farewell, and then Prior appeared, foreshortened, running down the steps.

On Vao there was a custom that when a bastard was born some leading man on the island adopted the child and brought him up as his own. The boy called him father, and grew up surrounded by love and care and then, when he reached puberty, he was given the honour, as befitted the son of a great man, of leading in the sacrificial pig, one of the huge-tusked boars in which the wealth of the people was measured. He was given new bracelets, new necklaces, a new penis wrapper and then, in front of the entire community, all of whom knew what was about to happen, he led the pig to the sacrificial stone, where his father waited with upraised club. And, as the boy drew near, he brought the club down and crushed his son's skull.

In one of his father's churches, St Faith's, at Maidstone, the window to the left of the altar shows Abraham with the knife raised to slay his son, and, below the human figures, a ram caught in the thicket by his horns. The two events represented the difference between savagery and civilization, for in the second scenario the voice of God is about to forbid the sacrifice, and will be heeded. He had knelt at that altar rail for years, Sunday after Sunday, receiving the chalice from his father's hands.

Perhaps, Rivers thought, watching Prior's head bob along behind the hedge and disappear from view, it was because he'd been thinking so much about fathers and sons recently that the memory of the two sacrifices had returned, but he wished this particular memory had chosen another moment to surface.

Part Two

SEVEN

29 August 1918

Bought this in a stationer's just off Fleet Street quite a long time ago. I've been carrying it round with me ever since unused, mainly because it's so grand. I bought it for the marbled covers and the thick creamy pages and ever since then the thick creamy pages have been saying, Piss off, what could *you* possibly write on *us* that would be worth reading? It's a marvellous shop, a real old-fashioned stationer's. Stationers', second-hand bookshops, ironmongers'. Feel a great need at the moment to concentrate on small pleasures. If the whole of one's life can be summoned up and held in the palm of one hand, *in the living moment*, then time means nothing. World without end, Amen.

Load of crap. Facts are what we need, man. Facts.

Arrived in London to find no porters, no taxis, and the hotels full. Charles Manning on the platform (the train was so late I was sure he'd've gone home), offering, as a solution, the room he rents in Half Moon Street, 'for the nights when he works late at the office and doesn't want to disturb the household'. Oh, c'mon, Charles, I wanted to say. It's *me*, remember? I was all for trudging round a few more hotels, but he was limping badly and obviously in pain *and* pissed off with me for going back when I could have been comfortably established in the Min of Mu chasing bits of paper across a desk, like him. (He'd go back to France tomorrow if they'd have him.)

When we got to Half Moon Street we went straight upstairs and he produced a bottle of whisky. Not bad (but not what he drinks himself either) and I waited for him to do what everybody else would do in the circumstances and collect the rent. He didn't, of course. I'm plagued with honourable people. I thought, Oh, for Christ's sake, if you haven't got the gumption to ask for it bloody do without. I was feeling tired and sticky and wanted a bath. After ten minutes of swishing soapy water round my groin and whisky round my guts I started to feel better. I had a quiet consultation with myself in the bathroom mirror, all steamy and pink and conspiratorial, and went back in and said,

Right let's be having you. Over the end of the bed. He likes being dominated, as people often do who've never had to raise their voice in their lives to get other people running after them.

Then we went out to dinner, came back, Charles stayed a while, long enough to introduce me to Ross – extraordinary man, rather Chinese-looking, and not just physically, a sense of a very old civilization. I shook his hand and I thought I'm shaking the hand that . . . Well, there *is* the connection with Wilde. And I felt at home in this rather beleaguered little community. Beleaguered, because Ross thinks he's going to be arrested, he thinks the utterly disgusting Pemberton Billing affair has given them *carte blanche* to go ahead and do it. He may be exaggerating the risk, he looks ill, he looks as if he goes to bed and broods, but one or two people there, including Manning, don't seem to rule out an arrest. A comfortable atmosphere in spite of it. Soldiers who aren't militarists, pacifists who aren't prigs, and *talking* to each other. Now *there's* a miracle.

But then – Birtwhistle. He's a don at Cambridge, very clever, apparently. Curiously, he actually prides himself on having a broader grasp of British society than the average person, i.e. he pokes working-class boys' bottoms. Might even be true, I suppose, though the heterosexual equivalent doesn't pride itself on broadening its social experience whenever it nips off for a knee-wobbler in Bethnal Green. Ah, but these are *relationships*, Birtwhistle would say. Did say. Lurve, no less. And yet he spoke of his working-class lover – his WC – in tones of utter contempt. And he didn't succeed in placing me, or not accurately enough. So much for the broader grasp. I played a rather cruel convoluted game with him afterwards. Which satisfied me a great deal at the time, but now I feel contaminated, as I wouldn't have done if I'd kicked him in the balls (which would also have been kinder).

Manning – after we'd had sex – became very strange. Great distances opened up. Partly because he hadn't intended it to happen – or didn't think he had – and partly just because I'm going back and he isn't. Two inches of sheet between us – *miles miles*. I was glad when he went and I'm even more glad he's not here now. Very few pleasures in sex are any match for a narrow bed and cool, clean sheets. (A post-coital reflection if ever I heard one.)

30 August

Collected my coat today. I'm not even going to write down how much it cost, but it's warm and light and it looks good, and I need all of that.

Mooched round the rest of the day doing nothing very much. Dinner at Half Moon Street in my room. Saw Rivers afterwards. Had made up my mind not to ask what he thought about my going back – and specifically not to ask if he thought I was fit – then asked anyway and was predictably irritated by the answer.

I had a very clear perception while we were talking – I suppose because I've been away for a while – that his power over people, the power to heal if you like, springs directly from some sort of wound or deformity in him. He has a lot of strengths, but he isn't working from strength. Difficult to say this without sounding patronizing, which isn't how I feel. In fact for me it's the best thing about him – well the only thing that makes him tolerable, actually – that he *doesn't* sit behind the desk implicitly setting himself up as some sort of standard of mental health. He once said to me half the world's work's done by hopeless neurotics, and I think he had himself in mind. And me.

Got to the station with an hour to spare and Manning showed up. I wished he hadn't but there he was and of course we had one of these awful station conversations. The ripples between those going out and those staying behind are so bloody awful the whole thing's best avoided. However, we got through it, looked at each other through the window with mutual relief and then away we went. Or I went.

Arrived here (Folkestone) in the middle of the night, exhausted. There's something about railway stations, and I've been in a lot of them recently. The goodbyes all get trapped under the roof and suck the oxygen out of the air. No other reason for me to feel like this.

Saturday, 31 August

Woke tired. But got up anyway, not wasting time – 'wasting time', 'killing time' start to be phrases you notice – lying in bed, and sat on the balcony for a while watching the sun come up and decided to do what people always think about doing, and then think again and go back to sleep: I decided to swim before breakfast. So down to the beach. Hovered on the shingle by the waterline, told myself not to be so feeble, etc., and plunged in. Water pearly grey, absolutely bloody freezing, but, after the first shock, total exhilaration. I stood for a while afterwards up to my knees, feeling the surge and suck round my legs, neither in the sea nor on the land. Marvellous. Still the slanting light of early morning. Worm casts on the beach very prominent, the sun casting vast shadows from little things, and I thought of the beach outside Edinburgh where I made love to Sarah for the first time. Went straight back and wrote to her. Then walked through town, giving myself small treats, chocolates, etc. and avoiding other officers.

Saw Hallet with his family, looking quite desperate. All of them, but I meant Hallet. Poor little bugger's had a station goodbye that's lasted for *days*. I waved and passed on.

On board

People playing cards below deck, but there's quite a heave on the sea, and I'd rather be out here watching it. Great bands of pale green in the wake, laced with thick foam, and terns hovering, riding rather – only the most fractional adjustment of their wings needed to keep them motionless. And they come quite close.

Watched the cliffs disappear. Tried to think of something worthy of the occasion and came up with: *The further out from England the nearer is to France*, and then couldn't get rid of the bloody thing, it just ran round and round my head.

Hallet came up and stood a few yards away, not wanting to intrude on what he took to be a fond farewell to the motherland. In the end I gave in, we sat down and talked. Full of idealism. I'd rather have had the Walrus and the Carpenter.

It's very obvious that Hallet's adopted me. Like one of those little pilot fish or the terns for that matter. He thinks because I've been out three times before I know what's going on. Seems a bright enough lad. I wonder how long it'll take him to work out that *nobody* knows what's going on?

Sunday, 1 September

Étaples marginally less brutal than I remember it, though still a squad of men passed me running the gauntlet of the canaries, who yelled abuse in their faces much as they always did. And you think, All right it has to be brutal – think what they're being toughened up *for* – but actually that misses the point. It's the *impersonality* that forms the biggest part of the sheer fucking nastiness of this place. Nobody knows anybody. You marshal men around – they don't know you, don't trust you (why should they?) and you don't invest anything in them.

Same feeling, in a milder form, between the officers. We sleep in dormitories, and it's the same feeling you get on big wards in hospitals – privacy sacrificed without intimacy being gained.

Hallet's in the next bed. He sat on his bed this evening and showed me a photograph of his girl – fiancée, I should say. His parents think he's too young to marry, which he fiercely objects to, pointing out that he's old enough for *this*. Of course I don't think he's old enough for *this* either, but I don't say so. Instead I told him I'd got engaged too and showed him a photograph of Sarah. And then we sat smiling at each other inanely, feeling like complete idiots. Well, I did.

Wednesday, 4 September

Time passes quickly here. Enough to do during the day, and a fair amount of free time. But the atmosphere's awful. The mess has scuffed no-colour lino – the colour of misery, if misery has a colour – and a big round table in the middle, covered with dog-eared copies of *Punch* and *John Bull*, exactly like a dentist's waiting-room. The same pervasive fear. The same reluctance to waste time on people you're probably never going to see again anyway.

I get out as often as I can. Walked miles today, great windswept sandy foothills, and a long line of stunted pines all leaning away from the sea.

Saturday, 7 September

Posted to the 2nd Manchesters. We leave tomorrow.

It's evening now, and everybody's scribbling away, telling people the news, or as much of the news as we're allowed to tell them. I look up and down the dormitory and there's hardly a sound except for pages being turned, and here and there a pen scratching. It's like this every evening. And not just letters either. Diaries. Poems. At least two would-be poets in this hut alone.

Why? you have to ask yourself. I think it's a way of claiming immunity. First-person narrators can't die, so as long as we keep telling the story of our own lives we're safe. Ha bloody fucking Ha.

EIGHT

Rivers turned to watch the sun swelling and reddening as it sank, a brutal, bloody disc, scored by steeples and factory chimneys, obscured by a haze of drifting brown and yellow smoke.

He'd come out to walk on Hampstead Heath because he was feeling ill, and needed to clear his head before settling down to an evening's work, but it wasn't helping. With every step he felt worse, muscles aching, throat sore, eyes stinging, skin clammy. By the time he got back to his lodgings, he'd decided to miss dinner and go straight to bed. He knocked on the door of Mrs Irving's private apartments, told her he wasn't feeling well and wouldn't be in to dinner, and glimpsed through the open door the portrait of her dead son that hung above the mantelpiece, with flowers beneath it and candlesticks on either side.

Going slowly upstairs, pausing frequently to lean on the banister, Rivers thought about what he'd just seen: the portrait, the flowers. A shrine. Not fundamentally different from the skull houses of Pa Na Gundu where he'd gone with Njiru. The same human impulse at work. Difficult to know what to make of these flashes of cross-cultural recognition. From a strictly professional point of view, they were almost meaningless, but then one didn't have such experiences as a disembodied anthropological intelligence, but as a man, and as a man one had to make some kind of sense of them.

Once in bed he started to shiver. The sheets felt cold against his hot legs. He slept and dreamt of the croquet lawn at Knowles Bank, his mother in a long white dress coming out to call the children in, the sun setting over the wood casting very long, fine shadows across the lawn. The shadows of the hoops were particularly long and fearful. He'd been awake for several minutes before he realized he was trying to remember the rules of mathematical croquet, as devised by Dodgson, and actually feeling *distressed* because he couldn't remember them. Then he realized that although he was now fully awake he could still see the lawn, which meant his temperature was very high. Always, in a high fever, his visual memory returned, giving him a secret, obscurely shameful pleasure in being ill. He wouldn't sleep again – he was far too hot – so he simply lay and let his newly opened mind's eye roam.

On the *Southern Cross*, on the voyage to Eddystone, he'd stood on deck, watching the pale green wake furrow the dark sea, reluctant to exchange the slight breeze for the stuffy heat below deck.

At one of the stops a group of natives got on, the men wearing cast-off European suits, the women floral-print dresses. A few of the women had naked breasts, but most were obviously missionized. A pathetic little remnant they looked, squatting there, part of the small army of uprooted natives who drifted from one island to the next, one mission station to the next, and belonged nowhere. At first sight all mission stations seemed to be surrounded by converts, and the uninitiated always assumed these were converts from *that* island. Only later did one become aware of this uprooted population, travelling from one station to the next, most of them from islands where the impact of western culture had been particularly devastating.

He squatted down beside them, and, as he expected, found enough knowledge of pidgin to make conversation possible. He'd devised a questionnaire that he used on occasions when it was necessary to extract the maximum amount of information quickly. The first question was always: Suppose you were lucky enough to find a guinea, with whom would you share it? This produced a list of names, names which he would then ask them to translate into kinship terms. And from there one could move to virtually any aspect of their society.

When he sensed they were getting tired he paid them their tobacco sticks and stood up to go, but then one of the women caught his arm and pulled him down again. Poking him playfully in the chest, she retrieved two words of English from her small store: 'Your turn.'

The questions were posed again and in the same order. When he told them that, since he was unmarried and had no children, he would not necessarily feel obliged to share his guinea with anybody, they at first refused to believe him. Had he no parents living? Yes, a father. Brothers and sisters? One brother, two sisters. Same mother, same father? Yes. But he would not *automatically* share the guinea with them, though he might *choose* to do so.

The woman who'd pulled his arm looked amused at first, then, when she was sure she'd understood, horrified. And so it went on. Because the questions were very carefully chosen, they gradually formed an impression – and not a vague impression either, in some respects quite precise – of the life of a bachelor don in a Cambridge college. Hilarity was the main response. And if the questions had led on to more intimate territory? If he'd been able, or willing, to lay before them the whole constricting business of trying to fit into society, of living under and around and outside the law, what would have been their reaction then? Laughter. They'd have gone on laughing. They would not have known how to pity him. He looked up, at the blue, empty sky, and realized that their view of *his* society was neither more nor less valid than his of theirs. No bearded elderly white man looked down on them, endorsing one set of values and condemning the other. And with that realization, the whole frame of social and moral rules that keeps individuals imprisoned – and sane – collapsed, and for a moment he was in the same position as these drifting, dispossessed people. A condition of absolute free-fall.

Then, next day, after a restless night, he and Hocart transferred to a tramp steamer for the last stage of the journey, and there he met the logical end product of the process of free-fall – the splat on the pavement, as it were – Brennan.

Smells of engine oil and copra, of sweaty human beings sleeping too close together in the little covered cabin on deck. Above their heads, offering no clear reference point to northern eyes, foreign constellations wheeled and turned.

Brennan slept opposite, his profile, under a fringe of greying curls, like that of a Roman emperor's favourite run to seed. He snored, gargled, stopped breathing, gargled again, muttered a protest as if he thought somebody else had woken him, returned to sleep. On the other side of the cabin was Father Michael, trailing behind him the atmosphere of the theological college he'd not long left behind – cups of cocoa and late-night discussions on chastity in other people's bedrooms. Then Hocart, looking much younger than twenty-five, his upper lip pouting on every breath.

Rivers supposed he must have slept eventually, though it seemed no time at all before they were stretching and stumbling out on deck.

The deckhands, emerging from their airless hellhole next to the engine, swabbed passengers down along with the deck. They finished off with a bucket of cold water thrown full into the face so that one was left gasping and blinded. Brennan stood, eyes closed, one hand resting between his plump breasts, a hirsute Aphrodite, water dripping from his nose, his foreskin, the hairs on his wrinkled and baggy scrotum. It was impossible to dislike somebody who brought such enormous zest to the minute-by-minute business of living.

As the sun rose, beating down on to the steaming deck, they began the day-long search for patches of shade. Father Michael and Hocart came close to quarrelling about the record of missionaries in the islands. Hocart was the product of a Victorian vicarage, and something of a rebel. Michael obviously thought he'd fallen among atheists, or worse. Brennan listened to the argument, scratched his neck, then gathered phlegm in his throat, a rich, bubbling sound – his zest for life became a bit much at times – and spat it on the deck, where he inspected it carefully, and Rivers, cursing his medical training, found himself inspecting it too. 'I knew a missionary once,' Brennan said, with a look of placid, lazy malice. 'Didn't speak a word of the language – just sets up shop – Jesus saves. And then he starts to get worried 'cause they all come flocking round but he can't get the buggers to kneel down. So down on his knees he goes. "What's the word for this?" Well *you* know and *I* know,' Brennan said, turning to Rivers, 'there's only one thing *they* do kneeling down. Come next Sunday, bloody great congregation, up he stands – raises his arms.' He looked at Michael and, in an amazingly pure counter-tenor, sang, 'Let us fuck.'

A bray of laughter from the open door of the engine-room where the skipper stood, wiping his fingers on an oily rag.

'I wish you'd leave Michael alone,' Rivers said to Hocart after the others had gone below deck.

'Why? He's an arrogant little –'

'He's a baby.'

But Hocart, a baby himself, saw no need for mercy.

After dark, packed round the rickety table on which they ate their dinner, there was no escaping each other's company. Elbows jarred, knees joggled, the leather seats tormented patches of prickly heat. Much covert and not so covert scratching of backsides went on. The skipper joined them for the meal, but contributed little to the conversation, preferring to be amused in silence. His trade had made him a connoisseur of social discomfort.

Brennan, sensing that Rivers liked him, embarked on what threatened to become his life story, interspersed with swigs of whisky and great breathy revelations of dental decay. He showed Rivers a photograph of his three naked brown babies tumbling over each other in the dust. Behind them, face, neck and breasts covered in tattoos, stood a young girl. 'She must be from Lepers Island,' Rivers said.

Brennan took the photograph back and stared at it. 'Yeh, that's right. *Bitch.*'

He seemed about to say more. Rivers said quickly, 'I didn't realize you'd been in the New Hebrides.'

'Started there.'

He'd started as a 'blackbirder', as so many of the older traders had, kidnapping natives to work on the Queensland plantations, and he was frank about his methods too. Make friends with them, invite them on board ship, get them drunk and Bob's your uncle. By the time they come round they're out at sea and there's bugger all they can do about it. Used to give the girls a bit of a run round the deck, mind. We-ll why not, they're all gunna get their arses fucked off when they get to the plantations anyway. 'Do you know,' he went on, leaning across the table in search of somebody to shock, and fixing on Michael, though Hocart's expression might have made him the more obvious choice, 'you can buy a woman – *white*, mind – for forty quid in Sydney?'

'I'd've thought forty quid was a bit steep,' Hocart said.

'*Buy*, man, I'm not talking about fucking rent.'

'So why didn't you?'

'Nah,' Brennan said morosely, swishing whisky round his glass. 'Years on their backs.' He turned to Rivers. 'Half way through the honeymoon you'd be pissing hedgehogs backwards. *He* knows what I mean,' he said, jerking his thumb at Rivers.

'We all know what you mean,' Hocart said.

The skipper leant forward, smiling a positively old-maidish smile. 'How about a nice game of cards?'

And then there was no further talk, only the creaking of the spirit-lamp above their heads, and the plump slap of cards on the table. Rivers, amused, watched Hocart slowly realize that when confronted by a dwindling stock of coins, Father Michael cheated and Brennan didn't.

Next morning – a small triumph for Melanesia – Father Michael, who'd hitherto crouched over a bucket to wash, stripped off with the rest of them, his white arum lily of a body with its improbable stamen looking almost shocking beside Brennan's.

The conversation that morning meandered on amicably enough, as they leaned together, sweating, in their patches of shade, until a smudge of blue-green on the horizon restored them to separateness.

By late afternoon they'd moored by a rotting landing stage on Eddystone, and clambered ashore to supervise the unloading of their stores. Rivers was used to missionized islands where canoes paddled out to meet the incoming steamer, brown faces, white eyes, flashing smiles, while others gathered at the landing stage, ready to carry bags up to the mission station for a few sticks of tobacco or even sheer Christian goodwill. A cheerful picture, as long as you didn't notice the rows and rows of crosses in the mission graveyard, men and women in the prime of life dead of the diseases of the English nursery: whooping cough, measles, diphtheria, chicken pox, scarlet fever – all were fatal here. And the mission boat carried them from island to island, station to station, remorselessly, year after year.

Instead of that – nothing. Nobody appeared. Rivers and Hocart waved till the steamer dwindled to a point on the glittering water, then lugged the tent and enough food for the night up to a small clearing a hundred yards or so above the beach. Spread out below them was the Bay of Narovo. The village, whose huts they could just see between the trees, was also called Narovo.

'Aren't we a bit close?' Hocart asked.

'We don't want to be *too* far away. If we're isolated we'll be frightening. The wicked witch lives in the *wood*, remember.'

'What do you suppose they'll do?'

Rivers shrugged. 'They'll be along.'

By the time they'd erected the tent the swift tropical darkness was falling. After sunset the island breathed for a moment in silence; from the bush arose the buzz of different insects, the cries of different birds. Rivers was intensely aware of the fragility of the small lighted area round the tent. He kept peering into the trees and thought he saw dark shapes flitting between the trunks, but still nobody appeared.

After a meal of tinned meat and turnipy pineapple, Hocart said he would lie down. He looked utterly exhausted, and Rivers suspected he might be running a slight fever. Shrouded in his mosquito net, Hocart talked for a while, then switched off his torch and turned over to sleep.

Rivers sat at a table immediately outside the tent, trying to mend the oil-lamp which was smoking badly. A small figure alone in the clearing, in a storm of pale wings, for every moth in the bush appeared and fluttered round the light. Now and then one succeeded in finding a way in, and there was a quick sizzle, a flare, more smoke. Rivers shook out the charred corpse and started again. An oddly nerve-racking business, this. Working so close to the light, he was almost blinded and could see virtually nothing even when he raised his head. He was aware of the thick darkness of the bush around him, but more as a pressure on his mind than through his senses. Once he stopped, thinking he heard a flute being played in the village. He sniffed the oil on his fingers, wiped his chin on the back of his hand, and sat back for a rest, his retinas aching as they do after an optician has shone his torch on to them. He took his glasses off and wiped them on his shirt. When he put them on again he saw a figure had come out from among the trees, and was standing on the edge of the clearing. A man in early middle age, white lime streaks in his hair, around the eye sockets, and along the cheek and jaw-bones, so that it seemed – until he caught the glint of eye white – that he was looking at a skull. He sat absolutely still, as the man came towards him. Alone, or apparently alone. He indicated the other chair, thinking it might be refused, but his visitor sat down, inclined his head slightly, and smiled.

Rivers pointed to himself and said his name.

A thin brown hand raised to his shell necklace. 'Njiru.'

They stared at each other. Rivers thought he ought to offer food, but the only food easily available was the remains of the pineapple, and he was chary of breaking off the encounter by going into the tent to look for it.

Njiru was deformed. Without the curvature of the spine he would have been a tall man – by Melanesian standards very tall – and he carried himself with obvious authority. In addition to the shell necklace he wore ear-rings, arm rings and bracelets all made of shells, and somehow it was immediately apparent that these ornaments had great value. His earlobes, elongated by the constant wearing of heavy shells, almost brushed his shoulders when he moved. The eyes were remarkable: hooded, piercing, intelligent, shrewd. Wary.

They went on staring at each other, reluctant to start exploring their shared resource of pidgin, aware, perhaps, even in these first moments, of how defective an instrument it would be for what they needed to say to each other.

Suddenly Njiru pointed to the lamp. 'Baggerup.'

Rivers was so surprised he laughed out loud. '*No*, no baggerup. I mend.'

Njiru was the eldest son of Rembo, the chief who controlled the most important cults on the island. Because of his deformity, he'd never been able to compete with other young men, in canoeing, fishing, building or war. By way of compensation, he'd devoted himself to thought and learning, and, in particular, to the art of healing. His abilities would have made him remarkable in any society. On Eddystone, his power rested primarily on the number of spirits he controlled. The people made no distinction between knowledge and power, either in their own language or in pidgin. 'Njiru knows Mateana' meant Njiru had the power to cure the diseases caused by Mateana. Similarly, Rivers was told within a few days of arriving on the island that Njiru 'knew' Ave. Without in the least understanding the significance of what he'd been told, he repeated it to Njiru. 'Kundaite he say you know Ave.'

A snort of derision. 'Kundaite he speak *gammon*.'

He was by far the best interpreter and – when he chose – the most reliable informant, capable of making rigorous distinctions between what he knew and what he merely supposed, between evidence and hypothesis. But he did not generally choose to share information. If knowledge was power, then Njiru kept a firm grasp on his. Indeed, at first he would do no more than translate passively what others said. In particular, he acted as interpreter between Rivers and Rinambesi.

Rinambesi was the oldest man on the island, the liveliest, and, after Njiru, the most vigorous. He seemed immune to the apathy and depression that many of the younger islanders seemed to feel, perhaps because he lived so much in the glories of the past. Like very old people the world over, he was hazy about yesterday's events, but vividly remembered the triumphs of his youth. He'd been a great head-hunter once, ferocious enough to have secured the rare privilege of a second wife. His memory for the genealogies of the islanders was phenomenal, and this was chiefly what brought Rivers to him. And yet, time and time again, the flow of information faltered, though it was not immediately obvious why.

Sexual intercourse between unmarried young people was very free, though 'free' was perhaps the wrong word, since every act had to be preceded by a payment of shells by the young man to the girl's parents. After marriage complete fidelity was required, and one expression of this was that one must never utter the name of an ex-lover.

All the women's names in Rinambesi's generation had to be left blank. Looking at the row of cards in front of him, Rivers turned to Njiru. 'This fellow make fuck-fuck *all* women?'

A gleam of amusement. 'Yes.'

Rivers threw the pencil down. Rinambesi, grinning toothlessly, was making a deeply unsuccessful attempt to look modest. Rivers started to laugh and after a moment Njiru joined in, a curious moment of kinship across the gulf of culture.

A thread-like wail from the baby Njiru held in his hands, one palm cradling the head, the other the buttocks, a morsel of black-eyed misery squirming in between.

Her name was Kwini and her mother was dead. Worse than that, she'd died in childbirth, which made her an evil spirit, likely to attempt to reclaim her child. The body had been dumped at sea, a bundle of rags strapped between the breasts to fool the mother into thinking she had her baby with her, but still . . . Kwini's failure to thrive was attributed to her mother's attempts to get her back.

She certainly *wasn't* thriving: skin hung in loose folds from her thighs. Rivers looked round the circle at her grandmother's wrinkled dugs, the flat chest of her nine-year-old sister, the highly developed pectoral muscles of her father. He asked what she was being fed on. Mashed-up yams softened by spit was the answer. The tiny hands clawed the air as if she would wring life out of it.

Njiru passed the leaves he was holding several times between his legs and then, stretching to his full height, attached them to the rafters at the gable end, where the scare ghost shivered in the draught. 'Come down and depart, you ghost, her mother; do not haunt this child and let her live.'

'*Will* she live?' Rivers asked.

He had his own opinion, but wanted to know what Njiru would say. Njiru spread his hands.

On their way back to Narovo, Rivers questioned him about the ghosts of women who died in childbirth. This was not a rare form of death, since the custom was for women to give birth alone, and there was no tradition of midwifery. Such ghosts could not be named, he already knew that. In the genealogies they were referred to as evil spirits. It had startled him at first to be told quite casually that such and such a man had married 'an evil spirit'.

They were called *tomate pa na savo* – the ghosts of the confining house – Njiru explained, and they were dreaded, since their chief aim was to ensure that as many other women as possible should die in the same way.

One ghost in particular inspired dread: Ange Mate. She was more powerful, more vengeful than any other ghost of the confining house. Rivers had been taken to see Ange Mate's well, a hole in the ground which had once been a living spring, now choked with coconut husks. Still, he sensed there was something more that Njiru was reluctant to tell him. 'What does she *do*?' he wanted to know. It puzzled him that the men were obviously frightened of her, if it were true that the *tomate pa na savo* selected women as their victims.

Reluctantly, Njiru said she lay in wait for men, particularly for men who fell asleep on the beach at Pa Njale. 'But what does she do?' A ripple of amusement among Njiru's retinue, a strange response in view of the obvious terror she inspired. Then he guessed. When Ange Mate came upon a man sleeping she forced him to have sex with her. 'Is he good-fellow after?' Rivers asked.

No, seemed to be the answer, he suffered from a long list of complaints, not the least of which was a disappearing penis. Rivers would have liked to ask about the psychological effects, but that was almost impossible. The language of introspection was simply not available.

By the time they reached Narovo, the sun was low in the sky. Rivers went down to the beach, following the narrow bush path that petered out into fine white sand. Hocart's head was a dark sleek ball, far out, but then he saw Rivers, waved and shouted.

Slowly Rivers waded out, looking down, rather liking the dislocation the refraction of the light produced, the misalignment of knees and feet. As usual he was joined by a shoal of little darting black fish who piloted him out into deeper waters – always a moment of absolute magic. Behind him, the bluish shadows of rocks crept over the white sand.

After their swim they lay in the shallows, talking over the events of the day. In the rough division of labour they'd mapped out between them, death, funerary rites and skull houses belonged to Hocart, ghosts, sex, marriage and kinship to Rivers, but it had already become clear that no division really made sense. Each of them was constantly acquiring information relating to one of the other's specialities.

Hocart, though, was in a mood to tease. 'Why've I got death when you've got sex?' he wanted to know. 'Ghosts and sex don't go together. Now ghosts and *death* . . .'

'All right, you can have ghosts.'

'*No* . . .' Hocart began, and then laughed.

Not true anyway, Rivers thought. On Eddystone ghosts and sex *did* go together, or so at least it must seem to men who fell asleep on the beach at Pa Njale and woke between the ravening thighs of Ange Mate.

They lay in silence, almost too lazy to speak, as the shadows lengthened and the sun began its precipitate descent. Nightfall on Eddystone was abrupt, as if some positive force of darkness in the waters of the bay had risen up and swallowed the sun. At last, driven back to shore by the cooling water, they snatched up their clothes and ran, laughing, back to the tent.

Mbuko was dying of a disease caused by the spirits of Kita, and had no more than a few hours to live.

Kita, Njiru explained, causes a man to waste away 'till he too small all bone he got no meat'. Certainly Mbuko could not have been more emaciated. He looked more like an anatomical drawing than a man, except for the persistent flutter of his heart under the stretched skin. He lay on the raised wooden platform that was used for sleeping, though nobody else now slept in the hut. Njiru said they were afraid. Outside, bright sunshine, people coming and going. Now and then a neighbour would look in to see if he were still alive. 'Soon,' the people sitting round would say, indifferently, shaking their heads. Some were obviously amused or repelled by his plight. '*Rakiana*' was the word one heard over and over again. *Rakiana*. Thin.

Even Njiru who, within the framework of his culture, was a compassionate man (and we can none of us claim more, Rivers thought), seemed to feel, not indifference or contempt exactly, but that Mbuko had become merely a problem to be solved. Njiru looked across the barely breathing heap of bones at Rivers and said, '*Mate*.'

'*Mate*' in all the dictionaries was translated as 'dead'.

'No *mate*,' Rivers said, breathing deeply and pointing to Mbuko's chest.

There and then, across the dying man, he received a tutorial, not unlike those he remembered from his student days in Bart's. *Mate* did not mean dead, it designated a state of which death was the appropriate outcome. Mbuko was *mate* because he was critically ill. Rinambesi, though quite disgustingly healthy, still with a keen eye for the girls, was also *mate* because he'd lived to an age when if he wasn't dead he damn well ought to be. The term for actual death, the moment when the *sagena* – here Njiru breathed in, slapping his belly in the region of the diaphragm – the 'something he stop long belly' departed, was *mate ndapu*. In pidgin, 'die finish'. 'Was the *sagena* the same as the soul?' Rivers wanted to know. 'Of course it wasn't,' Njiru snapped, nostrils flaring with impatience. Oh God, it was Bart's all over again. *Heaven help the unsuspecting public when we let you loose on them.* The problem with Mbuko, Njiru pressed on, as with all those who fell into the power of Kita, was that he couldn't die. He seemed to be making a very creditable stab at it, Rivers thought rebelliously. Kita could 'make him small', but not kill him. '*Kita pausia,*' Njiru said, stroking Mbuko. 'Kita loves him?' Rivers suggested. No, Njiru would know the word. Kita was nursing him.

Njiru hung malanjari leaves from the gable end of the hut where the scare ghost shivered in the draught, and began chanting the prayer of exorcism. His shadow came and went across the dying man's face. At one point Rivers got cramp in his legs and tried to stand up, but the people on either side of him pulled him down. He must not walk under the malanjari leaves, they said, or he would waste away and become like Mbuko.

Hocart came into the hut, edging round the walls, keeping well clear of the malanjari leaves, until he reached Rivers. Now that all eyes were focused on Njiru, Rivers could take Mbuko's pulse. He shook his head. 'Not long.'

Scattered all round were bits of calico and bark cloth streaked with mucus, with here and there a great splash of red where Mbuko had haemorrhaged. Now gobs of phlegm rose into his mouth and he lacked the strength even to spit them out. Rivers found a fresh piece of cloth, moistened it with his own saliva, and cleaned the dying man's mouth. His tongue came out and flicked across his dry lips. Then a rattle in the throat, a lift and flare of the rib-cage, and it was over. One of the women wailed briefly, but the wail faltered into silence, and she put a hand over her mouth as if embarrassed.

Rivers automatically reached out to close the eyes, then stopped himself. Mbuko's body was bound into a sitting position by bands of calico passed round his neck and under his knees. He was tied to a pole, and two men carried him out into the open air. Rivers and Hocart followed the little group down the path to the beach.

The body was propped up, still in a sitting position, in the stern of a canoe, his shield and axe were placed beside him, and he was quickly paddled out to sea. Rivers waited until the canoe was a shadow on the glittering waters of the bay, then went back to the hut and gathered together the stained cloths, which he buried at a safe distance from the village. As he scraped dry earth over the heap of rags, he felt an intense craving to scrub his arms up to the elbow in boiled water. That would have to wait till he got back to the tent. For the moment he contented himself with wiping his palms several times hard on the seat of his trousers.

He went back to the beach, where a disgruntled Hocart lingered by the waterline. They had both been hoping that this death would shed light on the cult of the skull. Instead . . .

'They don't keep the skull,' Hocart said.

As they watched, the paddlers in the canoe tipped the corpse unceremoniously over the side, where it sank beneath the water with scarcely a splash.

Rivers shook his head. 'I'm afraid what we need is a proper death.'

NINE

Wyatt had embarked on some interminable anecdote about a brothel he'd been to in which there was a whore so grotesquely fat you got your money back if you succeeded in fucking her.

Prior rested his cheek on the cold glass of the train window, glancing sidelong at the doubled reflection of cheekbone and eye, and then deeper into the shadowy compartment with its transparent occupants laughing and gesturing, floating shapes on the rain-flawed pane.

A roar of laughter as the story climaxed. Gregg, happily married with a small daughter, smiled tolerantly. Hallet uneasily joined in. One young lad brayed so loudly his virginity became painfully apparent to everybody but himself. Only Owen made no attempt to disguise his disgust, but then he hated 'the commercials', as he called them.

They'd been on the train for three hours, jammed together on slatted wooden seats, stale sweat in armpits, groin and feet, a smoky smell of urine where some half-baked idiot had pissed into the wind.

Five minutes later the train slipped into the dark station, a few discreet naphtha flares the only light.

Prior walked along to the trucks, where the men were stirring. Strange faces peered blearily up at him as he swept the torch across them, shading the beam in his cupped hand, so that he saw them – not figuratively but quite literally – in a glow of blood. They were not his, or anybody's, men, just an anonymous draft that he'd shepherded a stage further to their destination.

This section of the train had stopped well short of the platform, and there was a big drop from the truck. Repeated crunches of gravel under boots as men, still dazed from sleep, grappled with the shock of rain and windswept darkness. Marshalled together, they half stumbled, half marched alongside the train, on to the platform and through into the station yard where, after an interminable wait, guides finally appeared, their wet capes reflecting a fish gleam at the sky, as they gesticulated and gabbled, directing units to their billets.

Prior saw his draft settled in a church hall, said goodbye and wished them luck. Their faces turned towards him registered nothing, subdued to the impersonality of the process that had them in its grip.

Then he was free. Felt it too, following the guide through unlit streets, past that sandbagged witch's tit of a cathedral, along the canal accompanied in the water by a doddering old crone of a moon.

The night, the silent guide, the effort of not slipping on broken pavements, sharpened his senses. An overhanging branch of laburnum flung a scattering of cold raindrops into his eyes and he was startled by the intensity of his joy. A joy perhaps not unconnected with the ruinous appearance of these houses. Solid bourgeois houses they must have been in peacetime, the homes of men making their way in the world, men who'd been sure that certain things would never change, and where were they now? Every house in the road was damaged, some ruined. The ruins stood out starkly, black jagged edges in the white gulf of moonlight.

'Here you are, sir.'

A gate hanging from its hinges, roses massed round a broken pergola, white ruffled blooms with a heavy scent, unpruned, twisting round each other for support. Beyond, paths and terraces overgrown with weeds. Lace curtains hanging limp behind cracked or shattered glass; on the first floor the one window still unbroken briefly held the moon.

The guide preceded him up the path. No lock on the door, black and white tiles in the hall – a sudden sharp memory of Craiglockhart – and then a glimmer of light at the top of the stairs and Hallet appeared, holding a candle. 'Come on up. Mind that stair.'

Hallet had got his sleeping-bag out and arranged his belongings carefully in a corner of what must once have been the master bedroom. His fiancée's photograph stood on a chair.

'Potts and Owen are upstairs.'

Prior went to the window and looked out at the houses opposite, fingering the lace curtains that were stiff with dried rain and dirt. 'This is all right, isn't it?' he said suddenly, turning into the room.

They grinned at each other.

'Bathroom's just opposite,' Hallet said, pointing it out like a careful host.

'You mean it works?'

'Well, the bucket works.'

Prior sat down abruptly on the floor and yawned. He was too tired to care where he was. They lit cigarettes and shared a bar of chocolate, Prior leaning against the wall, Hallet sitting cross-legged on his sleeping-bag, both of them staring round like big-eyed children, struggling to take in the strangeness.

It'll wear off, Prior thought, lighting a candle and venturing across the landing to find a room of his own. It'll all seem normal in the morning.

But it didn't. Prior woke early, and lay lazily watching the shadows of leaves on a wall that the rising sun had turned from white to gold. He was just turning over to go back to sleep, when something black flickered across the room. He waited, and saw a swallow lift and loop through the open window and out into the dazzling air.

On that first morning he looked out on to a green jungle of garden, sun-baked, humming with insects, the once formal flower-beds transformed into brambly tunnels in which hidden life rustled and burrowed. He rested his arms on the window-sill and peered out, cautiously, through the jagged edges of glass, at Owen and Potts, who were carrying a table from one of the houses across the road. He shouted down to them, as they paused for breath, and they waved back.

He would have said that the war could not surprise him, that somewhere on the Somme he had mislaid the capacity to be surprised, but the next few days were a constant succession of surprises.

They had nothing to do. They were responsible for no one. The war had forgotten them.

There were only two items of furniture that went with the house. One was a vast carved oak sideboard that must surely have been built in the dining-room, for it could never have been brought in through the door; the other was a child's painted rocking-horse on the top floor of the house, in a room with bars at the window. Everything else they found for themselves. Prior moved in and out of the ruined houses, taking whatever caught his eye, and the houses, cool and dark in the midday heat, received him placidly. He brought his trophies home and arranged them carefully in his room, or in the dining-room they all shared.

In the evenings he and Hallet, Owen and Potts lit candles, sitting around the table that was Owen's chief find, and with the tall windows, the elaborately moulded ceilings, the bowls of roses and the wine created a fragile civilization, a fellowship on the brink of disaster.

And then ruined it by arguing about the war. Or Potts and Hallet argued. Potts had been a science student at Manchester University, bright, articulate, cynical in the thorough-going way of those who have not so far encountered much to be cynical about. The war, he insisted loudly, flushed with wine, was feathering the nests of profiteers. It was being fought to safeguard access to the oil-wells of Mesopotamia. It had nothing, absolutely *nothing*, to do with Belgian neutrality, the rights of small nations or anything like that. And if Hallet thought it had, then Hallet was a naïve idiot. Hallet came from an old army family and had been well and expensively educated to think as little as possible; confronted by Potts, he floundered, but then quickly began to formulate beliefs that he had hitherto assumed everybody shared.

Prior and Owen exchanged secretive smiles, though neither probably could have said of what the secret consisted. Owen was playing with the fallen petals of roses he'd picked that afternoon. Pink, yellow, white roses, but no red roses, Prior saw.

'What do *you* think?' Potts asked, irritated by Prior's silence.

'What do I think? I think what you're saying is basically a conspiracy theory, and like all conspiracy theories it's optimistic. What you're saying is, OK the war isn't being fought for the reasons we're told, but it *is* being fought for a reason. It's not benefiting the people it's supposed to be benefiting, but it *is* benefiting somebody. And I don't believe that, you see. I think things are actually much worse than you think because there isn't any kind of rational justification left. It's become a self-perpetuating system. Nobody benefits. Nobody's in control. Nobody knows how to stop.'

Hallet looked from one to the other. 'Look, all this just isn't *true*. You're – no, not you – *people* are letting themselves get demoralized because they're having to pay a higher price than they thought they were going to have to pay. But it doesn't alter the basic facts. We *are* fighting for the legitimate interests of our own country. We *are* fighting in defence of Belgian neutrality. We *are* fighting for French independence. *We* aren't in Germany. They *are* in France.' He looked round the table and, like a little boy, said pleadingly, 'This is still a just war.'

'You say we kill the Beast,' Owen said slowly. 'I say we fight because men lost their bearings in the night.' He smiled at their expressions, and stood up. 'Shall we open another bottle?'

Alone that night, the smell of snuffed-out candle lingering on the air, Prior remembered the bowl of pink and gold and white roses, but did not bother to recall Potts's and Hallet's arguments. This house they shared was so strange in terms of what the war had hitherto meant that he wanted to fix the particular sights and sounds and smells in his mind. He felt enchanted, cocooned from anything that could possibly cause pain, though even as the thought formed, a trickle of plaster leaked from the ceiling of the back bedroom where a shell had struck, the house bleeding quietly from its unstaunchable wound.

In the mornings he went into town, wandering round the stalls that had been set up in front of the cathedral to sell 'souvenirs'. So many souvenirs were to be found in the rubble of the bombed city that trade was not brisk. Prior saw nothing that he wanted to buy, and anyway he had a shelf of souvenirs at home, mainly collected on his first time in France. He'd thought of them often at Craiglockhart as Rivers probed his mind for buried memories of his last few weeks in France. Souvenirs, my God. When the mind will happily wipe itself clean in the effort to forget.

On the way home he saw Owen and Potts ahead of him, and hurried to catch them up. Owen had found a child's lace-trimmed surplice in the rubble near the cathedral and wore it as a scarf, the cloth startlingly white against his sunburnt neck. Potts hugged a toby-jug to his chest, stoutly refusing to admit it was hideous. They turned off the road and cut through the back gardens, entering a world that nobody would have guessed at, from the comparative normality of the road.

A labyrinth of green pathways led from garden to garden, and they slipped from one to another, over broken walls or through splintered fences, skirting bramble-filled craters, brushing down paths overgrown with weeds, with flowers that had seeded themselves and become rank, with overgrown roses that snagged their sleeves and pulled them back. Snails crunched under their boots, nettles stung their hands, cuckoo spit flecked a bare neck, but the secret path wound on. Hundreds of men, billeted as they were in these ruined houses, had broken down every wall, every fence, forced a passage through all the hedges, so that they could slip unimpeded from one patch of ground to the next. The war, fought and refought over strips of muddy earth, paradoxically gave them the freedom of animals to pass from territory to territory, unobserved. And something of an animal's alertness too, for just as Owen pushed aside an elderberry branch at the entrance to their own garden, his ears caught a slight sound, and he held up his hand.

Hallet was in the garden, undressing. Dappled light played across his body, lending it the illusion of fragility, the greenish tinge of ill-health, though he was as hard and sun-tanned as the rest of them. As they watched, not calling out a greeting as by now they should have done, he stepped out of his drawers and out of time, standing by the pool edge, thin, pale, his body where the uniform had hidden it starkly white. Sharp collar-bones, bluish shadows underneath. He was going to lie down in the overgrown goldfish pool with its white lilies and golden insects fumbling the pale flowers. His toes curled round the mossy edge as he gingerly lowered himself, gasping as the water hit his balls.

They strolled across the tall grass towards him and stood looking down. Legs bloated-looking under water, silver bubbles trapped in his hair, cock slumped on his thigh like a seal hauled out on to the rocks. He looked up at them lazily, fingers straying through his bush, freeing the bubbles.

'Enjoying yourself?' Prior asked, nodding at the hand.

Hallet laughed, shielding his eyes with his other hand, but didn't move.

'I'd be careful if I were you,' Owen said, in a tight voice. 'I expect those fish are ravenous.'

And not just the fish, Prior thought.

'Anybody want some wine?' Potts asked, going into the house.

They drank it on the terrace, Hallet lying in the pond, till it grew too cold.

'You know they might leave us here,' Owen said, squinting up into the sun.

'Shut up!' Potts said.

Everybody touched wood, crossed fingers, groped for lucky charms: all the small, protective devices of men who have no control over their own fate. No use, Prior thought. Somewhere, outside the range of human hearing, and yet heard by all of them, a clock had begun to tick.

*

11 September 1918

I don't think it helps Owen that I'm here. And it certainly doesn't help *me* that he's here. We're both walking a tightrope and the last thing either of us wants or needs is to be watched by somebody who knows the full terror of the fall.

At Craiglockhart we avoided each other. It was easy to do that there, in spite of the overcrowding. The labyrinth of corridors, so many turnings, so many alternative routes, you need never meet anybody you didn't want to meet except, now and then, in Rivers's room or Brock's, yourself.

Two incidents this week. We were all in town together and we saw wounded being rushed through the streets – some of them quite bad. Hallet and Potts stared at them, and you could see them thinking, That could be me, in a few days or weeks. Looking at the bandages, trying to imagine what was underneath. Trying not to imagine. Fear: rational, proportionate, *appropriate* fear. And I glanced at Owen and he was indifferent. As I was. I don't mean unsympathetic, *necessarily*. (Though it's amazing what you leave behind when the pack's heavy.)

The other was at supper last night. Hallet was cockahoop because he'd found some flypaper on one of those stalls in the cathedral square. Ever since we arrived we've been plagued by enormous wasps – Owen thinks they're hornets – and by flies, great, buzzing, drunk, heavy, angry, dying bluebottles. And Hallet had solved it all. There was this flypaper buzzing above our heads, revolving first one way, then the other, with its cargo of dead and dying. The sound of summer on the Somme.

I stuck it as long as I could, then climbed up on to the table and took it down, carried it right to the end of the garden and threw it away as far as I could. A pathetic effort – it described a shallow arc and fluttered to the ground. Hallet was quite seriously offended, and of course completely bewildered.

'Don't blame *me* if you all get tummy upsets,' he said.

Owen started to laugh, and I joined in, and neither of us could stop. Hallet and Potts looked from one to the other, grinning like embarrassed dogs. They obviously thought we'd cracked. The trouble is neither of us can be sure they aren't right. When I noticed the absence of red roses, I looked at Owen and saw him noticing that I'd noticed. It's no use.

★

My servant, Longstaffe

I chose him at bayonet practice. He was running in with blood-curdling yells, stabbing, twisting, withdrawing, running on. I thought, My God, *textbook*. Nothing of the sort – I've realized since that what he was actually doing was *once-moreing* unto the breach at Agincourt.

I had a word with him. He knew why, of course, and he wanted the job. Not a bad life, officer's servant, if you have to be here at all. He told me he'd been a gentleman's gentleman before the war and that clinched it. Later, when we were waiting for the train to Amiens, he owned up. He was an actor. The nearest he'd ever got to being a gentleman's gentleman was playing a butler at the Alhambra, Bradford. A larger part than it sounded, he was anxious to point out, because in this particular production the butler did it – a departure from convention that so little pleased the inhabitants of Bradford that the play had to be taken off after seventeen days.

Perhaps he was sure of me by then. Actually I found all that even more irresistible. Phoney gentleman's gentleman, but then I'm a fairly phoney gentleman myself.

An ironing board of a body, totally flat. Interesting gestures, though. He's the only *man* I've ever known to open doors with his hips. Perfectly plain, nondescript features. No Wanted poster would ever find *him*, but also this curious feeling that his face could be anything he wanted it to be, even beautiful, if the part required it. And burningly ambitious. Knows tracts of Shakespeare off by heart. A curious, old-fashioned romantic patriot, though I don't know why I say that, there's plenty of them about. Hallet, for instance. But then they don't all quote, 'We few, we happy few, we band of brothers,' as he did, quite without embarrassment, the other night while I was getting ready for bed. I said very sourly indeed that a more appropriate quotation for this stage of the war might be: 'I am in blood stepped in so far that should I wade no more . . .' His leap across the room was rather remarkable. He'd slapped a hand across my mouth, and we were staring at each other, dumbstruck, before either of us had time to think, his face chalk-white and I suspect mine as well, each trying to remember what the penalty is for smacking an officer in the gob. Quite possibly death.

Since then we've both gone very quiet, retreating behind the barriers of rank, which are as necessary to his protection as to mine, though not retreating quickly enough. Like the French lines at Agincourt, the barriers have been thoroughly breached.

Friday, the 13th September (No bloody comment)

We're not going to join the battalion. The battalion's coming here to join *us.* I suppose this explains this curious out-of-time holiday we've been having. Ended today, anyway. Rode round inspecting billets.

Weather also changed, which makes the other changes somehow more tolerable. Wind and rain, lowering grey clouds.

Saturday, 14 September

Watched the Manchesters march in, streaming rain, wet capes. Shattered faces, bloodshot eyes. Been having a bad time. One or two faces I recognized *from last year.* Before that? I don't think so. Nobody talks about the losses. What they moaned about, sitting on bales of straw, peeling socks off bloody feet, was the absence of fags. They'd been rolling their own in bits of paper, torn-up envelopes, anything, no tobacco of course, had to smoke weeds they picked by the side of the road and dried by tying them to their packs whenever the sun shone. I've written to Mam and Sarah and everybody else I can think of, begging for Woodbines.

Sunday, 15 September

Joined battalion. Adjutant a nice worried-looking man who suggested I might be battalion Gas Officer (which reveals a sense of humour not otherwise apparent). Marshall-of-the-Ten-Wounds was there, striding up and down, talking loudly. Everything about him – skin, gestures, expression, posture, voice – bold, free, coarse. Unscrupulous? Perhaps, I don't know, at any rate he doesn't care. Enjoys life, I think. By temperament and training a warrior. Bold, cunning, ruthless, resolute, quick of decision, amazingly brave – and if that's a human being then a human being isn't what I am. He's spent his entire adult life gravitating towards fighting – impossible to imagine him leading any other sort of life.

Last night, our last night in Amiens, there was a great storm, flashes of sheet lightning, wind buffeting and slogging the house.

I'd just got to bed when I heard a strange rumbling from above. Hallet appeared in the doorway, white-faced and staring. Only starlight to see by and the whole house with its broken windows so draughty the candle kept being blown out. We got an oil-lamp from the kitchen. Hallet said, 'Is it the guns?' I said, 'Of course it bloody isn't, it's coming from upstairs.'

The stairway leading to the upper floor and the nursery is narrow. We got to the nursery door, paused, looked at each other. Hallet's face illuminated from below had bulges under the eyes like a second lid. I pushed the door open and a blast of cold wind from the broken window hit me. All I saw at first was movement at the far end of the room and then I started to laugh because it was just the rocking-horse rocking. The wind was strong enough to have got it going, I can't think of any other explanation, and its rockers were grinding away on the bare wooden floor.

It ought to have been an anti-climax, and at first I thought it was. We moved the thing away from the window, out of the draught, and went downstairs still laughing, telling Potts, who peered round the door of his room, there was nothing to worry about, go back to sleep, but in my own room with the lamp out I lay awake and all night long that rumbling went on in my head.

TEN

They didn't have to wait long for their proper death.

Ngea was a strong, vigorous man, the most powerful chief on the island after Rembo. Everything to live for, apparently, and yet, as one saw so often in Melanesia, he was not putting up a fight. He lay in his hall, watching the scare ghost turn and turn in the draught, and his life lay, it seemed to Rivers, like a dandelion clock on the palm of his open hand.

His condition was so bad that, at one point, Emele, his wife, and the other women began to wail, the long, drawn out, throbbing, musical wail of the women, but then the sick man rallied slightly and the wailing was abandoned.

Rivers said goodbye to him, promised to see him again tomorrow, though he knew he wouldn't, and walked back to the tent. It was dark by the time he got back, and the green canvas of the tent glowed with the light of the lamp inside it. Hocart's shadow, sharply black and elongated, reached hugely over the roof. Rivers pushed a heavy weight of damp washing aside and went in.

Hocart was sitting cross-legged on the ground, with a pencil held sideways in his mouth, typing up his notes. 'I had to retreat because of the midges.'

'Midges?'

'Whatever.'

Hocart was careless with quinine, careless with the mosquito nets. Rivers threw himself down on his bed, clasped his hands behind his head and watched him. After a few seconds Hocart pulled his shirt over his head, and fanned himself with a sheaf of blank pages. As always the heat of the day was trapped inside the tent, and their bodies ran with sweat.

'You've lost weight,' Rivers said, looking at the shadows between Hocart's ribs. '*Rakiana*, that's the word for you.'

'Well,' Hocart said, round the pencil. 'Just as long as your pal Njiru doesn't start trying to put me out of my misery . . .'

'Is he my pal?'

A quick glance. 'You know he is.'

They worked for a couple of hours, ate some baked yam pudding that Namboko Taru had made for them, worked again, then turned off the lamp.

An hour or so later Rivers heard the sound of footsteps approaching the tent. Hocart had fallen asleep, one raised arm shielding his eyes, the pressure of the pillow pushing his cheek and mouth out of shape. Enough moonlight filtered through the canvas for the shadow of the passer-by to stalk across the inside of the tent. A minute later another, taller shadow followed.

Mali? Mali was a girl of thirteen who'd recently retired to the menstrual hut for the first time. When she'd re-emerged, five days later, arrangements for her defloration were already well in hand. A young man, Runi – he'd be about eighteen – had paid her parents the two arm rings that entitled him to spend twenty consecutive nights with her, and had decided – it was his decision, the girl had no say in the matter – to share the privilege with two of his friends.

Runi was considered a bit of a pest. Only the other day he and his two closest friends – presumably the two he'd invited to share Mali – had climbed some kanarium trees and pelted their unfortunate owners with unripe nuts. Rivers had been reminded of Rag Week. The old people grumbled, and then said, what can you expect, young men cooped up on the island sitting about like old women, instead of being off in their canoes, as they ought to have been, burning villages and taking heads.

Whispers, quite close by. A startled cry, almost a yelp, then grunts, groans, moans, a long crescendo of sobbing cries.

Hocart woke up, listened. 'Oh God, not again.'

'Shush.'

There was a belief on the island that a girl's defloration is never the first time, because her first bleeding means the moon has already lain with her. The men denied they believed it, insisting it was just a story they told the girls to reassure them, which at least implied a certain tenderness. He hoped so. She looked such a child.

A few minutes' whispering, and the grunts began again. What it is to be eighteen. Another cry, this time definitely male, and footsteps coming back.

'One down, two to go,' Hocart said.

'You realize for the rest of their lives they won't be able to say each other's names?'

No reply. Rivers wondered if he'd drifted back to sleep but when he turned to look, caught the gleam of eye white under the mosquito net. More footsteps. Another shadow climbed the far wall of the tent. A short pause, whispers, then the gasps began again.

Rivers sighed. 'You know, Rinambesi says when a chief dies the last thing that happens, *used* to happen, rather, is a great head-hunting raid, followed by a feast, and all the girls are available *free* to all the warriors. And not reluctant either, apparently. They run into the sea to greet them.'

'Head-hunting as an aphrodisiac?'

'Why not?'

'They seem to be doing all right without it,' Hocart said, as the moans got louder.

'No babies, though.'

The genealogies made grim reading. Families of five or six had been common three or four generations ago. Now many marriages were childless.

The last shadow came and went. Rivers supposed he must have slept, because it seemed no time at all before the grey early morning light made the mosquito nets as stark and sinister as shrouds.

Fowl-he-sing-out was the pidgin term for this pre-dawn hour, and the fowls had started, first a bubbling trickle of notes, always the same bird, he didn't know its name, rising to a frenzy of competing shrieks and cries. But this morning there was a new noise. At first he lay, blinking sleepily, unable to attach meaning to it, but then he realized it was the wailing of women, almost indistinguishable at this distance from the sound of flutes. And he knew Ngea was dead.

They arrived at Ngea's hall to find the corpse bound into the sitting position, propped up against a pillar. A stout stick had been strapped to its back, keeping the head and neck more or less erect – a sort of external spine. Ngea had been bathed and dressed in his best clothes, the lime on his face and in his hair freshly painted, bunches of riria leaves, a plant forbidden to men in life, fastened to his necklaces. Beside him sat his widow, Emele, not crying or wailing with the other women. Very calm, very dignified.

While the women rocked and wailed Njiru was systematically destroying the dead man's possessions, with the exception of the axe which he had set aside. One rare arm ring after another was smashed. Rivers squatted beside Njiru, and asked, in a low voice so as not to disturb the mourners, why they had to be destroyed.

'You make him no good he go Sonto. All same Ngea he stink, he rotten, bymby *he* go Sonto.'

The wailing went on all day, people coming from across the island to bid Ngea farewell. Towards evening – surely, Rivers thought, the disposal of the corpse could not be much longer delayed – Njiru hung a bunch of areca nuts from the rafters by the scare ghost, took down a cluster and held it out in front of them all. He waited till the last wail faltered into silence and every eye was on him, before he began to pray. 'I take down the portion of the chiefly dead.' He bowed towards the corpse, which gazed back at him with glazed eyes. 'Be not angry with us, be not resentful, do not punish us. Let them drink and eat, break coconuts, open the oven. Let the children eat, let the women eat, let the men eat, and be not angry with us, you chiefly dead, oh, oh, oh.'

The curious sound, half howl, half bark, that ended prayers on Eddystone. Njiru put a nut in his mouth and ate it. The people kept glancing nervously at Ngea, but Njiru went round the circle, offering the cluster of nuts to each person in turn. Every man, woman and child took one and ate it. Even a small child had a tiny crunched-up fragment forced into its mouth.

Ngea, without further ceremony, was slung on to a pole and carried off 'into the bush', they said, though in fact they took him to the beach, where he was placed in a stone enclosure – an *era* – with his axe and his shield at his feet. Still propped in a sitting position, his head kept erect by the stick, he looked out over the low stone wall, westwards, to the sunset. Food was left with him, and food for his mother and father, the 'old ghosts'. Once, Njiru said, and there was no mistaking the bitterness in his voice, a slave would have been killed at this moment, and the head placed between Ngea's feet. Njiru glared at Rivers, as if he held him personally responsible for the abolition of the custom. 'Now no all same.'

Next day Rivers went to Ngea's hall to offer his condolences to Emele, and was confronted by an extraordinary sight. A wooden enclosure had been built inside the hall, similar in size and shape to the stone *era* in which Ngea's corpse had been placed, but with higher walls. Inside this enclosure, knees bent up to her chin, hands resting on her feet, in exactly the same position as the corpse of her husband, sat Emele. She had been there, it seemed, all night, and from the expression of agony on her face it was clear cramp had set in.

A number of widows squatted round the enclosure, looking like stumps of wood in their brown bark loincloths. Many of them were his regular informants on such topics as sexual relations, kinship, the arrangement of marriage. Rivers mimicked Emele's cramped position, and asked for the word. *Tongo polo*, they said reluctantly, glancing at each other. *Tongo polo*, he repeated, making sure he'd got the inflection right. But his efforts to speak their language were not received with the usual maternal warmth. He thought they looked nervous.

'How long?' he asked, crouching down again.

But they wouldn't answer, and when he looked round he saw that Njiru had come into the hall and was standing just inside the door.

Before Ngea's death Njiru had agreed to take Rivers and Hocart to see the cave at Pa Na Keru. It was situated near the summit of the highest mountain on the island, and it was a morning's walk, the early stages through thick bush, to get there. Rivers was inclined to think Ngea's death would lead to the postponement of the trip, but when he emerged from the tent the following morning it was to find Njiru, surrounded by a much larger retinue than usual, waiting for him.

He gave them leaves to wear to protect them from the spirits of the mountain, and the whole group set off in good spirits, laughing and chattering, though they fell silent in the late morning as the ground sloped steeply upwards and the muscles of thighs and back began to ache. The path up the mountain, like all the paths on the island, was so narrow that they had to go in single file.

A solemnity had settled over the gathering. Rivers watched the movement of muscles in the back ahead of him, as they toiled and sweated up the slope. Before them was a massive rock-wall with a cave set into it, like a dark mouth. They slipped and slithered up towards it, sending showers of small pebbles peppering down behind them. The final slope was encumbered with big rocks and boulders, and other, flatter stones, some of them sharp. It was near noon, and their shadows had dwindled to ragged black shapes fluttering around their moving feet. One of the men picked up a stone and threw it at the cave mouth to scare away the ghosts. Rivers and Hocart were the only people there never to have visited the cave before, and they were not allowed to approach until Njiru had prayed that they might be protected from disease. While the prayer went on they watched the others bob down and disappear under the hanging wall of rock.

The cave was low but surprisingly deep, deep enough for the far end to be hidden in shadow. A flat stone near the entrance was called the ghost seat. This was where the new ghost sat and occasionally, to pass the time, drew on the walls. Further in, on the cusp of darkness, was another boulder where the old ghosts sat. 'All old *tomate* come and look new *tomate*,' they were told.

Rivers turned to Njiru and pointed to the seat of the old ghosts. 'Man he stink, he rotten, bymby he go Sonto. Why him no go Sonto?' he asked.

Njiru spread his hands.

Various marks on the wall were interpreted as being the drawings of the new ghosts. Hocart started sketching the marks and recording the identifications he was given. A man, a spirit, pigs, a war canoe.

Njiru wanted to pursue the matter of the old ghosts. He did not himself believe, he said, that there were ghosts in the cave. It was a, a . . . His patience with pidgin ran out. A *varavara*, he concluded. As nearly as Rivers could make out, this meant a metaphor, a figure of speech. Increasingly now, when they were alone, they tried to understand concepts in the other's language, to escape from the fogged communication of pidgin. The language barrier was more formidable than Rivers had initially supposed, for in addition to the ordinary dialect there was the 'high speech' of ritual, myth and prayer. There was also, though he had not been permitted to hear it, *talk blong tomate*: the language of ghosts.

While talking, they had unconsciously wandered deeper into the cave. Now Rivers touched Njiru's arm and pointed to a narrow slit in the back wall. They had to clamber over fallen rocks to reach it, and when they did, it seemed to be too small to admit even a very thin man. Once, Njiru said, the cave had been 'good fellow' right into the centre of the mountain, but then an earthquake had dislodged part of the roof. Rivers knelt down and peered into the darkness. If he crawled he was sure he could get through. And he'd brought a torch with him, not knowing whether the cave would be dark or not. He turned on his back and wriggled through, catching his arm, feeling a wetness that he thought might be blood. On the other side he stood up tentatively, and then stretched his arms high above his head. He had a sense of immense space around him. The cave was big. He was reaching in his back pocket for the torch when he realized Njiru was following him through. He put his hand into the hole, trying to shield the other man's deformed back from the jagged edge of the rock.

They stood together, breathing. Rivers shone his torch at the floor and cautiously they moved deeper into the cave. He put a hand out and touched something that slithered away under his fingers, then swung the torch round, a weak sickly ring of yellow light that revealed what for a second made him doubt his sanity: the walls were alive. They were covered in heaving black fur.

Bats, of course. After the first jolt of fear, it was obvious. He directed the torch at the ceiling where more bats hung, thousands of them, hundreds of thousands perhaps, little sooty stalactites. As the torch swept over them, they raised their heads, frenzied little faces, wet pink gums, white fangs, all jabbering with fear.

Moving very slowly and quietly, not wanting to disturb them further, he again shone the torch at the ground, so that they stood, disconnected feet and legs, in a pool of light. He shouldn't have been startled by the bats, because he knew – Njiru had mentioned it – that in the old days it had been a regular outing for the men of Narovo to go and hunt bats in the cave at Pa Na Keru. But then one day, or so the legend said, a man took the wrong turning and, while his companions wound their way *out* of the mountain, his every step was leading him deeper into it. At last he stumbled upon another exit, and made his way back to the village, but, though he'd been missing less than a week, he returned an old man. He stayed with his mother for three days, but then his face turned black and he crumbled away into dust.

Nobody had followed them into the inner cave. Hocart was busy with his drawings and the islanders were presumably afraid of the legend. Was Njiru also afraid? If he was, he didn't show it. They could hear talk and laughter only a few feet away, in the outer cave, but their isolation in this hot, fur-lined darkness was complete.

This was the first time he'd been alone with Njiru since Ngea's death, and Rivers wanted to talk about Emele: partly because any ceremony connected with the death of a chief was important, but partly too because he felt concern for the woman herself.

'*Tongo polo,*' he said.

He felt Njiru withdraw.

'How long?' he persisted. 'How many days?'

Njiru shook his head. 'Man old time he savvy *tongo polo*, now no all same.'

The last words were accompanied by a dismissive chopping movement of his hand, not intended to make contact with anything, but his fingers clipped the end of the torch and sent it clattering to the ground, where it continued to shine, a single yellow eye focused on them in the darkness. Then the walls lifted off and came towards them. Rivers barely had time to see the beam of light become a tunnel filled with struggling shapes before he was enclosed in flapping squeaking screaming darkness, blinded, his skin shrinking from the contact that never came.

He stood with eyes closed, teeth clenched, senses so inundated they'd virtually ceased to exist, his mind shrunk to a single point of light. Keep still, he told himself, they won't touch you. And after that he didn't think at all but endured, a pillar of flesh that the soles of his feet connected to the earth, the bones of his skull vibrating to the bats' unvarying high-pitched scream.

The cave mouth disgorged fleeing human beings; behind them the bats streamed out in a dark cloud that furled over on to itself as it rose, like blood flowing from a wound under water. Eventually, shocked into silence, they all turned to stare, and watched for a full minute, before the stream thinned to a trickle.

Inside the cave, Rivers and Njiru opened their eyes. Rivers was not aware of having moved during the exodus, indeed would have sworn that he had not, but he discovered that he was gripping Njiru's hand. He felt . . . not dazed, dazed was the wrong word. The opposite of dazed. Almost as if a rind had been pared off, naked, unshelled, lying in contact with the earth. Wonderingly, in the intense silence, they gazed round the grey granite walls, with here and there in the vastness black squares of baby bats hung upside-down to await their mothers' return.

*

A shaft of sunlight struck his eyes.

'Sorry,' Miss Irving said, and pulled the curtain a little way back. 'What sort of night did you have?

'So-so.'

He seemed to have spent the entire night between hot, fur-lined walls and the fur had got on to his teeth.

'Here's your tea,' she said, putting the tray across his knees.

He drank it gratefully, sending out messages to various parts of his body to find out what the situation was. Ghastly, seemed to be the general response.

'Don't you think you should have a doctor?' She smiled at him. 'Doctor.'

'No. All he'd do is tell me to stay in bed and drink plenty of fluids. I can tell myself that.'

'All right. Ring if there's anything you want.'

'Would you mind drawing the curtains?'

The darkness reminded him of the cave. All night he'd had bats clinging to the inside walls of his skull. But now at least there was a breeze, the curtains breathed gently. But he was still too hot. He kicked off the covers, unbuttoned his jacket and flapped the edges, ran his tongue round his cracked lips. Hot.

The sun beat down the moment they left the cave. It was past noon, but the hard bright white rocks reflected heat into their faces. They walked more slowly on the way back, Rivers intensely aware of Njiru walking just ahead of him, though they did not speak. Near the village they began, by mutual consent, to lag behind the others. Hocart turned to wait, but Rivers waved him on.

They sat down on an overturned tree trunk covered in moss. The sun crashed down, beating the tops of their heads, like somebody hammering tent pegs into the ground. And yet even in these sweaty clothes, the shoulders of his shirt thickly encrusted with bat droppings, Rivers had the same feeling of being new, unsheathed.

They sat tranquilly, side by side, in no hurry to begin the mangled business of communication. A slight breeze cooled their skin.

'*Tongo polo,*' Rivers said at last, because that's where they'd left off. How long? he asked again. How many days?

A bright, amused, unmistakably affectionate look from Njiru. There was no fixed time, he said, though eighteen days was common. His grandmother had observed *tongo polo* for two hundred days, but that was exceptional because Homu, his grandfather, had been a great chief. The men of Roviana blew the conch for her.

Blew the conch? Rivers asked. What did that mean?

A short silence, though not, Rivers thought, indicating a reluctance to go on speaking. At that moment Njiru would have told him anything. Perhaps this was the result of that time in the cave when they'd reached out and gripped each other's hands. No, he thought. *No.* There had been *two* experiences in the cave, and he was quite certain Njiru shared in both. One was the reaching out to grasp each other's hands. But the other was a shrinking, no, no, not shrinking, a *compression* of identity into a single hard unassailable point: the point at which no further compromise is possible, where nothing remains except pure naked self-assertion. The right to be and to be *as one is*.

Njiru's grandfather, Homu, was famous for having taken ninety-three heads in a single afternoon. Through his grandmother he was related to Inkava, who, until the British destroyed his stronghold, had been the most ferocious of the great head-hunting chiefs of Roviana. This was his inheritance. Rivers glanced sideways at him, close enough to see how the white lime flaked on the taut skin of his cheekbones. Njiru was speaking, not out of friendship – though he felt friendship – but out of that hard core of identity, no longer concerned to evade questions or disguise his pride in the culture of his people.

The blowing of the conch, he said, signifies the completion of a successful raid. He turned and looked directly at Rivers. The widow of a chief can be freed only by the taking of a head.

ELEVEN

Monday, 16 September 1918

We live in tamboos – a sort of cross between a cowshed and an outdoor privy. Corrugated iron walls and roof – bloody noisy when it rains, and it's raining now – carpeted with straw that rustles and smells and gleams in the candle-light. Fields outside – perfectly reasonable fields when we arrived. Now, after last night's heavy rain and the constant churning of boots and wheels, there's a depth of about eighteen inches of mud. The duckboards are starting to sink. Oh, and it gets into everything. The inside of my sleeping-bag is *not* inviting – I was tempted to sleep outside it last night. *But*. Mustn't complain. (Why not? The entire army survives on grousing.) In fact mud and duckboards are about the only familiar things left.

I've got a permanent feeling of *wrongness* at the nape of my neck. Exposure's the right word, I suppose, and for once the army's bad joke of a haircut isn't to blame. We're out in the open all the time and I'm used to a war where one scurries about below ground like a mole or a rat. (Rats thrived on us – literally. We must have devastated the moles.) It occurred to me last night that Rivers's idea of my using myself as a test case – the football he told me to dribble across – has one fundamental flaw in it. Same loony – different war. As far as I can make out, Rivers's theory is that the crucial factor in accounting for the vast number of breakdowns this war has produced is not the horrors – war's always produced plenty of those – but the fact that the strain has to be borne in conditions of immobility, passivity and helplessness. Cramped in holes in the ground waiting for the next random shell to put you out. If that *is* the crucial factor, then the test's invalid – because every exercise we do now is designed to prepare for open, mobile warfare. And that's what's happening – it's all different.

I told Rivers once that the sensation of going over the top was sexy. I don't think he believed me, but actually there *was* something in common – racing blood, risk, physical exposure, a kind of awful *daring* about it. (Obviously I'm not talking about sex in bed.) But I don't feel anything like that now. There's, *for me*, a nagging, constant apprehension, because I'm out in the open and I know I shouldn't be. New kind of war. The trouble is my nerves are the same old nerves. I'd be happier with a ton or two of France on top of my head.

Day was spent on general clean-up. The men's reward was compulsory games. I stood obediently on the touchline and yelled and waved. A cold grey day. The ball seemed to fly across the lowering sky like a drenched, heavy, reluctant bird. The men were coated in mud, plumes of steam rising from their mouths. All tremendously competitive, of course – 'C' against 'D' – and curiously unreal. Street-corner football played in the spirit of public-school rugby. I stood and watched my red-faced, red-kneed compatriots charging up and down a social No Man's Land. But at least officers and men play together – it's the only informal contact there is outside the line.

At half-time some of them stripped off their shirts and the steam rose from their bodies, red and white, chapped hands and faces, as they stood panting. Jenkins waved at somebody off the pitch and for a moment his face was turned towards me, greenish eyes, red hair, milky white skin blotched with freckles, I had to make an effort to look away. Mustn't get the reputation of 'having an eye for Tommy'. Bad for discipline. Though I don't know what the fuck else there is to look at.

That's the other change: the men's expressions. That look on Jenkins's face as he turned to wave. Before, there were basically two expressions. One you saw at Étaples, the rabbit-locked-up-with-a-stoat look. I've only ever seen that expression in one other place, and that was the Royces' house. Family of four boys in the next street to us. Their father used to make them line up every night after he'd had a few pints, and lift their shirt-tails. Then he'd thrash them with a ruler on their bare bums. Every night without fail. One of them asked once, 'What's it for, Dad?' And he said, 'It's for whatever you've done that you think you've got away with.' But my God they could fight. One of them was the bane of my life at school.

The other expression was the trench expression. It looks quite daunting if you don't know what it is. Any one of my platoon could have posed for a propaganda poster of the Brutal Hun, but it wasn't brutality or anything like that. It was a sort of *morose disgust*, and it came from living in trenches that had bits of human bone sticking out of the walls, in freezing weather corpses propped up on the fire step, flooded latrines.

Whatever happens to us it can't be as bad as that.

Wednesday, 18 September

Today we went to the divisional baths, which are in a huge, low barn. For once it was sunny and dry and the march, though long, was not too tiring. They weren't ready for us and the men sat on the grass outside and waited, leaning on each other's knees or stretched out on the grass with their arms behind their heads. Then it was their turn.

The usual rows of rain butts, wine barrels, a couple of old baths (proper baths). The water any temperature from boiling to tepid depending on where you were in the queue. They take off their clothes, leave them in piles, line up naked, larking about, jostling, a lot of jokes, a few songs, everybody happy because it's not the dreary routine of drills and training. Inside the barn, hundreds of tiny chinks of sunlight from gaps in the walls and roof, so the light shimmers like shot silk, and these gleams dance over everything, brown faces and necks, white bodies, the dividing line round the throat sharp as a guillotine.

One of my problems with the baths is that I'm always dressed. Officers bathe separately. And . . . Well, it's odd. One of the things I like sexually, one of the things I fantasize about, is simply being fully dressed with a naked lover, holding him or her from behind. And what I feel (apart from the obvious) is great tenderness – the sort of tenderness that depends on being more powerful, and that is really, I suppose, just the acceptable face of sadism.

This doesn't matter with a lover, where it's just a game, but here the disproportion of power is real and the nakedness involuntary. Nothing to be done about it. I mean, I can scarcely trip about with downcast eyes like a maiden aunt at a leek show. But I feel uncomfortable, and I suspect most of the other officers don't.

Through the barn, out into the open air, dressing in clean clothes, a variety of drawers and vests, most of them too big. The army orders these things to fit the Sons of Empire, but some of the Sons of Empire didn't get much to eat when they were kids. One of the men in my platoon, barely regulation height, got a pair of drawers he could pull up to his chin. He paraded around, laughing at himself, not minding in the least when everybody else laughed too.

Watching him, it suddenly struck me that soldiers' nakedness has a quality of pathos, not merely because the body is so obviously vulnerable, but because they put on indignity and anonymity with their clothes, and for most people, civilians, most of the time, the reverse is true.

March back very cheerful, everybody singing, lice eggs popping in the seams of the clean clothes as soon as the bodies warm them through. But we're used to that. And I started thinking – there's a lot of time to think on marches – about Father Mackenzie's church, the huge shadowy crucifix on the rood screen dominating everything, a sheaf of hollyhocks lying in the chancel waiting to be arranged, their long stems scrawling wet across the floor. And behind every altar, blood, torture, death. St John's head on a platter, Salome offering it to Herodias, the women's white arms a sort of cage around the severed head with its glazed eyes. Christ at the whipping block, his expression distinctly familiar. St Sebastian hamming it up and my old friend St Lawrence on his grid. Father Mackenzie's voice booming from the vestry. He loved me, the poor sod, I really think he did.

And I thought about the rows of bare bodies lining up for the baths, and I thought it isn't just me. Whole bloody western front's a wanker's paradise. This is what they've been praying for, this is what they've been longing for, for years. Rivers would say something sane and humorous and sensible at this point, but I stand by it and anyway Rivers isn't here. Whenever a man with a fuckable arse hoves into view you can be quite certain something perfectly dreadful's going to happen.

But then, something perfectly dreadful *is* going to happen. So that's all right.

Sunday, 22 September

Morning – about the nearest we ever get to a lie-in (I've been up and on the go by 5.30 every day this week). Wyatt's shaving and there's a voluntary service starting just outside. Smell of bacon frying, sound of pots and pans clattering about and Longstaffe whistling as he cleans my boots. Hallet's on the other side of the table writing to his fiancée, something that always takes *hours* and *hours*. And the rain's stopped and there's a shaft of sunlight on the ground and the straw looks like gold. The razor rattling against the side of the bowl makes a pleasant sound. The ghost of Sunday Morning at home – roast beef and gravy, the windows steamed up, the *News of the World* rustling as Dad drops half of it, the Sally Army tuning up outside.

> Onward, Christian soldiers,
> Marching as to war,
> With the cross of Jesus
> Going on before.

Twenty – perhaps a few more – male voices in unison. Longstaffe's singing the alternative version:

> Forward Joe Soap's army
> Marching without fear
> With your brave commander
> Safely in the rear.

He boasts and skites
From morn till night
And thinks he's very brave,
But the men who really did the job
Are dead and in their grave.

Sung very cheerfully with great good humour. We're all looking forward to Sunday dinner, which is roast beef and roast potatoes. I'm famished. And there is *not* going to be a gas drill during this meal. I *know*.

Tuesday, 24 September

Bussed forward. Men sang all the way, in high spirits, mainly I think because they didn't have to march.

Thursday, 26 September

The nearest village is in ruins. Extraordinary jagged shapes of broken walls in moonlight, silver mountains and chasms, with here and there black pits of craters thronged with weeds.

Some of the other villages aren't even ruins. You're not supposed to mention the effects of enemy fire, but a lot of this is the effect of British fire so perhaps I *can* mention it. Nothing's left. We passed through one village that hadn't a single wall above knee height. Old trenches everywhere, tangles of rusting barbed-wire, rib-cages of horses that rotted where they fell. And worse and worse.

The men, except for the one or two I remember from last year, are still reserved. Sometimes when they're alone at night you hear laughter. Not often. They guard the little privacy they have jealously. Most of the 'devotion' people talk about is from officers – *some* of the officers – to the men. I don't myself see much sign that it's reciprocated. If they trust anybody they trust the NCOs, who're older, for the most part, and come from the same background. But then I wasn't born to the delusion that I'm responsible for them.

What I am responsible for is GAS. Either the Adjutant wasn't joking or if he was it's a continuing joke. My old nickname – the Canary – has been revived. Owen for some reason is known as the Ghost. Evidently when he disappeared into Craiglockhart – and I suspect didn't write to anybody because he was ashamed (I didn't either) – they concluded he was dead.

Gas drill happens several times a day. The routine lectures aren't resented too much (except by me – I have to give them), but the random drills are hated by everybody. You're settling down for the night, or about to score a goal, or raising the first forkful of hot food to your lips, and *wham*! Rattles whirl, masks are pulled on, arms and fists pumped, and then the muffled hollow shout GAS! GAS! GAS! Creatures with huge eyes like insects flicker between the trees. What they hate – what *I* hate – is the gas drill that comes while you're marching or doing PT or bayonet training, because then you have to go on, flailing about in green light, with the sound of your breathing – In. Out. In. Out. – drowning all other sounds. And every movement leeches energy away.

Nobody likes the mask. But what I have to do is watch out for the occasional man who just can't cope with it at all, who panics as soon as it comes down over his head. And unfortunately I think I've found one, though he's in my company which means I can keep an eye on him.

The attitude to gas has changed. It's used more and feared less. A few of the men are positively gas happy. OK, they think, if a whiff or two gets you back to base and doesn't kill you, why not? It's become the equivalent of shooting yourself in the foot and a lot harder to detect.

At dinner I told Hallet and Potts that four years ago we were told to protect ourselves from gas by pissing on our socks. You folded one sock into a pad and used the other to tie it over your mouth and nose. They gaped at me, not sure if I was serious or not. 'Did it work?' asked Hallet. 'No,' I said. 'But it didn't half take your mind off it.' And they both laughed, quite relieved, I think, to know I was only having them on.

It used to give you spots round your mouth. Not that that was our main worry at the time.

And today was pay day. After an afternoon spent crawling running falling crawling again across wet fields, the men were so caked in mud they looked as if they were made of it. Tired, but pay day's always good, even if you've nothing to spend it on, and they were chattering, jostling, laughing as they queued. Then the rattles whirred. A groan went up – (with the real thing there isn't time to groan – more practice needed) and then the usual routine: clenched fists, pumping arms, GAS! GAS! GAS!

They went on queuing. Mud-brown men standing in mud, the slanting rays of the sun gilding the backs of their hands, the only flesh now visible. I was sitting next to Hardwick, ticking off names on the list. One man, waiting immediately behind the man who was being paid, turned his face a little to one side, and I saw, in those huge insect eyes, not one but two setting suns.

Friday, 28 September

Since yesterday evening there's been a continuous bombardment. All the roads forward are choked, drivers stuck in the mud, swearing at each other, a flickering greenish-yellow light in the sky and every now and then the whine and thud of a shell. A constant drone of planes overhead, all going one way.

We move forward tonight.

TWELVE

Rivers walked along the path between the tent and Narovo village, the full moon casting his shadow ahead of him. All around were the scuffles and squeals of the bush, the scream of some bird that turned into a laugh, then silence for a moment, more scuffles, more squeals, the night-long frenzy of killing and eating.

Once in the village he went straight to Ngea's hall, stooped and went in. The scare ghost shivered at his approach.

The women were asleep, the widows who tended Emele. He tiptoed past them, and knelt down, calling, 'Emele! Emele!', an urgent whisper that caused one of the widows to stir and mutter in her sleep. He waited till she settled before he called the name again. When there was no reply he pushed the door open and there, curled up in the prescribed position, back bent, hands resting on her feet, was Kath.

'Kath, Kath,' he said. 'What on earth are you doing here?' And the movement of his lips woke him up.

He sat on the edge of the bed, peering at his watch. Four o'clock, never a good time to wake. His throat was very sore. He swallowed several times, and decided what was needed was that good old medical stand-by, a glass of water.

In the bathroom he blinked in the white light, caught a glimpse of himself in the looking-glass and thought, My God, is this really what you've done to yourself? He took a moment to contemplate baggy eyes and thinning hair, but he wasn't sunk so deep in neurosis or narcissism as to believe an overhead light at four a.m. lays bare the soul. He drank a glass of water and went back to bed.

Despite the hour the curtains let in a little light, starlight, he supposed, there was no moon tonight. It was curiously reminiscent of the light in the tent on Eddystone. He beat the pillows into a more comfortable shape, and tried to get back to sleep.

'Leave the flap open,' Rivers said.

It had been hotter than usual, an oven of a day in which people and trees had shimmered like reflections in water. The earth outside the tent was baked hard. He watched a line of red ants struggle across the immensity, a group at the rear carrying a dead beetle many times their own size.

Hocart emerged from the tent. 'I don't think I can face sleeping in there tonight.'

'We can sleep out here if you like. As long as you're careful with the net.'

The remains of their evening meal lay on the table. Neither of them had felt like eating much.

'What do we do?' Hocart said, sitting cross-legged on the ground beside Rivers. 'What do we do if they come back with a head? Or *heads*, God help us.'

Rivers said slowly, 'Logically, we don't intervene.'

'Logically, we're dead. Even if we decide we won't tell the authorities, how do they know we won't? From their point of view, the only safe thing to do is –'

'Obey the law.'

'Get rid of us.'

'I don't think they'll do that.'

'Could they?'

'Well, yes, probably. The point is, it won't happen, there isn't going to be a head.'

'But if –'

'If there is we'll deal with it.'

A long, stubborn, unconvinced silence from Hocart.

'Look, you know what the penalties are. If they go on a raid there's no way the British Commissioner isn't going to hear about it. And then you've got a gunboat off the coast, villages on fire, trees cut down, crops destroyed, pigs killed. Screaming women and children driven into the bush. You *know* what happens.'

'Makes you proud to be British, doesn't it?'

'Are you suggesting head-hunting should be allowed?'

'No.' Tight-lipped.

'Good. When these people were taking heads they virtually depopulated Ysabel. It *had* to be stopped.'

'So how are they going to get her out?'

Rivers hesitated. 'I don't know. She can't stay in there for ever.'

What he secretly thought, but was superstitiously afraid of saying, was that the situation would end in Emele's suicide. He could see no other way out.

The following morning he went to see Namboko Taru. She'd become very fond of him (and he of her) ever since his miming of alternating constipation and diarrhoea had kept her amused while Njiru removed the *nggasin* from her belly.

She and her friend Namboko Nali had been bathing in the sea and their hair smelled of salt water. Taru's scrawny brown arms were folded across her breasts as she sat, with her back against the wall of her hut, steaming gently in the sun, while hens stepped delicately around her, pecking the dust. He sat beside her, admiring the gleam of dull emerald in the cockerel's neck feathers, as the village came slowly to life.

After a few minutes' gossip he started asking her about love charms, the subject they'd talked about at their last meeting. Three other women came out and listened. He got out his notebook and took down the words of the charm Taru supplied, aware that more than the usual amount of whispering and giggling was going on. Taru offered him betel to chew, and thinking, What the hell, who needs teeth? he accepted it. The women giggled again. A little while later Taru offered him lime, and to humour her he let her draw white lines on his cheekbones. The giggling was now almost out of control, but he pressed on to the end of the charm, at which point it was revealed that the words only became efficacious if the man accepted betel and lime from the woman's basket.

He laughed with them, and by the time they'd finished they were on such terms that he felt he could ask them anything. Even about Emele and *tongo polo*. Taru vehemently denied there was any question of suicide. Suicide, *ungi*, was totally different. Taru and Nali had helped Kera, the widow of the previous chief, to kill herself. She had tried poisoning herself with tobacco and that hadn't worked. And then she'd tried to hang herself, but the bough had broken. So they'd held a pole for her, high above their heads, and she'd twined a strip of calico round her throat and hanged herself from the pole. Garrotted more like, Rivers thought. It would not have been a quick or an easy death. What decided whether the widow would *ungi* or observe *tongo polo*? he asked. It was her choice, they said.

Returning to the tent, he found Hocart lying outside, having spent the first part of the morning washing clothes. He was asleep, or resting, with his arms across his face shielding his eyes from the sun. Rivers put his foot on his chest and pressed lightly.

Hocart peered up at him, taking in the white lines on his face. '*My God*.'

'I think I just got engaged.'

A bubble of laughter shook Hocart's ribs. 'Lucky woman.'

Sleeping was difficult, because of the heat, even after they'd taken their beds outside the tent. Sometimes they gave up altogether, and went to lie in the shallows, where the small waves, gleaming with phosphorescent light, broke over them.

Rivers had become obsessed by Emele. Wherever he was, whatever he was doing, the thought of the woman cramped inside the enclosure, inside the hut, followed him until he saw every other aspect of life on the island in the shadow of her imprisonment.

In the mornings he would go down to bathe and watch the canoes go out, foam flashing from the paddles, a wordless song drifting across the water: '*Aie, aie, aie*.' All vowel sounds, it seemed to be, no consonants. And then the smack of water being slapped to lure bonito into the nets.

It was still idyllic. His own happiness did not lessen, but always, now, there were these two points of darkness: Emele cramped in her enclosure; Ngea rotting in his *era*. Once he walked up the path on the other side of the beach, unable to explain his desire to see Ngea, for the facts of physical decomposition neither fascinated nor frightened him. A corpse was something one buried or dissected. Nothing more. And yet he needed to see Ngea.

The smell reached him when he was no more than half way up the path. He pinched his nostrils, breathing through his open mouth, but even so a few yards further on he had to abandon the attempt. A black cloud of flies, so dense it looked solid, rose at his approach, heat made audible. He backed away, as much as anything because they reminded him of the bats in the cave, and that experience, the sense of being unshelled, peeled in some way, that had seemed so positive at the time, now made him afraid. He was open to whatever might happen in this place, open in the way that a child is, since no previous experience was relevant.

The heat continued. From mid-afternoon onwards there was a curious bronze light in the sky, which became brownish towards evening, as if even the air were singed. Occasional flicks of wind teased the outermost branches of the trees, but did not disturb the intense brooding stillness.

Rivers slept uneasily, waking finally at 'fowl-he-sing-out', aware of having heard a new and different sound. He lay and listened and was just about to turn over and try to snatch an extra hour when it came again: the brazen blare of a conch shell.

He was on his feet and outside the tent in a matter of minutes. The bush distorted sounds, bouncing echoes back, but then he was aware of the crash of hurrying footsteps through the undergrowth, people running down to the beach. He shook Hocart awake, and followed the crowd, holding back a little, not knowing how secret this was, or how much it might matter that he was witnessing it.

He saw Njiru at the water's edge, draped in a white cloth, with a staff in his hand, looking out over the bay.

A canoe was heading in, quickly, paddled by Lembu, and in the stern was a bundle of some kind. He was too far away to see what it was, but an *ah* went up from the crowd, and suddenly, the women and girls began running into the sea, prancing like horses until they reached a depth where they could cast themselves forward and swim. Clinging to the canoe's side, they escorted it into the shallow water, and Lembu got out, everything about him shining, teeth, hair, eyes, skin, and hauled the canoe up the beach. He walked back to the stern, unwrapped the bundle, and dragged the contents out on to the sand. A small boy about four years old.

Rivers walked down to the canoe, since nobody seemed to care whether he saw this or not. The child's face was tear-stained, streaked with dirt and snot. He was not actually crying now, though irregular hiccups shook his thin chest. As people surged towards him and stared, he moved closer to his captor, resting one grubby hand on Lembu's naked thigh.

Rivers went up to Njiru. 'Is that your head?' he asked, unaware that he spoke English, not pidgin.

'Yes,' Njiru said steadily.

He took the child from Lembu and, surrounded by excited, smiling people, carried him up the beach path to the village. Rivers followed, but kept well back as the crowd gathered outside Ngea's hall. Lembu blew the conch as they entered the village, and again inside the hall. After a while Emele emerged, hobbling, resting her arms on the shoulders of Taru and Nali. Lembu and Njiru followed her out, and there was general rejoicing, except from the small boy, who stood alone at the centre of the throng, his eyes like black bubbles that at any moment might burst.

THIRTEEN

4 October 1918

What can one say? And yet I've got to write something because however little I remember now I'll remember less in years to come. And it's not true to say one remembers nothing. A lot of it you know you'll never forget, and a few things you'll pray to forget and not be able to. But the connections go. Bubbles break on the surface like they do on the flooded craters round here – the ones that've been here years and have God knows what underneath.

The night of I *think* the 1st (dates go too) we lay all night in a trench one foot deep – the reward of success because this was a *German* trench. Another reward of success was that we had no British troops on our left, we'd raced ahead of them all. I think I'm right in saying we were the only units that broke through the Hindenburg line *and* maintained the position. It was dark, early evening, deep black, and we expected a counter-attack at dawn. Until then there was nothing to do but wait, both intolerably cramped and intolerably exposed, enfilading machine-gun fire on three sides. 'Cramped' isn't a figure of speech either. The trench was hardly more than a scraping in the earth. Any careless movement and you'd had it. And for a lot of the time we wore gas masks, because there'd been a very heavy gas barrage put down by our side and it lingered. The whole area smelled like a failed suicide attempt, and I kept hearing Sarah's voice saying about Johnny, *It was our own gas, our own bloody gas.* In spite of all the drills some of the men were slow to put their masks on, one or two had bad reactions, and then Oakshott decided to have a panic attack. I crawled along to him, not past people, over them, one eel wriggling across the others in the tank, and tried to calm him down. I remember at one point I burst out laughing, can't remember why, but it did me good. There's a kind of angry laughter that gets you back to the centre of yourself. I shared a bar of chocolate with Longstaffe and we huddled together under my greatcoat and tried to keep warm. And then the counter-attack came.

Two bubbles break here. Longstaffe sliding back into the trench with a red hole in his forehead and an expression of mild surprise on his face. And the bayonet work. Which I will not remember. Rivers would say, remember *now* – any suppressed memory stores up trouble for the future. Well, too bad. Refusing to think's the only way I can survive and anyway what future?

The whole thing was breakdown territory, as defined by Rivers. Confined space, immobility, helplessness, passivity, constant danger that you can do nothing to avert. But my nerves seem to be all right. Or at least no worse than anybody else's. All our minds are in flight, each man tries to reach his own accommodation with what he saw. What he did. But on the surface it's all jollity. We're marching *back*, through the same desolation, but towards safety. Another battalion has leap-frogged us into the line. And every time my right foot hits the ground I say, *over, over, over.* Because the war's coming to an end, and we all know it, and it's coming to an end partly because of what we did. *We* broke through. *We* held the position.

5 October

I think the worst time was after the counter-attack, when we lay in that trench all day surrounded by the dead. I still had Longstaffe by my side, though his expression changed after death. The look of surprise faded. And we listened to the wounded groaning outside. Two stretcher-bearers volunteered to go out and were hit as soon as they stood up. Another tried later. After that I said, No more, everybody keep down. By nightfall most of the groaning had stopped. A few of the more lightly wounded crawled in under cover of darkness and we patched them up as best we could. But one man kept on and on, it didn't sound like a human being, or even like an animal, a sort of guttural gurgling like a blocked drain.

I decided I ought to try myself, and took Lucas with me. Not like going over the top used to be, *climbing* out of the bloody trench. Just a quick slither through the wire, barbs snagging the sleeves, and into the mud. I felt the coldness on my cheek, and the immense space above, that sense you always get when lying on the ground in the open of the earth as a ball turning in space. There was time to feel this, in spite of the bullets – which anyway frightened me less than the thought of having to see what was making that sound.

The gurgling led us to him. He was lying half way down the side of a flooded crater and the smell of gas was stronger here, as it always is near water. As we started down, bullets peppered the surface, *plop, plop, plop,* an innocent sound like when you skim a flat stone across a river, and bullets flicked the rim where we'd been a second before and sent cascades of loose earth down after us. The gurgling changed as we got closer so he knew something different was happening. I don't think he could have known more than that. I got right up to his feet, and started checking his legs for wounds, nothing, but then I didn't expect it. That sound only comes from a head wound. What made it marginally worse was that the side of the head nearest me was untouched. His whole frame was shaking, his skin blue in the starlight as our skins were too, but his was the deep blue of shock. I said 'Hallet' and for a second the gurgling stopped. I gestured to Lucas and he helped me turn him further over on to his back, and we saw the wound. Brain exposed, a lot of blood, a lot of stuff not blood down the side of the neck. One eye gone. A hole – I was going to say *in* his left cheek – where his left cheek had been. Something was burning, casting an orange light into the sky which reflected down on us. The farm that had been one of our reference points. The underside of the clouds was stained orange by the flames.

We got a rope underneath him and started hauling him round the crater, up the other side, towards our trench and all the time I was thinking, What's the use? He's going to die anyway. I think I thought about killing him. At one point he screamed and I saw the fillings in his back teeth and his mouth filled with blood. After that he was quiet, and it was easier but then a flare went up and everything paled in the trembling light. Bastards, bastards, bastards, I thought. I heard a movement and there on the rim of the crater was a white face looking down. Carter, who, I later discovered, had come out entirely on his own initiative. That was just right. More than three and we'd have been getting in each other's way. We managed to drag him back through fire that was, if anything, lighter than before, though not intentionally I think. Too little mercy had been shown by either side that day for gestures of that sort to be possible.

We fell into the trench, Hallet on top of us. I got something damp on my face that wasn't mud, and brushing it away found a gob of Hallet's brain between my fingertips. Because he'd gone quiet on the last stretch I expected to find him unconscious or dead, but he was neither. I gave him a drink of water. I had to press my hand against his face to get it down, because otherwise it slopped out of the hole. And all the time I was doing it I was thinking, Die can't you? For God's sake, man, just *die*. But he didn't.

When at last we were ordered to pull back I remember peering up at the sky and seeing the stars sparse and pale through a gauze of greenish light, and thinking, Thank God it's evening, because shells were still coming over, and some of them were falling directly on the road. At least we'd be marching towards the relative safety of night.

The sun hung on the lip of the horizon, filling the sky. I don't know whether it was the angle or the drifting smoke that half obscured it, but it was *enormous*. The whole scene looked like something that couldn't be happening on earth, partly the sun, partly the utter lifelessness of the land around us, pitted, scarred, pockmarked with stinking craters and scrawls of barbed-wire. Not even birds, not even carrion feeders. Even the crows have given up. And I stumbled along at the head of the company and I waited for the sun to go down. And the sodding thing didn't. IT ROSE. It wasn't just me. I looked round at the others and I saw the same stupefaction on every face. We hadn't slept for four days. Tiredness like that is another world, just like noise, the noise of a bombardment, isn't like other noise. You see people wade through it, lean into it. I honestly think if the war went on for a hundred years another language would evolve, one that was capable of describing the sound of a bombardment or the buzzing of flies on a hot August day on the Somme. There are no words. There are no words for what I felt when I saw the setting sun rise.

*

6 October

We're far enough back now for officers from different companies to mess together again. I sit at a rickety little table censoring letters, for the post has arrived, including one for me from Sarah saying she isn't pregnant. I don't know what I feel exactly. I ought to be delighted and of course I am, but that was not the first reaction. There was a split second of something else, before the relief set in.

Letters arrive for the dead. I check names against the list and write *Deceased* in a firm bold hand in the top left-hand corner. Casualties were heavy, not so much in the initial attack as in the counter-attacks.

Gregg died of wounds. I remember him showing me a letter from home that had big 'kisses' in red crayon from his little girl.

Of the people who shared the house in Amiens only a month ago, Potts is wounded, but likely to live. Jones (Owen's servant) wounded, likely to live. Hallet's wounds are so bad I don't think he can possibly survive. I see him sometimes lying in the lily pond in the garden with the golden fish darting all around him, and silver lines of bubbles on his thighs. More like a pattern than a picture, no depth to it, no perspective, but brilliantly clear. And Longstaffe's dead.

The Thane of Fife had a wife: where is she now?

I look across at Owen, who's doing casualty reports with a Woodbine – now blessedly plentiful again – stuck to his bottom lip, and his hair, rather lank at the moment, flopping over his forehead. For days after the battle he went round with his tunic stiff with blood, but then I had blood and brains on me. We must have stunk like the drains in a slaughterhouse, but we've long since stopped smelling each other. He looks like one of the boys you see on street corners in the East End. Open to offers. I must say I wouldn't mind. He looks up, feeling himself the subject of scrutiny, smiles and pushes the fags across. I saw him in the attack, caped and masked in blood, seize a machine-gun and turn it on its previous owners at point-blank range. Like killing fish in a bucket. And I wonder if he sees those faces, grey, open-mouthed faces, life draining out of them before the bullets hit, as I see the faces of the men I killed in the counter-attack. I won't ask. He wouldn't answer if I did. I wouldn't *dare* ask. For the first time it occurs to me that Rivers's job also requires courage.

We don't even mention our own dead. The days pass crowded with meaningless incident, and it's easier to forget. I run the ball of my thumb against the two first fingers of my right hand where a gob of Hallet's brain was, and I don't feel anything very much.

We are Craiglockhart's success stories. *Look at us*. We don't remember, we don't feel, we don't think – at least not beyond the confines of what's needed to do the job. By any proper civilized standard (but what does *that* mean *now*?) we are objects of horror. But our nerves are completely steady. And we are still alive.

Part Three

FOURTEEN

SHEER FIGHTING
BOTH SIDES PAY THE PRICE
HUNS WAIT FOR THE BAYONET

Prior would have been in that, Rivers thought. He picked the paper up from his breakfast tray and made a real effort to concentrate. It was clear, even from this gung-ho report, that casualties had been heavy. No point checking the casualty lists yet: individual names took at least a week to come through. But he could probably expect a field postcard in the next few days, if Prior was all right. He'd sounded fine in his last letter, but that was ten days ago.

Reading it, Rivers had felt the stab of envy he always experienced on receiving letters from men serving in France. If the wretched war had to happen he'd rather have spent it with Marshall-of-the-Ten-Wounds than with Telford-of-the-Pickled-Penis. He tried to focus on the details of the engagement, but the print blurred before his eyes. And his boiled egg – though God knows what it had cost Mrs Irving to buy – was going down like lead. He really thought he'd be sick if he forced any more of it down. He took his glasses off, put them on the bedside table and pushed the tray away. He meant only to rest a while before starting again, but his fingers slackened and twitched on the counterpane and, after a few minutes, the newspaper with its headlines shrieking about distant battles slipped sighing to the floor.

Ngea's skull, jammed into the *v* of a cleft stick, bleached in the sun. A solitary bluebottle buzzed in and out of the eye sockets and, finding nothing there of interest, sailed away into the blue sky.

On his way down to the beach to bathe, Rivers paused to look at the skull. Only a month ago he'd spoken to this man, had even held his hand briefly on parting. No wonder the islanders wore necklaces of pepeu leaves to guard themselves against *tomate gani yambo:* the Corpse-eating Spirit.

Later the same day he saw the little boy whom Lembu had brought back from Ysabel squatting listlessly outside Njiru's hut, poking about in the dust with a small stick. He was not crying, but he looked dazed. The story was he'd been bought, but Rivers was not inclined to believe it. In these islands – still, in spite of the abolition of head-hunting, warrior communities – not even the poorest family would willingly part with a son. Abduction was more likely. He watched the child for several minutes, wanting to go to him, and yet knowing the appearance of a strange white man would only terrify him more.

'Are they going to kill him?' Hocart said, lying sleepless in bed that night.

'No, they won't do that – they'd have to kill us too.'

'Perhaps that wouldn't worry them.'

'The Commissioner's response to it would.'

But after Hocart was uneasily asleep, twitching and muttering, Rivers lay awake, thinking that if the islanders wanted to get rid of them it wouldn't be too difficult. White men died of blackwater fever all the time, and no doubt there were poisons that mimicked the symptoms. You only had to look at Ngea's skull to know that by the time the next steamer put in there wouldn't be enough of them left to make investigation possible. Moreover, the next steamer would be Brennan's, since he was the local trader, and, confronted by any sign of trouble, he'd simply skedaddle as fast as possible. No, they'd just have to wait and see, and be cautious.

Next morning, when he arrived in the village, the little boy had gone.

They were invited to witness the placing of Ngea's skull in the skull house. Njiru officiated.

At dawn they were woken by the screams of pigs being slaughtered, and all morning columns of smoke had risen from the cooking fires. It was noon before the ceremony started, the sun crashing down on shoulders and heads, the heat intensified by two fires, the sacrificial fire on the hearth in front of the skull house, and the common fire where Rivers and Hocart sat along with people from the village and the surrounding hamlets. Rivers looked out for the small captive boy, but could not see him. Beside him Lembu was plaiting a creeper which he used to tie Ngea's jaw-bone to his skull, before placing a diadem of shells round the cranium and other shells in the sockets of the eyes.

Across the fire, moving figures shimmered in the heat. A woman with a baby in her arms, Nanja, whose own child had died in the confining house and who was now nursing Kwini, the emaciated baby whom Rivers had first seen with Njiru. The child worried at the nipple, guzzling and snuffling – already her wasted thighs had begun to fill out. She would live, he thought, and the idea cheered him for, to western eyes, the stacked-up skulls made disturbing companions.

Njiru raised Ngea's crowned skull above his head, and a silence fell, broken only by the careless cries of the children, but they were some distance away. Rivers could follow most of Njiru's prayer without need of an interpreter. 'We offer pudding, we offer pig, to you the ghosts. Be propitious in war, be propitious in the sea fight, be propitious at the fort, be propitious at the burning of the thatch. Receive the chiefly dead . . .' Here Njiru placed Ngea's skull in the house. 'And be you propitious and smite our enemies, oh, oh, oh!'

It was a prayer for success in the great head-hunting raid that ought to have concluded the mourning for the dead chief. The *Vavolo*, the Night Festival, at which all the young women were free – *tugele* – to all the returning warriors. But the raid would not happen. The prayer could not be answered. Njiru put pork and yam pudding in the sacrificial fire, whose flames burned dull in the sunlight. Then he took the remains of the pudding and walked round the stones that encircled the clearing, placing a mouthful of food on each stone. The stones were called *tomate patu*, stone ghosts, and were erected as memorials to men who died and whose bodies could not be brought home. Rivers watched him go from stone to stone.

Head-hunting had to be banned, and yet the effects of banning it were everywhere apparent in the listlessness and lethargy of the people's lives. Head-hunting was what they had lived for. Though it might seem callous or frivolous to say so, head-hunting had been the most tremendous *fun* and without it life lost almost all its zest.

This was a people perishing from the absence of war. It showed in the genealogies, the decline in the birth rate from one generation to the next – the island's population was less than half what it had been in Rinambesi's youth – and much of that decline was deliberate.

Against the background of such despair might not the temptation of taking one small head in honour of a dead chief prove irresistible? Raids, no, they couldn't do that, the punishment was too severe. But who was to miss one small boy?

Rivers ate the baked yams and pork offered to him, but remained thoughtful. Once he looked up to see Njiru on the other side of the fire, a tall, lean, twisted shape wavering in the column of heat, and surprised on the other man's face an expression of – bitterness? No, stronger than that. Hatred, even.

Kundaite could interpret *talk blong tomate*: the language of ghosts. Sometimes, he said, a meeting was held on the night the old ghosts arrived to take the new ghost back to Sonto with them, and he would question the ghosts and the people would hear them speak. Would this be done for Ngea? Rivers asked. Kundaite didn't know, he wasn't sure, he didn't think so. Would it be done if we give you ten sticks of tobacco? Kundaite nodded. He was given five and promised the other five the following morning. Would they hear Ngea speak? Hocart asked. No, was the reply. 'Ngea he no speak yet. He all same small fellow piccanini.' Kundaite, grasping his tobacco sticks, seemed to be worried. 'Don't tell Njiru,' he said at last.

They all met at sunset in what had been Ngea's hall, and sat cross-legged around the fire. It had been made with green sticks and smoked badly. They coughed, their eyes watered, they waited, nothing happened. Outside it was totally dark, for the moon had not yet risen. Nanja brought in dry sticks, feeding them into the fire skilfully, one by one, until the flames crackled and spurted. Kwini cried and Nanja jiggled and soothed her. Older children sat big-eyed in the firelight, and Rivers felt his own eyelids grow heavy, for he had been up since dawn walking miles in the heat. He blinked hard, making himself look round the circle. Emele – Namboko Emele as she must now be called – was there, wearing brown bark cloth without lime or necklaces. But not Njiru, a surprising absence surely, since he'd placed Ngea's skull in the skull house.

Kundaite came in and sat beside the door in the side of the hut. At a word from him the torches were extinguished, though Rivers could still see people's faces clearly, leaping and shining in the firelight. Silence fell, and deepened, and deepened again. Kundaite closed his eyes and began to moan beneath his breath. Rivers watched him sceptically, wondering whether the attempt to induce a trance state was genuine or merely histrionic. Abruptly, Kundaite seemed to come to himself. He put three sticks of tobacco in the fire as a sacrificial offering, saying casually that the ghosts were on their way from Sonto. A long silence. Nothing happened. Somebody suggested the ghosts were afraid of a dog that was lying by the fire. The animal raised its head on hearing its name, decided there was nothing to worry about and settled down again with a sigh. Others said the ghosts were afraid of the white men.

Rivers's back and thighs were aching from the squatting position. Suddenly Kundaite said, 'Listen, the canoes.' It was clear, looking round the circle, that they were hearing the swish of paddles. Joy and grief mingled on every face. Emele started the musical wailing characteristic of the women, but stopped when Kundaite held up his hand.

A tense silence. Then somebody whistled. The sound was curiously difficult to locate. Rivers looked round the faces, but could not see who was making the sound. The people began calling out names, familiar to him from the genealogies, each person calling the name of a relative who had recently died. Some not so recently. Namboko Taru called for her grandmother. Then the name Onda was called and somebody whistled again. Rivers could see Hocart also looking round the room, trying to locate the whistler.

A discussion about the white men followed, the ghost's whistles being translated by Kundaite. Who were the white men? Why were they here? Why did they want to hear the language of ghosts? Did the ghosts object to the white men's presence? Kundaite asked. 'What do we do if they say "yes"?' Hocart asked, not moving his lips. 'Get out quick.'

But the ghosts did not object. Onda, whistling, said he had never seen white men. Kundaite pointed to Rivers and Hocart. Onda, apparently satisfied, fell silent. Kundaite's father, also called Kundaite, came next and asked for tobacco. The living Kundaite put his last two sticks in the fire, saying, 'Here is tobacco for you, Kunda. Smoke and depart.' Namboko Rupe, Ngea's mother, spoke next, saying she had come to take Ngea to Sonto. Other relatives of Ngea followed. At last Kundaite said that Ngea himself was in the room.

A deeper silence fell. Rivers felt the hairs on his arms rise. Namboko Emele began to wail for her husband. Kundaite said, Don't cry. He's going to Sonto. Ngea's mother said, He must go now. He must blow the conch and come to Sonto. By now the room was full of whistles, slithering up and down the walls and all across the floor. At times the sounds seemed almost to be a ripple running across the skin. Namboko Emele began to wail again, and the other women joined in. 'Don't cry,' Ngea's mother said again, through Kundaite's mouth. 'I have come to take him to Sonto.' Then, Kundaite said, Ngea blew the conch. Everybody in the room, except Rivers and Hocart, heard it, and then the whistles faded and there was silence save for the musical wails and cries of the women.

*

Ten years later, throwing off hot sheets, Rivers reflected that the questions the ghosts had asked had all been questions the living people wanted answered. What *were* the white men doing on the island? *Were* they as harmless as they appeared? *Why* did they want to hear the language of ghosts? *Was* it possible the spirits might be offended by their presence?

At Craiglockhart, Sassoon, trying to decide whether he should abandon his protest and go back to France, had woken to find the ghost of a dead comrade standing by his bed. And thereafter, on more than one occasion, shadowy figures had gathered out of the storm, asking him, Why was he not in the line? Why had he deserted his men?

The ghosts were not an attempt at evasion, Rivers thought, either by Siegfried or by the islanders. Rather, the questions became more insistent, more powerful, for being projected into the mouths of the dead.

Walking back to the tent, a circle of torchlight swaying round their feet, their shoulders bumping as they tried to stay abreast on the narrow path, Rivers and Hocart talked about the seance. A silly word that didn't seem to suit the occasion, but Rivers couldn't think of a better.

'Who was whistling?' Hocart asked.

'I don't know.'

The occasion had moved him in a way he'd never expected when they sat down by that fire. They talked about it for a while, getting the sequence of events clear in their minds, for they had not been able to take notes. Then Rivers said, 'Njiru wasn't there.'

'No, I noticed that.'

Back at the tent Hocart said, 'Shall I light the lamp?'

'No, don't bother. Not for me anyway. I can't wait to get to bed.' He was unbuckling his belt as he spoke, rubbing the skin underneath where trapped sweat prickled. He kicked his trousers to one side and lay down on the bed, only to cry out as his head came into violent contact with something hard and cold. Hocart came in with the torch, his face white behind the beam. On the pillow, indenting it as Rivers's head would have done, was an axe. Rivers picked it up and held it closer to the light. The carving on the handle was rather fine by the standards of the island, and there was a knot, a flaw in the wood, close to the blade.

'Somebody must have left it behind,' Hocart said uncertainly.

'Well, yes, obviously.'

'No, I mean by accident. Whoever it is, he'll be back for it in the morning.'

'I hope not,' Rivers said dryly. 'It's Ngea's.'

'Are you sure?'

Rivers indicated the knot in the wood. 'Yes, I remember this, I noticed it when they put it in the *era* with him.' He stroked the blade. 'No, I'm afraid we've been asking too many awkward questions. We're being warned.'

FIFTEEN

10 October 1918

Back into corrugated iron privies again, which are dry but in other ways less comfortable than dug-outs. Owen has somehow managed to stick a portrait of Siegfried Sassoon to the wall of his. Sassoon in distinctly Byronic mode, I should say – not the Sassoon *I* remember, legging it down the main corridor at Craiglockhart with his golf-clubs on his back, hell-bent on getting out of the place as fast as possible. I stood and stared, gawped at it. And suddenly I was back in Rivers's room, watching the late afternoon sun glint on his glasses during one of his endless silences. Rivers's silences are not manipulative. (Mine are. Always.) He's not trying to make you say more than you want, he's trying to create a safe space round what you've said already, so you can think about it without shitting yourself. White net curtains drifting in on the breeze. *Pok-pok, pok-pok,* from the tennis courts, until somebody misses and the rhythm goes.

Owen said, tentatively, something I didn't quite catch. Something to the effect that we 'old Craiglockhartians' must stick together. Once that would have made me puke. I always felt, watching Owen at Craiglockhart, that there was some kind of fantasy going on, that he was having the public-school education he'd missed. I always wanted to say, it's a loony-bin, Owen. Who do you think you're kidding? I don't feel that now – perhaps because Craiglockhart was a shared experience of failure, and the past few weeks have expunged it for both of us. Wiped it out in blood, you might say, if you were histrionic, and I am. And not our own blood either.

Would that remark deserve one of Rivers's silences? I don't know. Sometimes I used to think he was back with his fucking head-hunters – he really does love them, his whole face lights up when he talks about them – and that gives him a slightly odd perspective on 'the present conflict' as they say.

I've been recommended for the MC for going out to bring Hallet in. I'd have been like a dog with two tails three years ago. Hallet's still alive, anyway. More than a medal, I wish somebody would just tell me I did the right thing.

11 October

Today we all had to stand up in front of the men and promulgate a new order. 'Peace talk in any form is to cease immediately in the Fourth Army.'

The brass hats needn't worry. Some of the men were sitting on bales of straw cleaning equipment while one read aloud from the paper: Austro-Hungarian Empire collapses, peace imminent, etc. Jenkins, a wizened weasel of a man (*must* be over age, surely), hawked the accumulated phlegm of four long years into his mouth and spat on his rifle. Then he went back to polishing it. Can't think of a better comment.

And yet. And yet. We all, at some level, think we may have made it, we *may* be going to be all right. At any moment now the guns may stop. Oddly enough it doesn't help.

We spend our time in the usual way while 'at rest'. Baths, change of clothes, general clean-up, exercises, compulsory games, church parade. Oh, and of course, *gas drills.* A lot of the men are coughing and hoicking and wheezing because they were slow putting on their masks. And perhaps deliberately in some cases; perhaps some people thought they'd get sent back. If so, they've been thoroughly disillusioned, and the proof is the endless cough, cough, cough, cough that accompanies all other activities. Owen irritated me profoundly by saying it was their own fault. He put *his* mask on in time, he's all right, he says. I'm afraid I let fly. The only person round here who has the right to be smug about surviving a gas attack is me. ME.

When we got here we found a new draft had arrived from Scarborough. They're sitting around at the moment, expecting to be welcomed, though so far they haven't been. Difficult to say why the other men avoid them, but they do. Heads too full of battle to be able to cope with all those clean, innocent, *pink* faces. A couple of them I remember. One particularly useless boy, the bane of Owen's life at the Clarence Gardens Hotel, until he upset some hot soup in the CO's lap, after which everybody, including Owen, found him a lot more tolerable. Waiters, drummer boys. They sit around, when they're not being chivvied from one place to another, most of them dejected, miserable. Frightened. A few strut up and down – hard men – real killers – and succeed only in looking even more like baby thrushes than the rest.

12 October

Parcels arrived today. Shared out fags in parcels intended for the dead and wounded. Tempers immediately improved. A lot of niggling administrative jobs connected with feeding men from the new draft into the companies. Get flashes from the battle while I'm filling in forms. The man I bayoneted. What worries me is that he was middle aged. Odd really – it's supposed to be golden youth you mourn for. But he was so obviously somebody who should have been at home, watching his kids grow up, wondering whether brushing his hair over the bald patch would make it more or less obvious, grumbling about the price of beer. And yes, you *could* see all this in his face – with some people you can. Some people do look exactly what they are. *Fuck it.*

Meanwhile more exercises. Route marches. We feed our faces on precisely adequate quantities of horrible food. Bread now has potatoes in it. (Makes an interesting combination with the wood chippings.)

15 October

Last night we were entertained by The Peddlers, the whole battalion, and a few officers invited over from our neighbours on the left. Among whom was Marshall-of-the-Ten-Wounds, now acting Lt Colonel, who applauded every turn with childlike glee. Exactly what you wouldn't expect him to do. At the end of the evening, when things are allowed to get a bit slushy, somebody sang 'Roses of Picardy':

Roses are flowering in Picardy
But there's never a rose like you.

Not a bad voice – it soared over the privies and the tents, the columns of smoke from the fires – and I looked along the row and there was Marshall with great big fat tears rolling down his cheeks. I envied him.

16 October

Bainbrigge's dead. I remember him in the oyster bar in Scarborough a couple of nights before we left. We were all pissed, but Bainbrigge was pissed enough to quote his own poems (than which there is no pisseder). He was talking to Owen, saying real anti-war poems ought to celebrate what war deprives men of – wait for it – 'Beethoven, Botticelli, beer and boys.' Owen kicked him under the table, for my benefit, I think. A wasted kick.

More new arrivals from England yesterday. And I've been transferred to a tent, just as the weather's laying on the first real taste of winter. The misery of sleety rain under canvas. Not that we spend much time under it. We're out all day doing route marches, column into line, consolidation, etc., etc. And gas drills.

But now it's evening. The men are leaning against their packs or each other's knees, aching legs allowed to sprawl at last, writing to wives, mothers, girlfriends. Perhaps even one or two to Beethoven & Co. I said I wasn't born to the delusion that I'm responsible for them. True. (True I wasn't born to it, true it's a delusion.) But I wouldn't like it to be thought I didn't care. So. Going round the group nearest to me. Wilson's got a fucking great nail sticking up through the heel of his left boot. We've all had a go at it: hammers, pliers, tent pegs, God knows what. Still it sticks up, and since it breaks the skin he's quite likely to get a septic sore, unless I can find him another pair of boots. Which ought to be easy, but isn't. Unfortunately, the septic sore won't be enough to get him out of the line if we have to go back there. It'll just exhaust him, make every step a greater misery than it need be.

Oakshott, who's sort of on the fringes of the group – he's taken to not talking to people – is well on the way to cracking up. (I should know.) The thing is he's *not* windy, he's a perfectly good soldier, no more than reasonably afraid of rifle and machine-gun bullets, shells, grenades. (Let's not ask ourselves how afraid that is.) He isn't even windy about gas, though inevitably it comes across like that. He's just terrified of the *mask*. I don't know what to do with him. Once or twice recently I've noticed him lagging behind in gas drills, and I've noticed myself letting him get away with it. Which I mustn't do. If *he* gets away with it, they'll all start.

Next to him, in front of him rather, is Moore. Moore's wife spent the evening of the Friday before last in the lounge bar of the Rose and Crown (I know it well) in the company of one Jack Puddephat, who has a good job at the munitions factory (same one Dad works at) and brings home five quid a week. Moore's sister-in-law, a public-spirited soul, was kind enough to write and tell him about it.

Heywood's kid has tonsillitis and the doctor's all for whipping them out. Heywood's all for leaving well alone, but the letter he's writing now won't get there in time.

Buxton's missus is expecting their first. The birth doesn't seem to worry her, but it terrifies him. His own mother died in childbirth, and he's convinced himself the same thing's going to happen to her.

Jenkins writes the most incredibly passionate love letters to his wife. They've been married since before the Flood, but obviously nothing's faded. I get erections reading them. Nothing else I've done sexually has filled me with such shame. In fact it's the only thing that's ever filled me with *any* shame. He *must* know they're censored, and yet still he writes, page after page. Perhaps he needs to say it so much he somehow manages to forget that I read them first? It's the mental equivalent of the baths. Here I sit, fully clothed as it were, knowing my letters to Sarah *won't* be censored. I suppose random checks are carried out on officers' letters, but at least it's done somewhere else, and not by people you have to see every day.

Peace talk goes on whether orders forbidding it are promulgated or no. On the night we heard the Germans had agreed to peace talks there was a great impromptu party, officers and men together. Everybody sang. And then next day in *John Bull* there's Bottomley saying, No, no, no and once again no. We must fight to the bitter end. (*Whose* end?) *I don't want any more talk about not being out to destroy the German nation – that is just what I am out for . . .*

But it doesn't wash with the men. Not this time. In fact some of them have taken to going to the latrines waving copies of *John Bull*.

Nobody here sees the point of going on now.

*

18 October

But others do. We leave here today, going back into the line.

SIXTEEN

October rain spattered the glass. Outside in Vincent Square golden leaves were trodden in the mud. Rivers stopped coughing, put his handkerchief away, and apologized.

''S all right,' Wansbeck said. 'I should be apologizing to you. I gave it you.'

'At least I can't give it back,' Rivers said, wiping his eyes. 'In fact you and I are about the only two round here who can't get it.'

'Things are getting pretty bad, aren't they? I mean, on the wards. I don't suppose I could do anything to help?'

Rivers looked blank.

'Lifting patients. It just seems bloody ridiculous a great big chap like me sitting around doing nothing while some poor little nurse struggles to lift a twelve-stone man on her own.'

'It's very kind of you,' Rivers said carefully. 'But I really don't think the authorities would allow it. In any case you're not doing "nothing".'

Silence. The hint was not taken up. Rivers forced himself to open his shoulders, knowing his tension was communicating itself to Wansbeck, though it was only the tension of driving himself through a long day while still feeling very far from well. 'How have you been?'

'Smell's gone.' A flicker of amusement. 'I know it wasn't there, but it's still nice to be rid of it.'

'Hmm, good.' What pleased Rivers even more than the vanished smell was the hint of self-mockery. The one expression you never see on the faces of the mentally ill. 'When did that happen?'

'Just faded gradually. I suppose about the middle of last week I suddenly realized I wasn't worried about it any more.'

'And the dream?'

'It isn't a dream.'

'The apparition, then.'

'Oh, we still see quite a bit of each other.'

'Do you ever miss a night?'

A faint smile. 'You mean, does *he* ever miss a night? No.'

A long silence. Rivers said, 'It's difficult, isn't it, to talk about . . . beliefs?'

'Is it?'

'I find it so.'

Wansbeck smiled. 'What a very honest man you are.'

'I wanted to ask if you believe in life after death?'

A groan, followed by silence.

It *is* difficult, Rivers thought. He could list all the taboo topics on Eddystone, but in his own society it seemed to him the taboos had shifted quite considerably in recent years. It was almost easier now to ask a man about his private life than to ask what beliefs he lived by. Before the war . . . but one must beware of attributing everything to the war. The change had started years before the war.

'No,' Wansbeck said at last.

'You had to think.'

'Yes, well, I used to believe in it. I was brought up to. I suppose one doesn't like to have to admit it's gone. Faith.'

'What changed your mind?'

A flare of the eyebrows. Rivers waited.

'Corpses. Especially in cold weather when they couldn't be buried. And in summer in No Man's Land. The flies buzzing.'

They rose from Ngea's body in a black cloud.

'It needn't have that effect, though, need it? What about priests keeping a model of a skull on their desks? Because it reminds them of their faith.'

Or Njiru. Man he stink, he rotten, bymby he go Sonto. A simple, casual statement of fact.

'Well, that's the effect it had on *me*. I'd like to believe. I'd like to believe in the possibility of – you're right, it *is* embarrassing – redemption.'

Silence.

'Anyway,' Rivers said, when it became clear there would be no more, 'you don't believe that the apparition is the man you killed? You don't believe it's his ghost?'

'No, though I'm not sure I'd believe that even if I were still a Christian.'

'So what is it?'

'A projection of my own mind.'

'Of your guilt?'

'*No*. Guilt's what I feel sitting here, I don't need an apparition. No, it's . . .' A deep sigh. 'Guilt as objective fact – not guilt as *feeling*. It's not . . . well, I was going to say it's not subjective, but of course it has to be, doesn't it?'

'It's the representation to yourself of external standards that *you* believe to be valid?'

'Yes.'

'What language does it speak?'

A blank look. 'Doesn't. Doesn't speak.'

'What language would it speak if it spoke? Yes, I know it's an irrational question but then the apparition isn't rational either. What language would –'

'English. Has to be.'

'So why don't you speak to it?'

'It's only there for a second.'

'That's not the way you described it. You said it was endless.'

'All right, it's an endless second.'

'You should be able to say a lot, then.'

'Tell it my life story?'

Rivers said gently, 'It knows your life story.'

Wansbeck was thinking deeply. 'All right. It's bloody mad, but I'll have a go.'

'What will you say?'

'I have absolutely no idea.'

After Wansbeck had gone, Rivers sat quietly for a few minutes before adding a note to the file. Sassoon had been much in his mind while he was speaking to Wansbeck, Sassoon and the apparitions that gathered round his bed and demanded to know why he was not in France. Also, another of his patients at Craiglockhart, Harrington, who'd had dreadful nightmares, even by Craiglockhart standards, and the nightmares had continued into the semi-waking state, so that they acquired the character of hypnagogic hallucinations. He saw the severed head, torso and limbs of a dismembered body hurtling towards him out of the darkness. A variant of this was a face bending over him, the lips, nose and eyelids eaten away as if by leprosy. The face, in so far as it was identifiable at all, was the face of a close friend whom Harrington had seen blown to pieces. From these dreams he woke either vomiting or with a wet bed, or both.

At the time he witnessed his friend's death Harrington had already been suffering from headaches, split vision, nausea, vomiting, disorder of micturition, spells of forgetfulness and a persistent gross tremor of the hands, dating from an explosion two months before in which he'd been buried alive. Despite these symptoms he had remained on duty (shoot the MO, thought Rivers) until his friend's death precipitated a total collapse.

What was interesting about Harrington was that instead of treatment bringing about an elaboration of the nightmares, so that the horrors began to assume a more symbolic, less directly representational form – the normal path to recovery – something rather more remarkable had happened. His friend's body had begun to reassemble itself. Night after night the eaten-away features had fleshed out again. And Harrington talked to him. Long conversations, apparently, or they seemed long to him on waking, telling his friend about Rivers, about life at Craiglockhart, about the treatment he was receiving . . .

After several weeks of this, he awoke one day with his memory of the first hour after the explosion restored. He had, even in his traumatized state and under heavy fire, crawled round the pieces of his friend's body collecting items of equipment – belt, revolver, cap and lapel badges – to send to the mother. The knowledge that, far from having fled from the scene, he had behaved with exemplary courage and loyalty, did a great deal to restore Harrington's self-esteem, for, like most of the patients at Craiglockhart, he suffered from a deep sense of shame and failure. From then on the improvement was dramatic, though still the conversations with the dead friend continued, until one morning he awoke crying, and realized he was crying, not only for his own loss but also for his friend's, for the unlived years.

Wansbeck's predicament was worse than either of these cases. Siegfried's apparitions vanished as soon as he agreed to give up his protest and go back to France. The external demands the nocturnal visitors represented, and which Siegfried himself believed to be valid, had been met. Harrington had been enormously helped by the discovery that he'd behaved better than he thought he had. From that moment on, his recovery had been one of the most dramatic Rivers could recall. Neither of these outcomes was available to Wansbeck, who'd fought a perfectly honourable war until one action had made him in his own eyes – and in the eyes of the law – a criminal. Almost everything one could say to console him either obscenely glossed over the offence or was in some other way insulting, and would have been instantly recognized as such by Wansbeck. A lesser man would have borne this better.

Rivers wondered whether Sassoon and Harrington had been *too* much in the forefront of his mind while he was listening to Wansbeck. At best, on such occasions, one became a conduit whereby one man's hard-won experience of self-healing was made available to another. At worst, one no longer listened attentively enough to the individual voice. There was a real danger, he thought, that in the end the stories would become one story, the voices blend into a single cry of pain.

And he was tired. Because of the flu epidemic he'd been on duty for thirty of the last forty-eight hours and he was on duty again tonight too. Sighing, he reached for an envelope, took out an X-ray and clipped it to the screen.

A skull stared out at him. He stood back and looked at it for a moment, one lens of his glasses illumined by the lighted screen, the other reflecting the rainy light of a November afternoon. Then he reached for the notes.

Second Lieutenant Matthew Hallet, aged twenty, admitted 18 October with bullet wounds to the head and to the lower jaw. On admission he was incapable of giving an account of his injuries, and the only information brought with him was a small card saying he had been wounded on 30 September.

So he was now twenty days post-injury.

A rifle bullet had entered just to the left of the inner canthus of the right ear and had made its exit directly above the insertion of the left ear. The wound of entry was marked by a small perfectly healed scar. The wound of exit consisted of a large irregular opening in the bone and tissues of the scalp, and through this protruded a suppurating hernia cerebri which pulsated.

Oh God.

He had so far said nothing spontaneously. When directly addressed he responded, but his speech was incomprehensible. The wound to his lower jaw made it difficult to determine whether this represented a deficit in the power of using language, or whether the failure to communicate was entirely or primarily mechanical. He showed some understanding of speech, however, since he had responded to simple questions, when asked to do so, by movements of his unparalysed hand.

Somewhere at the fringe of Rivers's perception was the soft sound of rain continually falling, seeming to seal the hospital away from the darkening afternoon. It had rained incessantly since early morning, the darkness of the day somehow making it even harder to stay awake. He took his glasses off, rubbed his eyes, and turned to the window, where each raindrop caught and held a crescent moon of silver light.

'Do you suppose it's ever going to stop?' Hocart said, turning over restlessly in the gloom of the tent.

It had been raining ever since they'd found Ngea's axe, not restrained English rain but a downpour, a gurgling splatter that flooded into the tent no matter how hard they tried to keep it out. Possibly it was stupid to stay inside at all, though difficult not to when even a five-yard dash into the bush to pee meant you came back with hair plastered to your skull and a transparent shirt sticking to your chest.

They lay and watched it through the open flap, a solid wall of water through which the not too distant trees could be glimpsed only dimly, a wavering blue mass beaten hither and thither by a wind that blew in sudden spiteful squalls. Hocart, in his frustration, had been kicking the roof of the tent where it sloped steeply down over his bed, and his muddy footprints now added to the general squalor and smell. Hot wet bodies, hair washed daily but only in sea water, salt drying to a white scurf on the surface of the skin. The only escape was into the sea, where total immersion relieved the misery of wet.

On the fourth day the rain eased slightly. Rivers stepped out into the clearing and saw Njiru coming along the path towards him, for once without his retinue.

Rivers had been wondering whether to mention the axe, and had decided not to, but as soon as he looked at Njiru he knew it was essential to bring it out into the open.

'Blong you?' he said, holding it out.

'Blong Ngea,' Njiru said, and smiled.

But he took it, putting it into the string basket he carried slung over one shoulder. Rivers heard the chink of one blade on another as it hit Njiru's axe. It was important to be totally steadfast at this moment, Rivers thought. He and Hocart were probably the only white men in the archipelago, apart from the missionaries – *some* of the missionaries – who didn't carry guns. They didn't carry knives either, though on an island covered in dense bush a machete would have been useful. Nothing that could possibly be mistaken for a weapon. And they went barefoot, as the natives did. Harmlessness was their defence, not guaranteed to succeed by any means, but guns would have made the job impossible.

Njiru had come, he said, because one of the oldest skull houses on the island was being rebuilt, and he had to go to say the prayer of purification over the priest. Would Rivers like to go with him? Of course, there was no question.

They set off, Njiru remarking at one point that it always rained when a skull house was being rebuilt because '*tomate* he like bathe all time 'long fresh water'. Soon the narrow path and the steamy heat made conversation impossible. Rivers watched the movement of muscles under the oiled skin, wondering, not for the first time, how much pain Njiru suffered. He was a mystery in many respects and likely to remain so. He was not married, for example, this among a people to whom the concept of celibacy was wholly foreign. Was that because his deformity caused the girls or their parents to regard him as a poor catch? But then in island terms he was both wealthy and powerful. Did he himself feel a disinclination for the married state? And what had the impact been on a small crippled boy of knowing he was the grandson of Homu, the greatest of the head-hunting chiefs? It was worse, Rivers thought, smiling to himself, than being the great-nephew of the man who shot the man who shot Lord Nelson.

None of these questions could be pursued. It was not lack of words merely, but a lack of shared concepts. The islanders seemed hardly to have discovered the idea of personality, in the western sense, much less to have contracted the habit of introspection. Njiru was one of the most powerful men on the island, perhaps the most powerful. To Rivers and Hocart it seemed abundantly apparent that he owed his position to quite exceptional intelligence, vigour and resolution, but such qualities were never mentioned by the islanders when they attempted to explain his position. His power was attributed entirely to the number of spirits he controlled. He 'knew' Mateana. And above all, he 'knew' Ave. *Njiru knows Ave*. One of the first things he'd been told, though he hadn't understood the significance of the statement then, and perhaps did not fully understand it even now.

In view of that chink of blade on blade, what accounted for this sudden change of attitude? He was reasonably certain it was Njiru who'd put Ngea's axe in the tent. He hadn't even pretended surprise when Rivers offered it to him. And yet here he was, being apparently helpful and co-operative, actually inviting him to be present at an important ritual occasion. But then he was like this, one moment clamming up completely, even ordering other people to withhold information, and yet at other times easily the best informant on the island. Standing over them sometimes to make sure they got every detail of a ritual, every word of a prayer *exactly* right.

The inconsistency probably reflected Njiru's doubts about the reality of his own power. Others were persuaded by it, but he was capable of standing back and asking himself the hard questions. Why, if he controlled the spirits, why, if the rituals did everything he claimed for them, were the white men still here? Not Rivers and Hocart, whom he liked and respected, but the others: the government that forbade the taking of heads though the people lived for it, the traders who cheated them, the plantation bosses who exploited them, and, most of all, the missionaries who destroyed their faith. If you can't prevent such things happening, what is the actual value of your knowledge?

And so he swayed to and fro: sometimes guarding his knowledge jealously, sometimes sharing it freely, sometimes spitting it out with a bitter, angry pride, sometimes almost with gratitude to Rivers, whose obvious interest in what he was being told seemed to confirm its value. And then again he would sheer off, ashamed of ever needing that confirmation.

A stormy relationship, then, on Njiru's side, and yet the mutual respect went deep. He wouldn't kill me, Rivers thought. Then he thought, Actually, in certain circumstances, that's exactly what he'd do.

By the time they reached the turning off the coastal path, the sun was at its highest point. Sweat tickled the tip of Rivers's nose, producing a constant frenzy of irritation. His groin was a swamp. At first the darkness under the trees was welcome, after the dreadful white glare, but then a cloud of stinging insects fastened on the sweat.

Abruptly, they came out into a clearing, sharp blades of sunlight slanting down between the trees, and ahead of them, rising steeply up the slope, six or seven skull houses, their gratings ornamented with strings of dangling shells. The feeling of being watched that skulls always gave you. Dazzled by the sudden light, he followed Njiru up the slope, towards a knot of shadows, and then one of the shadows moved, resolving itself into the shape of Nareti, the blind mortuary priest who squatted there, all pointed knees and elbows, snails' trails of pus running from the corners of his eyes.

The furthest of the skull houses was being repaired, and its occupants had been taken out and arranged on the ground so that, at first sight, the clearing seemed to be cobbled with skulls. He hung back, not sure how close he was permitted to approach, and at that moment a sudden fierce gust of wind shook the trees and all the strings of votary shells rattled and clicked together.

Njiru beckoned Rivers to join him and, without further preliminary, began the prayer of purification, rubbing leaves down Nareti's legs from buttock to ankle.

'I purify at the great stream of Mondo. It flows down, it flows up, it washes away the poisonous water of the chiefly dead. The thatch is poisonous, the rafters are poisonous, the creepers are poisonous, the ground is poisonous . . .'

Among the skulls laid out on the ground were several that had belonged to children. Children loved and wept over? Or children brought back from Ysabel and Choiseul and sacrificed?

'Let me purify this priest. Let him come down and pass under. Let him come down and step over. Let him not waste away, let him not get the rash, let him not get the itch. Let him be bonito in the sea, porpoise in the sea, eel in the fresh water, crayfish in the fresh water, *vape* in the fresh water. I purify, I purify, I purify with all the chiefs.'

Njiru's voice, which had risen in pitch, dropped on the final words.

Always in Melanesia, the abrupt transition from ritual to everyday life. Njiru was soon chatting and laughing with Nareti, then he summoned Rivers to follow him. A short path led to Nareti's hut and there, squatting in the dust, having the remains of lunch licked off his face by a dog, was the small boy whom Lembu had brought from Ysabel. Healthy, well-fed. Unbruised, Rivers saw, looking closely, not happy, but then that was hardly to be hoped for. He watched him for a few minutes. At least the dog was a friend.

He was to assist Nareti, Njiru said. When he grew up he would be a mortuary priest in his turn. An odd fate, to spend one's life tending the skulls of a foreign people, but at least he would *have* a life, and perhaps not a bad one, for the mortuary priests became wealthy and enjoyed considerable respect. This taking of captives had been the custom even in the days of head-hunting, Njiru explained. He was in one of his communicative phases. Some of the 'heads' taken on a raid were always brought back alive, and kept for occasions when they might be quickly needed. A sort of living larder of heads. Such captives were never ill-treated – the idea of deliberate cruelty was foreign to the people – and indeed they often attained positions of wealth and honour, though always knowing that, at any moment, their heads might be required.

On their way back across the clearing Njiru stopped, selected the central skull from the middle row, and held it out to Rivers.

'Homu.'

Rivers took the skull, aware of the immense honour that was being done to him, and searching for something to say and the words to say it in. He ran his fingers round the occiput and traced the cranial sutures. He remembered a time at Bart's, holding a human brain in his hands for the first time, being amazed at the weight of it. This blown eggshell had contained the only product of the forces of evolution capable of understanding its own origins. But then for Njiru too the skull was sacred not in or of itself, but because it had contained the spirit, the *tomate*.

He looked at Njiru and realized it wasn't necessary to say anything. He handed the skull back, with a slight inclination of his head, and for a moment their linked hands grasped it, each holding the object of highest value in the world.

The bullet caused gross damage to the left eye as it passed backwards in the direction of the temporal lobe. Left pupil fixed, cornea insensitive, eyelid droops, no movement of the globe except downwards. Eye blind because of rupture of the choroid and atrophy of the optic nerve. Yes. *A tendency to clonus at the right ankle joint . . .* All right.

Switching off the lighted screen and replacing the notes in the file, Rivers glanced at the cover and noticed that Hallet was in the 2nd Manchesters. He wondered if he knew Billy Prior, or whether, if he did, he would remember.

SEVENTEEN

19 October 1918

Marched all day through utter devastation. Dead horses, unburied men, stench of corruption. Sometimes you look at all this, craters, stinking mud, stagnant water, trees like gigantic burnt matches, and you think the land can't possibly recover. It's *poisoned*. Poison's dripped into it from rotting men, dead horses, gas. It will, of course. Fifty years from now a farmer'll be ploughing these fields and turn up skulls.

A huge crow flew over us, flapping and croaking mournfully. One for sorrow. The men didn't rest till they'd succeeded in spotting another.

Joy awaits us, then.

The unburied dead, though not cheerful companions for a march, had one good result. A boot for Wilson. Getting it wasn't pleasant, but once the debris left by the previous owner (*of* the previous owner) had been cleaned out it did well enough. He looks happier.

Men very cheerful for the most part, a long singing column winding tirelessly along (but we've a long way to go yet!). I found myself thinking about Longstaffe. Not dead three weeks, and yet he rarely crosses my mind. In Tite Street, three doors down from Beattie's shop, there was an old couple who'd been married over fifty years and everybody thought when one of them went the other would be devastated. But when the husband died the old lady didn't seem all that upset, and hardly talked about him once the funeral was over. In spite of all the young male vigour around here – and my God it's bloody overwhelming at times – we're all in the same position as that old woman. Too close to death ourselves to make a fuss. We economize on grief.

Later

Men bivouac in the open, but the officers are in dug-outs, the remains of an elaborate German system. The dug-outs are boarded off, but behind the planks are tunnels which reach back very deep. You can put your eye to a gap in the boards and look into darkness and after a while the eyeball begins to ache from the cold air. The extraordinary thing is everybody's slightly nervous about these tunnels, far more than about the guns that rumble and flicker and light up the sky as I write. And it's not a rational fear. It's something to do with the children whom the Pied Piper led into the mountain, who never came out again, or Rip Van Winkle who came out and found that years and years had passed and nobody knew him. It's interesting, well, at least it interests me, that we're still afraid in this irrational way when at the same time we're surrounded by the worst the twentieth century can do: shells, revolvers, rifles, guns, gas. I think it's because it strikes a particular chord. Children do go into the mountain and not come back. We've all been home on leave and found home so foreign that we couldn't fit in. What about after the war? But perhaps it's better not to think about that. Tempting fate. Anyway, here comes dinner. I'm hungry.

20 October

Another mammoth march. Lousy rotten stinking job too, rounding up the stragglers. Forget leadership. This is where leadership ends and bullying starts. I heard myself hassling and chivvying like one of those bloody instructors at Étaples. Except at least I'm *doing* what I'm bullying other people into doing.

I turned on one man, mouth open to give him a really good blast, and then I saw his face. He was asthmatic. That tight, pale, drawn worried look. If you're asthmatic yourself you can't miss it. He might as well have been carrying a placard. I fell in beside him and tried to talk to him, but he couldn't talk and march at once, or creep rather – he certainly wasn't marching. That's the thing about asthma: it creates the instant brotherhood shared humanity routinely fails to create. I got him into the horse ambulance, well propped up, gripped his wrist and said goodbye. I doubt if he saw me go. When you're as bad as that nothing matters except the next breath.

The curious thing is as soon as I saw his face, my own chest tightened, just because I'd been reminded of the possibility, I suppose. So far, touch wood, there's been no trouble. But I'm a bit wheezy tonight.

Singing very ragged by mid-afternoon, a lot of men marching in silence, it had become a test of endurance. But then suddenly, or so it seemed – we'd been marching half asleep – we found ourselves with green fields on either side, farmhouses with roofs on, trees with branches, and civilians. We'd marched right through the battlefields into what used to be securely German-held territory. Women. Children. Dogs. Cats. I think we were all amazed that the world had such creatures in it. A lot of wolf whistling at the girls, and nobody inclined to be fussy. 'Girl' soon stretched from fourteen to fifty.

I'm writing this at a kitchen table in a cottage. Outside is a farmyard with ordinary farmyard noises. Honking geese are a miracle. Though we move on again soon. They're questioning civilians in the next room, Owen's French coming in handy. And at this table, until a few weeks ago, a German officer sat and wrote letters home.

*

22 October

Still here, but not for much longer. We move on again later today. Not even the pouring rain that puckers the surface of the pond – with its official ducks and unofficial moorhens – can remove the feeling of serenity I have. Chest a lot easier, in spite of the damp.

24 October

More marching. I have visions of us marching into Berlin at this rate. Nearest village was shelled last night. Five civilians killed. When did we stop thinking of civilians as human? Quite a long time ago, I think. Anyhow, nobody's devastated by the news. And yet the people round here are friendly, we get on well with them. Only there's a slight wariness, I suppose. They hated the invasion, nobody doubts that, but the Germans were here a long time. An accommodation of some sort was reached. And the German troops in this area anyway seem to have been very disciplined. No atrocities. The respectable young ladies of the village are very respectable young ladies indeed, despite having spent four years in the clutches of the brutal and lascivious Hun. And the shell-holes that lie in the orchards, fields and roads round here – great gaping wounds – were made by *our* guns. The bombardment was very heavy at times. Some of the children run away from us. And yet we're greeted everywhere with open arms.

Still can't get used to ordinary noises, especially women's and children's voices. It must feel like this coming out of prison.

25 October

Owen is to be court-martialled. Mainly because he speaks French better than anybody else and all the local girls make a bee-line for him, not just thanking him either, but actually *kissing* him. I caught his eye while all this was going on, and thought I detected an answering gleam. Of irony or whatever. Anyway the Great Unkissed are thoroughly fed up with him and have convened a subalterns' court martial. Shot at dawn, I shouldn't wonder.

Wyatt, meanwhile, is visiting a farmhouse on the outskirts of the village where lives an accommodating widow and her equally accommodating but rather more nubile daughters. At this very moment, probably, he's dipping his wick where many a German wick has dipped before it. (A *frisson* wasted on Wyatt, believe me.)

But this morning I saw a woman in the village with sunlight on her hair and one of those long loaves of bread in her arms and there was more sensuality in that moment than in all Wyatt's humping and pumping. Out of bounds, of course. Perfectly respectable housewife doing the shopping.

26 October

This morning I went to one of the local farms to sort out a billeting problem. The woman who runs the farm had accused some of the men in 'C' company of stealing eggs. They denied it vociferously, but I'm sure she's right. After calming her down and paying her more for the eggs than they were worth, I noticed a boy with red hair staring at me. Not staring exactly, but his eyes met mine longer than was strictly necessary. About sixteen, I suppose. Perhaps a bit older. He was walking across the yard clanking a bucket of pig swill, and after I'd taken leave of Madame (his mother, I *think*) I followed him into the fetid darkness, full of snuffling and munching, pigs rooting round with moist quivering nostrils, trotting towards him on delicate pink feet. After he poured the swill in they squealed and guzzled for a bit, then raised their heads, watching us calmly from under long fine white eyelashes as they munched. I scratched their backs and tried to talk to him. Chinks of sunlight came in through gaps in the tiles, a smelly greenish wetness under foot. He spoke rapidly and I got very little of it – schoolboy French no use at all. I spun back-scratching out as long as I could, then departed, wondering how much of that initial look I'd imagined.

Nothing particularly attractive about him – dead white skin, splodgy freckles, curious flat golden brown eyes – not that it bothered me. After two months without sex I'd have settled for the pigs.

I met him again later, near the church. There's a lane runs past the churchyard, a low stone wall on one side, a canal on the other, one of the many canals that run through this area. A rather dank gloomy stretch of water, listlessly reflecting a dense white sky, fringed by willows with limp yellow leaves. He was sitting with his big, red, raw-knuckled hands clasped between his knees. The red hair glowed in the greyish light, not bright red, not auburn, a dark, flat, burnt-looking colour.

He was very obviously lingering. He greeted me with a smile and tapped his mouth, making smoking movements. I gave him a Woodbine and stood by the canal, a few feet away, looking up and down to make sure we weren't being observed. He made smoking movements again and pointed to the packet. When I didn't immediately respond, he pointed again and said something *in German*. I thought, My God. Have you really got your head stuck so deep in the fucking pig bucket you don't know which army's up the other end? I suppose it should have disgusted me, but it didn't. In fact it had the opposite effect – I'd have given him every packet I possessed. I handed them over and he got up and led me into the trees. It took a while finding somewhere sufficiently screened. I showed him what I wanted. He leant against the tree trunk, bracing himself on his hands. I pulled down his trousers and drawers and started nosing and tonguing round his arse, worrying at the crack to get in because the position hardened the muscles. A smell of chrysanths left too long in water, then a deeper friendlier smell, prim, pursed hole glistening with spit and, on the other side of that tight French sphincter, German spunk. Not literally – they left a bit longer ago than *that* – but *there* nevertheless, the shadowy figures one used to glimpse through periscopes in the trenches, and my tongue reaching out for them. I thought,

> Oh ye millions I embrace you,
> This kiss is for the whole world . . .

Suddenly it struck me as funny, and my breath made a farting noise between his buttocks and he tried to pull away, but I held on, and fucked him, and then turned him round and sucked off his quite small stubby very purple cock.

And then we parted. And I've been neurotically running my tongue round my lips feeling for sores ever since.

27 October

Everybody finds these marches gruelling. I spend a lot of my time on foot inspections. Some of the men have blisters the size of eggs. And my own feet, which were not good this morning, are now *very* not good.

But we're in decent billets tonight. I've actually got a bed in a room with roses on the wallpaper, and a few left in the garden too. Went out and picked some and put them in a bowl on the kitchen table in memory of Amiens. Big blowsy roses well past their best, but we move on again today so I won't be here to see the petals fall.

29 October

Arrived here under cover of darkness. Village wretched, people unsmiling, dazed-looking, not surprising when you think we were bombing them to buggery not long ago.

There's a rumour going round that the Austrians have signed a peace treaty. The men cheered up when they heard it, and they need cheering when you look at their feet. Nobody here can understand why it's still going on.

I lay in bed last night and listened to them in the barn singing. I wish I didn't feel they're being sacrificed to the subclauses and the small print. But I think they are.

Thursday, 31 October

And here for a while we shall stay. The Germans are dug in on the other side of the Sambre-Oise Canal, and seem to be preparing to make a stand.

The village is still occupied, but houses in the forward area have been evacuated and we're crammed into the cellar of one of them. Now and then we venture upstairs into the furnished rooms, feeling like rats or mice, and then we scurry back into our hole again. But it's warm, it *feels* safe, though the whole house shakes with the impact of exploding shells, and it's not good to think what a direct hit would do. Above ground the Germans have chopped down all the trees, but there's a great tangle of undergrowth, brambles that catch at your legs as you walk past, dead bracken the exact shade, or one of the shades, of Sarah's hair. No possibility of exercises or drill or anything. We lie low by day, and patrol at night, for of course they've left alarm posts on this side of the canal, a sort of human trip-wire to warn of an impending attack. Cleaning them out's a nasty job since it has to be silent. Knives and knobkerries in other words.

⋆

1 November

My turn to go out last night. One alarm post 'exterminated'. I hope it's the last. We crawled almost to the edge of the canal, and lay looking at it. There was just enough starlight to see by. A strong sense of the Germans on the other side, peering into the darkness as we were, silent, watchful. I had the sense that somewhere out there was a pair of eyes looking directly into mine.

The canal's raised about four feet above the surrounding fields, with drainage ditches on either side (the Germans have very sensibly flooded them). It's forty feet wide. Too wide to be easily bridged, too narrow from the point of view of a successful bombardment. There's no safety margin to allow for shells falling short, so men and equipment will have to be kept quite a long way back. Which means that when the barrage lifts, as it's supposed to do, and sweeps forward three hundred yards, there'll be about five minutes in which to get across the swampy fields, across the drainage ditches, and reach even our side of the canal. Plenty of time for them to get their breath and man the guns – though officially, of course, they'll all have been wiped out.

The field opposite's partially flooded already, and it's still raining. Not just rain, they've also flooded the drainage ditches on *their* side. From the canal the ground rises steeply to La Motte Farm, which is our objective in the attack. Uphill all the way. Not a scrap of cover. Machine-gunners behind every clump of grass.

Looking at the ground, even like that in semi-darkness, the problem became dreadfully apparent. Far clearer than it is on any of the maps, though we spend hours of every day bent over them. There are two possibilities. Either you bombard the opposite bank so heavily that no machine-gunner can possibly survive, in which case the ditches and quite possibly even the canal bank will burst, and the field on the other side will become a nightmare of weltering mud ten feet deep, as bad as anything at Passchendaele. *Or* you keep the bombardment light, move it on quickly, and wait for the infantry to catch up. In that case you take the risk that unscathed machine-gunners will pop up all over the place, and settle down for a nice bit of concentrated target practice.

It's a choice between Passchendaele and the Somme. Only a *miniature* version of each, but then that's not much consolation. It only takes one bullet per man.

They've chosen the Somme. This afternoon we had a joint briefing with the Lancashire Fusiliers on our left. Marshall-of-the-Ten-Wounds was there, surprisingly outspoken I thought, though you can afford to be when you're so covered in wound stripes and medals it's starting to look like an eccentric form of camouflage. He said his men stand *no* chance of getting up the slope with machine-guns still intact above them and no cover. Building a bridge in the open under the sort of fire we're likely to encounter is *impossible*. The whole operation's *insane*. The chances of success are *zero*.

Nobody argued with him, I mean nobody discussed it. We were just told flatly, a simple, unsupported assertion, that the weight of the artillery would overcome all opposition. I think those words sent a chill down the spine of every man there who remembered the Somme. Marshall threw his pencil down and sat with his arms folded, silent, for the rest of the briefing.

So here we sit writing letters. Supplies take a long time to get here, because the Germans blocked the roads and blew up the bridges as they withdrew. Nobody's been inside a proper shop for six weeks, so I keep tearing pages out of the back of this book and giving them to people.

Not many left now. But enough.

2 November 1918 2nd Manchester Regt. France

My dear Rivers,
As you'll have realized from my last letter, I'm still intact. Should this happy state of affairs not continue, I would be grateful if you would try to see my mother. She took quite a fancy to you when you met last year at Craiglockhart and you, more than most people, would know what to say. Or have the sense to say nothing, which was always rather your forte, wasn't it?

My nerves are in perfect working order. By which I mean that in my present situation the only sane thing to do is to run away, and I will not do it. Test passed?

Yours
Billy Prior

A chilly little note to send to someone who's done so much for me. Wrong tone completely, but there isn't time to get it right.

I daren't think about Sarah.

★

3 November

We're packed so tight in this cellar my elbow's constantly being jogged by people on either side. Cigarette smoke stings my eyes, I honestly believe if you ran out of fags here you'd just need to breathe deeply. But I've got enough to last, even after my spasm of generosity on the canal bank. Which this morning I reread, tore out and burned. Another canal bank meeting awaits – but this time the sort people approve of.

Curious day – it seems to have gone on for ever. We had another briefing at a farmhouse further along the lane. We were greeted by a little yapping terrier, still a puppy, black and white and full of himself, tucking one of his legs up as he ran so that at first I thought he was crippled, but the children in the house said no, he always runs like that. He quietened down a bit, but then got excited and started yapping again. Winterton nodded at me, and said, 'We can't have that.'

I shot it myself. I'm proud of that. In the trenches sometimes you'd be watching through a periscope and you'd see a German soldier – generally well back in the support lines – walking along believing himself to be safe, and he'd drop his breeches and settle down for a nice contented crap. You don't want to shoot him because there's something about the vulnerability of that bare arse, you feel the draught up your own crack, a moment of basic human empathy. So you point him out to the sentry and order the sentry to shoot him. That lets everybody off the hook – you haven't shot him, the sentry has, but only under orders.

But I shot the dog myself. I took him into the barn holding on to his collar. He knew something bad was going to happen, and he rolled over on to his back and showed me his puppy-pink tummy and widdled a bit, quite certain these devices for deflecting aggression would work. I tickled him behind his ear and said, 'Sorry, old son. I'm human – we're not like that.'

And I'm glad of the fug of human warmth in here, and not just because it keeps out the wind and rain. Those who've bagged themselves seats by the fire have steam rising from their boots and puttees. The rest of us just wiggle our toes and make do.

Having said I daren't think about Sarah, I think about her all the time. I remember the first time we met – that ludicrous wrestling match on a tombstone which in retrospect seems a rather appropriate start for a relationship so hedged in by death. And before that in the pub, plying her with port to get her knickers off, and she wanted to talk about Johnny's death and I didn't want to listen. Loos, she said. I remember standing by the bar and thinking that words didn't mean anything any more. Patriotism honour courage vomit vomit vomit. Only the names meant anything. Mons, Loos, the Somme, Arras, Verdun, Ypres.

But now I look round this cellar with the candles burning on the tables and our linked shadows leaping on the walls, and I realize there's another group of words that still mean something. Little words that trip through sentences unregarded: us, them, we, they, here, there. These are the words of power, and long after we're gone, they'll lie about in the language, like the unexploded grenades in these fields, and any one of them'll take your hand off.

Wyatt sleeps like a baby, except that no baby ever snored like that. Hoggart's peeling potatoes. Mugs of chlorine-tasting tea stand round. And somebody's chopping wood and feeding it to the fire, though it's so damp every fresh stick produces darkness, sizzling, a temporary shadowing of faces and eyes and then the flames lick round it, and the fire blazes up again. We need a good fire. Everybody's coughing and wheezing, a nasty cold going the rounds. I'm starting to feel a tickle in my throat, hot and shivery at the same time. I think of rats on the canal bank with long naked tails and the thought of that cold water is definitely not inviting. But we sing, we tell jokes and every joke told here is funny. Everybody's amazingly cheerful. The word I'm trying not to use is fey. There *is* an element of that. We all know what the chances are.

And soon I shall turf Wyatt out of that bunk and try to get some sleep.

Five months ago Charles Manning offered me a job at the Ministry of Munitions and I turned it down, and said if I was sent back to France . . . 'If if if if – I shall sit in a dug-out and look back to this afternoon, and I shall think, "You *bloody* fool."'

I remember sitting on the stiff brocade sofa in his drawing-room as I said it.

Well, here I am, in what passes for a dug-out. And I look round me at all these faces and all I can think is: What an utter bloody fool I would have been not to come back.

EIGHTEEN

Brown fog enveloped the hospital. Coils of sulphurous vapour hung in the entrance hall, static, whirled into different patterns whenever somebody entered or left the building. He'd gone out himself earlier in the evening to buy a paper from the stand outside Victoria Station, a brisk ten-minute walk there and back, a chance to get some air into his lungs, though air these days scorched the throat. The news was good. At any moment now, one felt, the guns would stop and they would all be released into their private lives. They all felt it – and yet it almost seemed not to matter. The end that everybody had longed for was overshadowed by the Spanish influenza epidemic that had the hospital in its grip. If somebody had rushed along the corridor now opening doors and shouting, 'The war's over,' he'd have said, 'Oh, really?' and gone back to writing up notes.

He looked at his watch and stood up. Time to go up to the ward.

Marsden was trying to catch his eye. He'd had the impression that morning, during his ward round, that Marsden wanted to ask something, but had been deterred by the formality of the occasion. Rivers had a quick word with Sister Roberts – the staffing situation for this duty was particularly bad – and then went and sat by Marsden's bed, chatting about this and that while he worked himself up to say whatever it was he wanted to say. It was quite simple. He'd overheard a junior doctor talking to a colleague at the foot of his bed and had caught the phrase 'elicited the coital reflex'. Did this mean, Marsden wanted to know, that he would *eventually*, he stressed, hedging his bets, not *now* obviously, *eventually*, be able to have sex again? 'Have sex' was produced in a flat, no nonsense, all-chaps-together tone. He meant 'make love'. He meant 'have children'. His wife's photograph stood on his locker. Rivers's neck muscles tensed with the effort of not looking at it. No, he said slowly, it didn't mean that. He explained what it meant. Marsden wasn't listening, but he needed a smoke-screen of words behind which to prepare his reaction. He was pleating the hem of the sheet between his fingertips. 'Well,' he said casually, when Rivers had finished. 'I didn't really think it meant that. Just thought I'd ask.'

One incident; one day.

Faces shadowed by steel helmets, they would hardly have recognized each other, even if the faint starlight had enabled them to see clearly. Prior, crouching in a ditch beside the crossroads, kept looking at the inside of his left wrist where normally his watch would have been. It had been taken away from him twenty minutes ago to be synchronized. The usual symptoms: dry mouth, sweaty palms, pounding heart, irritable bladder, cold feet. What a brutally accurate term 'cold feet' was. Though 'shitting yourself' – the other brutally accurate term – did *not* apply. He'd been glugging Tincture of Opium all day, as had several others of the old hands. He'd be shitting bricks for a fortnight when this was over, but at least he wouldn't be shitting himself tonight.

He looked again at his wrist, caught Owen doing the same, smiled with shared irritation, said nothing. He stared at the stars, trying to locate the plough, but couldn't concentrate. Rain clouds were massing. All we need. A few minutes later a runner came back with his watch and with a tremendous sense – delusional, of course – of being in control again he strapped it on.

Then they were moving forward, hundreds of men eerily quiet, starlit shadows barely darkening the grass. And no dogs barked.

The clock at the end of the ward blurred, then moved into focus again. He was finding it difficult to keep awake now that the rounds were done, the reports written and his task was simply to *be there*, ready for whatever emergencies the night might throw his way. Sister Roberts put a mug of orange-coloured tea, syrupy with sugar, in front of him, and he took a gulp. They sat together at the night nurses' station – there were no night nurses, they were all off with flu – drinking the too strong, too sweet tea, watching the other end of the ward, where the green screens had been placed round Hallet's bed. A single lamp shone above his bed so the green curtains glowed against the darkness of the rest of the ward. Through a gap between the screens Rivers could see one of the family, a young boy, fourteen, fifteen years old perhaps, Hallet's younger brother, wriggling about on his chair, bored with the long hours of waiting and knowing it was unforgivable to be bored.

'I wish the mother would go home and lie down,' Sister Roberts said. 'She's absolutely at the end of her tether.' A sniff. 'And that girl looks the hysterical type to me.'

She never liked the girls. 'Is she his sister?'

'Fiancée.'

A muttering from behind the screen, but no discernible words. Rivers stood up. 'I'd better have a look.'

'Do you want the relatives out?'

'Please. It'll only take a minute.'

The family looked up as he pushed the screens aside. They had been sitting round this bed off and on for nearly thirty-six hours, ever since Hallet's condition had begun to deteriorate. Mrs Hallet, the mother, was on Hallet's right, he suspected because the family had decided she should be spared, as far as possible, seeing the left side of Hallet's face. The worst was hidden by the dressing over the eye, but still enough was visible. The father sat on the bad side, a middle-aged man, very erect, retired professional army, in uniform for the duration of the war. He had a way of straightening his shoulders, bracing himself that suggested chronic back pain rather than a reaction to the present situation. And then the girl, whose name was . . . Susan, was it? She sat, twisting a handkerchief between her fingers, often with a polite, meaningless smile on her face, in the middle of the family she had been going to join and must now surely realize she would not be joining. And the boy, who was almost the most touching of all, gauche, graceless, angry with everything, his voice sometimes squeaking humiliatingly so that he blushed, at other times braying down the ward, difficult, rebellious, demanding attention, because he was afraid if he stopped behaving like this he would cry.

They stood up when he came in, looking at him in a way familiar from his earliest days in hospital medicine. They expected him to *do* something. Although they'd been told Hallet was critically ill, they were still hoping he'd 'make him better'.

Sister Roberts asked them to wait outside and they retreated to the waiting-room at the end of the main corridor.

He looked at Hallet. The whole of the left side of his face drooped. The exposed eye was sunk deep in his skull, open, though he didn't seem to be fully conscious. His hair had been shaved off, preparatory to whatever operation had left the horseshoe-shaped scar, now healing ironically well, above the suppurating wound left by the rifle bullet. The hernia cerebri pulsated, looking like some strange submarine form of life, the mouth of a sea anemone perhaps. The whole of the left side of his body was useless. Even when he was conscious enough to speak the drooping of the mouth and the damage to the lower jaw made his speech impossible to follow. This, more than anything else, horrified his family. You saw them straining to understand, but they couldn't grasp a word he said. His voice came in a whisper because he lacked the strength to project it. He seemed to be whispering now. Rivers bent over him, listened, then straightened up, deciding he must have imagined the sound. Hallet had not stirred, beyond the usual twitching below the coverlet, the constant clonus to which his right ankle joint was subject.

Why are you alive? Rivers thought, looking down into the gargoyled face.

Mate, would have been Njiru's word for this: the state of which death is the appropriate and therefore the desirable outcome. He would have seen Hallet as being, in every meaningful way, dead already, and his sole purpose would have been to hasten the moment of actual death: *mate ndapu,* die finish. Rivers fingered his lapel badge, his unimpaired nerves transmitting the shape of the caduceus to his undamaged brain, his allegiance to a different set of beliefs confirmed without the conflict ever breaking the surface of consciousness.

He took Hallet's pulse. 'All right,' he said to Sister Roberts. 'You can let them back in.'

He watched her walk off, then thought it was cowardice not to face them, and followed her down the corridor, passing Mrs Hallet on the way. She hesitated when she saw him, but the drive to get back to her son was too strong. Susan and the younger brother followed on behind. He found Major Hallet lingering by an open window, smoking furiously. A breath of muggy, damp, foggy air came into the room, a reminder that there was an outside world.

'Pathetic, isn't it?' Major Hallet said, raising the cigarette. 'Well?'

Rivers hesitated.

'Not long now, eh?'

'No, not long.'

In spite of his terseness, tears immediately welled up in Major Hallet's eyes. He turned away, his voice shaking. 'He's been so brave. He's been so bloody brave.' A moment during which he struggled for control. 'How long exactly do you think?'

'I don't know. Hours.'

'Oh God.'

'Keep talking to him. He *does* recognize your voices and he can understand.'

'But we can't understand *him*. It's terrible, he's obviously expecting an answer and we can't say anything.'

They went back to the ward together, Major Hallet pausing outside the screen for a moment, bracing his back. A muttering from the bed. 'You see?' Major Hallet said helplessly.

Rivers followed him through the gap in the screens and leant over to listen to Hallet. His voice was a slurred whisper. 'Shotvarfet.'

At first Rivers could only be sure of the initial consonant and thought he might be trying to say 'Susan', but the phrase was longer than that. He straightened and shook his head. 'Keep talking to him, Mrs Hallet. He does recognize your voice.'

She bent forward and shyly, covered with the social embarrassment that crops up so agonizingly on these occasions, tried to talk, telling him news of home, Auntie Ethel sent her love, Madeleine was getting married in April . . .

Susan had that smile on her lips again, fixed, meaningless, a baboon rictus of sheer terror. And the boy's face, a mask of fear and fury because he knew that any moment now the tears would start, and he'd be shamed in front of some merciless tribunal in his own mind.

Rivers left them to it. Sister Roberts and the one orderly were busy with Adams who had to be turned every hour. He sat in the night station's circle of light, looking up and down the ward, forcing himself to name and recall the details of every patient, his tired mind waiting for the next jerk of the clock.

The glowing green screens round Hallet's bed reminded him of the tent on Eddystone, on the nights when the insects were really bad and they had to take the lamp inside. You'd go out into the bush and come back and there'd be this great glow of light, and Hocart's shadow huge on the canvas. Safety, or as close to it as you could get on the edge of the dark.

On their last evening he sat outside the tent, packing cases full of clothes and equipment ranged around him, typing up his final notes. Hocart was away on the other side of the island and not due back for hours. Working so close to the light his eyes grew tired, and he sat back rubbing the inner corners; he opened them again to find Njiru a few feet away watching him, having approached silently on his bare feet.

Rivers took the lamp from the table and set it on the ground, squatting down beside it, since he knew Njiru was more comfortable on the ground. The bush exuded blackness. The big moths that loved a particular flowering bush that grew all round the tent bumped furrily against the glass, so that he and Njiru sat in a cloud of pale wings.

They chatted for a while about some of the more than four hundred acquaintances they now had in common, then a long easy silence fell.

'Kundaite says you know Ave,' Rivers said very quietly, almost as if the bush itself had spoken, and Njiru were being asked to do no more than think aloud.

Njiru said, almost exactly as he'd said at the beginning, 'Kundaite he no speak true, he savvy *gammon* 'long *nanasa*,' but now he spoke with a faint growl of laughter in his voice, adding in English, 'He is a liar.'

'He *is* a liar, but I think you do know Ave.'

He was reminded suddenly of an incident in the Torres Straits when Haddon had been trying to get skulls to measure. One man had said, with immense dignity, 'Be patient. You will have all our skulls in time.' It was not a comfortable memory. He was not asking for skulls but he was asking for something at least equally sacred. He leant forward and their shadows leapt and grappled against the bush. 'Tell me about Ave.'

Ave lives in Ysabel. He is both one spirit and many spirits. His mouth is long and filled with the blood of the men he devours. Kita and Mateana are nothing beside him because they destroy only the individual, but Ave kills 'all people 'long house'. The broken rainbow belongs to him, and presages both epidemic disease and war. Ave is the destroyer of peoples.

And the words of exorcism? He told him even that, the last bubbles rising from the mouth of a drowning man. Not only told him, but, with that blend of scholarly exactitude and intellectual impatience for which he was remarkable, insisted on Rivers learning the words in Melanesian, in the 'high speech', until he had the inflection on every syllable perfect. This was the basis, Rivers thought, toiling and stumbling over the words, of Njiru's power, the reason why on meeting him even the greatest chiefs stepped off the path.

'And now,' Njiru said, lifting his head in a mixture of pride and contempt, 'now you will put it in your book.'

I never have, Rivers thought. His and Hocart's book on Eddystone had been one of the casualties of the war, though hardly – he glanced up and down the ward with its rows of brain-damaged and paralysed young men – the most significant.

He had spoken them, though, during the course of a lecture to the

Royal Society, and had been delighted to find that he didn't need to consult his notes as he spoke. He was still word-perfect.

A commotion from behind the screens. Hallet had begun to cry out and his family was trying to soothe him. A muttering all along the ward as the other patients stirred and grumbled in their sleep, dragged reluctantly back into consciousness. But the grumbling stopped as they realized where the cries were coming from. A silence fell. Faces turned towards the screens as if the battle being waged behind them was every man's battle.

Rivers walked quietly across. The family stood up again as he came in. 'No, it's all right,' he said. 'No need to move.'

He took Hallet's pulse. He felt the parents' gaze on him, the father's red-veined, unblinking eyes and the mother's pale fierce face with its working mouth.

'This is it, isn't it?' Major Hallet said in a whisper.

Rivers looked down at Hallet, who was now fully conscious. Oh God, he thought, it's going to be one of those. He shook his head. 'Not long.'

The barrage was due to start in fifteen minutes' time. Prior shared a bar of chocolate with Robson, sitting hunched up together against the damp cold mist. Then they started crawling forward. The sappers, who were burdened by materials for the construction of the pontoon bridge, were taking the lane, so the Manchesters had to advance over the waterlogged fields. The rain had stopped, but the already marshy ground had flooded in places, and over each stretch of water lay a thick blanket of mist. Concentrate on nothing but the moment, Prior told himself, moving forward on knees and elbows like a frog or a lizard or like – like anything except a man. First the right knee, then the left, then the right, then the left again, and again, and again, slithering through fleshy green grass that smelled incredibly sharp as scrabbling boots cut it. Even with all this mist there was now a perceptible thinning of the light, a gleam from the canal where it ran between spindly, dead trees.

There is to be no retirement under any circumstances. That was the order. They have tied us to the stake, we cannot fly, but bear-like we must fight the course. The men were silent, staring straight ahead into the mist. Talk, even in whispers, was forbidden. Prior looked at his watch, licked dry lips, watched the second hand crawl to the quarter hour. All around him was a tension of held breath. 5.43. Two more minutes.

He crouched further down, whistle clenched between his teeth.

Prompt as ever, hell erupted. Shells whined over, flashes of light, plumes of water from the drainage ditches, tons of mud and earth flung into the air. A shell fell short. The ground shook beneath them and a shower of pebbles and clods of earth peppered their steel helmets. Five minutes of this, five minutes of the air bursting in waves against your face, men with dazed faces braced against it, as they picked up the light bridges meant for fording the flooded drainage ditches, and carried them out to the front. Then, abruptly, silence. A gasp for air, then noise again, but further back, as the barrage lifted and drummed down on to the empty fields.

Prior blew the whistle, couldn't hear it, was on his feet and running anyway, urging the men on with wordless cries. They rushed forward, making for the line of trees. Prior kept shouting, 'Steady, steady! Not too fast on the left!' It was important there should be no bunching when they reached the bridges. 'Keep it straight!' Though the men were stumbling into quagmires or tripping over clumps of grass. A shell whizzing over from the German side exploded in a shower of mud and water. And another. He saw several little figures topple over, it didn't look serious, somehow, they didn't look like beings who could be hurt.

Bridges laid down, quickly, efficiently, no bunching at the crossings, just the clump of boots on wood, and then they emerged from beneath the shelter of the trees and out into the terrifying openness of the bank. As bare as an eyeball, no cover anywhere, and the machine-gunners on the other side were alive and well. They dropped down, firing to cover the sappers as they struggled to assemble the bridge, but nothing covered *them*. Bullets fell like rain, puckering the surface of the canal, and the men started to fall. Prior saw the man next to him, a silent, surprised face, no sound, as he twirled and fell, a slash of scarlet like a huge flower bursting open on his chest. Crawling forward, he fired at the bank opposite though he could hardly see it for the clouds of smoke that drifted across. The sappers were still struggling with the bridge, binding pontoon sections together with wire that sparked in their hands as bullets struck it. And still the terrible rain fell. Only two sappers left, and then the Manchesters took over the building of the bridge. Kirk paddled out in a crate to give covering fire, was hit, hit again, this time in the face, went on firing directly at the machine-gunners who crouched in their defended holes only a few yards away. Prior was about to start across the water with ammunition when he was himself hit, though it didn't feel like a bullet, more like a blow from something big and hard, a truncheon or a cricket bat, only it knocked him off his feet and he fell, one arm trailing over the edge of the canal.

He tried to turn to crawl back beyond the drainage ditches, knowing it was only a matter of time before he was hit again, but the gas was thick here and he couldn't reach his mask. Banal, simple, repetitive thoughts ran round and round his mind. *Balls up. Bloody mad. Oh Christ.* There was no pain, more a spreading numbness that left his brain clear. He saw Kirk die. He saw Owen die, his body lifted off the ground by bullets, describing a slow arc in the air as it fell. It seemed to take for ever to fall, and Prior's consciousness fluttered down with it. He gazed at his reflection in the water, which broke and reformed and broke again as bullets hit the surface and then, gradually, as the numbness spread, he ceased to see it.

The light was growing now, the subdued, brownish light of a November dawn. At the far end of the ward, Simpson, too far gone himself to have any understanding of what was happening, jargoned and gobbled away, but all the other faces were turned towards the screens, each man lending the little strength he had to support Hallet in his struggle.

So far, except for the twice repeated whisper and the wordless cries, Hallet had been silent, but now the whisper began again, only more loudly. *Shotvarfet. Shotvarfet.* Again and again, increasing in volume as he directed all his strength into the cry. His mother tried to soothe him, but he didn't hear her. *Shotvarfet. Shotvarfet.* Again and again, each time louder, ringing across the ward. He opened his one eye and gazed directly at Rivers, who had come from behind the screens and was standing at the foot of his bed.

'What's he saying?' Major Hallet asked.

Rivers opened his mouth to say he didn't know and then realized he did. 'He's saying, "It's not worth it."'

'Oh, it is worth it, it *is*,' Major Hallet said, gripping his son's hand. The man was in agony. He hardly knew what he was saying.

'*Shotvarfet.*'

The cry rose again as if he hadn't spoken, and now the other patients were growing restless. A buzz of protest not against the cry, but in support of it, a wordless murmur from damaged brains and drooping mouths.

'*Shotvarfet. Shotvarfet.*'

'I can't stand much more of this,' Major Hallet said. The mother's eyes never left her son's face. Her lips were moving though she made no sound. Rivers was aware of a pressure building in his own throat as that single cry from the patients went on and on. He could not afterwards be sure that he had succeeded in keeping silent, or whether he too had joined in. All he could remember later was gripping the metal rail at the end of the bed till his hands hurt.

And then suddenly it was over. The mangled words faded into silence, and a moment or two later, with an odd movement of the chest and stomach muscles like somebody taking off a too tight jumper, Hallet died.

Rivers reached the bedside before the family realized he was gone, closed the one eye, and from sheer force of habit looked at his watch.

'6.25,' he said, addressing Sister Roberts.

He raised the sheet as far as Hallet's chin, arranged his arms by his sides and withdrew silently, leaving the family alone with their grief, wishing, as he pulled the screens more closely together, that he had not seen the young girl turn aside to hide her expression of relief.

On the edge of the canal the Manchesters lie, eyes still open, limbs not yet decently arranged, for the stretcher-bearers have departed with the last of the wounded, and the dead are left alone. The battle has withdrawn from them; the bridge they succeeded in building was destroyed by a single shell. Further down the canal another and more successful crossing is being attempted, but the cries and shouts come faintly here.

The sun has risen. The first shaft strikes the water and creeps towards them along the bank, discovering here the back of a hand, there the side of a neck, lending a rosy glow to skin from which the blood has fled, and then, finding nothing here that can respond to it, the shaft of light passes over them and begins to probe the distant fields.

Grey light tinged with rosy pink seeps in through the tall windows. Rivers, slumped at the night nurses' station, struggles to stay awake. On the edge of sleep he hears Njiru's voice, repeating the words of the exorcism of Ave.

O Sumbi! O Gesese! O Palapoko! O Gorepoko! O you Ngengere at the root of the sky. Go down, depart ye.

And there, suddenly, not separate from the ward, not in any way ghostly, not in *fashion blong tomate*, but himself in every particular, advancing down the ward of the Empire Hospital, attended by his shadowy retinue, as Rivers had so often seen him on the coastal path on Eddystone, came Njiru.

There is an end of men, an end of chiefs, an end of chieftains' wives, an end of chiefs' children – then go down and depart. Do not yearn for us, the fingerless, the crippled, the broken. Go down and depart, oh, oh, oh.

He bent over Rivers, staring into his face with those piercing hooded eyes. A long moment, and then the brown face, with its streaks of lime, faded into the light of the daytime ward.

AUTHOR'S NOTE

The reader may wish to know more about some of the historical characters encountered in this novel.

Colonel Marshall-of-the-Ten-Wounds was killed attempting to cross the Sambre-Oise canal, having led his men 'without regard for his personal safety'. He was awarded a posthumous VC.

James Kirk, who paddled himself out on to the canal to give covering fire, was also awarded a posthumous VC.

Wilfred Owen's MC, for gallantry in capturing an enemy machine-gun and inflicting 'considerable losses' on the enemy at the battle of Joncourt, was awarded after his death.

Rivers drew on his Eddystone data in several published papers, but the major joint work he and Hocart planned was never written. His notebooks are in the Rare Manuscripts Department of Cambridge University Library.

Njiru, Kundaite, Namboko Taru, Namboko Emele, Nareti, Lembu and the captive child are also historical, but of them nothing more is known.

The following works can be unreservedly recommended:

W. H. R. Rivers by Richard Slobodin (Sutton Publishing, 1997)

Memories of Lewis Carroll by Katharine Rivers, with an Introduction by Richard Slobodin (Library Research News, McMaster University, 1976)

Collected Letters of Wilfred Owen (Oxford University Press, 1967)

Wilfred Owen by Jon Stallworthy (Oxford University Press, 1974)

Owen the Poet by Dominic Hibberd (Macmillan, 1986)

Wilfred Owen, The Last Year by Dominic Hibberd (Constable, 1992)

Wilfred Owen's Voices: Language and Community by Douglas Kerr (Clarendon Press, 1993)

Wilfred Owen, Poet and Soldier by Helen McPhail (Gliddon Books in association with the Wilfred Owen Association, 1993)

READ MORE IN PENGUIN

READ MORE IN PENGUIN

A CHOICE OF FICTION

No Night is Too Long Barbara Vine

Tim Cornish, a creative-writing student, sits composing a confession: an admission of a crime committed two years ago that has yet to be discovered. 'A dark, watery masterpiece ... suffused with sexuality, which explores with hypnotic effect the psychological path between passion and murder' – *The Times*

Peerless Flats Esther Freud

Lisa has high hopes for her first year in London. She is sixteen and ambitious to become more like her sister Ruby. For Ruby has cropped hair, a past and a rockabilly boyfriend whose father is in prison. 'Freud sounds out as a clear, attractive voice in the literary hubbub' – *Observer*

One of the Family Monica Dickens

At 72 Chepstow Villas lives the Morley family: Leonard, the Assistant Manager of Whiteley's, his gentle wife Gwen, 'new woman' daughter Madge and son Dicky. Into their comfortable Edwardian world comes a sinister threat of murder and a charismatic stranger who will change their lives for ever. 'It is the contrasts that Dickens depicts so rivetingly . . . she captures vividly the gradual blurring of social divisions during the last days of the Empire' – *Daily Mail*

Original Sin P. D. James

The literary world is shaken when a murder takes place at the Peverell Press, an old-established publishing house located in a dramatic mock-Venetian palace on the Thames. 'Superbly plotted . . . James is interested in the soul, not just in the mind, of a killer' – *Daily Telegraph*

In Cold Domain Anne Fine

'A streamlined, ruthlessly stripped-down psychological family romance with enough plot twists and character revelations to fuel a book three times as long, as wicked and funny as anything Fay Weldon has written. Anne Fine is brilliant' – *Time Out*

READ MORE IN PENGUIN

A CHOICE OF FICTION

Mothers' Boys Margaret Forster

'Margaret Forster has a remarkable gift for taking huge social issues and welding them into minutely observed human dramas that are perfect portraits of the way we live now . . . The story grips and the heart bleeds for these good mothers who are, like all mothers, never good enough' – *Daily Mail*

Cleopatra's Sister Penelope Lively

'A fluent, funny, ultimately moving romance in which lovers share centre stage with Lively's persuasive meditations on history and fate . . . a book of great charm with a real intellectual resonance at its core' – *The New York Times Book Review*

A Private View Anita Brookner

George Bland had planned to spend his retirement in leisurely travel and modest entertainment with his friend Putnam. When Putnam dies George is left attempting to impose some purpose on the solitary end of his life. 'A beautiful book that one is impelled to read at one sitting and finishes with a deep sense of sadness' – *Evening Standard*

The Constant Mistress Angela Lambert

Laura King is a liberated, intelligent and successful woman. Although she has never married, hers has been an active and emotionally fulfilled life. Suddenly, at the age of forty-four, she learns that she is suffering from a rare liver disease and has only a year or two to live. In typically flamboyant style, Laura invites her ex-lovers to dinner . . .

The Rose Revived Katie Fforde

When May teams up with Sally and Harriet, it is the best day's work she's ever done. Each of them needs money, badly. Which is why they are reduced to working for Quality Cleaners under the watchful eye of 'Slimeball' Slater. When they discover it is *them* being taken to the cleaners, they set up as an independent team – and that is when things really begin to take off.

BY THE SAME AUTHOR

The Man Who Wasn't There

Twelve-year-old Colin has been brought up entirely by women. He knows little about his father except that he must have fought in the war. Viv, his mother, gritty, lively but totally absorbed in her boyfriend, refuses to talk about him, and Colin turns to films for images of what his father might have been. When this fails he begins to imagine his own film, a highly charged drama set in occupied France. Then the man in black, a character in his film, appears in real life, and the game of make-believe takes on a deadly urgency.

'Beautifully written, original and memorable' Susan Hill

'We get a sense of the thinness of the walls – where, indeed, they exist at all – between reality and fantasy, sex and violence, the funny and the decidedly not so. And always there is this writer's unerring ear for dialogue, about the nearest equivalent to absolute pitch our current fiction provides' *Guardian*

'Colin's catharsis . . . and its aftermath, are handled with a mastery of eeriness which, as well as her depiction of post-war provincial life, show the writer at her best' *Sunday Times*

The Regeneration Trilogy *is also published in three separate volumes.*